THE KING'S ORCHARD

James O'Hara, born in Ireland, educated in Paris, lands in Philadelphia in 1772 in search of the great American adventure. He is impressed with the business and social life of the city and emotionally stirred by his meeting with a beautiful girl, but he is singleminded in his determination to explore this young country. Driven by a desire to reach the frontier, he sets off across the mountains to Fort Pitt where he soon makes a name for himself in the fur trade and on the battlefields as a Revolutionary officer.

At the close of the war he brings his lovely bride over the mountains in an ox-wagon filled with treasures from her home to a log house in the King's Orchard, a little haven of beauty in the embattled land around Fort Pitt. During his successful and ever-changing career, the one thing that stays constant is his love for his beautiful wife, Mary.

THE KING'S ORCHARD

AGNES SLIGH TURNBULL

A New Portway Book

CHIVERS PRESS
BATH

First published in Great Britain 1964
by
Collins
This edition published
by
Chivers Press
by arrangement with the author
at the request of
The London & Home Counties Branch
of
The Library Association
1985

ISBN 0 86220 553 0

British Library Cataloguing in Publication Data

Turnbull, Agnes Sligh
  The king's orchard.—(A New Portway book)
  I. Title
  813′.54[F]   PS3539.U76

  ISBN 0–86220–553–0

Printed and bound in Great Britain by
Redwood Burn Limited
Trowbridge, Wiltshire

TO

THE MEMORY OF

MY FATHER AND MOTHER

"And yet they, who are long gone, are in us,
as predisposition, as burden upon our destiny,
as blood that pulsates, and as gesture that rises
up out of the depths of time."

RAINER MARIA RILKE

Acknowledgements

My first and deepest thanks go to Agnes Starrett, Editor of the University of Pittsburgh Press, for suggestions to me that I use James O'Hara as the subject of a novel.

During the writing I have been encouraged by the steady interest of Mr. and Mrs. Harman Denny and Mr. and Mrs. James O'Hara of Pittsburgh who introduced me to family treasures relative to my work, the Dennys being direct descendants of James O'Hara.

I regret that it is impossible to give credit to all the many sources from which I have drawn material, but I wish to mention three with my especial gratitude: *Pittsburgh: The Story of a City* by Leland D. Baldwin; *General James O'Hara, Pittsburgh's First Captain of Industry*, a master's thesis by Eulalia Catherine Schramm; and *Background to Glory: The Life of George Rogers Clark* by John Bakeless.

A.S.T.

Chapter One

The first thing he thought of as he set his feet upon American soil was the weather! After the scudding rains and mists of Ireland's County Mayo and the dank dawns and often darker noons of Liverpool, all topped by as stormy a crossing as the Atlantic could churn up, he stood upon the planks of the Philadelphia wharf and looked in astonishment at the sky. It was the colour of the Virgin's own robe, with only a lacy white cloud here and there to break the richness of the blue; while over all was the golden effulgence of the sun.

"I can't believe it," he said under his breath, "I can't believe it, *in October!*"

But it was true. There was even a certain serene assurance about the brightness, as though it was an accustomed thing not easily disturbed or driven away. There was also a pervasive beatitude in the warmth itself which not only comforted the bones but lifted the spirits. James O'Hara smiled, lighting up his long, handsome face. He had suddenly remembered a line from the old pamphlet he had discovered in a secondhand book-store and had brought with him. It was the prospectus written by William Penn nearly a hundred years before about his "Holy Experiment, Philadelphia." *The place lies six hundred miles nearer the sun than England,* the Quaker had written ingratiatingly.

"So that's it!" young O'Hara thought with a chuckle. He had come across the seas with the pull of adventure in his heart, steeled to face the perils of a new world, but never expecting the welcome of this beautiful autumn midday. So, still smiling as though at a fair presage, he took a firmer grip upon his baggage which looked like—and was—that of a gentleman and began to move along the busy wharf.

He had made no friends of his own age on the crossing, partly because he was reserved by nature but largely because all the other young immigrants seemed to have come steerage while he

7

had journeyed upper class. He had held a few conversations with older men whom he met daily but for the most part had read, walked the deck on the few hours when it was possible to keep his balance, and slept, as though storing up energy for what might lie ahead.

One of the men who had interested him was, he gathered, what in Great Britain would be called an iron master, Mark Bird by name. He was a man perhaps in his sixties, who apparently enjoyed the young Irishman's company and often sought him out for a chat. O'Hara was a keen, almost voracious listener as the talks went on. Bird was evidently a man of wealth, having not only *furnaces* but a pack of hounds as well.

"Have you ever hunted?" he asked the young man one day.

"A few times. Only on visits to my cousin who is keen on it."

"Uh hmm," Bird said, eyeing him with new respect. "May I ask where you intend to settle over here?"

"I don't know yet, sir. Not till I've looked around a bit."

"Does the frontier attract you?"

"It does, rather."

"Pretty rough going out there. And there's always the devil to pay with the Indians one way or another. As to that," he added slowly, "even if you decide to stay in the East, there may be trouble enough for everybody in a few years."

"What do you mean, sir?"

"You haven't heard about it?"

"Nothing that seemed serious."

The older man smiled grimly. "Well, you probably wouldn't, but over here there are a lot of people saying, 'To hell with the King,' and saying it pretty loud. That wouldn't be a popular cry in the old country."

"You mean there could really be a break with the Crown? On what grounds?"

"Well, it's hard to put it in a nutshell but you'll hear it little by little. Let me just say we've had our noses rubbed in the muck and we're tired of it. We're an upstanding lot in the Colonies and the air here smells free. After you've drawn it in for years—— Well, I don't mean to scare you out." He laughed. "It's not too late to go back."

O'Hara did not return the laughter. "I never heard of an Irishman running away from a fight," he said soberly, "but that certainly wasn't what I came over for. There's one thing I'd like to ask, though I believe you've already made it clear. If it should ever come to *war*, you mean you'd stand against the King?"

"Well, let's just say I'm an American first and last no matter what comes. Of course the troubles may all smooth out. We've got some good men working on them. Ben Franklin and others. But," he added, lowering his tone, "in my furnaces right now we're making a few cannon balls, *just in case*."

The night before they landed Mr. Bird had spoken to him again. "Do you know anyone in Philadelphia?"

"Not a soul. I've got a letter though from my employer in Liverpool to a Mr. William Carson, a Scotsman."

"Good," said the older man. "I know of him. I've been thinking, though, that if you give up the frontier idea and decide to stay in the east I'd be glad to have you come up and have a look at our furnaces. The Birdsboro Iron Works is the name, and the village is called Birdsboro. Anyone in Philadelphia can tell you how to get there. We're on Hay Creek that runs into the Schuylkill —just up the river. I could give you a job and maybe a day's hunting to boot."

"That's more than kind of you," O'Hara said. "I wouldn't be too good at the hunt but I'll surely remember about the job. I thank you, sir, for your interest in me." There had been a warm handshake between them as they said good-bye.

O'Hara now, with his letter of introduction in his safest pocket, still smiled as he stepped into the cobblestone street, for he faced a neat, new, clean little town. With the remembrance of worn old cities strong within him, especially the dark, decrepit buildings edging the Liverpool piers, he looked in amazement at the bright and tidy thoroughfare which here ran along the wharf. The houses were mostly brick, some, he could see, three stories high with iron grille-work decoration, but all pleasant, habitable, and fresh in the sunlight. There was still another contrast to the old world ports which he sensed at once. Here there was no salt in the air and no ocean breeze blowing. For there was only the broad, placid flow of the Delaware River to bear its shipping from the seven seas to Philadelphia's doorsteps.

As he stood looking at the buildings before him his eye caught a swinging sign in bold colouring from which the words *the Crooked Billet* beckoned. He knew his first move was to get established in a tavern before presenting himself and his letter to Mr. Carson, but he hesitated a moment while he surveyed the street.

It fairly bristled with other hostelry signs. From where he stood he could make out: *The Pewter Platter*, *The Star and Garter*, *King Henry on Horseback*, and *The Indian King*. But he had the strong Irish feeling for omen and coincidence. He decided to stick to the first sign he had seen and so went up the scrubbed stone steps and through the door into the Crooked Billet.

The bar-room which he entered seemed dark at first after the brilliant sunlight without, but it was, withal, a cheerful place. There was much polished brass about the wide fireplace and a settle at the side, worn smooth with use. Tables and chairs stood waiting for the later influx of customers, a dart-board showed invitingly in one corner and a row of beer mugs hung from their hooks on a rafter above the bar. A man in a leather apron and full-sleeved shirt came through a door at the back and grinned at O'Hara.

"What'll you have, friend?" he asked.

"Could I get a room, please?"

"I'll have the master, Mr. Hastings, in to see you about that. I just pulls the beer! I'm Sam," he added still grinning and disappeared.

The master proved to be tall, thin and pock-marked, with cheerful eyes which now studied the young man.

"You wish lodging?" he said.

"I'm James O'Hara. I've just landed and don't know yet what I'll be finding to do. I would like a room until I learn my way round a little."

The older man sized up his clothes and his luggage.

"Irish, then?"

"I was born there."

"Green or orange?"

"Orange. My family's divided on that. I might say I'll gladly pay you a week in advance."

There was a sudden noise of loud voices just outside the tavern and then two men entered apparently on the verge of a fight. From the dark bearded one a torrent of French issued, accompanied by threatening gestures; his companion, slightly shorter and sandy, clutched a heavy load of pelts, cursing eloquently as he fended off the other's efforts to grab the furs.

O'Hara jumped up. "*Arretez! Arretez!*" he cried. The Frenchman, startled at hearing his own language, stepped back and directed his angry discourse to the young man who listened carefully, putting a question now and then.

"What's eating at him?" the other man said. "Why is he trying to steal my pelts?"

"He says these are his pelts. That you picked up the wrong bundle in the trading store. He says if you'll check them over you'll see they aren't yours. I think the man is honest."

"The devil he is! They're all slippery, these Frenchies. Well, I'll take a look to satisfy him."

He opened an end of the bag bundle which was contained in a deer skin and then straightened in surprise.

"May I be a dead Injun if he ain't right! I hadn't any fox skins that colour. We both set our packs down at the store about the same time but when I saw who was back of the counter to-day I grabbed mine—as I thought—and hustled down here until Clark himself is in. Tell this to Frenchy, young fellow. . . ."

"O'Hara, and just now landed, Mr. Elliott," Hastings introduced.

"Well, O'Hara, tell this man how it happened and that I apologise. And tell him not to make a trade until Clark is in the store. That other fellow there will cheat him as sure as there's an eye in a goat. I've got to get back now and see to my own pack. But give these two both a beer to wet their whistles while I'm gone, Hastings. And thank you, young man. I think you saved me a drubbing."

As O'Hara and the stranger sat at the bar the French flowed apace between them; when they had finished their beer, still conversing, they moved over to the corner where the big bundle of furs lay. The Frenchman opened it up, displayed each skin, evidently explaining its value. O'Hara kept questioning him, until at last he put the pelts back into the deerskin, fastened it with leather thongs and then, with a wave to Hastings and a hearty hand grip to his new friend, shouldered it up and departed.

Hastings came at once from behind the bar.

"Now, I'd like a few words with you. In English," he added, laughing. "I'll be glad to give you lodging but suppose you explain yourself a little. It's not every day that an Irish Orangeman turns up here, speaking French like a native."

O'Hara laughed too. "It's no mystery," he said. "I was born in County Mayo, Ireland, but my father's in the Irish Brigade in France so I went to school there. That's about the way of it. Except that for years I've had a wish to come to America, and here I am!"

"Good enough," Hastings said. "Come along upstairs then,

and I'll show you the rooms. I've one at the front facing the
river, and one at the back over the garden. You can look at them
and take your pick."

"Sight unseen I'll choose the back one. I've been working in
Liverpool the past two years and I've had my fill of ships. The
garden will be a nice change."

"So be it, then," Hastings said.

He led the way into a passage and on up narrow stairs to a
larger hall at the top with rooms the length of it. He opened the
last door in the rear and O'Hara stepped inside with him. The
young man looked at the stout bed, the high dresser, and desk
with satisfaction, but when the shade was raised revealing the
garden below he could hardly restrain his delight. His mother,
however, had grounded him well in the Bible and the words of
the wise man ran at once through his mind:

*It is nought, it is nought, saith the buyer, but when he goeth his way
then he rejoiceth.*

So now he said, merely, "This room will do very well, I think."

Hastings had evidently expected more praise for he went on to
speak of the garden.

"It's Sam's work," he said, "and for its size I think it's a pretty
nice one. Of course now the *best* of the flowers are gone but there's
still a goodly showing for October. And the colouring of the trees!
That must be new to you?"

"It is. It's astonishing."

"Sam's my cook, too, and a good one, I may say, if you're
planning to have meals here. He was indentured to me for twenty
years but after he nursed me through smallpox I made him a free
man. So we keep bachelor's hall together. Well, I hope you'll be
comfortable."

"I'll be that," O'Hara answered. "Would you be knowing a
man named William Carson here in the city?"

"I do, indeed. He's one of our influential citizens and a rich
one. Are you connected with him?"

"I have a letter of introduction, that's all. I thought I'd go
to see him at once, towards the back end of the afternoon."

"Then you'll not be supping here, I doubt. Carson never
lets anyone leave his house hungry. It was that way as long as his
wife lived and it's still the same. You'll find he has a pretty little
daughter," Hastings finished with a smile.

O'Hara passed this over as though it was without interest.

"This trading business," he said. "From what the Frenchman told me it must be a good one."

"One of the best if you like to get mixed up with the Indians. For my part I prefer to keep as far away from them as possible. And keep my *hair*," he added with a chuckle.

They settled the lodging terms and then O'Hara, left to himself, gloated upon his new surroundings. He liked the small room with its substantial furniture and his spirits soared as he looked again at the garden. It was bordered by gold and scarlet trees, the like of which he had not seen before, and as Hastings had pointed out there were still blooming flowers between the edgings of box. *And in October*, he thought again, in amazement.

It was his nature to do promptly what was to be done, so, after Sam had brought him a can of hot water, he washed carefully at the small stand, arranged his clothes in the drawers and the press, then put on a fresh shirt and stock and a plum-coloured waistcoat, assured himself that he had the precious letter of introduction and, at four o'clock, planning to avoid family tea-time, he started out to wander a bit before going to the address on the envelope. Once out in the streets he marvelled again at the little city in which he found himself. It all had a look of fresh neatness. None of the heavy grime of centuries rested upon it. Sensitive as he was to a prevailing atmosphere, he felt a young, brisk confidence in the air. The people he passed confirmed this. He thought he might be stretching a point, yet the feeling persisted that a certain cheerfulness of spirit went with the general youth of the town.

He paused occasionally; once before a sturdy red Georgian building with 1724 on the gable and *Carpenter's Hall* below the date; once with interest at a place called *Rickett's Circus* on Chestnut Street; and at greater length at the market in the street of that name. Here in the open air under a colonnade were displayed geese, pheasants, rabbits, hams and small pigs hanging from their hooks while below were receptacles of fresh fish and baskets of every kind containing all the kindly fruits of the earth! It was a place that suggested good and bountiful living, and O'Hara savoured the scene with zest. Beyond, as he went along the street was a large flat-board wagon with two oxen in the shafts. A man suddenly fell into step beside him, carrying a heavy basket of hams and flitches from the market.

"Just loadin' up," he remarked. "Be leavin' at daybreak."

"Where are you going?" O'Hara asked.

"West," the other said, as though surprised at the question.

"You mean the *frontier*?"

"That's right, if the wheels stay on. I've been aimin' to do it this good spell."

"Any special place?" O'Hara pursued.

"Fort Pitt if we can make it. That's about the jumpin'-off spot in the west right now. I want to pick me up some spare land. Gettin' too crowded round here."

Impulsively O'Hara held out his hand.

"Good luck to you," he said. "I may head out that way myself."

"Stranger here, ain't you?"

"Just landed from the old country."

"Want to join up with us? Two wagons of us are goin' an' we got room for another able-bodied man. You look like you could hold your own in a tough spot. That is, if you had them fancy clothes off you."

O'Hara laughed and shook his head. "I thank you kindly but I'll be staying round here a while till I feel my way. But good luck to you again."

"We'll mebbe run into each other out there. My name's Silas Porter."

"Mine's James O'Hara."

The other waved and passed him with his basket. After a few steps he looked over his shoulder.

"Can you shoot straight?" he called.

"Pretty fair," the young man answered.

"You have to be better than that if you're goin' into the wilderness. Injuns an' rattlers don't give you a second chance." And with another friendly salute he reached his wagon.

O'Hara continued his saunter thoughtfully until five-fifteen, then he addressed his steps towards the Carson home. When he reached it he stopped, his heart beating faster. This was evidently an abode of wealth. The three-story building was brick, painted yellow. The wide steps led to a pillared entrance and the great brass knocker gleamed in the sun. He climbed to it slowly and struck it with a hand that hesitated in spite of him. He wondered about his welcome in a house like this.

A manservant opened the door. "Yes?" he queried over a long nose.

"I've a letter to Mr. William Carson. Would he be at home?"

"I'll tell him. Will you come in and have a seat in the hall, sir?"

It was a wide hall with an Oriental rug filling it. A gold-hinged Chinese chest stood along one wall with a heavy mirror above it. In its reflection O'Hara saw an oil painting of a beautiful woman and a child over his head. His eyes were still fixed on the portrait when the servant returned.

"He'll see you in the library, sir. Just come this way."

The man who rose to greet him had the big frame, rugged features and ruddy cheeks of a Scot. His eyes were keen but they had a fine twinkle.

"Come away in," he said heartily. "You wished to see me?"

"I'm James O'Hara, sir, just landed to-day from the other side. I have a letter to you from my employer in Liverpool—John McNeil."

"Ah, I'll give you a double welcome then. McNeil and I were boys together in Scotland and we've always kept track of each other. Sit you down while I see what he has to say."

He pointed to one of the fireside chairs and reached for the letter. When he had finished it he looked pleased.

"Well," he began, "in all the years I've known McNeil the greatest praise he's ever given anybody or anything was that it *was not too bad.* He's gone a little further with you so I know he must feel pretty strongly. He says your main interest is in some form of business."

"That's right, sir."

"I'm a business-man myself, forty years a merchant, so I know the field a little. Suppose, though, before we talk about positions and such, you tell me about yourself. McNeil says nothing about you except your qualifications. The name O'Hara hardly sounds *Scotch.*"

They both laughed. "I'm as Irish as Paddy's pig, sir," O'Hara began, "as far as my blood goes. The family's lived in County Mayo for generations and I was born there, around Tyrawley. But my grandfather Felix got sick of the Irish troubles and went into the French service. He was a major in Dillon's regiment of the Irish Brigade, and my own father John was born in France and went into the Brigade too, when he was old enough, so he's always had one foot there and the other in Ireland where he married my mother. It sounds a bit mixed up, I fear, sir."

"But very interesting. Go on."

"I lived in Ireland with my mother when she was there and with relatives when she was with my father, till I was twelve, then he wanted me to come to France to go to school so I went to the college of St. Sulpice till I was eighteen—and you know the rest."

"St. Sulpice, eh? You started out then for the priesthood?"

"Oh, not at all. The college is divided. It has a secular, classical course, too. Besides, I'm *North* Ireland."

"Theologically as well as geographically?"

"I guess you can put it that way."

"Good! Then for two years you've been in Liverpool in McNeil's shipbroker's office and now you're going to have a try at America."

"I've had an urge to come this long while, and I like the feel of it even after a day."

"I was just twenty when I came over myself, and I've never regretted it. And as to Philadelphia, it's the finest place you could settle. That's your intention, I take it? I can help you here, you know."

O'Hara moved in his chair a shade uneasily.

"That's good of you, sir, but I'm not rightly decided. You see it hasn't been my idea just to exchange one city for another. I'd like to get into the *new* country, the wilderness, the frontier, whatever you'd be calling it. It sounds presumptuous but I'd like to help build a *new* city instead of settling down in one that's already built."

"In other words you want adventure."

"Well, I'm young, sir."

"True enough. And there's this, I must admit. If no young men were willing to head for the frontier the country would be at a pretty standstill. But yet . . ."

He was interrupted by a clear young voice.

"Fa—*ther!*"

"That'll be my daughter, Mary," he said. "She's only thirteen but she's had to be mistress of the house since her mother died. *In the library,*" he called back.

In a second a girl appeared in the doorway, and seeing the stranger, hesitated there for a moment.

"Mary, this is young Mr. O'Hara, fresh over to-day from the old country."

She came nearer and made a graceful curtsy, as O'Hara rose and bowed.

"Your servant, ma'am," he said smiling, being pleased to use the words he would have employed towards an older woman.

When she looked up, smiling in her turn, O'Hara felt a rush of hot blood to his head. She could have been sixteen at least. The young breasts showed delicately full beneath the tight bodice. Her manner was poised and her face . . . O'Hara, growing up in France, was not without knowledge of women; however, it had all been to him purely physical and superficial. He had never before been emotionally moved in the way he was at this moment. For this girl—this child—had a beauty that arrested him. Her long lashes were dark over eyes blue as Irish flax; her features were as purely cut as a cameo; and the curls tied up on her head were auburn bright.

"Sit down both of you," Mr. Carson was saying in a voice a shade less hearty than before. His eyes were fixed quizzically upon the young man but the kindness of his expression did not change.

"Mr. O'Hara here," he said, addressing Mary, "has been working in Liverpool two years for my old friend John McNeil, who sent a letter by him. Now he's going to be a business-man when he decides where to settle, though already . . ."

"Oh, Mr. O'Hara," Mary exclaimed, her face lighting up, "you couldn't find a place in the country as delightful as Philadelphia! Isn't that so, Father? Have you told him how wonderful it is?"

"I believe he fancies the frontier."

Mary gave a little shudder. "Oh, surely not." Her eyes dwelt upon his elegant plum-satin waistcoat. "I can't picture you fighting Indians. And besides, if it's business you're interested in, there's no place better than right here with Father to help you get started."

She paused a moment and then, "I do love my city," she added.

"That is plain to see," O'Hara answered, "and I have a strong feeling of admiration for it even in this one afternoon. Of course I'll make no decisions to go west until I've learned all the possibilities here if your father . . ." he smiled and bowed to Mary ". . . and perhaps you, too, will teach me more about it."

"It's a bargain then," Mary cried. "Father can take you round the merchant houses and I'll show you the gardens—too bad it's so late—and make you acquainted with society. For we have that too, haven't we, Father?"

Mr. Carson's face had a touch of pride. "We do, indeed. Many people fresh over are surprised to discover that our men know how to dine and our ladies to dance even in the Colonies. And speaking of dining, you'll do us the honour to sup with us this evening?"

"The honour will be mine, sir, and thank you."

Mary rose quickly. "I'll run and tell Isaac to lay an extra place, while you go on, Father, telling him why he should stay here."

O'Hara's eyes watched her go, but as he turned he tried to keep his expression casual.

"Did I understand you rightly that your daughter is only *thirteen?*"

"That's true, though I know she seems older. Of course all our girls here grow up early, but Mary has matured incredibly since her mother's death. I need not add," he said, looking keenly at the young man before him, "that she is my chief treasure and I guard her accordingly."

O'Hara's face coloured slightly. "She is worth guarding, sir," he replied simply.

"But now," Mr. Carson went on, "I'll try to put in a nutshell why our city at the present at least is the most important one in the Colonies. First, there's our port. You've seen that for yourself. Then we've got a sort of strategic inland position. We've got iron and anthracite coal all around us for manufacturing. And maybe as important a factor as anything else in our growth has been our *tolerance.*"

"I beg your pardon?" O'Hara questioned.

"That's right. I said tolerance. William Penn started it and the plain fact is, to put it on the lowest level, it's been *profitable.* The Quakers have a mystic streak in them but they're damned good business-men and when other towns in other colonies ran them out, they came here and a lot more so-called heretics besides. And they all brought their skills with them. It's been good for the city. Well, as I can, I'll show you round."

The supper which followed soon was dazzling to O'Hara. The dining-room furniture was more elegant than any he had ever seen even in the home of his elderly cousin, Lady O'Hara in Tyrawley; the crystal chandelier with its dozens of lighted candles threw wine-coloured pools on the dark mahogany table; the silver gleamed. At the end of the table opposite her father, sat the girl Mary, now in rose brocade.

"Mr. O'Hara was educated in Paris," Mr. Carson said as Isaac passed the platter of fried chicken.

Mary gave a cry of delight. "*Paris!*" she echoed. "Oh, I want to go there even more than to London. Please tell me what it's like. Were you fond of it?"

"Yes, quite. I lived there for six years. But to describe it—that's a bit hard. You will have heard or read anything I could tell you, I'm sure."

At her look of disappointment he was apologetic.

"I was in school, you see, and pretty young. I don't believe I was very conscious of what you might call the historic beauty of the city. We had to work hard and when we had holidays we usually . . ."

"Yes?" Mary prompted.

"Well, we usually made for the *Bois*, you know, that's the great park, to get out of the city. It's a pleasant spot." He suddenly laughed, showing a row of strong white teeth. "One thing we often did there when the weather was fine was to take a row-boat across the lake to a cheap little café on the other side. The tables were set close to the water and the ducks used to come right up to our feet to be fed. We had names for them and bets on which one would be the quickest and get the most food. . . ."

He stopped, embarrassed. "You ask me to describe *Paris* and I tell you about feeding ducks! I am sorry."

"But I liked that," Mary said.

"More real, I should say, than if you had described Notre Dame's 'storied windows richly dight,' " Mr. Carson added.

"That's Milton," Mary put in. "Father's always quoting him."

"Well," Mr. Carson defended himself, "I'm a business-man but I do a bit of reading too, and I've always maintained that if a man knows Milton and Scott he can hold his own."

Before O'Hara could answer Mary broke in excitedly. "How stupid of me not to think of it before! You must speak French, then," she said to him.

"Well, naturally. I . . . I mean I had to."

"Why, Father, I must introduce him to Mary Vining and they can talk together! She speaks the most perfect French, everyone says, and she's so beautiful and witty. She lives in Delaware but she spends a great deal of time here. And she's coming up in two weeks for Anne Bingham's ball!"

The girl's eyes suddenly shone, as she gave an exclamation of delight. "Oh, here is the most wonderful idea! You see, Mr. O'Hara, I'm not really as old as I look." She paused innocently, as though to let the great confession sink in. "So while I've *known* all the older girls all my life, like Peggy Shippen and Peggy Chew and Mary Vining and Anne Bingham, Father hasn't thought it seemly for me to go to the balls before. Until this one. My very first. And now, since I want you to see our society anyway, and since Father was going to take me and call for me himself, if . . . *if you could escort me* . . ."

She blushed a rosy red as she looked pleadingly from one to the other. O'Hara's reply was immediate. "I would be greatly honoured, ma'am!"

Mr. Carson's face was sober as he watched the young people for a moment.

"With your permission, sir, of course," O'Hara added quickly.

"I think we will accept your offer, Mr. O'Hara," he said, "though I must remind my daughter that it is the gentleman who asks the privilege of escorting a lady."

Mary laughed as though she knew her father's reproof was not too sharp-edged. "He thinks I'm bold," she said. "But I'm not really. I'll call upon Anne Bingham to-morrow and see about an extra invitation. She'll be very surprised that I'm going to have a real escort. And pleased for me, too. Oh, Mr. O'Hara, I think you must have come straight from heaven!"

"Perhaps I have just arrived there," he said gallantly. And then, carefully avoiding even a glance again at Mary he gave most respectful attention to Mr. Carson's conversation until dinner was ended.

As soon as he felt it was proper O'Hara made his adieux. It was settled that he would meet Mr. Carson at the latter's office the next afternoon and be shown something of the business life of the city.

"By the way, where are you stopping?" Carson asked.

"At the Crooked Billet."

"Good house. You'll be well looked after. As a matter of fact Ben Franklin stayed there once himself."

When O'Hara said good-bye to Mary, he made his best bow and kissed her hand. All at once the poised young lady vanished and the little girl appeared as she giggled delightedly.

"Oh, I like *that*. Did you see, Father? No one ever kissed my hand before!"

They parted at the library door but as old Isaac was showing him out O'Hara heard laughter and running footsteps behind him.

"Mr. O'Hara!" Mary was calling, "it's so funny for me not to think of it before, but *can you dance?*"

He laughed back at her. "All French schoolboys have to learn that," he said. "Your steps here may be a bit different but I'll be doing my best."

Back in his room, he prepared for bed quickly, standing for a moment naked, flexing his muscles. As a boxer would have said he "stripped well." The full strength of the limbs did not hint beneath his clothes. There was a clean vigour about his body with its white Irish skin which would have struck any athlete. In college he had managed exercise with some sparring bouts, and even during his time at the shipbroker's he had walked miles every day, after office hours. He came of a hardy breed and his bare frame showed it.

He put on his bedgown and with a sigh of comfortable young weariness settled himself to review his evening with satisfaction. He had expected help from Mr. Carson because of his letter of introduction, but he had received more than the promise of this; there had been added a warmth of friendship as well. As to the girl . . . He recalled now his first feeling at sight of her with a kind of sane superiority. Odd, that sudden rush of hot blood he had felt. It was her unusual beauty that had impressed him of course and he could continue to enjoy that even if she was only a child. Yes, a pretty, charming child who would be an entertaining companion and be also of the greatest use in acquainting him with the social side of the city. At twenty his pulse quickened at thought of a ball. While deep within him he knew he still craved the adventures of the wilderness it was only common sense to study all the possibilities of Philadelphia first. But before dropping off he suddenly thought of the man with the wagon. Fort Pitt, he had said, was the jumping-off place in the west. *Ah, I might be having a look at that one day myself*, he thought. Then he fell asleep to dream that a laughing voice behind him kept calling, "Can you dance?"

The next afternoon in Mr. Carson's office the latter outlined his plans. It was to take his young protégé to meet some of the most successful business-men of the city so that he could feel for himself the strong commercial pulse of Philadelphia.

"And we'll start, I think, with Robert Morris, one of our most ambitious young men. Only now in his late thirties. He was born in Liverpool but came over here when he was in his teens."

He stopped and eyed O'Hara keenly.

"Funny thing. The two of you don't look unlike when I come to think of it. Also Morris made his connection with the Willing counting-house when *he* was just twenty. You'll see he's done pretty well."

They went out through the warehouses which interested O'Hara more than the well-furnished office. But Mr. Carson did not stop to comment upon the great boxes and bales piled up on every side.

"I'll save my own business for the last," he said as he noted O'Hara's interested glances. "I'm starting you at the top as it were. This young Morris is amazing. When he was only twenty-one he helped found our stock exchange and he's been in the thick of money affairs ever since. You might fancy banking," he added.

"It's possible, that," O'Hara returned seriously.

"About to-morrow," Mr. Carson went on. "I have a busy day. Can you amuse yourself? I'll be able to take you around any time following that. And you must come in soon and have a dish of tea with us."

"I'll be fine," O'Hara said, "and thank you. You mustn't be making a burden of me and besides I'm wanting to have a good look about the town. As to tea, I'll be very pleased to come when it's convenient."

They entered the big counting house and passed between rows of clerks standing behind their tall desks until they reached Morris's office. Here the young men smiled at each other at once, for there *was* a certain resemblance between them. They had the same wide-set eyes, the same lengthy nose, the same generous mouth all in a long face. They got on well from the start, beginning with Liverpool and progressing to finance. Mr. Carson left them together and they talked for an hour.

"If you're really interested," Morris said at last, "I think I can offer you a job. It would be at the bottom, but the rising is good here for the worthy ones. You'll let me know?"

"I'll do that, and my deep thanks to you. It's been a pleasure to meet you."

"I have a feeling we'll hear of each other again, whether you take to 'counting or not," Morris said.

"The same thing occurred to me. Would you be knowing a trading store with a man named Clark at the head of it?"

Morris looked at him quizzically. "So?" he said. "A little interest in *Indian trading*?"

O'Hara coloured. "A bit, maybe."

"It leads you nowhere, you know."

"Wouldn't that depend on where you're heading for?"

Morris laughed. "You're a deep one," he said, "and I'd like to know you better. I can direct you to Clark's and keep me posted, will you, on what you decide?"

The big trading store was like nothing O'Hara could have imagined: a barnlike building with a rough plank floor and rows of heavy wooden tables ranging along two sides and part of the front upon which lay the bundles of furs. Across the back of the room was another long, wide counter, one end evidently reserved for accounting and the rest given over to a display of clothing, trinkets and geegaws. The smell of freshly dried skins lay heavy on the air mixed with a reek of tobacco and sweaty unwashed bodies. Several traders stood about waiting their turn to have their pelts weighed while two others were poring over the table of knick-knacks. O'Hara watched it all avidly. He listened as the skins were checked and appraised by the man at the front, Clark apparently. There was somehow in the atmosphere the breath of the untamed forest; there was an emanation of struggle and danger and conquest. He turned suddenly and went out into the street.

For two hours he walked and thought, unmindful of the passing scene. He was about to make a decision that would mould the rest of his life. The logical one of course would be to stay in Philadelphia. His whole bent was towards business in some form, and here he would have Mr. Carson's mature guidance. Here (he felt it!) he, too, might become successful even as Robert Morris already was. Moreover, a job had even now been offered him. Above and beyond all this there was a certain small new cry within his heart. If he stayed here he would be near the young Mary whose beauty had so strangely disarmed him. As time passed and she grew older. . . .

But there still moved upon him another compulsion, that irresistible impulse which had begun back in the old country as he had heard of the new world's slow progress westward through the wilderness. It was this, he now knew clearly, which had made him cross the sea. It was this urging, unformed then, almost unrecognised, which had brought him hither. Was he now to disregard it? Could it be, perhaps, his *destiny*? And if so would a strong man turn his back upon it?

At long last he raised his head which had been bent forward in deep concentration, squared his shoulders and headed back towards the Crooked Billet. While with wisdom he realised that such contacts as the one to-day with Robert Morris and with the other businessmen Mr. Carson was planning for him to meet could be valuable to him later in one way or another, he must not go on under false pretences.

At supper that night with Hastings and Sam in the back room of the Crooked Billet he confided to them his decision.

"Well, trading's the big business out at Fort Pitt, I hear. At least that's what Elliott tells me. He's in it up to his ears and making some money too."

"I'd like to meet him again," O'Hara said.

"Oh, he'll be around. Usually drops in of an evening for a pint. He can tell you what you want to know. Of course, I think you'd be smarter to stay right here in Philadelphia."

"How's your shootin'?" Sam asked abruptly as he got up to bring in the pudding.

"Pretty good at mark. My father's a soldier and he saw to that, but at moving objects I'm not so sure."

"We'll have to practise you up," Sam said. "There's lots of movin' critters in the wilderness, I've heard tell. You can try your luck out in the garden. I'll throw some *objects* up in the air for you an' you can aim at 'em. Eh, Mr. Hastings?"

"Good idea. Have you a rifle?"

"No, but I'll get one."

"Well, Sam will put you through your paces. He shoots as well as he does most things. And talk to Elliott. He thinks Fort Pitt out there has a chance to grow. Not much to it now, of course. I gather that's where you're really heading for?"

"That's right. I hardly know why, myself, but it is."

That evening O'Hara sat in the taproom, listening and observing. There was plenty of rough men's talk, but there was also serious discussion of the state of the Colonies, with reference to the Crown. Something like a deep growl of dissatisfaction could be heard beneath the words. Dark words, some of them.

It minds me of Mr. Bird on shipboard, O'Hara thought. *I must be writing to him, for I doubt I'll not be going to see him now.*

It was nearly ten when Elliott came in. Upon seeing O'Hara he came across to him at once.

"Well, well! My rescuer! Glad to see you again. How's the maggot bitin' you anyway?"

They talked till midnight. Elliott was delighted to pour out his information.

"A good town this, but after I've been here a week or so, I get a feelin' cramped. Now Fort Pitt. Not much of a place yet and it's had plenty troubles, God knows, but it's on the edge of things. Room to grow and grow she will if I'm any judge. There's a point of land it runs right down to where these two big rivers meet— the Allegheny and the Monongahela. That's where the fort is, sittin' right there like a tomcat eyein' two tabbies, kind of sure of itself in spite of everything. Pretty little grove of apple trees along one side called *The King's Orchard.* Anyway right now Indian tradin's the big business there and I'm glad you've decided to get into it. And if you'd like to join up with me on my next trip I'll be pleased to have you."

Before he left they had discussed practical details: clothes, horses, ammunition, the trade supplies. Elliott had also inquired about his marksmanship and approved Sam's plan.

"I'll give you a look-in while you're at it," he said. "Mebbe give you some hints. When a cat's ready to jump from a tree at you, you have to be damned quick on the trigger."

"*Cats?*" O'Hara echoed in surprise.

"Painters. Fancy name is panther but we say painters over here. Bad customers no matter what you call 'em. We don't run into too many, though," he added encouragingly. "Of course," and his tone was serious, "this whole trading business ain't child's play. Mebbe you ought to think it over twice."

"I'm prepared," O'Hara answered simply.

The next morning before O'Hara had left his room, Sam, grinning widely, delivered a note.

"Ole Isaac from Mr. Carson's brought it an' is waitin' outside for an answer. Smells good," he added.

O'Hara opened the small missive with a slightly quickened pulse. The writing was delicate as was the scent of lavender.

Dear Mr. O'Hara:

If the weather holds and the day be fine will you drive with me on the morrow afternoon at two to Bartram's Garden of Delight and return here for a dish of tea after. Father says he can continue escorting you around on the day following. Kindly send reply by Isaac.

Respectfully,
Mary Carson

This timing could not have suited him better, considering his recent decision. He could now impart it to Mr. Carson over the tea-table. As to the drive? He went to the tall desk at once where he had put paper and a quill when he came. Honoured Madam (he wrote, a small smile quirking his lips at the phrasing) I shall be most happy to present myself at your home to-morrow at two and thank you for your gracious invitation. (Signed) Your humble servant, James O'Hara.

The weather held. The next afternoon was pure gold, and warm. When he reached the Carson house he saw a low barouche drawn up before the door with a driver in the front seat; a few minutes later he himself was handing Mary into the back seat and settling himself beside her. If possible, he thought, she was prettier in the full sunlight than she had been at the candlelit table. She was dressed in a full-skirted pink dress with velvet laced bodice, a bewitching poke bonnet of the same colour, with a small dun-coloured cape thrown over her shoulders. Her eyes were bright and merry.

"The Garden of Delight is so beautiful!" she said. "Mr. Bartram started planting it long ago and now it's known even in Europe. When you've seen it, and attended the ball, you'll surely admire Philadelphia."

O'Hara said nothing, content to watch the changing light on her face and listen as she chatted on.

"It's four miles out along the Schuylkill and a pretty drive. Oh, I went to Anne Bingham's yesterday and she is pleased indeed that you will escort me to the ball. It's to be in their town house. And such a mansion! Just wait till you see it. Mr. Bingham's the big West Indian merchant and he married Anne when she was only sixteen."

"Would you fancy the thought of marrying young?" O'Hara found himself asking.

"I don't know," she said. "In two and a half years I'll be sixteen. But I'd have to love any man very much to leave my father."

Mary turned again to the subject of the Garden.

"Mr. Bartram has such a knack with all growing things. One curiosity you'll see is a big cypress tree that grew out of a riding whip!"

"Oh, come, come!" O'Hara laughed. "You needn't tell me stories like that!"

"But it's *true*," Mary said earnestly. "Mr. Bartram brought the whip home once years ago from Delaware and for an experiment he planted it. You'll see the tree."

When they reached the Bartram place Mary led the way at once around the stone house to the Garden. O'Hara had come with small interest in what he might see of plant life; his main desire had been to be with Mary again. Now, however, he drew in his breath with astonishment and even rapture. For here, edging winding walks and behind box borders seemed to his untrained eye what must be every variety of tree and shrub in the world. Before Mary could begin her descriptions an elderly man in wide trousers and a leather apron came up the walk that led from the river.

"Oh, here is Mr. Bartram himself," she said.

He smiled at her. "Well, Mary, thee can't keep away from the Garden. And who is thy friend?"

O'Hara took to the old man at once after the introductions, and the feeling seemed to be mutual for Bartram insisted upon leaving his work at cider making to become their guide. He took them first to his cider mill by the river which he had hewed out of stone himself. There they tasted the freshly-made juice, O'Hara for the first time. Then he showed them slowly through the Garden, speaking of the unusual summer flower varieties now dormant for the winter, then of the more famous trees: the riding-whip cypress, the Christ's Thorn, sent him from the Holy Land, the Ginkgo, the Ohio buck-eyes, the Kentucky coffee trees, the great yellow-wood with its eight-foot stem, and the oak beside the house.

"Thee may have heard of André Michaux, the French botanist?"

"Just the name," O'Hara answered.

"We are in correspondence and he says this must be known as *Bartram's Oak* because I raised it myself from an acorn," the old Quaker said with pride.

As they bade good-bye at last, O'Hara tried to speak his thanks.

"I have never seen such beauty, Mr. Bartram. I shall treasure this hour in my mind. Your Garden of Delight."

"We'll come again," Mary called brightly as the barouche moved off.

"And you've seen the Garden at its poorest," she said eagerly as they drove on. "Imagine the beds filled with flowers in bloom! And some of the trees and shrubs too! That big yellow-wood is covered with hanging creamy clusters in May! What a sight! We'll come out then."

"Mistress Carson," O'Hara said, "there is something I must tell you. I have already settled upon the frontier."

The brightness left her face. "Oh, no! You couldn't decide so soon! Before Father's shown you round as he plans. Surely you can't mean it!"

"I'm afraid I do. It's a strange thing working in me. Do you know the word *destiny*?"

"Of course," Mary said with spirit.

"It's like that. I felt it even before I came over. I wanted to get into the newest end of the country and grow up with it, sort of. Help to build it. I'd like to feel that some day . . ." he hesitated, but her eyes were so tender . . . "that some day my name might be remembered for that."

To his astonishment the eyes into which he was looking filled with tears.

"But I like you so," she said innocently. "Somehow I was sure you would stay. And it's dangerous out there. You may get killed by the Indians!"

"I'll try to see them first," he said gently. "You mustn't worry. And of course I will be back in Philadelphia from time to time. Only not to stay."

"You won't leave till *after the ball*?"

"No, I told this Mr. Elliott I'm going with, that I'd be waiting for that. I haven't all my preparations made yet anyway."

Mary drew a small breath of relief but was quiet the rest of the way back. She was still quiet as she poured the tea. Mr. Carson was genial, talkative and eager to hear the immediate news of the Garden trip. Then he brought the conversation around to the interview with Robert Morris.

"He was very kind. I liked him immensely and he offered me a job," O'Hara said in answer to the older man's question.

"Fine! I was going to introduce you to William Bingham next but if Morris will take you, then if I were you I would look no farther! Just my own advice. Of course, you . . ."

O'Hara's firm voice broke in. "Mr. Carson, I can't thank you enough for your kindness, but I feel I must follow my first impulse, attractive as this city is. I've met a man, an Indian trader, William Elliott by name. He is willing to take me with him on his next trip clear out to Fort Pitt. I have decided, rather quickly at the last, to go with him."

Mr. Carson took a long sip of tea before he answered. "Well,

well," he said at last, "I had a feeling this might be the way you would end but I was hoping to show you more of the advantages here before you made up your mind. Well, well, you're young and strong and eager to prove your mettle. I fear, though, I've been of no use to you."

"But you have," O'Hara said eagerly. "I came here a stranger in a strange land and you made me welcome and gave me friendship —you and Mistress Mary. I'll go my way with a stronger heart because of that!"

"I've heard of this Elliott. A pretty good man I gather with the Indians. That is, if anyone can be sure of dealings with them."

"Father!" Mary's cry was piteous. "*Don't* talk about Indians. I can't bear it. And Mr. O'Hara's not leaving till after the ball!"

"Oh, good! Then I'm still saved from a late night. You must drop in often between now and the time you set out. Can you stay to sup with us this evening?"

"I thank you but Mr. Hastings and Sam are expecting me, and I meet Elliott again to-night to go on with our planning."

He made his thanks and adieux and kissed Mary's hand.

"When I'm camping in the wilderness," he said to her, "I can be thinking of The Garden of Delight."

The next ten days were filled to the brim with activity. O'Hara rose early and put in an hour of marksmanship after breakfast with his new rifle. Another in the late afternoon was supervised by Elliott. It was hard work for both hand and eye but progress was steadily made. In the intervening hours the young man spent time in the trading store, studying the furs and gradually making his own purchases. The Indians, he was told, were always eager for shirts, leggings, beads, powder, wampum and tobacco, along with any knick-knacks that might attract the eye. He spent much time picking out the latter articles: a little mirror, a doll, a ribbon, a bauble on a chain . . . He slowly built up his own wardrobe, under direction, and last of all bought a horse which he named *Pitt*, a fine beast with a good pair of eyes and a strong if undistinguished pack-horse. He left his money reserves in the care of Robert Morris after telling him his decision.

On his visits to the Carsons' there was a new tone of intimacy due to his imminent leave-taking, just as at the Crooked Billet, Hastings and Sam all but belaboured him with kindness and advice. By the time the night of the Bingham ball rolled around the preparations were finished.

He dressed with the greatest care that night with Sam, grinning widely, assisting. After the wash, there was clean underclothing, then a rose satin waistcoat and black knee breeches he had brought with him. The silver knee-buckles had been an ancestral gift from his cousin, Lady Mary O'Hara on his eighteenth birthday. He had bought in Philadelphia a new and elegant lace stock and a dark woollen cape lined in white satin, a pair of dancing pumps and a white wig with a queue. Finally caparisoned, he knew even from the small mirror that in looks at least he could hold his own with the other male guests. Sam and Hastings, admiringly, let him out the house entrance so he would not need to thread his way through the tap-room customers.

Mr. Carson had offered his carriage which was waiting. Old Isaac, in a trembling pleasure, greeted O'Hara at the door and ushered him into the hall where Mr. Carson waited too, holding a red cloak.

"Well, very handsome, Mr. O'Hara! Mary has the notion of us being here when she comes down the stairway. Ah, here she is!"

They both caught their breath a little for Mary came slowly, her head maturely poised, every movement assured, all in purest white from powdered hair to satin slippers. She looked like a vision—or a bride. Only her face was aflame with excitement and colour. When she reached the hall she curtsied.

"How do I look, Father?"

"Very lovely, my dear," he said, forgetting his Scottish reserve of praise.

"And Mr. O'Hara?" She was smiling at him with eyes coquettish beyond her years.

O'Hara could not speak. So he bowed low, placed the cloak about her shoulders, and offered his arm.

"Well, have a fine time now," Mr. Carson said, as they moved towards the door. "Take good care of her, O'Hara, and come home in reasonable time. Don't stay till the end of the rout. It could go on till dawn, you know, and Mary's too young for that."

"I'll remember, sir. You need not worry."

In the carriage Mary was excitedly gay.

"It's wonderful, past believing," she said, "that I'm going to a ball at last and with an escort. I hated the thought of being left there by Father and maybe not having a partner for the dances. The older girls are all kind to me but they'll be busy dancing themselves and could easily forget me."

"Even then," O'Hara said, "I think you would have had your share of attention." He could feel her soft body against his shoulder and the hot blood rose again in him.

"You think so? Then you do feel I look . . . nice?"

"That is too small a word," he said. "Before the evening is over, I'll tell you how you look!"

The Bingham town mansion stood in a garden of three acres. As they turned in the drive the lights from the great house shone out over the wide portico and the tubs of orange trees and exotic plants which bordered it. Lackeys waited to help the guests alight and more footmen were in attendance at the front door, showing the ladies and gentlemen to their respective dressing-room. When O'Hara and Mary met again, divested of their cloaks, they were both flushed with youthful excitement.

"I told you it was elegant!" Mary whispered as they started up the wide marble stairway.

"But I never dreamed of anything like this," he returned.

The great ballroom and the drawing-rooms were on the second floor and already the music was rippling out like a banner. In the main drawing-room where Mr. and Mrs. Bingham were receiving their guests, O'Hara was conscious of the carpet beneath his feet, its pile inches deep, and his quick eye recognised the French wall-paper and the Italian frescoes! The luxury it all represented amazed him. This was not Paris nor an Irish lord's castle. This was *the Colonies*!

He bowed low over Mrs. Bingham's hand, noting her charm. He had seen her affectionate greeting to Mary and also the look of pride and devotion on her husband's face.

"He dotes upon her," Mary said as they passed on. "If I ever get married I want my husband to be just like that to me."

"That could easily happen, I should think," he answered.

The ballroom was a maze of handsomely dressed men and women. Mary looked about eagerly to recognise someone she knew.

"I didn't think there would be such a crowd," she said. "I wanted to introduce you to Mary Vining and some of the others."

"Don't worry," he said smiling, "I'm quite content. Isn't this a minuet that's starting?"

"Can you dance it?" she asked eagerly.

"I would like to try."

"It's not hard. My teacher told me to keep thinking, *coupé*, high step and balance, and then over again. You know about *coupé*?"

"Yes. I've practised it a little. Shall we find our places?"

Mary was grace itself and O'Hara did not do badly. The music rippled and tinkled from the harpsichords; the violins streamed out their delicate melody; and under the glittering chandeliers the dancers swayed and stepped, their powdered heads now and then all but touching, then retreating again in the rhythm of the movements. . . .

It was not till midnight that a pause was made for supper. O'Hara had caught sight of Robert Morris's tall form and Mary had spied several of her friends during the dancing, so as they made their way to the dining-room where the bountiful collation was spread, they found themselves in the midst of laughing groups. With the confusion of voices it was only possible for O'Hara to talk for a few minutes with Miss Vining but each found surprised pleasure in the *French* of the other. Mary kept bringing more of her friends into the circle until O'Hara had met the Misses Chew and Miss Peggy Shippen and their escorts. He noticed the interested looks of a number of the young men as they turned towards Mary and after supper a little rush of popularity seized upon her. He did his duty by several of the young ladies and then retired to an alcove to chat with Robert Morris. They both found their eyes straying frequently to the figure in white which stood out from the coloured satins and brocades about her.

"A new star in the firmament, I see," Morris said thoughtfully after a time. "Do you really mean that is the Carson girl? I thought she was but a child."

"She's thirteen but extremely mature."

"In a city of beautiful girls I would say the others must soon look to their laurels. So, you're ready for your journey?"

"Yes. We set forth the day after to-morrow. My thanks to you again, Mr. Morris. And now I must meet my young charge and have her safely home before it's too late. This is her first ball."

"Your role of guardian must be a pleasant one. And my good wishes to you again. You may have chosen well. Sometimes when the counting-house seems particularly close and musty, I long for a breath of the wilderness myself."

O'Hara waited at the edge of the dancing floor until Mary's partner brought her to him, leaving her with a lovelorn bow.

"I'm afraid we must go now," O'Hara said. "As it is, your father may not be pleased at the hour."

Mary's lips pouted for an instant and then she smiled. "I know. You promised. Oh, it's been the most *wonderful* evening, beyond anything I could have imagined. And I could have had plenty of partners, just as you said. But I liked you best. There's one thing I must show you before we leave. It will only take a minute." She drew him into the hall. "It's Anne's *Greenery*. Come this way."

They went to the end of the hall where Mary pushed a half opened glass door. Inside, the walls of the room were draped with vines, while feathery ferns rose from the floor on all sides! Mary stood against the green background, the pale light from the hall touching her whiteness.

"Isn't it pretty?" she asked.

Suddenly O'Hara moved close, took her in his arms and kissed her with all his strength. For a moment she seemed to melt, yielding, into his embrace. Then she drew back, her eyes wide and frightened.

"Mr. O'Hara! What made you do . . . such a strange thing?"

His face was crimson. "I'm ashamed," he said. "I hope you can forgive me. Please forget that it ever happened. We must go now and prepare to leave."

They spoke no more to each other as they made their adieux and descended the marble stairway. But once in the carriage Mary's voice quivered.

"I'm tired," she said. "All at once I'm *so tired*."

O'Hara put his arms about her gently and drew her close. Her head drooped against his shoulder. It had been the lovely young white line of her throat, like a dove's breast, he thought, that had overcome him.

"I'm so very sorry that I startled you back there," he said. "It was because you looked so beautiful and I . . . like you so much."

Mary raised her head. "It was that?"

"It was that. Will you forgive me?"

She settled again with a little sigh. "I wish you weren't going away."

"But I'll come back again. I promise you."

They found Mr. Carson in the hall in not too good a humour. "You call two o'clock a reasonable hour, Mr. O'Hara?"

"I apologise, sir, but supper was not served until midnight and after that several young men . . ."

B

"I believe I could have had partners till dawn, Father," Mary broke in. "I'll tell you all about it . . ."

"Not to-night," Mr. Carson said firmly. "Say good-bye to Mr. O'Hara and up to bed with you. I'll hear the news to-morrow."

O'Hara bowed over her hand and kissed it. "Thank you for the privilege of escorting you," he said.

"I had a most pleasant time," she answered primly and turned to the stairs. Neither had said good-bye. At the landing she stood for a long moment, looking back. Mr. Carson did not notice, but O'Hara did.

On the second morning after the ball O'Hara stood, dressed for the journey in deerskin leggings and jacket, looking around the small room that had come to seem like home. He had arranged with Hastings that he would keep it for the present, so now his fine clothes were in the chest and closet and certain small treasures like the silver knee-buckles were locked in the drawer of the desk. He was ready to go. Sam had carried his packs down to the tap-room where Elliott was waiting. The horse Pitt and his pack-horse were tied at the door. He was taking these few moments to be alone and think of his situation. He was setting forth upon new and probably perilous adventures; drawn to this way of life by an indescribable inner compulsion; within three weeks from the sunny day he had landed, he had made his decision; he had in that short period come in a measure to know this city, met some of its most important businessmen, danced at one of its most fashionable balls. And strangest of all, he had for the first time in his young life kissed a girl as a man and a lover.

"My God!" he spoke aloud, and in his tone there was only a reverent awe. "Things do move fast in this new country!"

Chapter Two

But in the shadowy and mysterious forest time did not pass so quickly. Elliott had chosen the southern route for his own reasons, without explaining that there were certain additional hazards along the way, the chief being the more impenetrable forest. So now, after the first two weeks they progressed slowly on the faint road, if road it could be called, occasionally hacking down fresh undergrowth which blurred the trail.

O'Hara, quick-witted, eager to learn, watched the trained woodsman constantly and began to master the secrets of his craft. Elliott conducted himself entirely by the subtle signs of nature: thickened bark on a tree, the direction and length of shadows, the course of the streams, the snapping of a twig or scud of leaves which might indicate game, the changes in the sky which foretold the weather, and every variation in the smoke's rise and drift from the fire. Dusk fell early upon the forest floor and then the two men hobbled their own and the two pack horses, chose a wide spreading tree, and settled for the night. They had had dry weather so far which made a fire no problem with plenty of brushwood about.

One thing had surprised and pleased O'Hara; that was his increasing fondness for the beast Pitt. It was a new experience to him to own an animal and he knew for the first time that peculiar intimacy that can obtain between a man and the horse he constantly rides. Pitt now responded to his voice, whinnied at his approach, and nuzzled against him as he stroked the soft, starred nose. As to Elliott he could not say his feeling for him was that of a developing affection as with Pitt, but at least there was a growing respect. Two men living together in the wilderness come to know the quality of each other even while they are still strangers. O'Hara soon knew that Elliott in spite of his picturesque profanity was a decent man. One night as they leaned against a tree, smoking their pipes by the fire, the subject of women came up.

"I was in love once," Elliott said, "but I fought it. I'd never bring a woman to the frontier."

Something inside O'Hara felt unaccountably like a stone.

"Why not?" he asked. "There must be women there."

"Not mine," said Elliott sharply. "I've seen too much." After a moment's pause he added, "The Injuns won't violate a woman but they'll scalp her or knock her baby's head against a tree in front of her. I've seen that and a lot more. The frontier's no place for women and a man's a damned selfish brute to bring one here."

"But they come, don't they?" O'Hara pursued anxiously.

"Oh, sure they come. Sure they do. God knows why, for no man's worth it, but women are made queer. Well, I guess I'll turn in. Which in this case means turn *over*," he said with a laugh and closed the conversation by drawing his blanket about him.

But as the nights passed Elliott became more and more willing to talk. O'Hara was especially eager to learn about two subjects: the Indians in general and Fort Pitt in particular.

"You know," he said one night, "I've never laid eyes on an Indian. If we run into some on our way as you say we're going to, I won't know whether they're the kind to shoot at or parley with."

"If we have any luck," Elliott reassured him, "the ones we meet will be anxious to trade as we are. The Delawares I know are friendly an' if we swing round through Western Virginia as I'd like to, the Cherokees and Catawbas there are pretty easy to deal with."

He paused for a long minute before he went on. "I've been in this business about ten years and I still don't know how to describe Injuns to you. They have a big grievance against the whites, sure. This was all their country. You can understand them for wantin' it back. But it's their treachery, an' their *cruelty* that's beyond belief. You'll find a regular settler won't even talk about it. He just shoots. 'Course once in a while you run into a good Injun. There's old Logan, the Mingo, an' Cornstalk, he's a Shawnee, an' White Eyes. He's a Delaware an' the best of the lot. I've met him and I'd trust him. But even if chiefs like them are friendly they can't keep a whole tribe in bounds. So the fightin' goes on and the whites keep on thinkin' the only good Injun's a dead one. An' damned if I blame them."

He eyed O'Hara as though he feared to frighten him with the whole truth and decided to lighten his touch.

"I saw a sight one day, 'pon my soul! Last time I was at Fort Pitt I went out to the Nine Mile Run on an errand an' I stopped in at a Colonel Proctor's. Well, sittin' there by the fireplace was an Injun big as life an' twice as stuck-up, an' handsome as the very devil if I must say it. He was all decked out in scarlet cloth with a hat thing trimmed with gold lace. Never saw such a get-up, leastways not on an Injun. Colonel Proctor says, nice an' polite, 'Guyasuta, this is Mr. Elliott, the trader.' He kinda bowed his head like a king on a throne, an' I mumbled something. He speaks English if he wants to, but he had an interpreter with him, fellah by the name of Simon Girty! An' I'd trust the Injun as quick as I would him, by the way. Never liked the cut of his jib, somehow. Eyes too sharp. You'll run into him sometime."

"Well, what else about this Guyasuta?" O'Hara asked eagerly.

"Oh, I haven't seen him since. The Colonel said he was off up New York way to see Sir William Johnson about some treaty or other. Guess that was why he was so fancy. This Sir William is up to the ears in Injun affairs. Has an Injun wife I hear. As to that, George Croghan, the King of the Traders, they call him, married a Mohawk! So, there you are! The whole Injun business is too big an' mixed up to explain all at once. There have been treaties an' treaties an' massacres an' massacres. Well, don't get scared. I've got along with them so far."

"This Guyasuta," O'Hara said, "I believe I'd like to be meeting him."

"Be like you will," Elliott answered, "if you set out to. He's the big chief of the Senecas an' he's around. Always tryin' to make a treaty with somebody or other, an' then stirrin' up bloody hell the next thing. The settlers hate his hide. I've heard though," he ended thoughtfully, "that if he ever takes a man for a friend, he sticks to him. But I wouldn't know about that."

At the end of their third week's travel, the monotony broke. They had been riding through a glory of falling colour which Elliott had explained to his woodland novice. Richest of all were the red oaks, while amongst them the beeches sent down showers like yellow arrowheads. Lower came the purple and rose leaves of the pokeberries, and here and there the spice bushes, yellow and fragrant as incense, with their own dark red berries which Elliott explained the Indians used to cure a fever.

"They work too," he added, "for I've tried them. Got sick once on the trail an' I believe they pulled me through."

The excitement came at the end of a cool day which now had

the sharp promise of frost in the air along with the faint hint of the last witch-hazel blooms. The sunset was beginning to die when Elliott, listening sharply, raised his hand and they both reined their horses. A moon had risen and spilled a pale light upon the trail and the encircling mountain ridges. Suddenly from a hillside came a loud bellowing. Elliott turned back beside O'Hara.

"I'll be damned if that ain't a bull moose after a mate. He's a bad-tempered brute at best but when he's ruttin' he's a devil on the loose. He's in a bad way now, the poor bugger. Late in the season for him, too. Listen to that!"

Not two hundred yards away there rose a long mooing call.

"That's the cow," Elliott said softly. "She's answerin' him."

Then he gripped O'Hara's arm and pointed in front of them. A large black bear crossed the trail some distance beyond them, apparently attracted by the lady moose's proximity and the thought of fresh meat. He moved noiselessly into a thicket below the riders, unaware of their presence, as the wind was blowing towards them. But it had served the cow-moose well also for her love-answers ceased and it was evident she had slipped away at the scent of danger. Elliott already had his rifle drawn and bade O'Hara do the same.

"There may be a fight here if the bull moose comes on. We'll just sit tight unless the wind changes."

The moose came on, lured by the answering love-call which had sounded so enticing and then died away. He reached the edge of the sparse thicket and saw the bear.

"That bear hasn't got a chance," O'Hara whispered, as he peered to see the huge bulk of the moose with its six or seven feet spread of antlers.

Elliott only moved his head and kept his rifle at the ready.

The bear, apparently angered at the loss of his prey and feeling himself invaded on his own ground, threw himself back upon his haunches and prepared to fight.

"It's the moose that doesn't know what he's up against," Elliott whispered back.

Even at their distance the two men could see the contest in the moon's white light. With a bellow of rage the moose reared on his hind legs and struck two driving blows with his sharp front hoofs. But just as he did so, the bear slid forward and parried them with his forearm, thowing the moose off balance. For a second he was on his knees but it was long enough. With a coughing roar the bear swung his left paw in one mighty blow to the neck of the moose just back of the cheek-bone. There was a snap and the great beast rolled over, and was still.

"That done it!" said Elliott, taking careful aim. His shot rang in the air and the bear, the victor, his triumph short-lived, reared for a moment and then fell.

O'Hara felt his heart turn over. "That was a mean thing to do," he said hotly. "After the fight that bear put up, I think you might have let him get away! Would he have attacked us?"

Elliott laughed. "I doubt it," he said, "if we'd minded our own business, but lad, we can't use *sentiment* in the wilderness an' we can use that bear-skin some cold night. The moose is the biggest piece of luck, though. There aren't too many of them around. Just a few straggle down from the north, and their skins are a prize. Stronger an' tougher than deer. Well, I'd better get to work."

He was off his horse, hobbling it and drawing his hunting knife from his belt in a matter of minutes.

"I'd rather do this job by daylight but by then Mother bear or some other animal might have come for a moose meal so I think I'll get on with the skinnin' now."

O'Hara followed him along the trail and finally into the thicket. There was for light an afterglow in the sky and the full moon rising. He felt upset and squeamish and the next half-hour increased his discomfort.

Elliott began with the bear, parting the thick pelage and with quick, deft strokes of the knife, cutting from the throat to the tail and then carefully down the inside of each leg to the foot.

"Tell you one thing about a bear," he said conversationally as he worked on, "clumsy gait he's got. But don't ever let that fool you. There's no man livin' can keep ahead of a bear on foot, and many a hunter's found that out to his sorrow. Say, O'Hara," he said later, "go back to my pack, will you, an' bring me that bag of salt. I can't cure these skins, of course, so we'll just have to trade 'em green."

He had begun upon the moose when O'Hara, consciously loitering, came back with the salt.

"Watch it!" Elliott said sharply as the other set the bag down casually. "My God, man, that stuff's more precious than gold in the Back Country. Tell you what. If anybody ever thinks of a cheaper way to get salt out there than by pack-horse over the mountains his fortune's made. Hate to use any of this for the skins but I have to. Come on, now. Get your knife out an' I'll give you a lesson."

O'Hara had to turn aside several times but he stuck it through. The two skins were finally spread out and Elliott, carefully, gingerly, took small handfuls of salt and rubbed the crystals into each raw hide. Then, after two slabs of the meat had been secured, the two men carried them and the pelts back to the trail and unhobbled the horses. Elliott had said they'd better ride on for perhaps an hour before they ate and settled for the night.

"There may be a lot of visitors to the thicket an' we might as well be out of the way. We'll throw the skins over the pack-horses."

So they moved on through the now quiet forest, leaving the scene of the struggle behind them. O'Hara kept swallowing frequently, still with an uneasy stomach. As he had watched the traders in the Philadelphia store handling the pelts he had smelled the wilderness upon them and vaguely sensed conquest, but it had not been acute knowledge. He had not then been an eyewitness to the fury of a lovesick moose, the courage and skill of a bear, and the death of them both.

Elliott was unusually cheerful. When an hour had passed he reined in a small clearing and soon set about making a fire and starting supper, while O'Hara attended to the horses. He was unusually tender with Pitt and felt some easement as the animal waited for his caresses and rubbed his nose against him. All in this evening the whole animal world had changed for O'Hara, and while Pitt was in the upper level, he was still of it. Would he himself, the young man thought, ever be able to skin a fresh kill as casually as had Elliott? Or should his own place have been in the counting-house after all? A little later, he began to feel more normal. They each had two thick strips of flitch with their johnny-cake to-night, and after some hot coffee and a pipe the dark world of the wilderness looked brighter.

It was when they were making their way up the first mountain that Elliott sniffed the air. "Snow to-night! I can always smell it. But if it ain't too deep we'll plout through all right. We ought to hit a half-face pretty soon. Huntin' camp," he explained. "I an' another fellah built it once."

The cold sharpened, the snow fell and the men woke chilled in the night to take turns mending the fire. Once O'Hara sneaked an extra stroud from his pack to throw over Pitt's back. In the morning it was a white world and heavy going. But Elliott had been right about the hunting camp; by sundown they reached it, thankfully.

"Look at that!" he said proudly as they drew up to it. "We did a damned good job if I do say it! Even our pile of leaves is still in there!"

O'Hara studied it with interest. A huge log formed the back with stakes set along the sides growing taller towards the front. Cross slabs made the roof, sloping to the back, and moss and bark filled the chinks. The whole front was open but deep inside was shelter. They brushed away the snow, and got a fire going with handfuls of leaves. Then between them they spread the moose skin carefully over the top.

"Now, my lad, we'll lay on the bear skin an' cosy is the word."

It was strange to O'Hara how true Elliott's optimism became. Their wet deer clothes dried out quickly by the fire, then moving back after their meal they found themselves surprisingly warm and comfortable.

"Now the way I figure it," Elliott said, "we've been goin' slow and steady from daylight till sunset, makin' I'd say about eight mile a day—three weeks, twenty-one days . . ." He took a dirty almanac from his inner pocket. "I'd say we'd get to Fort Pitt the middle of December at the latest. One thing I always think about crossin' these mountains. You're always goin' *down* on one side of them!"

All at once he grinned kindly at O'Hara. "You've been itchin' to get there an' mebbe when you see it you'll wish you were back in Philadelphia. Not much to look at in a way and yet—them two rivers aren't meetin' there for nothing. That's what this Colonel Washington thought when he was a young fellah. Lieutenant, he was then, from Virginia. He was sent up to meet the French along the Ohio and tell them to get the hell out. An old trader I know was with him then. He said this Washington rode down to The Point in what's Pittsburgh now, looked both ways an' said, 'This is the place for a fort.' So these Virginians begun it after he left. He didn't get anywhere with the French."

"So?" O'Hara prompted with interest.

"Well, the French got there, told the Virginians to go back where they come from and then finished the fort themselves an' called it Duquesne. The English kept tryin' to get it back but it wasn't till old Iron-gut Forbes took hold that they won. My hat's off to that one. Sick unto death all the time he was gettin' the road cut through for his army an' carried on a litter the last of the march, but he had the spirit! They said when he got in sight of the fort he yelled, 'I'll sleep there to-night or in hell!' An' by God, he did. I mean he took the fort and named it Pitt for the Prime Minister, an' that's the story."

"And there's been no more trouble after that?"

Elliott laughed heartily as he got up to rebuild the fire.

"Listen to him!" he said, returning to the bear skin. "My lad, when you've been out there a while you'll learn there's *always* trouble. When I got there for the first time ten years ago there was plenty. All the Injuns had got up on their hind legs an' were makin' war. Bad. There was a fellah commandin' the fort then, Captain Ecuyer, his name was. He took to Injun fightin' like a duck to water. He had every cabin in the town burnt so the Injuns couldn't hide in them an' then he brought every livin' soul into the fort. I just got in in the nick of time."

"I hadn't pictured it as so large," O'Hara said in surprise.

"Pretty good size. Of course it's been added to. Well, this Ecuyer organised everything. Every man an' woman had a job. Look-outs all the time, day an' night. Then he collected all the beaver traps and crowfeet ones too an' put them along the top of the one rampart that wasn't finished! Pretty smart for just an *army officer* to think of!"

Elliott smoked thoughtfully, remembering.

"He tried his best to keep things clean but we had some sickness. Couple of cases of smallpox. There's a kind of bridge between the fort and the stockade. He made a little hospital there under it. One day some Injuns came up under a white shirt flag to parley. What a pack of lies they had to tell! Said all the tribes were comin' at us an' it was just their friendship for the whites that made them come to warn us. They told Ecuyer to take all his people and get out of the fort as fast as he could and *get away* before they was all massacreed."

"What did he do?"

"Stood there cool as a cucumber and lied right back at 'em. Said we were just fine. Plenty ammunition, plenty to eat and he'd hold the fort against all the Injuns in the forest. Said three armies were right then on the way to us in three different directions, and they could get right back an' tell their chiefs that. Then he. . . ."

Elliott paused, and glanced at O'Hara before continuing.

"Then he did the damndest thing. He told them he'd like to give them a present to show his regards for them, and didn't he take two blankets off the smallpox beds and hand out to them! He just smiled an' told them to get the hell out but when he come back into the fort, he wasn't smiling. 'Hope it works fast,' he said."

O'Hara's face was aghast. "You don't mean that an English army officer did an unspeakable thing like that?"

"Don't get excited," Elliott said. "Mind Ecuyer had seen plenty. There had to be forays sent out, to cut spelt and get game an' so on. We was always covered but still every once in a while the copper skunks would sneak up an' we'd lose a man or two. An' what they did with them wasn't pretty. We'd find them afterwards. An' plenty other reports came in. Ecuyer hated the Injuns something bitter. 'I could watch every one of them roast in hell,' he said once. Well, I didn't mean to give you such a harangue. Things are pretty quiet right now, or were when I left. But that fort has had plenty blood spilled over it. I haven't told you the half."

"But the town? You say this Ecuyer burnt all the houses?"

"Oh, it's all built up again. That was nine—ten years ago. Log cabins ain't hard to raise. There's quite a little town there now. It's a lot nicer in the spring when the King's Orchard's in bloom. That's a bunch of apple trees down towards the fort. Women bring seeds over the mountains when they come an' make little gardens round their houses too. I always fancy a garden."

And that night for the first time O'Hara dreamed of Mary as she had driven with him out to John Bartram's in her pink dress and poke bonnet. He was telling her he must leave and he could see tears on her cheeks as she said, "But I like you so!"

Even in the cold morning the dream persisted in his breast like a warm and fragrant flower, so he spoke little to Elliott for fear the reality of words might dispel it. Elliott, noting his silence, was concerned.

"I oughtn't to have gabbed so much last night. I should have held my whisht. But what I told you's past an' gone. Mebbe things will be better from now on. Don't take it too serious."

"I was very much interested," O'Hara told him, but said no more.

There had been a high wind towards morning which had shaken most of the snow from the tree branches and drifted the

trail so their progress was slower than usual. It was in the afternoon
when O'Hara's tender dream had melted away, and he was riding
tensely, peering sharply about him as he had learned to do, that
he saw the danger ahead. On a heavy branch under which Elliott
must pass in a few seconds there crouched a great tawny beast,
ready to spring. There was no time to call out and the sound might
be fatal. O'Hara reined Pitt, raised his rifle and fired. The painter
fell in the snow so close to Elliott's horse that the animal vaulted
and reared in fright. Elliott was overcome with shock and
embarrassment.

"Damn my gizzard," he said, "how did I come to miss that!
You'd think I'd never been in the woods before! Which limb was
he on?"

O'Hara pointed it out. They were both off their horses now,
looking at the panther.

"Got him in the head, too," Elliott said admiringly, then he
held out his hand. "Thanks. You're a good man to travel with."

O'Hara looked with tremendous pride at the creature before
him. Because of his own quickness and skill he had saved Elliott's
life. The jaws of the painter were open and the great claws bared.
But over and above the ghastly threat of the animal's power was
its beauty! The huge cat lay there, its tawny pelage unblemished,
the delicacy of the soft yellow tinted hair within the ears, the grey
of the throat and the pale yellow below the neck, contrasting with
the darker *tenné* coat.

"Big one," Elliott was saying. "About eight foot from nose to
tail tip I'd guess. Well, here's a pelt we weren't expectin'. Would
you like to try your hand? You shot him. We can clear away a
little snow here an' let you get to work."

"You go ahead," O'Hara said. "I think I'll watch. I'm not
too sure of myself yet," he added, allowing his double meaning to
go unexplained.

As Elliott's sharp, quick knife stripped away the fur O'Hara
steeled himself to look on, his eyes still full of admiration for the
animal itself.

"This is the most beautiful creature I've ever seen," he said.

"Reckon it is," Elliott answered. "All of 'em are. But the
Injuns think they've got the devil in them. *Dark spirit*, they call it.
An' I'll tell you a funny thing about the meat. It's whiter than
chicken an' tastier than pork but most hunters an' settlers out here
won't eat it unless they're starvin'. It's crazy but I can't myself.

I s'pose the Injuns started it with all their devil talk. Well, do you mind if we don't make a supper of it?" he laughed.

"But what about the skin. Will no one want that either?"

"Oh, that's a different story. There's no rug prettier than a painter hide. You'll get a nice trade for this one an' it's all yours."

Before they slept that night Elliott spoke his thanks again. "Good man!" he repeated, "good man! I had my doubts about you but you're shapin' up all right."

And with this praise hugged to him, O'Hara felt his heart warm even though the wind blew cold.

In general, however, the weather favoured them by not growing any worse. By early December they were over the last mountain and Elliott had begun to talk about the Indian village at which they would eventually stop, and to explain that the furs most wanted were *beaver* skins. "For the dandies' hats, you know."

"If we get enough there," he decided, "to make the trip worth while, I think we'll head right into Pittsburgh and let Virginia go. Depends of course on how many traders have been there afore us but I've got along pretty well with this clan so they've mebbe saved me some. Wouldn't be surprised if you make out with them too. You've got a good grin when you use it. How about learnin' some of their lingo?"

"Fine," said O'Hara. "I've been thinking about that. I believe," he added modestly, "that I have an ear for languages."

"You may even get a little use out of your French. Some of the older Injuns picked it up when the Frenchies held the fort. Well, now, let's see."

Each evening thereafter, huddled under their blankets on the bear skin with the painter pelt over their knees and that of the moose stretched from a tree to two stakes above them, the lessons went on. Elliott was amazed.

"Damme' if you don't do pretty near as good now as I do!" he said one night. "They know some English but it tickles them when you can talk a little Injun." He raised his head and sniffed the air. "I don't like the smell of this," he said. "Snow again, as sure as a skunk has a stink. If I mind my bearings there's a settler's cabin about a day's jog ahead of us. I've passed it before but I never needed to stop. Looks like we might have to to-morrow."

"Would they take us in?"

Elliott laughed. "Law of the frontier," he said. "Every traveller welcome, 'specially in a storm. It's give an' take though.

They're lonely as the devil, most of these familes, an' a stranger's a gift from heaven. Gives 'em something different to think about."

"Have they—extra rooms?" O'Hara asked in surprise.

"My God, listen to him!" Elliott laughed again. "Were you expectin' *beds*? What you're damned glad to do is to lie down on the floor with your feet to the fire. Well, we can see what to-morrow brings."

It brought the worst weather they had had. The cold was bitter and the predicted snow came not as a soft drifting shower, as before, but as a biting drive of tiny particles with a hard wind behind them. It did not block the trail but it stung the face and blinded the eyes and was particularly distressing to the horses. As O'Hara felt Pitt lag beneath him he tried with every tone and caress to encourage him. For himself he felt worn out and utterly miserable. He could see Elliott peering anxiously through the sleety mist as the day wore on. Suddenly he gave a yell, as the first dusk seemed imminent.

"There it is! There's the cabin! You can see a light!"

O'Hara saw it too. Hardly a flame, but a dim something that was not darkness. They both urged the weary horses on to where a right-hand break between the trees led them to a clearing and a log dwelling. The men dismounted stiffly and Elliott pounded at the heavy door. They could hear voices within and then the sound of a wooden bolt being drawn back and the latch string pulled out. A heavy-set unshaven man still perhaps in his thirties opened the door enough to look cautiously out.

"Well, strangers," he said.

"Could you give us shelter for the night?" Elliott asked. "We're pretty well tuckered with the weather."

"Aye, it's bad. Come in. Come in."

"What about the horses?" O'Hara asked anxiously. "Would there be shelter for them too?"

"Aye, there's room in the shed. My stable's pretty small. Wait there."

He shut the door and came out again wearing a hunting coat and cap. "Round this way," he said, leading them past the cabin to where a small neat stable stood with a lean-to shed beside it.

"Just about room for my horse an' cow in there, but the shed here will keep the snow off your beasts," he said, beginning to move some rough farm implements to the side.

"Got feed?"

"Yes. Just about enough to last to Pittsburgh."

"I'm glad. Mine's runnin' kinda low. Well, come on into the house when you get them fixed up. Bad night an' no mistake!"

O'Hara blanketed Pitt, wiped his face, patted him and left him to eat his meal. The horses all seemed well and full enough of life now. Even the shed was certainly an improvement over the raw outdoors.

Once in the cabin O'Hara looked around him with interest. Though he was to see many more like it, this was his unforgettable first. One large room served for all needs. Above the big fireplace hung a rifle on elk's horns, while over the fire itself on the great crane a kettle of mush was boiling. Stirring it stood a youngish woman, thin except where the heaviness of her body proclaimed a soon to be born child. As the travellers, exchanging introductions, came up to the fire to warm themselves, the woman burst into tears.

"Now, now," her husband said irritably, "don't start that again! She's been bawlin' so much this last week we might 'a' been flooded out. Think shame of yourself now," he added to the woman.

"I'm sorry," she said, struggling for control. "It's just that I'm clean done out. An' when I think of what's ahead of me . . . the little one here," pointing to a baby on the mat, "she can't even walk yet an' . . ."

"Ach," her husband said harshly, "you'd think to hear you, you're the only woman ever raised a passle of young 'uns. Now let's get some mush an' no more of this bletherin'."

Elliott's voice rose, calmly casual. "Tell you what, ma'am, the way it is. When a man sets out to make him a place in the wilderness he has to chop down every tree himself, an' get the stumps out before he can plant him a little patch of corn. Then he has to build a cabin an' a stable with his own hands an' he feels done out pretty often. Yes, sir. Then he gets him a pretty little wife like you an' she raises him a family an' *she* gets done out. But before you know it these here children will be big enough to help you an' you can sit an' spin like a queen. So don't you worry, ma'am. Things'll go fine for you."

They ate, crowded on two rough benches at the hewn log table. The wooden noggins held the hot mush and there was milk to go with it.

"I never tasted anything so good in all my life, ma'am,"

O'Hara said to the woman. She had brightened a little and her smile showed what a pretty girl she had been.

"It's only mush," she said, "but we've got plenty, so just eat up."

There was a bed at either end of the cabin. The four older children from the seven-year boy to the two-year-old, were put into one, with a stroud and a couple of coats over them. The present baby was put into the other bed where the parents presumably would sleep on either side of it later. The four adults on the settle and a bench drew near the fire which the man, John Forsythe, had quickened with new logs.

"Well, O'Hara,' Elliott said, "this feels pretty good, eh?"

"It feels wonderful. I haven't been so comfortable since I left Philadelphia!"

The woman looked at him in wonder. It was frontier custom not to ask too many questions so this was her first knowledge of where they had come from.

"You've been to Philadelphia?" she asked.

"Yes, ma'am. I was there three weeks after I came from the old country. Do you know the city?"

"But I came from there," she said hardly above her breath. "Tell me how it looks now so I can picture it again."

O'Hara had been moved by the experience of the evening. He had borne the rigours of the weather; he had been a party to the tragedy of animal mortality; but, here was the human element of the wilderness and he was shaken by all the implications of what he had seen. He looked from the woman, her slight form braced against the hard settle, her arms encircling her unborn child, to the other two men, sitting silent as though waiting too. He made a quick decision.

"I'll tell you all about my three weeks there," he said smiling.

It was not for nothing that he had had an excellent classical education. His narrative flowed vividly; his descriptions were dramatic. He began at the wharf itself, then passed to the Crooked Billet with Hastings and the ever-grinning Sam, to his first meeting with Elliott, and then his dinner at the Carsons' with detail upon detail: the rugs, the paintings, the silver-laden dining-table. He told of the city streets as he had walked them; of the Garden of Delight and last of all, *of the ball*! Here he let himself go and, all at once in the rude log cabin in the forest there seemed to be the golden blaze from crystal chandeliers, the sheen of silk and brocades, and powdered heads that bowed and receded and then bowed again in the dance, while the wind moaning over the cockloft became the music of the violins. O'Hara described it all except Anne Bingham's *Greenery*. It and what happened there were for his heart alone. When he had finished no one spoke for a moment, but the woman's eyes shone and a faint colour had risen in her cheeks. Her husband's face was softened too.

"I can picture it all to myself now," she said. "Over and over I can think about it. Thank you, Mr. O'Hara."

"Got so interested I forgot to make up the fire," Forsythe said with gruff praise.

Elliott was profanely pleased. "I'll be damned," he said, "if this fellah doesn't keep surprisin' me all the time. Here he's come over three hundred miles with me an' let me do all the talkin' and now he breaks out, layin' it off like a preacher or a Philadelphia lawyer."

But it was the woman's eyes that gave O'Hara a glow in his heart. He and Elliott went out ostensibly to see to the horses while the couple got themselves to bed. Then they returned, bolted the door, drew in the latch string and settled with their blankets on the floor. But O'Hara lay awake for a long time watching the shadows on the wall, considering the drama he had witnessed. "This," he thought, "is the way a new country is settled. There has to be this hardship for the man, this bitter pain for the woman, this peril for them both and for their children." For the rifle across the elk's horns spoke eloquently of that. Elliott was snoring comfortably and at last O'Hara too fell asleep.

In the morning there was early noise and confusion as the children, tousled and none too clean, milled about the room. There was also a good smell of frying flitch with strips of cold mush sputtering in the fat.

"Now eat hearty," Forsythe told them. "We had pigs an' right now up in the cockloft we've got enough hams and flitches to run us into summer. So, don't hold back."

They ate the good hot food with zest and then said their thanks to their hosts. O'Hara had slipped out to the stable as soon as he woke and opened his pack. He had noted the children's uncombed hair and that of the woman, drawn tightly back in a braid but otherwise uncared for. Now, after the other two men had gone out, he drew forth from the folds of his hunting shirt a comb and a small mirror, and held them out to Mrs. Forsythe.

"Maybe you'd care for these," he said. "It's a small return for all you've done for us."

She took the comb first in a sort of wonder. "I haven't had a one for more than six months! The young 'uns broke my last one. Oh, I don't know anything I'd rather have. I can fix myself up a bit now, and them too. It does raise the spirits. Are you *sure* . . ." she began anxiously.

"Perfectly sure. And here's something else for you."

She took the small mirror into her hand and slowly, very slowly and with fear looked into it. The excitement had coloured her cheeks, her eyes were blue and her hair still brown, for youth had not completely left her. She lowered the mirror suddenly.

"I . . . I supposed likely I looked . . . worse," she faltered.

"Every nice-looking woman should have a looking-glass," O'Hara said lightly.

She followed him to the door, clasping her treasures.

"I'll make out now," she said. "I thought I was at the end of my string, but I'll make out now, thanks to you, sir."

"And thank you, ma'am, and good luck to all of you!"

He found Elliott discussing the Indians with Forsythe.

"Didn't want to ask you in front of the Missus. Had any trouble?"

"Been pretty quiet," the settler said. "Course you never know what they may be up to by spring. But as long as the snow lies we're safe enough. The nearest ones to us are a passle of Delawares. They've got a village along the banks of the Allegheny . . ."

"That's just where we're headin' for," Elliott said, "to do a little tradin'."

"Devil of it is we never know what might hit us. Well, we all just hope for the best an' keep goin'. Same as you, I guess."

The two travellers rode side by side from the cabin back to the trail.

"I've got my belly nice an' full an' my feet warm for once so I think I can hold out the rest of the way," Elliott said.

"Me, too," O'Hara agreed. Then he added, "Do you know when that woman has her baby she'll have six children *under seven years?* I asked her."

"Yep! He ought to sleep in the stable for a spell, that fellah. Well, you know my views on women out here."

"Will there be a doctor or . . . a midwife or anyone to help her when her time comes?"

"Hell, no. She'll get through or she won't. Chances are with this many she will. But sometimes . . ." He hesitated, then went on.

"Once I helped a man bury his wife. She'd died tryin' to have her seventh. I happened along. The ground was frozen and he needed an extra pair of hands. An' before we were done he asked me if I knew where he could find another woman. It made me sick to my stomach, sort of. I told him he could damned well find his own wives an' kill them off too. Course he was in a hard spot. I guess I shouldn't have said it. But him askin' me right at that time . . . Well, you gave that little body back there something to keep her cheered up. I felt like I was at that *ball* myself. Must have been quite a rout."

"It was that," O'Hara answered, and then they reached the road and rode on single file as before, the younger man's face serious and set.

It was a grey, cold afternoon with a sullen sunset reflected in the broad waters of the Allegheny when they reached the Delaware village. The track from the main trail was only roughly broken so they came slowly upon it, giving O'Hara a chance to study it as they approached. There were the clustered tepees as he had expected, with an ordered look of settlement about them. Smoke rose from the top of each with a welcoming suggestion of warmth and cooking. At each side of the dwellings were wide fields with what seemed to O'Hara tall black sticks emerging everywhere from the snow.

"What are the black poles for?" he asked Elliott as they drew rein together.

He laughed. "Don't you know corn stalks, man, when you see them? Oh, I forgot you don't raise corn in the old country. You see the settlers cut down the stalks for fodder but the Indians don't go in for horses so they just let them stand after they gather the ears."

He came closer to O'Hara. "I hardly need remind *you* about manners an' it sounds crazy but you get on better with these sons of bitches if you're polite to them."

"I'll remember," O'Hara said smiling. "What do we do now?"

"We wait. They'll have seen us from the time we left the road, but it will be a while before someone comes out."

It seemed, indeed, to O'Hara a long time. Then with great deliberation an old man dressed in a deer-skin tunic came from a tepee and walked, unsmiling, towards them. Elliott dismounted at once and leading his horse went to meet the Indian. He bowed and spoke and the old man raised his hand in greeting and then looked inquiringly at O'Hara.

"Come on," Elliott encouraged him. "Try your French on him. He's Magataw, the chief here."

O'Hara approached the Indian, bowed deferentially and said, "*Bon soir, monsieur. Comment allez-vous?*"

"*Bien, bien,*" the man replied thickly at once and motioned them to come in.

It was supper time and only a few Indians were outside, but these all recognised Elliott and spoke in friendly fashion to him. Their guide led them to a tepee which he indicated was his own, bidding one of the young men see to the horses. He held the deerskin flap while they stooped and entered. O'Hara blinked hard in the smoke but soon saw an elderly squaw in a heavily-beaded tunic stirring a pot over the central fire, and another Indian man, tall and remarkably handsome, standing at the side.

"My God, that's Guyasuta!" Elliott said under his breath.

There were brief introductions and then they all sat down in a circle around the fire while the squaw dipped out the stew and handed them their portions. It was hot and filling but not tasty and O'Hara had difficulty getting his second helping down. Each time he raised his eyes he found those of Guyasuta fixed upon him. When the food was consumed the general silence was broken. In a mixture of English, Indian, and bits of French the strangers told of their journey and Elliott inquired about the trading prospects. Their host, now in high good humour after his meal, said they must all sleep first to make their brains sharp for the next day's bargaining. Guyasuta volunteered in a few words that he had just been to see the great Delaware chieftain, White Eyes, and was bringing friendship news to the Delaware brothers here from his own tribe, the Senecas.

"The hell he is," Elliott said softly out of one side of his mouth to O'Hara.

After the men had sat about smoking their pipes for some time, while the squaw finished her work and stretched out on one of the side beds made of boughs and skins, Elliott spoke of their packs and he and O'Hara went outside to fetch them. All was quiet around the village.

"This Guyasuta," O'Hara said, "what a remarkable-looking man!"

"You've got your wish about meeting him an' he seems to like you all right for he never takes his eyes off you. I don't know what the devil he's here for but he's usually up to no good. If he's making soft talk to the Delawares, he's got some scheme in mind, sure as shootin'. Well, our packs will be a little safer in with us."

"And . . . and you think we're safe in there ourselves?"

"Oh, sure, sure. They won't harm a man that's broken bread with them an' trusts their hospitality. Besides, they know me. I've never cheated them yet."

When they returned to the tepee Guyasuta and the chief were in earnest conversation which stopped abruptly. Their host pointed to the bed on the other side of the cabin from his own, indicating that Guyasuta preferred to sleep on the floor by the fire. When Elliott protested, there was only a signal of polite finality from the two Indians. It had therefore been arranged.

"It is wise," the chief said in his own tongue, which Elliott interpreted, "that we seek sleep early so that we may be prepared for the new day."

He went to his own side and lay down on the end of the bed, his feet touching those of his wife. There were plenty of blankets and pelts for all to place both under and over them, and cushions of deer hair for further comfort. In a few minutes all were settled, Guyasuta's great length beside the fire.

As in the Forsythes' cabin O'Hara could not go easily to sleep. The air was heavy for one thing, with the smoke, the odour of cooking and another new smell which he would learn later was peculiar to the Indians. He lay looking about him, his eyes picking up various features of the dwelling. He stared at the bark lining the tepee, placed with skill; at the weaving frame along with the cooking utensils; at the heavy bunches of dried herbs and grasses hanging from one of the poles; at the fireplace set in a depression in the centre and outlined with cobblestones. From this his eyes sought the man who lay beside it. Almost at once Guyasuta turned his head and looked at him. In this mutual gaze they were now for the first time alone, sharing some strange affinity. In an unconscious reaction O'Hara smiled. There was no change of expression on the Indian's face for a second, then he, too, smiled, raised his hand in a slight gesture and turned back to the fire.

"I believe I've got me a new friend," O'Hara thought with surprise as he fell asleep.

The next day began early, before O'Hara was properly awake. There was stir and noise now throughout the village and evidently excitement over the coming of the travellers. In the rough shed where the horses had been tied there were drying shelves around the sides. With the horses turned out there was room for the trading to begin. Elliott and O'Hara spread forth their wares, and one by one the Indians came with their pelts. O'Hara had made his own selection and now discovered it was good. Beads, vermilion, tobacco, neck ornaments for the women, combs, three more looking-glasses . . . He soon discovered these latter were the most valuable. He watched Elliott making his own trades and copied his technique.

"Beaver," Elliott would say firmly when presented with fox. "I have to have beaver!"

The Indians stared with greedy eyes at the bright array of trinkets, then slowly went back to their wigwams and returned with the beaver skins. Elliott accepted a few fox and lynx along with them but when the trading was over both men had a good bundle of the popular pelts.

At the very end, Elliott produced the moose skin and with a dignified speech of thanks, presented it solemnly to their host.

"We thank great Magataw for food, for beds, and always we will be his friends."

O'Hara's quick ear had already caught on to more of the Indian patois so he added a thank you and farewell of his own. There was an almost jovial leave-taking as the old man was apparently overcome with pleasure at his gift. Before the travellers left Elliott inquired about Guyasuta who had not been seen all morning.

"He leave before sun," Magataw explained.

With final reciprocal gestures of goodwill the travellers set off, their packs now built up high upon the pack horses.

"Well, that was a good haul," Elliott announced with satisfaction. "We'll just make a bee-line now right into Pittsburgh. I hated to part with that moose skin but it always pays to leave them thinking they got the best of it. Either of us will be welcome another time."

It was four o'clock on a cold, sunny day when they reached their journey's end. O'Hara, tensely excited, scanned the towering white hills that rose to the south and west, and then fixed his eyes upon the little town itself as they rode slowly through it. He had prepared himself for disappointment but he felt none. This was indeed the frontier, but there was evident everywhere the strong, determined business of living: the smoke from more than half a hundred chimneys, the men and women going about their errands from house to house along the snowy tracks, the fort and its imposing bastions, with the broad, rolling rivers half glimpsed at its feet; this town, he felt, was the habitation of people who had come to stay.

"We'll go first to the tavern," Elliott was saying, "an' get ourselves fixed up. Semple's. He's a good soul but his wife has a sharp tongue. Never see much of her, though. Sticks to the kitchen. He keeps a very good house, considering. Has to be for pretty often a big wig from Philadelphia or somewhere comes through on business. It's up here on the hill. Doesn't look too bad, does it?"

"It looks very good to me," O'Hara answered. And indeed it did. A large, spreading log structure on a slight eminence overlooked the rest of the town. There were plenty of stumps at the front with rings for tethering the horses, so the men tied up their beasts, unfastened their packs, stamped off the snow and entered by the heavy front door. The big room O'Hara saw did not have the polished look of the Crooked Billet taproom but it did have the same comfort: the great, blazing fire, the chairs and tables for the guests, a good smell of cooking food, and a well stocked bar at one side. A short stout man with red apple cheeks and longish white hair around a bald crown greeted them.

"Mr. Semple, this is James O'Hara fresh from Ireland, trying his hand at a little Indian tradin'. Can you put us up?"

"Aye, aye, aye. I've got rooms. From Ireland, you say?" turning to O'Hara.

"Originally. I've been two years working in Liverpool just before I came over."

"Well, well! I came from Scotland myself when I was a younker. You'll find the place here full of Scotch-Irish. Tough as hickory knots. Made for the frontier. Give them a psalm-book in one hand and a rifle in the other an' the devil himself couldn't beat them. So now, I'll wager you could do with a quick meal, couldn't you?"

"All we've had to-day is a bit of jerk for our breakfast. I got some from the Delawares back yonder. But we're hungry enough now to eat a live polecat!"

"Right. I'll tell Sally in the kitchen to set you up something. Would you like a wee drop to wet your thrapples first?"

The men drank the whisky neat, standing close to the fire, the warmth within and without slowly thawing their chilled bodies. Then they sat down to a hot dish of fowl and dumplings which Sally, broad, weathered and full of talk, ladled out to them. When she had left them, Elliott leaned over to his companion, and spoke in a low tone.

"I just thought of something. To-night if you'd like . . . I mean if you'd want . . . Oh, hell, you know what I mean. I can tell you the best place to go."

O'Hara coloured. "No, thanks, I believe not," he said.

"No offence. Just thought I'd mention it. Tell you what *I'm* going to do to-night. I'm going to toast myself, rump an' stump, in front of that fire an' 'wet my thrapple' as our friend Semple puts it, a good few times an' then go up to a *real bed* an' sleep till the last trump or thereabouts."

"I suppose they have quarters for the horses too?" O'Hara asked.

"Oh, sure. Semple has a big stable an' plenty of fodder an' feed. He has a boy here who attends to the beasts."

"I'll look in on Pitt," said O'Hara, "after I take a walk. I'd like to see the fort before dark."

"Well, look your fill to-night if you want to but you can see it all better to-morrow."

O'Hara's room was small and very chilly. There was a bed, however, with a big feather tick and decent sheets and it seemed to the young man fit for a king's palace. He opened one pack, hung up his few clothes on hooks along the wall, pushed the pelts into a corner, and then putting inside his shirt a quill pen and some paper, he went down again and out into the cold. It was the delicate hour of the winter's day when sunset drifts into twilight. The stars hung now purely shining for all lovers, above a gold and rose afterglow in the sky, and the moon-blue snow below. In the air was the faint sound of rolling waters.

O'Hara hurried down the little rise of ground, past log cabins with a poor light coming through their greased paper panes and on impetuously to The Point where he slowed up and looked intently about him. There on the side of the Allegheny with their tracery of bare branches stood the trees of what must be the King's Orchard; there was the main fort itself, plainly to be seen along the banks of the Monongahela. It had not been for naught that Elliott had drawn a rough diagram in the half-face cabin by the firelight. O'Hara knew his lesson well: left the Monongahela, right the Allegheny, while at their meeting stretched the broad waters of the Ohio, the *Beautiful River*, Elliott said the Indians called it.

He went nearer the fort. Pitt, named for the Prime Minister, fourteen years old this month, he had been told, strong looking, bastioned like a star with its look-outs and gun holes, could hold a guard of over two hundred men, Elliott said. There must be a good many there now for O'Hara could see lights and hear shouts, and suddenly a song! About four hundred yards away, he estimated, stood the older fort, Duquesne, finished and manned at last, as he had heard, by the English. Wooden palisades now surrounded it and between it and the other stood a small redoubt.

O'Hara felt a pricking of the skin as he looked at the scene. More even than in the settler's cabin in the forest he felt the mortal struggle, the spilt life-blood, and the stubborn courage by which this new country was being born. And now he, a stranger from hoary cities three thousand miles away, caught up mysteriously in the web of fate, was to be a part of it! He turned slowly about, his eyes on the little town lying for the moment at peace.

"I'm not sorry I came," he thought. "I don't believe I'll ever be sorry."

Once back in the tavern after assuring himself that his horse was comfortable, he spoke to Mr. Semple.

"Would you be having any ink I could either buy or borrow?"

"Aye, I've got a bit ink though not too many call for it. It's dear though. A wee bit bottle will cost you a shilling."

"I'll take one," said O'Hara. "Is there a post or a messenger going back to Philadelphia any time soon?"

"One in the morning. Give me your letter, laddie, and I'll see he gets it. That will be two shillings more. For the post."

O'Hara with his small container of ink went to one of the farthest tables. There were a number of men including Elliott in the tavern now eating or drinking but he felt entirely removed from them all as he spread out the paper, dipped his quill and sat in thought. Then in his best hand he wrote: *Mistress Mary Carson, Honoured Madame:*

When he had finished he read it all over, consideringly. He *had* to tell about shooting the painter, for when the skin was properly cured he intended to send it to her for a rug. The description of their night with the Indians would relieve her from the dread she had voiced concerning them. He had written more or less lightly about the visit at the settler's cabin. She would like the part about the comb and the looking-glass. It was his last sentence which he questioned. *During the nights on the journey when we had to endure the severe cold I thought of my hours with you and felt warmed in spite of the weather.* Was this too much to say? Should he rewrite the whole missive, leaving this out? He sat there, thinking.

Then suddenly with what was almost a gust of passion he signed himself, *Your most obedient and humble servant, James O'Hara,* folded the letter and sealed it.

Chapter Three

If the new world's sunshine in October had been startling to O'Hara, that which greeted him this December morning in Pittsburgh was much more so. The snow lay deeply upon the town, covering the roofs of the raw log cabins and warehouses with curving windrows and topping the sharp posts here and there with tufts like tow; the icicles hung glittering and unbroken from the eaves; the cold was intense, yet over it all the sun shone strongly, steadily benign. The young man, stepping out on the tavern porch for a moment before breakfast, liked the thought of this. A bright day had met him at Philadelphia, another welcomed him now to the frontier. With expectancy strong within him he went in again to the roaring fire and the smiling face of his host.

"Well," said Mr. Semple, "and how did you sleep, laddie?"

"Like a top. This is good air here."

"And plenty of it! We're about ten below zero this morning. Well, draw up to the table and get some breakfast under your belt. Elliott still asleep?"

"I guess so. I didn't disturb him."

"Aye. Best not. He don't like to be roused. Works hard and rests hard, that fellah."

He sat down opposite as Sally set a plate of bacon and eggs before O'Hara, smiling archly at him as she did so.

"Don't mind her," Semple said, when she had left. "She's forty if she's a day but she makes sheep's eyes at every man that comes in. Have you any definite plans for yourself now that you've got here?"

To his surprise O'Hara spoke confidently. "First of all," he said, "I'm interested in this fort. I'm astonished at its size. Last night I had only a twilight glimpse of it. Now I'd like to see it all. Then I want to get to know the proprietors of a trading store. Learn what I can about the business and as soon as possible, set out for myself."

"Good!" said Semple. "At least you know what you're after. And I s'pose Elliott's warned you it's no soft job, the trading?"

"Yes, but I'm prepared to face it."

"Aye. If a man wants eggs he must put up with the cackling. About the fort now. I watched it being built. Captain Harry Gordon, he was the engineer, stayed with me at my old place. Oh, it was a beautiful sight that fort when it was just finished. Aye, but it was! Ready for a garrison of a thousand men and officers. That was the day of its glory. Never been quite the same since."

"What happened? War?"

"Floods," he said. "The one in '62 was the worst. Even the oldest Injun couldn't remember one as bad. When these two rivers out here go into spate there's a watery rampage for sure. So, a good deal of the earth works were washed out and considerable damage done one way or another. But it's still a mighty fine strong spot anybody would find if he had a mind to tamper with it."

From the smaller room behind the main one there came the sound of loud voices rising to a pitch of anger. Mr. Semple drew a prodigious sigh as he rose from his chair.

"Trouble again," he said, "and it looks to me as if we're in for plenty more. Come along. I may need an extra fist."

O'Hara followed him curiously. At one side of a billiard table two men were arguing with violence.

"Why, you blasphemous, treasonous dog!" the one was yelling. "The King's the King! We're bound to support him! In the old country you'd hang for this kind of talk!"

"But we're not in the old country, I tell you. We've got one of our own and nearly tore our livers out to get it. And the King has no right to tax us to pay for his damned dirty war in Europe that we'd nothing to do with. I say to hell with the King and let's get on with our own business here."

"Nobody in my presence will say that, and me a loyal subject of the Crown!" the heavier of the two men shouted as he lunged out at the other's jaw.

It was a matter of seconds before the two were embroiled in deadly earnest. O'Hara, in spite of the seriousness of the fight he was watching, was filled with amusement at Semple's tactics.

"Gentlemen, gentlemen!" the latter cried, landing a skilful blow first at one man and then the other, "Gentlemen, I beg of you, *stop, desist*! "(Two more well aimed punches which found their mark.) "This is a peaceful house!" (*Right, left!*) "I will allow no fighting . . . Give the big fellow a good one, O'Hara," he said finally in an aside when it was evident the two fighters were growing winded. "I'll take care of this one."

O'Hara gave his best which was good indeed to the man indicated while Semple landed a *coup de grâce* on the other. After a few minutes the two men, dazed, bloody and groggy, regarded each other from the chairs where Semple managed to install them after he had got them up from the floor.

"Good, gentlemen!" he said. "Good! You were wise to stop. Now you've had it out, you can be friends. But just remember there must be no fighting in my tavern. Tell Sally to fetch a basin of cold water, son," he said in a low voice, following O'Hara to the door, "then you go and take a nice walk. I'll swab them up and give them a good dram of whisky and they'll never be clear that we were in on it at all. That's the only way to handle the thing though. If they're both knocked out soon, there's not likely to be trouble after. Thank ye, laddie!"

O'Hara did as he was bid and then walked out into the crisp bright air. Now in full day he could see the town clearly, and the great spreading pentagon which was the fort. Tremendous! Amazing! England must have expected a long and bitter fight with the French to have caused her to build such a bulwark here in the wilderness. And then her ancient enemy had fired their old stronghold at General Forbes's approach, as Elliott had told him, and in the light of its ruins marched away and never came back! Strange. But, O'Hara mused, governments had misjudged situations before and poured out money needlessly, and probably would again. He wished his father could see this masterpiece of defence, though. For floods or no floods, it still stood a supreme achievement for any country, let alone a backwoods colony, and he was determined to see it all as soon as possible. He could then write a full account back.

He walked to the edge of the great ditch where he had stood the night before, reasoning that in all likelihood someone would come along to cross the bridge into the fort enclosure and perhaps be willing to act as guide. In this plan as in everything, O'Hara felt a compulsion for prompt action. He waited for an hour and then his reward came. An officer, perhaps in his late thirties, with a height above his own, broad shoulders and a friendly countenance, came up to the bridge from the town. He nodded pleasantly and was starting across when O'Hara spoke.

"If you please, sir, would it be possible for me to go into the fort? I'm new here and I'm very much interested. My name's James O'Hara," he added, "a couple of months over from the old country."

The other reached his hand.

"Captain William Grant, at your service. We're not very busy here, just now, as you may have heard and I'll be glad to show you around. I'm pretty proud of the fort, some parts of it, especially," he smiled. "So take a good look from here and then we'll go inside."

"The man I travelled with coming from Philadelphia told me a bit of the history of it but I wasn't prepared for anything so large."

"Biggest the British have built anywhere on the frontier. Covers seventeen acres here at The Point. Of course that's including the out-works. Inside the ramparts it's about two. Well, now! You get a good view here of the Bastions and the walls between. These next the town as you can see are faced with brick, but the whole thing is what we call a *dirt* fort. Earth works are easier to keep up and the best protection you can get from gunfire."

The Captain paused to laugh.

"We've got one figure about that which always gets an argument from strangers. The dirt for this fort was dug out of this ditch you see before you, and it amounted to, X cubic yards! I've had plenty officers come out here and say it couldn't be done with picks, shovels and wheelbarrows. And I always say you're damned right it couldn't, only it *was* done. Well, let's go on in."

They crossed the bridge over the ditch and the drawbridge beyond.

"We still take this up at night," Grant explained. "We've had no trouble with the French this long time but the Indians, like the Biblical poor, are always with us. Blast their hides."

Inside the gate the Captain led the way to the centre of the open space from which he could point in all directions.

"You see," he said, "the simplest way to explain this to you is that we start here with a five-sided parade ground bordered by five rows of buildings which in turn are protected by the five high mounds of earth shaped like ramparts. These long buildings are the barracks for the officers and men. The little log one where we came in is the storehouse for flour, by the way. The brick house here to the right is the Commandant's home. Underground are storage supplies, casemates for powder, the guard house, and so on."

"My father's a soldier with the Irish Brigade in France and I'll be writing him of this. I wish he could see it."

"Be sure to note the brick pavements by the barracks," the Captain laughed. "They were my idea. Now, for the Bastions —they have different names but they're all alike so you need see only one. We'll go into the *Monongahela* to give you a good view of the rivers."

He led the way up a narrow ramped access which brought them out at the top of the defence. O'Hara drew a long breath and for a moment could not speak. He could feel the Captain's eyes on him.

"Quite a spot, eh?" the latter said.

At their feet rolled the deep, still waters of the Monongahela, white-spotted now with patches of ice. Across from it rose a steep sheer mountain of snow. To the right between low-lying banks rushed the swifter Allegheny, shaking off its ice as a dog sheds water, hastening on to its marriage with its neighbour river and the great consummation at The Point itself. Then on and on after their union flowed La Belle Rivière, the Ohio, on and on widely bending, sweeping into the far wilderness!

"I've never seen anything like this," O'Hara said at last. "And I've seen many rivers."

"There *isn't* anything else like it," the Captain agreed. "It's unique. And I often think that long after this fort is gone and forgotten there will be something else important here . . ."

"I was thinking that myself," O'Hara said quietly.

"At the tip of The Point itself is where the old Fort Duquesne stood. Right below us here you can see a small redoubt we built about eight years ago. A block house.[1] Good tight little structure with plenty of rifle holes. But if you look clear back over the fort, you'll see my special pride. The King's Gardens! Of course I can point out only the location now under the snow but the trees outline the walks and the thick block of them there along the Allegheny are the fruit trees—the King's Orchard."

"I spotted that last night from what Elliott told me."

"Of course the floods did a lot of hurt but we've come back

[1] This block house still stands.

pretty well these last years. We don't need so many vegetables now since the garrison's small, but I've seen the time we set out ten thousand cabbage plants! Our worst trouble after the floods and the Injuns have been the grasshoppers. They're a curse and no mistake. You know a gardener's always hoping for *next season*, and I can't wait. I want to plant more flowers this spring if the seeds come through. Well, I hope this has given you a little idea of the fort. Come again any time you like. There aren't many parades to see this weather. The men just hole up in their barracks."

"You've been more than kind and I thank you for your time and your courtesy. Captain Grant?"

"Yes."

"I'd like to ask you a question. Just before I came here this morning there was a fight at Semple's Tavern where I'm staying——"

Captain Grant interrupted with a chuckle. "Did Semple stop it in his usual fashion."

"He did."

"I watched him at it once. Funniest thing I ever saw. It always seems to work, though."

"It's the cause of this quarrel I wanted to ask you about. One man was for the King and the other was against him. Something about taxation. I heard a bit about this on shipboard. Is it serious?"

Captain Grant's face lengthened. "I'm damned if I know," he said. "We hoist the Union Jack every Sunday over this fort on the Flag Bastion. I'm a British officer," pointing to his uniform, "and I've never thought over the years that I could be anything else. But now . . ."

He paused and looked out over the river. "Two years ago a Colonel Washington was out here. Stayed at Semple's, by the way. He was interested in buying some land. He came to the fort and we had a long talk. He's a good man and a fine soldier. He's been round here different times when there was trouble. He was with Braddock when he was sent out to take Fort Duquesne from the French and then later with Forbes. This Braddock was an excellent general, by the way, but he didn't know anything more about Indian fighting than a rabbit, so his army was wiped out except for what this young Washington saved. The Indians were on the French side you see. When Forbes came out, he knew what he was doing.

But you've maybe heard all this. Well, Colonel Washington told me there's a lot of restlessness along the Atlantic coast—at Boston especially, over this taxation business. But he trusts it will calm down. Said he was going back to his place in Virginia and farm and hope for the best. *But* he added something that I've thought over pretty often since, for I admire the man. He said if it came to the pinch he'd certainly stand with the Colonies. So I don't know. Guess we'll all have to cross that bridge when we come to it. *If* we come."

As O'Hara turned to go, the Captain spoke again.

"The queer thing is that in spite of all the hardships and dangers the people *like this country*! Maybe they're just land hungry and there's plenty of it here, God knows. But no, I think it's more than that. Take me, now. When I was first sent over to America I fairly prayed to get back to England. Then little by little I began to feel at home. Even out here on the edge of the wilderness there's something in the air . . . something that makes you feel an inch or two higher than you are. And of course there's adventure and excitement. Odd thing, though, you know. Well, keep your ears open. You'll likely to hear more about all this, I imagine, rather than less."

As O'Hara walked back to the tavern, the sun was higher and the snow glistened. On the rough, rutted tracks through the town there was now plenty of activity: a rider who looked as though he might have crossed the mountains; a pair of hunters evidently setting forth for game; some straggling Indians in their beaded skins; a settler's wagon rattling over the bumps; and here and there a woman in full linsey skirt and shawl making her plodding way with a basket on her arm. He noted now particularly the squat warehouses along the Allegheny. These would likely be the trading stores. The cabins, comprising what Elliott last night had called the High Town, were more on the Monongahela side above the fort. To south and west towards the white hills, and on and on beyond them stretched the unclaimed wilderness.

All at once he felt shaken by a realisation of the country's immensity. He thought of the neat gardens, the farms, the estates even, which he had known in the old world. They now seemed, in memory, puny, niggardly, limited, *pent*, in contrast to the unimaginable vastness here. Even the rough settlement partook of the freedom of the wild. And a desire for ownership rose in him like a lust.

c

"I'll buy some land soon," he decided. Then with his quick smile he added aloud, "And I've an idea I'll keep on buying it!"

When he re-entered the tavern he saw a small crowd gathered before the fire where a man was talking in frightened tones.

"That's what my brother said it must have been. A mad wolf. He's down with pleurisy, my brother is, so I came here to get help. We just landed there about two mile back a few days ago, me an' my family. Come from Philadelphy. My brother says there's only one cure he knows of for me. It's one of *these pills*. He says he's heard there's a Doctor Marchand, a furriner, over on Sewickley Crick that has them. I got to get one. I *can't die* an' leave my family just when I've brought them out here. If someone would just ride there with me an' show me the way . . ."

The speaker turned his white face and saw O'Hara on the edge of the group. Recognition struck them both at once. O'Hara remembered him as the man storing his wagon at the market.

"It's you, then!" the stricken man exclaimed. "I'm Silas Porter an' I told you in Philadelphy we couldn't fail to meet out here. I'm glad to see a face I know even if I don't mind your name."

"O'Hara!"

"That's right. I'm in bad trouble. You mebbe heard. . . ."

A man spoke. "About this pill he talks about, Mr. Semple. Have you heard of it? Is it any good?"

Semple chose his words carefully. "We've all heard of it out here and I've known two men who took it and didn't . . . didn't get . . . I mean they got well. Far as I'm concerned if I was bit by a mad wolf I'd take anything I ever heard tell of, so I would. And they do say this pill has some power, some way."

"I'm nice and rested now so a ride won't hurt me, I guess, an' I know the way to Sewickley Crick. I'll go for your pill, Mr. Porter. You just show me the road to your brother's cabin so I'll know how to get back to it. Then you get right in there an' keep warm an' comfortable." It was Elliott who spoke.

There were tears in Porter's eyes.

"I can't ever thank you. You see I feel all right so far but they say the . . . the effects come on sudden after a few days. Would you be ready to start now?"

"Have a bite to eat first," Semple broke in. "That'll be my contribution. Sit you down, Mr. Porter, and you, Mr. Elliott. You can't set forth on an empty stomach."

"I think I'll be going with you," O'Hara said to Elliott quietly. Elliott was not a smiling man but he smiled now.

"Well, now, a little companionship along the way might be real nice. It isn't too far. About twenty miles or better, I'd judge. We'll strike out along the Monongahela till we hit the Yonghigheny and the Sewickley branches off it. You're sure you want to come?"

"Of course I'm sure," and this time O'Hara smiled.

They ate quickly, with Semple interrupting several gruesome tales of mad wolf bites and preventing other incipient ones by a steady flow of loud conversation about the weather, the chance of floods, the coming dance at the Commandant's house and the latest perfidy of the Indians.

When the men had finished eating Elliott and O'Hara went to their rooms to put extra clothing under their hunting shirts and breeches, collect their rifles and two blankets apiece. The stable boy brought round the horses, O'Hara making sure Pitt had been fed. Provisions for themselves and the beasts were fastened behind the saddles and the three set off with all the men in the tavern waving them good luck from the porch.

They allowed Porter to lead the three miles to his brother's cabin. As he dismounted there he thanked them again, his lip trembling.

"Did anyone get the wolf?" Elliott asked a little hesitantly.

"No, it got away. That's what's worryin' my brother. The boys have to go to the stable to feed the stock . . ."

"Can they shoot?"

"Aye, can they! Both of them."

"Good. Tell them not to go out without a rifle. And you keep yours handy and a hunting knife too. Well, don't worry now. We'll be back soon."

"You think the wolf might still be around?" O'Hara asked as they rode on.

"Could be. We'll keep our eyes skinned. I'll pick out the trail an' watch ahead. You keep looking round. And be ready. This is one of the worst things that can happen out here and to think that poor cuss ran into it almost as soon as he landed."

"Is it like a mad dog?"

"Only worse. No one knows why, but just once in a while a wolf goes mad. Then he seems to make straight for human habitation. Over on Chartier's Creek once there was one tried to jump right into a cabin. It don't happen often so everyone gets sort of careless. Out here you have to forget about lots of possibilities or you'd go crazy, I guess."

"But this pill. Do you believe in it?"

"Danged if I know. Some say it's not worth a swallow, but I met up with one man who swore he was cured by it. He was bit by a mad dog an' he never got rabies. So, that's why I had to make this trip. Give poor Porter there any chance there is. The doctors, what few we've got on the frontier, don't seem to know anything but bleedin' for a mad bite, an' that never helps. Well, we'll see."

Near sundown they ate from the food Sally had given them and fed the horses. The moon was bright and the Indian trail they were following beside the river recognisable from recent tracks.

"We'll keep on as long as we can," Elliott decided. "We can't get lost and the doctor's cabin, I've heard, is the first one on the crick. Thank God there's no wind."

The horses plouted patiently on through the snow, no sound above their movements except a soft flow of water and an occasional breaking twig in the frost. They stopped now and then for a few minutes during which O'Hara dismounted, patted Pitt's nose, stroked his flanks and rubbed his knee joints. It was, Elliott figured, about nine o'clock when they sighted the light of a cabin.

"This must be it," he said as he directed his horse towards it.

In response to a knock on the door a bearded, past middle-aged man holding a candle opened it a little way and peered out.

"Yes, what is it?" he inquired with a heavy accent.

Elliott told him briefly of their errand. He did not open the door farther.

"I'll get a mat for you to stand on," he said, "my wife is particular about her house. Wait."

In a few moments he was back, opened the door and spread a worn mat just inside. Elliott and O'Hara placed their snowy shoe packs carefully upon it.

"Now you say a mad wolf, yes? That makes the worst hydrophobia of all. I will get you the pill."

"You think it will cure him, Doctor?"

He nodded and then shook his head. "That is the answer. Yes—no. I got these from an old doctor in Switzerland. I bring them with me to this country. Not many times I have reason to give them. When I do mostly they help. Sometimes not. But there is nothing else I know to do for a mad bite. So I give the pill and hope to God. I get it for you."

It was a very large pill, brown in colour. The doctor wrapped it very carefully in a bit of linen cloth.

"Take care," he said to Elliott. "Where will you carry it for safety?"

"Next to my skin," he said, "and I'll tighten my belt you can be sure."

"There is one thing you must tell this man with all your strength. He must take no liquor, *none,* for two weeks. If he does the pill will not work. I cannot tell you why. I only know it is true. Will you start back at once mebbe?"

"Our horses are tired. We'll rest till near daylight if . . . if you . . ."

The doctor shook his head as they all three looked about the room. There were woven rugs on the floor, there were cushions on the settle; the table had been rubbed smooth, on the mantel was a pewter candelabra and a vase—this was not a settler's cabin.

"I . . . I have no place, I am sorry. My wife . . . but in the stable is a big pile of hay and in it is almost like feathers . . ."

"We have blankets and thank you very much. What is the fee for the pill?"

He glanced over his shoulder and then spoke low. "For this, one pound, *if the man gets well.* If not, there is no fee. That is fair, yes? A pound is not too much for a life. If not, nothing."

"You will trust us to bring you the money if the man gets over this?" Elliott asked wonderingly.

"My friend, when two men ride through this weather to help another, I'm sure they can be trusted."

They thanked him and went back into the night. The stable stood clear in the moonlight and in a few minutes they had the horses in the shed and they were burrowing into the hay.

"If I just don't roll over an' squash the damned pill," Elliott said as he touched it carefully through his shirts. "I'll sleep on my back to be sure. But if this Porter gets well he'll never have a pound to pay for it."

"I can manage it," said O'Hara.

"We can go halvers. You know that doctor fellow's scared to death of his wife. If I had one I'd be good to her but I can tell you I wouldn't let her boss me."

For answer strangely enough O'Hara laughed. "Oh, I guess

there could be women who would wind their husbands round their little fingers and the men would like it!"

"Speak for yourself," Elliott rejoined. "Ugh, it's cold! As between hay an' feathers I'll stick to the feathers. Punch me when you wake, will you? We ought to start off early as we can."

They reached the cabin of Porter's brother about two hours past noon the next day. A young boy answered their knock and motioned them to enter, but inside they stopped, transfixed. The whole family of perhaps a dozen people of all ages were kneeling upon the floor. Even the sick man in the bed lay with his hands clasped above him. A woman with a rather beautiful face, now fixed and white, spoke.

"We are at prayer . . ."

"Did you get the pill?" Porter broke in hoarsely.

Elliott drew it from his bosom, removed it from its wrappings and held it out to him.

"Careful with it! Swallow it right away."

"Hand me the whisky bottle, Abigail," Porter said taking the large pill nervously into his hand.

"No," Elliott ordered sharply. "You're not to touch a drop of liquor for two weeks or the pill won't work!"

"I'll be damned," came from the man on the bed, "the cure's worse than the disease!"

"He will take no liquor," the white-faced woman said quietly, bringing him a noggin of water. Then she resumed her position on the floor. "Will you both join us in prayer, gentlemen?"

O'Hara fell at once upon accustomed knees. Elliott stood for a moment and then awkwardly assumed the same position. Through the sudden silence the voice of the woman rose in an agony of supplication.

"O Lord God we come to Thee in our time of peril. Save Jonas, oh, spare him! Grant that the poison in his veins may be driven out. O Lord God, hear our prayer . . ."

O'Hara looked up. The woman's white face was raised as she went on, straining, beseeching, imploring, compelling the very heavens to bend to her need. At last, apparently at the limit of her strength, she opened her eyes and rose as if exhausted. The rest got up at once and the wife of the cabin set some food on the table before the strangers. Then with what cheerful heartiness they could muster Elliott and O'Hara said their good-byes.

"You'll be fine," Elliott said to Porter. "That pill will do the job. As to the wolf, if he hasn't come back again by now, don't worry. He's off to hell an' gone. And don't think this thing happens often. The folks here will tell you it don't."

O'Hara shook hands quietly with the man on the bed who reported he was feeling better every day.

Porter followed them to the door. "I can't ever thank you," he kept repeating, with tears in his eyes.

When the men were out on the trail again Elliott spoke.

"I never heard the beat of that! If Porter gets well I'll never know whether it was the prayer or the pill cured him! You'd have thought the Lord was right in the room the way that woman talked to Him. Do you take much stock in this prayin' business, O'Hara?"

"I've always been taught to," he said.

"I wouldn't know how to go about it, myself. 'Course once or twice when I've been in a pretty tight spot I guess I said *something* but I doubt if the Lord would pay much attention to a greenhorn. But that woman back yonder! She was on pretty close terms with the Almighty, I'd say."

They got back to the tavern in time for supper. Tired and cold they stood by the roaring fire and gave Semple the news. He had a bit for them also.

"The Indian agent got in just a little while ago—I mean McGill."

Elliott was surprised and pleased. "Now that's fine," he said. "I'd like O'Hara to meet him. I didn't think it was time for him to be round here again."

"It ain't but he says he got wind the Senecas have their backs up about something and he wants to talk to Girty about it before he goes out among them."

"What's an *Indian agent*?" O'Hara asked curiously as they climbed the stairs to their rooms.

"Just about what it sounds like. The Government appoints men to keep the peace between the Injuns and the whites. The big agent for all these parts is George Croghan. King of the Traders, they used to call him. But McGill is sort of assistant. Younger, you know. He's a good fellah but I think he's pretty sick of his job. He's a family man an' this business keeps him stravaigin' all over the wilderness about as bad as a trader. We'll have a talk with him."

As a matter of fact they all ate their supper together. McGill was a mild-mannered, stocky man with a pair of shrewd eyes. He seemed glad to see Elliott and eager for a chance to talk.

"I can see," Elliott said after the conversation had been general for some time and O'Hara had listened with interest and answered the stranger's questions, "I can see," Elliott repeated, looking at McGill, "that you've got something in your craw. Out with it, man!"

"I've got plenty," he said. "I'm about ready to give up the whole job. You can listen to this and tear your hair."

He drew an official-looking letter from his inner pocket.

"These are our latest instructions from the honourable members of the Assembly:

Resolved: That it be recommended to the inhabitants of the frontiers and to the officers at all the posts there to treat the Indians who behave peaceably and inoffensively, with kindness and civility and not to suffer them to be ill-used or insulted."

"Oh, my God!" Elliott groaned. "So you're to go to a man whose wife was scalped last year while she was out weeding her flax, and whose boy was captivated by them and say, 'Be kind to the Injun. He meant no harm.' "

McGill drew a long sigh and went on.

"The trouble is, as you very well know, that you can't tell how soon a *peaceable* Indian is going to put his tomahawk through your skull. But listen to this. This riled me even worse:

Employ for a reasonable salary a minister of the Gospel to reside among the Delawares and instruct them in the Christian religion.

Now that I will not do and Croghan agrees with me. And I'll tell you why. There was a young fellah just graduated from the New Jersey College at Princeton, a preacher. He was bound he was going to convert the Indians. It was his *mission*, he said. He went to a camp of them in the Kittochtinney Valley. A friend of mine is agent there and he told me about it . . ."

"How's your supper, gentlemen?" Semple broke in as he approached their table.

"Fine," the men chorused at once.

"You need to fill your bellies after your cold rides," he admonished as he passed on.

"Well, this young fellah I was speaking of preached to them and they listened like they believed every word. Sat like they were spellbound, drinking it in, he said. He'd studied up on their dialect and they all knew some English. And at the last he *baptised* them, every last one of them. Yes, sir. He came to report to my friend, just walking on air. 'I've been given souls for my hire,' he said. 'The Lord has used me as his instrument to save these poor savages from hell-fire and bring them into the kingdom.' He was beside himself with joy. And you know what those God-damned Injuns did two weeks after? Rose up and massacreed every white for miles around and the young preacher into the bargain!"

He took a long drink of whisky. "So, I'm not hiring any minister to go among the Delawares. If any one wants to go, his blood won't be on my head."

"You're right," Elliott said, "but what will you say to Congress?"

"Nothing. Those men sit back there safe and comfortable on their fat arses and they don't know any more about the real situation out here than a babe unborn. They *pity* the Indians. Well so do I in lots of ways. A good many settlers have taken their lands and not paid the Indians a cent nor has the Government. It's a shame and I've tried my best to remedy it. But the trouble is you can't *trust* an Injun. You pity him to-day and to-morrow he scalps you. I'm going to get out of the whole business by another year if I can."

Both men suddenly turned and looked at O'Hara. McGill seemed really concerned.

"You're new here and going out to trade. I shouldn't have talked like this in front of you. But this I'll say and Elliott here will bear me out. The traders are almost always safe. The Indians are glad to see them. They want the wares and if you're *honest* with them they'll do you no harm. That right, Elliott?"

"That's what I've found, like I told O'Hara. An' he's got a big thing in his favour. He can pick up their lingo like anything."

"Good! That's what they like. And you see, it's the settlers they attack mostly. Bitter about losing their lands, you know, and they don't discriminate much on who paid them and who didn't. And as to that, most of the settlers feel the land's as much theirs as anybody's. So it goes."

"What's up with the Senecas?" Elliott inquired.

"I'm not sure. That's what I want to talk to Girty about. Run into him since you got here?"

"No, an' I don't care if I never do."

"Why, what's bitin' you at Girty?"

"Oh, I dunno. He's got an Injun look to me. Mebbe he lived amongst them too long."

"Who's Girty?" O'Hara asked with interest.

"He's a chap that got captivated by the Senecas when he was just a shaver and he grew up with them. Then about eight years ago at the end of Pontiac's war he was released as a hostage."

"Yes, an' he tried to get back to the Injuns," Elliott put in.

"Well, he'd got used to living with them. He's helped me out as interpreter more than once these last years. He lives near Pittsburgh now. What about a game, gentlemen? I could do with a little diversion. Billiards or cards, eh?"

"Play billiards?" Elliott asked O'Hara.

"A little."

"Go ahead you two while I toast my toes. Sometimes I think I'm gettin' old. When you're done I'll give you a game of cards. No exercise for the legs in that."

O'Hara liked McGill. They played with about the same skill and were beaten cheerfully by the other two men who joined them. They stood then in the back room going on with their conversation before returning to Elliott.

"When do you start out?" asked McGill.

"I'm not sure. I've only just come and I must get to know a trading firm first." He smiled. "And Elliott tells me I have some school work to do!"

McGill laughed. "Oh, I know what that is. I had to learn it myself once so I could settle disputes.

1 Fall Buck	a Buck
2 Does	a Buck
4 Foxes	a Buck

and so on. You see I still know my trader's arithmetic. Well, best of luck to you, and don't take my harangue in there too much to heart. We're in different lines of Indian business, and you're in a very profitable one. Shall we settle for cards now if Elliott's ready?" As they neared the door he added thoughtfully, "The thing about the Indians is that they can neither be ignored nor wished away."

The next day O'Hara met the heads of the biggest trading firm in Pittsburgh: Simon & Campbell. Simon was tall and lean, Campbell, tall and stout, both Scotsmen. The big warehouse made the one in Philadelphia look small, but it had the same wild smell of pelts pervading it, and on the long tables at one side a bewildering variety of objects for the traders' use in their bartering. O'Hara moved slowly along, studying the assortment, for Elliott had left him after a word of introduction and at the moment both Simon and Campbell were busy. Here in great numbers were kettles, brooches, mirrors, ribbons, penknives, coat buttons, vermilion, crosses, jews'-harps and countless trinkets which he could not name. On one table clothing was piled: shirts, stockings, caps; on another strouds and blankets. This building in which he found himself was, he knew, the centre of an enormous industry which extended into the depths of the dark forests of the new world on the one hand and far across the sea to the old one on the other, where a beaver skin might make a rich and shiny hat for a young man of fashion. He had seen those beaver hats and admired them, without dreaming that one day he himself would be trading in strange and dangerous places to secure the skins to make them.

When the proprietors were free he went to speak with them. They sized him up with practised eyes and apparently were satisfied with what they saw.

"How soon do you want to set out?" Campbell asked.

"As soon as you think I'm ready," O'Hara smiled. "Mr. Elliott suggested I should wait till after Christmas."

"A good job too," Campbell went on. His face was round and suggestive of plenty of meat and drink. "We have a bit of old country good cheer at the season. The woods are full of wild turkeys and they make fine dinners. We have some singing through the street and the Commandant always has a dance in the fort Christmas Eve. You're young. You'd better have a bit pleasure before you tackle the forest, eh?"

"What I would like to do if I may is to come here every day for a little while to observe and listen. I might learn a good deal from other traders as they come and go."

"There's nothing to stop you," Simon said in his more serious voice. "Just keep from under foot and you can watch what goes on as much as you like. And meanwhile learn the *Buck* table. We've got an extra copy here, haven't we? We keep making them for our traders."

He dived among the papers on a desk behind the counter and produced a sheet, which he handed to O'Hara. "You study that till you know it by heart. You can't hesitate in front of an Indian or he'll get the best of you."

"Thank you very much," O'Hara said, "and I can assure you I'll learn it."

"Come in again whenever you want to," they called after him as he left.

Once in the tavern he sat down in a far corner and opened the paper on which he saw what McGill, the agent, had called the "Trader's Arithmetic." He read the careful, spidery writing slowly: It began:

1 Fall Buck[1]	a Buck
2 Does	a Buck
2 Spring Bucks	a Buck
1 Large Buck Beaver	a Buck
2 Doe Beavers	a Buck
6 Racoons	a Buck
4 Foxes	a Buck
2 Otters	a Buck
2 Summer Does	a Buck

With a fierce concentration O'Hara studied his lesson only to find at the end of an hour that he was not yet perfect. This was going to take practice. Below this list was an even longer and perhaps more important one for the trader, for it dealt with the price for trade goods:

1 stroud	4 Bucks
1 Blanket	4 Bucks
Brass Kittles	1-10 Bucks

He stopped a little dazed. This would demand quick thinking. It would take *sixteen foxes*, then, to buy a stroud or *eight otters* to buy a blanket. As to the kittles! A faint uneasiness swept over him which even the rigours of the wilderness had not produced. But he dismissed it. Other men had mastered this equivalence. Certainly he could also. But he decided with Christmas now only two weeks away he would wait until after that to set forth.

A few nights later, a dark, thick-set young man entered the tavern and sat down with a mug of ale opposite O'Hara who was waiting for Elliott. There was a certain magnetism about the stranger's eyes and a power, half friendly, half malevolent, about the large striking head which now raised suddenly.

"Stranger here?" he inquired.

"Yes."

[1] This is the origin of the American slang expression "a buck" as the equivalent of a dollar.

"My name's Girty."

"Mine's O'Hara."

"Irisher?"

"Yes."

"My father was an Irishman. A trader an' a devil for drink he was. He got killed by an Injun back at Paxtang . . . Oh, so here's McGill and our fine friend Elliott. He thinks he's better than God, that one. Elliott, I mean."

The two men had come from the back room, stopped to speak to Mr. Semple and then advanced towards the table. McGill's greeting was hearty.

"Well, Girty! I've been trying to get my sights on you. How are you?"

"Pretty fair. How's yourself? And Mr. Elliott?"

Elliott mumbled something and sat down next to O'Hara. McGill began at once on his business.

"I'm on my way out to the Senecas and I felt I'd like to see you first. Know how things are out there?"

"Oh, so—so. Guyasuta's got the wind up, I guess. An Indian I know was in town last week and he stopped to see me."

"What's wrong with Guyasuta?"

Girty shrugged. "Oh, same old story. He feels the whites have cheated them. So they have. He's off now to see Sir William Johnson up in New York State but he'll be back soon. You know the way *he* covers the ground. Then you'll have to do some smoothing down, I reckon."

"I only wish I knew how."

"Well, a little money, a few presents, a little soft talk . . . it all helps."

O'Hara leaned forward. "You know Guyasuta then?" he said to Girty.

"I ought to. I lived ten years with the Senecas."

"What is he like?"

"Why are *you* interested?"

O'Hara glanced at Elliott, but the latter spoke for himself.

"We stopped at the Delaware town as we were coming in. The old chief there has always been friendly to me so he kept us the night with him and Guyasuta was there too. O'Hara here took a fancy to him," he added with a short laugh.

"Guyasuta was *there*"? The words sprang from Girty automatically.

"Don't ask me why," Elliott rejoined.

Girty collected himself at once. "Oh, he gets together with them once in a while I guess. So you liked the Chief," he said to O'Hara. "There ain't many that do I can tell you."

"Well, I did," O'Hara maintained. "I felt I would like to know him better. He's got a strong face," he added.

Girty looked at the other young man with interest.

"I'll tell you one thing," he said. "If he likes you an' takes you for a friend he'll keep you for life. If he's your enemy it ain't so good for you. He never changes one way or the other."

"Does he speak English?"

"Fine!" Girty answered, "but he don't like to. Usually takes me along to the conferences to interpret. It looks big, an' besides he and I can chew things over in Injun without the rest knowin' what we say."

"Girty," McGill said, "could you come out along with me to the Senecas? I would appreciate it and of course I'll pay you. Your presence would be a big help. I think I'll have a talk with some of the half-chiefs before Guyasuta gets back. Maybe I can soften them up a bit. But I'd like to have you along. How about it?"

"Why, I guess mebbe I could go. I'm just doin' a little tradin'. Just when the maggot bites me. When do you want to start?"

"The sooner the better."

"Except that you can't be sure everything's settled until you've seen Guyasuta."

McGill considered. "Maybe you're right at that. How soon do you suppose he'll be back?"

"Oh, the way he goes, I'd say if you set out in a couple of weeks by the time you'd get to their town he'd likely be there too. He'll cut across like the crow flies."

"It wouldn't spite me to be keeping comfortable here at Semple's for a bit longer. And I can make the round of the Delawares while I wait. So maybe I'll do that. That would bring us till after Christmas. I can count on you, then, Girty?"

"Sure, I'll go. I won't take any sides, mind, but I'll interpret if you ever need any help. What are *you* plannin' to do, young feller?" he suddenly asked O'Hara.

"Trading, when I think I'm ready," he answered.

Girty laughed. "There'll soon be more traders than Injuns in the woods," he said. "'Course it's about the best you can do out here unless you take up land. Well, since I've wet my whistle I guess I'll be gettin' along. Good night, gentlemen."

During the next two weeks O'Hara went daily to the trading store and at night studied his "Trader's Arithmetic" until he was letter perfect. With Elliott to put him sharply through his paces, trying his best to entangle him, O'Hara became confidently expert. Meanwhile he was growing more and more familiar with the life of the town. He went back several times to see Captain Grant at the fort, young Pittsburgh's crown and reason for being, realising now that, paradoxically enough, it was because of the bristling cannon and rearing Bastions that a few gentler aspects of life were present in the stormy triangle. For, as Captain Grant told him, there *were* a few satin petticoats lifted above the mud and snow of the streets just as there was an occasional bright waistcoat or well-queued wig in the tavern. O'Hara himself had overheard two men one night over their bowl of rum argue as to the merits of Johnson or Hume; and travellers of consequence came and went.

For the most part, though, he saw this outpost of the Back Country for what it was: a dirty, dangerous, exciting mixture of muddy bordering waters and snowy streets, of ill-clad soldiers, rough traders, Indians and storekeepers; of express riders flinging wearily from their horses; of fighting wagoners; of messengers fraught with evil report or good; but most important, of a few steady stalwart pioneer citizens who had put their roots down firmly as they built their log cabins and in so doing had simply and unconsciously planted a city.

During his conversations with Captain Grant, as they stood on the Monongahela Bastion or sat in his small office in the barracks, more of the fort's history unfolded before him.

One day Grant slowly filled his pipe. "I guess you know the story of our siege here under Captain Ecuyer."

"Yes. Elliott told me that."

"Good man he was, Ecuyer, but there came a week when we knew we couldn't last much longer. Supplies were practically gone. Unless help came from the East soon . . ."

He paused until O'Hara prompted him.

"Well," he went on, "we were in despair. If we had to surrender it would be torture and death. Then, early one morning before daybreak . . . you know at that hour in the forest there is a great silence. We've no song birds west of the mountains. It's what you could call a 'breathless hush.' And that moment one of our sentries heard, faintly, away off, the sound of *drums*."

There was a catch in the Captain's throat as he went on. "If I live to be a hundred I won't forget that sound. Every man, woman and child in the fort were soon awake and listening, standing like statues. We all knew what it was. It was Colonel Bouquet drumming his way through the forest to our rescue."

"And he saved the fort?"

"Oh, yes. The Indians had heard the drums before we did, of course, with *their* ears. They got all the force they could muster and went out and met Bouquet about twenty miles east of here at Bushy Run. He had a strong little army. Two Scots regiments. The Black Watch for one. You know the fighters they are!"

"I do, indeed."

"Then he had a battalion of Royal Americans and about four hundred or more Rangers. Even so, it was a battle! But at the end the Indians broke and ran. A regular rout. You know what the Scotsmen said when they got here? What they minded more than the Injuns was the *heat*. It was fearsome that day and of course they'd never known anything like it in the old country. Well, there's a story for you. As a matter of fact the ground here's soaked with them. Come back when you want another."

As the Yuletide approached new emotions and old memories thronged upon O'Hara. He thought of the Christmases he had known in Paris as a schoolboy and most tenderly of the older ones in Tyrawley, Ireland, when his mother was alive. What happy days! How carefree his heart! For the first time a bitter sweep of homesickness overcame him as he wondered how he came to be here at all in this wilderness of a strange land! And then all at once he knew that the real longing within him was not for either Paris or Tyrawley. It was for Philadelphia. For the Carson home hung with holly and pine. For the mistletoe in the hall and the fire blazing, and the table spread, as he knew it would all be. And for *Mary*!

He had received no reply to his letter, but there had not yet been time. The worst of it was that he might have to start off before an answer came. Then it would be many weeks, indeed perhaps months before his eye could see the precious communication, for he was sure she would write. And of course he would send her another letter before he left. He had already dispatched the precious

panther skin, now all shining beauty, by a special express rider
with a brief note fastened within the bundle:

> *For Mistress Mary Carson*
> Merry Christmas though this may come late.
> I hope the rug will feel soft to your feet
> on cold nights, with best wishes from your
> most obedient servant, James O'Hara.

He wondered if his phrasing might seem indelicate as though
he were thinking of the skin beside her bed. For he was. He liked
thinking of it there. Well, he hoped she would take no offence.

The tavern now took on an atmosphere of near gaiety. Even
Mrs. Semple relaxed her customary grimness and helped put up
the pine around the walls. A tremendous supply of logs for the
fire promised warmth aplenty, and as Mr. Semple supervised the
stacking of it inside and out, his cheeks quivered with excitement
and goodwill. Odours of cooking and baking filled the rooms and
covered the pungent reek of soaking spilt liquor from the heavy
oaken tables and the kegs along the wall. There was even a *tree*,
dragged in by Hatch, the stable boy and set up, with much loud
suggestion and jesting, near Semple's counter-desk. Sally came
with a basket full of strings of corn to toss over the boughs and a
few little ornaments she'd made of old newspapers which she stuck
on the ends of the sprays, as Hatch stood on a stool to help with the
high ones. Everyone pronounced the effect quite fine, and O'Hara,
as he praised, felt the past returning. Especially he found himself
thinking of his mother. She had been dead now six years but she
was vivid in his memory. She had been small and quick and pretty
with smooth dark hair, Irish eyes and lips that laughed easily. She
had called him *Shamus* with soft teasing, and managed without
pressure to hear his confidences as he sat on a sofa in her bedroom
before she went asleep. She had questioned a little but mostly
listened, weighed and offered practical advice on many subjects,
some of which he would not have discussed with his father. Once
when he had confessed even then that he had a longing to go to
the new world she had paled. Even he, a teenage boy, could see
the colour ebb in her cheeks. But after a moment she had spoken
in her usual voice.

"Shamus," she said, "my old grandmother used to say that if
a man didn't follow the deep driving desire of his heart when he
was young he was no good for anything ever after. If there comes

a time when you feel you must cross the sea, then go you must, and even if it breaks my heart, I'll bless you."

She had not been there to give her blessing but somehow he had felt it just the same. So now as the Yule approached his mind kept glancing from Paris to Tyrawley, to Philadelphia, and back to the busy tavern with its increasing holiday custom and its atmosphere of lusty zest for living that seemed to belong to the raw new town and warm it under its drifted snow. He had already received an invitation to the dance at the Commandant's house on Christmas Eve. Elliott and McGill also. Captain Grant had evidently taken care of that. And while it would be a far cry from Bingham's ball and while he would not have any emotional interest in any ladies present, he was young with an occasional bored moment and so was looking forward to the event.

The day before Christmas a man and a boy entered the tavern with an air of excitement, their faces beaming. They edged through the group of talkers to Semple's desk, whereupon that gentleman gave one look and uttered a yell.

"It's worked!" he called out. "The pill! It's cured you! Damned if it hasn't!"

Jonas Porter joined in the shout. "That's right," he said. "I'm a well man. They say after two weeks you're safe and it's past that. I came to see the men that fetched me the pill."

Mr. Semple was already looking about the room.

"Elliott! O'Hara! Come here!" he shouted. "They're around somewhere. Just hold on a minute."

Elliott appeared from the back room and O'Hara from upstairs where he had been considering what he would wear to the dance. As they recognised Porter they fell upon him, making him tell his story over and over. How he had waited, hardly daring to sleep for fear . . . how he had thought the two weeks would never end, but now, look at him! Fine and fit as a man could be. He drew his benefactors a little to one side.

"I was so scared that day you left me the pill I never thought to say did it cost anything or how much? I thought me an' the boy here would ride over to this doctor's an' thank him an' if there was a charge . . . Just one pill you'd think wouldn't be much . ."

He looked at them anxiously and Elliott cleared his throat.

"Well, now, his fee is sort of queer, you might say. He said if you . . . if you didn't get well it would be nothing. If you came through all right it would be a pound."

"A . . . a *pound*!" Porter's face blanched.

O'Hara spoke quickly. "I have a little money I'm not needing at the moment. I'll lend you a pound and give you five years to pay it back. Agreed?"

The colour came slowly back to Porter's face. He drew a long breath. "You really mean five years to pay?"

"That's right. I expect to be round here that long. As to the big fee you see it was for your *life*, actually. So you mustn't begrudge it, or," he added shrewdly, "spend it on anything else. We guaranteed to take the money back to the doctor if you got well."

"I'll take it. I give you my word. Just tell me the way and the boy an' me, we'll set off early in the morning with it."

He left with the pound in his pocket, his thanks multiplied by the loan.

"I'll never be sure," Elliott said, "whether it was pill or prayer. But I guess they could work together. Anyway, we did a good job, O'Hara. Let's have a drink on the head of it."

As he dressed for the dance that night in the second best shirt and knee breeches he had brought with him, O'Hara mentally checked his preparations for setting out the day after the morrow. Pitt was in fine fettle and also the pack-horse he had bought in Philadelphia. In his room at this moment was the large bundle of trading wares he had selected with care. Since most of them were small articles he figured he had enough for several months' trading. He had picked up much information from his days at Simon & Campbell's, and even learned more dialect from Girty who seemed to have taken a fancy to him. Indeed it had been decided that he would start out with Girty and McGill but part from them before they reached the first Seneca encampment since their business and his would not mix well. He glanced towards the corner where his rifle and hunting knife lay ready. His stomach still felt queasy as he thought of skinning an animal, but if he was hungry enough . . . He would have a good supply of jerk in any case and the men said the Indian villages were not too far apart. As far as he could prepare himself he was now ready.

When he reached the fort that night in company with Elliott and McGill he was surprised at the general stir all about them. Men and women, most of them singing at the top of their voices, were crossing the drawbridge into the Pentagon where Captain Grant met them in the parade ground and directed them towards the Commandant's house. Here there was a blaze of candlelight, a roaring fire, and a hearty greeting from their host, a tall man in his sixties with piercing black eyes. There was apparently no mistress for the home and the large room had the rather bare air of a bachelor's headquarters. Most of the furniture, in any case, was now moved towards the walls to leave dancing space.

O'Hara surveyed the scene with keen interest. As to dress, there was variety. Red, gold, and white uniforms on the officers, deerskin shirts and pants in predominance among the other men, with a few knee breeches like his own and McGill's. The women, he noted, were mostly of early middle-age with only a few young girls and a handful of smaller ones. Most of them were dressed in linsey-woolsey skirts and basques, with a white handkerchief crossed at the neck, but as the Captain had said, here and there was evident a fine silk petticoat!

The room was soon well filled and alive with talk and laughter. Suddenly the Commandant gave a signal for quiet.

"Ladies and gentlemen, guests, I wish to welcome you and to say we will now start the first dance. Pick your partners, please, and make up your sets. Mr. Craig here, will call the figures. All right, you musicians, get ready to strike up."

O'Hara then noticed three older men in the corner, one with a fiddle, one in uniform with a fife, and one with what looked like a battered wooden flute. The latter and the violin had probably been brought across the mountains with sacrificial care, and he guessed the fifer might belong to the fort's band. There was a stirring mêlée now as the men and women paired off and formed small groups, into one of which O'Hara was propelled by Elliott. He found himself partnered with a buxom woman in her forties perhaps, who grabbed his hand and smiled delightedly at him.

"This is a big night for us," she said. "We don't often get a dance except at weddin's and house raisin's and then there ain't room like this."

"But I don't know how to do this," O'Hara demurred. "I'll maybe spoil your fun."

"Not a bit," she said cheerfully. "You'll learn quick. Just listen to the calls and follow me."

All at once the music started with a shrill, rollicking tune and Mr. Craig on a chair began to shout his commands.

> *"First couple out to the right!*
> *Around that couple and take a little peek.*
> *Back to the centre and swing your sweet.*

Around that couple and peek once more,
Back to the centre and circle up four.
Right and left through and lead right on. . . ."

O'Hara floundered through the steps guided by his partner who though far from slim was surprisingly light on her feet and bounced her way through the dance with a contagious enjoyment which began to touch O'Hara too. It was a far cry from the minuet and the waltz but there was here a reckless abandon in the shrill rhythm of the music, the beat of the feet, the clasp of the hands, the violent swinging of warm body pressed to warm body . . .

"This set's just about over now, listen!" his partner whispered as Mr. Craig's voice grew louder.

"Home you are with a balance all,
Swing around eight and swing around all,
Go up the river and cross the lake,
A grand Allemande and a grand chain eight!
Hurry up gents and don't go slow
And meet your honey with a promeno!"

When everyone stopped for breath the men mopped their faces and the women sought the chairs to rest between dances. Everyone was gay, hilarious even, as though lifted completely above the harsh rigour of daily living by the exhilaration they had just experienced. O'Hara was sensitively aware of this, and a mingled pity and respect touched him as he watched. The guests at Mrs. Bingham's ball with the powdered wigs, lace jabots and brocaded satin were not subduing a wilderness and making the far reaches of the new world fit for habitation. *These* were the men and women, these upon whom his gaze now brooded! These had met peril and steeled themselves against it; but in so doing had not lost sight of the fact that happiness is an integral ingredient of the human heart. So when the opportunity came, they could fling their shoulders high and stamp and swing and revel in their evening's pleasure, even though the men's faces were beaten and weathered by the elements and those of the women older than their years from hardship.

Elliott seemed to be amusing himself with one of the younger women but McGill came over.

"Well, how do you like the backwoods dancing?"

"It rather took my breath away at first but I caught on to it a little. By the end I was beginning to enjoy it."

"Here comes Captain Grant to check on you!" he said after some minutes.

"You got on first rate," the latter began when he came up. "I was watching you. Quite a contrast from a ballroom, but I can tell you it stirs up the blood better than a minuet. Or is that an advantage for us bachelors?" he added laughing. "Oh, here we go for the next dance. Come on. Grab a partner!"

It was one of the little girls this time but O'Hara was pleased. She was younger than Mary but that same light of early innocence on the face reminded him of her.

"You'll have to help me," he whispered smiling.

"Oh, I *will*," she said, taking his hand.

The musicians struck up again, Mr. Craig shouted from his chair vantage and a delirious wave of sound and flying movements swept the room.

> *"Stand up straight and simmer down eight,*
> *Swing on the corner like swingin' on a gate,*
> *And then your own if you ain't too late!"*

When the third dance ended the Commandant invited his guests into the dining-room where great bowls of spicy negus waited. No one minded that noggins were often passed from lip to lip. The main thing was that there seemed no end to the bounty. Their host and Captain Grant dipped and dipped and even the women kept coming back, though apologetically, for more. The lemons which gave the delicious and unaccustomed tang had been brought, they knew, over the mountains from the east and before that in ships from Spain! This was the treat of the year and thirsty throats made the most of it.

When all had well drunk and they had returned to the main room a shout above the general clamour rose from one of the men.

"How about a few kissin' games now?"

Bedlam followed with the men's heavy voices seconding the suggestion and the woman's half-hearted disclaimers all but drowned in the general confusion. The fiddler settled it.

"Here we go!" he called. "Make up your rounds for 'Oh, Sister Phoebe'. " And he began to play.

Quickly the men started pulling the women and girls into the circle amid much coy and feigned reluctance on their part. McGill spoke to O'Hara.

"I don't feel like kissing games. As a matter of fact I'm sort of homesick to-night. I think I'll make my manners to the Commandant and go back to bed."

"I'll go with you," O'Hara said promptly.

"Why, you're a young blade," McGill looked at him in surprise. "Why not stay and have the fun? . . . Well, we can watch the first round, anyway."

The two circles were moving now with everyone singing including the man in the centre of each. The words and plaintive cadence of the old English folk song had been borne without loss across the stormy Atlantic; carried indestructible over the mountains to be heard now in the western wilderness and then to be borne along the Monongahela, the Allegheny, the Ohio, south and north and still on into the deeper unknown; for the frail echo of a song's lilt, the fragile memory of a rhyme were among the settlers' few imperishables.

So, now they sang:

> *"Oh, Sister Phoebe, how merry were we*
> *The night we sat under the juniper tree,*
> *The juniper tree, I, oh!*
> *Take this hat on your head and keep your head warm,*
> *And take a sweet kiss, it will do you no harm,*
> *But a great deal of good, I know."*

Each centre man grabbed a woman and brought her into the middle of the ring where he kissed her with quick heartiness. Then he stood there alone waiting to choose a partner for the next kiss while round and round flew the linsey-woolsey skirts and the buckskin breeches as the rhythm quickened. Some of the older women sat along the walls, watching, but the men of all ages had joined the circles.

"Well, that's the way it goes. They'll keep this up for a good while and then go back to the dancing till morning. You're sure you want to leave now?" McGill asked.

"Yes. I'll go with you to the Commandant. I think Elliott must be going to stay it out."

"Oh, him! He won't leave till the last dog's shot! When he gets started there's a surprising amount of ginger in him."

When the two men emerged from the fort the little town was quiet and dark, except for the faint candle glow behind the tavern windows. O'Hara glancing behind him was surprised to see sentinels with their rifles ranged around the Bastions.

"Why, they have look-outs posted!" he exclaimed.

"Ah, yes," McGill agreed. "This would be a fine night for an Indian raid with nearly every able-bodied man at the dance. There's something you have to get used to, O'Hara. Out here there is *always* danger!"

On Christmas Day O'Hara slept till past noon, missing his breakfast, but appearing in his white shirt and breeches when Mrs. Semple pounded the gong for dinner. There was small variety possible in the daily fare, but now the table groaned with platters of venison, wild turkey and dumplings, corn pone and a pudding for dessert! And all this with plenty from the kegs along the wall to wash it down. Gradually an air of robust well-being filled the room and toasts were drunk indiscriminately to the King, the Colonies, the Prime Minister and Benjamin Franklin! Suddenly O'Hara found himself on his feet.

"To Pittsburgh!" he cried. "And may a great city stand one day where we are now!"

A roaring outburst followed the toast, both from those whose interests were in agreement with it and from those who were now mellow enough to drink to anything.

As the afternoon wore on towards the sunset, O'Hara sat at the farthest table where the western colours could be seen through one of the two glass windows in the town, and wrote his second letter to Mary. When he had finished, he dusted and sealed it, and then sat with it in his hand as though by the prolonged contact it might carry more of his love. For he knew with every passing day that love it was. He sat now, planning the future with the wholly illogical and unreasoning confidence of youth. He must of course wait a few years for Mary to grow up. It need not be many. She had spoken herself of girls she knew who had married at sixteen! Now, as with everything, his determination had been swiftly and strongly made. He would build a house for her in *The King's Orchard*. No other place would be fair enough. While he had not yet seen the trees with their springtime bloom and autumn fruit, even the bare boughs now were to him a frame for the bridal home! Somehow he would bend events to his will so that he would own a portion of this plot, the name of which delighted him. And the town would grow, even as his toast implied. *Their* town, his and Mary's. They would help build it.

So he mused, watching the rose and gold of the winter sky burn with beauty above the hills of snow. And again, strangely he thought of his mother. When he was a small boy he had watched and listened as *she* sat at a west window in the sunset, playing sentimental old songs on the small pianoforte. There was one which he had particularly loved without knowing why. He could still hear her laughter as he begged for it.

"Oh, Shamus! You are the funny lad! Why do you like that song? You can't understand it. You're not old enough!" But of course she always sang it for him.

The melody now ran clearly through his mind, but most of all, the words.

> *Have you seen a white lily grow*
> *Before rude hands had touched it?*
> *Have you marked but the fall of the snow*
> *Before the earth hath smutched it?*
> *Have you felt of the wool of the beaver,*
> *Or swan's down ever?*
> *Or have smelt of the bud of the brier,*
> *Or the nard in the fire?*
> *Or have tasted the bag of the bee?*
> *O so white, O so soft, O so sweet, so sweet,*
> *so sweet is she!*

He sat on, smiling to himself. He was old enough to understand it now.

Chapter Four

It was breaking spring when O'Hara returned to Pittsburgh. He had not expected the trip to last so long, but while there had been delaying hardships a-plenty and some dangers, in the main it had been successful. The pack-horse and Pitt, too, were laden with skins and within himself there was a feeling of buoyancy. He was now a seasoned trader. His particular gifts had stood him in good stead. His quick ear had picked up enough of the dialects to assist greatly in the conversations and he had found that many of the older Indians remembered some French from the days when France held the lake forts.

He did not know that his wide smile showing the rare complement of strong white teeth had all but bewitched the Indians. Because they warmed to his friendliness O'Hara had felt no fear. He had eaten with them, slept with them, listened by the fire to their tales of hunting and war, making out what he could; traded honestly with them and honestly sympathised with their complaints. Their lands, their hunting grounds were going. More and more the white man was taking them. What would be left for the red man? Ah, what indeed, he thought, as he made his way through the depths of the forest between villages, the tales of Indian massacres receding from his mind as his heart kindled towards his new friends.

There had been some touching incidents. Once when he was snowed in at a Delaware settlement for nearly three weeks the chief, who had evidently taken a strong fancy to him, had suggested that he remain and be adopted into the tribe. If he would do so they would give him a maiden to wife. She was brought in, before O'Hara in his embarrassment could reply. He had hated himself for his fleeting thought of desire, for the girl was beautiful, like a slim, bronzed flower. She stood meek and yielding with the faintest smile, as though beneath her impassive façade there lay a warmth of eagerness.

The chief dismissed her and O'Hara mustering all his diplomacy explained that however much he was honoured by the proposal, and admired the lovely maiden, he must pursue his work as a white man just as the chief continued his as an Indian. Also he added shyly that there was a girl of his own race whom some day he hoped to marry. The chief had accepted the explanation with composure and without rancour, and they had pledged friendship in any case.

Indeed O'Hara had wondered as he had first set out whether the Indians might have the embarrassing custom of some primitive tribes of offering their women to passing guests as a courtesy. But he soon learned that the red man guarded their wives and daughters as jealously as the white man. Indeed, more carefully if anything.

It had been in the Shawnees that O'Hara had taken the deepest interest. In the first place the great chief, Cornstalk, was in their village when he reached it and while he had heard of the man briefly from Elliott he was entirely unprepared for the actual encounter. Cornstalk was taller than Guyasuta though not as handsome, with features less finely cut; but his bearing was one of such regal dignity that O'Hara was amazed. Besides this, his English was fairly good and he seemed glad of a chance to speak it; there was from the start a fine rapport between them since their ideas could be freely interchanged. A dozen questions in O'Hara's mind could now be broached.

"If it is not impolite," he had said, "I would like to know all I can learn about your way of life, the small things as well as the big."

And the chief was pleased. "Not many white men care to learn of us," he said.

So he displayed his war bonnet made with eagle feathers, symbols of power; he produced two wampum belts, red for war, white for peace; he showed him how they made their colours; red from what O'Hara knew was red iron-oxide, ground in small mortars and mixed with grease; black from charcoal, white from gypsum, yellow from clay. He explained how the inner bark of the swamp ash was made into string and how the women powdered Indian corn so fine it became a powder to heal sores. He told how a hunter prepared for a real hunt. Here his English failed him, but O'Hara gathered from highly descriptive gestures that he drank purges, took emetics, had a sweat and then bathed in water to which sweet fern had been added. Cornstalk broke some of this from a great bunch hanging from the roof, and handed

it to O'Hara. Even when dry there was in the fronds a woodsy
perfume.

"By this means," Cornstalk went on, "the animals do not smell
the hunter as he comes. They smell forest."

One set of burning questions in O'Hara's mind he forbore to
ask. These dealt with the scalps hanging like a grisly frieze around
the chieftain's wigwam. Cornstalk saw the young man's eyes
fastened upon them one night and spoke slowly.

"You would like to know more of this custom?" he asked.

"Yes," said O'Hara, "if you care to tell me."

Cornstalk smoked for a few minutes in silence then waved an
arm towards the trophies.

"Not all from white men," he said. "Many from Indian
enemies," and he smoked a while longer. Then he began carefully
to speak.

"This," he said, touching his own scalp lock with its decorative
feathers, "has man's power in it. Everything the man is, what he
will do and what he will be is all in the scalp lock. When I take one
from an enemy that power all comes into me. You see?"

O'Hara nodded.

"So—many scalps, much power."

"They are not all the same size," O'Hara commented hesitantly.

Cornstalk touched his own head, clipped close except for the
scalp lock.

"With most Indians it is easy to get. With white men's heads
covered with hair we take all to make sure."

That night O'Hara's sleep was not as sound as usual.

The Shawnees were slow, deliberate traders and O'Hara did
not hurry them. Instead he waited, observed and listened and,
he hoped, became their friend. His reward at the end of his stay
was more than beaver skins. By Cornstalk's own invitation he
witnessed an adoption ceremony which had to him remarkable
overtones. A young Mohawk was being taken into the tribe,
for what reason O'Hara could not discover though it became plain
the custom of adoption was a familiar one. He had taken his
place with the group of onlookers with pleasant anticipation, a
feeling soon dispelled.

Between two rows of warriors armed with wooden bats, sharply
pointed sticks and knives the young brave ran the gauntlet while
O'Hara, whose stomach had perforce grown stronger, again found
himself sickened. The Mohawk stood finally and with difficulty

at the end of the lines, his face impassive, his eyes like steel and his body battered and bruised, the flesh hanging here and there in strips. The warriors nodded approval and proceeded to the bloodletting which was not pretty to watch but not as painful certainly for the young man as the gauntlet. Then the whole group raised their voices in a chant that thrilled O'Hara to the bone. He could make out only occasional words, but when the new young Shawnee had been led away by the squaws after word to receive, as he was given to understand, rest and care (Egad, he needs it! thought O'Hara) he made bold to ask Cornstalk if he would translate the Adoption Song.

Once again the request for information pleased the chief. He began to intone the words slowly to which O'Hara listened in amazement.

"Ho! Ye sun, moon, stars, all ye that move in
the heavens, I bid you hear me!
Ye Winds, Clouds, Rain and Mist,
Ye Hills, Valleys, Rivers, Lakes, Trees and Grasses,
Ye Birds, Animals and Insects,
Ho! All ye of the Heavens, All ye of the Air,
All ye of the earth,
I bid ye all to hear me!"

O'Hara had been brought up in a religious atmosphere. The small Book of Common Prayer which his mother had given him on his twelfth birthday had crossed the sea with him, and now, the paths of the wilderness. He had not read from it on this trip, indeed had brought it along, he feared, as a sort of talisman, but now he hurried to his pack to look up what he was sure was there. With the small volume in his hand he leafed through the Order of Morning Prayer and stopped at one of the Canticles. The various sentences leaped from the page:

O ye Sun and Moon,
O ye Stars of Heaven, O ye Showers and Dew,
O ye Winds of God, O ye Dews and Frosts,
O ye Mountains and Hills,
O all ye Green Things upon the earth,
O ye Fowls of the Air, O ye Beasts and Cattle . . .
Bless ye the Lord.

Strange, strange that the words he had heard sung from a child in quiet Christian churches should have been so nearly duplicated in the savage rite he had just witnessed! What vital affinity with the universe ran through the spirits of all men, savage or civilised, whether they were calling on the forces of nature alone or through them to God himself!

He was, as a matter of fact, thinking of this now as he rode on his last lap through the budding greenery of the trees on his return to Pittsburgh, intensely conscious of the beauty about him; the afternoon sun brought out the soft blush running up the stems of the sassafras and sumac and lighted the springing sweet fern with which he had already become acquainted, and the thick dark tangle of bushes he did not know by name. There was lonely silence, there was always danger, but there was a curious peace also, for now he felt at home in the forest. So he rode on confidently into the little town, wondering first if a letter awaited him, and second whether the King's Orchard would be in leaf.

Pittsburgh looked very different from his last memory of it. The snow was gone as though it had never been, the buildings looked more crude than they had with their white covering but the trees were burgeoning and would soon soften the general outlines even more than the snow had done. He stopped first before the warehouse of Simon & Campbell, tied the horses and went inside, keeping a wary eye meanwhile upon his skins. Only Simon was there but he gave a hearty welcome.

"Well, well, how did you make out?"

"Not too badly, I think. Would you be kind enough to give me a hand with the pelts?"

Between them they carried the packs into the counter, the piles being greater even than O'Hara had thought.

"Well, well," Simon said again, "you have got a good few. Of course we can't tell much until we weigh them."

He concentrated then on the scales while O'Hara watched carefully and waited. All at once Simon looked up.

"I'll tell you," he said, "this will take a while and my partner will check when he comes in. Why don't you get along to Semple's and get some supper. I'll wager Sally's cooking will set pretty well after your trip. How long have you been gone now?"

"Nearly three months."

"Oh, you'll need a bit rest up. Trading's hard work. Come in, then, in the morning and we'll settle accounts."

O'Hara didn't feel entirely easy but he had his own list of skins and supposed all would be well. Besides he had a consuming desire to get to Semple's desk as fast as he could. As he rode up the slope to the tavern his heart lifted, for the King's Orchard was, indeed, in leaf!

Semple received him like a returning son.

"My word, laddie, I'm glad to see you! There's no way to know whether a trader's alive or dead while he's out on his rounds. Why, you look braw enough, that's sure. Did you have good hagglin'?"

"Pretty fair, I think. It's good to be back. Would there . . . would there be a letter for me?"

Semple grinned widely. "I've smelt it many's the time since it come. Lavender. My guess is it's not from *your father*! Off with you then, up to your room now and see what she says."

O'Hara, scarlet, took the little missive, tried to smile and hurried off as he was bid. Once in his room his fingers were clumsy on the seal. It was not only that they were work hardened but there was a tremor in all his frame. Finally the paper with its delicate writing lay open to his eyes.

Dear Mr. O'Hara:
   The rug is the most beautiful present I have ever received. I have it beside my bed and each time my feet touch it I think of you. (And sometimes in between.)

He had to stop there to ease the pounding of his heart. Then he read it all through and then again . . . and yet again! He could not see the words often enough. She described the two fine routs she had been at with no lack of partners but wished withal that he had been there. One had been given by Peggy Shippen and was most elegant. Her sister Elizabeth and her husband had come for Christmas. They had decorated the rooms with greens and lud, but they looked lovely. There was mistletoe in the hall and she got kissed betimes but she paid small attention. There were different kinds of kisses. Father was well but he and all the men were always talking politics now about how badly the ministry in London was acting towards the Colonies and she supposed they meant the King. She was going to Miss Jayne's Young Ladies' Academy and was learning French and would he please be very careful about the Indians and send a letter when he could? She signed herself, *Your sincere friend and well-wisher, Mary Carson.*

O'Hara smiled tenderly, his face alight. Then it clouded. The trouble with him and his *Dear Delight* as he had begun to call his love to himself, thinking of their visit to the Garden, was that the distance between them not only separated them physically but made even the exchange of letters so infrequent. He would write to-night and hope for a speedy express. He raised the letter to his lips, smelled the delicate lavender fragrance again and then put it next his heart.

The following weeks were quiet compared to the ones he had just passed. He realised now that he was more tired than he had ever been in his life. Semple explained that this weariness was common to even the most experienced traders; so comforted by this O'Hara slept for days, coming down only for dinner. His settlement with Simon & Campbell had been satisfactory, and yet he had a slight feeling of uneasiness, especially as they had pressed him to take part credit instead of money. It was only after insistence that he received cash in full for his skins. He determined to visit the other warehouse before he set off again. Elliott was still out and McGill had returned to the East on his own errands. Simon Girty dropped in often of an evening, professing real admiration for O'Hara's new proficiency in the Indian dialects and his general attitude towards the "Red Brethren" as he termed them.

"They ain't bad, the Indians, when you get to know them. Take me, now. I'd as lieve live with them as with white men. I'd have stayed on with the Senecas if Bouquet hadn't made them give up all their hostages after Pontiac's war. That was about nine years ago. Before that we'd roamed all over the wilderness north-west of the Ohio. Good life, when you're used to it." His black eyes looked far away.

One evening as they sat together over their noggins Girty began to speak only in dialect. O'Hara, eager to learn, listened hard and replied as he could. Girty explained the similarities and the differences, corrected O'Hara's mistakes and after a couple of hours, grinned at his pupil.

"By God, you've got the twist of it!" he said. "I'll tell you something. I know McGill is stepping out soon. You'd make a damned good Indian agent."

"*Agent?*" O'Hara echoed, amazed.

"That's what I said. If you go out again, don't stay too long. Something might come up."

"Who would recommend me?"

"McGill and I get on pretty well. I'll put a flea in his ear next time he's back about the dialects. But I know he likes you and he wants to get shed of the job."

O'Hara went one day to the other big trading store to meet its proprietor, Devereux Smith and was at once drawn to the man. Simon & Campbell were both pleasant enough if *canny* but Smith was a man of parts with a good mind and a breadth of vision. His interests went beyond the financial. He too, O'Hara found, expected Pittsburgh to grow and wanted to be a witness to, a partner even, in this development. They talked for hours, Smith, slender and greying, yet with a youthful face listening attentively to all the younger man had to say.

"My interest has always been in business," O'Hara told him. "I refused an Ensign's Commission that my cousin Lord Tyrawley would have got for me in the old country, and went into a ship-broker's office instead when I was through school. I wanted to learn business methods. I don't know what I'll be doing here later on, but . . ."

Devereux Smith looked shrewdly into O'Hara's eyes.

"I know," he said. "You'll be Pittsburgh's first captain of industry!"

Then they laughed together and somehow the friendship was sealed.

"You get on with the Indians?"

"Fine," said O'Hara. "And I've got the hang of their dialects. I seem to have an ear for them."

"Wonderful! So you'll go out this next time for us? Ephraim Douglas is my partner."

"I will that, and thank you. I'm all cleared up with the other firm."

"You know," Smith said meditatively one day, "I see a good many men from the East as they drop in here. They bring disquieting reports. One of my best friends here, John Ormsby, goes so far as to say we're going to have war. Next year or the next. He's an old soldier—he was out here with Forbes—and he's sure it's coming."

"Are you?"

"Afraid so. But we live a day at a time and there's always room to hope. I mention this because you're new and hardly had a chance yet to become a real American."

O'Hara smiled. "It doesn't take long."

"Good! When would you like to make your next trip?"

"As soon as my horses and I are completely rested."

"I need a man to go out to Kaskusky for a few months. It's a

D

good sized Indian town near the junction of the Mahoning and Shenango rivers and a proper place to work out from and keep an eye on our affairs. How does that strike you?"

"Sounds interesting. I could stay the summer, but I want to be back by late fall. I have some business east at Philadelphia then." He hoped his cheeks did not redden.

"You may need a little different articles of trade out there," Smith went on. "More traps, files, knives of all kinds and brass wire, for instance. And plenty of jews'-harps, whistles and bells. The jews'-harps have taken the Indians by storm. But I'll fix you up."

The next week O'Hara set out on his second trading trip but not before he had walked in the King's Orchard breathing deep of the sweetness which filled the air like a light drifting incense. *It's a bridal fragrance*, he said to himself. *And one day I shall bring my bride to this very spot when the apple trees are in bloom.*

Then he started again through the dark impenetrable forest which covered the hills and banks, crossed by occasional paths, touched humanly here and there by a band of Indians, a settler's cabin, or a canoe on the silent rivers, as he journeyed to Kaskusky.

It was early November when he returned with the sumac and sassafras now bright red, laden again with peltry and alive with his accomplishment. Smith was congratulatory in the extreme as he heard the full report and looked over the skins.

"I'd hate to lose you as a trader," he said, "but you'd make a fine Indian agent. It's pretty good pay. I'll speak up for you if I have the chance."

Elliott was now back at Semple's and the two men met with hearty pleasure. When O'Hara said he intended soon to leave for Philadelphia Elliott scratched his head and opined he wouldn't mind going along.

"Got a little business there," he said. "Ought to see to."

"So have I," O'Hara replied casually.

They travelled this time without the pack horses and by Forbes Road, which, built of military necessity, ran along the high ground to avoid alike ambush and swamps.

"Why the devil didn't we take this route going out to Pittsburgh?" O'Hara asked irritably one day.

Elliott gave him a shrewd sidewise glance. "You'll always be a better man for going on the trail I took you," he said.

"So! You were proving me then?"

"Might be. An' you stood up pretty damned well, I must say. In our business you can't know too much about the forest an' there ain't always a Forbes Road to travel on when you're a trader."

It was late afternoon on a mild December day when they reined their horses and tied them in front of the Crooked Billet. Everything inside was just the same: the comfortable taproom, the friendly Hastings, Sam's grin. O'Hara hurried up to his old room and penned a note:

Mr. William Carson, Honoured Sir:
Within the hour I have arrived in Philadelphia, lodging at the Crooked Billet as before. I should like to pay my respects to you and Mistress Mary if I may at your earliest convenience. Would it be possible for me to call upon you this evening? I shall eagerly await the kindness of your reply.
Your most obedient servant,
James O'Hara

When Sam had been dispatched with the missive O'Hara nervously laid out his best clothes, checked on his knee-buckles, and brushed his thick blond hair vigorously, wondering how he would look with a queue. It would not be practical of course for the wilderness, and he had stopped short of powdering up till now. But he longed to be at his best to-night if . . . A tap at the door made his heart jump in his breast. Sam grinned with pleasure as he presented a note and received a benefaction for the same. O'Hara opened it hurriedly.

Dear Mr. O'Hara:
My daughter and I will be at home this evening and would be pleased to have you sup with us at eight of the clock if you care to do so.
My best compliments, sir,
William Carson

When he reached the house, he felt that he had never been away except for a certain strength and assurance within him which he had not known before. He shook hands with the old serving man and was shown into the library where Mr. Carson rose to greet him warmly.

"Welcome back to Philadelphia!" he said. "Have you decided the East is best after all?"

"I'm afraid not exactly that, sir, but I'm delighted to be here."

"It's a year isn't it since you left? Well, we must hear all the news of your wanderings. Ah, here is Mary!"

She stood in the doorway, dressed again in rose, but changed by the twelve-month into new beauty. Fourteen now and a woman in her form at least. O'Hara felt himself trembling as he went to meet her and bow over her hand. She smiled sweetly upon him.

"You've *grown*," she said. "Isn't he taller, Father? Could that be?"

"I knew a young man that grew out of his wedding suit," Carson said. "In height, that is. I guess most men grow out of theirs in the other direction."

Then they all laughed together and sat down before the brightly burning logs. At first O'Hara listened to their news, gently deflecting questions about his own affairs. When supper was announced Mary looked up at him archly.

"You can't put us off all evening, Mr. O'Hara. After we sup you must tell about shooting the panther and all the rest of it, Indians, too. I promise to be brave as I listen but hear it I must."

So, when they were back again in the library, O'Hara spoke of the strange year that he had lived since seeing them. His powers of description were good and his listeners' eyes, especially Mary's, encouraged him. He told of the trip out, the fort, the town of Pittsburgh and the months of trading. He found himself presenting the Indians as a completely friendly and hospitable race in spite of the large question on Mr. Carson's countenance!

"Then you really weren't in any danger after all?" Mary exclaimed delightedly. "Unless it was from the panther," she added.

"I managed pretty well," he answered, and she didn't seem to notice any evasion.

The problem of seeing Mary alone loomed large in O'Hara's mind. He was constantly made welcome at the Carson home, to tea or supper when he feasted his eyes upon his Delight, but found that by accident or design her father was always present. The weather had changed, snow had fallen and the suggestion of either a walk or a drive would seem rather ridiculous, so O'Hara chaffed as he got through the days, filling them with what small business he could, hoping always for the opportunity he craved. He did his banking, renewing acquaintance with Morris, roamed the streets, or sat restlessly in the tavern.

One day the taproom door flew open and a rider entered. His whole bearing indicated news.

"Well, boys," he shouted, "the fat's in the fire now!"

"What's up?" came from all sides.

"Give me a dram to warm me up an' I'll tell you . . . Well, here it is," he went on when Sam had rushed him a noggin. "The English have had three shiploads of tea in Boston harbour for weeks. The authorities there tried to get it sent back on account of the tax. When they got nowhere with their petitions, a crowd of Bostoners fixed themselves up like Indians, got on the boats and pitched all the tea into the harbour! Now, can anyone say we're not in for trouble? I'm on my way to give Mr. Franklin the message. Just stopped for a drink." He threw some money on the counter and was gone.

O'Hara left the uproar of the taproom at once though it was an hour before tea-time at the Carsons'. Once there, he told Mr. Carson what he had heard and the two sat with grave faces, discussing the matter.

"It's bad, this," Mr. Carson said. "You see it's been one long series of irritations and when at last there's one too many . . ."

"Surely there will be reasonable men both here and in England."

"When troubles edge towards the breaking point it seems as though reason disappears. Oh, I haven't lost faith. I hope and I pray, but sometimes in the dead of night . . ."

His face suddenly looked old.

"I think of Philadelphia if . . . if war should actually come. I know half the best families here would stick with the Crown. God help the rest of us."

"Mr. Carson," O'Hara said, "I wish to speak to you upon an entirely different matter when I have this opportunity. There is something as an honourable man I must tell you. I love your daughter."

Mr. Carson's jaw dropped as he started upright in his chair.

"I cannot believe I heard you aright!"

"You did, sir. I have loved her from the first time I saw her. It happens that way sometimes to a man. It was so with my own father, he said. I am asking your permission to tell her."

"She is still but a child! I cannot have her burdened by any such declaration at her age!" His voice was sharp.

O'Hara spoke slowly, considering each word.

"You do, I think, know something already of my character.

I have ambition. I believe Pittsburgh because of its location will grow into a city as time goes on. I intend to grow with it. I hope one day to be a man of ample means. Right now I do not know whether I can return to Philadelphia even as often as once a year. I will do my best, you may be sure. But my own work and the times are both uncertain. This is why I wish to tell Mistress Mary now of my feeling for her. I cannot go back for another year or perhaps more without doing this. Surely it cannot harm any girl of any age, sir, to know that a man loves her."

"You would not, of course," Mr. Carson said slowly, "try to exact any promise from her?"

"I will not," O'Hara said. "Much as I should want to. But I would like your permission to see her alone. You may be certain I shall in no way abuse the privilege."

For what seemed an unconscionable length of time Mr. Carson sat in thought. At last he spoke.

"You have been manly and honest, O'Hara, and for that I respect you. I will not try to disguise from you the fact that if you were planning to remain in Philadelphia or anywhere in the East rather than in the western wilderness, I would view your suit with more favour. Indeed the very thought of Mary's ever going to live under the rigours of the frontier, makes me shudder. Surely you can understand that."

"But it will not always remain the frontier, sir. And if Mary should ever later on . . . become mine, I would guard her happiness with my very life. As I have told you I greatly desire your permission to speak to her of what is in my heart. But it is only fair to add that I intend to do so anyway."

The faintest smile crossed Carson's sober face. "You are a young man of determination, but I can't say I care much for any other kind. So, since I have little choice, go ahead and talk to her. But remember, I shall do the same."

"That is a father's right. But I thank you for your kindness, sir. Perhaps after supper to-night? Since Mary was gracious enough to ask me to stay on the evening."

"I'll leave you alone, then. Only be sure you are not importunate. I will not have her disturbed. Please remember she's but fourteen."

O so white, oh so soft, oh so sweet is she! ran through O'Hara's mind. "I will remember."

They heard the reverberation of the heavy knocker on the

front door, voices, and then the butler appeared with a businesslike envelope in his hand.

"Sam brought this over from the Crooked Billet, if you please, sir. He said it was marked 'Important' and mebbe Mr. O'Hara ought to have it at once."

"For you, then," Carson looked surprised.

"If you will excuse me," O'Hara said, as he opened the seal. He read, and read again, his face flushing with pleasure.

"Good news, I should say?"

"Very, I think, and startling at that. It's my appointment as an Indian agent."

"Well, well, *well*!" Carson said. "Why, that's quite a job, I know. Your first recognition then! I congratulate you. How did it come about?"

"I'm a bit puzzled myself, but I think it was like this. A Mr. McGill, who has been an agent and wanting to give up the job, was out at Semple's Tavern in Pittsburgh a year ago and I got to know him. I've had a little luck learning the Indian dialects and I think he heard about this after my first trading trip perhaps and recommended me. I must say I am very pleased."

"Where did the letter come from?"

"It's from a Mr. Duncan, a member of the Assembly. It was sent out to Semple's It must have got there just after I left and Mr. Semple sent it right on by express rider."

Mr. Carson rose and shook hands. "This calls for something stronger than tea to celebrate," he said. "I am amazed and delighted that you have achieved a real office so soon. This will mean travel?"

"Yes, a great deal. A trader can pick his tribes. A Government agent must go about among them all. I will have part of the Pennsylvania and Ohio area, as this states."

"There will be danger?"

O'Hara smiled. "There is a certain peril in crossing the ocean and yet one does not hesitate to board ship. I'll take a chance on the danger."

Mary had been out at an afternoon party and now came with a small rush into the library, her cheeks crimson from the frosty air as her bonnet and cloth muff. She was excited.

"Oh, Father and Mr. O'Hara, have you heard the news of what happened up in Boston? Some men dressed up like . . ."

"We've heard, my dear."

"Everyone's talking about it, even on the streets! They're calling it the *Boston Tea Party* and that's very funny, isn't it?" She giggled delightedly.

"I'm afraid not," her father said, "but run along and get ready for our own tea. We'll speak of this further."

It was nine-thirty when Mr. Carson, with an odd look upon his face, excused himself on the plea of letters and left the young people to themselves. Mary was surprised.

"He always does his letters at the office," she said.

"I asked him as a favour if I could have a little time with you, alone."

"You did?" A soft blush slowly rose in her cheeks and deepened as she saw O'Hara's eyes full ablaze fixed upon her.

"W . . . why, Mr. O'Hara?"

"Because," he said gently, "I have something to tell you."

"A secret?" she smiled.

"If you wish. Do you remember the day last year when we visited Mr. Bartram's *Garden of Delight*?"

"Of course."

"Ever since to myself I have called you my *Dear Delight*."

"Oh, I like that," Mary exclaimed. "Is that the secret?"

"No, I want to tell you that I . . . I love you."

"After being away so long?"

"I loved you before I left and every minute since I've been gone. I expect to love you all my life."

She raised her beautiful eyes to his and her face was covered with light.

"Oh, Mr. O'Hara, I'm so surprised, but I'm *so* glad. I'm sure I must love you too. I think about you so much and when I first saw you here when you came back, I felt so queer and so . . . *quite* different from the way I feel towards Father."

"That is as it should be," O'Hara said, smiling with tender assurance.

He crossed over to her wing chair, sat down on the arm and drew her close. His head bent to hers.

"May I kiss you?"

"As you did that night in the Greenery?"

"Yes."

"Oh, please do. I won't be startled now."

It was a long time before he released her. His face was one burst of joy.

"And now," he said, "we must talk about our marriage—not for a while of course—but it will be wonderful to plan for it!"

"*Marriage?*" Mary's eyes were filled with a frightened surprise. "Oh, I wasn't thinking of marriage, Mr. O'Hara."

He was gently tolerant. "We must wait a year or two but when two people love each other as we do, they eventually marry, of course. So let us speak of it anyway."

Mary looked up at him piteously.

"Mr. O'Hara, are you coming back to live in Philadelphia?"

His face paled a little. "No," he said. "I have cast my lot in with Pittsburgh and I must be staying there."

"But don't you see? I *couldn't* go out to the frontier. I couldn't leave all this," sketching a motion towards the luxurious comfort around her. "And my father and my friends and the city here. I would be terrified of the Indians and . . . and all the wild life there."

She went on, plaiting and then smoothing a fold of her satin skirt.

"What I was thinking of was that we would go on loving each other and writing letters and being together—like this—when you would come back. Would that not be . . . enough?"

He looked into her innocent young face and felt a mist in his eyes. "Yes," he said gently. "That will be enough for several years perhaps. And then we can talk it all over again. Just to know you care for me will warm my heart wherever I am."

"Oh, I'm so glad!" she said. "You frightened me a little. But you must remember, Mr. O'Hara, that I could never go west and live in Pittsburgh."

His assurance was a little dimmed but in the breathless joy of the caresses he put his doubts behind him. He told her of his new appointment and explained that his duties might keep him away for more than a year. He could not be sure.

"But you will write often and tell me everything you are doing?"

"Of course and you must also."

"Aren't you proud of being an Indian agent so soon?"

"I am! I've never felt so proud over anything except . . . that you love me. There's one matter though I must prepare you for."

"What is that?"

"I'm going to see the member of the Assembly to-morrow who sent me my papers. He may tell me I have to get back to Pittsburgh at once."

"Oh, *no!* Not before Christmas . . . *and the holiday rout?*"

"I hope not. But, my Dear Delight, a man must go where and when his business takes him. If he put a ball before his work he wouldn't be much of man, would he?"

"I suppose not," she said slowly, "but how can I bear you to leave so soon?"

"We'll make the most of every minute. Will you come for a walk with me to-morrow, even in the snow? The paths are clearing wonderfully."

"Oh, yes, Mr. O'Hara. I'll go anywhere with you!"

"*Anywhere?*"

"In Philadelphia," she amended, smiling a bit roguishly. "You mustn't catch me up like that."

O'Hara's fears were justified. He was urged to return to Pittsburgh immediately and take up his new duties. There was always unrest among the Indians here or there and he was told that the reports coming east in regard to his success with the dialects as well as his friendliness with the red men made it advisable that he should start work at once. The possibility of coming war with the British made this unusually important, for the Colonies must make every effort to keep as many of the tribes as allies as possible. One question, Mr. Duncan, the Assembly member, asked him.

"We have judged from various sources that you as of the present wish to become an American. In the case of a conflict with the Crown, may I ask for a frank statement of your position?"

"My allegiance will be to the Colonies. I pledge it."

"Good!" said his questioner. "Then get out west as fast as you can to make the savages feel the same way. Have you met Croghan?"

"Not yet, but I've heard of him of course. An Irishman like myself," he smiled.

"Amazing man. Getting on a bit now and more interested in his large land holdings than anything, so you may not run into him. But as a trader he was King and as Deputy Indian Agent he got closer to the Indians, especially the Iroquois, than any other man except Sir William Johnson up in New York State. They've worked a good deal together. Both have Indian wives, by the way. You will be in a general way under Alexander McKee who is taking over Croghan's Deputyship. Hope you get on, and all success to you! The times are ticklish."

Before he left Philadelphia O'Hara went to a silversmith's and purchased a delicate gold brooch in the shape of a heart. There was a diamond in the centre and on the back he had the jeweller engrave J. O'H. to M. C. He would have liked to add *with love* but feared her father would object. At the end of his last evening at the Carsons' he gave it to Mary before his final good-bye. Her surprise and joy in the gift put an end to her imminent tears.

"It's *so* beautiful," she kept repeating, turning it this way and that, looking at the initials and exclaiming over the diamond. "And oh, Mr. O'Hara, I like . . . love you so!"

"Would you not say James, or perhaps Shamus which is the Irish for the name? My mother called me that."

"It sounds a little strange to me but I'll say *James* if you would like me to and you must say *Mary*. I *wish* you didn't have to go!"

"Not half as much as I do, but it must be, I fear. Good-bye, my Dear Delight."

A last kiss on the soft young lips and he was gone out into the winter street to make his way to the Crooked Billet and complete his preparations for the journey. Elliott had been greatly pleased over the appointment and insisted that he had finished his business and would return along to Pittsburgh; so once again they set forth together.

As O'Hara rode on he felt upon himself the hand of destiny even more than on his first trip. While of an intensely practical nature he had also, in his Irish blood, something of the mystic and the philosopher. His thinking was mature beyond his years, just as was the depth and certainty of his love. He pondered now on a thought that had come to him before. He believed that in the greater matters of life the mind must fling itself forward beyond the present data and grasp as a possession that which lay beyond. Surely this was the only way to success. So as the dusk of the forest finally closed in again upon the travellers, O'Hara felt the premonitory challenge of eventful years lying just ahead and the up-leaping of his own powers to meet them.

Chapter Five

On a bright afternoon in early May 1775, a weary rider flung himself from his horse at Semple's Tavern and brought the news that the farmers of Massachusetts had surrounded the British redcoats in Boston! The war, then, had begun.

O'Hara had arrived in Pittsburgh the day before after a long stretch in the wilderness. He had come back this time with a limited sense of accomplishment. The Delawares and the Mingoes and perhaps the Cherokees he felt would stick with the Colonies or remain neutral. Of the Shawnees in spite of his own friendly relations with Cornstalk, he was not so sure. There had been constant warfare the last two years between them and the settlers who had been pouring into the rich Kentucky region which the Shawnees regarded as their own. A delegation of them had even come to Pittsburgh to remind Alexander McKee, the present Deputy Superintendent, that this white encroachment below the Kanawha River was a flagrant violation of solemn treaties. O'Hara had been present and listened. So did McKee; but the latter was powerless to offer redress. He could only condole with the Indians and counsel patience.

This local war then had continued until at last the Shawnees were beaten back. For something had gradually happened to the settlers. Instead of scattered, anxious men, each prepared to defend his own cabin and family, there had developed a common courage, a kind of determined cohesion which increased their fighting strength. This, while they did not know it then, was to help render them more nearly invulnerable in the great revolutionary struggle yet to come. But while they had actually bested the Shawnees for the time being, the deep bitterness on both sides remained.

O'Hara at his various listening posts had heard tragic if isolated stories. The son of Daniel Boone, whose fame he knew, had been killed by the Shawnees. On the other hand the family of Logan the Mingo, the unfaltering friend of the whites, had been cruelly murdered, and Logan with a number of ardent young Shawnee warriors had wreaked a terrible vengeance. So it had run. O'Hara knew now that on the fringes of any so-called *conventional* war, if there could be such a thing, there would be the blot of unspeakable savagery.

With all this in the back of his mind he listened to the tumult of voices in the tavern for it was but a short time after the arrival of the express rider until the room was filled. When he could be heard, Samuel Semple spoke.

"There must be a meeting called! We've got to prepare resolutions as to where we stand."

"There's no two places to stand," a man shouted. "We're all on our side, ain't we?" he ended somewhat ambiguously.

A roar of approval went up.

"We've still got to have a meeting and get things organised. It's all very well to cry *liberty* an' such but mind you there will be fightin' too."

"Let 'er come! We've got rifles."

Devereux Smith raised his hand to be heard.

"I suggest we hold a mass meeting of all citizens for the expression of public opinion. How about next Tuesday, that's May the 16th. That ought to give time to send the word round. If we have too big a crowd for here we can meet in the meadow."

"How about the fort?" someone cried.

"That's British, you fool. We can't talk free there," another answered.

There was continued shouting and arguing, much drinking and even laughter, in spite of the serious matter under consideration; then the day was agreed upon for the general meeting and gradually the group thinned out. O'Hara sat at one of the tables with Devereux Smith and his friend, John Ormsby. The latter kept shaking his head sadly.

"A sorry business, this! A sorry business. I knew they'd been getting itchy up Boston way, and hell might break loose any time. The fact about Pittsburgh itself is that we haven't had too much cause to complain. England's been pretty decent about sending us help when we asked for it. But we've started a new country and we'll all have to stick by it. How about you, my boy?" he asked O'Hara.

"I'm with you," he said. "I can't quite explain it to myself, but I'm here and I intend to stay. At whatever cost," he added.

"Good," said Ormsby. "And I think, Smith, that it would be a good idea to have a few resolutions ready *before* the meeting. We might get Hugh Brackenridge on to it. He's a lawyer. We'll get nowhere if we wait for the crowd to put forth suggestions."

"I think you're right. Tell Semple how you feel and I'll talk to Brackenridge. By the way, O'Hara, you and Brackenridge ought to be pretty congenial. He's just lately come to settle here and hang out his shingle. Quite a scholar. Graduated from New Jersey College back at Princeton about four years ago. You'll be sure to be running into him soon."

After supper O'Hara walked out in the May evening. The King's Orchard was in bloom and a gentle breeze blew from the rivers, but in spite of the beauty around him his heart was sad. There had been a number of letters awaiting him when he returned yesterday. One had been from an Irish solicitor with the news that his elderly cousin, Lady Mary Tyrawley, had died and left him a legacy. Of course he would appreciate the money, but he felt real grief. Lady Mary had come next to his mother in his heart. He had visited her from his small boyhood on, and had loved the big country house, the stabling where the riding horses lived, the big hound Nicanor with the long silken ears who sat close to his mistress at meals and watched with melting eyes for the titbits handed him. The room where O'Hara had always slept had had a sloping ceiling that seemed somehow to enfold and caress him; out of the dormer window could be seen the lovely ragged water meadows and a bit of the river beyond. Over her domain as over her young relative, Lady Mary, tall, handsome and reserved, had exercised firmness mingled with kindness. Now, the thought that stabbed O'Hara through his memories was that during his years in America he had written her so seldom! And to her, old and lonely, letters would have meant much. Why had he not sent them? It was an anguished question which he could not answer.

But there was another and sharper ache in his heart. There had been three letters from Mary, each moving him with the charm of her recounted days, and her words of affection. But in each she had managed to mention her fear of the frontier. While this was in relation to himself it meant also that she shrank from even the thought of its dangers and hardships. With almost superhuman effort he had managed to get back to Philadelphia the year before, only to find Mary a little older, a little more beautiful, and himself more hopelessly in love. Even without Mr. Carson's frank talk with him then, he could not fail to be aware that Mary was fast reaching the stage when many admirers would besiege the Carson home. Would her feeling for him be wiped out by the ardour of other present lovers while he was far away? He was afraid he could not get back east now for he was sure he would be sent out at once to deal with the Indians as best he could since war had really begun.

The war. On top of everything else the war. While he knew he was no coward he had no stomach for fighting. If there was only some other way he might serve the Colonies! Well, he came of a soldier line and he must carry on as best he could.

Through the gathering dusk he looked at the fort. Even that depressed him. For in the three years and a half that he had been in Pittsburgh the great fortress had fallen into a mild disrepair. Its first brilliant glory had departed. The earth works here and there were crumbling, the bastions had breaches, the draw-bridge looked rusty and unsafe. He thought of going in to see Captain Grant but in the light of the present news he decided against it. So he continued walking along the paths in the King's Gardens while the darkness which suited his mood closed in. When he made a sudden turn about he all but ran into another man.

"I'm sorry, sir. I was thinking and didn't know there was anyone near."

The other man had a pleasant voice. "No harm done," he said. "I was doing a little thinking myself. Sometimes it comes easier while you walk. My name's Hugh Brackenridge."

"Why, this is a coincidence. I heard you mentioned only an hour or so ago by Devereux Smith! He said I'd soon be running into you but I didn't expect to, literally. I'm James O'Hara."

"Well, I've heard of you too and from the same source. That ought to be a proper introduction. I've just come to Pittsburgh within the last months and I gather you've been away during that time. I've got me a cabin along the Monongahela. Would you care to come with me there and continue our thinking out loud?"

"I would like nothing better. I'm depressed to-night and I dreaded going back to the tavern. Thank you for the invitation!"

The young men made their way to the group of log cabins above the river at one of which Brackenridge stopped. The door was open and a large candle burning on the table.

"I only went out for a breath of air. I've been working all evening. Sit down and let's take stock of each other. My word, I'm glad to meet a young man who can handle the King's English!"

O'Hara sized up his host with pleasure. A tall, slender chap with a broad scholarly brow and serious eyes but a mouth mobile and friendly.

"Well, now, O'Hara, tell me about yourself first. When I start they say it's hard stopping me!"

O'Hara laughed and sketched his background briefly as well as his years in the new world. Brackenridge listened intently.

"I had an upbringing as different from that as day from night. Pioneer farm boy beyond the mountains, dead set to go to college. I got my first Latin and Greek from a minister in return for doing chores. Walked thirty miles to do it."

He paused and smiled. "I'll tell you one of my darkest hours. Just to give you an idea. I had borrowed a copy of *Horace* from this Reverend Blair and one morning when I went out early to milk I took it along intending to read a little in the quiet when I'd finished, so I laid it on a stump. When my pail was full I heard a yellow-breasted chat I'd been listening for, so I set down the milk and went looking for it. When I came back the cow had chewed up *Horace*! *There* was a tragedy."

O'Hara's face was more compassionate than he realised.

"But," Brackenridge went on, "I managed. I taught school when I was fifteen and finally got to New Jersey College and oh, it was like heaven to be there. The studies and the friends! One of my classmates was a chap named James Madison; we all feel he'll be a statesman one day. And Philip Freneau was another. He's a poet already but he'll be a better one. I think you'll be hearing about these two, at least, as time goes on. We had a little Whig literary club and we amused ourselves writing satires against the Tories. Philip and I wrote a long poem we called 'The Rising Glory of America'." Hugh laughed. "We didn't leave much out. Discovery, settlement, growth, the future. I read it at the commencement exercises and the people seemed to like it."

"Could you repeat some?" O'Hara asked eagerly.

Brackenridge looked abashed. "There," he said ruefully, "I knew I'd talk too much. It's the lawyer in me, I guess."

"No, please. I really want very much to hear the poem. Even a little."

Brackenridge still looked embarrassed but finally stood up.

"I'll say a few lines from the end. Can do it better standing." He declaimed in a strong voice:

> *'Tis but the morning of the world with us*
> *And Science yet but sheds her orient rays.*
> *I see the age, the happy age, roll on*
> *Bright with the splendours of the midday beams,*
> *I see a Homer and a Milton rise*
> *In all the pomp and majesty of song,*
> *Which give immortal vigour to the deeds*
> *Achieved by Heroes in the field of fame."*

O'Hara clapped loudly. "That's fine!" he said. "That's real poetry. I congratulate you! And thanks for saying it for me."

"It sounds different, somehow, here than in Princeton. Rather young and bumptious, but we meant it when we wrote it. And," he said, leaning forward, his dark eyes intense, "it *is* the morning of the world for us here in America. Everything is before us! Only we've got to be free."

They talked then of the war that had really begun, of the part they might have to play in it and of the meeting set for the next Tuesday.

"Smith came right over to see me about that and I've been working this evening on the Resolutions. You see, one of the men can have them tucked in his shirt tail all the time and after the Committee confers, can bring them out and no one in the crowd will know that they aren't spur of the moment proceedings. You know why I didn't go east to practise law?" he added suddenly.

"Why?"

"Because I think there's a big future for this little Pittsburgh."

"So do I. That's why I came myself. Business is what I foresee."

"Well, once the war's over you can go ahead with your industry and I'll dream of something better than coon-skin academies. A university some day. Why not? You know what my life's motto is? *Liberty and Learning.*"

When the young men finally parted, it was with a warm handshake and O'Hara went back to the tavern strangely comforted.

The next Tuesday was fair and warm and a surprising number of men gathered in the meadow above the Monongahela. Amidst the noise and confusion a committee was finally named: John Ormsby, John Campbell, Edward Ward, Samuel Semple, Thomas Smallman and Devereux Smith. And after a short conference the latter read out to the crowd the *Resolutions.*

"Resolved unanimously that this Committee have the highest sense of the spirited behaviour of their brethren in New England and do most cordially approve of their opposing the invaders of American rights and privileges to the utmost extreme."

"Yea! Hurray! Hurrah!" yelled the crowd.

There was a further Resolution that the Standing Committee should secure such arms and ammunition as were not employed in the actual service and deliver them to any captains of independent companies who would apply for them.

More cheering, more speeches, more cheering, and then gradually the meadow cleared. But the excitement was far from over. From back in the woods a dozen or more men carried a thirty-foot pine tree, stripped of its branches. This they set up in the centre of the village and proclaimed it the *Liberty Pole*. Whisky was rolled by the barrel from Suke's Run and when night fell a huge bonfire was built to light the scene. Excited pandemonium reigned. People joined hands and danced around the pole, singing, shouting, swearing. The pent-up emotions of restricted lives now found expression. O'Hara and Brackenridge were in the circle which constantly grew and heaved in the glow of the bonfire.

When at last they agreed they had had enough, they dropped out and went into the tavern where the older men were toasting "liberty" and once in a while, confusingly enough, "His Majesty King George the Third, God Bless Him."

"A thought struck me when the Resolutions were being read," O'Hara told his new friend. "That was the suggestion of the *Independent Companies*. I've just inherited a bit of money and I wondered if perhaps I could fit out a company with it when the right time comes. The legacy was from an old cousin I was fond of. She was a spirited old lady and I have an idea she would like it to go to the cause of liberty and independence."

"I haven't an extra sixpence to bless myself with," Hugh said mournfully. "I'll have to give my help some other way."

They talked till late, glad of the congeniality of their youth and ideals. But in the morning the message O'Hara expected came. He was to set out again at once for the Shawnee territory, by way of the Delawares, giving the latter encouragement and support as he went. It would be his longest and most important trip. He wrote to Mary, more ardently than he had ever done before, explaining his difficulties, lamenting his separation from her and begging her to keep the most dear and special place in her affections for him even though other young men desired her friendship. It was all he could say, he decided, as he sanded the words torn from his heart, and sealed the letter ready to send by the next express rider.

He had been five days out on his new journey when he reined Pitt suddenly one afternoon. He noticed with the keen eyes he had developed, a small pile of sticks, the kind of smokeless fire the Indians built. An Indian or a group of them was therefore near. He sat motionless looking sharply about in all directions. Suddenly he saw the figure of a man leaning against a tree, his glazed eyes looking back at him. It was Guyasuta! He jumped from his horse, and holding the bridle advanced quickly to the Indian who looked up at him wonderingly.

"O'Hara," he muttered through swollen lips.

"You are sick. What is it?" O'Hara asked quickly.

"Snakebite," the old man said. "Rattler, very bad. Water. I can hear stream."

So could O'Hara. He tethered his horse, got one of his cooking pots and hurried in the direction of the sound. When he returned Guyasuta drank with great parched swallowings. O'Hara then wet a large handkerchief and placed it on the sick man's head.

"Now, let's look at the bite," he said. "On the leg?"

He had not far to search. Under the loosed deerskin legging the leg was swollen to twice its size. The small tragic red marks were plainly visible. He had received some instructions from Elliott on snake bites. If possible and in time the wound should be sucked. He asked Guyasuta, knowing he himself could not have reached the spot, making his lips form a sucking sound.

"Mebbe too late. You're not afraid?"

"No," said O'Hara. "I'll try."

"You have food?"

"Yes."

"Bring some. Wash poison out of mouth first with water, then eat food and spit out."

O'Hara provided for his own safety, then applied his lips to the wound though he feared the poison had now spread. A faint shudder went through him but he persisted without hesitation, spitting out the venom if he had caught any, then the water, then the chewed food.

Guyasuta looked at him with yearning eyes between the retchings that shook him. The strange bond established in the Delaware chief's wigwam that far away night seemed now indissoluble.

"Brave man. Good man," muttered the Indian. "You know *pocoon*? Bloodroot?"

" I think so."

"Find some." The words were faint.

O'Hara searched with an anxious heart. He was afraid the Indian was dying, and he himself for the first time was feeling the horrible danger of rattlers. He watched his every step for fear he would see the flashing loop of a black and yellow neck. After a short time he came upon a clump of bloodroot which Elliott had once told him was an Indian cure. He pulled it up, root and all and went back to Guyasuta. The heavy perspiration still dripped from him and he was retching desperately. Weakly, as he could get breath he directed O'Hara.

"Mash root and . . . lay . . . on . . . bite."

It was not difficult to do, and in a few seconds a moist mass was spread on the leg.

"Mash leaves. Put water on. I drink. . . ."

This too was done. O'Hara kept bringing fresh water from the stream, bathing the hot face and hands, and finally persuading the Indian to lie down with a rolled blanket for a pillow. The soft, sifted afternoon light finally began to fade. O'Hara ate his supper of jerk and water, and as the night fell, spread his other blanket on the ground beside Guyasuta and sat close. The Indian had stopped retching now and seemed drowsy. Whether this was a good sign or not O'Hara did not know. He kept feeling the improvised poultice of bloodroot and when it became hot from the fever he placed a new, cooling one on the wound. Once Guyasuta spoke in his own tongue but O'Hara knew the words.

"My son. My son," he said.

Towards morning O'Hara too fell asleep. When he woke at daylight with a start, Guyasuta's eyes were open and watching him. It was evident that the fever was down.

"I get well now," the Indian said simply.

O'Hara remembered that with a snake bite the outcome was not long in the balance. He felt an almost unwarranted sense of thankfulness and pleasure.

"Good! Wonderful!" he said smiling at his companion.

He examined the leg. The swelling had gone down quite

appreciably. The clean blood of the victim and his own ministra-
tions had evidently overcome the poison. He felt happier than he
had for weeks, and Guyasuta's words of the night before made a
warmth in his lonely heart.

It was the work of a few minutes to shoot a squirrel. The
skinning and cleaning took longer but he had become expert.
The fire had been built first and now the pieces were soon bubbling
in the pot. With a pinch of the precious salt he carried and a bit
of jerk to dip in the broth, there was soon a tasty breakfast. Guyasuta
ate ravenously. O'Hara guessed he had not done so for some days.
After the meal was over the facts all came out. The chief had been
making his way on foot alone through the forest as he liked to do
when he was overtaken by a sudden sickness. His head was heavy,
he said, his stomach full of pain. He had made a fire but had not
strength to hunt or to cook. While in this dazed weakness he had
trodden on the rattler. He seemed greatly ashamed of the happening for to him it was an evidence of carelessness—a quality which
Indians did not tolerate in the woods especially. All he was able
then to do was to sink down under the tree where O'Hara had
found him.

When he urged O'Hara to go on and leave him there to gain
some strength, the young man flatly refused. So, the two through
the pleasant days and the more quiet nights were close together,
the strange tie which neither could explain growing stronger. Each
in their conversations tried honestly to present the problems of his
race. O'Hara told of the war and Guyasuta shook his head sadly.

"If the white men fight even their *King* for this country, they
will want it all. Then what will the poor Indian do? My heart is
heavy."

"Could you not make your Mingoes and Senecas help the
Colonies in this war? The white men would repay you!"

Guyasuta shook his wise head again.

"I have made many treaties. They have been broken like
rotten sticks. But what I can do to keep the peace, I will do."

When O'Hara found he would not be more specific he dismissed
the subject and turned to forest and Indian lore. He spoke once
of Simon Girty and Guyasuta looked off through the trees.

"Sometimes with a man you need eyes here," he said pointing
to his forehead, "and eyes here," he added, touching the back of
his head.

"So!" O'Hara said in surprise.

When at last travel was possible, O'Hara put the Indian on his own horse and walked beside him to the nearest friendly village some ten miles away. Their parting was touching in the extreme to O'Hara, for Guyasuta said again half under his breath, "My son. My son!" And the young man wrung the chief's hand as he would have his dearest white friend's.

As he went on his way to fulfil his newest commission, O'Hara thought to himself, *No matter what happens after this, I have now had what is probably the biggest experience of my journey.*

There had been, however, near the end of his homeward trip an incident that shook him more than he liked to admit. He had stopped at a little Indian settlement on the Muskingum to stay the night with John Heckwelder, the Moravian missionary whom he had met once at Fort Pitt. Just after they had gone to bed an Indian runner arrived with a message for Heckwelder. O'Hara overheard the words in amazement.

"Get our friend O'Hara out of town immediately as eleven warriors from Sandusky are well on their way to take or murder him."

"I can't believe this," O'Hara burst out. "Why would any Indians want to murder *me*? I've been friends with them."

"I'll get you a guide as fast as I can, but there's no answer to your question," Heckwelder said, adding, "And I've lived among them for a long time."

When the guide, a handsome young Indian named Anthony, stood before them he looked O'Hara in the eye.

"Do you trust me?" he asked.

"I do," O'Hara said. "So let's be off."

They walked through the woods towards the Ohio along devious paths, O'Hara leading Pitt. When daylight broke Anthony stole to the river at intervals until at last he spied two white men cleaning out a canoe on the opposite shore.

"Here," he said, "you had better cross. We daren't call to them. Can you swim it?"

"I think so. If my horse can."

"Oh, they can always swim, the horses."

When he had thanked his guide O'Hara spoke to Pitt, stroked his nose affectionately and led him into the stream. The river was quiet and not too wide at this point, but still it was a chilled and exhausted man and horse that reached the other side. The men they had seen so intent upon their work had finished it and gone into the house during the crossing and after a few muffled shouts as he neared the shore, O'Hara had thought best to save his breath for swimming. Once at the house there was a pioneer welcome and after a hot breakfast and a drying out before the fire he went on his way but with knitted brows.

"Maybe it's not well to be over confident," he muttered to himself.

So it was April almost two years after he had left it, when he was again at Fort Pitt. He made prompt report of his travels to Alexander McKee and also to General Hand, then Commandant at the fort which was now considered Colonial property. He found that some time earlier Guyasuta along with Captain Pipe, a Delaware chief, The Shade, a Shawnee, and several others, had been there for a Conference and had promised neutrality at least; O'Hara hoped that his influence had helped bring this about.

But there was so much important news of the war itself to catch up on that for days he talked of little else to Semple, Smith and Brackenridge. Colonel George Washington of Virginia, they said, had been appointed Commander in Chief of the Army by the Congress and all agreed he was the best man.

"He stayed here once, mind, at my very tavern. Well, well, you never know what any traveller will turn out to be!" said Semple complacently.

There had been a dispiriting first winter for the Continental Army up at Cambridge, by all reports; then that next spring while General Howe was holed up in Boston watching as a cat does a mouse, a lot of heavy guns had been miraculously brought down from Ticonderoga through three hundred miles of blizzard and thaw and mounted on Dorchester heights overlooking the city. This had turned the score. Boston became untenable and Howe had taken to his ships. But of course he'd try to strike elsewhere. New York, maybe? Or Philadelphia.

From then on though things had gone badly for General Washington. Mostly defeat or withdrawal: Long Island, Manhattan, White Plains. He had ferried his army to New Jersey and finally had reached the Delaware. As the tellers went on with the story at this point, each man broke in excitedly upon the other's version of how on a cold snowy night the General had taken his army over the river amid the ice and captured Trenton! If only, they all lamented, he could have followed up this victory with another at once! But, report had it, his men were poorly fed and

more poorly clad—many of them without shoes in the snow—
and General Howe was pressing hard upon them. At last word
they were quartering in a place in New Jersey called Morristown.

But the greatest piece of news was in connexion with what was
called *The Declaration of Independence*, written and approved the
summer before. The newspapers which the express riders had
brought over the mountains at the time had carried copies, and
this first night after O'Hara's return, he and Hugh Brackenridge
pored over one in the latter's cabin.

"It's the best writing I've ever read," Hugh said. "There's
some question yet who was responsible but one rider said people in
Philadelphia were sure it was a young Virginian by the name of
Thomas Jefferson. It's a wonder to me they didn't let Franklin
do it. But," he added thoughtfully, "he'd have put a joke or a
quip in somewhere and Congress couldn't take a chance on any
levity with this. Read it! I want to listen."

O'Hara read it slowly aloud: " 'When in the course of human
events it becomes necessary for one people to dissolve the political
bonds which have connected them with another and to assume
among the powers of the earth . . .' "

He read it through, but on the last sentence his voice caught.
The eyes of the two young men were misty.

" 'And for the support of this Declaration we mutually pledge
our lives, our fortunes and our sacred honour.' "

"You see that cut the tie forever," Brackenridge said. "There's
a sadness about it but we daren't think of that now. You know
Congress and General Washington were still trying for peace with
the King when something happened a year last spring they hadn't
bargained for. Ever hear of Fort Ticonderoga?"

"Just the name."

"Well, it's pretty strategic. Stands on the border of New York
and Vermont, dominating the water route to Canada. Without
orders or a by-your-leave two American officers, an Ethan Allen
for one and a Colonel Benedict Arnold pushed right up to it and
captured it! That showed the King that the Colonies meant business, you see, and things went on from there in earnest."

"Benedict Arnold?" O'Hara repeated in surprise.

"Yes. Know anything about him?"

"I had a letter just yesterday from a girl I know in Philadelphia.
She mentioned that one of her older friends was—well—very much
interested in this Colonel Arnold."

"Yes? Did she mention her name?"

"Peggy Shippen."

"Prominent people, I hear, the Shippens. Devereux Smith told me they're one of the families there that lean to the Tory side, and there are a good many more, I guess. Well, what are you going to do now?"

"Raise my company, I hope. Unless . . ." he hesitated, "unless I should go back to Philadelphia first."

"Ah," Hugh smiled, "so that's the way the wind blows, eh?" O'Hara nodded.

"I've got my own girl picked out from back home, but I have to earn a little more before I can think of marriage. Well, good luck to us both, and to the girls, as well. It's not an easy life for a woman out here."

At the sharp spasm of pain that passed over O'Hara's face Brackenridge looked concerned.

"Is that the trouble?"

"The most of it."

"I'm sorry. I always talk too much. Don't worry, though. Love breaks down all barriers."

"I hope so," O'Hara answered.

As a matter of fact he was desperately unhappy. Along with the letter from Mary which had awaited him had been one from her father. It was kindly but very firm. Mary, he said, was now seventeen. It was right and natural that many eligible young men should frequent their house and constitute her escorts in the social life of the city. He had talked again with her and found that she felt she could never go to live on the frontier. If then, O'Hara was still determined to make Pittsburgh his home it would seem advisable for him not to see Mary again. While it was true that she now cared for him, it was inevitable (with no disrespect to O'Hara) that she would get over it and eventually marry within the sphere in which she had been brought up. After each of O'Hara's visits, she had been for some time unsettled and unhappy. So, from the standpoint of a father, he felt that the visits should cease. He would always have the greatest interest in Mr. O'Hara's career and with all good wishes, etc. . . .

O'Hara sat in his room and read this over with something like physical pain in his heart. He was a reasonable man and so could understand Mr. Carson's attitude. His one hope during the last two years had been that the strength of his own love and an increasing warmth of feeling upon Mary's part would overcome her reluctance to the thought of the frontier and, as Hugh had put it, break down all barriers. He had now but two choices. One was to go to Philadelphia and against Mr. Carson's wishes storm his home and Mary's heart, thereby perhaps bringing unhappiness to her and anger to her father. The other was to pour out his longings to her in his letters as he had been doing—fortunately they had not been forbidden—and *wait*. Oh, hardest, most unbearable of all human burdens! To wait. And in his love to compel her by the very power of the thoughts he would send out to her, to remember him and hold him dear.

There was of course one other course which strangely enough he did not even consider seriously. This was to leave Pittsburgh for good and return to the East. When the idea passed fleetingly through his mind, he spoke aloud to himself.

"It's one of the laws of love that a wife's place is with her husband wherever that is. So it will have to be with me."

But at the same time he clenched his hands. *I will not despair and I'll never give up*, he thought.

He wrote to Mr. Carson, making no reference to the matter of his letter, merely stating that he regretted greatly that since he was about to raise and captain a company for frontier service it would be impossible for him to return to Philadelphia at this time. With kindest remembrances to him and to Mistress Mary, he remained his most respectful and obedient . . .

The next day after a more or less sleepless night he made the rounds of the most important men in the village including General Hand, who was now out of British uniform. With a determined expression on his lips and a strange light in his eyes O'Hara explained that he wished to purchase a section of the King's Orchard. At first he met with surprised resistance but he persevered. He had money, *hard money* and it was scarce. By the end of the third day he was the possessor of a plot of land along the Allegheny, in the midst of the apple trees. Devereux Smith, who had been appointed to consummate the deal, was curious.

"What the devil do you want this particular spot for?" he asked. "You've got all that other property."

"I intend to build a house here when the war lets up a little."

"Ah, hah! If you're getting a nest ready you must have the bird picked out."

"Perhaps," O'Hara replied, but with such reserve that there

were no further questions. At least he felt he had in this instance thrown his dreams and intentions forward far beyond the date in hand, as a strong man should do. There was a power, he believed, in this active faith.

The matter of raising a company took more time than he had imagined. The problem of the settlers round about was that in enlisting for general service they were leaving their homes unguarded. O'Hara felt their position keenly. It was to him a marvel that *any* man under existing conditions would volunteer for new perils while his family was left to face alone the constant old ones. But their love of liberty was a fire in their bones and with it an incurable thirst for adventure.

"You'll get your men," Semple encouraged O'Hara. "There's a good few enlisting now in the Eighth Pennsylvania for the regular army. It's the Scotch-Irish hereabouts you can count on. I'll tell you about them, laddie. As I always say, give a Scotch-Irishman a bible, a bottle of whisky and a rifle and he'd beat down the gates of hell itself."

By the first of October a company of forty men had been formed and outfitted. For frontier fighting there was no uniform, only the regular hunting shirt and deerskin breeches. There were, however, two other necessities: ammunition and boats. For the assignment given O'Hara by General Hand was to proceed with his company down the Ohio to Fort Randolph on the Kanawha River at the Virginia border, there to protect the countryside, to hold the Indians in check and to prevent them from making any contact with British forces.

Ammunition was not too plentiful but with his money and business acumen, O'Hara managed to secure a goodly amount. So much that after the party had left, General Hand and Captain Grant wondered uncomfortably how this had been achieved. There were a few good boat builders in Pittsburgh and samples of their workmanship were always moored along the rivers. O'Hara bought two large, stout "flatboats," laded them with the food supply, goods for Indian trading, ammunition, and finally his men.

Through the bright, early haze of an October morning the boats pushed off, heading down the Ohio, with a friendly group of interested well-wishers on the shore waving them farewell. One of these was Hugh Brackenridge. He had said his real good-bye the night before almost with tears.

"I'm no woodsman, O'Hara," he lamented. "I'm not physically

strong. What little I have to recommend me is up here," touching his forehead. "I'd be worse than useless in frontier fighting and I hate myself for it. They might use me as a chaplain. I guess I didn't tell you I started out for the ministry before I changed to the law."

O'Hara had comforted him. "Don't forget," he said, "that brains are better than brawn. You'll find your work and do it well. Just be here when I get back. Don't forget!"

As the boats moved slowly down the great Ohio, O'Hara was overcome with the unimaginable loveliness of the new scenes. The great river wound among wooded hills, each bend bringing a more striking panorama into view. Herds of buffalo, elk and other deer could often be seen standing in the shallows and upon the shining water itself here and there were fleets of ducks, geese or snowy swans. The men had soon discovered also the riches beneath the water and had caught large perch and bass.

One never-ending pleasure to O'Hara was the quick flame-like flashes among the already colouring forests: the scarlet, green and gold plumage of flocks, apparently, of parakeets! And once pigeons flew overhead in such numbers as to darken the sun! Everywhere the impression was first of incredible and primeval fecundity, and second of unutterable loneliness. For there were no towns along the banks, no settlers' cabins, no Indian villages. All had withdrawn to less exposed sites. So the flatboats moved on in the great silences until it seemed as though the men were lost in the lush and unbelievable beauty of an empty world.

At night, as O'Hara lay looking up at the stars, he thought of Mary's last letter which he carried next his heart. The scraps of war news in it were discouraging as had been the fuller reports brought to Pittsburgh by the express riders. Mary wrote that her father thought people in general were not concerned enough over the war. Peggy Shippen, of all her friends, talked most about it for she still was interested in Colonel Benedict Arnold. He had had the only real victory lately. They said he had built a fleet of ships from raw timber up at Lake Champlain and with them had checked an invasion from Canada. Peggy bragged about him all the time and it looked as though she might be in love, but the way she flirted, even with General Washington himself when he had been there, was a caution. Of course she would flirt with anybody. Over the last lines of the letter O'Hara pored though he knew it well by heart.

I am wondering what you will be doing in the war and what danger you may be in. I say a prayer for you every night.

Your true friend,

Mary Carson

This said so much and yet so distressingly little. Only *his friend* after all that had passed between them? How much restraint her father had already put upon her he had no way of knowing. She would before long have his last letter telling of his new title— for a *Captaincy* had been automatically accorded him—and of the proposed trip to Fort Randolph. How long he would have to stay there he could not say. But if there should be any way of sending a letter, he told her, he would surely write. And then he sent his love, as he put it, unchanged and unchanging.

When at last the boats reached the mouth of the Great Kanawha River they moved up to the fort itself. And a sorry-looking place it was! No one, least of all O'Hara, had been prepared for its general decrepitude. A half-dozen men in worn frontier dress greeted them with subdued cheers.

"We could yell louder all right, but we don't want to stir up any trouble."

"Have you had much?" O'Hara asked.

"Plenty," one of the men said. "You see most of the fellahs round here have gone off to join the Ninth Virginia an' that leaves the families pretty unprotected. We'll get back a-kitin' to ours now you're all here. We've been prayin', I tell you, that help would come for we'd been told Governor Pat Henry had sent for it. Well, you can bet your boots you're welcome."

And so the months of the company's duty began to roll. They all fell to at once to rebuild the fort and established themselves in what semblance of comfort was possible. Patrols went out daily in all directions to scout for Indians. O'Hara knew the necessity for this. It was indeed what they had been sent out here for, but as he explained one night to his men, he himself had always had peaceful relations with the Indians both as trader and agent. He had never killed a red man and only once had felt his own life was in danger from them. He urged his men to go slow, to be sure any Indians they caught sight of were indeed enemies. But in two weeks' time three of his men had been killed. From then on the eyes of the recruits were like steel and their lips shut tight. They shot first thereafter and O'Hara said no more. He did decide however, to do some trading himself. He found a half-dozen men, bored sufficiently to be willing to take one of the boats down a little farther and across the river. Then with a white cloth fastened to the top of his rifle and a big trader's sack over his arm he advanced alone into the forest. As he had surmised, they had not been unobserved. Very soon a group of Shawnees were around him. He talked to them in their own tongue, urged them to stop their forays on the other side, and then set forth his wares.

When the time for actual barter came he was adamant: he didn't want furs; he wanted *powder*. By what devious means the Indians got powder no one was ever sure, but they usually had it. There was now heated and angry discussion while the tempting array of goods lay spread before their eyes. When they made their refusal, O'Hara nodded and quietly began putting the gay strouds, the trinkets, the jews'-harps, the vermilion and the rest back into his sack. At once there was an outcry and more consultation. In the end the trade was consummated and when the boatload returned safely to the Kanawha with a goodly supply of powder O'Hara could sense the rising respect among his company.

"But why wouldn't they just shoot you or tomahawk you and keep the goods and the powder both?" one man asked.

"I honestly don't know," O'Hara answered. "They are used to trading for one thing and though you won't believe it, they have certain principles that govern their actions."

"Principles!" The men shouted in derision, but O'Hara stood firm.

"I mean that. Besides, some of them may have recognised me or my name. I've been around among the Shawnees a good deal."

"An' what sort of principle makes them come across here an' plunder an' kill every family they can find?"

"They were once promised this land by a treaty, down through Kentucky, and the whites didn't keep their word."

"By God, that's news to me," one man said. "What'll we do now, then? Just sit here an' let them swarm over the countryside?"

"No," said O'Hara, "I've warned them now and told them to pass the word. As to us, we'll have to go on doing what we're here for."

One day in late December they had a visitor, a tall young man with bright red hair. O'Hara brought him up to the fire with eager hospitality. Whatever his reason for coming he presented a welcome diversion. Besides, O'Hara liked the man on sight.

"Clark," the stranger was saying. "George Rogers Clark is my name. I just thought I'd have a look at your fort here."

"I'm James O'Hara. Captain," he added, laughing a little at the incongruity.

Clark joined him. "Oh, I can beat that, as of the last weeks. I got promoted to Lieutenant-Colonel! But . . . you're not native here, are you, Captain?"

"Irish once. American now."

"Fine! Well, I guess you've been round enough to know titles don't do you a damned bit of good in wilderness fighting, eh, men? Nice to have at soirées and things like that."

There was an engaging mixture of hard strength and friendship about the stranger, with humour thrown in.

"Well, I suppose you'd all like to hear the latest war news," he said.

The men who were there at the moment gathered close.

"I'm just fresh from Williamsburg with the Governor so I got it straight. And some of it's good for a change, Dad Drabit! Burgoyne has surrendered to our General Gates up at Saratoga!"

There was a wild burst of cheers.

"The rest isn't quite so fine. General Washington and his army are at a place called Valley Forge in Pennsylvania and they're in a devil of a bad way. Not enough clothes for half of them in this weather and short rations. And why in the name of God should this be? They're not too far from Philadelphia. People there have enough and why can't they share it? Hasn't Washington got a Quartermaster that's worth his salt? I can't understand it, but all the messages that get through say the men are suffering something terrible. Howe's in Philadelphia. The Congress has moved out to a place called York, to be safe. Hah! Well, I guess that's about all I know."

O'Hara could see Clark's eyes upon him with an intentness that was disconcerting. When the men present had gone out on their various duties Clark spoke.

"I'd like to talk with you where we'd be sure to be alone. Other scouts likely to be returning here?"

"Yes."

"Could we go out and find a nice soft log anywhere to sit on?"

They went out laughing, and into the deep wood behind the fort where they finally settled on a fallen tree.

"I'll try to be as brief as I can," Clark began.

"I've got an idea and it's burning a hope in me. This is it. As I see it, we've got to capture Kaskaskia and Vincennes or the British may come smack down between them from the north and then all the Kentucky area and Virginia too would be wide open for them. See? If we can take Kaskaskia we'd cut off some of Detroit's provisions and get command of the two big rivers. It would help control the Indians and might even win them over to the American side. Then," he added, "Vincennes later."

"I wish I knew the geography of this better," O'Hara said regretfully.

"Oh, I can help you on that." Clark took a bit of pencil and paper from his pocket and quickly drew a rough triangle of south-flowing rivers with Kaskaskia on the lower Missouri at the left and Vicennes on the Wabash to the right. He sketched in the Ohio flowing towards and joining the Wabash and then the uniting of all the waters at the point of the triangle where they became the Mississippi.

"Do you get the picture?"

"Very clearly. But why not Vincennes first?"

"Has to be the other way," Clark said. "Now. I've just been with Governor Patrick Henry and told my plan. He approved of it but he didn't like the idea of sending a force a thousand miles from their eastern base. But luckily for me Tom Jefferson was there at the time and he and two others spoke up for me."

"You know Thomas Jefferson?" O'Hara asked with interest.

"I've known him since I was born," Clark said. "Our planta-tions join. He's some older than I am. Another red-head, by the way. Say, how old are you?"

"Born in 1752."

"Why, Dad Drabit, so was I!"

They slapped each other's shoulders in a kind of jubilation.

"I thought when I met you there was a kinship between us," O'Hara said.

"Me too. And now for the most solemn promise you've ever made. Can you keep what I've told you locked inside you? Not a word to any man?"

"I can and I will."

"Good. I trust you and I'll need you and your men. Will you join me?"

"When?"

"Probably not till spring. I'm going north, up round Fort Pitt now to do some recruiting. It'll be tough work in any case but I daren't let the men know all they're getting in for. On the face of it, it's for the defence of Kentucky. That's what the Governor told the Assembly or they wouldn't have approved it."

"But it's not true."

"True as far as it goes. True enough for war-time. We are going to defend Kentucky but we're going to do it by invading the enemy's country and smashing him there. Are you really interested in the expedition and in any case will you keep the secret on your honour?"

"Yes, to both," O'Hara said slowly as they rose and shook hands. "The only thing is that we were supposed to go on down towards the Ozark in the spring."

"Just hold on here till I come. You're pretty much on your own, aren't you?"

"Oh, yes," O'Hara smiled. "Not much supervision possible here."

"Then wait for me and don't let an Injun pick you off in the meantime."

"*Eh bien!*" O'Hara said without thinking, as he smiled.

The effect of the words on Clark was electric. He grabbed O'Hara's shoulders.

"Don't tell me you know some French!"

"I was educated in Paris."

Clark's face was a study of amazement and delight.

"The Lord sent you," he said. "I know about as much French as you could wad a gun with and my men don't know that much. Kaskaskia and Vincennes are full of Frenchies, so you see what it'll mean to have you along."

"And you would have gone on with this without anyone who spoke French?"

A wide and most infectious grin spread over Clark's face.

"I'll tell you how I have things figured out. In any big project like this there's seventy-five per cent damned hard work, twenty per cent bluff and five per cent luck! I take chances. When I have to. Only now for the love of heaven, stay alive till I get back here to meet you!"

Before he left O'Hara asked a favour.

"When you finally leave Pittsburgh would you bring any letters for me that may be there? At Semple's Tavern."

Clark looked at him keenly.

E

"This undertaking I'm interested in is going to be hard as the devil and plenty dangerous. I'll not think ill of you if you go about your own affairs instead of joining."

"But you feel it's going to be important in helping win the war?"

"I do, by God!"

"I'll be with you, then. But," he smiled, "don't forget the letters."

They parted with something like affection: two strong handsome young men, the same age, and nearly the same height, but more important, with much the same qualities of courage and determination.

At Fort Randolph winter crawled its way to spring, monotony punctuated by rifle shots and death. O'Hara developed the habit of watching the sky at night, naming the stars he knew, noting the silvery vapour of light in the Milky Way, the splendour of Orion, and most of all, the unimaginable remoteness and energy of Sirius, the Dog Star. All this beauty brought some comfort and even occasional exaltation to his lonely heart. For in addition to his desperate longing for his love he brooded often upon the death of Cornstalk who had been murdered early that fall in this very place. He remembered the Indian's kindness; the days and nights they had spent together; and he grieved for his friend. As to his men, he had the feeling that they, like himself, would welcome any change and ask few questions when Clark's boats finally reached the Kanawha to pick them up.

This came to pass on the 18th of May. Clark had succeeded in raising a force of 150 frontiersmen, and twenty settlers' families had joined for protection on the river journey. O'Hara's flatboats fell into line with the others and they all floated downstream. Clark had sent orders ahead for as many men as Kentucky could send to meet him at Dennon's Lick but there were, alas, very few when they got there. However, to make up, among them was Simon Kenton, known all through the Back Country as the most expert scout of them all. He, as their pilot now guided the little fleet to the Falls of the Ohio, after they had dropped the settlers at a spot called Corn Island. It was the day after they had shot the rapids at the Falls that Clark suddenly began feeling inside his shirt as he and O'Hara were talking.

"Dad Drabit, I forgot your letter! Here, take it. If the inside's as sweet as the outside smells you'll be all right."

There was, then, only one. But while it carried the perfume of lavender as usual, O'Hara's heart felt like lead as he read it.

For it was a cool little note, telling briefly of Philadelphia in war-time and ending with the statement that since she could not know where he was she felt it might be better if she did not write again. For the present. And she returned to the formal "Mr. O'Hara," in her salutation. His despair this time was absolute. She had accepted her father's dictum then without a struggle, and his own great love had been of no avail. One fact rose at once to his mind. On this wild and desperately dangerous adventure upon which he was embarking he would now have no fears. The fatalism of the frontier enveloped him. If death came, what did it matter when life had lost its sweetness and its hope. Under cover of darkness that night he tore up the letter and dropped it into the river, his heart drowning with it.

The little fleet of boats went on without mishap while Clark cheered his men and planned his strategy. Suddenly as they neared Massac where he intended to leave the boats and march overland to Kaskaskia they spied a canoe gliding towards them with one man in it. As they drew near they recognised him as one of the settlers, William Linn. He handed Clark a dispatch which he said had reached Corn Island soon after the boats left: *France had signed an alliance with the United States*. Here was unbelievable bolstering to the morale of the little force before their plunge into the wilderness! Clark's idea was to take the fort at Kaskaskia when he got there, frighten the French including the acting Governor Rocheblave, out of their wits, and then gradually show leniency. Now with this trump card up his sleeve he had something with which to dazzle them when he was ready.

They left the boats in a little gut near Massac and began to march single file through the forest, treading soft as Indians. O'Hara, his heart still heavy, found a certain comfort in the comradeship of these intrepid men, calm and casual in what he felt must be extreme danger.

"Aren't there Indians around here?" he asked Clark one day.

Clark grinned. "They're *all* around. Tribes of them. But I've got to take the chance. We'll get through," he added cheerfully. "The worst trouble now is that by another day we'll have nothing to put in our bellies."

It was true. They had to travel light and supplies were soon exhausted. There was, however, one saving fact. This was the

berry season in Illinois: dew berries, blackberries, and wild rasp-
berries hung in ripe plentitude and the men fell upon them with
zest.

"Why can't we shoot a deer or some game?" O'Hara asked
softly one night, with hungry curiosity as he and Clark talked
together.

Clark explained patiently. On the frontier, especially through
the Virginia and Kentucky areas, almost anyone could tell the
sound of one rifle from another. The Indians were good at this.
If they heard shots now they would know they were from white
rifles and get the little company's location at once.

"I'll tell you a story," Clark said. "Back in Kentucky there
was a girl that thought her husband was dead. Been gone two
years. Indians got him. Well, on just the day she was going to
marry again a shot was heard in the woods and she screamed,
'That's John's rifle.' And by God, it was. These fellahs here . . ."
He stopped and looked over his sleeping men, sleeping that light
sleep of those in danger whom a mere breath can arouse. "These
fellahs know their rifles like their own souls and they can shoot
them like . . . well, the ones from Virginia and Kentucky have
a saying that they never shoot a squirrel except *in the left eye*. That
tells you!"

O'Hara became more and more convinced as they proceeded
that although Clark acted as though he had started upon this
expedition with a sort of debonair casualness, he had in effect
prepared the way beforehand with all the skill of an intelligence
officer. There must have been scouts and "spies" sent out earlier
to make maps and advise on the route; and when they finally came
to the Kaskaskia River there were in care of a French farmer
enough boats to take the men across.

"These boats just *happened* to be here, I assume?" O'Hara asked
with a twinkle.

"Guess so," Clark answered, unperturbed.

The farmer was helpful. He spoke to O'Hara who translated.
Yes, Kaskaskia had been keeping spies out but had learned nothing,
he believed. There were a great number of men there but the
Indians had generally left. The largest house inside the fort was
that of Lieutenant-Governor Rocheblave.

They ferried across the narrow river and waited for night.
Clark's decision was to attack at once, leading part of his men to
take the fort, the rest waiting for a signal to attack the town.

As midnight neared Clark with Simon Kenton, O'Hara and a small group slipped up to the fort. To their amazement they met with no resistance at the gates. They found Rocheblave's house and got in. When the Lieutenant-Governor woke it was to see himself surrounded. On one side of his bed stood a young man six feet tall with bright red hair. This was George Rogers Clark. On the other stood a second red-haired six-footer. This was Simon Kenton. At the foot stood several more husky, dirty bearded men with rifles ready.

It was easy to take Rocheblave into custody but the gallant Virginians left Mme Rocheblave undisturbed in her chamber only to find next day that most of the official British papers were missing!

"Dad Drabit," Clark said then, "we shouldn't have been so damned polite."

As soon as the fort was secured that night, Clark gave the order that he wanted all hell to break loose in the town. O'Hara at the head of the few Virginians who knew a little French, tore through the streets in the van of the company, shouting that Kaskaskia was now taken and anyone leaving his house would be shot down. As a matter of fact no shot was fired but the Americans kept up a fiendish uproar all night long, seizing all the village arms, setting patrols, demanding food, and otherwise behaving like conquerors.

And so Kaskaskia fell to Clark and the nearby town of Cahokia mildly surrendered soon after. Within the fort the officers relaxed a little. The one whom O'Hara liked best was Captain Leonhard Helm, probably sixty but sound as a nut. He was a jolly man with Rabelaisian humour and a good education, as learning went, known amongst all the company for his favourite drink of apple toddy. Now, during this brief military hiatus, Helm sat by the fire and prepared his drink, expounding on the recipe as he did so.

"To a gallon of apple brandy or whisky you add one and a half gallons of well-sweetened hot water, a dozen large apples, nutmeg, allspice, cloves, a pinch of mace and a half-pint of *good rum*."

As he spoke he drew from his inmost shirt little papers of spices and a small bottle of rum.

"I was afraid I might be killed for this on the march but the Lord preserved me. I got the whisky and apples here in the town," he added. "Now we'll let this stand three days, then heat it up with a hot poker and you'll taste a drink that has, shall we say, some *authority*."

O'Hara had a question and he decided to ask Helm.

"This capture of Kaskaskia," he said quietly. "It was so *easy*."

Helm turned around and stared at him. "Easy!" he said, and then he laughed. "I doubt if there's another man in the whole Continental Army that would have dared to do what Clark did. At any minute on that march we could have been surrounded by Indians and killed or tortured, every man-jack of us. We made it, and we had luck at the fort here, of course, but don't ever call the whole thing *easy*."

Clark came in and grinned at Helm, as he stirred his brew.

"Well," he said, "I've got the inhabitants scared of my very shadow. Now I'll begin being gradually lenient and they'll think we're pretty good fellahs. There'll be some tough work ahead with the Indians, though, as they come in. I'll have to bamboozle them some way. Then . . ." his red hair seemed to bristle as his mouth set grimly ". . . the big trip."

"To Vincennes?" asked O'Hara.

"To Vincennes. Are you sticking with us? There's not much else you can do now, is there, Dad Drabit?"

"In any case, I'm sticking," said O'Hara.

Chapter Six

All his life through, though it contained other dangers and hardships, O'Hara was to shudder as he thought of that march to Vincennes! Then along with this tremor of memory there would come a grin of amazement and satisfaction. It had been incredible; it had been impossible; but Dad Drabit, as Clark would say, they had done it!

The moment Kaskaskia was under complete control Clark began his preparations for the larger enterprise. It was most necessary for him and his small army to remain there while he dealt with the surrounding Indians; but he must find at once what the situation was at Fort Sackville in Vincennes. For this latter information he sent Simon Kenton, the intrepid scout, with Shadrach Bond, another expert woodsman, to cover the 240 miles that lay between. They left on 6th July, just two days after Kaskaskia had been captured. While waiting for their return Clark began his great game of bluff with the Indians, which O'Hara watched with fascinated interest and took part in whenever possible. Kaskaskia was surrounded by tribes on good enough terms with the French but unfriendly to the Americans. Clark had a ridiculously small force compared with the number of his adversaries, so concealing this fact as best he could he put on his show. With an air of utter confidence, almost indifference, he met the chiefs as they came in like a conqueror not to be trifled with. He let slip amongst the French the delightful lie that a huge army was even now at the Falls of the Ohio on their way to join him before he attacked Vincennes. This rumour was soon passed on to the Indians.

When Bond returned he reported that Kenton had joined up with Daniel Boone and gone on to raid the Indian country to the north-west, but as to Vincennes itself they had, dressed in blankets, looked the place well over, been undiscovered, and decided that no alarm of Clark's proximity had reached it. There were no regular troops there and no concentration of Indians.

"Why don't we start off then at once?" O'Hara asked Clark one night.

"Can't do it," Clark said. "Not till I get these Injuns here under my thumb. If we leave now, as likely as not they'd swarm up behind us on the march and that would be the end of us. I'll get them," he added. "I'll scare the hides off them yet!"

And next day the village priest, Father Gibault, now completely won over to the Americans, came with a proposition. He was accustomed to going once or twice a year to Vincennes, to shrive his flock there. Dr. Laffont, the physician, also made an annual trip. Why could they not go now together and by judicious diplomacy, win the French populace over to the Americans without the need of marching troops? To Clark and his officers this sounded only too fine, considering the few troops they had! The good Father, while emphasising that he would indulge in no secular manipulations himself, yet hinted delicately that in his spiritual conversations with his parishioners he could give strong suggestions, while Dr. Laffont could pursue his efforts in the open. The Indians on the outskirts of Vincennes knew them both and were friendly to them. The plan seemed at least reasonable so Clark bought them two horses and on 14th July they set off into the wilderness with two friends who might be useful and one of Clark's own men added as a spy to see that no double-dealing went on.

"Looks too good to be true," Clark said to O'Hara, "but, Dad Drabit, it just might work. Luck's been with us this far, anyway. And we can't take a chance on *missing* a chance."

In the stillness of the nights, sometimes under the luminous stars, sometimes along by the fire in Rocheblave's former house, the two young men talked together as young men will, lightly of life and death, seriously of adventure and ambition and occasionally hesitantly when stars or fires burned low—of love. Clark so far was emotionally untouched though his feeling was intense as to what the right wife could mean to a man.

"Now take my mother," he said once. "She married my father when she was fifteen, went to housekeeping in a little cabin he built himself right on the frontier and had ten children. She's got five officer-sons in the war this minute and as proud as the devil over it. Now if I could ever find a girl like her!"

O'Hara, his heart torn with his love and his despair, longing for the release of a shared confidence, still found himself unable to speak of Mary. And somehow as he tried to picture her delicate beauty in a log cabin, her slender body worn by birth pains and hard work as a frontier woman's must, his heart failed him. Who was he, *what* was he, to steal her away from comfort and safety? So, he, too, in these talks spoke of love only in the abstract and if Clark's discerning eye sometimes watched his tense face curiously, there was no question asked.

Early in August, Father Gibault, Dr. Laffont and their companions returned with good news. Their diplomacy, secular and spiritual, had been crowned with success! The people of Vincennes, with no strong attachment for either side had agreed to cast their lot with the Americans. A few were holding the ramshackle fort and it only remained for Clark to take over. A handful of men would be enough, they declared jubilantly.

"It looks all right so far," the colonel said somewhat dubiously to his officers that night as he scanned them. "If old Hamilton just keeps his ass on his seat out at Detroit."

A growl went up from the men, a fierceness of anger, a consuming hatred the like of which O'Hara had never seen before.

"I'd give my life to capture the Hair-Buyer," a man said.

"So would we all. Do you think he's up to something now?" It was Helm who spoke.

"Don't know," Clark said. "I've had a spy or two out there and they got the idea he's planning to set off to attack Fort Pitt."

"*Fort Pitt?*" O'Hara echoed, more moved than he would have believed possible.

"Well, they couldn't be too sure. They were damned smart to get there and back with their lives. Williams and Hurley went."

The men made no comment. They had learned that Clark with all his casualness had his feelers out everywhere. So when a man or two were suddenly missing for a time no one questioned the absence.

"I want the best officer among you to take twenty-five men and go to Vincennes and hold the fort. I'll come on if I have to, but if I don't it's all to the good. I've got plenty to keep me busy here. For this job I'll pick you, Helm."

There was a murmur of approval. Everyone liked the jovial Helm and respected him. He was a trained Indian fighter and a soldier of resource.

"Select your own men, Captain, from the enlisted," Clark went on. "You'll know what to do when you get there. Have a sharp eye out for the British, keep the populace happy, smooth down the Indians, and see that the guns all work. They've got one field gun at least, Gibault says."

So the force set off with Captain Helm putting the little papers containing his remaining spices carefully next to his skin. The ground then was not swampy, the rivers not flooded, for it was still August. It was felt that the trip would be easy.

Meanwhile the work at Kaskaskia went on. O'Hara had not only become official interpreter but also in a sense "quartermaster." With his shrewd business ability he procured in divers ways the supplies needed by the troops. On Clark's part there were two great problems: always the Indians, who were gradually being won over. Clark amazed them and in a sense delighted them with his cool courage. "The Big Knife," as they called him, was a man they could understand. As his stories grew in magnitude and bravado the chiefs became more and more respectful. With his own men Clark faced trouble. They had enlisted for a short term, now up; they were far away in strange country; they were sick and tired of everything; they wanted to go home. Like a juggler Clark tossed up for them a dozen good reasons why they should stay on. So, as winter advanced the original troops were still there. However, a new and great anxiety had developed. The encouraging messages from Helm had stopped. Because of this Clark sat up till all hours with O'Hara, walking the floor, talking, pondering.

"It's Hamilton I'm afraid of, and if Helm can't get a man through to me, I won't try a messenger from this end. He wouldn't have a chance. At least I'll wait a little longer. Listen to that goddamned rain!"

For it was falling, falling, now, constantly, often mingled with snow and sleet upon the flat and all too receptive Indian lands.

"Now, this fellah, Hamilton . . ." O'Hara began.

"One of the Crown's fine officers," Clark said through his teeth, "and Dad Drabit, he may be a gentleman from the skin out, but he's connived with the Indians and given them presents if they brought in white scalps ever since he's commanded Detroit. That's why he's called the *Hair Buyer* and there isn't a man on the frontier that doesn't hate him like . . . like . . . oh, the devil's too nice a word."

"*A British officer! Are you sure?*"

"My fine young friend, in this country you have to learn to swallow a lot without choking."

"But this Hair-Buyer business makes me sick at my stomach! I don't believe I'll sleep too well to-night."

"I can't sleep *any* night just now."

It was not until the end of January when the tension was becoming unbearable, that the news came in a most unusual and circuitous way by the arrival of one Francis Vigo, a St. Louis merchant, thoroughly pro-American. He had gone to Vincennes in the interest of his business and found the fort and the town itself taken over by General Hamilton and his troops! Captain Helm had had only a few faithful men with him in the fort at the last, it appeared, and the British had seized it without firing a shot.

"And what about Helm now?" Clark asked anxiously.

A smile broke over Vigo's swarthy countenance.

"He's on his parole not to leave his quarters or try to send word to you. And in the meanwhile it would seem the Governor's taken a great fancy to him and they drink a kind of *toddy* together."

In spite of the grievous news a roar of laughter went up from all the men listening.

Vigo went on with his report. He would guess that Hamilton must have close to five hundred men, and the fort had three field guns and two swivels.

"He thought I was so innocent, he told me his plans even. The season now is too bad, he says, but next spring he will attack Kaskaskia. When I left he made me swear a solemn oath I would not communicate with you *on my way home to St. Louis!* And I didn't by God! I went there first and came right back!"

Again the throaty laughter rose and Clark slapped Vigo warmly on the back. "Good man!" he cried. "Smart man! We can't even try to thank you. But we'll give you the best we have for your supper and a bed to sleep in to-night."

When Vigo was gone in the morning Clark and his officers held a council of war. The situation could not have been blacker. The prairie from Kaskaskia to Vincennes was now either freezing water or half-frozen mud all the way; the weather, winter cold; their force small; the whole idea of making the march under present conditions, fantastic.

As against this there were these other facts; Hamilton would never dream of suspecting an attack now, which was mightily in their favour, while by spring if he united the northern and southern Indians and came upon them here in full strength he would be irresistible. Then not only would Kaskaskia fall but there would go Kentucky and Virginia too! This was the threat that sharpened the decision of the men as they listened to their leader.

"I tell you," Clark said, "we have only one course. We've got to attack Hamilton in his own quarters and at once. For," he added, "if we don't take him, he'll take us as sure as you have a gut in your belly."

"Oh, no, he won't," yelled one fellow. And a chorus of angry shouts joined him.

O'Hara, listening, said nothing. The plan seemed suicidal, and his heart was very heavy. Clark, catching sight of his sober face, winked, and the unquenchable optimism of his friend raised O'Hara's spirits a little. After all, why should they *not* gamble upon this last and wildest chance of all? If he could be certain that a letter awaited him back at Semple's Tavern, perhaps he would now know more fear for his own safety. But Fort Pitt itself seemed a limitless distance away, and Philadelphia as far removed as heaven.

That night as they had their usual talk O'Hara knew the young colonel was serious enough in spite of his insouciant wink.

"I've got to play-act this time," he said, "if I ever did. So if you see me struttin' round like a turkey cock you'll know the reason. All the same," he said half under his breath, "I'd bind myself seven years a slave to have five hundred troops!"

"What do you really think of the situation then?"

Clark eyed him shrewdly. "Can you take it straight?" he asked.

"I wouldn't be surprised."

"Well, it's about as bad as anything could be this side of hell. But we've got no alternative. And," he added flinging up his head, "the whole business somehow suits me to a T. I like danger. I like taking a chance when I have to. It brings out all the . . ."

"Red in your hair," O'Hara finished grinning.

"Right!" They laughed together.

"One thing all this campaign has done for me, is to give me a friend," O'Hara said seriously. "I've meant to speak of this before."

"Same with me. Well, we're one year's children, as the old women say, maybe that's why we've kind of stuck together. You've helped me in more ways than your French, O'Hara."

They shook hands in a rare display of affection, then each turned somewhat shamefacedly to his bed.

The play-acting went on gloriously. To see Clark's superb confidence no one would have guessed there was a difficulty in the way. Hamilton, from his swagger, was as good as captured. The troops braced to it; the local women thrilled to it when a detachment came from Cahokia to join up; Kaskaskia raised its company too, and there was a feast to celebrate the general leave-taking. On 5th February Clark with his force of a hundred and thirty men and a dozen pack-horses set out. Each man had his own normal material equipment: a rifle, a knife and a tomahawk; and on the spiritual side the friendly Father Gibault had graciously granted absolution to Catholics and Protestants alike! Thus caparisoned in body and soul as it were, the men plunged into the rain and the mud.

It was soon evident that the march was going to be worse than anyone had dreamed. The inundation was so deep in places that the men were often up to their arm-pits in water, trying desperately to keep their powder and rifles out of the wet as they slogged along. Day or night they were never dry and never warm. The things that kept them going were that first they were physically hard as nails, and second, that Clark's high spirits and invention never failed to raise the morale. The men were allowed to shoot at game as they passed, since they were too far from Vincennes for the sound to matter and there were no Indians in that immediate vicinity. This meant that there was a feast of good hot meat every night in the pots even though the camp was on wet ground. There was also entertainment in the way of games and imitated Indian war dances. In addition to this enlivening by night Clark and his officers kept going about amongst the men by day, shouting and encouraging them and running as much through the mud and water as any of them.

On the 13th they reached the bank of the Little Wabash and here the difficulties just past seemed small by comparison with those facing them. Ordinarily the Little Wabash was narrow with a good strip of land between it and the Main Wabash river. Now, because of torrential rains the two streams had joined higher up, submerged the ground between and now presented a wide turbid expanse to the gaze of the wet, cold, weary men. O'Hara eyed his friend, the young colonel, inquiringly.

"Now what?" he asked.

"Well, this might be enough to stop any set of men not in the temper we are, but Dad Drabit, we're pretty tough!"

He sent most of the men to camp on the higher ground above the river while a small group built a pirogue. When it was finished several men paddled out in it with instructions, somewhat the same as Noah's dove, to find some dry land, but in their case *to report it anyway*! They did, but oddly enough it was the truth! A tiny island reared itself in the midst of the wide morass. As they all started for it an unusual incident proved inspiriting. A drummer boy from Cahokia found the water too deep for his short legs and began to float the drum with himself upon it! As the laughter spread he started singing comic songs, as the men propelled his strange craft for him. When O'Hara called Clark's attention to this the colonel laughed loudest of all.

"Just what we needed!" he said. "Any diversion is welcome, by God!"

The next morning on their tiny island the men heard the distant boom of the gun at Fort Sackville; by two o'clock they were on the banks of the big Wabash, nine miles below Vincennes, wet and cold as usual but now hungry into the bargain. This river could not be waded and they had but two boats. To divide the men as would be necessary with part on one side during the ferrying and part on the other was dangerous to the point of extremity but there was no other way. One more chance had to be taken. By evening they were all over the river but as the red morning sun rose they saw, still ahead of them, a flooded plain! Morale was cracking for the men's stomachs were empty. Clark went out himself and measured the water. "Only up to my neck," he whispered to O'Hara and Bowman, one of his best officers, when he came back.

"But we're six feet or over," O'Hara said anxiously. "What about the shorter men?"

"God help them. We've got to go on. Every one of you here around me do just what I do."

He wet his hands, poured a little powder on them and blackened his face like an Indian in war paint, then giving the Indian war whoop which they all knew only too well, he plunged into the water. Without a word the troops followed him.

Of the whole ghastly trip the last stretches were the worst. Weak, cold and starved, the men, trying again with desperation to hold their rifles and powder horns above the water, waded up to their chins, clung to trees as they appeared or floated on occasional logs. The two canoes picked up those sinking from utter exhaustion. Finally, more dead than alive, they landed, some dropping half in and half out of the water, on a dry woodsy spot of about ten acres in plain sight of Vincennes! The great march was over. All they had to do now was to give battle to a force probably four times the size of their own!

But as they thawed out at the carefully screened fires, or, in the case of the weakest ones, were walked up and down until the numbness went out of their legs, something like spirit returned to them. Nothing to come could be as bad as that which they had passed through. The sun shone, and at this very moment a canoe load of squaws on their way to Vincennes was captured quietly along with nearly a quarter of buffalo meat, corn, tallow and kettles. The men soon drank broth on their empty stomachs and were once again invincible.

"The holy angels must be just swarmin' around you," one solemn soldier told Clark.

"When I get time, I'll thank them," he grinned.

In the ponds near the town they could see ducks swimming and a few hunters out shooting at them. The thought of roast duck sent the saliva trickling over many a bearded chin. O'Hara with three Frenchies was dispatched to capture one of these hunters and bring him back. It did not prove hard. The man was evidently impressed with O'Hara's manner and elegant Parisian French and came peaceably.

"We've got to put the fear of God in him now," Clark said to O'Hara. "You do the translating. He seems to listen to you."

The orders were quickly given. The man was to go back to Vincennes, pass the word quietly that the Illinois army was here to take the fort. The people were to stay in their houses. The women were to have food ready to feed the soldiers. Did he know a man named Captain Bosseron? He did. Good! Better than best! He was to tell Bosseron, who was really anti-British and a friend, to find some way to get a message to Captain Helm that the Virginians were here. And if he, the hunter, warned Hamilton, he would be executed.

"Make that strong!" Clark told O'Hara.

"*Exécuté*," O'Hara repeated.

The villagers were to remain tranquil and Bosseron was to bring to Clark any extra powder he had. By a careless wave of his hand towards the woods back of them Clark conveyed the impression that it too was full of troops. So the hunter set off and the men waited. Anxiously. But not for long. Bosseron himself came with powder and good news. Hamilton suspected nothing. He and Helm were having their nightly game of piquet. The message to Helm had been taken by a Mrs. Henry whose husband was also a prisoner. The garrison had been working hard all day on repairs and were now resting. What more could Clark want? What indeed, Dad Drabit!

Bosseron went back to his anomalous position and Clark's little army moved up to Vincennes, seized the main street silently and put out guards. There was nothing conspicuous about those who entered the town. After they had washed the black from their faces they looked like any other woodsmen or French Canadians who were always moving about. Even with the first burst of firing the fort remained quiet, Hamilton no doubt blaming it on one of the shooting sprees that the Indians or the French often engaged in.

It was at this point that a few of the enlisted men approached Clark with a request. It was practically certain that as Helm sat at the game, his toddy was simmering on the hearth. Couldn't they fire into the chimney, knocking the clay and plaster down the flue into the mug? For the sport of it? It was exactly the type of thing that tickled Clark's fancy; also although it would waste some ammunition it would send troop morale soaring and he wasn't sure just then how much might be needed before they were through. He gave consent. Some time later when Hamilton realised he had an enemy at his gates, a volley hit the chimney and the anguished voice of Captain Helm rose above the noise of battle.

"You rascals! You've ruined my toddy!"

Clark's men, all expert riflemen, were ordered to pour in the hottest fire possible from different directions, then cease and indulge in great laughter, shouting and noise to bewilder the enemy and make him think fresh troops were constantly being brought up. Between the gaps in the log fort the Virginians could pick any form that showed itself, and from the trench where Bowman had managed to instal himself and a fair number of men, it had been possible to knock out the British big guns in the first hour. All through the night the noise, shouting and firing of the Virginians gave the impression of a large army. By four o'clock Clark sensed that the number of Hamilton's force while several times larger than his own, had still been exaggerated and that the complete security felt before had not added to its effectiveness now. Clark also knew that his own boldness, bluff and ingenious pretences were once again going to work.

About nine o'clock he told his officers he was going to ask for surrender. Some writing equipment was secured and Clark settled on a stump behind a wide tree to his task.

"Can you spell, O'Hara?" he asked.

"Pretty well," O'Hara smiled.

"Watch me then, for I can't. And I'll bet the old Hair-Buyer can spell like the devil. All right, let him, Dad Drabit!"

When the message was completed after corrections it read as follows:

Sir:

In order to save yourself from the impending storm which now threatens you I order you to immediately surrender yourself up with all your Garrison Stores Etc. Etc. for if I am obliged to storm you may depend upon such treatment justly due to a Murderer beware of destroying Stores of any kind or any papers or letters that is in your possession or hurting one house in the Town for by heavens, if you do there shall be no Mercy shewn you.

G. R. Clark

This, under a white flag of truce, was sent into the fort, and at once all firing ceased. During the lull the Virginians went in groups for a hot breakfast in the town, the first real meal they had had in days. The Governor's answer was brief and elegant.

Gov. Hamilton begs leave to acquaint Col. Clark that he and his Garrison are not disposed to be awed into any action Unworthy of British subjects.

H. Hamilton

When hostilities began again they were heavy. Clark's men refreshed by their good meal were ready for action in earnest. Some of the crack Virginia riflemen began shooting into the fort from two directions with a hot cross-fire. By noon the fort was quiet. The great gate was unbarred and a man emerged under a white flag who wore what could only be described as a grin. It was jolly Captain Helm himself! He brought the news that Hamilton was ready to give up if the terms were acceptable.

When the two companies of the Illinois regiment finally drew up to the fort gate to receive the surrender of the British garrison, Hamilton eyed them in bewilderment.

"But where is your army, Colonel?" he asked in a strange voice.

"This is it, Governor," Clark said smiling.

The men talked the moment over that night, Clark, Helm, O'Hara and Bowman. They all agreed that when Hamilton turned his head aside there were tears in his eyes.

"And why mightn't there be?" Helm said. "He had enough men to take you if he had only known how small your force was. He's swallowed a bitter pill, yon one, but he's still got his hair on, that's more than he deserves."

"I don't know whether he could have won anyway," O'Hara said. "The British aren't used to fighting men who shoot a squirrel only through the left eye!"

There was laughter and jollity and many a recounting both of all that had gone on upon the ghastly and incredible march and inside the fort itself as Helm waited and hoped. Of one thing they were all convinced. Vincennes could have been captured in no other way.

The men were quartered in the town after the fort was garrisoned, and O'Hara, in a house where the French flowed pleasantly around him, slept for two days from utter exhaustion. When he finally woke and stretched with vigour in spite of sore muscles he knew that he was more of a man than he had ever been even after his Indian journeys. He was now hardened, seasoned, *toughened* not only in body but also in mind. He collected his original company of whom there were now but twenty-nine and prepared to go back at least to Fort Randolph, or, as he hoped, to Fort Pitt. He had done what he had promised Clark he would do and could now leave honourably. The Indians around Vincennes, quick to sense change of masters, kept pouring in and had to be dealt with. O'Hara stayed on a little longer to be of what service he could with the dialects, and then on a bright March morning set off overland with his men.

He and Clark had had strangely little to say on their last night together.

"Your best bet is to head for Corn Island and pick up some boats there," the colonel said. "I wish you felt like coming on to Detroit with me. That'll be my next move."

O'Hara shook his head. "Sorry, but I must get back now. I'm not really a soldier of fortune, you know."

"You've made a damned good try at it, I'd say. I'm going to

need more men. I may have to go back to Fort Pitt myself later to recruit."

They stood as they had at their first meeting: two strong young men, their eyes on a level, born the same year on opposite sides of the Atlantic and thrown together by fate to help work out a new nation's destiny in the American wilderness. They wrung each other's hands hard and said no more.

The journey back by contrast to the one just past was uneventful in the extreme and when they reached Fort Randolph there was a letter for O'Hara left by some traveller giving instructions from General Brodhead, now Commandant at Fort Pitt.

"Another new one," O'Hara muttered but he smiled over the message. Since his force by now must be small, the general wrote, he was to check on the Indian situation around the countryside and if satisfactory, he was to return with his men to Fort Pitt by the end of the summer.

October was in full flame when they finally reached the last waters of the Ohio. The men were eager to scatter to their various homes before a new order sent them off to join the Eighth Pennsylvania or perhaps the Ninth Virginia. Their joy in their return was natural, but O'Hara was surprised at the quick anticipation of his own heart. He sharply quelled the thought of a letter and concentrated upon the dubious pleasure of being again in the only home he had. He looked over the rolling rivers, the fort, the bright-coloured wooded hills, the little town itself. Nothing was changed except that now no redcoats showed among the deer-skin suits. He hurried from the wharf along the dusty street to Semple's, but before entering the tavern he went to the stable to see Pitt. The horse whinnied with joy and nuzzled against him. O'Hara laying his cheek to the soft velvet nose, spoke to him tenderly. There were worse friends than a horse.

Samuel Semple was in his usual place behind his desk-counter, but at sight of O'Hara came forward with both hands outstretched.

"Bless my stars and garters!" he shouted. "We get so damned much bad news in here that I can't believe the good when I see it with my own eyes. Welcome back, laddie. We've lost track of you altogether. Where all have you been?"

"It's a long story but a pretty important one, I think. Suppose I wait . . ."

"Right. I'll pass the word to Devereux Smith and young Brackenridge and a few and we'll hear it all to-night. Agreed?"

"Gladly. It's good to be here. Is . . . are there any letters for me?"

Semple looked embarrassed and made a show of fumbling about his desk. "Now come to think of it, I don't believe there is. Everything gets held up in war-time."

"Right!" said O'Hara. "I'll have a look at my room now."

He had thought he was prepared for this blow, but he was not. Deep down below all his determined sophistry, he knew now that he had not given up. That, indeed, it was this slim but unquenchable hope rather than the blackness of despair which had steeled him through the sufferings of the Vincennes march. He had lied when he told himself he believed he had lost Mary forever. That was only that the contradiction might eventually be the more sweet. Now, the lie had become the bitter and desperate truth. If after these long months she had not written then she had indeed meant what she implied in her last letter.

He looked about the familiar room and then flung himself upon the bed. His body was tired enough, but it was his heart that was more spent. Over and over like a throbbing in his brain came a line from Spenser which he had read as a schoolboy and which had persistently come to him as he struggled through the freezing waters.

When shall this long weary day have done,
And lend me leave to come unto my love?

He fell at last into a troubled sleep and woke startled from a dream of drowning as the great gong was beat for supper. He tidied himself quickly and went downstairs. Here was Hugh Brackenridge waiting for him, one great smile of welcome. Smith came in soon and John Ormsby and they settled to eat.

"Semple says you're to save your story till later so everyone can hear it together. We've had a bare hint of it from a scout who came through and we're pretty eager to get the whole of it. My word, man, you look thinner but very fit, I must say," Brackenridge appraised.

Hugh looked thin himself. His brow seemed higher and whiter and his eyes more dark. O'Hara guessed that his lack of fighting strength still was a bitterness to him.

"But what about news from the East?" O'Hara questioned. "Tell me what's been happening in the war. I'm away behind. The last I heard was over a year ago about General Gates capturing Ticonderoga. Wherever that is," he added laughing.

They all began at once and then settled to more intelligible turns. O'Hara knew of the terrible winter at the Valley Forge, but had not known that the British General Howe had all that time been comfortably ensconced in Philadelphia, fêted and dined by the Tory families; that he had resigned a year ago in May, been replaced by Sir Henry Clinton who had orders to evacuate the city and get his forces to New York.

"Of course," Smith said, "they're smart enough to see that's the best harbour on the coast and they can bottle up the Hudson River from there. On his way across New Jersey Washington's army fell on him, Clinton, that is, and there was a pretty hot battle from all reports at a place called Monmouth. But we won."

"And what's happened since then?" O'Hara asked eagerly.

"Well, you know how a war drags on. A wearisome business, it is."

"There's *Stony Point* this summer," Hugh put in eagerly. "We must tell him about that."

"Go ahead," said Smith, "though I doubt if that fight did much more than give a general a nick-name. When we didn't hold on to the fort what the devil did we take it for? Well, go on, tell him."

Stony Point, Hugh explained, was on the west side of the Hudson, held first by the Americans, then taken over by the British in May. One night in July a General Anthony Wayne, who hailed from somewhere in the Philadelphia area, attacked the fort with about thirteen hundred picked troops and the garrison surrendered.

"And it seems, the way he stormed the place as if he wouldn't stop at hell itself, made his men call him *Mad Anthony*, and now I guess everybody's saying it. Must be quite a man."

"But I still don't understand the whole thing. He took that fort the 16th of July with all this flourish and then evacuated it two days after. That doesn't make sense to me. But who can make sense out of a war? You heard about the alliance with France last year?" Smith questioned.

O'Hara told them the way the news had been brought to them on the river by the man in the canoe.

"But you haven't likely heard of the young Frenchman that's come over to help us. Just in the spirit of liberty. No other reason. Quite a young fellah with a title too. Marquis, isn't it? Name's La Fayette. He was in this battle of Monmouth we were speaking of and we hear General Washington's quite taken with him. Well, I guess that brings you about up to date."

"Of course the Indian wars in New York State had been bad, bad," Ormsby put in. "All the Iroquois except the Oneidas and part of the Tuscaroras have sided with the British and murdered and plundered like mad. This August a General Sullivan, we hear, went up with a big force and just about wiped them out. For once the whites gave as good as they got, I guess. A bloody business! The worst they say there's ever been. You heard about Girty?"

"No. What about him?"

The men all spoke at once.

"Defected! A year ago this spring! Went over to the British! Lock, stock and barrel, and been doing the devil's own work with the Indians ever since. Everyone now calls him the *White Savage*."

"I can't believe it!" O'Hara burst out.

"I can," said Smith. "I never liked the cut of his jib. He had an Injun look to him. Well, he's with them again now, and up to all their dirty tricks."

O'Hara was speechless. Somehow this news of Girty which Clark had either not known or not thought of repeating, hit him very hard. He had been friendly with the man and had not thought ill of him.

"Congress is back in Philadelphia," Hugh went on, "and they've voted half pay for seven years after the war to all officers and a bounty of eighty dollars to each soldier. I guess," he added, his face falling, "it's helped enlistment."

"So Philadelphia is free now?" O'Hara asked from a tight throat.

"Oh, yes," Smith said. "General Washington put a General Arnold in charge there just after Clinton left. Benedict Arnold his name is. He cuts quite a dash, we hear. Drives round the city with a carriage and four, dines out when not entertaining himself and just this last spring married a Philadelphia girl about twenty years younger, they tell me. A Miss Shippen. Of course her family are Tories but I guess in society they all mix! From what I can hear that was the case even when the British were there. Well, I guess that's about all the news, O'Hara. Things are sort of quiet this fall but there can be a flare up any time. What we want now is to hear your story. Eat up, fellahs and let's get to it."

O'Hara hadn't counted on so large an audience but Semple

had passed the word amongst the other tables so when supper was ended fifteen men drew their chairs and benches forward to listen. He was embarrassed but he felt an obligation upon him to tell them all, for Clark's sake. Also because of the old feud between Western Pennsylvania and Virginia over their border line, he must tell now of the courage of the Virginians and Kentuckians as well as those who had been recruited from around these very parts.

"Stand up where we can all see you," someone shouted.

So O'Hara stood and hesitantly at first, then in full confidence, told the main story while the listening men scarcely breathed. It was a long recital but the men sat motionless until it was done, then to O'Hara's surprise they each came forward to shake his hand. He had never felt so much an American as in that moment.

He went back with Brackenridge to his cabin later and they drew close again.

"How's the law going, Hugh?"

"Not too badly. It's unbelievable how many little jobs come along. There's the matter of wills, for example. These times make men think of them. Not much money in that but it all counts up. Of course when I can help a poor man out in any way there's no charge. What are you going to do next?"

O'Hara shook his head. "Haven't an idea. I'll report to Brodhead to-morrow. He sent for me to come back."

"Good man, I hear. They change commandants here every time the wind blows. I wish you could stay in Pittsburgh, but where honour calls . . ."

"There's one thing I find I can do better than shooting a gun, though I've mastered that fairly well. At Kaskaskia I took over the job of getting supplies for the men. I thought I might just mention that to Brodhead."

"By all means. Quartermastering, isn't it? From all I hear they can do with some good ones. Our army's had pretty slim pickings. How . . . how are things on the personal side?"

O'Hara shook his head. "I've never felt so lost," he said.

"Don't give up, man. *Amor omnia vincit.*"

"I wish I could think so," O'Hara said.

The next day he went to the fort to call upon General Brodhead, whom he found businesslike but pleasant and eager to hear his tale.

"You *did* take off with Clark without special orders but I guess results justified it," he said when O'Hara finished.

"Colonel Clark is a difficult man to say *no* to, General."

Brodhead laughed. "I know only too well for I've tried it. Now, what I want you to do is to go back east to headquarters with papers to General Washington. We need clothing and supplies desperately for our soldiers out here. Reports say this is going to be the coldest winter in years. I know His Excellency will be eager to hear of the Vincennes campaign and who better to tell him than you who were on it? When you get through your recital I've an idea our requests will be granted. Not," he added hastily, "that Washington doesn't do his best all the time, but he's got the hardest job in the world. A *mortal* hard job," he added.

"When should I start?" O'Hara asked.

Brodhead stroked his chin. "Right now," he said, "our army's up around West Point, Washington and Clinton sort of eyeing each other across the Hudson but both apparently afraid to move. My sources of information are good. Have to be. Towards the end of November Washington intends to bring his troops down to a place called Morristown, where he wintered last year. Why don't we say you will leave in about two weeks' time."

"Right, sir. But where is this Morristown?"

"In New Jersey. If you go straight to Philadelphia, you can get directions there."

When O'Hara set forth once again, his face towards the East, his feelings were mixed. He was greatly honoured by his commission, and thrilled at the thought of meeting the Commander-in-Chief. He was now rested and physically alive and the feel of Pitt under him once more was inexpressibly good. But on the other hand, his heartache increased as the miles were covered on the now familiar Forbes Road over the mountains. If he were only in truth going unto his love as the poem said! He had decided to see her if this was possible even though he realised that the very sight, if that were all, would be the torture of a knife in the wound.

He rode through the glory of the last days of Indian summer, the brilliance of the foliage still a surprise to his old-world eyes, stopping occasionally to gather some of the late grapes which grew luxuriantly where there was fallen timber, or beside the smaller water courses, where the crab apples turned golden and fragrant on the ground amongst the autumn leaves. These varied his meals of game or the eternal jerk and water and made him think of the Carson dinner table with its great bowl of fruit and glow of candlelight. In his nightly camps he pondered upon the vulnerability of the human heart. As to his own body it had endured unimaginable sufferings of strain, cold, hunger and distress, and had survived and triumphed. But the heart. O God, the heart! It could not be hardened or *seasoned* as the body in its anguish. According to the immutable law by which Nature had ordained the mystery of love for her own vast purpose of continuance, the heart must remain tender, violate, susceptible to deadly wounds. Unhealing.

He had much else to think upon as the days passed for the mildness of Indian summer left in a sudden bitter wind and the first snow began to fall. There had been rumours in Pittsburgh of a hard winter and the present discomforts tended to support the prophecy. He had blankets and now a trained woodsman's skill, so he built his fires, rubbed Pitt's knees and endured the cold. Often he mused upon Girty and his shocking defection. He thought of Guyasuta and wondered what part he was taking now in the war. Girty knew him well. Could the *White Savage* have persuaded the *Red* to follow him? He wished ardently that he could have seen his Indian friend before he left Pittsburgh, but in these times that would have been difficult. He wondered, too, if he could locate Elliott while he was in the east. His old travelling companion, according to Semple, had left for Philadelphia as soon as they heard it was evacuated.

So the miles were finally covered and he drew rein again at the familiar Crooked Billet. One way to secure directions to Morristown had occurred to him. As Philadelphia was now, he must tread carefully between the Revolutionist sympathisers and the Tories. One man he knew he could trust. This was the Mark Bird he had met on shipboard who was even then in 1772 making cannonballs at his foundry "just in case." He had not seen him since, but he intended to see him now.

In the old taproom he was given a hearty welcome before the big fireplace. Hastings looked older and a bit haggard and let no word slip as to his own leanings, probably for business purposes. Sam was the same, friendly, grinning and eager to talk, but O'Hara was cautious even though at the moment there were no other customers present.

"And what have you been up to since we saw you?" Hastings inquired.

"Oh, a little of this and that. There's plenty to keep a man busy in and around Pittsburgh. It's good to get back to civilised life for a change, though. What all has been going on here?"

"Plenty. And yet it's surprising how much we've gone our own way at that. We had General Howe for a while running things as though the war was only meant for balls and routs, then Clinton for a short time and now the English are gone and our own General Arnold is in charge. He and Miss Peggy Shippen were married in the spring. That set the town by the ears."

"So?"

"Oh, yes. Quite a whirlwind courtship. He's a widower, much older, but they tell me he's got a way with him. Must have, to catch a belle like Miss Peggy."

"Could you direct me to the Bird Iron Works at Birdsboro?" O'Hara said abruptly.

Hastings looked surprised. "I can. That's at Hay Creek just up along the Schuylkill a little way. Have you decided to come east for a job?"

O'Hara laughed. "No, I'm a fixture on the frontier, I guess, but while I'm here this time I want to make a long-delayed call on Mr. Bird. He was very kind to me on the ship coming over."

He could not relax in his room as he did before. He longed to ask for news of the Carsons but the words would not come. Instead he had supper with Hastings and Sam and filled his talk with Indian tales to which they listened avidly. The next day he set out for Birdsboro and reached it by early afternoon. There before him were the great foundries, there the little town of workmen and on the hill beyond, the spreading manor of the owner.

Like Hastings, Mr. Bird seemed older by more than the inter-vening years and for a moment, looking sharply at his guest who had been shown into the drawing-room, he did not recognise him. Then as O'Hara introduced himself recollection returned in a rush, and there was a warm greeting. O'Hara did not wait but told him quickly the purpose of his call, apologising as he did so for not accepting the kindness of his invitation long before.

"Of course I can direct you to Morristown," Mr. Bird said, "and you'll find the roads pretty fair. However, I suggest that you spend the night here and in the morning I can send one of my grooms to ride with you. He knows the way and it will save you time as well as give him something to do. He's lame and couldn't go into the army. Have you got a good horse?"

"The best," O'Hara smiled. "Pitt and I are real friends."

"*Pitt!*" Mr. Bird's eyebrows went up. "I assume, though, you've broken your British ties?"

"Absolutely."

In the quiet of the library after dinner O'Hara summarised in brief for the older man all that he had done since his landing in the country on that bright autumn day seven years before. Touching the highlights, helped by Mr. Bird's perceptive questions, he gave a good résumé, climaxed with a quick account of Clark's exploit. Mr. Bird drank it in and his face lightened.

"This is good news," he said. "I'm on the edge of things, too old to fight, more's the pity. But we make the balls for the soldiers to shoot. It's something, anyway."

"A tremendous something, I should say."

"At any rate, O'Hara, your visit is heaven sent. I've been low in spirits. I've been discouraged and you have been like a bracing gust of cold air to blow away the vapours. We've had some bad times." He shuddered. "That winter our army spent at the Valley Forge was enough to make every man desert! But General Washington! There's the main reason we still have a chance. I envy you your interview with him."

They talked on till midnight.

Very early the next morning O'Hara said good-bye to his host with something like affection, and with the young groom beside him rode off by way of Trenton and Newark for Morristown. Once there they spent the night at Arnold's Tavern (where mine host at once boasted of the fact that it had been the General's Headquarters the year before) and at the earliest hour next day which he deemed suitable O'Hara dismissed the groom with thanks and a benefaction and then made his way past The Green, now snowed over, to the substantial, widespreading white house on the edge of the little town, now the temporary home of His Excellency. Just across the road was a group of log huts inhabited, Arnold had told him, by the General's Life Guards. He approached the front door, noting as he did so the beauty of the curving fanlight and the narrow, corniced windows bordering the entrance, and stated his business to the sentry. The door was at last opened to him by a handsome young man of perhaps twenty who looked carefully at O'Hara's papers and then conducted him through to the great kitchen-living-room at the back.

"His Excellency is busy in his study just now so you may have to wait a little, and this is the warmest place in the house. I am Colonel Alexander Hamilton," he added, "Aide to the General. And glad to meet you, Captain O'Hara."

When he withdrew, O'Hara looked about him with delight. He had not seen such a kitchen since he left the old country; the great fireplace with pots and cranes and skillets; the spinning wheel and reel at the side ; the grandfather's clock, the work tables and rush-bottomed chairs all about. There were servants attending to their work, paying no attention to him. Probably many such messengers as he waited there. Once a pretty, plump, brown-haired little woman came in, gave a few firm orders and left with a half smile in his direction. He wondered if this might be Mrs. Washington.

When he was finally shown into the general's study, O'Hara found his knees weak as water and his heart beating fast. The man at the tall secretary rose with true Virginia courtesy.

"Captain O'Hara, sir, you have made a long journey. Will you be seated?"

"Your Excellency, sir," O'Hara managed as he bowed, "I thank you."

His immediate impression was of the General's great height— about six feet three, he would judge—then the broad shoulders beneath the gold epaulets, the strong steady face with its high brow, large nose and wide, firm mouth. He had anticipated much and was not disappointed.

"I had word from General Brodhead that I might expect you. I gather you come with certain requests but in return are prepared to recount to me some news I very much desire. Is this correct?"

"Substantially so, I believe, Your Excellency."

"Well," said the general, "suppose we let the requests wait until you have told your story. I know the mere fact of the capture of Vincennes. You can imagine how much I will relish complete details. Will you proceed, Captain?"

"It's a long story, General."

A faint bitterness crossed the older man's face. "I have time to hear it all. Unfortunately too much time just now."

As O'Hara plunged once more into his account he realised he was telling it this time with a difference. There was now no need for selectivity. Because of the intent interest in the face before him he omitted nothing. As he had lived it, so he told it, fluently, descriptively, pouring it all out now to the one who most needed to hear it. Only once did his voice break a little: when he told of the point at which they had had to abandon the horses to their fate and go on without them. The general spoke.

"You are fond of horses, Captain?"

"Very, sir."

"So am I. My mare Betsy and my gelding Nelson . . . like a part of my own body when under me."

"I understand that." The two looked at each other with quick sympathy.

"Go on, Captain, if you please."

There was a lightening of the tension occasionally when the general smiled. Over the young drummer boy and Captain Helm's toddy, in particular.

At the end O'Hara said, "I wish I could present Colonel Clark to you more clearly, sir."

"I think you have done so, Captain." Adding, with a twinkle, "Dad Drabit."

For what seemed like a considerable time Washington sat quiet. O'Hara, watching him, thought to himself, *this man would always be good company, even if he said nothing.* But at last the general spoke.

"I can't thank you sufficiently for this clear, dramatic account of a remarkable campaign. My spirits have been lifted so much more by it—so immeasurably much more—than by the incomplete and conventional reports I would otherwise have received. Now I wish to inquire into a remark you made concerning the time spent at Kaskaskia. You said you managed to secure provisions for the troops while there?"

"I did, Your Excellency."

"You found this work congenial?"

"Very much so. More than soldiering. My interest has always run to business."

The general was threading his large-boned fingers together as he considered.

"We've had serious problems everywhere with our provisioning. Just now I badly need a quartermaster for our hospital at Carlisle, Pennsylvania. A good day's ride from Philadelphia. Will you take this position, Captain?"

"I will, Your Excellency."

The lack of hesitation seemed to please the general. "Good! My only orders are to secure what the men need there by lawful purchase, if possible, if not—by any other means. This is war. Do you understand?"

"I do, Your Excellency," O'Hara smiled.

"I will do what I can about money. It is tight, very tight. And now, about the requests from General Brodhead?"

O'Hara presented them, adding details from his own observation. The general's face fell into heavy lines as he sighed.

"The trouble is that most of our own men here need clothing. My army camped now in Jockey Hollow just a little to the west of here are, many of them, in a bad way. But I'll write General Brodhead that I'll do what I can. No man can do more. I'll notify him, also, of your new assignment and you, too, must have your orders with you."

He turned quickly to the secretary and wrote for some moments, then he rose and handed the papers to O'Hara.

"My thanks again for the Vincennes account which has not only interested me but encouraged me. Can you go soon to Carlisle?"

"Within a few days, Your Excellency."

"Good. It's bad enough for well men to suffer, but harder still for the sick. My best wishes go with you."

O'Hara bowed again as he said good-bye to the Commander-in-Chief, but not from the routine courtesy of soldier to general. He knew he was in the presence of a great man and his soul made obeisance too. He spoke of this as he talked for a moment with Colonel Hamilton before he left.

"He's so strong, so utterly good, he seems more than human."

Hamilton smiled. "He's all you say, but he's human enough too. He's got a temper and how he can swear! When occasion demands," he added.

"So?"

The colonel looked both ways. No one was near. "At Monmouth one of the generals disobeyed orders and nearly lost the battle. I was there. Well, His Excellency just cut loose and the air was blue! It did the men a lot of good, too, I guess. In any case he's the greatest man we've got and I'm proud to serve him."

O'Hara rode directly back to Philadelphia as the bitter cold continued, and on the evening he reached the Crooked Billet again, he supped quickly and then in his room dressed with the greatest care in spite of a pounding heart and unsteady fingers. He brushed his hair almost with violence, since the life he had recently lived had not improved its texture, and fastened it at the back with a rich black bow. He chose his finest white stock with the lace ruffles, his plum-coloured satin waistcoat, his silver knee-buckles! In all the details of his dress, at least, he could do his love no more honour. Then, clothed for the street, he started on the familiar walk to the Carson house.

In spite of the alleged inuring of his body he felt an actual weakness overtake him as he climbed the steps. He bit his lips hard as he sounded the great knocker. The old manservant opened the door, looked startled and then smiled as he ushered the guest into the hall and took his hat and cloak. It was this smile that steadied O'Hara as he waited to be received. Suddenly he saw Mary at the upper landing! She had evidently heard nothing and was descending slowly, her face sober, her eyes downcast. All at once she looked up, stopped, and then gave a cry.

"Mr. O'Hara! James!"

She started down precipitously while O'Hara rushed forward and caught her into his outstretched arms as she tripped at the last stairs. They stood then, her head pressed to his breast as sobs shook her, his face against her hair.

"My darling! My darling! My dear Delight!"

There was a sound behind them and they both looked up. Mr. Carson stood there in the library doorway.

"Father!" Mary cried. "I did my best to please you. I tried, oh, I tried so hard! But I couldn't forget him!"

"So I see," Mr. Carson said quietly.

Then because he was a gentleman as well as a father he came forward and held out his hand to O'Hara.

"I see," he repeated, "that a mere parent cannot stop the course of true love. Come in, come into the room, my children."

But once there, he did not stay long. After the briefest questions and answers he left them to themselves.

"I'll be in the drawing-room, O'Hara, when you go."

"It may be quite late, Father," Mary put in.

"Very likely," he said with a smile. "Very likely."

There was so much to tell of all that had happened during the cruel intervening months but for a long time they said nothing but words of love as he held her close. Then with a strange joy they poured out to each other the anguish of their former fears.

"I thought never to see you again!"

"I was sure you didn't care!"

At last when their hearts were absolved they began upon the events which they had not shared. O'Hara gave a highly expurgated account of his exploits, emphasising the lighter incidents and the crowning success at the end. He told her, too, of his interview with General Washington and his new appointment.

"Carlisle?" she said incredulously. "Oh, that's not so far away. You can come to see me, often perhaps?"

"What could hold me away, now?"

And then it was Mary's turn to tell about Philadelphia in the war years.

"There was such gaiety while General Howe and all his officers were here, you wouldn't believe it," she began, "but last winter I didn't go to the routs. It seemed wrong when our men were in such dreadful straits at the Valley Forge. Then last May the biggest affair of all was held, the *Meschianza*, and Father felt I should go to that. The army was not really suffering at the time and he thought I would never have a chance to see the like again. And I never will," she added.

"What was it like?"

Mary drew a long breath. "I wish I *could* describe it. You see it was a sort of farewell to General Howe and his young officers paid for it. I guess most of them are very rich young men. One of them, whom everybody liked even though he was a Britisher, was Major André. He planned it. I went with Becky Franks and her brother. Oh, *everybody* in society was there. It was on 18th May, and I'll never forget that date. First of all, everyone went up the river on barges with flags and decorations and bands playing like a water pageant, until we came to Walnut Grove, that's the Whartons' estate. Then we got out and walked through files of troops to the jousting field."

"To the *what?*"

"I knew you wouldn't believe that but it's the truth! There was a real jousting field with grandstands and marquees all around. Then the Knights came riding out. Seven *Knights of the Blended Rose* with red and white favours and seven *Knights of the Burning Mountain* with yellow and black."

"And they actually jousted?"

"It was mock, of course, for their lances were blunt, but every now and then a horseman was unseated. At the last a herald announced that the honours were even and everyone went into the ballroom and danced. Then at ten there were fireworks on the lawn. Oh, I *loved* that! And at midnight the supper was served. *Four hundred and thirty covers laid.*"

O'Hara whistled softly.

"It was like a dream! Pier glasses around the walls with all the candelabra and hundreds of tapers reflecting in them. And the costumes! And the colours! Do you know," she added, "Father heard that the silks alone for the Meschianza cost *fifty thousand pounds.*"

"Incredible! Wicked!" he said, his face stern. "And some of our men with no shoes for their feet."

"I know. There was strong feeling, but no one could do anything. Except Allan McLane," she laughed. "He was so mad about it that he got his dragoons together and they made bombs out of iron pots filled with powder and rode round the British outposts and threw them every which way at dawn. We danced until four, and everyone was just getting home then."

"Good man, McLane!"

"I know the Meschianza was all wrong and yet, you won't think ill of me?"

"As if I could!"

"Well, I'm so glad I was there. It is something to remember always. Like a vision. I'm glad that Major André planned it."

"He's the young officer you said everyone liked?"

"Oh, yes. No one could help it. He's so charming and friendly and gay. Do you know, he painted all the scenery for the Southwark Theatre last winter? Some young Tory helped him. And I really think he's in love with Peggy Chew."

"And she?"

"I know she likes him very much. Before he left he wrote her a little poem. It's not actually a love poem so she read it to a few of us. I remember the last verse. Would you like to hear it?"

"Of course."

"He said that when the war was over if he got back to Cliveden, that's the name of the Chew place . . .

> Say, wilt thou then receive again
> And welcome to thy sight,
> The youth who bids with stifled pain
> His sad farewells to-night.

It sounds so pathetic somehow, doesn't it?"

"War is always tragic," O'Hara said, and then asked about the Arnold-Shippen wedding.

Mary did not approve of it. General Arnold was too old for his bride, was a widower and lame from a wound.

"Not that I would hold his lameness against him, it just all

F

seems unsuitable. But I'm more worried about another of my friends. Do you remember Mary Vining? The girl who speaks French so well?"

"Yes, I do remember her. We talked in French quite a little at the Bingham ball. What about her?"

"She's so clever and witty and beautiful and admired and . . . I think she and General Anthony Wayne are in love, *and he's married!*"

O'Hara was serious. "That's not good. Not good at all. You're probably mistaken. Why do you think such a thing?"

"Because," she said slowly, "because they look at each other the same way you and I do."

Finally even by lovers' time O'Hara felt he must leave. After the last long kiss Mary stood with him by the library door and gently fingered the gold buttons on his waistcoat, her eyes downcast.

"In all this evening," she said, "there is something you have not asked me."

"I know," he answered.

"Why not?"

"I've been afraid."

"I think perhaps it would be safe to ask me now."

"Mary!" His voice broke on the words. "Will you marry me when the war is over and come to live with me in Pittsburgh?"

She raised her eyes then and the shining glory in them made his own mist over.

"Mr. O'Hara," she said, "I will go with you to the world's end."

Chapter Seven

The little town of Carlisle lay cosily asleep under its Cumberland Valley snow when O'Hara reached it early one afternoon after his hundred and twenty mile ride from Philadelphia. He had an immediate feeling of satisfaction as he looked about him. This had not the raw frontier aspect of Pittsburgh nor yet the civilised urbanity of Philadelphia. Rather it reminded him in the modest comfort of its stone cottages blocked around the open square, of villages he had seen in the old country. His quick eyes noted the quarry on the hill beyond, where evidently most of the building material came from; he could see a small church spire, a brick edifice that looked as though the law might be administered there; two unmistakable taverns, and on the edge of the town a long low barracks turned hospital. He rode there at once to present his credentials and look the place over.

The physician in command was a Colonel White, a harried-looking man of perhaps sixty who grasped O'Hara's hand in relief.

"I had word you were coming," he said, "and if you can help us here you're as welcome as spring. Sit down," he indicated his bare office, "and I'll give you the picture. We need everything and I guess I needn't tell you that to apply to Congress and wait till they vote on it and then *get* it here . . . well, I've given up on that. We'll have to depend on local supplies."

"I surmised that from General Washington's orders," O'Hara smiled.

"The thing I must tell you at the start is that this is a good little town. Patriotic to the core, but it's been about bled white. When the war broke, nearly every man in it enlisted. Take the Butler family. He was a gunsmith and when all his five sons joined up he did too. When the neighbours tried to remonstrate his wife said, 'Let him alone. Every man that can shoulder a musket ought to be in this war. I'll make out somehow.' That's their spirit. Brigadier General Richard Butler is one of their boys. He's with General Wayne right now and of course General Irvine hails from here."

"I've heard of them."

"Oh, you'll find fine folks in Carlisle, but they're all hard up. They can't help us. And the farmers . . . well, it's winter and they need their stock. So, you'll have a hard job. Come along now, though, and I'll show you the place."

O'Hara had seen death and danger but this tour of the so-called wards left him shaken. This, then, was the aftermath of war; these were the men who had not escaped cleanly for either life or death. They looked up at him with anguished eyes and he looked back at them with a grim determination. Here was a job to do, a big one, and he meant to do it.

In the first place the building was cold. While most men had beds of a sort there were still many on the floor on straw pallets, and the straw under the coarse covering was thin. There were not enough blankets; there was not enough nourishing food; there were not enough medical supplies; and of course, as Colonel White told him, not enough help. O'Hara sat down again in the office and concentrated upon the problem, his heart working with his head.

"I'll begin to-day," he said at the end of their conversation, "where I can. I'll get a load of straw somehow. And I'll get some beef killed at once. You must need a lot of broth."

"My God, yes," the colonel said.

"I'll work with you," O'Hara said, getting up. "I'll do my best. I went to see Dr. Benjamin Rush before I left Philadelphia and he helped me get a few medicines . . ."

The other gripped his arm. "Any chloroform?"

"Two bottles."

A long sigh escaped White. "I'm a merciful man by nature, I think, but we've had to do some pretty bad things without chloroform. I've been delaying some operations. Now they can come to-morrow."

O'Hara went out to where Pitt was tied and brought in the box he had carried in his blanket roll. The doctor accepted it as more precious than gold.

Back in the town proper O'Hara worked fast as was his wont. He arranged for lodgings at the Green Tree Inn and after explaining his mission to the owner secured the names of a dozen farmers in the neighbourhood. Though it was now mid-afternoon he was bent upon getting at least a load of straw to the hospital before night. As he came out again on the steps he stopped short. *Elliott* was just tying his horse at one of the stumps! He looked up and nodded as though they had met the day before.

"My word, but I'm glad to see you!" O'Hara exclaimed. "Where under heaven did you come from?"

"Well, I've been here and there," Elliott said with his usual bland evasiveness. "Fact is, I heard you had been around Philadelphia and Hastings told me you had this new job so I decided mebbe I could be of some use." He looked straight at the question in the other's eye. "I'm a fairly good man as long as I'm on a horse but I've got a leg that would give out in half a day's march. That's why I'm not in the army. Single man an' all, I know it looks bad. But that's how it is. Could I give you a lift in your quartermastering?"

"*Could you!*" O'Hara responded. "You're heaven-sent, my friend."

He poured out the needs of the hospital and his plans for the rest of the day and they rode off together when Elliott insisted he didn't need food for a few more hours. The first farmer was hesitant. He had his own problems; he could hardly make a living; he had been in favour of the war but felt when men enlisted they ought to be prepared to take whatever . . .

O'Hara broke in coldly. "I want the load of straw now, immediately. And to-morrow I want you to kill a beef. If you co-operate you'll be paid. If you don't I'll take them anyway. Order of General Washington. Now, let's get at the straw. We'll help you load it." The man who spoke was young but the authority in his voice was mature enough, and the farmer knew when he was bested. Besides, the word *Washington* held magic. O'Hara talked as they worked, but now ingratiatingly, entertainingly.

"It's good you have an Irish tongue in your head," Elliott remarked on the side.

When the straw was ready the farmer accepted his pay, and promised, if grudgingly, to kill a beef next day. His son drove the load and Elliott and O'Hara rode ahead. The sunset sky was now a cold pale violet and the wind was bitter.

"I've got to get some more heat in that place," O'Hara said. "There's just one fireplace in each of the big rooms . . . you'll see, and the poor devils at the opposite ends don't get any warmth at all. And I'm going to get more blankets if I have to strip the town," he added grimly.

When they reached the hospital it was almost dark. An orderly came out, looked at them in amazement, told them to unload the straw in the shed, then went to call his superior. When White appeared in a cloak, a lantern in his hand, he, too, stared, astonished.

"Well, you do work fast, Captain. I hadn't expected any results so soon. Some of these fellows have their bones sticking into the floor and they'll bless you for this. The last Q.M. here didn't bother much about anything."

"I intend to bother, Colonel, and if you'll direct us a little we'll build up the pallets right away. Of course this straw will be cold. How about that?"

"Straw warms in a hurry and we'll put the fresh next the floor. We'll all lend a hand here. Tell the cook and his boy to come out," he said to the orderly.

They worked fast, all of them, carrying in great armfuls of the straw from which they had shaken the dust as much as possible. O'Hara and Elliott helped lift the men to the side on their blankets as the pallets were piled high with the fresh bedding. In every case there were relaxed and grateful moans of relief as the patients finally felt the new softness under them. O'Hara studied each fireplace and the wood beside it.

"Enough here to keep good fires all night?" he questioned.

"We're often short of wood too," the colonel said.

"Why, the country round here is full of timber!"

"It's not the trees, it's the choppers. We have to ease along as best we can."

"You've plenty for to-night and to-morrow?"

"Oh, yes."

"Then use it freely. I'll get some choppers and Elliott here and I can swing an axe, too, if need be. This is a bitter cold night, Colonel, so don't skimp the fire."

"I've got the sickest men and all my chest cases in the warmest places but the cold does come in the cracks and no mistake."

"I'll try for more blankets to-morrow but now we'd better get along."

He saw the men's eyes following him as though they realised a new force was working for them. O'Hara smiled and raised a hand as he left the wards; the efforts in return touched his heart. He asked the colonel as he left what his next most pressing need was after the meat.

"Flour," he said, "*flour*, for God's sake!"

"Is there a mill near here?"

"Over the hill there only a couple of miles but the miller won't sell to us."

"We'll see," said O'Hara, as he said good night.

Once back at the inn he and Elliott had a late supper, then stretched their cold legs to the fire and settled to talk. There was much to catch up on. When their main events had been sketched in, Elliott's mind proved full of the defection of Pittsburgh's renegades.

"That somehow cut deep with me," he said. "Girty I always mistrusted some but I never thought of anything like this. A queer cuss, though. But Matthew Elliott, no relation of mine, thank God. For him to be a turncoat seems hard to believe. They can do us plenty damage, too. Girty, most, of course, damn his hide."

"Have you heard anything about Guyasuta?"

"Not lately. Saw him a few months back. He was upset. He told me he had meant to side with the Americans, but too many things had happened." Elliott drew a heavy sigh. "If the whites only had a clean conscience, but God A'mighty, after all they've suffered you can't blame them if they do a little killing for themselves. You like the old fox, do you? Guyasuta?"

O'Hara hesitated. "You may wonder at it, but I do." He told then the story of the snake-bite and the days in the forest.

"Every man to his taste," Elliott said. "Of course some of these fellahs like the great Sir William Johnson himself are married to Indians. Could you marry one, O'Hara?" he asked curiously.

O'Hara laughed and shook his head. "I'll tell you a secret, though. Mistress Mary Carson of Philadelphia has just done me the honour of promising to marry me when the war's over."

Elliott stared, dumbfounded, then clapped his thigh. "Well, I'm a dirty, stinkin' weasel if I ever suspected a thing! All the times I've been with you, too. You're a close-mouthed one, you are. So you're to marry *pretty Polly Carson*! That's what they call her, I hear, in Philadelphia. Do you call her Polly?"

"No."

"What then? *Mary?*"

"When I name her."

Elliott laughed. "I see. I won't quiz you on the pet words. What does she call you?"

"Mr. O'Hara, usually."

"Well, I'm damned pleased for you!" He held out his hand. "Congratulations, old fellah. Stick to quartermastering and you ought to have a whole skin when the war's over. It'll be back to Pittsburgh then, eh?"

"Right. I want to get a house started soon in the King's Orchard. Well, I see mine host is looking at us as though he doesn't want to set out fresh candles. We've worn these about to the stick. Shall we go up?"

As they climbed the stairs Elliott still kept muttering: "Pretty Polly Carson! Well, I'll be damned!"

The next days were full from dawn till dark. O'Hara had made his plans with businesslike acumen. Once he remedied the worst features of the immediate situation he would be free to pursue a normal routine of supply. Now, however, there had to be quick measures taken for there were too many avoidable deaths, the colonel told him, at the hospital. It was the worst winter in years and the ice and snow not only doubled the hazards of the sick but also the problems of the quartermaster. He and Elliott had first of all checked with the farmer about the beef. The latter had been as good as his word. The animal was killed, skinned and quartered. They left it to freeze for a day and went on, a hard, plodding ride to the mill. Here there was trouble. The miller, a short stout man named Cox, met them with a stare as cold as the weather. He had his regular customers, he was running a bit slack anyway, and *he had no flour to sell to the Government*! O'Hara sized him up and decided blandishment might work. He looked around with interest.

"Quite a little difference between mills here and the ones in France," he said consideringly.

"How so? *France!* What do you know about France?"

"Oh, I used to live there. We boys often went out to a mill in the country to get ourselves weighed and look around. Now *there*, the bands came down like this . . ."

In a few minutes' time Cox was watching and listening. O'Hara moved over the big, dusty floor, commenting and asking questions as he went. In another fifteen minutes he had skilfully switched to the war and the Vincennes campaign. Cox was eating it up and at the end he said slowly, "'Course, I might mebbe let you have a couple of sacks. That any help?"

"Very much," said O'Hara. "If you could make it three . . ."

They finally left with four, carefully carried in front of them.

"It's been a great pleasure to meet you, Mr. Cox. We don't

always run into a man so interested in events," O'Hara had said solemnly, as he offered his hand in parting.

"Well, you talk pretty good. Ain't hard to listen to you. Mebbe I can let you have a little more flour from time to time. That Clark must be quite a fellah!"

"I haven't told you the half yet."

As they rode back Elliott chuckled. "My lord, you buffaloed that one, all right. Good as a show to watch you."

"I thought from the look in his eye he couldn't be threatened, but there's always more than one way to skin a cat!"

In two days there was meat in the great pots and fresh bread in the oven. The flour on hand had been scant and mouldy at that.

"You see," the colonel explained glowingly, "if we can give the weakest men a good noggin of broth with decent bread broken in it, they've got a meal. And meat of course for the stronger ones."

"Have you salt?" O'Hara asked.

"Very little. Just enough to take the flat off. Congress bought it all up and Cumberland County's share for the duration was eighty bushels! So you can guess how much we have here."

"It's one of our big problems in Pittsburgh too," O'Hara said. "It's all brought over the mountains by pack horse and it's worth its weight in gold when it gets there. Have you had any eggs for the men?"

"*Eggs!*" the colonel echoed. "What are eggs? We've never seen them here."

"There ought to be quite a few hens round these parts waiting to do their duty for their country," O'Hara said, grinning. "We'll see."

He bought a farm sledge and a work horse, feeling Pitt should not be subject to the indignity of *hauling*, and with Elliott and himself on the seat, proceeded to comb the town for blankets. He greeted the women at their doors courteously, explained his errand, and at the end smiled, showing his wide white teeth. In most cases it worked. One blanket from a family and here and there a pillow. O'Hara had noted that many of the men now had only their worn uniforms rolled under their heads. At one door the woman did not return his smile.

"My only son died at Valley Forge. They were cold there, too." She gave him two coverlets.

They made the rounds of the countryside as the weeks passed, buying when the farmers would sell, stealing when they wouldn't.

Quietly over the snow the sledge often made its way in the dark of night. The horse was hitched to a tree near to a barn. Elliott and O'Hara with a covered lantern moved to the pig pen or the byre. Elliott did the sticking with his sharp hunter's knife and between them they dragged a calf, a pig, or a sheep back to the sledge. They found surprisingly little outcry from the beasts. As hunters they came upon their prey softly; the kill was swift; the leave-taking was cautious and the animals drowsed again.

Back of the hospital Elliott dexterously did the skinning, then there was a change of meat in the pots while the colonel and his aides gloried in the fact that the patients had never been so well fed.

"Gumption," Elliott kept repeating. "*Gumption!* That's what you've got, O'Hara."

Meanwhile O'Hara began to enjoy the town itself. As Colonel White had told him there were good people here, distinguished people, and while most of the men were away in the service, the women brought them close in their conversation. Little by little he grew familiar with the names of Irvine, Wilson, Armstrong, Blaine, Montgomery, and Denny. Of all the women he most admired Agnes Denny. She was not young but she was still beautiful with her fair complexion, bright sandy hair and blue eyes which reflected the energy and intelligence of her mind. Her favourite topic when O'Hara sometimes paused for a chat was her son Ebenezer who was with the Pennsylvania line. When she told of his being a dispatch bearer to Fort Pitt when he was only thirteen—six years ago—O'Hara gave a startled exclamation.

"What does he look like?" he asked.

"Like me," his mother laughed, "only his hair is redder."

"Why, I saw that boy out there! More than once. He was so young to be crossing the mountains alone. Everyone spoke of it."

"He shipped out for the West Indies after that and went to sea until he got an ensign's commission in the army and joined the First Pennsylvania. To think that you've seen him!"

"It's a pleasant coincidence to me. I hope to see him again."

"He wrote me a joke about himself. He's a good boy to write. When he joined his company he wasn't used to marching. All the walking he'd done for several years was pacing a quarter-deck. So one day when he was just about ready to drop Captain Montgomery—he's from here too—came up and whispered to him, 'Listen Eb, for the honour of old Carlisle don't disgrace yourself!' That kept him going. He's with friends for sure. Colonel Dicky

Butler comes from round here. We've always known him. But the man Ebenezer is always writing about is his general, Anthony Wayne. He worships that man."

"I keep hearing about him," O'Hara said. "I'd like to meet him, myself."

The most important stories heard, some of them over and over in the Green Tree Inn, from the farmers or from the women as he met them, were written back to Mary as he penned his loving missives to her three times a week. He wrote the most prideful tale with relish for it was about a woman. Carlisle had a heroine and no one would be long in the town without knowing it. This was *Molly "Pitcher."* She had been living in the family of General Irvine here until she left to join her husband, John Hays, with the Revolutionary troops in New Jersey. When he was wounded at the battle of Monmouth she fired his gun and then did an even greater service by carrying water on that hottest of June days to the wounded and dying. She had found a pitcher by the spring and this she filled over and over in full view of the British and held to the poor parched lips. "Molly, *pitcher!*" the men kept calling, and the name had stuck. Oh, O'Hara wrote Mary, the townsfolk would never forget this. Indeed, everyone, hearing of it, should remember, he added.

But the tenderest of all the Carlisle stories he saved to tell her in person. This was of Regina, the Indian captive. Something deep in his heart turned over as he thought of it. A dozen mothers in the town had made sure he heard it, and Mrs. Denny had taken from her Bible a bit of paper on which she had written the famous hymn and allowed him to copy the verse.

When the worst needs of the hospital had been met and some sort of routine established for the supplies, O'Hara left Elliott in charge and made a hurried trip to Philadelphia. In addition to the joy of again seeing his love, he wanted to consult her about the plans that he had worked on night after night for the house to be built in the King's Orchard. And when they finally pored over these together they were closer than they had ever been.

"This first house will have to be logs, but just wait! One day you'll have the finest home in Pittsburgh," he promised gaily.

Mary called her father to look at the design and O'Hara went over it again.

"I thought a good-sized parlour with a dining-table where we could eat when we had guests and then a very large kitchen-living-room with the cooking fireplace. You've no idea how comfortable and pleasant such a room can be! I modelled this a bit after the one I was in at General Washington's headquarters at Morristown. Then three bedrooms upstairs. Does it seem . . . I mean, sir, do you think this would be . . . be adequate for a start?"

Mr. Carson looked at their love-lit faces. "I think it sounds very commodious and I expect to come to visit you."

"And I can take all kinds of furnishings with me. Mr. O'Hara said we can have two wagons when we make the trip!" Mary said eagerly.

It was so sweet, so intimate to dwell upon the rooms which would contain their life together. After Mr. Carson had left them and O'Hara had put the plans back in his pocket Mary must needs see them all over once again.

"If only the war was finished!" she sighed as their one precious evening was finally drawing to an end. "Father says it may drag on for years yet. And you'll have to be in it somehow, won't you?"

"I am afraid so. But now when we're sure of each other everything seems so much easier. We must try to be patient. Oh, I almost forgot the story I saved to tell you."

Mary brightened. "I love stories. Is this one true?"

"Absolutely. Have you heard the name of General Bouquet?"

"I . . . think so."

"He won the battle of Bushy Run and saved Fort Pitt when the French and Indians were making trouble. Then he forced the Indians to return all their captives to Pittsburgh."

"Their what?"

"Their captives. The people they had taken back to live with them. Most of these were claimed by their families there but the rest Bouquet brought on to Carlisle. There's a square in the middle of the town and after sending the word round the countryside he had all the captives stand in the square . . ."

Mary had been sitting on a hassock at his feet. Something in her face made him reach down suddenly and draw her up to his knee, holding her close.

"There was a Mrs. Hartmann who had lost her little girl, Regina, when she was only seven and now eight years had passed. The poor mother could hardly wait to get to the square. She looked at each person there but couldn't see a trace of her child, and no one recognised her."

"Oh, Mr. O'Hara, I don't think I like this story."

"You will at the end. Mrs. Hartmann went to General Bouquet with the tears running down her cheeks and told him of her terrible disappointment. He thought for a minute and then asked if there was any song she had sung to her little girl that she might remember. 'There is one,' Mrs. Hartmann said, 'that I used to sing to her every night when I put her to bed.' 'Sing it,' the general said."

O'Hara drew a slip of paper from his pocket. "I copied this to read to you. Mrs. Hartmann stood there while everybody stayed perfectly quiet. Many people in Carlisle still remember all this, you see, and here is what she sang:

Alone, yet not alone am I,
Within this wilderness so drear;
I feel my Saviour always nigh,
He comes my weary hours to cheer,
I am with Him and He with me,
I cannot solitary be.

"And all at once a tall girl with her skin tanned like an Indian and her long hair hanging down her back rushed to Mrs. Hartmann and flung herself into her arms. It was Regina!"

O'Hara waited eagerly for Mary's comment. He could see she was moved for there were tears in her eyes. But when she spoke the words were not what he had expected.

"They don't still do that, do they?"

"What . . ." he began.

"The Indians. They don't still carry people off, do they?"

He made his voice very strong. "Why, dear Delight, this happened *sixteen years ago!*"

She seemed content, though even during their most tender farewell he fancied there was a shadow in her eyes. And all the way back to Carlisle he kept wishing that he had not told her the story of Regina, the captive maid.

The winter ended at last and spring flooded the valley; the Judas trees turned the woods to rose and the distant circling mountains were as blue as the skies above them. O'Hara took satisfaction in what he had accomplished. The sick men had been warmed and fed, and besides this, Colonel White said he had sent a letter to General Washington, commending the services of his Commissary. The war seemed to be shifting to the south and as the summer advanced O'Hara kept wondering what his next assignment would be. While he had grown fond of Carlisle his work here had lost something of its challenge and he found himself hoping for a larger post. Meanwhile he was eager to get back to Fort Pitt and arrange for the building of his house.

It was August before he went, leaving Elliott in charge again. It was an easy journey this time of year and at the end he felt once more as though he had come home. Nothing had changed except for a few houses along the Monongahela. He went about his plans promptly after an evening of good talk in the tavern with Semple, Hugh Brackenridge and Devereux Smith. They were all interested in his affairs and when they heard the log house was eventually to hold a bride they became excitedly eager to help. So, the next morning they all joined to pace off the ground and drive the stakes at the corners. Four apple trees would have to be sacrified but the rest would form the bower which O'Hara had particularly wanted for Mary's home.

Two elderly boat builders who he knew to be good general carpenters were engaged to put up the building, working on it as they could find time, and a copy of the carefully drawn plans was given to Devereux Smith who agreed to keep an eye on the work as it progressed.

O'Hara found his friends discouraged about the course of the war, Brackenridge most of all.

"It seems to me to be running slack, as far as we can learn. And it's hard to watch the women and children round the country here trying to get in their bit of harvest while their men are away. If only we were winning! The last we heard of a real engagement was when this Colonel Tarleton's cavalry cut ours to pieces down in Virginia. That was back in April. I guess Cornwallis has settled himself in the South and it will likely be hard to dislodge him. They say he's called 'the modern Hannibal'. "

"All right. Hannibal was beaten, wasn't he? I pin my faith on General Washington. If you could meet him, you would too."

"Hope you're right," Hugh said. "At least I'm glad your personal affairs are pointing towards a happy head. The war! The war! If there's ever an end to it."

"You're keeping busy, aren't you?"

"Oh, so-so. I'm doing some writing. I'd like to author a book some day on pioneer life. I guess it would turn out to be a kind of social satire. Then I still make a few verses." He laughed.

"I'll tell you my latest. I got so wrought up over this business of *duels*. We keep hearing about them every now and then from back east especially. I think it's the damndest silliest performance I ever heard of for two men to stand up and pot at each other over some trifle for their *honour*! Fiddlesticks! Well, anyway, here's my rhyme. I think I'll send it to one of the Philadelphia papers.

> *To fight a duel!*
> *I'd live ten years on water gruel,*
> *Rather than stand up and be shot at,*
> *Like a racoon that can't be got at.*"

So the young men laughed together as they said good-bye while agreeing that duelling should be outlawed. And O'Hara made his way back to Carlisle over the road that had now become familiar to both Pitt and himself.

He had been there barely a month before the news came that stunned the whole town and for a time shattered his own heart. The post rider told it first at the Green Tree Inn and then in the square where a crowd was not long in gathering. The word was that within a week's time General Benedict Arnold, hero and friend of General Washington himself, had turned traitor and gone to the British and his liaison man, Major John André, had been caught, unfortunately out of uniform, and hanged as a spy. So, the news.

O'Hara when he heard it could not speak. Voices were voluble enough all around him, exclaiming, lamenting, vilifying, questioning, but he made no answer to anyone. He went up to his room and shut the door. A shudder ran through him as he sat. Benedict Arnold, a *traitor*! The trusted general who had been given charge of West Point at his own request had been guilty of this black, this dastardly betrayal, and was safe now, the post had said, on a British ship lying in the Hudson! It was unbelievable. It was too ugly to be true.

And Major André! O'Hara felt the smart of tears in his eyes. Only a year older than he, himself, for Mary had told him so. The gay, the gallant, the friendly young man who had won all hearts, had painted the scenery for the Philadelphia theatre, had arranged for the Meschianza, had written the tender farewell verse to Peggy Chew which Mary had read to him, *hanged*. Oh, what would Mary's heart feel about all this, for Arnold's wife was her friend! Had Peggy been a party to the plot? The Shippens had always had strong Tory leanings, he knew. What would become of her now? And Major André. . . .

He could eat nothing at supper for the food choked him. Elliott was silent too. Oddly enough when they did speak it was to say the same words at once.

"Who can you trust?" And the saying of it together brought something like a smile to their faces.

Mary's letter when it came was almost incoherent in its distress. She longed for O'Hara, so they could talk of it all together. She had no relief in speaking with her father for he was so bitter. He even said the major deserved hanging! But as the girls talked it all over among themselves their sympathies went out to Peggy Arnold with her new baby and their tears were for John André. Oh, war was so cruel. And how long would it last? And what dangers might he, O'Hara, still have to face?

More bad news came belatedly on the heels of that of Arnold and André. Two thousand men under General Gates had been utterly routed by Cornwallis at Camden, South Carolina! The modern Hannibal indeed. Perhaps Brackenridge had been right. At least Gates was now ousted and General Nathaniel Greene, who stood next to Washington himself, was in charge of the southern campaign. O'Hara for the first time felt a vague discouragement. And the next word of a mutiny in the Pennsylvania line did not lift his spirits.

"Poor devils," he said to Elliott. "The wonder is there hasn't been mutiny before this, considering what the men have borne, and for the most part without pay."

"Congress ought to be made up of ex-soldiers," Elliott said savagely. "Then we might get some action."

And another winter passed, lightened for O'Hara only by the brief occasional trips to Philadelphia which were to him as cold water to a thirsty soul. Then with spring came the new appointment for which he had been hoping. In its character, however, it was an enormous surprise. Chosen by Washington, ratified by Congress, he was now Quartermaster to the Army in the south! He was to join General Anthony Wayne and his companies at York in May and proceed with them to Virginia, seeing to their provisioning from the point of contact on. A letter from Robert Morris came also, a friendly one, congratulating him upon his good work at Carlisle and explaining the financial details in connection with his new job. He might need warehouses for certain supplies though in the main he imagined the army would have to "live off the land." But he added, and this cheered O'Hara, he had the feeling that they were entering upon the last and winning stage of the war. He would lay his bets on Mad Anthony every time!

One thing O'Hara decided at once when he had recovered from the pleasurable shock of the news: he must have Elliott with him.

"We know how to work together," he said. "There's a new Commissary due here and since you insist on serving without pay, there's no appointment necessary. Will you come?"

So it was settled and early in May after leaving hospital affairs in good order they rode off once more together. Aside from the prospect of a big and challenging job, O'Hara's great anticipation was the meeting with Anthony Wayne. On his last tender trip to say farewell to Mary she had told him more about the general: his dash, his courage, his constant solicitude for his men, and of course , . . his love. Everyone in Philadelphia, that is in their social group, knew of this now, she said. The blaze in his eyes and the answering yearning in Mary Vining's whenever they met, simply could not be hidden. While his home was near Paoli and Mary's was in Delaware they were both well known in Philadelphia. Mary came up for all the balls, and Wayne had been a member of the Colonial Committee for Safety before the war. The odd thing was that they had never met until just before Stony Point. From then on their secret was all too manifest.

O'Hara's plan was to reach York well before the army and have some supplies ready when the men came. Using his tried methods of simple purchase, threat and cajolery he was able to secure a great quantity of smoked meats, cheese, flour and vats of lard from the wide and rich countryside. York itself reminded him of the old country even as Carlisle had done and the farms around it were beautifully fertile. He made the purchase of a warehouse of sorts and into this he and Elliott, working tirelessly with their helpers, arranged the stores in neat order.

"They'll have wagons with them," O'Hara said, "so we had better not buy more until we're sure how many we'll need. Do you feel nervous, Elliott?"

"Like a cat."

"So do I. I was a little too puffed up, I think, when my appointment came. Pretty sure of myself. And the devil always gets a kick in at you for pride. Now, I'm scared. It's a big jump from being Commissary at a hospital to feeding an *army*."

Elliott grinned at him and slapped his back. "You've been in tight places before. Don't worry. Your gumption will see you through."

One afternoon towards the end of May they heard the drums! In the moment O'Hara realised the difference between regular troops and the frontier sharp-shooters of the Vincennes campaign. The sound came nearer, rhythmic and compelling. Then in view on the dusty road came the officers on horseback and the soldiers in companies rank upon rank behind them. O'Hara made a quick decision. He and Elliott should be on horseback too, not standing in the dust like a pair of schoolboys when the officers approached. It was a matter of minutes until he was on Pitt, and Elliott mounted beside him. When the commanding officer drew up he knew at once that it was Mad Anthony Wayne. The general sat as well in the saddle as any man he had ever seen, with a fine figure and an easy grace. His grey eyes had a reckless light in them even here on the quiet road. Spirit, vigour, endurance were written upon his handsome face, vanity, too, perhaps but, even more clearly, honesty. He wore a bright blue coat with red lining and creaseless lambskin breeches, and he smiled as he spoke.

"Captain O'Hara, I take it?"

"The same, sir. Quartermaster at your service, with my helper, Mr. Elliott."

After the greetings the general looked keenly at O'Hara.

"I've heard of your good work in Carlisle, that you can even *steal* upon occasion. That cheered me up no end. We've had a bad time about provisions all through this war. My men are hungry right now. I suppose you haven't . . ."

O'Hara nodded. "We came on ahead and pretty well stripped the countryside. We have a sort of warehouse here. What about fried ham and flapjack for the men's supper?"

Wayne stared. "Do you mean that? Good God, the boys will be sure they got shot on the way and have gone to heaven! Just a minute, and then I'll go and see your stores."

It ended with the soldiers camping in the open field south of the town. The fires were started, the great skillets brought out, the cooks making use of the long trestle tables O'Hara and Elliott had built, and before long there was a smell in the air that made the men cheer.

When night fell the soldiers settled for sleep on the ground, their stomachs for once warmed and filled. There was plenty of sassafras in the woods and O'Hara had hired all the small boys in town to dig roots of it, so there had been sassafras tea with a bit of milk along with the supper. Even without sugar it was a palatable drink and one which the men would have had in their own homes. They gulped it greedily.

Elliott slept at once but O'Hara could not. As he walked to the edge of the encampment he saw another figure pacing under the stars. It was Anthony Wayne. When he saw O'Hara he signed to him and together they moved farther away.

"I wanted to talk to you when all was quiet," the general began, "but I didn't like to wake you up. My thanks again for that meal. It's put new spirit into the men . . . and me too."

"I'm glad. Of course you understand I can't manage one like that *every* night, but I'll do my best. I'm having some beeves killed to-morrow morning and dressed. Even though the meat will be fresh it ought to taste pretty good. How long before we leave here, General?"

"Let's see. This is the twenty-first. I plan to beat at daybreak on the twenty-sixth. Will that give you time to load your provisions?"

"Oh, yes."

"We have a nasty job to do to-morrow. I wanted to tell you this so you and your friend would be prepared."

"So?"

"Let's sit down," Wayne said. "I guess I should lead up to it. You heard, of course, about the mutiny in our line?"

"Yes."

"That was bad, bad. I did my best to dissuade the men. *I* knew what they had suffered. *I* knew their grievances were legitimate. But even granting that you can't have mutiny in the army. It threw a scare into all of us." His voice had been quiet but now it seemed to catch fire.

"And I maintain if it hadn't been for *Arnold*, the whole thing would never have happened. Damn him to hell! Did you know he's been in the south with the British *fighting against us*?"

"No. Oh, no!"

"Well, he is even now. I've known the man for years. Never liked him much, but I respected him as a brave officer. He was always in and out of quarrels though, making enemies. Of course, while he was commanding in Philadelphia he spent money like water, and there was plenty of criticism. And at last somebody brought a lot of more or less trivial charges against him to Congress and there was a court-martial. He was acquitted but with the order that Washington should reprimand him. That, I guess, was the last straw, for he's proud and touchy as the devil. Even though I heard that the reprimand was almost praise, he couldn't stand it. But, *treason!*"

Wayne only paused for a second and then went on.

"*I've* been bitter myself. Congress passed me over once in favour of General St. Clair. He comes from round your Pittsburgh way, doesn't he?"

"A little to the east. Ligonier, I believe. I've never met him."

"Well, he's the old-fashioned kind of general who leads his troops *from the rear*. And that's not my way."

"So I've gathered," O'Hara said, a smile in his voice.

"The trouble with St. Clair is that he's got too much Scots caution. Oh, well, the point is any man in the soldiering business has to take the bitter pills that come, swallow them and keep his mouth shut. But *Arnold . . .*"

He was quiet until O'Hara reminded him.

"You said something about a job to do to-morrow?"

"Yes. In a way it's all bound up with what I've been talking about. After the mutiny the troops were warned again that any deserter would be shot. Every man understood it but . . . we've got five back there now under guard to be executed at sunset to-morrow."

O'Hara could not speak.

"I ought to be hardened," Wayne went on. "I am, to death in battle. I've seen soldiers fall round me and it didn't faze me, for I was right there with them and knew I could be the next one, myself. But to line five decent men up and shoot them down like dogs . . . God, I have to watch it. *Order* it! One's just a young chap. Shouldn't wonder if he was running off to see his girl. Well, I thought I'd tell you, so you and Elliott could keep out of the way if you want to."

"Thank you, General. I . . . I appreciate your telling me."

"It's a hard necessity," Wayne answered and then the two sat on in silence with the Maytime night all about them. There was an almost full moon showering its white light; there was the scent of blossoms like a whisper, and the distilled essence of spring itself rising from the waking earth; there was a little warm wind moving amongst the new leaves like a caress. Were the five men who were appointed to die, now awake? O'Hara wondered. Were they watching their last moonlit night? Did the beauty of this their last springtime lie upon them now like an agony?

At length Wayne stood up and so did O'Hara. The general hesitated and then spoke in a low voice.

"I believe," he said, "that you and I have mutual friends."

"I believe we have," O'Hara answered.

Then, without saying more the two men made their way back to their own quarters.

The troops were subdued the morning after the executions and the noisy jollity of their first evening in York did not return before they got under way at daybreak on the twenty-sixth. From then on they skirted down along the Blue Ridge Mountains towards Fredericksburg. The plan, as O'Hara learned it, was to march to Virginia and join the Marquis de La Fayette whom Wayne described out of the corner of his mouth as "a statue looking for a pedestal." He admitted, however, that the young nobleman along with his intense ambition and love of liberty had the qualities of a good officer and would probably acquit himself well in this campaign.

"I can work with him, all right," he said.

O'Hara found his own duties discouraging as the weeks went on. The men were marching hard and were always hungry. The supplies in the wagons dwindled and the countryside through which they were passing was very different from the fertile farms around York. For this had been ravaged by the British with Arnold in the lead, and he had not spared the torch. Fields and barns were blackened ruins. The best cattle had been slaughtered or driven off and every good horse apparently impressed. Elliott was still his cheerful self but sometimes O'Hara in his desperation did not appreciate his friend's humour.

"Did you kill those two cows you said you found?" he asked Elliott one morning.

"Yes, we managed it. But I'll tell you how it was. It took four men to hold up each cow while we knocked it on the head."

They searched henhouses, taking all the chickens and eggs they could get their hands on, despite the owners' protests. This was small provender but better than nothing. With the helpers allowed him, he and Elliott shot hares and squirrels and every turkey buzzard they could bring down for the northerners didn't know they were scavengers and they helped fill the pots.

In addition to the burdens of his work something else bothered

O'Hara. He smiled grimly sometimes as he considered the contrast between this march and the one to Vincennes, for in this army there were women and a good many of them. A very few like "Molly Pitcher" were brave wives, but the majority were those who plied their ancient profession as casually here as anywhere else. One large, blowzy girl apparently had marked O'Hara for her own and gave him no peace. One night he woke to find her snuggled cosily against him. He shook her to her feet and gave her several resounding whacks upon her seat. She went off, he hoped in pain, crying, "Oh, Captain, you hain't got no heart."

The next day he spoke to Elliott.

"I've got another job for you."

"Not another hen roost, for God's sake," Elliott groaned. "It's taken me two days to get the lice out of me from the last one."

"No. This is serious. From now on you've got to sleep with me."

Elliott gazed at him and then grinned.

"Me lad, I'd as lieve sleep with a wet dog as with another man!"

"So would I. But listen."

He told his problem and Elliott found it amusing. "So, you're afraid of her, eh?"

"No, I'm not afraid, but I'm a decent man and I intend to remain so. And I won't have that filthy trollop hanging around me."

"All right. I s'pose I'll have to protect you. I'll lie near you but I won't get close."

"You'd better not," O'Hara said, and they both laughed.

One pleasant feature of the march to O'Hara was making the acquaintance of Ensign Ebenezer Denny of whom his mother had spoken so often. He was a friendly youth with a good sense of humour and when there was a chance he and O'Hara swapped yarns of both Carlisle and Pittsburgh. There were nights, too, when the camp was asleep, that Wayne seemed eager again to talk to O'Hara. Though they still avoided the intimate disclosures bound to come ultimately, there grew with each meeting a feeling of mutual respect and friendship. Moreover, Wayne told him many interesting bits of army news. Alexander Hamilton, for instance, whom O'Hara had met in Morristown, had hardly spoken to General Washington after the hanging of André, so he was no longer on the staff but again an officer of the line. Well, everybody had felt badly about André. Nathaniel Greene? *There* was a general for you! Quaker, too, believe it or not. He had a nice sort of slow grin but by God, he wasn't slow about anything else. The report was that when he couldn't get Cornwallis to stand and face him down here, he went after him, snapping at his heels. Good man, Greene.

Whenever Wayne spoke of Arnold his voice became hard as stone. "I'll tell you a pretty piece of gossip about him. He sent a letter to La Fayette about an exchange of prisoners or something and La Fayette wouldn't even open it. Sent the aide back with it. Arnold was second-in-command then to a General Phillips. Next day the aide came back with the letter and said Arnold was now commanding officer of the force as Phillips had just died. La Fayette still wouldn't touch the letter but the rumour went like wildfire that Arnold had poisoned Phillips to get the command! And I wouldn't put it past him."

"How do you hear all this?"

Wayne laughed. "Oh," he said, "that's the easiest thing in the business. We have couriers, scouts, runners. And spies. La Fayette has the best of those for he pays them out of his own pocket. He outfitted his men too. I wish to heaven I could. Our men look like scarecrows. Nothing but rags to their backs."

"And I wish I could feed them better!" O'Hara said regretfully.

Wayne clapped him on the shoulder. "It may not seem such good pickings to you but let me tell you they've had a damned sight worse. You're doing wonders in a hard jog. I've an idea things may get better a little farther south. By the way, I hear La Fayette has picked up English fairly well, but still you may be able . . ." He paused. "I mean . . . I understand your French is pretty fluent if we should need it."

"It's at your service. I'll be very honoured to meet the Marquis."

They met him just outside Fredericksburg where, with his gracious courtesy, he had ridden with a few troops in their fresh suits behind him, to greet General Wayne. It seemed a happy meeting and while the soldiers all rested the two generals talked. O'Hara stayed near to help with the language difficulties when he could. He liked the Marquis with his young, eager face and aura of unquenchable optimism. The news he brought was that Cornwallis was encamped around Richmond with his supply base at Williamsburg towards the sea, while the cocky little Colonel Banastre Tarleton (whom the Continentals hated almost as much as Arnold) was using his flashy cavalry to beat up the banks of the James River for forage. With Wayne's troops the Marquis said their own forces would now number over four thousand; Cornwallis had about five.

But the great news was that the French Admiral de Grasse was on his way from the West Indies with ships and almost an army of men. *That* ought to turn the tide! If he just got there, the Marquis added ruefully.

When the talk was over and La Fayette gone O'Hara said to Wayne, "I like that man. Maybe he's a bit vain but aren't we all?"

"True," said Wayne. "And we ought to forgive him anything because of what he's got the French to do for us. Well, it's on to Richmond now and for myself I'm red hot for a fight."

But Cornwallis had left when they got there, and the days ran on until the 4th of July, the nation's fifth independence anniversary. It was wet in the morning but cleared by noon and the men celebrated with a regular *feu de joie*, extra rum rations, and the best supper O'Hara could scare up. The provisioning was becoming a little easier now, but even so O'Hara was still discouraged and very tired. For one thing there had been no exchange of letters between him and Mary. The army messengers did not carry personal mail and there was no other means of communication. This was hard. He found that something of the energy and drive he had felt on the Vincennes campaign had gone out of him. Perhaps to be in the army and not of it was dispiriting. Like Wayne he might be unconsciously eager for action.

It came, for the soldiers at least, two days after the celebration. They had moved to a place called Greenspring where they discovered Cornwallis was already. Wayne ahead with his eight hundred picked Pennsylvanians mistook the van of the British for the rear and set upon them. Young Denny, who was close to him, reported it all later to O'Hara.

"A bullet went right through the plume of the general's infantry cap and I swear to you he just looked at the feather falling and then at the enemy and *seemed amused*!"

The hero worship on the young man's face was dazzling. "And when we could see we were in a trap with the British closing in on both sides what do you suppose the general did?"

"Ordered an attack," O'Hara smiled.

"How did you know, back here?"

"I know the man."

"Well, that's what he did. All at once he yelled, *Forward . . .
charge . . . bayonets!* So we did and the British evidently were
surprised and thought the whole army was behind us. They drew
back to reform and we retreated then in good order. It was getting dark anyway. But imagine a man who wasn't able either to
hold his ground then or fall back, saving himself by driving
into the enemy with his bayonets! Well, that's Mad Anthony for
you."

The hot weeks passed slowly. Watermelon season came and
the men feasted. The country generally was more fruitful and
O'Hara was less put to it to find provisions. He was still restless,
however, and often longed to talk to someone of what lay nearest
his heart. The opportunity came one Sunday in late August.
They were camping along the James River near the Byrd mansion.
There had been divine service that morning under the elegant
shade of the great trees; now it was night and he found himself
alone with Wayne, looking up at the stars.

"Let's sit down," the general said, as he had that night in
York. "Let's talk. You've never told me about your plans. I mean
with Mary Carson. Is everything . . . settled?"

O'Hara's voice was full of happiness. "Yes," he said. "It is
now, but I had a long time on tenterhooks. We expect to marry
as soon as the war's over."

"Live in Pittsburgh?"

"Yes."

"Will she be contented there? It's still pretty rough frontier,
isn't it?"

"That was the trouble at first, but now she's willing to go and
I feel sure I can make her happy. I'm having a house built there
in the King's Orchard. It's a really lovely spot. A big grove of
apple trees along the river. And there will be a few women she
can be friends with. Her own kind, you know. With it all, sometimes I'm anxious."

Something in the words made Wayne reach over and lay a
hand on his shoulder.

"Don't worry," he said. "When you're free to love each other
everything else will smoothen before you. Now with me . . ."

Even in the darkness O'Hara could feel a gathering of tension,
of anguish in the other. He thought of this man, smiling at his
falling plume in battle which meant he had missed death by a

hair's breadth; ordering the bayonet charge when defeat was upon him. He who sat next to him now, he knew, was not Mad Anthony, the intrepid general, but Anthony, the lover.

"It will ease me to talk about my own problem," Wayne went on. "You've probably heard it all anyway from your Mary. You see, I'm married. We were too young when it happened. Neither of us knew what we were doing. For years now we haven't been close. I never knew what love was until I looked into Miss Vining's eyes. Then we both knew."

He was silent and O'Hara waited, suffering with him.

"The thing is," Wayne finally said, "I'm a gentleman, I hope. I haven't much stomach for low compromise in morals. But I tell you as a mere man I would stoop to it because of the fire in me, but I couldn't ever ask it of her. So there we stand. Absolutely without hope." A terrible sigh was wrenched from him.

"What can I say to you?" O'Hara burst out. "Only that I feel for you from my heart. I had my own time of despair, you know. I wish I could . . ."

"There is nothing anyone can do. The reason we can't even *hope* is because the circumstances under which I would be free are those I could never wish for. Well, tell me about your plans with 'pretty Polly Carson.' She's a sweet young thing. How did you get to know her?"

So O'Hara told him of that first meeting, of the Garden of Delight, the Bingham ball and the years since. It comforted him to go over it all and strangely enough it seemed to interest Wayne without arousing envy.

"Yes, yes," he said. "That's the way it should be. Thanks for telling me. It's sweetened my own thoughts, somehow."

It was only a few nights later that the accident happened. A message came to Wayne from La Fayette, rather an excited message. Would the general have the kindness to come at once to discuss important strategic matters? De Grasse with his whole fleet and his men were arrived at the Chesapeake Bay. General Washington was on his way south to Williamsburg with his own army. The British had gone to Yorktown. It looked as though the end was in sight.

Wayne was immeasurably elated. At eight o'clock he bowed good night to Mrs. Byrd on the great portico. Shaved and powdered and handsome, wearing his cocked hat and dress sword he joined two officers and O'Hara who had been invited to go along to help with any language problems. They all mounted and rode off into the night, reaching the outskirts of La Fayette's encampment two hours later.

Out of the darkness came the challenge of a picket whose voice sounded frightened. Wayne answered with the counter-sign and prepared to ride on. But the sentry was evidently thinking of Cornwallis, Tarleton and the British raiders for he doubted Wayne's reply and fired. O'Hara saw a streak of red go past him and then saw the general sway in the saddle. They all called out then to save themselves from being riddled and rushed to help Wayne. They got him to La Fayette's quarters where a surgeon was called. He found the ball had struck the thigh bone and was evidently lodged behind it, though the agony of pain was all in the foot.

The following day the general professed himself able to talk plans, then insisted on getting back to his own quarters in the Byrd mansion. From then on he lay in bed, fuming and cursing. Of all humiliating accidents to be shot by one of their own sentries! Of all intolerable times to be laid up now with General Washington coming and three thousand French troops just landing! But one evening when O'Hara was visiting him in his room his mood was quiet and sombre.

"I don't like this, O'Hara," he said. "It's as if someone had stepped across my grave, as the old women say."

"Oh, nonsense!" O'Hara said. "If you'd got that wound in battle you'd have taken it as a matter of course and not tried to find an *omen* in it. You're really over the worst now."

And he was, for on the twelfth day after the shot he got dressed again in his best and limped to a carriage when he rode off to an elegant supper of welcome for the commander-in-chief. The next day he reported that things were really on the move at last. Cornwallis in Yorktown, the French fleet shutting him off from the sea, and all the Continental troops, it was hoped, soon to reach ground just in front of him. An electric thrill ran through officers and men alike as the march began.

The siege of Yorktown was to O'Hara the most thrilling experience of his life, more even than Vincennes, for here was not a backwoods battle but a conflict in which two large and trained armies confronted each other in a last desperate struggle which was to decide the destiny of a country, the country he himself had elected to make his own.

Between his arduous labours behind the lines when he, with Elliott and his helpers foraged for food to feed Wayne's troops, O'Hara watched keenly the preparations that went on. The first thing to be done as young Ensign Denny had reported to him was the building of a long line of trenches right before the enemy position, the first parallel it was called. Already over a thousand men were at work making breastwork baskets and filling them with soil, while as many more guarded them from sudden attack. In the main, things were quiet. The British fired a field piece now and then but the Continentals did not reply. For one thing all their artillery was not yet in position. The British regulars had full regimental bands and now often they could be heard playing; and when the wind was right the sound of singing came also. To O'Hara it had an eerie effect.

"Isn't Cornwallis scared? Doesn't he know this is *serious*?" he asked Wayne one day as the music was borne upon the air.

Wayne grinned. "We think my lord expects relief. He's just planning to sit tight until Clinton can get here and then all will be well. Of course that's not quite General Washington's idea."

The night of the 6th October was picked for the opening of the first parallel. It was just past full moon and if the sky was clear the men with their picks and shovels, only eight hundred yards from the British inner defences, would be easy to hit. But the clouds were kind, the firing did little damage and by dawn the trench was finished. Three days later with the artillery in place the Allied bombardment began and from then on never ceased. A second trench was dug still nearer the enemy; there were sorties by the British; a capture of redoubts by the Allies; but always, steadily, mercilessly, day after day, in light and in darkness, the endless pounding from the French and the Continental guns.

On the bright morning of the seventeenth, a drummer boy was seen mounted on a British parapet. Above the firing the sound was lost but everyone knew what it meant. The guns all grew quiet and then they could hear the drummer. He was beating the *chamade*, the call to parley, the sweetest music in the world to the ears of the Allied soldiers.

The surrender was carried out with dignity on both sides. On Hampton Road south of Yorktown the victorious armies lined up: the French in their white gaiters and coats, their epaulets and gold braid; and opposite them those glorious ragged scarecrows (as Wayne had called them), the men of the Continental Army of the

United States of America! The British general's sword was offered and returned; the British regiments came out, bands playing but colours cased, as they left their guns in a meadow nearby. The great war was won and O'Hara as he watched the ceremony felt a lump in his throat even as his heart rejoiced.

One episode of the day had brought bitter disappointment to young Ensign Denny. He told O'Hara about it that evening. A fort on the bank of the York River was to be formally given over and the new standard raised.

"Dicky Butler . . . I mean General Butler from Carlisle but I've always known him . . . well, Dicky was given the standard but he passed it to me. He said, 'Eb, I'm short and you're tall and besides this will be something nice for you to remember.' Well, I took it as proud as you please but just when we got inside the fort General Steuben grabbed it from me and raised it himself. I could have kicked him!"

"Come on, Eb," O'Hara said sympathetically. "Let's go celebrate a little and forget our troubles."

It was several days before he could talk to Wayne, then O'Hara began jubilantly, "Well, so we've won!"

"Damned if we haven't," Wayne agreed, but without enough enthusiasm.

"How soon do you think we can start back?" O'Hara asked eagerly.

Wayne looked at him with a strange expression.

"I don't know. General Washington has asked me to stay on . . . put it in a way I couldn't refuse as a soldier. I think you may get the same orders."

"Stay *on*!" O'Hara said, his voice unsteady. "Why should we have to stay on when the war's over?"

"The war's won but it's not over. There's a difference. General Greene's still down south and he may need some help before he clears things up. Besides we've nearly got eight thousand troops here even after the French that came up with de Grasse have gone back to their ships. You can't just say *scat* to an army that size and go off and leave it."

O'Hara turned his back. In all his life he had never known such a stab of disappointment as he felt at this moment. Ever since the drummer boy beat his *chamade*, he had been busy reckoning the time—in weeks and days—until he would again hold Mary in his arms and plan definitely for their wedding. And now. . . .

Wayne was speaking slowly. "After this we may be able to get letters through. That will be a help."

And all at once O'Hara felt ashamed. For him no matter when he got back, the heaven of his marriage lay before him; for Anthony Wayne there would be no such consummation of love. He turned suddenly and looked into the other man's eyes from which the reckless light had disappeared.

"Of course," he said, forcing a cheerfulness he was far from feeling. "We have to do our duty. And time passes. And there's one thing sure. When we finally get back to Philadelphia we'll both get a welcome that will be . . ."

"Worth waiting for," Wayne ended for him.

And even with an effort, the two men smiled at each other.

Chapter Eight

It was the month of May. The month of Mary! And the wedding day itself with sunshine, new verdure, and soft airs was as freshly beautiful as though just dropped from the hand of God. In a front room at the Crooked Billet with Sam to assist him, O'Hara arranged his newly powdered hair, tied it with a black satin bow, fastened his elegant lace stock, buttoned his rose satin waistcoat, and finally in knee breeches and long coat, gave a last fastening to the silver knee-buckles with hands that trembled. For it seemed past belief that time's slow march had actually brought him to this moment! He thought of that far-off conversation with Wayne when they had discussed the possibility of their being detained in the south. O'Hara then had considered the delay in terms of months. As a matter of fact it was more than two years and a half since the night when—as Mary had told him—the Philadelphia watchman making his rounds had called out upon the hour: *Past one o'clock and Cornwallis is taken! Past two o'clock and Cornwallis is taken! Past three o'clock* . . . For Colonel Teuch Tilghman who had carried the great news had ridden well. Mary had been awakened by this shout and had not slept at all after, as she said, her mind chanting its own paean: *Now he will come back soon, soon!*

But the weary wait had dragged on with only letters to solace their hearts, until at long last the duty was done and Wayne and O'Hara returned to Philadelphia together with the last of the troops. After the first rapturous reunion with his love, O'Hara had gone back at once to Pittsburgh to check upon the house. He had been more than satisfied. It stood, strong and not unpleasing in its simple design, in the midst of the apple trees. He had bought some necessary furniture to supplement that which Mary was bringing: an oak trestle table, straight chairs and two rockers for the kitchen, and a four-poster bed for the room upstairs. The great fireplace delighted him for the mason had done a fine job even to a decorative row of flat cemented stones below the mantel! The workmen had all apparently put forth special effort, which was touching, as was the welcome from his old friends, and their eagerness to be of help. Devereux and Mrs. Smith had found, they thought, the perfect cook-housekeeper for Mary, whom O'Hara at once interviewed and engaged. In addition to the middle-aged Prudence Bond, he had acquired a young indentured negro youth by the fascinating Irish name of McGrady, which amused O'Hara out of all reason. They had looked each other in the eye and liked what they saw. It was McGrady who knew the exact answer to his question as to when the apple trees would be in bloom, for O'Hara had planned over the years that he would bring Mary to the King's Orchard when the perfumed blossoms would surround her. And it was McGrady who promised to get the cooking utensils for the fireplace and later to purchase the food supplies which O'Hara listed for him. It was then early March so they reckoned the time carefully.

"The young lady, suh, ain't mebbe used to the frontier?"

"No. She comes from Philadelphia."

"We all gonna try to make her comfortable, suh. I looken out for her very special myself, suh." His speech still was richly southern.

His new master clapped him on the shoulder.

"I'm glad I found you, McGrady."

One thing lay heavily upon his heart as he started back again over the long but now familiar route. This was the news of the burning of Hannastown the July before! The little village about twenty miles from Pittsburgh had been important, with its law courts held in Robert Hanna's big tavern, its neat log houses and general air of respectability. There were prominent citizens, too: Colonel Proctor belonged there, so did Archibald Lochry, names known both east and west. On a sunny afternoon, so the report went, while most of the men were helping a neighbour harvest, the Indians had stolen upon the town. The women and children got to the fort and the men, fighting as they went, hurried there when the alarm reached them. By courage and by ruse they held the small stronghold so that there were only a few deaths and a few captives. But at the end the pleasant little village with all it held of patient building lay in ashes. All this was tragic enough but the part that distressed O'Hara immeasurably was that the leader of the raid had been *Guyasuta!*

"I can't understand that!" O'Hara had lamented to Devereux Smith. "I thought *Guyasuta* was a good Indian."

"There's just one good Indian, my friend," Smith said between his teeth. "That's a dead one."

So O'Hara had to hide his hurt and his questions until a later day.

Now, back in Philadelphia as he stood in the last hour of his bachelorhood, dressed for the greatest event of his life, his busy mind checking over the details of the last weeks here in the city when the preparations for the trip were in progress. Had he forgotten anything that would add to Mary's comfort? It had been his concern waking and sleeping. One wagon was already gone with the heavier furnishings in it; the second wagon, with its sturdy oxen, was standing now on the side street just beyond the Carson home. The hard seat had been upholstered with cushions. Under it were boxes and travelling bags, while in the back of the wagon were the Oriental rugs which Mr. Carson had insisted upon giving, and on top of them three feather ticks with pillows, sheets and covers. Over this O'Hara had spread a waterproof tarpaulin for use if needed but chiefly to keep curious eyes from looking upon what would be the marriage bed.

There was a clatter of hoofs below on the cobblestones and the sound of wheels.

"There you are, Mr. O'Hara! Carriage is waitin'. You're mighty handsome, I tell you. Anybody know you was a bridegroom just by lookin' at you."

"Thanks, Sam." He peered from the window. Christian Febiger, Mary's brother-in-law who was to stand with him at the ceremony, was looking up and waving. His wife Elizabeth, whom O'Hara had never met until this spring due to his short and infrequent visits at the Carson home, was to be Mary's matron of honour. He wrung Sam's hand now and looked his last at the house that had first sheltered him in the new country; then having already made his farewell to Hastings, he ran down the stairs and out into the bright sunshine. Febiger stood by the carriage handing him in as though he were royalty.

"To the Locust Street Presbyterian Church," O'Hara said to the driver.

"Don't you suppose I've already told him that?" Febiger asked.

O'Hara grinned. "On an occasion as important as this, it's best to leave nothing to chance." There had been one immediate

G

bond between the two young men for Febiger had served under Anthony Wayne at Stony Point and admired him greatly.

"We're to sit up front," Christian was saying now, "until Mary and her father come into the church. Parson Brown has given me all the directions. He says bridegrooms are too nervous to be trusted. Do you want to keep the ring or let me have it till the proper time?"

"I'll keep it if you don't mind. I have a feeling I'd rather no other hand touched it till I put it on her finger."

"All right. Relieves me of responsibility. O'Hara . . .?"

"Yes?"

"You know I wish you and Mary all the best in the world, even if . . . even though Elizabeth and I have been anxious about the match . . . afraid it's too big a step for Mary to take after the way she's been brought up and all that. But I do want to tell you now . . ."

"Yes?" O'Hara prompted again, his face grave.

"Well, since we've met you we feel better. If anyone can take care of her, I'm sure you will." He reached his hand and O'Hara grasped it without speaking.

Inside the church everything at first was quiet for the young men were early, then there began the sound of footsteps and rustle of stiff silks as the guests walked up the aisle and settled in the pews. Parson Brown sat solemnly upon the pulpit dais, his face ruddy above his white Geneva bands, his eyes fixed upon the door. O'Hara's heart was beating thunderously. Christian Febiger's words had struck him deeply. He knew Mary's family were concerned about her marriage to him; when he allowed himself to be objective, so was he. Her happiness, her very life was soon to be in his keeping, and while the most desperate perils of the frontier were now past there were still dangers . . . had he been honest enough about these? O God, had he because of the strength of his love in any way deceived her?

At last there were sudden movements in the back of the church, Parson Brown was coming down from his high chair to stand before the pulpit, Febiger was nudging him and rising, they were out in the aisle moving to join the minister . . . Then O'Hara looked back and all his doubts and fears vanished as a mist before the sun! For Mary in white ribbed satin, and a little veil of cloudy lace was coming towards him, a smile upon her lips! He went, in his eagerness, more than the prescribed steps to meet her, then her small hand clasped tightly in his strong one, they stood together repeating after Parson Brown the vows which made their union sacred and eternal.

The reception at the Carson home later was both elegant and gay. There were flowers everywhere and in the dining-room where an elaborate collation was spread, the silver gleamed and the crystal sparkled. To make up for Mary's disappointment at the lack of music at the wedding (Parson Brown felt it savoured of Episcopacy) three violinists in the wide hall sent waves of melody through the rooms, where an élite group of Philadelphians were gathered to do honour to the young couple. There was a constant flow of guests at once up the stairs to the front room where some of the wedding gifts were on display for an hour longer before they were packed according to prearranged plan and put into the wagon. The gift causing the most comment was the dozen cut champagne glasses from General Washington!

Judge Bingham spoke to O'Hara in the drawing-room about it. "Quite a signal honour for His Excellency to remember you in this way. May I ask how you became so close to him?"

"I hardly know," O'Hara admitted. "Of course he couldn't help but feel my strong admiration for him. Then he professed himself . . . satisfied with the work I did in the south."

"No special bond?" the judge kept pressing.

"Well, we found out we're both very fond of *horses*."

"Ah, could be that. Very likely. What about your own horse. Mary told my wife about him. Thinking of changing his name now?" The judge laughed.

"No more than Pittsburgh is thinking of changing its name," O'Hara replied smiling. "Pitt has been with me everywhere I've gone and he's to travel with us now, tied to the back of the wagon."

At the moment a tall, handsome man appeared in the doorway, his eyes searching the room. It was Anthony Wayne! Alone. O'Hara went quickly to meet him, and the two shook hands without speaking. What was there to say that they had not said to each other already?

"If you'll come to the library I think Mary is there at the moment . . . and some other old friends."

Mary Vining, beautiful in yellow silk that set off her dark hair and eyes to perfection, was in a small group by the window. She turned as if drawn, saw Wayne and coloured until her face was rose. So, thought O'Hara, no wonder everybody can tell what's going on. Wayne spoke to the bride, bowing low over her hand, greeted a few others and then made his way with great attempt at casualness towards the group in the corner.

When it was time for O'Hara and Mary to change from their wedding to their travelling attire, Christian Febiger with perhaps a little too much champagne, signalled for all to keep quiet while he gave, as he put it, his last instructions to the groom. O'Hara felt a moment's uneasiness but when Febiger's voice rang out it was in the old rhyme which he already knew.

> "*Lead her like a pigeon,*
> *Bed her like a dove,*
> *Whisper when you're near her,*
> *'You're my only love.'* "

There was general applause and laughter and raising of glasses which O'Hara and Mary acknowledged smiling, then she started upstairs with her sister Elizabeth, and O'Hara followed with Christian. Not, however, before he had seen Wayne and Mary Vining quietly slip out of the front door. Poor Anthony! he thought.

When they came down again O'Hara was in his uniform and Mary was all in dove grey with a tiny bonnet of the same material edged with white ruching. Practical, but oh, so becoming! There were exclamations from the ladies, admiring glances from the men, and then the good-byes at the doorway with good wishes floating after them as they reached the wagon now drawn up before the house. O'Hara lifted Mary to her place, sprang up beside her, taking the lines in his hand, and amid a chorus from the steps they drove off, with O'Hara's last glance for Mr. Carson. He had had a long talk with his father-in-law the night before, and now he raised his hand in what to the rest would seem merely a gesture, but which was really the expression of a vow; then the wagon rattled over the cobblestones and on out to the Lancaster road.

"I may cry a little," Mary said brokenly.

"I don't wonder. You've been so brave all day. Put your head on my shoulder and cry all you want. You'll feel better."

But in a short time she sat up again. "It was a beautiful wedding, wasn't it?"

"Absolutely perfect!"

From then on they went over all the details of the day including their own emotions, until suddenly they realised they were both very, very hungry.

"I was too excited to eat any of the lunch," Mary said.

"I too."

"And I really don't believe I had much breakfast."

"Same with me!"

They laughed and brought forth the big basket packed in the Carson kitchen which they fell upon with healthy young appetites.

At dusk O'Hara took off the big tarpaulin and folded it. Mary, looking back, saw the soft blankets and the linen sheets and pillow cases from her own bed!

"You've thought of *everything* for my comfort, James," she said later, when darkness enfolded them and they were ready to settle between the white linens.

"I tried to," he said.

As a matter of fact he had discussed with her in detail the arrangements for this night. They could by leaving earlier, reach a tavern of sorts, but he had tested it, found it noisy and none too clean. If they slept in the wagon now, as they would have to do many times later, they would actually have more comfort and certainly more quiet. Mary had voted for the wagon. O'Hara had explained that they would stop at the larger places as they came to them for hot meals and overnight if she wished. Also for supplies to carry them to the next inn. Between times there were cooking utensils, dry groceries and smoked meats slung underneath the wagon and he was an experienced wilderness cook.

Now they lay together and by the time the first half-hour had passed O'Hara had made love. But Mary was tense and distressed. "I wish there were some other way," she said with tears.

He gathered her to him, repentant. "I was too eager, too impetuous. You must forgive me, darling. I should have waited. I should have talked with you first. Please try to understand. I was swept away."

He began to talk to her then, gently, of many intimate things. Little by little she voiced shy questions and he answered them. Overhead the moon, almost to the full, rolled in splendour, while sweet fragrances stole upon their senses from the woods.

"*On such a night as this,*" O'Hara quoted once and Mary went on with the lines. They could not sleep as the hours passed. Perhaps it was because of the excitements of the day; perhaps it was because of an unconscious anticipation. For now O'Hara caressed her in new and tender ways until the tension all went out of her body and she moved closer as though seeking.

Before the darkness ended a strange and wonderful thing happened. Suddenly, softly, without apparent volition, they drew together; for him the desire of love rekindled; for her the hesitant, the fearful became all in the moment as a familiar warmth that stirred the pulses and flowed with yearning through every vein. She yielded now in utter giving until at the last she was overtaken by a tremulous rapture . . .

As the kiss ended, Mary lay breathing quickly, holding her lover as though she would never let him go.

"James," she whispered, "I didn't know . . . I didn't dream . . ."

"But this is what I've been trying to tell you, darling."

"I'm so glad it ended like this on our wedding night, aren't you, instead of . . . the other way?"

His cheek touched hers and now it was his tears that lay upon it.

"What is it?" she asked in alarm.

"It's the happiness," he said, "after all the long, long waiting . . . I feel as though I could hardly bear it."

"And now I'm truly your wife?"

"Truly, my dearest Delight. My wife! My own!"

With their bodies fulfilled and relaxed and a peace like heaven upon their hearts they fell asleep at moon-set, just before the dawn.

As the days passed they became aware of pleasant surprises. For one thing, for the first time they found *fun* in each other's company. Before, their visits together had been so brief, so fraught with doubts and fears and the shadow of coming separations that their conversations had of necessity been mostly serious. Now in the freedom of intimacy and of their new estate, O'Hara's native wit rose to its full flower and Mary's own delightful humour answered it. The woods echoed with their laughter. Sometimes of an afternoon he let the oxen rest for a little, and Mary then donned a blue wrapper which he particularly admired and lay down for a nap in the back of the wagon. One day she roused to find O'Hara near, an eager question in his eyes.

"In the day-time?" she demurred. "I don't think that seems quite . . . *delicate*."

He was immediately grave.

"You are right. Look at Pitt. His eyes are definitely disapproving. And that squirrel over there. He's been watching us with a very shocked expression. We must conduct ourselves with the greatest propriety, *especially* in the forest."

And then Mary's delicious laugh rang out, as her hand reached his.

There was so much to fill in from their backgrounds and neither could ever tire of hearing details of the other's life.

"One thing I want from my old home is a table," O'Hara said one day. "I've already written my sister, Katherine, and sent money for its shipment."

"Your *sister?*" Mary said in surprise. "Why, you never mentioned having one!"

"Maybe I didn't. But you see I never was much with her. She was in Ireland with relatives while I was years in France. At any rate I hope she sends the table. I tried to make it worth her while."

"What's it like?"

"It's lovely, as I remember it. Round, with an inlaid edge and *the feet are shamrocks!* I want it for our living-room. We could use it for special dining . . . I'm sure it would seat six. I'll keep after it until I get it," he added.

"Don't you ever give up on anything?"

He looked deeply into her eyes. "Not easily," he said. And they laughed again.

They were blessed by the weather. The days followed each other with dappled sunshine on their faces and around them the beauty of dogwood and Judas trees amongst the green. The nights were balmy with a fresh breeze carrying in it the breath of wild flowers; the Mayapples, sky rockets, trilliums and sweet fern. They could watch the stars through the opening above the road. The Milky Way was a silvery vapour. All of this was more than O'Hara had dared hope for and more than Mary had known to hope for. One thing only had disturbed her and this was the fact that O'Hara's rifle was always close beside him.

"Is there really danger then?" she asked anxiously.

He had tossed off the question.

"Why, I'm a frontiersman and a soldier. How would I feel without my rifle?"

What she did not know was that his keen eyes constantly watched the road and the woods beside them. One thing he feared was that a rattler would bite an ox's leg. A rider could usually circumvent this danger, but with these dumb, stupid beasts, as O'Hara always called them, it could be a threat. And one day it was. Mary was drowsing with her head against his shoulder and he himself was sitting relaxed, his feet braced against the wagon front-board, when suddenly he caught sight of a yellow and black looping neck, close, too close to the plodding oxen. The snake had evidently been concealed by the leaves that still lay on the cart track or he would have seen it before. He pulled on the lines; then throwing them to the floor, put one foot hard upon the ends, raised his rifle and took more careful aim than he ever had done before in his life. The snake, sensing its own danger, had coiled now. He fired and hit the coils; then as fast as he could he fired again, this time hitting the head. The oxen, frightened, were backing wildly with eminent threat of overturning the wagon. O'Hara used the whip until they moved forward again and passed over the rattler's body with Pitt and the pack-horse whinnying behind, and Mary sitting up straight, her face pale.

"Will you hold the lines now for a few minutes?" O'Hara asked her. "The oxen will behave but I want to keep a sharp look-out for a possible mate to that varmint."

They drove along quietly until O'Hara finally put his rifle down, took the reins, and leaned over to kiss her.

"Thank you," he said. "I think most girls would have screamed which wouldn't have helped matters much."

"In all the times I was planning for this trip . . . I don't know why . . . but I never once thought of snakes. Now I'll be terrified ever to get out of the wagon again!"

"No," he said. "I'll tell you something. You have never been out of the wagon that I didn't watch you every single minute. So you've nothing to worry about."

"Oh, James!" she said, embarrassment in her tone.

"It's necessary, dearest. And as to . . . well, nothing matters between us now, does it?"

"I suppose not," she said slowly.

But a little later he felt her hand slip through his arm.

"I do feel safe with you, *Mr. O'Hara!*"

They stopped overnight in Carlisle and he had to show her all the places familiar to him and take her to call on Agnes Denny, who mothered her at once and insisted upon giving her a lovely pewter plate as a gift for her new home.

"I've got another just like it for Eb's wife when he gets one. I wish he was here now. Do you know he seems to have his eye on Pittsburgh too. What's so special about it, I ask him. Isn't Carlisle good enough?"

"It would be for me," Mary said. "I could be happy here."

"God grant you may be happy wherever you are. The main thing for a woman, though, isn't the *place*, dearie, it's the *man*, and I think you've got a good one."

She poked O'Hara's ribs playfully. "Just see you deserve her for I can tell you have a treasure."

"I'm the one knows that better than anyone else," O'Hara said, "and I'll do my best."

As they left, Mary hugging her plate, Mrs. Denny called after her. "If you ever need any advice, dearie, on cooking or husbands or any other woman matters just write me a letter."

"I will," Mary promised laughing, not knowing how often over the years she was to keep her word.

The travelling grew more difficult as they reached the mountains and the oxen floundered slowly up the stony trails of Tuscarora, Sideling Hill, and Allegheny. There had to be frequent rest periods for the beasts and O'Hara fretted within himself, chiefly because Mary was growing tired. The constant jolting was wearing and she spent a good part of each day now, resting on the feather ticks in the back of the wagon. Once refreshed by this, however, she resumed her place on the high seat and eagerly went on with their endless conversations.

"About church now," she said one day. "You were good to be married in mine when you have a partly Catholic background."

He smiled. "I guess that description fits me. I don't go as far as Tom Paine but I do believe in freedom of religious thinking. Then, you see, I had an Anglican mother."

He told her then about the little prayer-book he always carried and how he had found an Indian rite almost duplicated in it. He would show it to her, he said, when they unpacked.

"There isn't a Presbyterian church in Pittsburgh yet, is there?" she asked.

"Not yet, but they're talking about building one. I imagine it won't be long."

"And you'll go with me to it, then?"

"Of course. And you won't mind if I lend a hand to the Catholics sometimes, will you? For my father's sake."

So their religious problems were settled on the back of the Laurel Mountain, the worst of the lot, "that bugbear" as General Forbes himself had called it as his men had toiled fearsomely in making the road over it twenty-five years before. But there was beauty enough in all conscience to offset the precipitous ascent, for the bushes that had given the ridge its name were now in full bloom. Masses, as far as the eye could see, of shiny oval-pointed leaves bearing the clusters of heavenly pink flowers, each tiny frilled cup a miracle of design. O'Hara plucked some for her day by day so she could enjoy them in her hand; and once when her bonnet was off, he tucked a bunch in her hair with an overwhelming effect, for he all but forgot to guide the oxen as he kissed her again and again.

Most of all now, though, in their talks he tried to prepare her for the Pittsburgh scene, the house itself, and the people she might care to know.

"I suppose Hugh Brackenridge is my best friend, at least nearest my own age. He has a brilliant mind and is an interesting talker and I fancy after his own bachelor cooking he'll be pleased to have dinner with us occasionally. Then there are the Smiths, older but very nice and the Craigs and the Nevilles . . . oh, I don't think you'll be lonely."

As to his own plans he had to answer a direct question from Mary.

"But what are you going to *do*, James, when we get there?"

He had hesitated, a strange thing for him. "I don't wonder you ask that but I have talked it over with your father. The Government owes me quite a good deal of money and I suppose I'll have to wait for that awhile. But one way or another from my trading and a little legacy and so on, I have some money in the Philadelphia bank, enough to keep us comfortable for some time. I intend to buy more lots. Pittsburgh is going to grow— I've always been sure of that—but you can't tell now in what direction, so I'm going to buy in *every* direction to make sure. Land is cheap now. Then I might have a store for a while. People are going to be coming west in great numbers for the soldiers are being paid off in land and they'll probably all come by way of Pittsburgh, so a store might be a good thing for a start, but I'll wait and see. Just trust me, Mary. Shall I tell you a secret?"

"Oh, yes."

He leaned close. "I intend to be a rich man some day."

"I wouldn't be surprised," she answered, "since you've made up your mind to it."

It was at the top of the last, the Chestnut Ridge, that O'Hara stopped the oxen and allowed Mary to look upon the magnificent panorama spread before them. The sun was just setting and a peculiar lambent light flooded the wide scene. The primeval forest still held place over much of it, but scattered here and there were small rolling fields of brown ploughed earth and the rising smoke of frontier cabins. Slowly, slowly, nature was being tamed to man's intent and this earnest of the future softened the wildness and touched the hearts of the two young people who looked upon it with hope.

"Oh, it's beautiful!" Mary exclaimed. And even as she spoke the western sky became an intolerable glory while luminous clouds spread towards them until the watchers became part of an Apocalypse, an opening heaven of gold that enfolded them.

Mary's eyes were wet with the wonder of it, and neither she nor O'Hara spoke much during their evening meal and the usual preparations for darkness. But they both knew without words that this night perhaps more than any since their first one, was made for love.

When Fort Ligonier was passed and then Greensburg, O'Hara realised that the end was only about six hours away and his heart grew anxious. Nothing he had told her could possibly prepare Mary for the actual sight of the place to which she was coming to live. Her own face was somewhat drawn as the last miles passed and when they reached the edge of the town it was white.

What she saw at first was a sprawling pioneer village of fifty or sixty log houses, some of them ramshackle, most of them unpainted; dirty streets in which here and there a drunken Indian snored beside a hog in a mud puddle; evidence round about of the altogether too primitive sanitary conditions; and facing them the muddy, irregular bank of the Monongahela!

O'Hara didn't speak. He could not, for never in his life had he felt such deathly fear. He drove on. The great fort came into clearer view with its old moat now a tiny lake in which ducks were disporting themselves. The King's Gardens were green and the apple orchard? His eager eyes sought for the blooms and his spirit fell still lower for there were only, he could see, the empty clusters from which the petals had fallen. He knew their journey had taken longer than he had foreseen but still he had hoped against hope that the blossoms would last. He turned into the narrow track that led to the house, and there it stood, sturdy and strong and all white from the many applications of limewash. He drew the oxen to a stop at the kitchen door, and still neither of them had spoken. Then he saw Mary raise her head and draw deep breaths. He had been too lost in his terrified absorption before to notice the overpowering fragrance upon the air, not that of the apple blossoms but something stronger, more sensuously sweet.

"*Locusts!*" Mary said in wonder. "We've a street lined with them in Philadelphia and I always walked back and forth on it every day to smell the perfume. Oh, James, you didn't tell me we would have *locusts*."

"I never thought of it," he said, his voice uneven in his sudden relief. "But there they are, a whole row of them along the river and just beyond them is the Allegheny itself. Hugh Brackenridge calls it 'the loveliest stream that ever glistened to the moon!' He's a poet, you know."

He had jumped from the wagon and was at her side ready to lift her down.

"We're here, darling. This is home," he said as his arms went round her.

The door which had been closed upon the coolness of the day was flung open now and Prudence Bond in a neat neckerchief and full apron stood smiling at them. She moved aside as O'Hara carried Mary over the threshold and set her down in the big kitchen. And all at once as they stood there together it *was* home. There was the great fireplace glowing before them like a happy heart! The pot simmered on the crane and good baking smells came from the side oven. Prudence had braided a rag rug during her weeks of waiting and it lay brightly in front of the big rocking chair. And against the long wall that had been bare when O'Hara last saw it stood a big walnut dresser, polished to satin, waiting for the bride's dishes. A paper lay on the lower shelf and O'Hara hurried to read it.

> Congratulations and good wishes from
> your old cronies of Semple's Tavern.

The names followed: Smith, Campbell, Craig, Neville, Brackenridge, Ormsby and of course Samuel Semple himself.

O'Hara was incredulous and deeply moved, and Mary exultant as she smoothed the beautiful wood.

"Was it really made here, in Pittsburgh, do you think?"

"Oh, we have some good craftsmen here, but wasn't it wonderful of my old friends to do this? And doesn't it give a *tone* to the kitchen, though? What about the other wagon, Prudence? Did it get here all right?"

"Aye, sir, and I had the things all set in the other room awaitin' you, all except the bedstids."

O'Hara drew Mary with him to see the big room, now safely and happily cluttered with the precious pieces of furniture.

"It wouldn't be large for Philadelphia but for here . . . it's not bad, is it? We can call it the parlour or drawing-room without stretching a point, can't we? And when McGrady comes . . . Oh, Prudence, where *is* McGrady?"

"He's sure to be here on the quick, sir, for everyone, most, has been watchin' for you. There's him now I'll warrant, runnin' like a killdeer."

McGrady entered breathless, evidently chagrined that he had not been on hand to greet them.

"I was up Grant's Hill, suh, but I taken the short way back."

"This is your mistress, McGrady, see you take good care of her."

McGrady's eyes were rolling white with admiration.

"Yes, ma'am. Yes, suh. I sure to, suh."

"Now," said O'Hara, with boyish exuberance, "you and I, McGrady, are going to clear out this room, then unpack the wagon out there, lay a rug down and get things back in place where Mrs. O'Hara . . ."

He stopped and looked at Mary and she looked back at him. Then he motioned the servants out and closed the door.

"That's the first time I've said it!"

"I wondered how long I'd have to wait," she answered demurely.

He held her close. "Do you like the sound of it?"

"It's very sweet," she said.

While the two men moved chairs and tables out of the parlour and then unloaded the wagon until they reached the rugs Mary sat in the kitchen listening as Prudence expatiated upon the merits of the new dwelling. O'Hara, overhearing her at one point, grinned.

"It's the finest in the town by far, that little privy is. As snug an' nice built as anybody could wish an' whitewashed to match the house even. There's not another to touch it. Most of them are poor contraptions and . . . I think shame to say it . . . some folks don't have none at all. You'd ought to go out, an' see for yourself, ma'am, how tidy a treat it is."

O'Hara kept busy at the far side of the wagon until he had seen Mary end her tour of inspection and come up the path again chuckling to herself. He knew the cause of her mirth. When he had seen the small edifice in March he had noticed that one of the workmen had carved two hearts joined with a piercing arrow on one of the walls. Now, he met Mary and asked in a low voice, "Did you like the decorations?"

"Oh, *you*!" she said roguishly and laughed aloud.

The most welcome sound in all the world, he thought after her white face when they had driven into town.

By supper-time the beautiful rose Oriental filled the parlour and Mary had directed the placing of the furniture. The wing chairs at either side of the fireplace, the small haircloth sofa along one wall with candle stands at either end of it, and opposite, a side table with a drop leaf and two rush-bottomed chairs.

"Over here," O'Hara said gaily, standing at the empty wall, "we can put my shamrock table when it gets here. Doesn't it all look homelike already? And to-morrow we'll bring in your boxes and you can unpack your little pretties and set them around."

Prudence, her voice full of awe, spoke from the doorway before Mary could answer.

"You *step* on that?" she asked, pointing to the rug. "You *walk* on it?"

O'Hara and Mary laughed together. "Of course. That's what it's made for!"

She shook her head. "Never seen nothin' like that before. You'd better explain careful to anybody comin' in or they'll never set foot on it, never! I'm afeared to even now when you say so."

They ate supper at the trestle table in the kitchen, with ravenous appetites for the good plain food: boiled flitch and potatoes with scraped horse radish root, hot baked raised cakes and berry jam.

"McGrady he's a great one to scrimmage round in the woods. That's where he got the radish roots. An' he picked the berries up round Grant's hill. I used a bit of the sugar you left, sir, to do them up. I hope it's all right with you," Prudence said a little fearfully.

"I couldn't be better pleased," O'Hara said, helping Mary again to the jam.

When they had finished he and McGrady again began work

upon the wagon for there was still much to unload. Mary, according to a gleeful command, stayed below so that the eventual surprise might be the greater. There was endless labouring up the stairs and the noise of moving and settling in the room above the parlour until dusk had fallen. Then O'Hara ran down and proudly escorted Mary to her chamber. She stood in the doorway and gave a cry of pleasure, for the room was large like the one below it with the floor filled richly now with the second Oriental in which blue, her favourite colour, predominated. The four-poster bed stood handsomely in place already made up, to Mary's amazement; opposite, her own dressing-table with the candle holders, and the small mirror miraculously intact!

"But look at this, Mary!"

In one corner stood a three-sided wash stand with tin bowl and pitcher!

"I had it made, and here, you see . . ."

He opened the small door below to exhibit an article for her comfort.

Mary suddenly dissolved in tears and leaned against him.

"It's all so much nicer than I expected. When we drove in and I saw the town first I thought my heart would break but now the house is so lovely, and to think it's mine, my very own! I mean *ours*," she added hastily.

O'Hara smiled. "It is yours, my dear Delight. I'm just going to live in it with you!"

She sank down on the side of the bed. "But I'm *so tired*!"

He was all solicitude. "Of course you are! You must get to bed at once. I'm about worn out myself and what must you be. Let's get settled soon for a good night's sleep for to-morrow will be an exciting day, I imagine. But first, come here to the window." He opened it, apologising as he did so for the glazed paper panes.

"I'm so very sorry I couldn't get glass for all the windows! I had a hard enough time to get it for the parlour ones alone. But some day . . . Look, darling!"

Through the May twilight they could see the wide, swift-flowing Allegheny, with a glimpse of the great Ohio beyond at The Point. Upon the air hung the heady-sweet fragrance of the locust blooms.

"Isn't it beautiful, the view?" he asked eagerly.

"To think," Mary said wonderingly, "I can see this every day instead of just roofs of houses! Can we leave the window open?"

"Of course. I'll run down and get a candle lighted and we'll be to bed in no time."

He had been struck by the anxious thought of a possibility. So he asked McGrady to sleep on a blanket on the kitchen floor that night and he agreed with his usual alacrity. He had already taken Pitt and the pack-horse to Semple's stable during supper, and later the oxen to be tied in the open space behind it.

"You fed the beasts well, as I told you?" O'Hara asked now.

"Yes, suh. I done everything you say. All the men round Semple's talkin' 'bout you gettin' here to-day with the Missus."

"I'll warrant they were," O'Hara said under his breath as he carefully drew in the latch string on the door and ran the bolt. When he got back upstairs with his candle, Mary was already in bed and half asleep. He undressed quickly, blew out the light, kissed her gently and then lay, listening. If what he feared took place there would be no doubt of his waking but he preferred to hear the first sign. He was glad McGrady was in the house; just in case, Prudence, too, was there, in one of the small back rooms. He lay, wondering if he should have stayed up. But then, most likely nothing would happen to-night.

But an hour later it began. First, shouts and yells he judged from the front of the tavern, then the ear-splitting, nerve-rending noise of rifle butts on pans, iron pots, and implements banged against each other, a weird cacophony of jangling, shattering sound. He leaned over and touched Mary.

"Darling, can you wake up?"

She roused, heard the noise and clung to him.

"Is it Indians?" she whispered, terrified.

"No, no, dear. Nothing to harm us. It's just a shivaree!"

"A . . . a what?"

"A shivaree. A crazy serenade they give newly married couples. But we'll have to get something on in a hurry for they always want to see the bride and groom. Just throw your dress on over your bed gown and I'll do the same. We'll go out on the front stoop for a minute and that will satisfy them. Then I'll have to give them a treat . . ."

McGrady was at their door with a candle even as O'Hara was pulling on his trousers and they could hear Prudence speaking her mind below.

"Hurry, dear. We want to get rid of them as fast as we can."

They waited beside the parlour front door until the noise was all around them, then O'Hara put the latch string out and slid the bolt. Holding the candle in one hand and Mary's in the other, he drew her out before the yelling crowd. He had, he supposed, seen as sinister-looking a group before but certainly Mary had not. In the light of the few wavering pine torches the rough faces and clothing of the frontiersmen must look as alarming to her as Indians. But there were other men scattered through the crowd also, he spotted at once. Even to him these were dangerous looking, for he knew they were keel-boatmen just off the river and they usually made trouble. Pressing close to the stoop were some of his own friends, Brackenridge apparently leading them.

"Smile at them, Mary, and wave," O'Hara urged her.

At once there was whistling and cat-calls and some shouted remarks he hoped Mary hadn't caught. He held up his hand for quiet and Brackenridge hammered out a tattoo to support him.

"Thank you, men, for this fine shivaree! My wife and I . . ."

"My God," yelled a man, "looks like the bridegroom wears a *night shirt*! Can you beat that? Seems like we ought to take it off him. We don't wear no *night shirts* on the frontier!"

There were ribald shouts, but once again Brackenridge pounded and O'Hara called at the top of his voice: "Hey, men, what we all want is a good drink of whisky right from Suke's Run. Get back to Semple's and I'll treat you all."

"Back to Semple's!" Hugh yelled and the other men of the town joined him. The crowd began to turn.

"Bring me my hunting shirt quick, McGrady. I'll have to go to the tavern, Mary, and treat them, but I'll be back as soon as I can, and you are perfectly safe. Just go to bed, and to-morrow we'll laugh over this. Prudence, see Mrs. O'Hara upstairs and McGrady bolt the doors. Don't worry, darling, I'll be with you shortly."

He jumped from the stoop and overtook Brackenridge and the others who were plainly concerned.

"We're sorry about this, O'Hara. We were just going to have a bit of fun like we always do when these keel-boaters joined up. They're always out to raise hell. I think if they get enough to drink they'll stick at the tavern, though," Hugh said.

"You've got a beautiful bride, O'Hara," Smith added, "if this hasn't scared her to death. There are a few rough customers in from trading too. Well, hope we can hold them down."

Inside Semple's there was milling about with noise and shouting.

O'Hara ordered the drinks and when the men had found places either beside the tables or on them with their noggins, there was a slight cessation.

"This fellah must be feelin' pretty good," one man yelled.

Loud laughter followed. "Wonder why he's feelin' so good?"

"Another drink, men?" O'Hara called above the uproar. "Another round, Mr. Semple!"

It was when this was nearly drunk that one frontiersman, a stranger, shouted, "What about puttin' the bridegroom to bed? Say, don't you think we ought to put him to bed now?"

A wild chorus of assent followed while O'Hara's blood froze in his veins. He had heard of this custom. He saw his friends slowly move closer but he raised his arm and managed to be heard.

"Not yet, fellahs. We got to have a little more whisky. Isn't this good stuff? Right here from our own distillery at Suke's Run. Come on, Mr. Semple, fill 'em up again."

Anything to gain time, he thought, even as he realised in desperation that he and the townsmen would never be a match for the lewd element of the crowd.

"Hi, O'Hara, give me a hand here, will you?" It was Semple calling.

When he was close enough, Semple said under his breath, "I'm goin' to start a fight an' by God this is one I won't stop. When things get goin' you sneak out the back room here an' leg it for home as fast as you can. That's it," he added in full voice, "just carry one of these jugs around. I've got plenty whisky, boys, so drink up now!"

It was only a few minutes until he stepped from behind his bar-counter and scanned the crowd carefully.

"I s'pose none of you keel-boaters would happen to be *Mike Fink*," he said.

One strapping man rose slowly, put down his noggin and shook himself.

"An' what would you be knowin' about Mike Fink?" he growled.

"Oh, no offence, no offence," Semple said amiably. "I just heard he was the best fighter on the river an' there wasn't a man could match him an' we haven't seen a good fight here for so long . . ."

The boatman came forward and pranced a few steps like a gamecock, then he took off his shirt and threw it behind him.

"Who's Mike Fink? I'll tell you I'm the best keeler that ever pushed a pole on the old Massassip! I'm a ring-tailed roarer! I'm half horse an' half cock-eyed alligator an' the rest of me is red-hot snappin' turkle! Whoop! I kin outfight, no holts barred, ary man on both sides the river from Pittsburgh to N'Awlins an' back ag'in to St. Louiee. Come on, you damned greasy b'ar hunters. Is there a one of you that'll stand up to me? I'm spilein' for exercise."

One huge frontiersman, as broad as the boatman, got up and stripped off his shirt.

"Come along, boys," Semple called. "Push the tables an' the chairs out of the way. Make room for the fight . . . make room now."

Brackenridge, Smith and the others had caught the significance of the ruse at once. With a great show of moving the furniture they managed with loud talking to form a protective screen in front of the door to the back room. O'Hara weaved in and out among them, apparently intent only on preparing for the coming fight, then dexterously slipped unnoticed between them and on through the back room and out the window, not even waiting for the usual exit by way of the kitchen. He ran as for his life, never stopping until, breathless, he tapped at his own back door. McGrady opened it instantly and locked it carefully after him.

"No trouble here?" O'Hara asked him, panting.

"No, suh. You had trouble where you was, suh?"

"A little. Think it's all right now. Just stay here, McGrady, and call me at the slightest noise. I don't need a candle."

He took his rifle from its hooks on the way. He would certainly not harm anyone but—if necessary a few shots might scare danger away. On the top stair he found Prudence crouched in the darkness.

"Thought I'd just wait till you was safe back, sir. She cried some soon after you left—just scared out of her wits, she was. She ain't used to the rough ways out here. But she went off to sleep like a baby at the last. Clean wore out, pore little soul."

"Thank you, Prudence, for staying with her. Everything will be safe now."

He went into the bedroom, closed the door, stripped to his night shirt, laid his rifle on the floor by the bed and crept in between the sheets. Mary did not waken. He moved his hand to touch her hair and felt that her pillow was wet. His heart ached within him. This, on her first night in their new home! He was not exactly a praying man but he prayed then with a craving intensity that life would not be hard for her and that naught would affright her again for a long, long time.

He lay tensely listening. Once in a while came the echo of shouting voices. Then after the best of an hour there was silence. The quiet was all enveloping so that he could hear the deep, throaty flow of the Allegheny. He drew a long breath, blessing Samuel Semple! At least Mary had been saved from intolerable embarrassment which to her sensitive soul would have been shame. He turned carefully, put an arm around his bride, and he, too, fell asleep.

In the morning the events of the night were like a bad dream when it is past. The sun poured effulgently, a gentle Maytime breeze was blowing with the breath of the trees along the river stronger than it had been in the darkness. Mary and O'Hara slept late and laughed from sheer happiness as they woke and looked at each other. After all they were young and in love and a bright new day was before them.

"I'm so sorry you were frightened last night at that crazy shivaree!" He tried to speak lightly.

"I guess it was because I was so tired and they *did* look so wild to me. But," she added, "as I think of it now it was a little bit funny too."

"Wasn't it?" he agreed quickly.

"Especially about your *night shirt*," she giggled.

"Oh, they may have rough manners, these frontiersmen, but most of them are good fellows."

"Did you treat them all," she asked.

"Oh, yes. I had to spend quite a little, but it was worth it." He looked at her as she drew her shift over her white shoulders. "Yes," he added. "*Well* worth it."

Before they had finished breakfast they had a caller. Hugh Brackenridge came in, was properly presented and urged to have something to eat. He sat down, curbing his eagerness and ate heartily, his eyes resting admiringly upon Mary as he did so.

"Do you know, Mistress O'Hara, this husband of yours was in such a hurry to get home last night he didn't wait to see the fight!"

"Ah," said O'Hara blandly, "there was a fight, then?"

"My word," Hugh echoed, "was there a fight! The biggest I'll warrant ever seen in Pittsburgh!"

"How did it come out?" O'Hara asked.

"Well, you see, Mistress O'Hara, there was this enormous keel-boater who gave the challenge and a fellah from the back-woods who's been out trading, about as big, took him up. We moved the furniture back," he glanced here at O'Hara who winked in return, "and then they were at it. Never saw anything like it in all my life."

"And who won?"

"Well, you won't believe me but at the end the trader did. The keel-boater was laid out flat. Semple threw a bucket of water on him and even that didn't bring him to. The other boaters carried him upstairs. Took four to do it. Everything got quiet after that. We'd all had enough for one night."

"Oh," Mary said with a small shudder. "I think a fight like that must be *terrible!*"

"Yes," said Hugh, "and yet I can think of certain occasions when it might be—well—useful, can't you, O'Hara?"

"It's possible," O'Hara rejoined calmly. "But now if we're all finished we'll have to show our things off, Mary. First of all, the dresser!"

"You approve of it?" Hugh asked eagerly.

"Oh, we love it," she said. "How wonderfully kind of you men to have it made for us. Mr. O'Hara is going to get my boxes in from the wagon this morning and then I'll unpack the dishes and set them in it. Shouldn't we take him into the parlour now?"

"By all means," O'Hara agreed. "We're really pretty proud of ourselves, Hugh. Mr. Carson, Mary's father, gave us two beautiful rugs and some furniture . . ."

He opened the door and Hugh stood looking with astonishment into the elegance before him.

"Great heavens above!" he burst out. "Why, it looks like a room back east! Isn't that what they call an Oriental?" pointing to the floor.

"Yes," Mary told him. "We have one in our bedroom too. My father's a merchant so he has the chance to get good ones. You really like it?"

"Whew!" he said for answer. "You'll have to expect the whole town to come to call when people hear about this. Only I'll warrant a good many will be afraid to step on the rug."

"Why, that's just what Prudence said," Mary laughed. "Won't you sit down now and be our first caller?"

"I'll come back another time if I may. I know you're both busy now. I just ran over early to tell O'Hara here about the fight. Since he didn't stay for it," he added with a side look. He held out his hand and bowed in a courtly way over Mary's. "It is the greatest pleasure to welcome you to Pittsburgh, ma'am, and I congratulate my friend here with all my heart."

"You are a bachelor, Mr. O'Hara tells me," she said.

"Unfortunately so."

"Then when you tire of your own cooking you must come and dine with us, mustn't he, James?"

"My dear lady, that is a most dangerous invitation—for you, I mean—but I'll try not to presume too much upon it. Thank you, though, very much indeed!"

O'Hara walked to the end of the lane with him, getting a few more details of the night before. But Hugh on the whole was grave.

"You're the very button on Fortune's cap, O'Hara," he said. "She's unbelievably pretty but it's more than that. Her manner, her charm! Her spirit shines out of her eyes. Well, you're one of the few men I know who deserves such a woman."

"No, no," O'Hara disclaimed violently. "Far from it. All you can say of me is that I *know* my good luck . . ." His voice was a bit unsteady. "And appreciate it to the full," he added. And then, "How are things with you?"

"Personal or professional?"

"Well, both."

"Personal couldn't be worse. I made an ass of myself a while back and will have to pay for it. Professionally I have hopes. I'm glad I settled for the law. I think there's a chance for a career here one day, though just to look at the place now nobody would believe it."

"Well, there have always been two of us who have had faith in Pittsburgh. Good-bye, Hugh. Come over often."

When the boxes were set into the kitchen, Mary in an enchanting ruffled apron (which was the cause of many private delays in the other room) began to unpack her "pretties" as O'Hara called them. There was a noble pair of brass candlesticks, two little lustre bowls and a Wedgwood teapot for the parlour mantel; and delicately embroidered cushions for the sofa. But to crown it

all there were draperies for the two windows which had real
panes of glass! O'Hara had given her the measure long before,
and now when he with McGrady's help had put up the fixtures
Mr. Carson had thoughtfully added, the soft folds of rose China silk
fell on either side of the framework to the floor, in bright contrast
to the white plastered logs. O'Hara himself was overcome by this
last touch of luxury.

"Hugh is right, Mary. We're going to have plenty of callers
when the word gets around. Of course I'll be proud as Punch to
show off the house, but most of all my wife! You won't mind a
deluge of visitors?"

"I'll love it," she said, her eyes sparkling. "To be hostess in
my very own house! Oh, there I go again."

"That's right," he said. "I like to hear you say that. First
and last it is *your* house. Now, I must get back to work."

They all worked to such good end that by supper it seemed
as though the log dwelling had been occupied for years! Enough
dishes to make a showing were ranged on the dresser shelves
with the rest in the cupboard opposite; the napery was in the
drawers; two turkey red cushions sat bright and inviting upon
the rockers; clothes and bedding were unpacked and put in the
closets upstairs; while all sorts of oddments and treasures were set
in their places. These included a bible and a volume of Shakespeare
on the side table in the parlour! At the last and making a small
ceremony of it, Mary set Agnes Denny's pewter plate upright in
the centre of the kitchen mantel.

"I think she would like it here where we'll be most of the time,"
she said. "I'll write and tell her."

The next morning O'Hara set out early on his own business.
With him there was always the conviction that a relation existed
between immediacy of action and ultimate success. He paid his
bill at Semple's first of all, thanking him again for his inspiration
for the fight, then went to the big trading store of Devereux Smith.
There he leaned upon the counter, drew in the familiar, heavy
smells of forest and fur and got the news of the town after they,
too, had gone over the details of the night before.

"Still interested in real estate, O'Hara?"

"I am, indeed. What's the latest on that?"

"Well, Isaac Craig and Stephen Bayard, you know, were, up
till lately, officers at the fort but now they've sort of gone into
partnership for the mercantile business though really I think to

deal in land and lots. They first bought three acres down at The Point between the rivers from the Penns and the last word I got was that they own the land now that the fort stands on!"

"The devil they do," O'Hara ejaculated.

"But," Smith went on, "we understand they're actually working for a Philadelphia firm, Turnbull, Marmie & Company is the name. They've all got their sights set on Fort Pitt. I reckon the whole place will have to be sold eventually but I'll hate to see it go."

"General Irvine still in charge?"

"Going back to Carlisle in the fall, I hear. Good man, though. Kept order, kept everything in repair, and such gardens! Well, anyway there's a bit more to this real estate business. The Penns hired George Woods from Bedford to come over and survey the town and what a pretty sight it is on paper! You wouldn't believe it! Streets marked out and named for the old settlers. *Smithfield* is one. Now put that in your pipe and smoke it!"

O'Hara laughed. "I'm impressed no end, especially since you deserve it."

"The lots look as neat as a checkerboard. You'd never guess there was a loose hog on any of them. And Craig told me he and Bayard have bought up thirty-seven!"

O'Hara whistled. "Where can I see this plan?"

"Oh, there are several copies around. As a matter of fact, *I've* got one myself. I was just waiting to bring it out!"

They pored over it together, discussing locations. "I'll be writing to the Penns to-night," O'Hara said. "Could I be borrowing this, just until morning? And then I've another matter I want your advice upon."

"Shoot! Advice is the cheapest of all commodities!"

"I've decided to set up in a store."

"A *store*! My word, man, won't that be quite a come down from all your other activities?"

"A little, perhaps. But I like any kind of trade, any form of business. And the point is I must do something at once. My idea would be to sell necessities, of course, but work in some luxuries too. I believe people would buy them. And there's going to be a regular tide of immigration out here now that the war's over."

"So you're going to settle down to be a storekeeper the rest of your life, eh?"

"Good lord, no! This is just for the present. I expect something much bigger to turn up. At least I have a feeling . . . But meanwhile I think I may be able to turn a fairly pretty penny with the store."

"Knowing you," Smith laughed, "I wouldn't be surprised. Well, there are a couple of vacant spots if either of them appeal to you. The ropewalk for one."

"What happened to Jake Hatch?"

"Well, you know his trade has always been mostly with the boatmen so he decided he'd give the river a fling. He sold out to the fellah down by the ferry and he's gone on the old *Massassip*, as our friend the other night called it. Oh, and Billy, the chandler, is gone. His wife got homesick and they went back east last month. His room is bigger but not in as good a location. Well, look them over."

As O'Hara was leaving he added another request with his thanks.

"I hope you'll bring your family over soon to see Mary. The Craigs and the Nevilles and a few more may wait a while. You know—propriety and all that—but I don't want her to get lonely."

"Don't worry," Smith said, "I can hardly hold my womenfolk back, so we'll be there."

Before he reached the door, O'Hara turned again.

"Have you heard anything about Guyasuta? Where he is?"

"He can be in hell for all I care. That's where he ought to be. That Hannastown business hit me hard. Mike Huffnagle was in the other day. It was in his field, you know, that the men were harvesting when it all happened. He says some of the folks went back east and of course I know some have gone through here on their way to the Ohio country. A pretty heart-sick business, the whole thing. Even *for the frontier*, it was bad, And if I were you I wouldn't make too many inquiries about Guyasuta."

By the end of the week O'Hara had rented the ropewalk. It was a long, low narrow building, but with a new floor and shelves along either side it would make an unusual but to him perfect store. His shrewd sense had at once informed him that by the time a customer had walked the length of it, her eye would have been caught up by many articles she had never set out to buy. I believe, he thought with a twinkle, I'll put the *necessities* at the back. He got hold of a carpenter and with his own help and that of McGrady the store-room was ready in a month. There was even some merchandise on the shelves, secured by O'Hara's own miraculous (and bordering upon the devious) methods: some things from a storekeeper in Greensburgh who was hard pushed to meet his creditors; a load from Bedford where there had been a fire; and some choice bits from other Pittsburgh stores which had been bought up by O'Hara's emissaries and then set up on his own shelves to the annoyance of their original owners. Orders of course had gone off to Philadelphia and also to New Orleans.

But while the store became a going concern as the summer weeks passed, the house in the King's Orchard had grown so rapidly in popularity it was like to die of it! They came, the rich (comparatively speaking) and the poor; the aristocrats of the town and the shabby toil-hardened women, starved for beauty. These latter appeared shyly at the kitchen at all sorts of odd hours, were received with warm kindness by Mary, taken to the door of the parlour, where they feasted their tired eyes upon its elegance, though, as had been predicted, could not be persuaded to set foot upon the wonder of the carpet. Afterwards they were urged to have a cup of tea at the trestle-table or perhaps in a red cushioned rocking chair where their tongues became loosed and they told Mary the problems of their lives and begged hungrily for details of her own back in Philadelphia.

One element of such visits afforded Mary and O'Hara riotous merriment.

"All of these women," she told him, "ask if they can go out and see the . . ." She pointed towards the small whitewashed edifice at the back. "I do believe they're more impressed by that than by the Oriental!"

"They'd probably rather have it," he laughed.

But at the other end of the scale came Pittsburgh's élite, to the parlour door, at four o'clock in the afternoon. These Mary received with dignity in one of her trousseau gowns, sat at the side table and poured tea into thin cups which Prudence in a white apron passed. It was not Philadelphia, but oh, it was close enough to make it apparent that a new young hostess had come to town who must be treated with respect. And Mary on her part reached eagerly out to these women who she knew would be her closest friends as time went on: Margaret Neville, Rachel Craig, Elizabeth Smith, Jessie Brison, the nearest to her in age, wife of the personable would-be young politician who like O'Hara and Brackenridge had a fixed faith in Pittsburgh. These and more she tried to

remember carefully and think of when the sight of the village itself
dampened her spirits.

One night she and O'Hara sat in the wing chairs facing each
other, he with tablet and pencil, she with a sock on the needles.
He was making out a new order and had found already that
Mary's advice was excellent. Indeed, he had been more and more
amazed by her good judgment in their daily affairs. So now he
read over to her what he had written as a beginning:

> 2 barrels sugar
> 6 casks sherry wine
> 1 keg allspice
> 6 half gallon coffee pots
> 12 blankets
> Soap and candles—amount to be filled in later
> 12 wash basins
> 12 sets knives and forks

"And what now do you suggest, Mary?"

"Well," she said thoughtfully, "I would add one dozen best
bibles, some thread, sewing silk, shoe buckles, writing paper,
looking-glasses if you can get them, some playing cards, and
six dozen finger bowls!"

"Darling, are you mad? *Finger bowls* out here?"

"Just what we need," she said. "You want some luxuries to
put on your shelves. These will give all the women who can't
use them something to talk about. And after I've had a dinner
party and used mine you'll find you have a rush sale on, from the
others. I know women! Oh, *do* order the finger bowls! It will be
fun!"

O'Hara laughed. "Well, that's one article I would have felt
we could do nicely without, but you may be right at that. It will
certainly make talk and that in turn makes business. Well, let's
finish the list to-morrow. I'm tired to-night."

He sat watching her. She had changed subtly during the
summer. Her beauty seemed enhanced, and there was added a
new poise, a gentle assurance, a trace of maturity.

"Oh, Mary," he burst out suddenly, "don't grow up too soon!"

She looked at him, her eyes bright with laughter. "*Grow up!*
Why, Mr. O'Hara, I'm a married woman, with a husband and
a house and a household and . . . and everything!"

The dark lashes rested on her cheeks which were now pure rose. *"And everything!"* she repeated softly.

For one second he sat as though stunned, then he crossed to her, knelt down and put his arms about her waist.

"Oh, my dear Delight . . . I can't believe . . ."

She cupped his startled face with her hands.

"Considering . . . I mean, in view of . . . I mean I don't think you should be *too* surprised if what I suspect is true!"

Chapter Nine

It was strange, Mary often remarked, that time passed more quickly here in Pittsburgh than it had back in Philadelphia. The days flowed into weeks and even the months were caught in the same swift current.

"It's because so much is happening, I guess," she said once, "and we always seem to be in the middle of it, somehow."

"Don't you like that?" O'Hara asked quickly.

"You know I do," she replied, laughing. "I never dreamed I would feel so important. Do you remember the night we sat on the bench under the locust trees beside the river and planned that the motto for our home was to be *hospitality*? It was just before little William was born."

"Yes," O'Hara said gravely, "I remember."

As a matter of fact his recollection of that evening and of the day and night that followed was still all too clear in his mind, for the primeval curse of Eve had fallen heavily then upon Mary's slender body. During the months before she had been completely well and happier than he had ever seen her, teasing him gently about his solicitude.

"Not that I don't love you for it all," she would say, "but there's really nothing to fear."

On the day when he sat in the parlour with Dr. Nathaniel Bedford, however, listening to the subdued cries and moans from the bedroom above, he was wild with it.

"I've got to go up there, Doctor!"

"No, no. That's no place for you. Prudence is as good as any midwife, and I'll go up again presently."

"But how long is this . . . this likely to go on?"

"Can't tell with the first one. Could be till to-morrow morning."

"My God! She couldn't stand that!"

"Oh, yes. Women do. Don't ask me how, but they get through it. Most of them."

O'Hara pounced. "What do you mean, *most of them?*"

"Well now, be reasonable. Considering the number of babies born there's not too much goes wrong. But of course once in a while . . ."

O'Hara leaped to his feet. "I'm going up," he said. "I certainly had a part in the beginning of this and I'm going to stand by her now at the end of it."

"Tut! Tut!" the doctor said. "Sit down and behave yourself. *I* know husbands. You're likely thinking now there'll never be another if it's like this, but when the baby's safe here you'll forget all about that and have your wife pregnant again in two or three months. I *know*. I've seen it happen too often."

O'Hara gave him one terrible look and made for the stairs while the doctor muttered, "Most cantankerous young man I ever ran into."

Prudence, on her way down, tried to fend him off.

"No, Mr. O'Hara. That ain't any place for you up there. The doctor's the only man . . ."

He pushed her aside none too gently and took the steps two at a time. At the bedroom door he paused a second to quiet the beating of his heart, before he went in. Mary lay, already white and spent, her face dripping with the sweat of her travail in the unseasonably warm May afternoon. As she saw O'Hara she reached her arms with a pitiful cry.

"Oh, James, you've come to me! Prudence said it wasn't seemly . . ."

"Seemly or not, darling, I'm here and I'll not leave you for a minute until this is all over."

"I can bear it better when I have you. Will it be . . . much . . . longer?"

"No," O'Hara lied stoutly. "Of course not. Oh, my dear Delight, hold on to me if it helps. Can you smell the locusts?" For the fragrance was sweet upon the air.

"No," she whispered weakly.

The anguished hours went on through the evening, through the night, until before the dawn Dr. Bedford's face was as grave as O'Hara's own. Then at daybreak with a last expulsive agony while Mary's arms held tightly around her husband's neck and his own supported her, the baby was born and a new cry was heard upon the earth.

"It's a boy," the doctor announced, now with calm assurance.

"A fine boy. Here you are, Prudence, clean him up and then they can have a look at him."

Mary lay unheeding, her eyes closed, small shuddering breaths coming from her. "Will she be all right?" O'Hara asked anxiously, without glancing towards his son.

"Yes, yes," Dr. Bedford smiled at him. "Let her rest a while. When she sees her baby she'll perk up fast enough. What about you? You'd better get yourself a good slug of whisky. You look as though you'd had the labour pains yourself."

When the new parents finally looked together upon the small creature born to them, O'Hara gave the name. Before this Mary had evaded any selection. "Let's wait," she always insisted. Now O'Hara spoke it plainly. "I would like to call him William Carson, if you are agreed."

"Oh, Father will be so pleased! But would you not like to have a *James*, after you?"

"Perhaps," he said smiling, "in due time." Then as though Dr. Bedford were listening, "*in due time*," he repeated with emphasis.

It was that fall that they had their first overnight guest. The second smaller room upstairs had been nicely fitted out, for the store was prospering as O'Hara's friends had predicted, and Mary's fine taste made good use of the money available.

In addition to the newly furnished bed-chamber another piece of fine living now graced their home: this was the Irish table which had come over sea and mountains in time for their first wedding anniversary. O'Hara was tremendously moved at sight of it, and Mary was thrilled beyond measure. She even knelt to caress the shamrock feet.

"There's such an elegance about it," she kept saying, "and such a difference from anything I've ever seen. I'm so *proud* of this, James!"

One afternoon when O'Hara was working in the store with McGrady a man walked in. It was John Wilkins from Carlisle. O'Hara wrung his hand for they met as old friends.

"What a surprise!" he said. "What brings you here?"

The other man looked grim.

"Glad to see you again, O'Hara, but I'm a bit discouraged. I decided a while back to move to Pittsburgh. More opportunity here, I heard, so I came ahead to spy out the land as it were before I brought my family. From what I've seen so far I think I'll stay in Carlisle."

O'Hara laughed. "Don't be hasty. I suppose you've noticed the dirt."

"*Noticed* it!" Wilkins exclaimed. "There's a hog in every mud puddle. There's a poor seedy look about the whole place. Plenty of taverns I can see with drunken Indians rolling out the doors and not the sight of a *church*. Is there one?"

"Not yet," O'Hara admitted, "but we . . ."

"What makes you think this town will ever be anything more than it is now?"

O'Hara drew him outside and pointed to the confluence of the two great rivers at The Point.

"That!" he said.

"Oh, you mean the location here?"

"I do. I doubt if there's a better one in the country outside of the eastern harbours. And look over there." He pointed across the muddy Monongahela to the hill which rose mountain high just beyond it. "That hill is full of coal. And some day . . ." His keen eyes narrowed as if he already saw into the future. "Some day I hope to get into manufacturing and if I do I'll use *coal*. I hope I'll be the first man to do it, but," he added laughing, "you can bet I won't be the last!"

"Well," Wilkins conceded slowly, "there may be something to what you say but I'm still quite disappointed in the town."

"Come home with me to dinner and we can talk it all over. I want you to meet my wife."

"Agnes Denny says she's a beauty."

"She's that and more. Have you engaged a tavern room yet?"

"No. I inquired for you and came right here."

"Good. We've got a guest room. I want to hear all about Carlisle so we'll make a night of it. Come back to the store now and I'll send a message to my wife to put an extra potato in the pot."

He dispatched two notes, as a matter of fact, with McGrady, the second being to Hugh Brackenridge.

Hugh: Come to dinner and help convince John Wilkins of Carlisle that Pittsburgh is more than a pigsty. Bring all your eloquence and *wear your best breeks*. J. O'H.

When O'Hara and his guest reached the house in the King's Orchard the latter's eyes opened wide. They became still wider as dinner was served in the parlour at the Irish table with Mary in a tight bodiced rose dress, O'Hara in a fresh vest and Brackenridge in *knee breeches!* The conversation was lively from the start. A skimming of national politics first; the necessity for a strong central Government with a President. Jefferson? Hamilton? Franklin perhaps? General Washington topped them all, they agreed. Hugh and Wilkins discussed pro and con the beginnings of a *party* to be made up of those who championed a Constitution. Alexander Hamilton and John Adams were at the head of it and if it finally got organised the members were to be known as *Federalists*.

"I'll join up with that," O'Hara said quickly. "I'm for a Constitution as fast as we can get one. Something's got to hold us together now or we'll fall to pieces. In spite of the *peâce*," he punned.

There was, indeed, between more serious topics a great deal of witty chaffing from Brackenridge and O'Hara and the recounting of jokes, the one from Wilkins, though, being pronounced the best of the evening.

"You remember, Mrs. O'Hara, when your husband went back east a year ago to do some buying for his store?"

"I surely do," Mary answered. "It was the first time we had been separated since our wedding."

"Well, he stopped overnight in Carlisle and a few of his old friends—Eb Denny, Dicky Butler and I—went to the tavern after dinner to visit with him. There were several strangers stopping there, officers, who joined the group. One of them, a right handsome young blade, spoke up and said to your husband, 'Captain, you talk of Philadelphia. Did you ever happen to meet pretty Polly Carson when you were there?' Of course Eb and Dicky and I were biting our pipe stems, waiting for the fun. 'Oh,' says your husband, 'you haven't heard that she married last spring?' 'The devil she did,' said this fellow. 'Who married her?' 'Why,' said O'Hara here, cool as you please, 'Parson Brown, I believe, of the Locust Street Presbyterian Church.' 'Come, come,' said the fellow, 'you know I don't mean that. Whom did she marry?' 'Well, if you must know, sir,' said your husband, 'she married *me!*' "

After the laughter Mary looked across the table.

"You never told me that story, Mr. O'Hara."

His eyes twinkled. "I guess I was afraid the man was one of your old beaux!"

"And there were plenty of them, I'll warrant, eh Mistress?" Wilkins said with admiration.

H

"Perhaps," Mary answered demurely, "but there was only one that ever mattered."

Hugh slapped the table. "By my faith, prettily spoken, that! For the thousandth time I congratulate my friend here."

With this, Mary rose, on pretext of attending to her baby, and left the gentlemen to their port. When they were settled finally in the easy-chairs, O'Hara gave Hugh a side glance and he began at once to speak of Pittsburgh and his own ambitions for it.

"Of course we do need a *church*!" he said.

Wilkins was at once interested.

"Now that's the thing I missed as I first looked around. You think there is the possibility of one?"

"Definitely," said O'Hara. "A group of us have been planning already. One of our most prominent families here are the Nevilles, but they're Episcopalians. However most of the others are Scotch-Irish and if you scratch their skins you know you'll find Presbyterians."

"The Penns reserved lots for the various congregations," Hugh put in, "and ours has a fine big tree on it which I picture standing by the side of the front door of the church. If you come to reside here, you would be of enormous help I know in promoting a building."

"It would certainly be a project of the greatest interest to me," Wilkins said slowly.

"Good!" said Hugh. "We'll count on you," as though Wilkins's coming was now assured. "But I have two other irons on the fire," he went on. "I want this town to have a *newspaper* and an *Academy*! I think I've got a Philadelphia printer lined up already, but he can't come out for another year. Then we'll have to have an editor . . ."

"Mr. Brackenridge, may I ask what your business is?"

"I'm a lawyer, sir."

"You mean you have enough work to keep you busy here?"

"Pretty much. And I'm not the only one either. You see, Mr. Wilkins, the *law* whether broken or kept is an integral part of the life of every civilised community. And, I might add, the degree of civilisation in any place depends upon the quality of the citizens and not," here he grinned at the older man, "upon the number of hogs running loose."

"You've hit me fair!" Wilkins said. "I judged hastily. But

you'll admit the general outlook here leaves much to be desired. But go on, Mr. Brackenridge. You speak of an *Academy*."

"Oh, that's the thing nearest to my heart. *Liberty and Learning!* That's my motto. You know the only type of school we have at the present? A Mrs. Pride opened classes for girls, spreading the word that she would teach needlework and *Reading, English and Knitting* if required! There's education for you. Well, I've got a beginning made for an academy though it may be several years before we can incorporate. I've got some trustees promised and we have our fingers on two lots between Second and Third streets, off Smithfield. It will be small at the start, but so was Princeton. Who knows but my little academy may turn into a University one day, too! That's what I like about being a part of a young, growing town. The possibilities of the future are unlimited."

The port was excellent. The men mellowed. As the hours passed Pittsburgh grew, industry developed, learning flourished, elegant brick houses took the place of ramshackle log cabins, great vessels left the docks to sail around the world . . . the picture grew more vividly real as midnight turned into morning. When at last Hugh got up to go Wilkins had reached a decision. He would find a place to live and bring on his family. O'Hara handed him his candle and wished him good night.

"I'll walk Hugh to the end of the lane to be sure he doesn't get lost in the city we've just built," he said grinning.

When they were out in the crisp autumn air under the apple trees he went on, "We've got ourselves a fine new citizen to-night. Thanks for your part in it."

"I've had too much port," Hugh said irritably. "My head is fuzzy and my legs aren't steady. For the love of heaven, you'd think my Scotch blood would take care of me better than this."

"You should have mixed it with a little Irish," O'Hara rejoined, grabbing his arm.

"What I want is a *wife*," Hugh burst out suddenly to O'Hara's surprise.

"Best wish in the world. Anyone in mind?"

"Yes, but it's hopeless."

"Don't ever say hopeless to me in matters of love," O'Hara said. "Do you want to talk about it?"

"Yes. Maybe it's the port, but anyway I'll tell you. A few weeks ago a farmer from out here, fifteen or twenty miles back, came to see me about a boundary dispute with his neighbour.

Well, I rode out one day to look over the land, and—the man had a daughter."

"Some men do," O'Hara murmured.

"Now the Lord never cut me out for a celibate. I've proved that in plenty of predicaments but I tell you, O'Hara, I never felt about any girl as I feel about that one. Just looking at her, mind you, I knew I wanted her for my wife. She's the opposite of Mary, dark instead of fair, but as pretty in her own way I think, and with such a spirit in her eyes! I think she felt something too, for if my blood was hot so were her cheeks. But . . . I'm trying to be sensible."

"*Sensible!*" O'Hara fairly shouted it. "When was a man in love ever sensible? What's wrong with you? Go after her and never stop till you get her!"

"It wouldn't work, O'Hara. She's completely unlettered. She can read and that's about it. All she knows is to milk a cow. And I've got ambitions. I'm going into politics. I want a nice home eventually and a wife who can preside at my table and speak the King's English. Put yourself in my place. You can see then that I must forget her. And yet . . . as we stood in her father's pasture looking at each other, something struck fire between us. So, you have my story."

The young men had stopped on the edge of the Orchard and stood now in silence. The little town itself was still except for the mournful tinkle of a cowbell occasionally from the field beside Suke's Run. At last O'Hara spoke.

"If I were you, Hugh, I would go back to see this girl. Often. Make sure that you love each other. If you do I'd marry her and then send her back to Philadelphia to a good school for a year."

"What an utterly mad idea," Hugh groaned angrily.

"No, it isn't. She has looks you say and a spirit that would indicate intelligence. Able to pick things up quickly. She probably has common sense and good womanly qualities. What she lacks is the outward polish. In the right kind of school she'd get this in a year. *You* know. Manners, speech, some social graces, with a little literature and such thrown in! Mary would know the right place. Well, if I had this problem that's the way I'd handle it."

"Do you suppose a girl would agree to such a plan?"

O'Hara chuckled. "You're not unattractive, Hugh, my lad. Marry her first and show her what love can be like. I think probably then she would do anything to please you."

"Well," Hugh said after a pause, "you're either a damn' fool or a genius, O'Hara. On second thought I believe you might be the latter. In any case I'll go home now and sleep on it."

"Can you make it back alone?"

"Oh, sure. The night air has cleared my head. If it hadn't, your suggestion would have knocked me stone sober. Thanks for everything. Good night."

The guest room, which Mary had so charmingly furnished, continued to be occupied with such frequency that the tavern keepers twitted O'Hara about stealing their custom. It was all in good sport, however, for it was generally conceded that élite strangers should be directed to O'Hara's store from whence they would eventually be taken to the house in the King's Orchard. This, not only for the greater comfort of the guests, but for the greater glory of Pittsburgh.

One stranger scared Mary out of her wits at first. Upon answering a knock at the kitchen door she saw a large man with a face so swarthy it was almost black, accoutred with four belts around him, two brace of pistols, a sword, a rifle over his shoulder, a pouch and a huge tobacco pipe! He introduced himself as General Peter Muhlenberg whom O'Hara had sent on to the house since he himself was detained at the store.

But the odd-looking man proved most entertaining. He was on his way to the Falls of the Ohio to locate lands in Virginia for the officers and soldiers of the Virginia line in Continental service. His interest in the Indians was deep-seated for his grandfather was Conrad Weiser who had held conferences with the red men forty years before! There was, naturally, much to discuss between him and O'Hara.

So the picturesque transients came and went, contributing as O'Hara and Mary agreed, a richness to their living and a new meaning to the hospitality for which they were growing famous.

One afternoon O'Hara came home to find Elliott sitting on the back stoop whittling a small horse. He glanced up and gave a characteristic greeting.

"Started this damn' thing on too small a piece of wood. Not going to have a tail for the beast."

"Elliott!" O'Hara exclaimed. "Man, I'm glad to see you! Where have you been all this time? When did you get in? Are you going to stay a while?"

"Hear you've got a store."

"Yes. It's not bad either and business is growing. Want a job?" He laughed as he said this, but Elliott was serious.

"My gammy leg's been kickin' up lately. I'm afraid I'll have to give up tradin'. But behind a counter now I might look right smart. You know I'm a devil with the ladies."

O'Hara sat down and threw an arm round his shoulder.

"You're always heaven-sent, Elliott. How do you know to turn up just when I need you?"

Elliott didn't answer this. Instead he looked up and smiled. "I've met the Missus an' I must say you've done yourself proud, O'Hara."

They ate in the kitchen and then settled comfortably afterwards around the fire, the men with their pipes. Mary with her knitting listening avidly to their stories, especially the ones of their first trip to Pittsburgh. Of those details she couldn't hear enough: the death of the moose, the shooting of the bear *and the panther* which still in rug form lay beside her bed. She let her knitting fall idle as O'Hara told of their night in the pioneer cabin where he had described the Bingham ball.

"I suppose," she remarked with a twinkle, "you didn't tell *everything*."

"Oh, I omitted a few details," he said, and even as they looked at each other Elliott did not seem to be shut out, as he joined in the laughter too, guessing the reason.

A closeness fell upon the three. When the fire grew low it was Elliott who got up casually and put a new log on, as though after long wanderings he had come home.

"Ever run into Guyasuta since I saw you?" O'Hara asked.

"Yep. Once. He mentioned you, by the way. Said he'd like to see you again, but didn't know whether he would be welcome."

"You heard about Hannastown?"

"Yes, I don't know how the old buck got into that but do you know what he's got in his craw now?"

"No more depredations, I hope," O'Hara said sharply.

"No, no. I think he's mebbe quietened down a little. He told me he's decided to settle over here across the Allegheny and spend the rest of his days there. I don't know how the town will take to that."

"Not very kindly, I imagine. Is he coming soon?"

"Not for a couple of years, he said. Ever seen him, Mrs. O'Hara?"

"No. I've just heard of him many times. What's he like?"

As the two descriptions continued they were decidedly at variance.

"A crafty-lookin' customer," from Elliott.

"A really noble face!" from O'Hara.

"Just plain Injun if you ask me."

"I think he's rather handsome! Oh, I guess you'd better wait till you see him, Mary," O'Hara added, laughing. "Then you can make up your own mind."

With the perceptiveness that constantly surprised and delighted her husband Mary sensed the bond between the two men, and when Elliott rose to go back to Semple's she held out her hand.

"I want you to know, Mr. Elliott, that you will always be welcome in our home."

He looked down at her, his keen eyes softening.

"Those are nice words, ma'am, for a lonely man to hear. I thank you."

The next morning he was at the store when O'Hara got there. By noon it seemed as though he had been there from the start. He ambled around, learning the stock, making suggestions, greeting customers in his easy fashion. In between busy moments he and O'Hara talked of Indian affairs which were in a bad way. In spite of the fact that peace was concluded and a treaty signed, the British still held fortified posts in the north and west, and the officers stationed there were evidently encouraging the Indians to stop the American advance if they could, for the attacks kept growing in number and ferocity all the time.

"Even here it's been too close for comfort," O'Hara said. "The settlers around have been having trouble, and a month ago a band of the Senecas, we think, tried to shoot up the fort! There aren't many men on duty there now but they managed to scare the Injuns off."

"What do you think it's going to be? More treaties an' speeches or an all-out war?"

"Both would be my guess. I hear some Commissioners have been appointed to go out and talk things over. But the trouble is, Elliott, there's too much right on each side to make the one or the other give way. Here are the Americans, veterans of the Continental Army, paid off in western lands instead of cash. They're going to go out there and claim them. And they should. The west has to be settled. On the other hand there are the Indians pushed

out of what they naturally feel are *their* lands. Never sure the
promises made to them will be kept. They've been fooled too
often. A bad business all around."

"And you think it'll be a big fight at the end?"

"I don't see how things will ever be quiet without."

"What if the Injuns win?"

"They can't in the long run but it'll be bloody bad in between.
I got word General Josiah Harmar is going to come out with
some troops to safeguard the Commissioners and then stay to take
command of the federal forces north of the Ohio. Elliott?"

"What?"

"I'm more glad than I can tell you that you're here. If I should
have to be away you could run the store and keep a watch over
Mary. I still think it's a miracle that you always appear at the
right time. Is it because you keep track of what I'm up to?"

"What makes you think you'll have to be away?" Elliott
parried.

"Oh," O'Hara grinned, "my prophetic Irish soul, and a few
hints in letters from back east. I may get mixed up with this
thing. Well, anyway, it won't be for a while, I imagine."

But the call came sooner than he expected in the shape of a
message from General Knox of the War Department, requesting
that O'Hara become contractor for furnishing provisions to
Harmar's western army as well as providing things "necessary for
the table and support of the Commissioners" during their negotiations with the Indians.

He read the letter to Mary who looked back at him with
astonishment and alarm.

"What would this mean, James?"

"Well," he said slowly, "it would mean the hardest appointment
I've ever had so far. To provision an army in the wilderness is a
tremendous undertaking. To collect the supplies will be difficult
enough but the transportation problems will be the worst. I
wonder," he added consideringly, "if it can partly be done by
boat."

"Will you be among the Indians?"

"Oh, yes, of course. Somewhat. The idea of having the
Commissioners go out is to talk with them and try to make treaties,
and I'll be with these men sometimes at least. I know the dialects."

"Will there be danger?" she pursued.

He smiled at her tenderly. "Dear Delight, there is always a

certain amount of danger in the wilderness. I suppose," he said, his visional eyes looking off beyond her, "that even when the country is built up with towns and cities there will still be dangers. Not rattlesnakes nor Indians but others. Why, darling, you laughed at me for thinking there might be danger for you in child-birth. Well, there will only be about the same degree for me in this project."

Mary had been sewing quilt patches together. She laid her work on the kitchen table and walked over to the fire, and stood, looking into it.

"It is settled then?" she said, without turning. "You have no choice in the matter?"

"I'm afraid not. After all, I've been an officer in the army. This order comes from the War Department. I couldn't respect myself much if I refused it."

He went over to her and took her in his arms. "Is it all right? I will have to be away, of course, but not for too long at a time. By the very nature of the work I'll have to come back to Pittsburgh often for supplies. So you see, it won't be too bad."

Mary met his eyes.

"You *want* to do this, James, don't you?"

He hesitated. "I needn't tell you that I don't want to be separated from you even for a little. But as to the work, I would like to try it. It's a tremendous thing they've asked of me. It's a challenge sure enough and I like the feel of that. Then— not to blow my own horn—it *is* a pretty big compliment. It implies the Government liked my work before. Yes, I want to do it if it's possible."

"And besides you are bored with the store."

He looked down at her in amazement. "How did you ever guess that?"

"I know you pretty well by now, Mr. O'Hara," she smiled.

"You're uncanny. Yes, I'm bored with the store even though it's doing well. Now, Elliott can look after it with McGrady's help and make himself a living and we'll still get some income from it. But about this contractor business, I'll naturally be honest, scrupulously honest, but I'm sure I'll still make money at it! Will it really be all right with you if I go ahead?"

She stood as she had done years ago in the library back home, twisting a button of his waistcoat.

"I told you once I'd be willing to travel to the world's end with you," she said. "Now I guess my part as a wife is to be content at home while you do the travelling. That's harder, but I'll try."

Events from then on moved so swiftly that even O'Hara with his predilection for speed was staggered. His own letter of acceptance was followed by others from the War Department, one from Robert Morris in Philadelphia relating to his salary and one from General Harmar.

But most thrilling of all was the information about the Commissioners themselves who under the protection of the troops would arrive in Pittsburgh in a month's time, before going on to their conferences at the western forts. For he learned then that among these men were Dicky Butler and *George Rogers Clark*! It was incredible, O'Hara told Mary jubilantly, that he was going to see Clark again and oh, certainly have him in their home. But in this new world it was the unbelievable which always happened! Clark did not write. He wouldn't. But Dicky Butler whom O'Hara admired deeply said in his letter that he and Arthur Lee, another of the Commissioners, had written to Robert Morris, the Secretary of Finance, to be sure there would be no slip-up, asking that "the articles which we have noted as necessary should be purchased by Mr. O'Hara, *in whom we can confide.*"

Mary read this aloud over and over and while her husband told her she was unduly proud it was evident that his own heart was warmed by the praise.

The work was heavy. In addition to the order for army provisions, the State, wishing to convince the natives that she could furnish the best assortment of goods for them, demanded that O'Hara procure a goodly supply of suitable articles for the Indians. So once more he was combing the other local stores and sending back to Philadelphia for brooches, arm-bands, knives, bridles, ribbons and finger-rings. He added coats, blankets and ruffled shirts from his own stock. All of these he packed, marked, numbered and placed in the back of his store until the arrival of the Commissioners.

When they came with their guarding troops, General Harmar elected to camp on the level ground on the other side of the Allegheny, and O'Hara ferried across at once to see them. His meeting with Clark was almost violent in its mutual delight. They gripped hands, they slapped each other on the back, they laughed uproariously in sheer pleasure.

"Dad Drabit!" Clark kept saying with his red hair rampant,

"if I ain't glad to see you, you old son of a gun! And when we're not up to our chins in water, either!"

O'Hara and Mary had carefully planned the entertainment they wished to give. It would be impossible to have *all* the Commissioners to dinner, so it was decided to invite Clark, Dicky Butler and Harmar for the meal itself at which Mary would be present. Then she would retire as she had done before and the guests from the town, General John Neville, Major Isaac Craig, Devereux Smith, John Wilkins and of course Hugh Brackenridge, would be asked to come in for port and an evening's talk.

"We can't have the wives," Mary said as they discussed it. "In the first place we haven't enough chairs and in the second place you men will be freer to visit without us. While you are away I'll entertain the women. I'll have teas and maybe a nice quilting party for them. So that will even it up."

"You're right, as usual," O'Hara agreed and proceeded at once with his invitations which were promptly accepted.

On the night itself Mary bloomed as she always did under excitement, the parlour was fresh from its extra dusting and polish and the Irish table bore with grace her finest china and silver. The dinner guests were all impressed, but Clark was ebullient. He was all over the house. He must see everything. Then he would come back to gaze at Mary.

"You've a fine place here and no mistake. And you've got a good man too. I've seen him in some tight fixes and he stood up mighty well. Whether he deserves anything as nice as *you*, ma'am, I wouldn't know. Dad Drabit," he added turning to wink at O'Hara, "you'd better behave yourself pretty good the rest of your life or I'll come back and knock the gizzard out of you."

Dinner was gay with many reminiscences of the war, some of which made O'Hara look a bit anxiously at his wife. But Mary took them all in good part and laughed with the rest. The one which amused them all the most was Clark's description of the night the Governor of Kaskaskia and his wife had wakened to find four men surrounding their bed.

"And of course we all looked like the devil," he said. "Dirty and ragged and beards an inch long. All of us over six feet and Simon Kenton and me with red hair sticking out all over to make us seem wilder. But you didn't look too smart yourself, O'Hara, as I recall."

When the laughter died down, he went on. "But the thing I never got over was how Madame Rocheblave foxed us. We took him right into custody but we left her by herself to get dressed and all. Felt that was only polite. And Dad Drabit, if she didn't steal all the British papers and we never did find them! Well, it taught me one thing. It don't always pay to be a gentleman."

When Mary rose at last to leave them the men bowed as low over her hand as though they were in a Philadelphia drawing-room. Then there were knocks both at the parlour and the kitchen doors and the guests from the town arrived. When General Harmar talked to O'Hara a few days later he spoke with amazement and pleasure of that evening.

"I had no idea," he said, "of the quality of your leading citizens here! The East couldn't produce any better. I think this town is going to grow, Captain."

The first conference was to be held at Cuyahoga on the bank of Lake Erie in November and O'Hara had finally decided that since the waterways did not quite connect he would have to transport everything by pack-horses and go across the country with the troops. He was working each day from dawn till dark, coming in at night exhausted, for a late supper during which Mary entertained him with little William's latest accomplishments, the town news or letters from the East. Agnes Denny wrote that Eb was definitely coming to Pittsburgh that fall; her father said that Philadelphia was moving now in its old groove, business fairly good, society very gay, politics on the rampage with him and most of his friends in favour of getting the Federalist party under way and a Constitution drawn up. Here in Pittsburgh the biggest excitement in Mary's eyes was that Hugh Brackenridge was actually *going to see a girl*! Out in the country!

One night when O'Hara came in late Mary was nowhere to be seen. Prudence merely said that Mrs. O'Hara was tired and had gone on up. He swallowed his food quickly and a bit anxiously, and hurried after, glad to be settled early for the night. When he entered their room Mary was sitting white-faced and fully dressed on the edge of the bed.

"Darling, are you sick?"

He went over to kiss her but she pushed him gently away. "No, I'm not sick," she said. "It's just that I would prefer to-night to be alone."

"Alone? You mean you don't want me to . . . to sleep here?"

"If you please."

"But why? Mary, what is it? You're not . . . not . . ."

"No," she said. "I am not. And I'm not sick. It is just that I would like to be by myself."

He stood staring at her, incredulous. Then as she gave no sign he turned, got his night things from the closet and moved towards the door. Here, he looked back.

"But darling, *what have I done? Tell me!*"

It was an anguished cry but it did not move her. She sat still as stone, and after a moment of waiting he went out. He lay down in the guest room, stricken, going over and over in his mind all he could remember of the past few days. They had been as far as he could recall, perfectly normal except for his longer hours and greater weariness at night. But Mary had seemed so understanding, and so really interested in all his efforts to get the flour, biscuit, candles, and the rest. She had even given him good advice on several occasions. More and more he was finding that she had business acumen, strange in a woman. She was her father's own daughter. But most mystifying of all was that their breakfast together on that very morning, while hurried, had been a happy one. They had laughed together over Elliott's remarks on the finger bowls of which there were now, according to Mary's original prediction, only a few left. Elliott after a hasty explanation from O'Hara did some experimenting on his own but was discouraged.

"Course, I'd never have any call to use one," he said, "but I couldn't get one of my big paws all in it, anyway. I guess they're just for the ladies."

Mary was still chuckling over this as he had said good-bye. He had been gone all day down the river at a gristmill to get more flour, so had not seen her until just now. Something must have happened during those intervening hours, but what, what could it have been, so grievous that she would not tell him? That she would *shut him out* with this devastating coldness.

But another thought finally pierced him. Could her present attitude represent the accumulation of hidden loneliness, fears, and even resentment at his leaving her? If this were true it would be the most serious of all reasons to combat. For how could he assuage these feelings without giving up the work he was now committed to do?

When he finally fell asleep from sheer exhaustion it was with a last thought that on the morrow everything would surely come right. There was always healing in the daylight.

But it was not so in Mary's case. She remained pale, stony, distant. To all his frantic questionings, to all his attempts at caresses, she withdrew into an impregnable silence.

At the end of the fifth day he could stand it no longer. He drew her, half resisting, into the parlour and shut the door. She sank down on the sofa and he stood before her.

"Mary," he said, "when we were married one of the vows you took was that you would obey me. As a gentleman I would never dream even of referring to that except in some extreme emergency. I feel it is that now. We can't go on this way. You will be sick and I will be ruined for I cannot, I will not leave you until this is cleared up between us. I ask you now to tell me exactly what is lying on your heart. *What happened?*"

She shook her head but his voice was stern.

"I expect you to answer."

She looked down at her hands as she kept threading them together.

"It was the day you were away down the river," she began slowly. "You know the new little Bake and Sweet Shop where the saddlery used to be?"

"Of course."

"The stoop is at the side instead of in front of the door. I went in to get some seedcakes as a little treat for your supper . . ." She swallowed with difficulty. "And as I was coming out I heard women's voices on the stoop. They couldn't see me and I couldn't see them. But I heard them."

"Yes?"

"I stopped right in the doorway when I heard one of them say, 'Poor little Mrs. O'Hara!'"

"What?"

"The woman said she'd never want a daughter of hers to marry a man who had been an Indian trader. She said . . . she said they all had a wife somewhere in the wilderness and even when . . . when they were really married to a white woman they would find a way to get back sometimes to . . . to the Indian. And the other one said . . ."

"Go on!" His voice was choked.

"She said, 'Look at O'Hara. He's going back amongst them now with these Commissioners and you can see he's happy as a

king over it. You'd think he'd be satisfied with what he's got,'
and the other one said, 'They're never satisfied.' And then I . . .
I ran through the store and out the back door. The man ran
after me for I dropped the seedcakes but I never stopped till I got
home. And that is . . . what happened." The tears were running
down her cheeks.

It was O'Hara's face now that was white; it was livid with
anger. The torrent of his words poured from him. Mary had
never heard him swear before. She heard him now. When he
finally checked himself he raised her to her feet.

"Look at me!" he said. "Look into my eyes."

She raised her own brimming ones to his.

"Mary, since the time I kissed you in Mrs. Bingham's Greenery
until our wedding night I never," he paused as though searching
for the right words to use before her, "I was never with a woman.
I will not insult us both by giving my oath on that. I think you
will accept my word," he added bitterly.

A great light flooded her face. "James!" she cried, reaching
her hands to him. "Oh, James!"

But he moved back, his own countenance unchanged.

"To think that you could believe this loose, evil gossip *about me*!
To question my life in this regard before we were married would
be bad enough. But for you to think that I would now leave you,
my wife, to go to the arms of *any* woman, let alone a savage, this
has cut me to the very quick."

"But the women sounded so sure! And I don't know about
. . . about men." Her voice was piteous.

"I'm not *men*," O'Hara said, still with bitterness, "I'm your
husband and you should never have doubted me."

He turned on his heel, went out of the parlour, shutting the
door with finality behind him, and went up again to the guest
room. This that he had just learned was worse than anything
he could possibly have imagined! He felt wounded beyond healing.
His pride in his own integrity had been destroyed, and his resentment was devastating. How could Mary, in the face of his utter
devotion, have been affected by the accusation in the first place?
But even though she was troubled by it, how could she have
believed it to the extent of refusing even to give him a chance to
speak in his own defence, until she was forced to do so? It seemed
to him in his anger that all his love up to this point had been
unavailing. He lay, drowned in a black misery.

Just beyond the King's Orchard as the night advanced, he could hear the rolling waters of the Allegheny for a high wind had risen. Then in an hour's time the rain came, beating against the many-layered paper window panes. He listened to the threat of the storm upon them and muttered, for a moment forgetting the grief of his spirit. "Some day I'm going to make glass!" And even as he voiced his resolution it brought to him the poignant thought of all Mary had given up in leaving her old life in Philadelphia for the one in Pittsburgh. She had brought her grace and beauty to the rough, sprawling, unkempt pioneer village and borne its limitations without complaint. Even with the joy of her child and the small diversions possible, he knew she had times of discouragement and loneliness for the friendships and surroundings to which she had been accustomed. He knew this because occasionally his cheek, moving against her pillow as he roused from his initial sleep, had found it wet as it had been on their first night here. But always in the morning her smile had once again made bright the place of their habitation. Oh, he had taken her cheerful acceptance of this life too much for granted!

But something else smote him sharply now, something he had refused to admit before because of his own hurt pride. He had cursed the women who had brought this unspeakable distress upon him and Mary; he had branded their words as loose and evil gossip, but he knew as he forced himself to honesty that beneath their exaggerations there was a strong element of general truth. Mary did not "know men" as she had said piteously, but he did, and he knew fur traders. He remembered, too, the night a certain chief had offered him his daughter in marriage, and that the girl was beautiful enough to quicken a man's desire. And he knew something else which he had never told Mary and never would. Elliott, in spite of all his words against the natives, had an Indian wife! If he stayed on in Pittsburgh there would be times when upon one pretext or another he would ride off into the wilderness and be swallowed up there for days or weeks . . .

Was it perhaps the existence of such burning facts as these below the women's speech that, unconsciously sensed, must have overwhelmed Mary's normal repudiation and seared her tender heart?

Suddenly he leaped to his feet and hurried to the door. Even as he opened it, above the wind and the rain, he heard the sound of sobbing. And there in the hallway was Mary, coming to him.

"James," she cried brokenly, "I can't *live* if you're angry with me!"

He picked her up, enfolding her small, shivering body in his arms. He carried her to their own bed and there beside her, cradled her against his heart while their tears mingled and the words, *Forgive! Forgive!* from each of them, were smothered by their kisses.

They had never been closer than on that night.

It was the beginning of the following week that the trip to Cuyahoga was begun. In the early morning the troops, the Commissioners on horseback and O'Hara with his pack train set out. He and Mary had said their last good-byes, but as she stood at the top of the kitchen steps watching him out of sight down the lane, he turned suddenly and came hurrying back until he stood below her, looking up into her face. All the tenderness, all the passion of their love had come flooding back, stronger than ever during the intervening days and nights, but his eyes now, at his departure, were still anxious. She kissed him very gently on the forehead, the eyelids, the lips as if in blessing.

"I'm glad it all happened," she said softly in final reassurance. "Before, perhaps I wondered a little without realising it. But now I *know.* I will always know. Hurry along now," she added with a brave little laugh. "The sooner you go, the sooner you'll come back to me!"

Chapter Ten

It was early evening of a hot July day the following summer when O'Hara rode out of the forest and into Pittsburgh on his fourth trip home. In spite of his eagerness to get to Mary he reined Pitt in for a minute at the edge of the Orchard and surveyed the town. There was a noticeable change, a pleasant one. John Wilkins, he knew, had been the chief instigator of it with Neville and Craig to back him up. Some of the usual roving hogs were now apparently in pens; the roads had been worked upon and presented a somewhat smoother, if dusty appearance; front yards for the most part were fairly neat and in many cases planted with flowers from the precious little seed packets brought over the mountains; and several log cabins had been whitewashed like his own! Behind it all rose Grant's Hill, always greenly pleasant, where the townspeople strolled of a Sunday.

"Well, well," O'Hara said to himself, "we're getting on a little and no mistake!"

He rode quickly down the lane, flung the reins over Pitt's head, and ran up the steps. The horse had long ago learned to stand, waiting his master's pleasure. Prudence appeared from the stairway and greeted him calmly.

"Oh, you're back, I see, sir. Well, the child has just gone off to sleep and the mistress is dining with Mr. and Mrs. Wilkins. I believe Mr. Brackenridge is there too. Have you supped yourself, sir?"

"Not a bite. Anything you happen to have will taste fine. I'll do some work at my desk until Mrs. O'Hara returns."

He went upstairs first to look at his boy, who stirred only slightly under his father's kiss, then came down and settled himself with his papers at his newest acquisition, a tall secretary which had been made in Pittsburgh. While he chafed under the delay in seeing Mary he would be glad to have a little start on his accounting which was always intricate and time consuming.

Except for the one big disaster last December he knew that his work had been praiseworthy and, in certain respects almost incredible, so his record-keeping while laborious, brought satisfaction too. But the remembrance of that one ghastly incident, error, accident, whatever it might be called, was still galling him.

It had happened on the way to Fort McIntosh where the second parley with the Indians was to take place. This post was situated where the Beaver River joins the Ohio and since there was of course continuous waterway from Pittsburgh to that point he had secured a large flatboat and loaded it heavily, but he felt safely, with the needed supplies. The weather had been sunny and only moderately sharp the first of the month but when they were well on their way they ran into bitter, freezing, deadly cold. The vessel was driven aground on a fish dam by the ice, with its broadside battered in. There was no way of getting it off with the weight it bore, two of the crew were already dangerously frost-bitten, and there was no hope of relief; so he had done the only thing possible. He had ordered thrown overboard twelve thousand-weight of flour, five hundred-weight of bread and biscuit, the rum, the soap, the candles and the rest! As the valuable stores, secured by him with unceasing labour and awaited with need by the troops and Commissioners, dropped into the icy river O'Hara's own heart had sunk with them. This was his first real failure and it was a desperately serious one.

It had been morning before the men were able to float the boat off the dam and get her battered remains to shore. Eb Denny, who had been sent out to join the Commissioners at Fort McIntosh, was with him, and seeing O'Hara's black mood had tried to comfort him.

"It was an accident, man. I can testify to that."

"They will say I should have started earlier."

"Well, why didn't you?"

"I was trying to get more flour. It's a hard job, Eb."

And there had been criticism. Plenty of it. Especially from Arthur Lee, one of the Commissioners. O'Hara had gritted his teeth and said nothing after stating the facts themselves. But he had made himself very clear to General Harmar. He pulled now from a secret drawer before him a paper which he reread for his comfort each time he got back home. It was a copy of the statements between himself and the general. His own concluded:

As these losses of provisions may probably be considered

under the fifth article of my contract with the Secretary in the War Office, and you being acquainted with the circumstances, I shall esteem it a particular favour if you will please to furnish me with the necessary certificate thereof.

The General's reply had been prompt to the effect that—

The above statement of facts relative to the loss of the contractor's boat and cargo is just and true agreeable to the best information that can be obtained.

So the War Office had accepted it, absolved him and the whole thing was pretty well forgotten now by everybody but himself. To him, in spite of Mary's wise comforting, it remained a scar in his memory. Well, he thought, I've been pretty lucky. I guess when a man gets to feeling too sure of himself the devil gets in a crack at him.

It was nine o'clock before he heard voices in the lane. He had eaten his supper, chatted a moment with McGrady—who always reported in the evening and now had taken Pitt to his usual stall in Semple's stable—and had covered several long sheets with his neat, careful writing and figures. He leaped to his feet now and went to the door where he could see John Wilkins and his wife with Hugh and Mary approaching the house. When he stepped out and down the steps to meet them Mary rushed towards him with a cry of joy and there was general exclaiming and welcome.

"Come in! Come in!" O'Hara said hospitably, even as he hoped they would refuse.

The Wilkinses did decline, but Hugh, when the others had made their farewells, entered the kitchen eagerly.

"Go ahead! Kiss her!" he said, applying himself to the fire. "Don't mind me. As a matter of fact . . ."

"Oh, James," Mary said as she finally released herself, "we have such news for you! Tell him, Hugh."

Hugh turned then, grinning from ear to ear.

"I'm about to become 'Benedick, the married man!' " he said.

After the medley of excited questions and answers they all sat down while Hugh told his story.

"Her name is Maria Wolf and you know the first of it, O'Hara, for it was your advice that brought it all about. I've been going to see her regularly, and a few weeks ago she promised to marry me and also to go to Philadelphia to school. In fact she agreed so

quickly to that that my feelings were hurt at first. Then I found it
was because she wants so much to be . . . be . . ."

"Worthy of you?" O'Hara prompted.

"Well, that sounds pretty bumptious but she does want to
fit in with whatever kind of life we may have. You know I'm
running for the Legislature and I've a pretty good idea I'm going
to be elected. If I am I'll be in the East too, and I can see her
betimes."

"Who's going to marry you?" O'Hara said.

"You might well ask! Parsons are as scarce here as hen's teeth.
But I've got on the trail of a young theolog from Princeton who's
roaming around. He's got some idea of converting the Indians.
You know, all that kind of business. So, next Tuesday he's going
to tie the knot. Just her father and mother there. Meanwhile,
blessings on your wife here!" He paused to look fondly at Mary
as she took up the tale.

"Prudence and I have been cleaning Hugh's cabin and fixing
it up a bit. Oh, it's such fun! And on their wedding night, James,
I thought we'd give them a supper. Just us. To invite more people
might . . ."

"Yes, that would embarrass her," Hugh said. "She's not
really shy, but you must remember she's had no advantages. She's
a fine girl, though!" Then he added, ruefully, "But guess what
she's afraid she's going to miss? *A cow!* My God, I want to be
good to her but I won't have a cow in my back yard. I hate the
dirty beasts. I had enough of them when I was a boy. Try to
convince her, Mary, that I'm much better than a bovine, won't
you?"

There was great laughter and handshaking and good wishes
as Hugh said good night. Almost immediately, however, he stuck
his head again in at the door.

"This will prove I'm in love all right, O'Hara! What do you
suppose I forgot to tell you? After working on the thing for nearly
three years, too. Listen to this!" He emphasised each word with
a pointed forefinger. "On the twenty-ninth of this month of July,
1786, there will be published the first issue of *The Pittsburgh Gazette*!
Put that in your pipe and smoke it."

Oh, the bliss of union after absence! Warm heart against
warm heart! Peace, even though transient, instead of the love-
laden fears born of danger or loneliness! And the unburdening
of all the mind had stored against the meeting. There was, indeed,

more than usual this time to talk about. Mary had much news from the East, the biggest being that her sister, Elizabeth, had a little son, Christian Carson Febiger!

"So the *Carson* name is getting its just due!" O'Hara observed.

Then there had been letters from old friends, one from Mary Vining which was very sad. She said she and Anthony Wayne had tiny snatches of happiness like spots of blue in a storm-swept sky but that after these brief meetings they felt worse than before. Her heart ached more for Anthony even than for herself, but what could she do? She had asked pitifully:

"What *can* she do, James?"

O'Hara was pacing the parlour floor as he listened. "Nothing!" he said emphatically. "Nothing! Wayne as a man and a gentleman has made the decision himself as he ought to do. She must abide by it."

"She says his hair has gone almost white. It will make him very handsome."

"I'm afraid he's paid a bitter price for his looks, then. Well, any more news of the social set?"

"Several girls have heard from Peggy Arnold in London. She has a second baby. But the general is terribly unhappy and quite bitter. He expected to be an important man there, and Peggy writes that nobody pays any attention to him."

"I could have told him that! The British respect an honest enemy but they'll have no truck with a traitor. Well, let's get back to Pittsburgh and pleasanter topics. Now, about Hugh's wedding. Did I understand you to say you were having them to supper on their wedding night?"

"Why, I thought so," Mary said innocently, "wouldn't you like that?"

"It isn't what *I* would like but I think they'd rather be by themselves that evening."

A flash of understanding recollection spread over Mary's face with a blush. "Oh, James," she said, "how stupid of me! I should have thought of that."

He smiled mischievously down at her. "Yes, I certainly think you should!"

"Prudence was talking to me the other day," Mary went on with a small giggle. "She says when a man *makes* too much over his wife it's likely to spoil her."

"Fancy that!"

"And that she knew a man once who was always hugging and kissing his wife like . . . well, she said she would mention no names."

"Very discreet of her."

"And that this woman got so spoiled and above herself she ran off with another man!"

"Well, well," O'Hara said, kissing her soundly, "I must really be more careful. And by the way, if Prudence opens up the subject again, tell her to mind her own business. Politely, but make the meaning clear. Get your hat now, dear, and we'll go out and have a look at the town."

They stopped at Hugh's cabin and O'Hara was amazed at the transformation. It was now *clean* with a couple of braided rugs on the floor; the books, English, French, Latin, Greek, set neatly on new shelves; a dresser along the wall back of the table; and two rockers and a settle beside the fireplace.

"I got the extra furniture cheap from a man who's moving on west to the Ohio country. What do you think of it?"

"It looks like a real home, Hugh," O'Hara said.

Mary had a few more touches to put upon the bedroom so the two men stood outside looking over the town and commenting on the changes a year had brought. A new growth had come upon it, a new era, indeed. The days of Indian trade which had supported it from its first cabins had almost passed. While there would, of course, still be some traffic in furs the chief business now was selling goods to passing travellers. For the movement westward was gaining momentum every month and Pittsburgh lay directly on the route to the farther lands. It was the last place where the immigrants could purchase supplies before they "jumped off," as it were, into the unknown wilderness.

"You'll hardly believe how many stores have sprung up," Hugh was saying, "even in the last few months. Nineteen we have now, by actual count! Two bakeries, a ropewalk, a gold and silversmith—though how he's going to make a living I wouldn't know. And of course the printshop. I want you to see that and meet my men. It's just back here at Ferry and Water. Can you come now?"

"Let's make it afternoon, shall we? I really ought to see Elliott first. Can you keep a secret, Hugh?"

"I've been known to."

"Well, I've got an idea. It may be years before I can carry it out, but when I can get shed of this contracting business I want to get into manufacturing. Some day *I'm going to make glass!*"

"Glass?" Hugh said. "Did I hear you right?"

"You did. I'm sick unto death of oiled paper window panes, and what's more to the point with me, so is Mary. They're a continual annoyance to her. I don't know how long it will be before I get to this but I plan about it every night out in the wilderness before I go to sleep. I'm going to buy up some land soon over here at the foot of Coal Hill. Good place, I figure."

"Well," said Hugh, "if you're set on it, I guess it's as good as done but may the devil admire me if it isn't the craziest scheme I've ever heard. Why the secrecy?"

O'Hara grinned. "I don't want any other man to get the idea first."

Hugh roared. "On that I think you're pretty safe. No other fool big enough, I'd say."

Mary came out and went on to do some shopping; O'Hara made his way to his own store and since there were no customers at the moment he and Elliott settled for a chat.

"How's business?" O'Hara asked.

"It's damned good. More strangers goin' through here now than you'd believe. We're makin' money."

"Well, that's the object. Do you think we could put prices up a bit?"

"I was just goin' to suggest that. You can check over things while you're here. How long are you stayin'?"

"Three weeks or more. I never know how long it will take to raise the supplies."

"Run any more boats aground?"

O'Hara gave him a sharp look and then laughed. "You're the only man I'd take that question from. It's still a sore spot. No, I've been pretty lucky these last months. I've been able to get cattle out there, one way or another, and that seems to impress the Commissioners. I needn't tell you it's a tough job though. It takes all the ingenuity I've got."

"How's the Injun business goin'?"

O'Hara shook his head. "I don't think it's going at all. And the worst of it is that it may be years before the Commissioners realise it. We've all gone from post to post while they've made treaty after treaty . . ."

"I can see it," said Elliott. "The Injuns all sittin' around in their best beads an' feathers an' noddin' an' takin' their presents an' goin' off, an' God only knows what's in their skulls."

"Right. Elliott, do you know about Gnadenhutten?"

"Yep. I know all about it."

"Why didn't you ever tell me?"

"We was both down in the south when it happened. By the time I got the story he was separated. It's all past anyway."

"I want to hear it. It's one of the pieces of this whole ghastly picture. Go ahead. I want to know."

"Well, to put it in a nutshell things had been pretty bad for the settlers round north an' a little west of here. Plenty killed. One man's wife an' children all taken; so after that, they got about eighty men together an' set out for Gnadenhutten on the Muskingum, where the Moravians lived. *They'd* all got converted somehow an' they was peaceful but the settlers found out that the warriors that did the depredatin' had their winter quarters in this village. To clinch it, when they got there, one of the men in the party who'd lost his wife found her clothes in one of their houses. They were pretty bloody. Well, I guess I know what *you'd* have done under them circumstances."

"I guess I do," O'Hara gritted.

"Well, they done it, all right. Killed every man, woman an' child of them. A fella that was along told me about it. Said he got pretty sick before they was through for them Moravians was prayin' to Jesus Christ while they died."

There was silence for a minute, then Elliott went on. "I s'pose you heard about the next raid out to Sandusky. Colonel Crawford's?"

"I heard what happened to him."

"I guess everybody has. An' while the Injuns were killin' him by slow torture Simon Girty was sittin' on a log watchin' it. Crawford kept beggin', 'Shoot me, Girty, for God's sake, shoot me!' An' this fella that got away said Girty just laughed an' said, 'Sorry, Colonel, I haven't got a gun.' An' I'll tell you what was back of *that*!"

"What?"

"Why, some good while ago, Girty took an' awful shine to one of Crawford's daughters. He went to the house one night full of business an' Crawford showed him the door, pretty definite. There was enough Injun in Girty to make him want revenge. He had to wait a while but he got it, all right. Well, there are a few more pieces for you. If you can fit them together you're a better man than I am."

"I think I'll go take a walk," O'Hara said, getting up. "Has everything been quiet round here? Indians, I mean?"

"Why, pretty much. Course we get some bad stories from the settlers as they come in, but here in town we've had no call to take our guns off the hooks."

"I worry about being away. Would you be willing to sleep in the house?"

"Sure. Only not in that fancy guest room. I can be mighty comfortable on the kitchen floor. I don't look for no trouble here at all, but if ever there was any, well as to your wife—my life for hers any time."

He held out his hand in a rare gesture and O'Hara grasped it, then stepped out into the sun, his eyes misty.

The wedding day was fine, bright and midsummer mellow. Mary had been busy since they had seen Hugh ride away, dressed in his best. At her suggestion their wedding gift was a pretty set of dishes from the store which she now arranged to their best advantage on the dresser. From her linens she made up the bridal bed, set on the mantel a pair of candlesticks from her own wedding gifts, and surveyed it all with satisfaction.

"From what Hugh told me confidentially," she said to O'Hara as he stopped for her, "this may seem almost elegant to Maria compared to her parents' cabin."

"Could be. It looks cosy enough. I hope the marriage goes well, for in a way I feel responsible."

The supper next evening for the newly-weds presented a problem. Should she, Mary asked her husband, array the table with her best Philadelphia silver and crystal which Hugh had often seen, or with her plainer settings in order not to overcome the bride by luxury unknown to her? They both decided that for Hugh's sake they should use the best they had to do honour to the occasion. So when the guests finally appeared *at the parlour door* (after being out of sight all day) they found a gleaming table awaiting them. Hugh's swift glance towards it justified the earlier decision.

Maria was in the main a pleasant surprise. She was prettier than either O'Hara or Mary had expected and on her the usual frontier linen dress and folded white neckerchief were becoming. Her dark eyes sparkled, she laughed easily and there was about her a certain alertness which bespoke an active mind. But her few remarks showed frequent lapses of English, her hands were rough and reddened by farm work and her movements had an uneasy awkwardness as though she was, quite naturally, embarrassed at meeting her husband's fine friends.

Dinner conversation was fairly easy with Mary keeping up a cheerful line of small talk and O'Hara and Hugh filling in with light comments as they could. The state of the refurbished cabin was discussed at length with Maria expressing her pleasure in it. But when they all sat down for the evening a heavy quiet fell. Mary with a side glance at her husband conveyed the fact that she had done all she could by way of verbal exchange; Hugh, the eloquent, the ever talkative, now sat in a sort of bemused and wordless surprise, with constant possessive glances towards Maria, while she in her turn was smilingly and continuously silent.

O'Hara cleared his throat and clutched at an inspiration.

"I've just thought of something," he said. "This would be a perfect time to present a problem I've been considering. Here is a lawyer and here are two intelligent ladies to voice their opinions. How about it?"

"Go ahead. Shoot!" said Brackenridge.

"It was Eb Denny who raised the question in my mind. You met him, Hugh, when he was going through here?"

"Yes. Fine chap."

"Mary liked him too. He is now with the Commissioners. Does your wife know of their work, and mine?" O'Hara asked.

"Oh, yes. I've told her all about it," Hugh said.

"Well, here are the facts. There was to be a parley at Fort Finney on the Miami River. Captain Beatty, the paymaster, got sick on the way down so he turned the money over to me and went back. I always have with me everywhere, a big line of articles for the Indians in case they are needed, so I picked out all the things I thought would interest the troops and after I had paid the men I spread out my wares in front of them. They bought everything I had! So, as Eb Denny pointed out, half in a joke, I brought back with me about the same amount of money I took out. Now, was there anything wrong in that? What do you say, Hugh?"

Brackenridge laughed and slapped his thigh.

"You're a good one, O'Hara. That was the neatest trick of the year. But," he went on seriously, "you were entirely within your legal rights. You didn't even urge them to buy, did you?"

"Heavens, no! They were all bored to death and they fell on the articles like children."

"Your prices were reasonable?"

"They were, indeed."

"Well, I give you a clean bill on that. You were just confoundedly clever to think of it. What do you say, Mary?"

"As long as the men were satisfied . . ."

"Oh, I give you my word they were! And now, Mrs. Brackenridge, what are your sentiments?"

Maria looked embarrassed, glanced towards her husband and shook her head.

"Oh, come," said O'Hara. "I would like to hear from you. Pro or con. Please!"

"Go ahead, Maria," Hugh said, "speak up!"

"Were the troops mostly married men?" she asked hesitantly.

"I imagine so."

"With families?"

"Very likely," O'Hara said, a faint colour rising in his cheeks.

"Their pay I s'pose usually went to their wives. It's awful hard, like, for a woman with her man away. An' her with little childer mebbe. So I thought . . ." She gave a frightened glance towards Hugh. "I just thought mebbe you shouldn't ought to have tempted the men to spend their money."

There was a second of hushed silence during which Hugh turned scarlet. But O'Hara went across suddenly to Maria and held out his hand.

"Thank you," he said, "for saying honestly what you thought. And I wouldn't be surprised if you came nearer the truth than the rest of us."

They all, except Maria, put forth a sudden effort at conversation on other subjects then, Hugh apparently feeling more responsible than before to carry his end of it. So he spoke now of the coming newspaper and the two young easterners, John Scull and Joseph Hall, whom he had persuaded to come from Philadelphia to Pittsburgh for this adventure.

"Hall isn't a very rugged man. I hope our winter here won't be too hard on him. Scull is tough as a nut. He'll carry the biggest load. Everybody is excited about the paper, but whether they'll pay their subscriptions remains to be seen. Well, it's a start anyway, like our church foundation. You've seen that, O'Hara?"

"Yes, John Wilkins and I inspected it yesterday. He's going

to work on the building himself. I wish I were here more to help. I'm glad it's going to be a sizeable structure. Even if it's only a log one with a good oak floor and walnut pews it will have some dignity. And I'm going to hold out for a good strong ceiling if I pay for it myself."

"I'm so glad they left the big oak tree at the front," Mary said. "I can picture people coming out of church in the summer and standing under it to discuss the sermon and . . . and everything."

"Chiefly the *everything*, I imagine," Hugh said, smiling, "but I stipulated that the tree should stand. Well, Maria, I think we must be leaving after a very delightful evening."

There were hearty good wishes and congratulations and Mary impulsively kissed the bride who whispered, "I'm glad you're going to be nigh-hand me. You can tell me things."

When the new couple were lost to sight in the summer darkness O'Hara turned to his wife.

"Well, what do you think of her?"

"I like her," Mary said slowly. "After a year in Philadelphia she'll be a very charming person. And I think she can stand up to Hugh if she needs to."

O'Hara laughed. "So you feel my friend might be a bit dictatorial?"

"Perhaps, but she'll manage him. The one thing I *didn't* like about her was her criticism of you."

O'Hara sobered instantly. "Well, frankly I didn't either but she may have been right. I didn't tell quite all the story. I had liquor to sell too. The general gave the troops permission to buy it and toleration to get drunk if it didn't interfere with their duty. Lord, how they responded! For three days there wasn't a sober man in the garrison. But there again I was within my legal rights. The general himself gave me permission to sell and at first I was pleased over the whole transaction."

He stopped and then said with a wry smile, "Until Eb Denny said, 'Well, O'Hara, between the wet and the dry you're going to take back as much as you brought.' And that was true, except for the officers' pay. It's hard for me to resist a chance to make money, if it's honest, and I made a good deal on this. But after Eb's speech I had a twinge of conscience, and Maria added to it."

They put out the downstairs candles and went up to their room. Once there O'Hara said, "Dear Delight, it's so illogical of me. I want *you* to criticise me when you feel you should, only . . ."

"Only you would rather I didn't?" she smiled.

"I'm afraid that's the amount of it. Let's just say I'll try not to give you cause."

On the evening of the twenty-ninth, a group of men gathered in the print shop at Ferry and Water streets with a bowl of negus as a treat on the table. There was of course Brackenridge himself, O'Hara, John Ormsby, Isaac Craig, Presley Neville, Devereux Smith, and John Wilkins, together with the two young printers, Scull and Hall. It was by way of being a send-off for the first issue of *The Pittsburgh Gazette*. Hugh did most of the talking.

"We want your support for this project and we hope you'll discuss it with all your friends. We intend to give you each a sample copy to-night so you can peruse it before you sleep." He pointed to the bench behind him where, neatly stacked, lay the first papers, four pages each, ten by sixteen inches in size, printed with care on the hand press the young editors had brought over the mountains.

"Each week we'll try to have some foreign news. Who of us wouldn't give half a guinea to know what is going on at Smyrna and Amsterdam or how many armies are on foot in Europe? Then closer home in our own state," he went on, "heretofore we haven't known much about what our representatives were doing. Like boys creeping into a haystack we could only see their heels while their heads were hid away amongst the cabals of Philadelphia. Well, we hope to remedy that, and to-night we invite you to give us suggestions for general subjects to be included. For most of our subscribers, as you know, have no reading matter except the Bible and an almanac and we trust the *Gazette* will be an educational influence in their lives."

The negus went down in the bowl as the men voiced their opinions. There should be articles on religion, politics, agriculture, essays in praise of this or dispraise of that . . .

"And don't forget," O'Hara said, "to sprinkle a few witty anecdotes through the pages to brighten them up."

The men all laughed for O'Hara's own lambent wit was more or less proverbial.

At the end of the evening there was one glass left for each man. Hugh raised his. "To the success of *The Pittsburgh Gazette!*" he said. And the men drank the toast with heartiness.

Until O'Hara left again with his supplies, his days were full from dawn till dark. But as he worked his mind was busy also on his own affairs. He wanted to buy up more lots. He pointed out to Mary one evening the sketch he had made of the Woods plan.

"Here at the fort is the apex, you see. Now, the only place the town can expand due to the rivers is at the back here on the legs of the triangle, as it were. So I'm going to buy up land at both sides in order not to lose out, no matter which direction the march of progress takes." He laughed as he said it.

"You're so clever, James."

"There's another thing. I wanted our first house to be here in the King's Orchard. A log one was all I could afford at the time but in a few years I can build you a bigger one."

"But I love this one."

"I know, but you'll love another one still more. There's no question in my mind but that the best residential section is going to be along Water Street. You know where Major Kilpatrick's house is now?"

"Yes. It's a nice one."

"Well, I hope to build one next to his, finer yet. The best for you, Mary."

She considered. "That would be along the Monongahela and I like the Allegheny so much better."

"So do I, really. But the view from the place I've picked out is worth the change in rivers. You see, darling, we will want a bigger house one day."

"You guessed then?" she said, surprised.

"Guessed what?" he asked quickly.

"I've been afraid of upsetting you but I think there is a chance for little *James* by another spring."

He stared at her in dismay.

"Don't look that way," she said. "Aren't you pleased?"

"The question is whether *you* are."

"But of course I am. I'm happy about it. I want a big family."

"Women are brave," he said under his breath.

"Don't worry. All my friends here tell me the second is much easier than the first. And I lived through that."

"But to be away from you so much just now! Oh, that will be distressing."

"Well," Mary rejoined, "it distresses me, too. But I'll tell you something, Mr. O'Hara, if it doesn't make you vain."

He leaned over and laid his cheek against her hair.

"I'd rather be married to you, even if you're away most of the time, than to any other man who was always with me."

They walked slowly along Water Street the next Sunday, past Major Kilpatrick's fine house.

"There," O'Hara said, "you see these lots just next to his? They're the ones I have my eye on. If you like the location I'll take an option on them at once. Look at the view!"

It was a nearer and more magnificent vista of the marriage of the rivers than they had from the Orchard and while the Monongahela did not have the clear swiftness of the Allegheny nor the bordering locust trees, it too, was a great rolling stream and edged by spreading sycamores.

"It's a beautiful spot!" Mary said.

O'Hara made an expansive gesture. "No more logs! A big frame structure is what I have in mind, with a stable and carriage house too. After all I've begun to make money and I expect to make a great deal more before I'm through. And," he added quickly, "in the doing of it I hope to serve my country and help my city grow. I'm really not as selfish as I sound."

As they walked back home Mary spoke seriously. "James," she said, "I wish you would take me into your confidence about your business affairs."

He looked at her in amazement. "Why, darling, it never occurred to me you would want to be bothered with such things."

"But I would," she said. "And it wouldn't be a bother. I might even be able to help you in some small ways. I'm not a merchant's daughter for nothing and I'm really rather good at accounts."

"I know that. I've seen your housekeeping ones. To-night, if you like, we'll sit down together and go over all my . . . my *assets*," he said, laughing.

At bedtime when they had finished, O'Hara looked up at her in mock gravity.

"It's not fair," he said. "It's definitely not fair."

"What isn't?" she asked in alarm.

"For any young woman to be as beautiful as you and still have a business head on her!"

The next morning early O'Hara went to see Dr. Bedford whose generous house stood along the Monongahela where Water Street ended in country. He had to wait a few minutes in the small office and while he paced the floor he stopped now and then to read again one of the framed diplomas on the wall as though to give him courage.

> *London, April 3rd, 1770* [1]
> These are to certify that Mr. Nathaniel Bedford
> hath diligently attended our Lectures on the
> Theory & Practice of Midwifery and on the
> diseases of Women and Children.

WM. MOORE   THOS. DEBMAN

When the doctor came in he was brisk, cheerful and discerning as usual.

"Well, you've done pretty well with your timing. Better than I expected."

"You know why I'm here?" O'Hara asked in surprise.

"My dear young man, it's written all over your wife as plain as a pikestaff. We doctors can read the signs. Now, what's bothering you at the moment?"

"It's my having to be away so much during these coming months," he burst out. "I'll have to go on with my contracting . . ."

"I should hope so. A man has to do his work and a woman has to bear the children. The Lord ordained it that way from the beginning. I don't quite see how you could further the matter now if you were at home. May be as well if you're away, as a matter of fact."

O'Hara removed some bills from his pocket and quietly slid them across the desk.

"I know a woman doesn't see the doctor until her . . . her time has come but in this case I wondered if you would be willing to stop in once in a while and check . . . just be sure everything is all right?"

Dr. Bedford as quietly slid the bills back towards O'Hara.

"Why, I'll do that, Captain. Always a pleasure to talk to your wife. I wonder if you know what a spot of brightness she makes in this town. Mrs. Bedford was at her quilting and what a party that was apparently! Just the *élite* there, of course. But your wife makes everybody welcome, high and low. I know, for I hear about it from some of these poor bedraggled critters when I go round amongst them. Do you know what they do when they get

---

[1] This diploma hangs now in Carnegie Library's Pennsylvania room in Pittsburgh.

to the end of their rope? Well, they go to your kitchen, Captain, and your wife gives them tea and talks to them and cheers them up and by the time they get home they think they've been to Philadelphia and back."

Dr. Bedford held out his hand.

"Glad to keep an eye on Mistress O'Hara. Maybe she'll give *me* a dish of tea betimes. So get along with your business. It's pretty important."

As O'Hara made his way from one gristmill to another along the rivers he had an idea one day. If he owned a gristmill himself and made his own flour he would have one steady source he could count upon. He could sell his output to the Government at the same price other mills charged *and*, here he smiled to himself, make a good deal of money doing it! He studied each mill at which he stopped and finally decided upon the largest of these about three miles down the Ohio. It was in good condition but the owner was not young and at that moment looked hot and weary. Would he be interested, O'Hara asked him, in selling the mill at a good price if he were kept on at a salary to run it?

"And with another man perhaps to help you," O'Hara added. "This is a pretty big job, and I think we could make it still bigger."

The miller stared at his questioner in amazement, then slowly, each feeling his way, the bargaining began. John West, the owner, showed O'Hara around the property, pointing out the great wheel, the smaller cogs, the solid granite foundation.

"My father built this mill," he said, "and I've kept it in good order. I dress my own mill stones," he added proudly, "but I'm getting along and no son to come after me!"

In the end O'Hara had the mill, or would have when he brought his first payment, and West was hard put to it to conceal his satisfaction. He would get an assistant and then would have to turn no grain away.

"No, no," O'Hara said, "never do that! I want the output of flour doubled if you can. We've got a market for it."

Within a few days of his leaving O'Hara had a strong feeling of accomplishment. Once again a great flatboat was loaded with supplies but at this season the waters would be safe. On his own account he not only owned a gristmill but he had bought ten lots on the legs of the triangle and had an option on the two on Water Street. Greatest food of all to his ambition was the purchase of a parcel of land at the foot of Coal Hill across the Monongahela.

There, he thought to himself, *as soon as ever I can get to it I'll start Pittsburgh's first real manufacturing. I'll make my glass if it breaks me!*

He woke very early the second day before he was to set off. He raised himself on one elbow and looked his fill at Mary's sleeping beauty as the first light came hesitantly through the oiled paper panes. Prudence was not yet stirring he knew, and yet his trained ear caught small sounds at the kitchen door. He threw his clothes on quickly and went down. It was Elliott.

"Get your gun, O'Hara. There's trouble an' I think we've got to go," he said in a low voice.

"What is it?"

"It's Porter. You know the fellah we got the pill for? He's over at Semple's an' he's as near crazy as he can get. His boy's took an' his wife . . ."

Elliott made a swift gesture across the top of his head. "He wants us to go back an' help him."

"What can we do now? The Injuns will be gone far enough by this time."

Elliott swallowed. "He wants us to bury his wife for one thing. He says he can't, an' his brother's laid up sick again."

"I'll be with you in a minute."

O'Hara went up to the bedroom and leaned over Mary.

"I have to leave early, darling. I'll be home as soon as I can. You go back to sleep."

He went down, took his rifle from its hooks and joined Elliott.

"Semple's up. He says he'll give us a bite of breakfast before we start."

The men did not speak again until they reached the tavern. Here they found Porter shaking as if from palsy and Semple trying to force whisky into him.

"Drink up, man! It'll settle you. You can't go on like this!"

O'Hara took the glass and spoke to the white-faced man before him.

"Porter, we're going back with you to do what we can. Try to pull yourself together." He held the glass close while he grasped one of Porter's hands in his own. "Drink it," he said, and then added to Semple, "Something hot if we can have it."

"We can't wait," Porter broke in. "They may come back and take her."

"No," Elliott said, "I can promise you, they won't do that.

We'll get on our way soon but we'll all need something in our bellies first."

During the meal, when even Semple was speechless, the silence was broken only once.

"She didn't want to come out here," Porter said quaveringly. "She only done it to please me because I was so set on it. She never wanted to come." And it was O'Hara's face then that turned white.

The three men rode through the dawn, tense and watchful, O'Hara beside Porter, Elliott behind. Little by little the distracted man told his story. It had happened the afternoon before while he had been in one of his cleared fields a little distance from the cabin. He had heard screams and come running. His wife lay dead, scalped, at the back doorstep; the boy was gone. At first he had been so sick he could do nothing even with the little children's terrified crying behind him. When he was able to stand up he had called and called for the boy until he realised that the Indians must have captured him. Then he had taken the younger ones over to his brother's and returned to sit by his wife's body until he had determined to come for help. Even now, as he finished, a hard retching shook him.

"What can I do now, Mr. O'Hara?" he asked when he could speak. "I'd take the little 'uns an' go back to Philadelphy to-morrow, but how can I leave my boy with the savages?"

"Don't think of this at the moment, Porter. We'll talk it all over later. Just keep a sharp eye out now to your right and ahead of us. We may be in plenty of danger ourselves."

But they reached the cabin in safety. Even before he had seen the ghastly work of the marauders at the back, O'Hara felt a sharp pang as he looked at the small home before him: the rude logs, felled and put together by a man's bare hands; the little clearing, wrested from the wild, with its precious crop; the signs of all the hardship of daily struggle against the threat and encroachment of the forest. Why? *Why* did men leave safety and comfort and cross the mountains for this? But even as he asked himself the question, his own heart answered it.

Elliott got off his horse and came close to O'Hara. "I've seen this before but you haven't. It ain't pretty. Keep your teeth tight shut and look away as much as you can."

They tied the horses and followed Porter around to the back step. There at the sight of what lay before them O'Hara turned quickly, a terrible nausea overwhelming him. With a tremendous effort of will he mastered it, gritted his teeth and fastened his gaze on the lower part of the woman's body. Elliott was taking charge.

"Have you got a clean sheet, Porter, or a blanket or anything?"

Porter brought a sheet, his hands shaking as he held it out.

"She'd just ironed yesterday."

"You go off to the clearing now an' work as hard as you can. We'll do what has to be done, an' then we'll call you."

They found a shovel and another digging tool in the small shed, and when they had selected a spot on the opposite side from the clearing, Elliott and O'Hara began their work. They dug the grave deep and when it was done they wrapped the woman's body in the sheet and lowered it as gently as they could into its resting place. O'Hara was thinking of her face, a lovely face indeed, as he had last seen it, raised in a white agony of supplication. Elliott was evidently remembering the same.

"She prayed hard enough to save him," he said. "But I guess there wasn't anyone round to pray for her when she needed it."

"There's got to be a prayer here to-day," O'Hara said. "There's got to be."

"Well, you'll have to make it, then. It ain't in my line an' you can't expect Porter to do it."

They filled the grave, making its surface flat with the forest floor, and then deftly with their hands scattering over it bits of dried leaves and withered acorns, moss and twigs that made the summer carpet. At the head of it they stuck a living branch. Except for that it was indistinguishable.

"I'll go an' fetch Porter now an' you can be thinkin' up something to say."

O'Hara's mind was distraught. To utter any words of his own before Porter and Elliott would be to him intolerable. And try as he would he could remember no other except the Lord's Prayer and he knew his control would not hold out for the length of that. Just as the others returned the last words of the burial service came suddenly to him.

The three men stood in silence beside the leafy bough. Porter drew a long shuddering breath and then straightened as though the outward sign of the inevitability of earth as the mother of all had in a measure steadied him. And then O'Hara spoke.

"May she rest in peace, and may light perpetual shine upon her soul."

They sat for a little while inside the cabin, needing the rest and the corn pone Porter offered them.

"It's the boy we've got to think of now," he said. "What can we do about my son?" The words were anguished.

"How old is he?" Elliott asked.

"Just bare eight."

Elliott looked off through the door.

"Tell you what we'll do. You've had about all you can take for one day. You get along over to your brother's an' stay there while O'Hara, here, and me hunts round in the woods to see if we can pick up a trail or anything."

They saw Porter, pathetically submissive, ride away, his face still stony white but his hands able to grasp the reins. When he was gone Elliott voiced his opinion.

"If that's all the age the boy is I'd say he's gone with his mother by this time."

"You mean they haven't captured him?"

"Doubt it. If he was older they'd take him all the way. But a little chap like this would likely cry an' if he couldn't keep up with them they'd knock him on the head an' go on. Leastwise that's the way they mostly do. If we go out through the forest, with any luck we'll find him."

"Ride or walk?"

"Have to ride. I'm afraid to leave the horses here. You see there may still be some of the devils lurkin' round. I don't just relish this job. If I was sure the little chap was safe dead . . ."

"What do you mean?"

"We wouldn't need to bother then. But they could have hit him an' . . . O'Hara, why don't you stay here an' behave yourself an' let me see what I can find. I've got nothing to lose, live or die, an' you've got a damned lot."

"You mean the child might be lying out there, still alive?"

"Well, there's a chance of it."

"Come on then. We've no time to waste."

They bestrode their horses and set off into the forest warily, every moment on their guard, watching for the faintest sign which might indicate which way the Indians had passed. They turned in this direction and that, their eyes sharp, their ears quickened. But there was only the strange pulsing sound which is not sound, the silence of the wilderness.

It was two hours later when Elliott got off his horse and peered at the ground. What he saw was only a folded leaf and a broken twig. He held up his hand and O'Hara joined him. Their long training gave them discernment as they walked slowly along, leading the horses. Other subtle signs appeared. They felt sure they were on the trail. And then, suddenly they found what they were seeking. The child's body lay to the side of their path, his small tear-stained face showing white against the forest floor. But the blow had been strong enough. There was no life in him.

It was O'Hara who carried him back in front of him on Pitt. It was his eyes that were wet as once again he and Elliott did their unspeakably hard task. When at last all was finished the two men rode over to the cabin of Porter's brother without speaking until they drew up at the door.

"You're better with words than me, O'Hara," Elliott said. "I guess you'll have to tell him."

But the telling was not as hard as they feared. Porter met them, his face distorted with anguish.

"You didn't find him?"

"Yes, Mr. Porter, we found him. We brought him back and did . . . what must needs be done. It was a blow that killed him apparently. I'm sure he knew nothing afterwards."

"He wasn't . . . not like her?"

"No."

Porter moved back and sank into a chair beside the table. "I guess I'm thankful it was that. If they'd taken him I'd never have slept thinkin' of him so little among the savages, mebbe abused, an' him lost an' homesick for his mother. Now, he's with her an' he's safe. I'll stand it some way."

He dropped his head upon his arms, his shoulders shaking, but no sound coming from him.

The family was stricken quiet but the woman set hot mush before Elliott and O'Hara, which they were glad to eat. Before they left Porter stood up to bid them good-bye.

"I can't even thank you for what you done to-day. I might ha' gone clear crazy if I'd had it to do myself. An' I've never paid you your pound yet," he added to O'Hara.

"Just forget it. I don't need it. What will you do now?"

"I'll take the little 'uns an' go back where I come from. I've a sister there will look after them. I'll mebbe wait till I can sell the cabin." His voice broke on the words.

"Oh, he'll sell it all right," his brother spoke from the bed.

"They keep comin' out here all the time. God knows why. Many's the time I've wished . . . 'Course if I didn't get these doncy spells every once in a while we'd get on pretty good, unless . . . unless . . ." His eyes rested on his brother and the words trailed off.

It was sunset now as the two men rode back along the river. They took the hours in silence as the darkness overcame them. It was when they entered the town that O'Hara reined Pitt while the words burst from him.

"Elliott, I can't do it! Not after all I've seen to-day. I won't go off and leave my wife and child in danger. I'll break my contract with the Government. Someone else can supply the troops. I tell you *I won't go!*"

There were only two lights visible in the little town. One was at the tavern, the other in a cabin where one could guess Dr. Bedford was ushering in a new life.

"Well now," Elliott drawled at last, "might be worth while to think this over a little. First place I can tell you this. I know the Injuns about as well as any man does an' I can promise you they won't come into the town here. Not now."

"What about Hannastown?" O'Hara asked sharply.

"All right. What about it? It wasn't a town like Pittsburgh is. The men there worked out in their fields. The day it was burnt every last son of a gun of them was out helpin' Mike Huffnagle take in his harvest. Now here there's business to keep the men in the town every day. The Injuns know that. Another thing . . ." He paused.

"Such as what?"

"Well, it's kinda hard to put. You an' me both believe these parleys an' treaties ain't goin' to solve the whole problem. But while they're goin' on they certain sure keep a good few Injuns round these parts out of mischief. A good many lives may get saved by them in the meanwhile. Do you get what I mean? An' you're a pretty big part of this treaty business. Well, go home an' think it over. An' don't forget I'm sleepin' in the kitchen every night you're away. If you go," he added.

O'Hara made no reply for a long minute, then he said, "You're a good man, Elliott."

"Same to you," Elliott answered and turned towards the tavern.

O'Hara dismounted quickly and handed him the rein. "Take my horse along, will you? I'll walk home."

The house was dark and silent when he reached it. He went

into the kitchen, lighted a candle and then stood by the fireplace leaning his head against the mantel. He was shaken as he had never been before in his life. The ghastly experiences of the day had stripped him of his normal strength. He felt too weak, too distraught to make a decision and yet it had to be made. Remade, rather, for his mind had been fully settled as he rode the miles between the cabin and the town. Yet he knew Elliott spoke the truth in so far as any man could apprehend it. He knew too, that his work was important and realised without vanity that no other man would be able to do it as well. General Harmar and the Commissioners had often told him this. The hard discipline of fact and of duty bore down steadily, irresistibly upon him as the minutes passed. He would have to go.

But even as he knew it he saw again the body of Porter's wife as it lay on the doorstep. Would he ever be able to forget that sight? He heard again Porter's words which had pierced his own heart: *She never wanted to come. She only did it because of me!*

"Oh God! Oh God! *Oh God!*" he cried aloud, and it was a prayer of supplication.

At last he blew out the candle, went softly upstairs and undressed in the dark. With his first movements near her Mary woke.

"James, are you back at last? I tried to wait up for you but I got so sleepy. Was it a hard day for you?"

He didn't reply at once and she asked him again.

"Was it a hard day, darling?"

"A little," he said, as he drew her close.

Chapter Eleven

Mary and her women advisers had been right. Little James entered this world with a minimum of trouble for his mother. O'Hara had planned his trips with care so that he would be home for the event and was now happy, proud and relieved.

"And I can go on and have my *six*?" Mary asked him roguishly.

He laughed. "I'm not Providence."

"You come close to it. I only hope," she added, glancing at the cradle, "that the times will grow settled and that there will be peace for our children to grow up in. How are things going now? Please tell me the truth. You always evade my questions."

"It's largely because I don't know how to answer. Most of the tribes come to meet with the Commissioners and there are speeches from our men and speeches from the chiefs, White-Eyes, Captain Pipe and so on. No sign yet of Guyasuta, by the way. Then the Indians take their presents and go off. The Shawnees are the ones we're most anxious to pin down to a treaty but they keep hanging back. General Harmar, I may say, is considerably discouraged. But, we'll see. Don't worry your little head about it all."

"How can I help it, when you're in the thick of it? I'd like to know more details about your work too. I thought you were taking me on as a partner in your affairs."

He bent over and kissed her. "I am," he said, "but in another line."

When they finished laughing Mary persisted in her questioning. "Can't you be specific about what you do? You come back here, are away most of the days and then leave, and that's all I know."

"Well, let's see. Maybe this would seem more concrete to you. As of the present the daily ration for each soldier is eighteen ounces of bread or flour. If I run short of that I use a quart of rice or a pound and a half of Indian meal. Then each man gets a pound and a quarter of fresh beef a day or a pound of salted beef or three-quarters of a pound of salted pork. When fresh meat is issued we have to provide salt to keep it and that means two quarts for every hundred rations. Soap is at the rate of four pounds per hundred rations and candles a pound and a half. So that's the way it is. I have to know how much is needed for each post for say, three months in advance, and provide it."

Mary's eyes were wide. "Somehow this makes me realise more than ever before what an enormous job it is and how wonderful you are, darling."

"I like business," he smiled. "If I didn't have to be away from home so much I'd really be enjoying all this. It's a challenge and no mistake. The easiest thing to provide is the liquor. When the officer orders it the men get half a gill of rum or whisky. That and the flour I can get around here, locally. The candles and soap come mostly from New York. The meat is the hardest. I intend while I'm back here this time to ride down into Kentucky and see if I can buy a herd of cattle. I can pick up some men there I know to take them out. I'd like to get them to Detroit and fatten them there. Of course there is always the problem, too, of pack-horses for the wilderness and boats for the rivers depending upon where we're heading. I should have told you that for every ration 1 receive one cent. As my contract says, 'for full compensation for the trouble and expense in issuing the same.' And it counts up, darling! I'm making money! Well, enough for now of my business. Let's look at my namesake."

More even than a year ago O'Hara was conscious of the changes in Pittsburgh itself and drank in the signs of growth and new activity. Flatboats and keelboats were more numerous along the wharf, new taverns and stores had sprung up it seemed on every corner, and on the cultural side, the Presbyterian congregation was now incorporated by legislative act, and the log building completed with the Reverend Samuel Parr installed as the first pastor. More extraordinary still perhaps was the incorporation of the *Pittsburgh Academy* with a fine list of trustees, a tract of five thousand acres in the wilderness and the block of lots bounded by Smithfield Street, Cherry Alley and Second and Third Avenues. Hugh Brackenridge was full of this latter triumph when he brought Maria over one afternoon to call upon the new baby and its parents.

Although Mary had prepared him somewhat O'Hara was still startled at the change in Maria. She wore a modish dress, was now free from embarrassment and self-consciousness, and made few slips in her English. Her bright eyes attested to the eager mind which had made her improvement possible. *So!* O'Hara thought to himself, *my suggestion was a good one.*

Hugh, as usual, was full of talk and filled in the news O'Hara had not heard.

"Yes, we've really made the first start for the Academy. In another year or two we'll get some sort of building ready and a principal and then we'll open."

"How was the Legislature, Hugh?"

"Oh, so-so. I enjoyed it and I suppose I'll always be in and out of politics. I'm changing my views though. At first I was a Federalist through and through. I wanted a strong central government like Alexander Hamilton, but I'm getting interested in this new Democratic-Republican party that Thomas Jefferson is starting. Well, at any rate the Constitution has been adopted. That's the biggest piece of news."

"Ah," said O'Hara. "That's wonderful. Now if we can elect a President . . ."

"Are you for Washington?"

"I certainly am. Who else could be thought of?"

"Well, I've heard John Adams spoken of here and there."

"Capable man but nothing to Washington."

"Of course after those dozen champagne glasses he gave you for a wedding present you'd have to stand by the general!" Hugh laughed. "Come on. Let's leave the girls to gossip while we look over the town."

Once outside the Orchard O'Hara turned towards The Point. The noble old Fort was falling steadily into disrepair. Its bastions were breached, its turrets toppling.

"Well, its glory has departed, sure enough," Hugh said meditatively, "and it can never be rebuilt. What the town needs now is a smaller fort near the centre which can really be manned in an emergency."

O'Hara looked at the great fortress with narrowed eyes. "Good bricks there. I think when the teardown really comes I'll buy them."

"I wouldn't doubt it," said Hugh. "What for?"

"This town could stand a nice neat row of brick houses. Give it tone. Yes, I think I'll see to that."

"Anything else on your mind at present?" Hugh's voice was ironical but O'Hara didn't seem to notice.

"Yes," he said. "I'm going to try to get a sawmill started while

I'm here. With all the increased building—boats and houses too—
the place can stand another one. Then later on when I can
manage it, I think I may build a brewery! Down here on The Point
wherever I can get the land. After all, drinkables are a big product
around these parts, and the one most easily marketed east or south.
Wouldn't you say so?"

"I'd say something more. There's a greater amount of drunkenness round here than the East would ever dream of. But O'Hara,
there's a little cloud gathering. No bigger than a man's hand yet,
but by crickey some day it's going to make trouble."

"What's that?"

"Taxes," he said. "We're a new country and we're in debt.
Back east they're sniffing round every corner to see how money can
be raised. I've heard more than one man say, 'What about all
this whisky coming in from the Back Country? How about an
excise on that?' Well, it won't come for a few years, maybe, but
some day, we'll be in for it."

"But the farmers can't send their wheat and rye back east as
grain! The only way they can market it is after they distil it!"

"I know. I'm only telling you what's in the wind. Come on,
and I'll show you what Marie has done to his new tavern this
summer. And I'll buy you a glass of whisky, speaking of the
stuff."

They moved slowly through the town, O'Hara stopping often
to greet those he passed: old Major Kilpatrick, still jaunty at ninety
with his knee breeches and cocked hat: Dennis Lochy, the blind
ballad singer who improvised a few lines for his benefit.

*"In songs and rhymes I'll sing the praise
Of Captain O'Hara all my days."*

O'Hara dropped some coins in his hat as Brackenridge muttered,
"Well, I've heard him do better."

"Probably with a better subject," O'Hara grinned, and then
he raised his hand in quick salute as General John Neville's commanding figure emerged from a store. It was a friendly meeting as
far as O'Hara was concerned. He summed up the Indian situation
in answer to the general's question and heard his plans for an
Episcopal church next to the Presbyterian. Hugh, meanwhile,
maintained an aloof silence. When they passed on O'Hara said,
"What have you got the wind up about Neville for?"

"I don't like him. He's too much the aristocrat for my stomach.
Then he's got such a damned clique around him. There's his son,

Colonel Presley, his brother-in-law Abraham Kirkpatrick, his son-in-law Major Isaac Craig, and his lawyer John Woods, my biggest rival, by the way. If they saw old Neville caught here *in flagrante delicto* they'd all swear he was back east at the time!"

"Come, come, Hugh! That's a nasty comparison for a man like the general!"

"All right, I'll withdraw it. But I will say they all make up a pretty strong little cabal if anyone had to buck them, politically. Well, here we are at Marie's. What do you think of it?"

O'Hara exclaimed with pleasure. He had seen the new tavern itself before but not the gravel walks with their bordering shrubs and early flowers. John Marie, with his French blood had both business and æsthetic sense, and here at the foot of Grant's Hill, which was the only *pleasance* the town could claim, he had built a spot of beauty. While the men were finishing their drinks O'Hara voiced his praise of Maria. He had hesitated before for fear it might reflect upon his first impression of her, but Hugh had evidently been waiting for his reaction.

"You notice a change in her then?" he said eagerly.

"I do. You have a very charming wife, Hugh. I congratulate you."

"And I thank you again, my friend, for your advice."

All the way back to the house Hugh extolled Maria's qualities. She was proving to be a great reader and he was helping her to continue her studies now under him as teacher. He was boyishly exuberant.

"What do men *do* who have stupid wives?"

"I really wouldn't know," O'Hara said, laughing. "Of course I fancy there are a few stupid husbands in the world too."

"Touché, old chap. Well, let's just say we're among the blessed."

Maria was ready to leave when they got back to the house and O'Hara stood at the kitchen step watching them down the lane, satisfaction upon his face. All at once Hugh turned.

"Mind your P's and Q's, O'Hara."

"What's that? What are you talking about?"

Hugh hurried back. "There! I'm glad I was the first to introduce you to the new catchword. Did you notice that board on the wall behind the bar at Marie's? Well, all the taverns have them now. When a man is drinking hard all evening and treating too, the tavern keeper writes his name on the board and puts *P* for pint and *Q* for quart after it and then checks how many of each he orders. When the number gets up he calls the man to the bar for a reckoning. So someone lately started the expression and it's spread like wildfire. No one ever says *Watch out!* or *Be careful*, now. They say 'Mind your P's and Q's.' Pretty good, eh?"

"Excellent," O'Hara said. "I'll take that one back to the troops!"

The gristmill was flourishing. The output had indeed doubled and O'Hara had engaged another man in the hope of increasing it still more. For his own flour he charged the Government exactly what he had to pay to other mills, and made a handsome profit doing it. The idea of a sawmill had been in his mind for some time. Now on this trip home he decided to put it into action. One of the many boat builders was an Irishman, Dennis O'Keefe, and on this afternoon when Hugh and Maria had left, O'Hara made his way towards the wharf. Dennis was a brawny man but, as O'Hara had sized him up before, he had brains as well and he *knew wood*. The plan proposed was simply this: if O'Hara put up all the capital would Dennis see to the building and operating of a sawmill? The Irishman stood for a moment as though stupefied, then he drew his hand across his brow.

"*Would* I?" he said. "It's the opportunity of me dreams an' me never expectin' it. I know how to go about it, Captain. I've been round sawmills off an' on all me life. I pledge you'll never be regrettin' this. When do we start?"

"At once," said O'Hara firmly. "I own a couple of lots down here. We'll take a look at them now, and then I'll order whatever machinery you'll need." His eyes roved over the forest clad hills beyond. "At least there is no shortage of raw timber."

That night Mary was able to be downstairs and she and her husband sat together in the parlour while once again he went over with her his assets, explaining just what money was with Robert Morris in the Philadelphia Bank, and how much he was leaving in one of the secret drawers of the desk for all her needs and any sudden demand of his own.

"I'm almost getting to be a banker, myself," he said. "General Harmar has asked me to keep some of his funds. They are in the other secret drawer, in an envelope bearing his name. You see, I do consider you my partner in everything, in spite of my little joke."

He told her then of the plan for the sawmill. "My idea is to develop a number of industries here. First of all, naturally, I want to make money. But along with that I want to stimulate business production. I want to make Pittsburgh grow and before I'm done I want to make some of those smug easterners take notice of the possibilities out here. I've got a far-reaching plan . . ."

There was a soft sound, less than a knocking, at the back door. O'Hara went quickly through the kitchen. On the back stoop in the darkness he could discern an Indian! For one quick moment a chill struck his heart; then he recognised the man before him. It was Guyasuta! With a cry of welcome he drew him into the kitchen, grasping the Chief's arms with his own.

"Where have you come from?" he asked, falling easily into the Seneca dialect.

Guyasuta looked at him impassively.

"You are glad to see me? Even remembering . . . Hannastown?"

O'Hara paused as he studied the strong figure before him. The face, while beginning to show signs of age, had the same nobility he remembered.

"Yes," he said slowly. "While I may be very sad at some of your actions, I am still your friend."

The Indian nodded. "And you are my son. I stay away because I fear you would not receive me. Now my heavy heart is light."

"Sit down," O'Hara said eagerly. "You must meet my wife. You must break bread with me at my own table. Oh, Mary?"

She came a little hesitantly but with a smile which her husband knew to be a brave one. He introduced the two and Guyasuta studied her without speaking for some moments. At last he turned to O'Hara and said in his own tongue, "She is beautiful as a young willow in spring beside the water courses!"

"I'm afraid she's a little tired now for we have a new baby. Why don't you go on up now, Mary, and I'll set some supper out for Guyasuta."

As she nodded assent O'Hara lifted her in his arms and carried her up the stairs. When he returned the old Indian wore a puzzled expression.

"How many days has your new child?"

"Eighteen."

Guyasuta shook his head. "When Indian baby has *two* days mother is chopping wood and waiting on husband. I have now two wives. Old squaw takes care of me by day. Food and clothes. Young squaw for nights. Indian ways are wise. Huh?"

O'Hara kept a sober face. "White men's customs are a little different. Now for some food."

He took down a flitch hanging beside the fireplace, cut generous slices for the long-handled skillet, brewed a pot of tea, and set out cornbread and butter from the cupboard. He could see the Indian's nostrils dilate at the good smell of the frying meat. When all was on the table Guyasuta fell upon the viands ravenously while O'Hara made a pretence of eating with him. When it was finished they both lighted their pipes.

"I am very glad to talk with you," O'Hara said in English. "I suppose you know what is going on in the West."

"A little," the Indian said, as O'Hara restrained a smile. He knew the system of communication among the red men was well-nigh perfect.

"We are honestly trying to make peace with your people. We are spending much, much money, much hard work to get treaties signed by all the tribes. Will you tell me what you think the result will be?"

Guyasuta smoked on as if he had not heard. At last he spoke.

"When white man first come he had *one fire*. Now he has *thirteen*. When he first come he say he want only as much land as a buffalo hide could cover. Now . . ." he gestured widely with his pipe. "Moons will rise and set and year will follow year and still he will take our land, and never keep a promise. What good is a treaty? Your men might as well come back home."

"There is only one other way."

Guyasuta slowly nodded his head.

"Your people then will fight?"

"We will do what we must."

"How will the *Six Nations* go?"

"As against the white man we all go together."

And then there was silence as the smoke slowly filled the kitchen.

When a heavy hour had passed in which O'Hara had felt there was nothing for him to say, Guyasuta again removed his pipe. He leaned over the table and touched O'Hara's arm.

"I have no son of the flesh. *You* are my son of the spirit. I come to-night to ask a favour. The lands beyond the Allegheny were once my hunting ground. I want to end my days there near to you and be buried there, by your hand. Will you promise me? You, I trust."

O'Hara looked startled but he slowly rose—as did the Indian—and held out his hand. Guyasuta looked at it for a moment and then grasped it.

"I promise on my honour to see to your burial as you request, if I live longer than you. And if in your old age you need care you will have it in my own home."

The Indian looked steadily into O'Hara's eyes, drew a deep breath, pressed the hand he held again and started to the door. Then he turned and with a faint relaxing of countenance pointed upstairs.

"Young love—best love," he said, and went out.

The next morning O'Hara told Mary all about the visit, including the details of the two wives. She pretended great alarm.

"I do hope as years go on his influence over you in that line won't be too great!"

O'Hara smiled. "I rather think I can stand up under it. But I did make a promise to him I probably shouldn't have without consulting you. He wants me to bury him across the Allegheny when the time comes, and I added that if in his old age he needed care I would give it to him in our house."

"Mercy!" Mary ejaculated. "I can't fancy having an Injun at my fireplace!"

"Don't worry. He'll probably be hale and hearty till he's a hundred. For some reason I have a great fondness for the old fellow. And he calls me his *spiritual son*. It touches me, rather. I hope you understand, dear."

"Of course. And I don't wonder he loves you. Oh, I wish to-day we wouldn't have any callers. Just us. You'll so soon be going again, won't you?"

"To Kentucky, yes. But I'll be back here after that. I'm with you, though, in hoping no callers come."

But they did. At least two. The first was a thin, unshaven man with worn clothes and his feet sticking out of his shoes, who remained on the stoop as O'Hara went out to talk to him.

"Captain," he began, swallowing hard in his embarrassment, "I'd think shame to come here like a beggar if I wasn't in awful need. I was a keelboater but I took lung fever an' it nigh did for me. Then the Missus has a new baby an' Doctor Bedford says we all ought to have a . . . a . . . bit more to eat an' it was him said to come to you an' tell you just how it is. 'Course he's helped us by not chargin' us an' a lot like us, but . . ."

"You did right to come," O'Hara said quickly. "You know my own store?"

"Yes, sir."

"I'll give you a paper for Mr. Elliott there and he'll give you groceries. Wait a minute."

When he came back he had some money besides the paper and Prudence was already putting bread and butter in a basket and ladling out soup from the big pot over the fire into a kettle.

"There!" O'Hara said as the man took his various gifts. "Carry this carefully. It will give you all a little food before you go to the store. And let me know if you get in a pinch again. Could you work now at something easier than keelboating?"

"I ain't too strong yet but I could do something. Captain, I need to work . . ."

"Well, when you go to the store tell Mr. Elliott I said to give you some little jobs, and we'll see what happens."

The man's eyes were wet with tears. "I can't thank you, Captain . . ."

O'Hara waved him off. "No need. We all have to help each other. Good luck and let me know how you get on."

When he told Mary about it she confessed she had often been tempted to give money aid to some of the women who seemed in hard plight, but had not been sure how he would feel about it. She did often press food upon them.

"In most cases probably food is best but if you ever find there is real need, feel free to give money too. You remember," O'Hara smiled, "the night we sat under the locust trees and agreed upon the motto for our home?"

"How could I forget? *Where friend and stranger, rich and poor, will be welcome*," she repeated, musingly.

"I believe I said 'the decent stranger uninterrogated,' " he amended, "and we've certainly stuck to it. I wonder how many travellers we've entertained over the years? And we've had plenty of elegant guests, too, like Colonel John May of Boston a few months ago."

"He told me he would write in his Journal that he had had an elegant dinner at Captain O'Hara's home!"

"I believe I'm more proud of our reputation for hospitality than of all my land holdings. And they're pretty considerable at the moment. But it's you, darling, who make it possible and I love you for it."

The other caller was a surprise and a pleasure. He came in early evening to the parlour door, his uniform neatly brushed, his hair freshly powdered, and the grey eyes in his slender handsome face sparkling. It was Ebenezer Denny.

O'Hara sprang to meet him. "*Eb!* How on earth did you get here? Come in ! Come in, man!"

Eb greeted Mary with smiling courtesy, settled himself comfortably in one of the wing chairs and looked content with life.

"What's up? Why are you back?" O'Hara kept asking.

"Give me time," Denny said, "and I'll tell you all my news. I'm here because I foxed the General into giving me a little furlough. Good man, General Harmar. If I ever have a son the General will have a namesake! Of course I have a message or two for the powers that be, back in Philadelphia. That's excuse enough on the surface, but what I really wanted was to get a few days in Carlisle."

"To see your mother, I take it?" O'Hara asked wickedly.

"Naturally," Eb answered. "To see her . . . and others."

"All right, we'll let it go at that. We'll give you our big news now and then I want to hear what's been happening at the Post. Could I bring the baby down, Mary, and show him off?"

"Oh, bachelors aren't interested in babies, dear!"

"Egad, they'd better be or the race might become extinct. Can I bring him? I'll be careful."

So little James was brought down, sleeping, by his father, examined shyly by Eb, pronounced remarkable in every respect, and conveyed, still sleeping, back to his cradle above.

"And now," O'Hara said urgently, "what's been going on? I can't wait longer to hear."

"Well," Eb began, "we've had the devil of a time—excuse me, Mistress O'Hara—with the Shawnees these last weeks. First of all they announced that a big delegation would come to the Council House to treat. It would be quite a thing, you know, the first real overture we've had from them, so the officers got together and decided we'd receive them royally. That we'd cook and serve them food, ourselves!"

"Oh, *no!*" O'Hara ejaculated.

"Well, you'd have known better but you weren't there."

"Wasn't *Clark* there?"

"No, he'd gone down the river. So, we went ahead and after the gun salute we brought out the food. You should have heard them hoot! 'The old women!' they said. 'The old women dressed up as soldiers!' "

"That's the way it is with them," O'Hara put in. "Only the *old* women do the cooking."

"Well, we found it out all right to our sorrow. They listened to Harmar, made a speech or two themselves, and then went off as sassy as you please."

"I'll wager they did!"

"Clark got back a few days later and just after that in marched the Shawnees again. Some of them recognised him and their countenances changed a little but their chief walked up to the table bold as brass and laid a wampum belt on it, mixed white *and black*. Peace and war, you know. Clark was standing there with a sort of cane he had cut from a thorn tree. Know what he did? He took his stick and skited the wampum belt off the table on to the ground and set his foot on it!"

O'Hara threw back his head and roared with laughter. "And his red hair bristled?"

"I swear it stood on end. Well, the damned—excuse me, Mistress O'Hara—Injuns left with their tails down and in a few days they came back and signed a treaty!"

Mary gave an exclamation of joy. "Oh, now the trouble's all over, isn't it? There won't be any real war?"

Eb started to speak but O'Hara quickly forestalled him. "That's what we'll hope for, certainly, isn't it, Eb?" Then he looked at his watch. "Dr. Bedford sets the rules here just now and we have to keep hours. Shall I take you up now, Mary? Then Eb and I can mull things over and have something to 'wet our thrapples' as Semple says, and even use a cuss word now and then if our feelings for the red brethren get the best of us. All right, dear?"

"You must take my love to your mother," Mary turned back to say to Denny. "I write her about all my problems as she told me to." She gave a little laugh. "She's advised me already how to make a mustard plaster and when to start a child on the Shorter Catechism and how to test pound cake by breaking a piece against your ear to see if it sings! You'll be sure to give her my message?"

"I won't forget. I know she likes to hear from you and I might add she was born to give advice. You should see what she writes *me*!"

When the men were alone with their whisky noggins they settled to serious discussion of the Indian affairs.

"I didn't say it in front of your wife but a few days after the treaty those sons of bitches fell on a little settlement just down the river and wiped it out. So, there we are again. Harmar's got his craw full and he'd like to get out of the whole thing if he decently could. But of course he'll stick till something's decided."

" 'If 'twere done when 'tis done, then 'twere well 'twere done quickly', " O'Hara quoted, musingly.

"How's that?"

"Oh, if we could be sure that a big battle would finish it all up, then we ought to get at it right away. It's this year after year prolonging, waiting, dillydallying, that frets me. I had a call from Guyasuta last night!" he added.

"No! What's *he* up to?"

"Oh, nothing particular that I know of. But he says we might as well bring our men back as far as treaties are concerned. He says the tribes will all join with the Six Nations in a war, and he evidently thinks it's inevitable."

"You know what Harmar told me out there? Congress is about to appoint General St. Clair as governor of the Western Territory!"

"No!"

"You don't care for the general?"

"Oh, he's a fine man I'm sure personally but I don't have much faith in his ability in Indian affairs. Eb, there's just one man who in my opinion could go out there and clear the whole mess up. Mad Anthony Wayne! You know his watchwords? *Silence, surprise and cold steel.* That's just what would do the trick. Congress may come to him finally but in the meanwhile they're just dumb enough to waste a lot of money and good men!" He sighed. "Oh well, if we will have a democracy we've got to put up with the frailty of our lawmakers."

"Better than a bad king at that, isn't it?"

"Oh, absolutely! I'm just restive at the moment. Selfishly so. I'd like to have the Indian business ended so I could get on with my own affairs. You know, Eb, when the old fort comes down there's going to be a chance to get some fine building material. Want to go in with me on that?"

"I'd like it fine. As soon as I'm free of a uniform I want to settle here and get into business and . . . and get married."

"Ah," said O'Hara, "how is little Nancy Wilkins of Carlisle?"

"As sweet as ever but young, too young yet."

"Well," O'Hara laughed, "that's a fault she'll get over. Take heart, Eb. I had to wait till Mary grew up. Now about this building idea of mine . . ."

They talked on till morning and in their plans a row of brick houses rose to replace log ones. "When the time comes, O'Hara, I'll be glad to be your partner in this. The idea 'likes me well,' as the saying goes. Now, I've got to get back to the tavern for I start on to-morrow."

"As to sayings, here's a new one started round here." And he told him about the *P's* and *Q's*. "Take that one back east with the compliments of the Back Country," he said as they chuckled together.

Day by day O'Hara had been negotiating as usual for the needed supplies; he had also taken up his option on the lots on Water Street for more and more he dreamed of a great spreading house there one day, in keeping with his growing family and his own ambitions. He often looked at the coat of arms which hung on the parlour wall. It signified his descent from the Barons of Tyrawley, the O'Hara ancestors of County Mayo, Ireland. The rampant lion looked back at him, he fancied, a little reproachfully. *You deserve better than logs behind you*, he would think, *and one day you'll have a place worthy of you, old fellow.*

The last night before he left for Kentucky to purchase cattle he and Mary for once had no interruptions. She lay curled up on the sofa and O'Hara sat in a wing chair beside her with the candle stand close.

"I've been so busy I haven't read the papers for two weeks," he said, leafing through them. "I wonder how Scull is getting on with his news. Hugh says the subscriptions are going well but people forget to pay for them."

"Read to me," Mary said. "I'd love that."

"All right. I'll just pick the lighter items for you. Oh, here's my own little advertisement:

Just received at the store of subscriber a complete cargo of West India goods, groceries and dry goods.   *James O'Hara*

"Simple and to the point," he commented. "But listen to this one:

Just received from Philadelphia to be sold by Wilson and Wallace at their store in Water Street, will dispose at reasonable terms for flour, beef, cattle, butter or cash: Coffee mills,

Testaments, Bibles, groceries, axes, saddlery, dishes, hats, sickles, tea kettles, ribbons, wash basins, muffin plates, wagoner's tools and many articles too tedious to mention."

"Well," O'Hara said, "that ought to pretty well cover it. Here's an item about *ginseng:*

A quantity of good ginseng wanted by the subscriber for which a generous price will be allowed in merchandise."

"What is ginseng?" Mary interrupted.

"Oh, it's primarily an American root, I guess, and there's a big trade going on in it round here. It's supposed to cure all manner of ills. And," he added, with a sly side glance towards her, "it's reputed to increase a man's sexual powers. I wondered whether I should get some."

"*James!*" Mary said with a shocked giggle, "you are really dreadful!"

"Just thought I'd inquire," he said imperturbably. Then he cried out, "Why, here's something I sent in myself months ago!"

"I didn't know you'd written anything!"

"Well, I didn't really. I got this out of an old London paper and thought Scull might use it, as an *Anecdote*. I'm strong for those. Listen. I think this is amusing.

Doctor Sheridan, the celebrated friend of Swift, always had his pupils to prayers in his school. One morning in the middle of prayers one boy saw a rat descending the bell-rope, and laughed aloud. When pointed out Doctor Sheridan was so angry he called him up and had his posteriors bared for the rod, when the witty schoolmaster told him if he could think of anything tolerable to say on the occasion he would forgive him. The trembling culprit addressed his master with the following beautiful distich:

> *There was a rat for want of stairs*
> *Came down a rope to go to prayers.*

Sheridan instantly dropped the rod and instead of a whipping gave him half a crown."

"Oh, that's wonderful!" Mary laughed. "Mark that and I'll look it over when I want to be entertained. But do go on reading."

"Now let's see:

"The famous horse DOVE will cover, this season at . . . Um . . . um . . . um."

"What was that?"

"Nothing. Just stable talk. No interest to us. But here's something! The first Pittsburgh Almanac is soon to come out, and ah, here's a poem! By Brackenridge, I'll wager. It's called *Poetic Blossoms by a Western Swain addressed to his Mistress*, no less.

> *Ye powers divine assist in softest lays*
> *My first attempt to sing my Anna's praise.*"

(He couldn't very well say Maria!)

> *"Sublime the theme, sublime ideas rise*
> *Depict the radiance of her charming eyes;*
> *Charmed by those eyes, in unison conspire*
> *All Ovid's softness and all Pindar's fire.*

"That's Hugh all right. No one else knows Pindar and Ovid. There's an article on Advice to Young Men, and one on Drunkenness. I don't think we need to read either of those. I see there's a negro wench offered for sale! I'm against slavery. You know what Hugh said one day? He said there were men around here who wouldn't for a good cow shave their beards on Sunday and yet would keep slaves and sometimes abuse them. Well, enough reading for one time, dear?"

"Perhaps, but I enjoyed it. Talk to me, now. Something I can think of when you are away."

O'Hara sat watching her. She had not yet regained her colour but the paleness enhanced rather than detracted from her delicate beauty. At last he spoke.

"Hugh's verse is very nice but it's not real poetry. It doesn't go to the heart. But I know one that does. Should I repeat it for you?"

"Oh, *do*, James. That would pleasure me greatly."

"One Christmas afternoon I was sitting in Semple's Tavern at sunset thinking of you, and an old song my mother used to sing came to my mind. I always liked it so much as a boy that the words have never left me. This is it:

> *Have you seen but a white lily grow*
> *Before rude hands had touched it?*
> *Have you marked but the fall of the snow,*
> *Before the earth hath smutched it?*
> *Have you felt the wool of beaver*
> *Or swan's down ever?*

Or have smelt of the bud of the brier,
Or the nard in the fire?
Or have tasted the bag of the bee?
O so white, O so soft, O so sweet, so sweet,
   so sweet is she!"

There were happy tears on her cheeks when he finished and his own were misted in tenderness.

The passage of some years could be described as the "slow and steady march of time." During other periods the months in their succession seem as swiftly moving as though driven by the very spheres, because of important events crowding upon each other. The latter was the way O'Hara felt about the years which followed that quiet night with Mary in the King's Orchard.

Through bitter weather in late January of 1789 he rode once again along the Forbes Road, this time on a horse other than Pitt who was now old. O'Hara was headed for Reading with a new and peculiar glow in his heart, for he had been selected as one of the Pennsylvania electors, who would vote for the first President of the United States! His own interests had of late years been so entirely wrapped up in business, that this honour, which might be termed political, had come to him as a surprise and an enormous pleasure. He had often wakened in the night, thinking of it. More than all his service in the War, this appointment made him an *American* through and through. He gloated upon this fact as he rode along, even as he saddened at thought of his native Ireland. For one item in the *Gazette* headed *Irish Affairs*, which he had lately scanned but had refrained from mentioning to Mary, was that by Royal Proclamation any soldier who persisted in tacking on the barracks the sign *No King and Liberty* would receive 500 lashes! And a note below had struck him even more forcibly. It was to the effect that any foreigner detected in having the book entitled *The Rights of Man* by Thomas Paine, should be indicted as a felon.

"Poor Ireland," O'Hara muttered as he rode along. "I'm glad I'm out of it! I'm glad I'm in a free country."

The Pennsylvania delegation with General Hand as chairman voted unanimously for General George Washington at their February 4th meeting, and O'Hara finally returned home with satisfaction and fourteen pounds, five shillings pay for his trip! But the experience had wakened a new idea within him. This great game of politics was a challenge too, and he liked any sort. He decided to run that year for Representative in the Assembly!

It was desperately hard to fit his campaigning in with his regular work as contractor for the Western army, but he applied all his great energies to the task. Mary encouraged him, for she was thrilled over the possibility of a year in the East; but Hugh Brackenridge was openly pessimistic.

"You haven't a chance, O'Hara, if you remain a Federalist. I tell you the Democratic-Republican party is the popular one. If you had changed . . ."

"I would no more change my politics than I would change my wife," O'Hara said shortly.

"All right. Have it your own way but you'll lose as sure as shootin'."

And he did. It was a bitter pill to swallow for he was accustomed to bending events to his will, but as it happened he had plenty of other matters just then on his mind. It was clear now apparently even to Congress, that the Indian troubles could not be solved by treaties; and General Harmar was ordered to make an expedition of war against the Maumees, the renegade Indians who were then infesting the frontiers. A thousand militia were ordered from Kentucky and five hundred troops from the Pennsylvania back counties.

And O'Hara, along with the other provisions, loaded two hundred and twelve horses with flour!

The Indians won; the losses were sickening; General Harmar resigned, and a new expedition was ordered under General St. Clair. Harmar on his way back stopped in Pittsburgh and he and O'Hara talked it all over.

"St. Clair's gathered up five thousand men, but what an army! Most of them are collected from the streets and the city prisons and hurried out to the West with no more knowledge of Indian fighting than rabbits. And his officers are as ignorant, except for Dicky Butler who has no confidence in St. Clair. My expedition was disastrous enough, but I predict St. Clair's will be a slaughter."

"There is just one man . . ."

"I know. I've recommended him to Congress."

"So have I."

Harmar's prediction was all too true. When the news of the next great defeat reached Pittsburgh, the town shivered with fear. The situation was now desperate. Running like a chant of death through the streets was the nasal voice of the blind rhymester, Dennis Lochy:

"Come gentlemen, gentlemen all,
Ginral Sincleer will remem . . ber . . ed be,
For he lost thirteen hundred men all,
In the Western Tari . . to . . ree!"

A few days later O'Hara helped draft an appeal to the President and was one of those who signed it:

In consequence of the late intelligence of the fate of the campaign to the Westward, the inhabitants of the town of Pittsburgh have convened and appointed us a committee to address your Excellency. The late disaster of the army must greatly affect the safety of this place. There is no doubt that the enemy will now come forward with more spirit and in greater numbers, for success will give confidence and secure allies.

We seriously apprehend that the Six Nations, heretofore wavering, will now avow themselves. Be that as it may the Indians at present hostile are well acquainted with the defenceless situation of this town. At present we have neither garrison, arms nor ammunition to defend the place. If the enemy should be disposed they would find it easy to destroy us. The safety of this place being an object of the greatest consequence not only to the neighbouring country but to the United States as it is the point of communication to the Westward it must be of the greatest consequence to preserve it.

The reply was speedy. General Knox of the War Department wrote Major Isaac Craig to procure materials for a picketed fort to be built in such part of Pittsburgh as would best cover the town and any stores kept there. And with this order old Fort Pitt died forever and the new Fort La Fayette was born.

O'Hara spoke again to Elliott. "Why don't you eat at the house too, when I'm away? I'll tell Mary and Prudence you're tired of tavern fare. How about it? I'd feel safer."

"Couldn't refuse good vittles."

"You know Guyasuta?"

"Sure. I know the old goat."

"He's my friend. If he should ever turn up at night, watch out. He'll be on a peaceful errand."

"If you say so."

"I do. But if any hostile Indians should ever come near . . . for God's sake, Elliott, aim straight."

"Well now," he drawled, "it ain't hardly necessary to tell me how to use a rifle. I've a general idea which end the shootin' comes out of. But I'll take care of things. I still think the Injuns will study a while before they come into the town here but the new fort's a help. It's goin' up fast, I tell you."

"How's the new man working out at the store?"

"Why, damned good. Takes to it like a duck to water. Oh, we'll get along fine here. But what do you think's goin' to happen now in the West? Something's got to be busted up, huh?"

"And pretty soon," O'Hara said grimly.

As a matter of fact several things happened in quick succession in that April of 1792. First, a quiet letter but one filled with potential significance came to Mary. There was a post office now in Pittsburgh and the inhabitants listened on certain days for the blast of the post rider's tin horn which announced the arrival of the mail. So on this day Mary, upon hearing it, had sauntered up to where the letters were dispensed and returned with her own which was from one of the Chew sisters in Philadelphia. She read its news eagerly as she walked along, and then at one sentence stopped in her tracks.

Mrs. Wayne, Anthony's wife, died last week at their home in Paoli, after a long illness. It is said he cared for her most faithfully. Only now of course we wonder . . .

Mary could hardly wait for O'Hara to get home that evening. She told him at once.

"Oh, James, it would seem so wicked to rejoice and yet how can we help it a little? Will you write him? Should I write Mary Vining?"

"I would say no to both," he replied thoughtfully. "It's a delicate situation. I think we should wait until we hear the facts from one of them. Of course if what I hope for comes true, we may see Anthony here before long."

The two appointments came close together: Major-General Anthony Wayne was chosen at long last to snatch victory from the Indian tribes of the west; and James O'Hara was appointed by the President with the advice of the Senate to be Quartermaster-General in the Army of the United States!

When the dignified certificate was received O'Hara and Mary pored over it that evening with pride on both their faces.

"This is the biggest thing that has come to me yet. I can't help feeling elated that His Excellency has such trust in me. You see this means that I'll be responsible not only for provisioning all Wayne's troops but for every post we have, even up into New York." O'Hara drew a long breath. "It will be a tremendous job, but somehow I think I can do it!"

"Of course you can," Mary agreed. "You can do anything! But I suppose this will mean you will be away from home more than ever?"

He looked steadily into her eyes. "I'm afraid that will be true, dear."

She managed a smile. "I'll try to do my part too," she said.

Although as beautiful as ever, Mary had changed in the last five years. Two more babies had come to her, very close together. One, little Butler, named for General Dicky whom O'Hara greatly admired, lay sleeping safely now, upstairs; the other, alas, lay in a tiny grave behind the Presbyterian church. "There are so many *little* graves," Mary had whispered piteously to her husband on that tragic day.

O'Hara had known a sharp grief at the time, but the rush of work and the lively children still in the house had dulled it. But he knew Mary's heart still mourned. It showed in the white silences that occasionally fell upon her and in the weeping that sometimes overtook her in the night when she clung to him. But, perceptive as he always was towards her, he realised that the sorrow had deepened her nature. She was no longer merely the lighthearted girl; she was a woman, and now essentially his help-meet. She had learned more details of his government work and his private business. She studied carefully the information he gave her, and was ready with practical advice now and then which, to his surprise, he found himself taking seriously. Of course due to O'Hara's native wit there was between them the same constant flow of laughter and small jokes; but each was finding new depths in the other as the years passed.

At once, as was his habit, O'Hara began to plan for his new duties. There must be, he realised, the erection of magazines and granaries for the storage of dry forage at various points; he would need to hire blacksmiths, wheelwrights and carpenters, and perhaps most important of all, secure a deputy quartermaster for each large post. He began this latter selection by talking with Major Isaac Craig. The news of his own appointment had soon swept Pittsburgh and O'Hara found the daily greetings of his neighbours tinged with new respect.

"You'll come out of this a *general*," Hugh predicted as he congratulated his friend.

"Just so *I come out of it*," O'Hara said, "I'll be willing to forgo the title."

"Um," Hugh was meditative. "You do get yourself into the damnedest jobs. This new one will be plenty dangerous one way and another, I suppose."

"Plenty," said O'Hara, "but I'm like Oliver Goldsmith, 'I have a knack at *hoping*.' Well, just don't give Mary the other idea, nor Maria either, for that matter," he added. "Women do talk together, you know."

His conversation with Major Craig was highly satisfactory.

"Isaac, will you Q.M. for me in Pittsburgh? I'll need a good deputy here. It will be a case of receiving and distributing the public stores as they come in. It's all going to be big business, Isaac."

"Well, I'm glad I don't have the whole responsibility. But I'll take over for you here, gladly."

They paid their respects to the old fort as they walked towards it, and discussed the new one. It would be the centre now for the supplies. O'Hara's eyes were fixed across the Monongahela.

"I'm going to tell you something, Isaac, which I've told only to Brackenridge and of course, my wife. When General Wayne finishes the Indian business I want to get into manufacturing."

The Major laughed. "You need something, of course, to occupy you. All you have now is a store, a gristmill, a sawmill, a tannery and plans, I hear, for a brewery here at The Point."

O'Hara made a deprecative gesture. "Oh, I like to keep Pittsburgh busy. But this other is my special dream. I own land over below Coal Hill. I want to put up a plant there one day to *make glass*."

"I'll be damned!"

"Is that so strange?"

"No. The surprising thing is I've thought of it myself."

O'Hara reached for the other's hand and gripped it. "*Good man!*" he exclaimed. "When we're ready to start, will you be my partner?"

The Major looked rather dazed. "You're a hard one to refuse, O'Hara. I guess I may as well agree to this too."

So the bargain was sealed.

A few evenings later there was a knock at the parlour door after supper, and there stood Major-General Wayne. *Mad Anthony!* Handsomer by far than either O'Hara or Mary remembered, with ruddy cheeks, chestnut brows and golden-brown eyes below the white hair. A great warmth of friendship enfolded them, with the pulsing undercurrent of the future's beckoning joys always present but never quite breaking through. There was all the general Philadelphia news to discuss though one name was not spoken. Then when all the light gossip was over Mary rose and extended her hand prettily.

"It's delightful to see you again, General. Of course we met on my wedding day but I was so excited then . . ."

"Of course you were. I've always heard that love is a great beautifier, and you, who needed least to prove it, have done so!"

"Oh, what a gallant speech! I thank you, General, and we'll expect you to-morrow night to dinner. Now I'll leave you both to discuss the big matters."

They were indeed big and the two men settled to them with stern faces. The troops would be arriving soon, and the westward march would begin. Wayne's questions came, sharp, intelligent, determined, and O'Hara answered them from his wider experience with the Indians and the wilderness. When the general rose to go at last a slight grimace of pain crossed his face.

"Do you remember that damn' fool sentry that shot me the night we were going to La Fayette's camp?" he asked.

"I do, indeed. Do you mean you still have trouble from it?"

"I do, a little. The doctors have probed around as if they were digging potatoes but they can't find the bullet. Still in the fleshy part of the upper leg, I guess. Oh, well, as long as it behaves itself there I'm all right."

He stood a moment as though uncertain how to proceed, then he said slowly, "Have you heard anything recently about my . . . family?"

"We have," O'Hara answered. "Mary had a letter from a friend in Philadelphia. I . . ."

Wayne raised his hand. "I do not wish to speak of that. It has its own sadness. But since you know my story I will tell you that when a sufficient time has elapsed Miss Vining's parents will announce our engagement and then . . ." All at once his golden-brown eyes fairly blazed with light. "As soon as I'm finished with this campaign, we will be married!"

O'Hara wrung his hand, still forbearing comment for fear

of choosing the wrong words, but he did say quickly, "Come, I'll walk along the lane with you. The apple trees are almost in blossom and there's a moon."

They went slowly and in silence through the faintly perfumed air with the pale light glancing upon the new, young leaves. O'Hara wondered if Wayne was thinking as he was of that other spring night at York when they had sat together and spoken of the soldiers sentenced to die the next day. He shook off the memory. At the end of the lane he said, "Anthony, this night is too beautiful to think of Indians! Let's just concentrate on whatever brings joy to our hearts, shall we?"

"Even so!" the general answered, smiling. "Even so."

They parted then, both strong, virile men in their early prime, tested in many fires and not found wanting. And both in love.

K

Chapter Twelve

If General Wayne's mission was a desperately difficult one: to win complete victory from the Indians who now were more than ever confident because of their successes over Harmar and St. Clair; throw the west open for civilisation; and indirectly compel the British to yield the posts they still held on the American side of the Great Lakes; O'Hara's problems loomed at first all but unsurmountable. He knew moments when the weight of his vast responsibility seemed crushing. But his years of experience in this particular field along with his natural determination and confidence bore him up. So he wrote firmly to Secretary of War Knox:

"I can now take the liberty of assuring you that no motive nor consideration can possibly interfere with the duties of my station, which I feel myself most religiously bound to execute agreeable to your instructions and my own judgment."

Thus, he dedicated himself to the task.

One of his first problems was that arrangements had to be made now for handling large sums of money. One early consignment of cavalry horses alone cost $25,000. O'Hara decided that not more than $10,000 should be sent to him at one time. Then he talked the matter over with Mary.

"These packets will come to *you*. You will open them, count the money, make a record of it and then turn it over to Major Craig. If I am out at a post at the time and need it there, he will forward it to me."

Mary was aghast. "*I* am to receive this money?"

"You are. I trust a great many people. Most of them in fact. But there is only one person in whom I have perfect and absolute confidence. Give you one guess," he added with his usual warm smile. "This way we will always have a double check. Now, can you ever say again you are not my partner?"

There was one personal matter to consider now when they were together. O'Hara was eager to have the big house on Water Street built as soon as possible.

"We're cramped here," he said. "Look at our family already, and I can't trust you not to add to it!"

"I hope to," she said demurely.

"So," he went on, "since you and I have already agreed upon the plans, I'll try to get the workmen started at once. I'll look things over from time to time when I'm back and it will give you something interesting to do, to supervise while I'm away. You're happy about it, aren't you?"

"Yes," she said slowly, "though I will always like the King's Orchard better than Water Street."

"Ah, but I have a surprise for you! How would you like it if we should keep this house? I'll use it for my office and we can come over to it whenever we wish. When the apple trees are in bloom, for instance."

She threw her arms around his neck. "Oh, James, you always read my heart."

Once more O'Hara rode through the trackless forests where danger always lurked, for he considered it his duty to visit all the posts at least once a year as he transacted his enormous business. There were the ever pressing and vexing problems of supplies and transportation, but even more wearing was the keeping of accounts for the War Department. In a leather package fastened to his saddle there were the long sheets upon which by candlelight in all sorts of strange places he wrote in his precise hand the endless records of money received and expenditures listed.

Wayne at this time was comfortably camped at a place he had named *Legionville* from the "Legion" he had organised. Word had come back to O'Hara that the general had inaugurated the strictest discipline with the troops. Two soldiers had been shot for sleeping at their posts (hard necessity, he would say again); whisky was forbidden in the camp; cleanliness and regularity of diet was insisted upon; there was drilling every day including the use of bayonet and sword; Wayne dined with his officers, carefully explaining to them all the details of the expedition; and most remarkable perhaps of all, he had secured the services of some friendly Choctaws and was using them to sow dissension among their hostile brethren.

These facts all helped to answer a question often put to O'Hara. Why did Congress not appoint George Rogers Clark to lead this expedition? Who knew the Indians better than he? O'Hara in answering tried to be fair to both his friends. Clark was the most

fearless, the most ingenious of leaders when his troops consisted of
a band of frontiersmen who could endure incredible hardships and
"shoot a squirrel through the left eye." But this battle that was
slowly but inevitably building up was one which would demand a
seasoned general of trained troops. The Indians now in their
warfare had come a long way from the time of Braddock, when they
shot arrows from behind trees! They had learned much of the art
of war and now, supplied by the British, had guns and bullets.

While O'Hara working with his various deputies was supplying
all posts, his greatest concern of course was for Wayne's encampment, as his neat records showed.

19404 lbs. flour	$1940.40
18750 lbs. fresh beef	468.75
9500 lbs. salted beef	1045.00
30 head beef cattle	440.00
1 yoke oxen	66.00
1 Brown steer	235.00
1 Kentucky boat 30 ft. long	41.80

And notations. *Furnish 270000 daily rations in advance on December
1st. Purchase 1400 more horses and equipment . . .*

O'Hara often thought with a wry smile as he scanned his
accounts that mere figures could not list the miles he had travelled;
the deals he had effected; the contracts made, broken and restored;
the difficulties with recalcitrant wagoners and boatmen; the
ingenuity (he admitted it!) by which he achieved the well-nigh
impossible. And with it all, while he tried to keep the thought
underneath, he realised he was making a great deal of money.

Upon one subject Wayne had twitted him playfully. O'Hara's
love of horses was ingrained. When he wrote the general anxiously
about the care of certain invalid dragoon horses Wayne had replied
that he believed O'Hara was more interested in *equus* than in *homo*.

But their letters were as a rule serious in nature and couched in
conventional language. They were both angry and frustrated when
Congress decided even now to attempt another parley and sent
Commissioners to Fort Erie to sue for peace! The result was that
the Indians gained the time they wanted, then refused to treat at
all, and the burden fell upon Wayne to see that the Commissioners
reached their homes with their scalps on their heads, for which
they formally gave him thanks.

In the fall of 1793 a new anxiety fell upon Pittsburgh and

especially upon O'Hara. A contagious fever had broken out in Philadelphia. Most of the clothing for the army came from there and an order from the War Department was received at once by Major Craig to open, air and repack all the bundles! The Pittsburghers were frightened. O'Hara came back when the news reached him, his heart torn within him. He felt he must help Craig but in doing so he forfeited the opportunity to go home. He spoke to Mary from outside their door, slept in the Fort and prayed as he had not often done. The reports from Philadelphia grew worse and then there were none at all. Secretary of War Knox had fled with his family to Boston, Major Stagg, also of the department, had gone to New York. so there were no communications from the War Offices. There was nothing to do but work, wait and hope.

O'Hara's great solace during these weeks was the sight of the new house on Water Street. "There must be *stabling*, too," he had once said to Mary. "That's what it's called in the old country. For I intend to have a nice place for Pitt to end his days in and also room for two carriage horses."

"Are we to have a carriage then?" Mary had asked in pleased surprise.

"Indeed we are. I fancy seeing my wife ride out on a summer day, holding a little parasol over her head. A coachman on the box, of course."

"Won't you be along?"

"On Sundays. Then we can pretend we're driving once more to the Garden of Delight! You had a pink dress on that day."

"I'll get another."

The house and stables were now finished, ready for the last painting and the planting of the grounds. The place had a spacious dignity even O'Hara had not expected and he thrilled with the pride of it. Inside beyond the wide reception hall there was a great drawing-room, a dining-room of generous dimensions and a library, with kitchen and pantries behind. Prudence had some misgivings about cooking on a *stove* but her devotion was such that she was ready to try anything. Besides there would be, of course, another servant. Over the stables were adequate quarters for McGrady who, while his indenture period was long since up, was a fixture in the family and a possible coachman.

" 'It likes me well,' as Eb Denny would say," O'Hara murmured as he went over his property.

New furniture had already been ordered, with the dining-room pieces a surprise for Mary. These, O'Hara had written his father-in-law, were to be the handsomest that money could buy and he and Mary's sister Elizabeth were to select them. He mentioned in his letter that their house in the King's Orchard, while modest, had already become famed for its hospitality; so it was his desire that the new dining-room should be meet to receive even the most distinguished guests.

By the end of November the epidemic had subsided as suddenly as it had come; the exiles returned to Philadelphia; mail began to come through bringing a letter to Mary from her father that all was well with the family; Pittsburghers relaxed as there was now no further danger of contagion from the army clothes; and O'Hara, scrubbed and brushed at the Fort, went to spend his last nights with Mary.

As he rode off again he was thinking seriously of his conversations with Brackenridge which had taken place here and there on street corners. Hugh was violently worked up over the proposed excise tax on whisky and its possible results.

"I tell you, O'Hara, these farmers around here are oiling their rifles. They mean business. They're going to fight this like hell. They've got David Bradford, a young Washington County lawyer, for their leader and when the time comes they'll stop at nothing, even to *invading Pittsburgh*."

"Oh come, Hugh," O'Hara had said. "Aren't you pulling the long bow?"

"I am *not*," he replied shortly. "I've studied this thing and the root of the trouble is far deeper than a mere quarrel over the excise. As these people see it, it's a stand by the Democratic, poverty-ridden West against the encroachments of the aristocratic Money Bags of the East."

"And may I ask where you stand on this?"

"Well, I'll answer indirectly and please keep it to yourself. General Neville is backing up the excise tax for all he's worth, and I was born to be an enemy of the general's!"

"Well, mind your P's and Q's, Hugh," O'Hara said with a grin.

"Mind your own. Oh, good luck, old man. I know you have enough on your mind just now without my bothering you with this. What a lot of problems there are in the world!"

There were plenty for O'Hara during that winter, and few visits home. By April he had to go to Philadelphia to await the passage of the Appropriation Bill in order to get more money and the chance to buy there in the city much that he needed for the west. It was good to see Mary's family again and exchange all their news. Christian Febiger, Elizabeth's husband and his own erstwhile groomsman, was going to ride back with him, on his way to the Legion. He was a soldier, eager to serve in this new crisis and most of all to be once again under General Wayne. Ever since Stony Point his admiration for Mad Anthony had mounted to near worship.

The Bill passed, the Secretaries of War and Treasuries were not only helpful but loud in their praises of O'Hara's work; and to his great relief he was able to secure certain supplies he needed for the western county right there and order them forwarded as quickly as possible without further intervention from him.

The ride back to Pittsburgh was one of the most beautiful O'Hara could remember. A soft blush was creeping up the stalks of the sumac and sassafras, the small green leaves were unfolding on all the trees, the tiny wood folk scampered about, and the fresh scent of new growth rising from the forest floor was all around them. It was a comfortable trip too, compared with those he made constantly to the various posts, for now the Forbes Road was well travelled and inns had sprung up along its route. A contrast indeed to the one upon which Elliott had taken him on his first journey west! Between stops, however, there were still long hours of forest solitude. One day O'Hara broke the silence.

"I've got a new bee in my bonnet, Febiger."

"I wouldn't doubt it from the news I get about you. What's this one?"

"Salt," said O'Hara laconically.

"*Salt?* What are you talking about?"

"Well, it's like this. Salt has always been most devilish expensive in our parts. It all has to be brought over the mountains either from Baltimore or Philadelphia with a very high freight rate. *We've* always been able to afford it ourselves, but there are plenty of settlers around and people in Pittsburgh too, who can't. I tell you there's still many a sprinkling of wood ashes used to take its place."

"Good lord! I never heard of such a thing!"

"You never lived on the frontier," O'Hara returned grimly. "Now I've found out on my trips around the posts that there is a big saltworks at Salina, New York, not far from Niagara. The Onondago works, it's called. If I could manage to get salt shipped from there I'm sure it would eventually be cheaper than from Baltimore."

"How would transportation be?"

O'Hara laughed. "Now you've asked the *real* question. All I would need to do, as I see it, would be to buy a good many wagons and teams, build a couple of vessels at the Lakes, improve a few roads and portages . . ."

"I think you'd better forget it!" Febiger said, highly amused.

But O'Hara knew that the idea once having entered his mind would never leave it. He added only one more comment now. "If I can ever bring this about it would benefit not only Pittsburgh but all of Western Pennsylvania."

By June a letter came from Wayne which was both amusing and pathetic. He said that the war had now assumed so serious a complexion that O'Hara should be with the Legion. That at the moment they had no deputy at Greenville, their present encampment, "except the most trifling thing, whose utmost stretch of abilities will not reach across the counter." O'Hara and Mary laughed over this together. But in a few days a more urgent message came. Wayne wrote that he considered O'Hara's presence there "indispensably necessary."

So there was another good-bye, this time fraught on O'Hara's part with the knowledge that the great battle, after the long skirmishes, preparations and delays, was at last about to be waged. And he would be there. The new house stood ready but the occupancy must wait perhaps until fall.

"Couldn't you take over a few linens and little things?" O'Hara asked. "I fancy Maria would like to help and it would give you pleasure to begin your moving in small ways. It will all have to be done sometime, you know."

"I think I would like that. Oh, James, don't you suppose it would be proper now to tell Anthony that I've heard from Mary Vining and that I send him my warm congratulations!"

"I'm sure it would. I'll have a good deal to tell him myself."

For the word in various letters from Philadelphia was that the social set was completely agog over the news of the engagement and coming marriage. All reports said Mary Vining had never been so beautiful, never so radiant, never, of course, so happy. She shone like a star in every group. Even the thought of an imminent battle did not seem to frighten her, the dangers of war being apparently less absolute to her than those of the unending bonds of honour had been. "My Anthony is invincible!" she had said once proudly.

As O'Hara held Mary for the last time before he left he wondered with pain in his heart if farewells would ever cease, if perils would ever end, for he knew, unlike Mary Vining, that no man was invincible.

When he finally reached the camp at Greenville on the Miami River he received a touchingly warm welcome from Wayne who looked tired and careworn but brightened immeasurably as he received Mary's message and heard O'Hara's further reports.

"I can hardly believe it!" he said with a sudden boyish smile. "And thank heaven we're coming toward a climax here at last, by the reports my spies bring in. You see we can't have a real battle until the Indians actually line up against us. So it's been skirmish after skirmish with nothing conclusive. My word, I'm glad you've come, O'Hara! This fellow here doesn't know a flapjack from the sole of his shoe." He laughed. "As a matter of fact I can't tell the difference either, as things are."

"I'm sorry about him. He was well recommended. Have you fared pretty well up to this?"

"Excellently. I think you've saved the army! I know what a job it must have been. One of those impossible things that somehow gets done anyway."

"I'll get to work at the Commissary at once."

"Oh no. Wait till morning. Come into my tent and let's talk. We both deserve that much respite."

So they talked again chiefly of happy matters: the wedding and where it would be; O'Hara's new house; details of dress for a military bridegroom; the charms of their respective Marys upon which each could expatiate with full sympathy from the other. As the hour grew late Wayne filled their noggins again with whisky. "Not good for the troops," he said with a twinkle, "but excellent for the general.

"As a matter of fact, O'Hara," he went on, "I don't see why we shouldn't admire ourselves a little! We damned well deserve it. I'm pretty proud of this last record. I've marched nearly four hundred miles through the country of the most watchful and most vindictive enemy! I've cut a road through the woods the entire way, a lot longer and more remote and more dangerous, too, than Braddock's ever was. We've built three forts and now at last we've got to a position where the issue is really going to be joined!"

O'Hara raised his cup.

"And *you*!" Wayne went on. "Look what you've done, man! You've supplied this army all the way, through practically insuperable difficulties. Without you the whole thing couldn't have happened!"

He raised his own cup. "Here's to us! As the Scotch say, '*Who's like us!*'"

O'Hara set to work at once the next day and with something of Wayne's own disciplinary powers, reorganised the Commissary department. There was food enough there if it was properly sorted and prepared. The staff soon learned they were now working under a master who meant business and improved accordingly. The meals at once grew better and Wayne spoke his satisfaction.

"Nothing puts spirit in an army quicker than decent food. I was growing desperate before, for in these next weeks I want to hold the men up to fighting pitch."

"More supplies ought to arrive any day now. I started them out weeks ago," O'Hara said. "One thing I want to ask. When the final engagement comes, be sure to put me in it. I can shoot as well as most."

"No," Wayne answered. "We'll need to eat after the battle, whenever it comes. You stick to your own job and the rest of us will attend to the shootin'."

"I feel rather a coward, staying in the rear."

"*You!*" Wayne laughed. "You're the last man I'd ever accuse of that. Besides, if it's any comfort to you, there won't be much safety anywhere at that time. And you can keep your rifle loaded."

O'Hara was amazed at the encampment itself, the neatness, the order! There were close to three thousand soldiers here but their movements were a pattern of disciplined training. He watched the bayonet drills with interest. *This* weapon was the one thing, he knew, against which Indians would not fight. Good old Anthony! He knew his job.

As the weeks wore on more supplies arrived and there was through the camp the murmur of full-bellied satisfaction. In addition, the reports from the spies indicated that the Indians were collecting in earnest some miles away along the Miami.

"We'll move up, now," Wayne told O'Hara, "and build another fort. The men can knock one up in a hurry. I think we'll name it *Fort Defiance*."

"You'll wait to build a fort?" O'Hara asked in surprise.

"It won't take long and it will be a good thing to have. I don't expect to *fall back* to it, but we might need it for the wounded."

The order to break camp and march was given early in August. O'Hara's work was in a way the heaviest of all, for the removal of Commissary and supplies was always a difficult one. He talked the night before with Febiger.

"If either of us should stub a toe in this business it might be wise to leave a few last words . . ." They took it lightly but certain messages from each were carefully written down.

"I'm sorry Eb Denny is missing all this. He was sent up to Fort Erie with a contingent some time ago. He'd like to be with Wayne, I know that."

"We all like to be with Wayne," Febiger replied.

The march was through the very heart of the Indian country but there were no incidents, further proof that the enemy was concentrating farther on. When the stop finally came, the fort, as Wayne had predicted, was quickly built: a rude log structure but capable of protection and defence. A thrill like that of a tingling nerve was now sensible amongst the men. In the officers' mess there was rejoicing. After their long, intolerable waiting there was to be decisive action at last. For the report of the scouts was that the Indians, probably about two thousand of them, were now lining up about five miles distant in regular battle array.

"Good!" Wayne gloated. "Couldn't be better!"

The order to march again was given early the next morning and the five miles were covered speedily with the army moving in its fighting positions, the Miami River to the right of them until they came upon a spot where a tornado had evidently swept through the forest, leaving twisted trunks and uprooted trees in enough profusion to impede the cavalry. Wayne, as always in the van, led the way around the fallen timbers, and when the army was all at last on level ground, formed his forces in two lines with cavalry leading the first. Suddenly the Indians opened fire upon the mounted men in front, so concerted and murderous as to drive them back to the main army. There was a rain of bullets from the Legion, only to be answered steadily by the Indians. O'Hara in the rear where he had been ordered to stay felt sheer terror grip him. "This is worse than Yorktown!" he kept muttering. "Much worse."

The Indians, though in more or less conventional formation, still practised their ancient art of deploying behind trees. The battle grew more and more merciless as the hours passed. Life or death, that struggle, with the Indians fighting at their last stand for their lands and their homes; and the Legion of the United States fighting for a country that would stretch from the mountains to the western sea.

At last O'Hara from his vantage saw what Wayne was about to do. He was sending one force to turn the right of the enemy, and another at the same time along the river to turn their left. And in the centre, there was advancing a heavy brigade with *bayonets fixed*, to press by direct charge, the enemy from their coverts.

The Indians could not withstand this mode of attack. They broke in utter confusion and were driven two miles in the course of an hour with, as O'Hara heard afterwards, dead bodies and British muskets scattered in all directions. Before the sun set their villages and cornfields were burned for miles around. The forty-year struggle with the red men was ended.

O'Hara had no time to talk as he supervised the hot supper the soldiers sorely needed. Meanwhile the wounded were taken back to Fort Defiance where General Hand, with the army now not as a military man but in his own profession as a doctor, ministered to them. Wayne and the other officers were seeing to the burial of the dead.

The last smouldering embers were dying out in the sky when O'Hara went into Wayne's tent at his request to join him at supper. The general looked white and exhausted but with a spark of triumph in his eyes.

"Well, it's over, thank God," he began.

"And what a victory!"

"Yes, I guess we'll call it the Battle of Fallen Timbers when we send in a report. Good a name as any. What a place that was! I'll tell you something O'Hara. I've fought my last battle. I think I've done my duty for my country. What I want now is to go home and get married and make love and lead the life of a country gentleman the rest of my days. I don't ever want to hear the word *war* again."

"I don't wonder. After to-day I certainly don't myself. But now you can leave soon for the east, can't you?"

Wayne stared at him. "Let's eat first and wet our whistles well, and then I'll tell you how the immediate future looks to me." As he moved an expression of pain escaped him.

"General, you're not wounded!"

"No, no. I don't know how I always escape. Mary says I'm 'invincible.' No, it's that damned old bullet that gives me a twinge sometimes. I'm fit as a fiddle, really. Just tired. Dog tired."

When they had eaten and drunk well, Wayne leaned back and began to speak slowly.

"You remember after Yorktown, O'Hara? Well, I'm afraid we're caught in the same way, now. The big battle is over, true, and I'm sure the Indians will never take concerted action again, but there are still a lot of them around. If we pulled out our troops completely now it would be unwise. I want to see a *real* treaty signed this time. One that will stick, and this time it may take a while. Then of course there is the matter of the judicious and orderly dispersion of several thousand troops. Poor devils! They all want to get home as much as we do. I don't let myself think how much longer I may have to stay. You'll get back sooner of course, but I will need you for several months more at least. How about it?"

O'Hara smiled. "I think I can still take orders, *Mon Général*."

"Do you remember after Yorktown when we had to accept delay I spoke one note of comfort?" Wayne asked.

"I'm afraid I don't. I guess my mind at the time was not too receptive to comfort."

"Well, I said that at least from then on letters would get through. And it's the same here, only better. It's amazing what work the messengers have done. So let's count on that. One pleasant fact to me is, I'm still *alive*."

O'Hara sobered as he looked into Wayne's eyes.

"After what I saw you doing to-day I can't account for it, but I give hearty thanks."

So the weeks went on. As the general had said, letters came with surprisingly regularity. A brief one from Brackenridge gave O'Hara the keenest anxiety. The "Whisky Rebellion," as it was now being called, had reached a point of near violence. Commissioners appointed by President Washington were in Pittsburgh, including Brackenridge himself, William Bradford, the Attorney-General of the United States, Thomas McKean, chief justice of the state supreme court, and Congressman William Irvine, once commander of Fort Pitt. On the other side were David Bradford and his fire-eating followers of Washington County, including the stiffest of those resisting the tax on their own distilled whisky. Brackenridge wrote:

> I trust you to keep this under your hat, O'Hara, but for the moment I'm running with the hare and the hounds both. My sympathies are with the western farmers, but I feel I can do more for them by appearing to side with the law until things get quieter. If the foxy Nevilles find me out, I'm as good as done for. The girls don't seem to realise the seriousness of the situation yet and I don't enlighten them. Mary, of course, is completely out of it since you are, yourself. Better stay there a while longer.

As a matter of fact Mary's letters were very cheerful. She and Maria were having the greatest pleasure in the leisurely move to the new house. It was becoming more and more like home to her and she really had to curb her feeling of *pride* in it. The house in the King's Orchard *did* look small now. And wasn't this strange when it had seemed ample before? She would never cease to love it because it had been their first home and was so relieved they were to keep it. She had started the older little boys on the New England Primer and had found them to be *so* bright. Little Butler had been left with a cough after the measles but Dr. Bedford said it often happened. She read his letters over and over and slept with the latest one under her pillow, and just exactly where *was* he now?

One night he sat at a camp table and wrote her in detail.[1]

Headquarters
Miami Villages
Oct. 3rd, 1794

My Dear Wife
I had the pleasure of writing you last from Cincinnati, on the 19th. Ultimo. On the 20th I left Fort Washington and on the 30th arrived at this place with my convoy in perfect order and very acceptable. This march was by no means disagreeable.

[1] The original of this letter is in possession of Mrs. E. H. Brereton, the great-granddaughter of James O'Hara.

The Army arrived here from Fort Defiance on the 17th of September, and the Legion is now employed in erecting a Fort which will be strong and regular. A Garrison of three Hundred and fifty will be left, and about the 15th the remainder of the Army will return to Greenville, and the business of my department being completed in the Quarter for six months, I shall then proceed to Fort Washington. This will probably be about the first of Nov. I shall in the meantime embrace every opportunity of writing you.

The intentions of the Indians yet remain a mystery, their long and total silence in respect to us is considered as very extraordinary. I am however convinced that they are awaiting the result of more refined and corrupt councils than their own, which may terminate in the confusion and disgrace of the Incendiaries concerned.

I am greatly concerned for the Doctor's state of health, and have some apprehension for Febiger, who would also be an irreparable loss to the whole connection, *hope for the best.*

I see your curiosity to know how far we are from any place.

I inform you that Recovery is one Hundred miles from Fort Washington, the General Course with 16 Degrees West, that here the Army faced to the Right and marched to Grand Glaize where Fort Defiance now stands, seventy four Miles and a half, General Course North, 10 Degrees East, and from that point the Army marched on the 13th Ultimo, ascending the Miami river forty eight Miles and a half, General Course, South, 69 Degrees West, and with the last Escourt I kept the old Course by Fort Recovery to this place which I reckon fifty four Miles from Recovery, then 24 Miles to Greenville, then 76 to Fort Washington, and about 500 to *home.*

It gives me a great deal of pleasure to hear that my dear little boys are such clever fellows and learn so well. I am in hopes my Butler will grow bold and strong with the change of the Season.

God bless you and them,
and preserve you, the
delight of your most
tender

James O'Hara

He got home in late November earlier than he had expected, on an Indian summer afternoon. He rode quickly through the town and dismounted, his heart beating fast, at his own door. Here Prudence met him.

"Oh, you're home, sir," she said with her usual calmness. "Well, the Mistress is over at the Big Place!"

He thanked her and hurried to Water Street. Before him stood the house of his dreams, painted white now, making it look even larger than it was, with the new grass still green upon the lawn and the young trees at the sides and back showing sturdy growth. He stood for a minute looking at the noble view of the rivers, then with his heart high, he bounded up the steps and opened the front door. There was no sound within.

"Mary!" he called. "Mary!"

There was a cry then and the sound of running feet and she threw herself into his arms, but not with the usual joyful welcome. She was crying as he held her, sobbing even.

"Oh darling, my Delight, what is it? Tell me!" His voice was terrified.

"It's your being away so long. I can't stand it. I've tried to be brave and do my part but it's been too hard, with all this Whisky War going on. James, they almost burned down this house!"

"*What?*" he cried.

"It's true. It was only Hugh that saved it. You know Major Kirkpatrick right next us here has been working with General Neville for the Government and the Whisky people hate him and they came one night, a crowd of them, to set fire to his house. And of course that would have taken this one. And Hugh came and talked to them. He said you were away, serving your country and they mustn't do this harm to you. And finally they went away. But they did burn the Kirkpatrick farm buildings up on Coal Hill. We could see the glare all over town. Oh, I've been so *frightened!*"

There were a few chairs already there and he drew her to one and held her on his knee, smoothing her hair as he tried to comfort her, making strong resolutions within himself.

"Darling, listen. You've been so brave, so uncomplaining these past years. But now my plans are going to be different. I will not leave you this time until all this *Whisky* trouble is over. And even after that I promise you my trips will be shorter. The big battle is won now and I can delegate more of the business to others. Would you care to hear a little piece of news?"

She raised her head and he wiped the tears away.

"I've been made *General* O'Hara. Do you like the sound of that?"

She kissed him for answer, her face suddenly all alight. "I never was so proud! How long have you known it?"

"Not long. I got word before I left the Post. As a matter of fact I feel a bit 'lifted' myself as they say in the old country. Well now, dear little *Mrs. General O'Hara*, would you join me in a tour of the house?"

So the tears and their own dark days of separation were once more forgotten, but Mary had a quick question.

"What about General Wayne? When will Anthony get home?"

O'Hara's face sobered. "I don't know," he said. "You see, he's just done a tremendous thing. He's made a complete conquest of the Indians for the first time in forty years. Now he naturally wants to oversee the Peace Treaty. He practically has to, and the Indians are delaying. We think they're waiting to see what the British will do about the forts they still hold. What do you hear of Mary Vining?"

"Oh, she's *so* happy, everyone writes me. So relieved he got through the battle safely. She pretended she wasn't worried but of course she was, terribly. Now she says when their happiness is so assured she can wait as long as she has to. The girls say she's doing the most exquisite needlework for her bridal chest. Well, I hope it won't be too long. Come now, and see the dining-room rug. Father sent it addressed to me, so I had it laid. And the furniture is all here in crates at the back of the store! Of course it was all sent to you, but since the rug is mine . . ."

"But dear Delight, everything I have is yours!"

"Oh yes, but I wanted us to be together when the furniture was set in. Can we have it done soon?"

"As soon as to-morrow we'll begin."

When they had made their tour and stood in front of the house ready to start back to the Orchard, Mary said slowly, "When this is all furnished as we plan I believe it's going to be even more beautiful than my old home in Philadelphia!"

O'Hara tucked her hand under his arm and gave it a little squeeze. "You musn't hate me for it, but that's been my ambition all along."

The next day before he began upon the furniture O'Hara felt he must learn for himself just how serious the "Whisky War" had been or indeed might still be. He could see the presence of strange troops in town and they filled him with consternation. He went first to talk with Samuel Semple, always a repository of information and common sense. He went into a couple of other taverns, where he asked a few questions but listened more, then he talked with Elliott. From it all he pieced together these facts. Alexander Hamilton, author and head of the Federalists, had apparently seen in the uprising of the Democratic western farmers, who resented paying a tax on the whisky they were selling, a fine chance to dramatise his own party with its emphasis on the control of the central government. So he had urged the raising of troops, marched them over the rough Alleghenies and fanned them out over Pittsburgh and the surrounding Monongahela country with the idea of ferreting out all traitors, Hugh Brackenridge suddenly becoming the chief! For the Nevilles had consciously or unconsciously misrepresented his behaviour in every way possible and were ready to see him arrested for treason.

When O'Hara stopped at the Brackenridge house Hugh met him with a very lopsided smile.

"Well, well, O'Hara! Glad to see you but you'd better not come in. I've been poison round here."

"I guess I'll risk it," O'Hara said, stepping over the threshold. "What the devil's been going on, Hugh?"

"Plenty. How much do you know already?"

"The background, but I want details. Go ahead, man. Out west I had no idea how serious it all was, for you especially."

"Maria's out doing errands so sit down and I'll let you have it. I wrote you my sympathies were with the farmers but I certainly stand for law and order. The Nevilles, though, twisted everything I did. I went out to Mingo Creek once to try to calm down a violent group there. And once when they came up here to shoot up the town I bought three barrels of whisky *out of my own pocket* to quiet them. But to the Nevilles I was 'consorting with the insurgents'."

"I can hardly believe this!"

"True, just the same. You know General Neville was one of the tax collectors and the farmers hate his hide. They came up one night to demand his papers. Of course he didn't give them and there was a little shooting. One good man, McFarlane, one of the farmers, was killed in the fracas. So things got worse."

Hugh's face was thin, O'Hara saw now, with dark circles under his eyes.

"You know Hamilton, don't you?" he went on.

"Slightly."

"Well, he came with the troops and had a little band of judicial inquisitors. General Henry Lee was at the head of the army, and damned if they didn't quarter him *on me!*"

"In this house?"

"Exactly. I guess they thought if he was here I wouldn't run away. Like young David Bradford did. I knew Lee years ago. I tutored him at Princeton, but I don't like him. Well, we did our best by him. I was pleasant as a basket of chips and Maria nearly killed herself cooking for him and waiting on him. And what do you suppose happened? Two weeks ago he told us that 'for the sake of retirement' he was moving to a less central part of town, and *left!* You can see what that made us look like. Maria was heartbroken after all her work and thinking she was helping me! I'd like to kick that fellow across the Alleghenies, even if I broke both legs doing it!" His voice was bitter.

"Well, what now," O'Hara persisted. "Have things quieted?"

"They had to. What could the farmers do against all those soldiers? But there's plenty of rancour still. They arrested sixteen men a few weeks ago at night. Didn't even let them get dressed entirely. Marched them out into the country, kept them in a pen out there for days till they nearly died of exposure and then found out that most of them had been falsely accused! How they missed me in that group I'll never know. Oh, there's been dirty work done. But as to me, want to hear the climax?"

"I needn't tell you I do."

"Just a week ago Hamilton summoned me for an interview. He's a reasonable man. We talked it all out and he ended by giving me a clean bill!"

"Thank God!"

"And they tell me old Neville nearly exploded when he heard of it. He talked about it everywhere and a man told me he said 'Brackenridge is the most artful fellow that ever was on God Almighty's earth! He's deceived everyone and now he's even put his finger in Hamilton's eye.' Not a bad epitaph, eh?" Hugh laughed.

O'Hara was sober. "This is all so much worse than I ever imagined. You've been through bad times, Hugh. I'm glad it's over for you, and that you're cleared. Mary told me how you saved our house. How can I ever thank you enough? You must have pretty well taken your life in your hand to do it."

"It was a tough crowd but they really listened when I expounded on you. If you'd heard me you'd have been convinced you're quite a fellah. They were dead set to fire something that night so they went up on the hill and burnt Kirkpatrick's farm buildings and a pretty blaze they made! Of course you know he's worked hand in glove with Neville."

"How is Maria now after all the anxiety?"

Hugh's face lit up. "She's feeling pretty happy that I've been cleared especially since now we'll be eligible for the ball. Has Mary told you about that?"

"Oh, yes. I heard the news last night."

"Well, if anyone deserves an invitation to this affair in honour of Lee, she does. There have been a good many social events the last couple of months but of course we've been out of them. And your Mary didn't seem to have much heart for going, with you away. Now we can go together and show off our pretty wives. They're planning their dresses already, I think."

O'Hara got up to go. "We're putting the new furniture over on Water Street to-day, so I've got to leave. I'm still stunned by all you've told me."

Hugh lowered his voice though no one was near. "There's one thing I didn't mention. It still haunts me. Just after the troops came when feelings ran pretty high, I looked out of the bedroom window one night and saw some dragoons advancing on my house here *with a rope*."

"You can't mean that!"

"I do. But I'll say this for the Nevilles. They headed them off. I guess even they decided they'd stop one short of hanging me! But it's not a pleasant memory. Oh, O'Hara, I'm ashamed never to have mentioned your big victory! What must you think of me?"

"I'll tell you all about that later. Just now I wanted to hear exactly what you've told me. My news will keep."

"When are they going to make you a general?" Hugh asked with a chuckle.

O'Hara coloured. "Well, as a matter of fact they've already done so."

"Ho! Ho! So, that's the reason you weren't afraid to come into my house. As a *general* you can . . ."

O'Hara's grey eyes shot sparks. "Take that back, Hugh!"

"My God, the man's touchy!"

"On some points, yes. Things like honour or friendship . . . Take that back!"

Hugh grasped his arms. "Why, you damned fool!" he said affectionately. "Surely you knew I was joking. But O'Hara, I'm glad you flared up like that. I'm good and glad. It comforts my heart after all I've been through. I've got one true friend in Pittsburgh, at least."

The moving to the Big Place, as Prudence called it, was accomplished in a week's time with McGrady and Elliott helping while Lewis, the erstwhile keelboater, kept the store. Other men in need of work were pressed into service so that a steady stream of loaded wagons traversed the short distance between the King's Orchard and Water Street, while from the store the heavy crates were transferred to the grounds at the back of the new house and opened there. O'Hara planned that the last things set in place would be the dining-room pieces, so that room was left empty for the time being.

It was Mary's decision to leave enough furniture in their old home so that it would not look *forlorn*, as she put it. The big secretary of course remained in the parlour and O'Hara had a larger and plainer desk set in to give more working space. The large wing chairs, now showing signs of wear, remained, with a couple of candlestands. But the beautiful table[1] from Ireland with its shamrock feet was the first thing to be removed to the new drawing-room, and above it O'Hara hung the Tyrawley coat of arms with a feeling of satisfaction.

"I think the old lion will feel more content here," he said to Mary.

The guest room in the old house was to remain intact. "We might have an overflow of visitors some time, or a stranger might need a bed," Mary said.

"Or," said O'Hara with great seriousness, "I might be working late in my office and decide it was too much trouble to go home and I'd just sleep there."

Mary looked up startled and then seeing the twinkle in his eyes, laughed. "Oh you!" she said. "What a tease you are!"

When it was time to say the last good-bye to the log house Mary's

[1] This table is now in the home of James O'Hara Denny, of Pittsburgh.

eyes were full of tears. "One reason I insisted upon keeping a bedroom here was that some time when the apple blossoms are out, or the locusts, perhaps we might come over ourselves for old sake's sake and stay the night," she said.

"We might," O'Hara said tenderly. "We might do just that." And then they kissed, as they closed the kitchen door for the last time and left the King's Orchard.

But in the great new house there was no chance for tears or regrets as its welcoming beauty surrounded them. For their first night there O'Hara had ordered fires in every room and plenty of candles lighted; so in the late afternoon he and Mary walked through their new domain in a gentle glow. The drawing-room had long yellow satin sofas which picked up the colour in the wallpaper that Mary had selected from samples sent from Philadelphia. The chairs were striped blue and gold and the candlestands and side tables were polished cherrywood. At the end of the room near the library stood a small spinet. Mary paused to finger the puckered blue silk pockets at each end.

"This is the best place for it, I think. For if we should ever have a soirée the violinists could stand here at either side and be out of the way."

When he felt the time was ripe O'Hara led her to the diningroom where for a moment she was speechless. It *was* unbelievably handsome! The long table with its eighteen chairs, the massive sideboard, and the serving table, all in richly carved mahogany. Prudence had to call them three times for supper before they could cease admiring; then they sat down at last with the children, in the big comfortable kitchen. Prudence was cooking over the open fire but promised to try the new-fangled stove soon.

"After all, a good, sound kitchen is the heart of the home," O'Hara said, looking about him, relaxed and content.

That night before she slept, Mary said, "Do you know, James, what I believe I like best in the whole house?"

"Me?" he suggested.

She moved her head on his arm with a little laugh. "Well, of course, *you*, but I mean the house itself. I think I'm most thrilled over the real glass window panes!"

"And the devil's own time I had getting them," he answered. "About half the first shipment broke coming over the mountains and when it was finally all here I found it had cost about as much as the furniture! But some day . . ."

"What do you mean, *some day?*"

"Oh, some day I hope everyone in Pittsburgh will have glass window panes."

Through the coming days O'Hara discovered that a delicious under-current of excitement was running through the conversation of the women who belonged to the town's élite. The main subject at tea or at casual meetings in stores or street corners was apparently the coming ball in honour of General Lee. Since no private house was adequate it was to be held in the new Fort and James Brison, prothonotary of Allegheny County, was the manager and would issue the invitations. Maria and Mary discussed their dresses and tried them on for masculine approval, before hanging them up, ready for the great night. The two couples were to go together and Maria's cheeks always flushed red with anticipation as they spoke of it, for the ball would be in the nature of a triumph and public vindication for Hugh.

Meanwhile O'Hara had gone to see Major Craig. They discussed in detail the great victory in the west and exulted over their own success with the supply lines, then O'Hara turned grave.

"There's something I have to say to you, Isaac."

"All right, say on."

"I'm a Federalist, as you and your immediate connections are, and I'm your friend and theirs. But I am also a friend of Hugh Brackenridge. He's been through a pretty little hell over this *Whisky Rebellion*, and I don't think all of you can take much satisfaction in what you've done to him. For myself, I don't like it."

"Well, well," the Major said, somewhat embarrassed, "you were away and couldn't know all the facts. But shall we just say it's past now, Brackenridge has been cleared by Alexander Hamilton, so let's get on to our own business."

"I had to make myself clear, Isaac."

"You have," he smiled grimly. "You usually do."

So, this being understood they fell to planning the future. "I doubt if we can really get started on our *glass* for another year or so," O'Hara said, "but at least we can be thinking about it. I heard that a glassworks near Philadelphia has a fine man as manager and I've made some inquiries. He's a William Eichbaum, a German. Family, glass cutters for generations. Now, why can't we at least keep a finger on him until we're ready? You write him, and ask his advice as to how to go about building a glassworks. That will flatter him and he'll remember our names. Sign mine with yours, will you, Isaac?"

"Easy enough. Good idea."

"As for me I've got something else I have to start on at once."

"What now?"

"I'm going to ship salt from the Onondaga works up at Salina, New York down to Pittsburgh."

"That's impossible!"

"I know it. That's one reason why the thing attracts me," he grinned. "We've got to find a cheaper way than getting it across the mountains and I tnink this will be it. Don't look so shocked. After what we've done these last two years in Quarter-mastering I should say it's reasonable to tackle anything, wouldn't you?"

"That depends very much upon who tackles it," said the Major.

A few days later the invitation to the ball arrived for *General and Mrs. James O'Hara*. They were both proud of the wording and happy over the prospect itself. "I'll have to check over my own wardrobe," he said, "and stop in at the wigmakers. My old one looks as though the rats might have been in it. Oh, from the way this reads we're invited to the dinner too! That *is* an honour."

"Then we can't go with Maria and Hugh, can we, for they won't likely be at the dinner. But we can meet them before the dancing starts. It's a wonder Maria hasn't been over. I'll run in to-morrow and we'll make final plans."

But before she had a chance to go, Hugh came there. His face was set.

"The invitations are all out," he said, "and the Brackenridges did not receive one."

"Oh, Hugh!" Mary cried in distress.

"It was James Brison! He had it in his own hands. And I'll tell you something. I'm not through with politics yet by a long shot, and if it's the last thing I do in this world I'll get even with him for this!" And he turned and walked out.

"This is cruel!" O'Hara said. "It's not just the disappoint-ment of missing a ball, though to Maria that will be great enough. But it's another blow to Hugh personally. I'm very sorry about this."

"Couldn't you do something, James? Couldn't you speak to Mr. Brison or General Lee or . . . or even to Mr. Hamilton?"

He shook his head. "I don't think so," he said. "It's not too good an idea to use your own spoon to stir another man's broth."

"This is going to take the pleasure out of it for us, too," she said mournfully.

And to a considerable extent it did, though the affair was the most socially ambitious in the town's history. O'Hara listened to many comments from the easterners to the effect that they had not expected such entertainment in the Back Country! He was glad to renew acquaintance with Hamilton and meet the other officers but his special gratification was in seeing Mary holding her own little court, as beautiful, he felt, as on the night of Anne Bingham's ball in Philadelphia. As the silks and laces and powdered wigs began to move to the strains of a minuet, however, O'Hara was thinking of the deerskin breeches and linsey-woolsey dresses he had seen rollicking in the square dance at the old Fort on his first Christmas Eve here, over twenty years ago. *Pittsburgh has really grown up*, he smiled to himself.

They left early. "When your heart is a little heavy, your feet seem a bit heavy too, don't you think, James?" Mary said on their way back. And as they passed the dark and silent Brackenridge house, he agreed with her. Once at home they went directly to their room where O'Hara lighted the fire and drew the small sofa of many memories close. There as they discussed the evening the thing took place which often happens between married people in love: they thought of the same thing at the same time! It was that *they* would give a party at which Hugh and Maria would be honoured guests!

"It won't be the same as being at the ball to-night but it will be something to salve their wound," O'Hara said.

"And we *should* give a housewarming in any case. Just for our particular friends, don't you think?"

"The *crème de la crème*!" he smiled.

"And just before Christmas we can have the house trimmed with pines. Oh, it will be beautiful. Let's plan!"

The fire had to be remade three times before they finally went to bed. But because of all their decisions Mary wrote the invitations one day in her delicate hand: *General and Mrs. James O'Hara will receive* . . .

And receive they did one evening the week before Christmas in the wide centre hall carpeted with roses and with the curving stairs behind them twined with greens. Movement and laughter and admiring voices filled the rooms as the logs in the fireplace crackled and flamed and the candlelight shone soft and golden from every mantelpiece and table.

There had been one anxiety in connection with the party. This was that the Neville "cabal," as Hugh called it, had to be invited. Not only, as O'Hara had pointed out to Mary, were they perhaps the town's first family, they were also his friends and Major Craig, the General's son-in-law, was his close business associate. Whether bringing the erstwhile enemies together in the confines of four walls would be disastrous or not, had remained to be seen. But as it turned out there was no open indication of feud. O'Hara did some clever manipulating as a host and the principals themselves kept out of each other's way. With it all, Hugh and Maria had reason for pride in their position that night, for it was patent to all that they were valued friends in the house. So the music from the violins and spinet flowed on in the drawing-room, the elegant buffet and hot spiced rum punch was dispensed in the dining-room, and the general gaiety continued without a break.

When Mary and O'Hara had bade the last guest good night, he put his arms about her. "Well, it was delightful, dear, wasn't it?"

She looked into his eyes. "You've given me *so much*, James!"

"Not a fraction of what you've given me! That is beyond price. But at least you're in your proper setting at last."

They moved slowly through the rooms, putting out the candles, placing the shields before the fires and recounting all the evening's successes.

"I'm sure we brought happiness to two of our friends with the party. If we could only know that Mary Vining and Anthony Wayne were together now how wonderful that would be! I was thinking of them as I dressed to-night. Surely he will be through in the west before too long, won't he?"

"I have no idea. One thing I do know. The general will always do out the duty."

"But the waste of it, when they could be married now after all the long delay. The terrible waste of time!"

"There's one thing you can always count on about *time*."

"What is that?"

"It passes."

And it passed swiftly for O'Hara during the months that made up the following year! Ever since the idea of transporting salt from New York State to Pittsburgh had entered his head, he could not rest until he had put it into execution. The situation was simply this. Money, as always, was scarce with most people and salt—that infinitely precious commodity, the preserver, the essence of all flavour, the very life of taste and appetite, lending zest to the palate and savour to all living—was brought now from the east or from Baltimore over the mountains by laden pack-horses for *eight dollars a bushel*! O'Hara was convinced that he could bring it from the Onondaga works to sell at half that price and make a good profit. But the difficulties in the way were stupendous. A whole transportation route would have to be built. Could it be done?

He went up to Salina right after the New Year and with his shrewd eyes narrowed and his contractor's invaluable experience to give him assurance, he began his negotiations. First for the salt itself and then, practically, for the barrels. He would reserve some in his contracts but he ordered others from a cooperage to his exact specification: "good pork barrels, with not less than twelve hoops on a barrel and not to be nailed with less than ten nails and to be delivered to Oswego in good order." Then, the route! Roads and portages would have to be improved and wagons bought; and there would *have* to be two small vessels built, one for Lake Ontario and one for Lake Erie!

He did not quail. The very magnitude of the task exhilarated him. He examined all the terrain; he drew precise plans; then he proceeded as he had done with all his other smaller undertakings. The idea and the entire capital were his own; but after that came the selection of capable men to take charge at each step of the way, with himself checking and overseeing both on the ground when he could, and from a distance when he could not. Relentlessly he pressed his plan; steadily the idea took palpable form; apparent impossibilities smoothed out; delays and discouragements were overcome, as the year grew older and at last, old.

By December O'Hara, back in Pittsburgh, stood at the wharf one bright, cold day to receive his first shipment of two hundred and fifty barrels of salt which had come safely by keelboat from French Creek down the Allegheny on the last stage of its long journey. It would sell at the rate of *four dollars a bushel*!

A crowd gathered as the keelboats were unloaded. Men and women with pans and pails waited jubilantly to buy the precious grains when the first barrel was opened. They shook hands with O'Hara and tried to express their thanks.

"This is a great day for us, General!"

"You're the only man could have done it!"

"No more wood ashes now!" one shabby woman said happily.

When the salt was finally removed to O'Hara's own store, he went back home to exult with Mary over his achievement. He had kept his promise this year to come back oftener, though the times with her had of necessity been short, except for one visit in the fall when a new baby had come to the big house on Water Street, this time a little girl. O'Hara had not known how greatly he desired a girl-child but now his whole strong being seemed to melt at the touch of the small rosebud creature. She had been named *Elizabeth* for Mary's sister and would soon be three months old. There was a newcomer also in the Brackenridge home, a boy! So, he was thinking as he walked briskly along, compared to the other events of the year the shipping of the salt could be reckoned as less important. But he would not belittle it. It had been a great and successful undertaking, a benefit to his town and to himself.

There was another reason still why this coming holiday season would bring joy to him and Mary. Vicarious but very real. Anthony Wayne had at long last been released from western service and would be back in Philadelphia by Christmas!

When O'Hara reached the house, pausing first as always to gloat over the handsome structure and the view upon which it faced, he poured out to Mary all the details of the scene at the wharf, and then with pencil and paper showed her just how much he himself would be making on the venture.

"Couldn't you bring the salt price down still further then?" she asked.

"Ah, my little conscience!" he said, laughing. "Later on when I've recouped the money I've had to lay out, I *will* bring down the price. But even now, don't forget I've halved it from what it used to be. Letters from the East to-day?"

Mary's face was aglow as she laid two before him. "They are both filled with news of Mary Vining. She's going to give a big dinner in honour of Anthony's return and they'll be married at the New Year! She is almost beside herself with joy, they say, and no wonder!"

"And imagine Anthony! I can picture what *he's* feeling."

They discussed their own holiday plans and decided to have a large afternoon reception just before Christmas instead of a soirée such as they had had last year. But, as Mary said, no matter what they did this would be an unusually happy time for many reasons.

It was two days before the party, merrymaking was in the air and the house was hung again with greens when O'Hara came in suddenly, his face white. He found Mary in the library and pressed her gently into a chair.

"Sit down, my dear," he said. "I've just had dreadful news. *Ghastly* news!"

She looked up at him, terrified. "What?" she breathed.

"Anthony Wayne died on the fifteenth out at Erie. On his way back!"

Chapter Thirteen

Pittsburgh was indeed growing up. True, there were still a few cows pasturing comfortably at the foot of Grant's Hill and an occasional hog running wild, but for the most part an almost urban decorum had replaced the raw frontier atmosphere of earlier days. Most of the log cabins were gone now with the frame and brick structures taking their place. When the old Fort was demolished O'Hara and Ebenezer Denny had used the bricks according to their plan, and with the neat row of dwellings they put up the number of houses rose to over eight hundred! At the same time O'Hara had bought the small block house," built by Col. Bouquet, in order that it might be a permanent landmark in the town. While the newer buildings were devoid of any architectural beauty and even lacked the picturesqueness of the old, their miscellaneous outlines were all softened by the profusion of locusts, sycamores, Lombardy poplars and weeping willows which had sprung up in the wake of the primeval forest.

Certain attributes of the Pittsburghers themselves were discernible to strangers who came there. These qualities may have derived from the prevalence of Scotch-Irish blood which, as always, had a large percentage of *iron* in it; or perhaps they were the result of the former bitter struggles with nature, the elements and the Indians, but there remained a core of strength, of determination and also of self-esteem quite removed from egotism, in these men who were founding a city.

The *Academy* was at last a flourishing concern and there were also several schools for younger children. A small courthouse had been built, and two more churches established, the Episcopal and the Methodist. The ironic comment by a traveller that in Pittsburgh "taverns were more plentiful than churches and whisky purer and stronger than the faith" could at this point be more successfully challenged. The King's Gardens were now largely covered with houses instead of vegetables and flowers as of old, but the Orchard, while somewhat smaller, remained. The keelboats still poled up and down the waters, with Mike Fink, after his congenial practice with Wayne's Indian fighters, continuing his supreme sway among the boaters. It was a colourful day when he visited his native Pittsburgh, making his rollicking rounds of the taverns, fighting any man willing to fight with him and some who weren't, testing their courage by first shooting tin cups off their heads and subsiding by night into hidden but quite as turbulent orgies!

There was another colourful spectacle, however, of a peaceful nature. Little by little the roads over the mountains had been improved and now even more anticipated in the town than the post rider's horn was the sound of the bells which heralded the approach of a Conestoga wagon! It *was* a beautifully impressive sight, for the wagon boxes were painted blue with the running gears red; above, flared the great white covering canvas. Six powerful coal black Conestoga horses, of a special breed, pulled the wagon and each was provided with hame bells so that the loud, ringing music of their chime became synonymous with safe arrival. It was not long before another catch phrase sprang into common use. "I'll be there *with bells*," one townsman would say to another.

Within the big house on Water Street the changes had been happy ones. There was to keep Elizabeth company a second little girl now, at O'Hara's insistence, *Mary*, and the boys were growing tall and strong. There was also a chambermaid and another kitchen helper for Prudence. In the stabling there were housed, besides the aged Pitt, a young riding horse and a spanking team of bays which drew the only carriage in the town! Mary prayed earnestly to herself as she rode out in it that she might be delivered from vanity and pride!

Their hearts still ached over the tragedy of Anthony Wayne's death, due, as they had learned later, to a flare-up of his old wound; and even more continuously for Mary Vining who, as the letters from the East told, had never left her home since the news came. She had been writing the invitations for the dinner of welcome when the word had been brought to her and she, too, had seemed to die then, though still in life.

Both O'Hara and Mary missed the Brackenridges who were living in Carlisle to be nearer the centre, for Hugh also had a title now. During the last big gubernatorial campaign he had worked zealously for Thomas McKean, who was elected. His reward was his appointment as justice of the state supreme court! It was a signal honour and the very position for which Hugh was eminently fitted. His fame had spread also because of the publication of the first two volumes of his work, *Modern Chivalry*, upon which he had been concentrating for years; so O'Hara felt sure that the old hurts in his heart were now pretty well healed. One evidence, however, that he still remembered them was that upon his appointment he had at once prevailed upon the governor to dismiss James Brison as prothonotary and replace him with one of Hugh's own relatives! So was the revenge complete.

While they missed Hugh and Maria, they now had the Dennys, who in a large measure took their place. Ebenezer had at last married his little flower-like Nancy Wilkins back in Carlisle, and had come with her to make their home in Pittsburgh. So O'Hara had a congenial friend and onetime comrade-in-arms with whom to smoke his pipe and exchange reminiscences, and Mary had another young bride to take under her wing. When they supped with the O'Haras it was often by common consent in the big home-like kitchen where Agnes Denny's pewter plate still graced the mantel.

But though O'Hara seemed the same to the casual eye as he walked the streets receiving respectful greetings from his townsmen and exchanging witty sallies with a favoured few, and while he checked with satisfaction upon his various industries, which now included The Point Brewery, he was, within himself, a seething mass of anxieties and nerves. For the first time in his life he could not sleep and woke up in the mornings tense and unrefreshed. The trouble was that he was now launched upon the greatest of all his undertakings, the fulfilment of his most cherished dream: the manufacture of glass. And the difficulties involved were more intricate, more overwhelming because of their unfamiliarity than any he had heretofore encountered.

He often thought of the night the idea had first come to him with force. It was as he lay in the guest room of the Orchard house, heartbroken and estranged from Mary, listening to the beat of the rain upon the oiled paper panes. He knew then that he must one day make glass for her, for Pittsburgh, and of course for himself. And now he was in the midst of it and for the first time in his life he had doubts of his own power to succeed.

They had begun, he and Isaac Craig as they had planned, by enlisting the interest of William Eichbaum, a Westphalian glass cutter considered the best in this country. His first demand while still in Philadelphia had been for samples of clay from the country-side around Pittsburgh to see if any was suitable for the making of *pots*. This took time. Finally Eichbaum admitted that one sample "was not amiss" and ordered the digging and ripening of twenty-five tons!

"Why doesn't the man come on out and oversee everything himself as we want him to do?" O'Hara had fretted. "I'll pay him! What's the matter with him, anyhow?"

But Eichbaum was canny. Until the O'Hara Glassworks were really started he would remain where he was. The next problem had been the location of coal. O'Hara had been determined from the first that this was to be the fuel instead of wood, but it took much time and labour to find a vein of sufficient depth.

"We'll be the first in the country to do this," he kept telling Craig, "so don't let's give up on it."

At last the proper depth was found and the factory itself built, at the foot of Coal Hill below Jones Ferry on the Monongahela almost opposite the point where the two rivers met. Then, at last, Eichbaum came on. O'Hara invited him to stay at their home until he became somewhat settled before bringing on his family, and had quite looked forward to the visit, but they had found him a difficult guest. He was a Continental gentleman of great refine-ment and regarded Pittsburgh with a patronising eye. He had left Germany for France in pursuit of his trade or *profession* as he termed it and had been most successful there, even to supplying some of the glass for the Palace of Versailles under Louis XVI! After the fall of the Bastille he had come to the United States but he still managed somehow to affect the air of the court. This all infuriated O'Hara who bore his own honours lightly and spoke to all, high and low, with the same easy friendliness. So annoyed was he that he would not speak French with Eichbaum though the latter kept urging it.

"Oh," O'Hara would say innocently, "my French is rather rusty. And besides, my wife does not speak it." He could see Mary turning her back on these occasions to hide her amusement. But the more he saw of Eichbaum the more convinced he was that the man knew his business. "And that's the only thing that matters," he told Craig.

O'Hara was still involved with government business though he was trying hard to be released from it; so the Major had to be the acting manager of the glassworks. When the building itself

L

was finished O'Hara stayed on in Pittsburgh until the furnace was built. This contained eight pots for window glass which, they hoped, would turn out three boxes to a blowing, each box containing one hundred square feet. Two pots of the furnace were to be used for the making of *bottles*. At this point O'Hara's spirits soared. He had engaged workmen, a few experienced ones from Philadelphia; he and Craig had learned much of the process themselves from Eichbaum, who seemed to be growing more and more interested; the coal was dug and waiting with a crew to keep it in supply; everything now, in fact, was ready for the great experiment. And O'Hara had to leave!

"This is one of the hardest things I've ever done!" he told Mary the night before he set out. "But I can't in all honour delay here any longer. Until I'm free from my contracting I can't take a chance on letting a post get low in supplies. I've got to inspect them. I think I'll be gone only a few weeks, and we'll celebrate when I get back! This is going to be a big thing, darling."

He had explained to her in detail the business arrangements, and as before, left in her charge the money to be paid out. As he rode off that next morning he watched the building beyond the river upon which the great hope was set. In a few days now smoke would be pouring from those chimneys!

But when he returned one late autumn day, his eager eyes saw the factory just as he had left it, the chimneys empty! He rode quickly to his own home, found Mary out but assured himself from Prudence that all was well there, then hurried to the ferry and on to the factory which stood now, cold, empty and silent. He found Craig and Eichbaum in the small lean-to office and burst in upon them almost with violence. "What happened? What went wrong?"

Craig shook hands and set a chair. "Now calm yourself, O'Hara. We're all disappointed, I can tell you. Explain it, Eichbaum."

"It was the clay," Eichbaum said, "I chose the best of the samples you sent me and I was sure it would do. It was not right. When we first fired the melting pots, they broke. New Jersey is the only place where I am *certain* the clay is right. It would have to be shipped in barrels over the mountains if you decide . . ."

"I have a feeling, O'Hara, that we should give up the whole thing. You know better than anybody else what that expense would be," Craig said.

O'Hara looked back at them in white astonishment and anger. "Give it up? What do you mean? I'll never give it up. We started out here to make glass and we're going to make it! Let's get the order in for the clay at once. Come on over to my office where we have better writing materials. We can send the letter by to-morrow's post."

"Have you any idea," Eichbaum said slowly, "of the amount of money you'll have to spend on this?"

"I don't care how much I have to spend. I guess I'm able for it. The only thing I'm interested in is getting on with it. Let's go."

Over in the house in the King's Orchard Eichbaum dictated the letter. In it the matter of haste was emphasised though at the best they all knew it would be four or five weeks before the clay arrived. When they had finished their consultations and Eichbaum had received permission to go back to his family during the interim, O'Hara detained him after Craig had left. He had a question which had risen in his mind on one of his solitary rides, along with a great resolution.

"Could you tell me," he asked now, "which glass manufacturing house in all Europe you consider the best?"

Eichbaum told him. "You're not thinking of *importing* glass if we fail here?" he asked.

"We're not going to fail. But thank you very much. Just curiosity," he added.

When he was alone O'Hara wrote a second letter, this one to the Westphalian Glassworks. In it he stated he was interested in purchasing the largest and finest crystal chandelier the house could make, with description and price to be sent him as soon as possible. For this was the idea that had come to him in the forest. He was now President of the Board of Trustees in the Presbyterian Congregation of which he and Mary were members. He was also the wealthiest man in the town. It would be fitting then for him to give a gift to the church, and what more suitable, more to his liking, than one of *glass*, glass in its most delicate and resplendent form. Practical, too, for the flickering light from the poor side sconces and the one candlestick on the pulpit left the room now in semi-darkness at any evening meeting. He sat picturing with pleasure the glorious change his gift would make, and then added a postscript to his letter, asking for a sketch along with the estimate and the approximate date at which the chandelier, if ordered, could be shipped.

As he left the King's Orchard for Water Street his heart, because of his new plan, was eased a little from the first bitter disappointment over the cold chimneys of the factory; besides, he would soon see Mary!

She was waiting for him in the library, eager as always, quick to comfort him for the momentary failures of his hopes, but full apparently of excitement.

"What is it?" he asked when he released her from his arms, "what's the big news?"

"How you do *know* me, James!"

"I should hope so, by this time. What's happened?"

"It's really quite extraordinary! Sit down and I'll tell you all about it. General Neville was over and he says that Prince Louis Philippe, Duke of Orleans, I think he called him, and his two brothers from France are touring the United States! They've been visiting in Philadelphia and are going down to New Orleans and will come by way of Pittsburgh!"

"Good heavens!"

"The letter came from General Washington addressed to either you or General Neville—of course he knows how much of the time you are away—asking if between you, you would entertain the princes. The Nevilles would like to accommodate them at night but the General wondered if you—we—would have them for the dinners, probably two, and make quite a ceremony of them. I think," she added, "that he is impressed by our dining-room."

"Indeed, he'd better be," O'Hara grinned. "Well, this *is* news with a vengeance. We've already had some pretty distinguished guests but these will top them all. When are they likely to arrive?"

"That's a difficulty. We can't be certain but General Neville says he thinks they may be on their way now and he will check on every wagon that comes in. So we'd better start on our arrangements right away. I do think it's thrilling, don't you?"

"Very much so! Now let's see whom we should have as the other guests with them. For the first dinner the Nevilles of course, and the Craigs, and perhaps the Devereux Smiths. He has French blood in him. Oh, I wish Brackenridge could be here! He's always such a dinner-table asset. Mr. Arthur of the Academy I would like, for he's versed in history and literature and a good conversationalist. And the Dennys certainly. Then we can have a second group for the next night. Well, you go ahead, dear, and plan your part of it. Needless to say we'll spare no expense. I'll invite the guests conditionally when we decide on them but I've an idea none of them will mind holding their time open!"

He paused considering. "Do you realise the Duke of Orleans is heir to the throne? I wonder why they are here. My guess would be that with all that's going on now in France they may feel it is wise to be as far away as possible for a time. The Duke's father was among those executed a few years back."

"Oh, how dreadful," Mary said. Then she added, "I suppose you will deign to speak French *with the Duke*."

"I may, if I remember any," he chuckled. "And who's the tease now?"

"I'm so glad I've just got new gowns from Philadelphia! If we have several dinners I can wear a different one each night."

The arrangements went forward apace. The house shone, for McGrady had been impressed to polish the brasses and the silver. There were still chrysanthemums in the garden and Mary decided upon a large bouquet on the Irish table and an epergne for the dining-room as soon as the date was fixed. Already on the buffet the decanters were filled with the best Monongahela rye and the finest Philadelphia sherry, Madeira and port. The food was planned, with O'Hara insisting upon something distinctively American. So, since the season was fall they settled on the main viands as roast turkey with baked apples stuffed with fresh sausage, Prudence's superlative cornbread and pumpkin pie for dessert.

"That will be practically an all-American menu for them, and they'd better like it!" O'Hara said. "Only I wish to heaven they'd soon get here. My lips are getting stiff on my smile of welcome!"

"And I'm so nervous I could jump out of my skin!" Mary said.

He was instantly all solicitude. "You mustn't be worried about the dinners. No prince is worth that. If you just smile at them they won't know what they're eating. Now do relax. I can't have you worn out over this."

But after another week the news came. General Neville sent over a note to the effect that the guests had arrived that afternoon and as they were very weary from the trip Mrs. Neville would serve a light supper and allow them to retire early. But on the next evening if convenient they would be pleased to dine with General and Mrs. O'Hara, and also on the one following.

The activity on Water Street began at once. The turkeys were secured, plucked and dressed for the oven. The pumpkins were cooked ready for the morrow's pies. The flowers were cut and put in water and Mary went about trying to make the already perfect house more perfect. O'Hara meanwhile informed his guests both for the first night and the second, and then on his return managed to get Mary to bed at a reasonable hour. They both woke early in the morning, however, with a strong inner excitement.

"It's almost treasonous for us to make so much over the fact that we're about to entertain royalty," O'Hara said dryly. "After all we live in a democracy where all men are born 'free and equal'. "

Mary's reply was not relative to any political philosophy. "I do hope you'll like the dress I'm wearing to-night. You haven't seen it yet for I've been keeping it as a surprise. It's cut in the very latest fashion."

"What colour?"

"Red. Red satin."

"Whew! That ought to raise the temperatures of our guests!" He laughed, easily.

Through the day the big kitchen was filled with delectable odours as Prudence and her younger helpers went about their preparations. McGrady had been well trained in waiting on table and Joseph, the coachman, was equipped to double as butler whenever occasion demanded. So the service was assured. Mary arranged the flowers and set the great table with O'Hara near, assisting when he could. The doilies of Madeira lace, the tall silver candelabra, and the crystal glasses and epergne added elegance to elegance.

"You were so right to order eighteen chairs," Mary said. "I would never even have thought beyond a dozen."

"What made you choose red?" he asked suddenly.

"For my dress? Oh, I don't know. It's a nice warm fall and winter colour and I've never had a red one before."

Mr. Cox, who taught a singing school two nights a week in the courthouse, had been engaged to play the spinet, bringing with him two violinists.

"Be sure to tell them this is not a musicale," Mary had reminded O'Hara. "We only want a soft background for the conversation, as the evening advances."

"I think," said O'Hara now, as he arranged the General Washington champagne glasses with some of their own on a silver tray, "that I'll tell them to start playing when these are passed.

They can wait in the library until then. Did I tell you I'm serving cider? The princes will be used, of course, to champagne and this will be different. I don't recall ever tasting cider in France."

At last everything was in readiness and it was close to the time when the guests would arrive. O'Hara was dressed in his best: a blue rounded dress coat, a rose velvet vest, and white satin breeches, fastened with his ancestral knee-buckles. He paced the hall floor nervously now, calling up to Mary who had been delayed because of a ripped flounce in her lace petticoat. It was the very moment of the hour when she finally came down the stairs. As O'Hara looked up at her his heart jumped. The lustrous red satin basque, dropping off the shoulders and cut to a very low point in the front, seemed moulded to her form. Her cheeks from the excitement were as scarlet as her gown, while the rest of her skin was as purely white as winter snow. The whole effect was ravishing.

She had just taken her place beside him when the great knocker sounded and Joseph opened the door to admit the Nevilles and the honoured guests, three young and distinguished looking men, the Duke of Orleans by far the handsomest. O'Hara greeted them warmly and saw them bow with a sort of startled admiration before Mary as they kissed her hand. The others came soon after and there was general talk in the drawing-room as the rye and sherry were passed and repassed. When Joseph announced dinner Mary led the way to the dining-room on the arm of Prince Louis Philippe with his next younger brother following with the daughter of Devereux Smith and the youngest with Nancy Denny, O'Hara himself taking in Mrs. Neville. There were subdued exclamations of pleasure as the great table with its glittering appointments came into view; the food, as course followed course, was beyond praise and the conversation throughout was bright and entertaining. Opposite him O'Hara could see Mary at the far end of the table, glowing and seductively beautiful in her red dress, smiling up at the princes on either side of her while they apparently could not for long turn their eyes away.

When the ladies retired to the drawing-room at last and the gentlemen were left to their port O'Hara moved to be nearer the princes and with an apology to the others began speaking to them in French. They thanked him for the courtesy and began eagerly to respond. He found, however, that they did not wish to dwell upon France and the tragic years that lay behind. After touching lightly upon Napoleon and the Egyptian campaign in answer to a remark of his, they came swiftly to a discussion of their visit in the United States. They had been agreeably entertained in New York but had felt most at home in Philadelphia. They had been to Mount Vernon and greatly admired General Washington. They had seen Niagara Falls, what a marvel! But most of all they wanted to ask questions about the new country here: its government, its political parties, the *Indians*, and finally about their proposed trip down the Ohio to New Orleans. O'Hara had long been a master of self-control so he chatted now with ease and charm.

When they rejoined the ladies the royal guests gallantly made a point of conversing with those whom they had not been near before: they professed themselves enjoyably regaled by the *cider* and found the soft music most pleasing, as it was. All in all as the evening ended there was writ large not only upon their faces but upon those of the other guests, that it had been an enormous success.

"I will find it difficult to wait for to-morrow night, Madame," the Duke said as he bowed over Mary's hand.

When the great door closed for the last time Mary turned, radiantly, to her husband. "It was perfect, wasn't it?"

"I think it went off well enough," he answered.

She looked at him anxiously. "You're tired, James. You've looked worn out ever since you started this glass business. I'll go now and thank the people in the kitchen and then we can go right up. Joseph and McGrady will see to the lights and fires."

He followed her slowly up the stairs, still in silence. Even in their own room when Mary dropped down on the little sofa he did not come to join her as was his wont but seemed to be busying himself at his highboy.

"What is the matter, James? Did anything go wrong? Please tell me."

He turned, his face flushed and stern.

"Yes, I'll tell you what was wrong. It was the way those men looked at you! I don't care if they are royalty. They're *Frenchmen* first of all. I could read every thought in their eyes and I could have killed them for it! And you, smiling up at them!"

"Smiling at them!" Mary echoed. "Why, you *told* me to smile at them. You said if I did they wouldn't know what they were eating!" Then she added slowly, in astonishment, "Why, James O'Hara, I do believe you are jealous!"

"Jealous!" he flared. "Of course I'm jealous. Every man is

if he's in love. And that Louis Philippe is so damned attractive!"
Suddenly a delicious sound filled the room. It was Mary's laughter.
She leaned her head against the back of the sofa and gave way to it
utterly while O'Hara stared at her.

"You find that so amusing?" he asked.

"Of course I do! And *so* nice! So wonderful!"

"I don't understand you," he said, amazed.

"Oh, any *woman* would understand. To think that I, past forty,
with four big children and my first grey hair pulled out to-day,
should have a jealous husband! Don't you see it makes me feel so
young and so . . . so *desirable!*"

His face softened as he came over and sat down beside her.
"Have I ever given you any reason to doubt the latter?" he said,
with his old smile breaking through.

"Mercy! I should say not! But you know any woman likes
admiration any time. We're just made that way. You do forgive
me for laughing at you?"

"As a matter of fact, I'm glad you did," he said slowly. "If
you had argued or reasoned or explained I might still have had
a little hurt in my heart. But when you laughed you drove it all
away. I'm sorry I spoke sharply. It's just because I love you so
terribly. Always have. Always will. But there's something I
have to ask you, darling."

"What is it?"

"I don't want you to wear that dress again."

"This *dress!* But it's so beautiful! I was sure you would like it.
Why don't you?"

"It's cut too low. It's too revealing."

"But that's the very latest fashion. I've had pictures from a
Philadelphia magazine. All the women are wearing them this
way!"

"Not you," he said. He bent swiftly and pressed his lips to
the curving white flesh. "This beauty is for me, alone. I won't
have it even suggested to other men's eyes!"

She looked at him in wonder. "I never thought of anything
like that. But I could . . . put . . . a . . . little . . . lace in the dress
I plan to wear to-morrow. If you insist."

"I'm afraid I do, and thank you."

It was a good while before they settled themselves for slumber
that night. O'Hara spoke once again.

"A man is a jealous beast," he said.

"And a woman is a vain thing," she replied.

Then they both laughed, kissed again and went to sleep.

There was a second newspaper in Pittsburgh now, this one, also of Hugh Brackenridge's sponsoring, called *The Tree of Liberty*. Scull, still editor of *The Gazette*, had according to Hugh become so partial to the Federalists that he did not give fair space to the political propaganda of the Democratic-Republicans. Hence, the new sheet, edited by young John Israel from Washington. Hugh's interest in fanning the life flame of the new journal was so great that he made fairly frequent trips back from Carlisle to see how all was going and to contribute in person his own vitriolic articles. O'Hara, knowing this, had haunted the office for the past two weeks hoping to hear that Hugh either had arrived or was expected. On this, the day of the second dinner for the visiting princes, he made one last call at the office and was hailed by young Israel at the doorway.

"He's here," he said, pointing to the back room.

O'Hara gave a shout and fell upon Brackenridge as he sat writing at a desk there. "I've had some great coincidences in the course of my life, but this is one of the best. How are you? How's everything? Can you come to dinner to-night with French royalty?"

They talked fast, catching up on all their news. Maria and the boy were well. They were all enjoying Carlisle. As to to-night's dinner, Hugh's eyes sparkled, until he thought of clothes.

"I've nothing to wear but what's on my back!"

"I can fit you out. We dine at eight, so get around to the house about seven. This is to be a smaller group so the talk can be general. My word, Hugh, I'm glad you got here. Working this afternoon?"

Hugh nodded. "Why?"

"Oh, it's the opening of the county fair and Neville and I thought the princes might like to see it, and go to the races. Couldn't you join us?"

"Too much to do here, I'm afraid. But I'll turn up at your house by seven. What about your *glass*, O'Hara?"

"No go for the moment, but I'm not giving up. I'll be through with my contracting in another month and then I'll devote my whole attention to it. See you then at seven!"

If possible the second dinner surpassed the first. The smaller number both in the drawing-room and at table would have made conversation more easy and intimate in any case but with Hugh present it became scintillating. There was plenty of laughter as the afternoon at the fair was discussed.

"And the *racing!*" the Duke exclaimed. "It was excellent. I was surprised that you have a Jockey Club here!"

"It's been in existence for several years," O'Hara replied. "We're just as eager to lose our money on the horses as they are in larger places. Makes us feel very cosmopolitan, you know."

Even as philosophy and politics were touched upon, the lighter note was preserved until at last Hugh began to dilate upon his idol Thomas Jefferson, and then his eloquence captured them all.

When the last good-byes were said Mary, in yellow brocade with a little white cascade of lace upon her bosom, looked up at her husband mischievously.

"Will you not say this time that everything was perfect?"

"Absolutely."

"And you're not jealous to-night?"

He shook his head. "Only proud. Proud as Lucifer."

O'Hara's position as Quartermaster of the United States had been ended some time before, and now at last and upon his request, his work as contractor for the armies was finished also. It gave him a strange feeling. The long, exacting burdensome weight of responsibility with its dangers and problems was now removed. He was, he kept telling himself with relief, a free man. Free to pursue his own interests and to live without interruption in his own family. But the custom of years could not be shaken off in a moment. Instinctively he found himself often considering transportation, or waking up at night in a sweat of fear because he must have forgotten to order *flour!* So he had upon him still the stamp of old anxieties in addition to the new ones pertaining to his great dream.

The precious clay from New Jersey was long in coming. Delay after delay was questioned, partially accounted for and then added to by another. Craig, Eichbaum, who was now back, and O'Hara stormed or swore according to their various natures—and waited. Meanwhile the workmen had to be paid to retain them.

One day O'Hara received a letter from the Westphalian Glassworks, containing a sketch of a chandelier. It hung from a circle with a double row of candles, below which were pictured a myriad of crystals. O'Hara studied it for a long time during which some of the new lines in his face seemed to smooth out. This was what he had in mind, and the price did not deter him. This would be his gift. He wrote the order, and then sat on in his office imagining the effect of the chandelier in the plain log church. It would transform it even in the daytime. But at night, lighted . . . He began, with a smile, to write out possible presentation lines, and finally after many tries came up with a sentence that pleased him because he found a faint humour beneath the words: *In token of a glowing desire to promote the lustre of this enlightened society.*

He chuckled over this and laid it in the drawer. He had decided to tell no one of the gift, not even Mary. He wanted particularly to surprise her at the last. He went out now taking quick look-ins at the tannery, the brewery, the sawmill, the gristmill and last of all the store. Elliott, a little more lame but blandly casual as usual, sat down for a chat.

"Well, how does it feel to be out of the woods permanent?"

"Pretty good. Only I'm still contracting in my sleep. The best part of the thing is that I won't have to be leaving my family now."

"Nice lot of children you got there, General."

"I'm pretty fond of them."

"Wonder to me is they've growed up so well with you away so much."

"They have a good mother."

"They have that. But them boys. They told me when you went off you left them *in charge.*"

"I did. Every time."

"Well by gum, they seemed to take it serious. That Butler. You know he's goin' to be the most like you."

"Think so?"

"He's got your wit. Ever hear about the day he whistled in school?"

"No, I don't believe I did."

"It was while I was stayin' at the house. They told me Butler whistled right in the middle of class. The teacher pounced on him an' asked him why he done it. An' he says as cool as you please, 'I was just whistlin' down my sums'. "

They laughed together and then Elliott went on. "An' them little girls of yours . . . well if they wanted my *skin* they could have it. They sort of make up to me for some things I've missed. By the way," he added as though there was a logical sequence, "your friend Guyasuta was round."

"Where?"

"Oh, he was down by the ferry the other day. He'll probably be to see you. I wouldn't know what's in his craw. He don't look too good to me."

"Sick, you mean?"

"Well, when an Injun's not up to snuff he gets the funniest damned colour. I've seen it often and Guyasuta's got it now."

"If you see him again tell him to come to me at once, will you? I wonder why he hasn't done so before. Could he be frightened out by the new house, do you suppose? Well, I must be moving along now." The man he had once helped came towards him as he got up. "Oh, how are you, Lewis?"

"I'm doin' real well, General, but there's something I'd like to tell you."

"Go ahead."

"I know you've helped a lot of people besides me but there's a family livin' near me now that's in awful bad straits. He's been sick an' she's just had another baby. Seems as if there's always a new baby."

O'Hara smiled. "Pittsburgh has to grow," he said.

"I know, but it's hard when there ain't enough to eat."

"All right. Now let's get to work on this. Elliott, get out your biggest basket and fill it up with groceries and Lewis, you take it now and one like it every day to this family till the man's working again. And here," he added, feeling in his pocket, "take a little money to them. Make them feel safer."

He waved away the thanks and started out, but looked back from the door. "And Lewis," he said, "when you hear of anyone else in real trouble, let me know."

He was concerned at the news of Guyasuta, especially since it reminded him of a decision made and temporarily forgotten to buy some land across the Allegheny. There, he had solemnly promised to bury the old Indian, and he must not be laid in alien soil. Besides the idea had occurred to O'Hara that they should have a summer home. A dank heat rose from the Monongahela during July and August; but up on the low bluff above the Allegheny there would be cooler days and evening breezes. He made his way now to the office of Devereux Smith.

When the two men late that afternoon crossed the ferry and rode their horses over the land beyond the river, O'Hara cried out in surprise.

"To think that I've lived all these years across from this spot and never actually seen it. This would be an ideal location for a house!"

"What! Another one?"

"A summer home," O'Hara explained. "Look at that orchard! Some long-ago hands planted that. Mary and I are rather sentimental about orchards, so this would delight her, I know. This tract could all become valuable farm land, Smith. I'm going to buy it. Will you arrange the sale?"

"How much would you want?"

O'Hara scanned the land around with a careful eye. The virgin forest had been cleared but there were good trees here and there in addition to the orchard. The ground was level and he knew what richness lay in the soil. In one way and another it would be a good investment.

"I would want some real acreage," he said. "About three hundred, I should think."

Smith whistled, and then they talked terms of sale. "I'll have to check on just who the proprietors of all this are at the moment. Some of it still belongs to the Penns, I think, but I haven't much doubt that it can be bought. You'll soon own this whole end of the state, O'Hara."

"I'll stop a pinch short of that, I guess," he laughed.

As they rode back to the ferry O'Hara reined his horse before a magnificent spreading oak tree, the finest he had ever seen.

"Not thinking of cutting that up for your sawmill, are you?" Smith asked.

O'Hara shook his head. He had decided that this spot should be Guyasuta's grave when the time came.

When he told Mary that night of the idea for a summer-house she was at first amazed and then gradually enthusiastic.

"It would be nice to have a real farm with plenty of outdoor space for the children. You say there's an *orchard?*"

"Quite a sizable one. If we get this place I'd like to give it a name as they do with homes in the old country. My word, it ought to be a lovely spot in the spring!"

Mary considered. "Why not *Springfield* then," she suggested.

"I like that!" he said decidedly. "I like that very much. Let's stick to it."

So to their amusement and satisfaction the O'Hara country estate had a name before it was even bought!

On a grey November day the first barrels of clay arrived. At once the factory became active. The workmen were rounded up; Eichbaum began his careful supervision of the making of the new pots; and Craig and O'Hara watched and lent a hand everywhere they could. O'Hara felt a vast elation. Now, all would surely go well. The excitement seemed to have spread even to the workmen, for they proceeded with unusual zeal. Too much, as was later proved.

It was not until late December that the pots were all completed. Now again the great furnace was put in blast and the result awaited tensely. O'Hara lay awake nights and felt his hopes unaccountably drowned in new fears. And his dark intuition proved correct. One after another the pots were lost, sometimes at the first melting. Eichbaum was strangely humble.

"The trouble must have been in the drying," he said. "The men were over eager. They didn't give the pots time enough. Perhaps I was too eager myself. I am sorry, gentlemen. I'm afraid this is a serious loss. What shall we do now?"

"We'll go ahead. We'll try again. What did you think?" O'Hara exclaimed. "Have you any new suggestions?"

"Yes. I would like another man who really knows the business to be secured to help me. I cannot oversee all the workmen myself, as I should. I've heard of a man back east, named Wentz. If we could get him as an operating foreman . . ."

"Do you know where to reach him?"

"I have his address."

"Then send for him at once. I'll write him also. Can you start things up here again until he comes?"

"I'd rather wait," Eichbaum said.

O'Hara drew a heavy breath. "So be it. We'll have to let the furnace go out again then, and lay the men off."

"You can still withdraw from the whole venture if you wish," Eichbaum suggested, looking at the others.

"We'll go ahead," they both said at once.

"Glad you're sticking with me, Isaac," O'Hara said as they left that night.

So another long wait began.

Christmas passed with outward merriment but, as far as O'Hara himself was concerned, inner frustration and Mary worried over him even as she tried to comfort him. On New Year's evening a low knock was heard at the back door which O'Hara opened himself. On the steps stood an Indian wrapped in a blanket. It was Guyasuta! O'Hara drew him quickly in out of the cold, seeing upon the ravaged once handsome face the peculiar pallor that was not pallor of which Elliott had spoken. He seated the old man by the fire and began to chafe the thin hands.

"I have come," Guyasuta said weakly, "as you told me to do."

"You are sick!"

The old man nodded. "I will not trouble you long."

Mary had come out and the Indian looked at her doubtfully. "You will not be angry?"

"Oh, you are welcome, Guyasuta," she said warmly. "And you must have food, now."

"Have you any corn-meal mush left, Prudence?" O'Hara asked. "Thin a little down to a gruel and put some sugar in it."

Then he and Mary conferred as to where they would put their guest. "He won't be comfortable in a fancy bedroom," O'Hara said with concern.

"How about my little sewing-room? It warms quickly and we could put the cot Butler used to sleep on, in it."

"That would be best. I'll go up with you . . ."

"No, you stay with him. The boys will help me. We won't be long."

So O'Hara waited until the older boys came down and then amongst them they half carried the Indian up to the room Mary had prepared. She had just now brought in one of her husband's own warm bed gowns. O'Hara signalled the others to leave, then removed the old man's blanket and started to take off his deerskin clothes. But Guyasuta shook his head, and lay down on the bed as he was, with a small grunt of relief at its comfort. O'Hara put more wood on the fire, drew the fresh blankets over him and saw that already he was asleep.

During the night each time O'Hara woke, which was often, he went in to make up the fire and check on the sick man's condition. He still lay motionless upon his back, eyes closed, but whether in sleep now or not, was not plain. In the morning he seemed weaker and reverted entirely to his own tongue.

"Would you like some of your people to come here to see you?" O'Hara asked anxiously. "Perhaps your wife . . . wives," he amended hastily. "Elliott knows where they live. He would go and fetch them."

The Indian shook his head. "All my long years I live with my own people. Now, I die with you."

He looked off across the room. "You have never harmed an Indian. You have been to all a friend. To me you have been as my son. From that first night when our eyes met. We have seen each other seldom but always I carry you in my heart. You feel this also?"

"I feel it also," O'Hara repeated.

"Then I am at peace."

When O'Hara went to the store that afternoon leaving Mary to watch the sickroom for an hour, he ran into General Neville.

"Well, so I hear you have Guyasuta with you!"

"Yes, I have."

"Do you not know that he was a prime leader at the awful siege of Fort Pitt in '63?"

"I do."

"And the chief leader at the burning of Hannastown?"

"I know that."

"And yet you dare harbour the old bastard in your own house?" His voice had risen in anger.

"And since it happens to *be* my own house, General, have you any objection?" O'Hara's eyes were cold.

Neville sputtered a bit. "Now, now, no real offence meant. But I certainly can't understand this situation."

"As a matter of fact, I can't myself. What I do know is that this man is my friend and I have an obligation to him which I intend to fulfil. Good day, General."

By another evening Guyasuta was very weak indeed. He had refused O'Hara's suggestion of Dr. Bedford with a determination that could not be questioned, so the hours passed and his pulse grew fainter. Elliott had been in and spoken in easy Seneca which the Indian had answered. Since he knew the time was near O'Hara told him gently of the land beyond the Allegheny, now his own, and the great tree there. From beneath it could be seen the meeting of the rivers. It would be a noble resting place.

"It is well," Guyasuta whispered, and by morning he was dead. The strange, tender, continuing bond between the Indian and the white man was now severed.

O'Hara's heart was heavy as he made the few necessary arrangements. The man who always dug the graves in the churchyard went out with him to be shown the spot under the oak tree. In the afternoon Guyasuta's body, wrapped in his own blanket and in another fresh one upon which Mary insisted, was placed in the undertaker's spring wagon; O'Hara with Mary and the boys, who had been deeply affected by all that had passed, rode in their own carriage while Elliott followed on horseback. This completed the small cortège.

When the grave was filled they all stood for a moment looking across at the icy rivers, as the wind moved among the bare branches overhead.

"I wish it could have been spring for him," Mary said softly.

"Perhaps it is," O'Hara answered. "That is what we do not know."

With the coming of Wentz, affairs at the glasshouse became both better and worse. To O'Hara and Craig he seemed a reasonable, capable man, with whom it was easy to get along, but for some reason not apparent on the surface he and Eichbaum took an immediate dislike to each other. They covered it, but the other men knew it was there, and felt the situation would not make for steady progress. However, Eichbaum needed Wentz; Wentz needed the job; so an armed truce prevailed.

The next great experiment of melting also failed, and Wentz was certain the trouble now was in the kind of *sand* being used. Eichbaum reluctantly agreed. It was decided then to secure samples from all the sand pits around, and let the furnace go out while the outcome of it all hung once again in the balance. The delay drove O'Hara into an inward frenzy. In all his tremendous undertakings heretofore, there had been along with the difficulties and discouragements a constant, steady movement of overcoming. Now, these blocking standstills to him were well-nigh unbearable. Mary watched him with keen anxiety for there was white at his temples now and the first lines in his face were growing deeper. One day she spoke seriously to him.

"James," she said, "have you thought that perhaps you may never have success with the glass?"

"I won't tolerate that thought! I will never give up on this. Why do you ask that? Don't you have faith in me?"

"Yes, I really believe that you will achieve what you've set out to do. But I also believe . . ." She stopped as though embarrassed.

"Go on," he said, looking intently at her.

"It's hard for me to put my feeling into words, but I think any man worthy of success should also be able to bear defeat. If it should come," she added.

He did not speak and she went on. "If you accept this possibility you can still try just as hard as ever to . . . to make the glass but maybe you wouldn't then be so tense, so . . . sort of bitter over the setbacks . . ."

He watched her for a moment and then still without answering turned as though to leave the house. She ran after him.

"James! I haven't offended you, have I?"

He smiled at her. "You couldn't offend me," he said. "I just want to get out by myself and think over what you've told me."

He walked along the river, keeping his eyes away from the factory. He knew himself to be a strong man, both of purpose and execution. He had had up till now what was perhaps phenomenal success. The idea of failure was foreign both to his nature and to his experience, and perhaps because of this he had grown to consider himself infallible and ready to war with any circumstances that threatened to prove him otherwise. This, he slowly realised, was less than good. This attitude, which had in it something at least of stubborn pride, was not one he would admire in another man. He thought again of Mary's words. If he now without bitterness could accept the possibility of failure in this his most cherished dream, perhaps the tension would indeed go out of him and he would once again be able to sleep at night as he used to do, and rise in the morning strong and willing to meet whatever the day brought. But more importantly, he might be a better and a humbler man.

He walked for an hour pondering this until he began to feel some of the strain leaving him. How wise Mary was! All through the years she had not only given him the joy of her love and her tender womanliness, but had supported him many times by the soundness of her judgment. She often made him think of his own mother who had seemed outwardly all feminine beauty, but who had an inner strength that he knew his father had respected and depended upon. He decided now to do his best to follow Mary's suggestion to which he had with difficulty reached agreement in his own mind. "But," he muttered to himself, "I'll still never give up while there is a shred of hope!"

He took a short cut through to the store, for a chat with Elliott always relaxed him. He found that gentleman swearing steadily as he wrestled with three large boxes which he said had just come in on the last horse train of freight.

"They're addressed to the store here so McGrady brought them over but what in hell's in them, O'Hara?"

O'Hara's heart leaped as he read the lettering on the boxes. They had come from the Westphalian Glassworks in Germany!

"If anyone asks you that, Elliott, just tell them you don't know," he said, laughing.

"Well, that'll be no damned lie. But I can't help wonderin' what you've been up to now. Ain't we goin' to open them, then?"

"Not yet. But don't worry. Next after Mary, I'll tell you what's in them."

When he got home he didn't refer to their recent conversation, instead he poured out his great secret and had the satisfaction of seeing Mary's delight in the idea. One thing he still withheld. This was his plan, conceived from the beginning, of making the gift synonymous with the first success in the glass manufacture. To this he would still hold, as long as he could.

The last slow, disheartening winter months passed. New sand was substituted for the old but *still* there were failures. O'Hara brought Wentz to his office one day to talk it all over with him in private.

"What is *wrong?*" he asked peremptorily. "I want the truth."

"Well, a good many things. We haven't got the best workmen, you know. Some from round here are just new to the trade. The last few failures have been because somebody bungled, but they're all learning."

"Should we try to get more workers from Philadelphia?" O'Hara asked.

Wentz shook his head. "Good glass-men are hard to come by. We'd have to break new ones in and even then we wouldn't be sure. Better stick to what we have."

"You think you've got the right sand at last?"

"I think so. We've had trouble with the coal, as you know. I'm convinced it *is* the best fuel but neither Eichbaum nor I have used it before and we have to learn how to adjust the heat. We had two failures because the pots got too hot."

O'Hara leaned forward. "Tell me, Wentz, honestly, whether you think I'll like it or not, do you believe we have a chance of ultimate success?"

"I do, if your money holds out."

O'Hara smiled. "That's my responsibility. What about yours?"

"It's a tricky business, General, but I don't see why we can't win out with it *sometime.*"

"Eichbaum seems pessimistic."

"Oh, that's his nature. Don't pay any attention to him. What I've got him to agree to now is to forget the window glass for the present and just keep the two melting pots for the bottles fired. If we can finally produce *one perfect glass bottle*, we've got it! We can go on from there and do anything we want."

O'Hara rose and shook his hand. "You've cheered me up, Wentz. Go ahead as hard as you can."

"I only hope we don't break up doing it, General."

"I'll manage," O'Hara said, smiling again.

On a late afternoon in April some sober Pittsburgh residents were astonished to see their first citizen now in his early fifties tearing hatless up from the ferry at a speed his own sons might have envied! James O'Hara did not slacken his pace along Water Street nor at his own front steps which he took two at a time. If the puzzled eyes of the neighbours could have followed him indoors they would have seen him rushing through the front hall.

"Mary! Mary! Mary!" he shouted.

She came in fright from the back of the house to see her husband throwing his arms wildly in the air and executing the steps of what she learned later was an Irish jig.

"We've done it!" he yelled. "We've done it! We've *won*! To-day we've made a perfect green glass bottle!"

Suddenly he sank down in one of the hall chairs with an expression, half wickedly gleeful and half ashamed.

"At a cost," he added, "as I reckon it, *of thirty thousand dollars!*"

The news swept the town and there were many callers at the house on Water Street that evening offering congratulations.

"Well, we hear you've done it again for Pittsburgh, General!"

"The first glasshouse west of the Alleghenies, we can say now!"

"We knew success would finally come, with you at the head of it!"

"And Major Craig says window glass will be made before too long."

For Craig came in for felicitations too, though all the town knew that it was O'Hara's foresight, capital and determination which had made the achievement possible. For the first time, that night, O'Hara spoke to Mary about her advice to him.

"I honestly tried to hold in my mind an acceptance of whatever might come, but the odd thing was that as soon as I'd done that I was surer than ever that we'd succeed! Odd, wasn't it?"

"Maybe that's the way it happens," Mary said, "and I'm so happy for you."

"Now, I'll get to work at once on the plans for the chandelier," he said jubilantly. "I was just waiting . . ."

"I surmised that."

"So? Who is it knows whom now?" he teased.

He confided the secret of the boxes to Elliott the next day and also to his associates at the glassworks for he wanted Eichbaum's help in assembling the piece. He sent notes by McGrady calling a meeting of the Trustees at his office for the following week. By that time he expected to know how long it would take to have the chandelier ready for hanging. Eichbaum came over to the store that afternoon after work, filled with curiosity and a marked irritation that he had not been told before this. But when the space there was cleared and blankets spread to receive the delicate contents he began to unpack the boxes with a skilled and sensitive hand, his enthusiasm rising above his former annoyance.

"So this was what you wanted the address for," he said.

"Yes," O'Hara answered, "but I planned to keep the matter secret for a while. Do you like what you see, so far?"

"Beautiful! Exquisite!" he exclaimed, gently unwrapping one prism. "But we must work here only when we have good daylight. Better to do only a little each afternoon than to rush it."

"How will you get it to the church? Will you assemble it all here and then take it over?"

Eichbaum shook his head. "The main part we'll put together here, but all the crystals I will want to hang in the church itself when the framework is already up. We can carry them over wrapped carefully in baskets, then if we three could work together, I'll attach them if you men hand them up to me. You won't want the public to see this for the first time until it's lighted, will you, General?"

"That's my idea. Could we have it all ready by the week after next?"

"I'm sure of it. You'll have to keep people out of this part of the store, though."

"I sorta think I can see to that," Elliott drawled.

"Shoot a few if need be," O'Hara suggested cheerfully, "I hope none of the pieces have been broken in the shipping."

"I don't think so. Not from the Westphalian works. This must have cost you a pretty penny, General."

"Well, well, if you give a gift, give a good one. And this, I hope, will last for a while."

O'Hara's spirits soared as the next days passed. Wentz had been right. After the first perfect glass bottle, the difficulties that had nagged and blocked them disappeared. The clay, the sand, the temperature had all now been finally proven correct. The blowing had always been the least uncertain part, for Eichbaum and Wentz (who now seemed almost congenial in their new success) were both experts as well as two young Philadelphia workers; so the bottles were steadily turned out as the chimneys smoked, the furnace glowed, and an air of assured activity filled the glass-house.

At the meeting of the Trustees O'Hara told of his proposed gift and the men were loud in their expressions of surprise and pleasure. They listened respectfully to his plan. The chandelier would be hung early the following week. Could there, following this, be an evening meeting at which time he would present it formally to the congregation who would then see it for the first time, lighted? His idea would be to have the meeting something less than purely religious under the circumstances, with a *talk* or *address* by someone, rather than a sermon. What were their views on this?

There was then animated discussion which O'Hara directed skilfully.

"Would you not have Reverend Barr take charge then?"

"By all means. He would preside, announce a hymn maybe to start with, offer prayer, and introduce all the speakers. That should give him enough to do."

After more discussion this was conceded. "But who would you get to give the address?" one man asked.

O'Hara brought forth an idea as though it had just occurred to him.

"Well now, let's see. What would you think of Reverend Arthur? He's President of the Academy and a born intellectual. He has a very easy, pleasant manner of speaking and I think he might give us an interesting talk. How does that strike you?"

After more discussion everything was settled exactly as O'Hara had previously decided it in his own mind.

"And now, gentlemen," he said, "I'm going to depend upon you to inform Reverend Barr upon the matter and allow him to set the evening. Any one will suit me. And also will you speak to Mr. Arthur about his part? I'm sure among you, you can arrange this all tactfully. I wish the church was big enough to invite the other congregations but I fear that would be impractical."

"Never fear," one man said. "When the news spreads we'll have a crowd, that's sure. Well, some can stand if they can't all get seats."

"Funny thing!" one of the Trustees remarked as the men were leaving, "for you to be giving this glass chandelier to the church at the very time your own works start going in earnest!"

"Yes," O'Hara agreed innocently. "Odd coincidence, isn't it?"

The work of assembly went on steadily in the back room of the store each afternoon. Eichbaum was in his element. His fingers seemed more and more to have the artist's touch as he handled the delicate crystals.

"Two rows of tapers!" he exclaimed one day as he lifted out the framework.

"Yes, it's going to make quite a light, I hope," O'Hara answered.

By Monday of the following week they were ready to begin work at the church. The meeting had been set for Thursday night at eight, so there would be no need of haste. Eichbaum had been relieved of all duties at the factory until the chandelier was completely hung and had now developed a possessive feeling toward it which was both amusing and touching.

"Would you rather have two of the men from the glasshouse over to help you hang the crystals?" O'Hara asked, as they left the store one day.

But Eichbaum shook his head.

"We've worked together with the unpacking, the three of us, and I'd rather go on that way. I want you there in any case, and this Elliott person has a surprisingly sure and gentle touch for an . . . an *uncultivated* man," he said.

O'Hara tried to hide a grin as he agreed.

The following day he met Mr. Arthur who was on his way to Water Street. "Come on back to the house, then," O'Hara urged.

"Let's walk as we talk," the older man answered. "It's a beautiful day. The apple trees are in bloom in the King's Orchard. Did you notice that?"

"Oh yes, I never miss them."

"Lovely fragrance. Essence of spring. Well, General, I hear we are to have a wonderful surprise next week."

"I hope it will be . . . pleasing."

"And I also hear that I, alas, am slated to make a speech. I feel honoured to be a part of the happy occasion but I don't know what to say. That was why I was on my way to see you. I wondered if you could suggest a selection from the Bible perhaps that I could use as a starting point? Oh, I know I'm not to preach a sermon, but I will have to have a *topic*. Do you have a favourite verse, for instance, General?"

O'Hara shook his head. "I'm not an Elder, Mr. Arthur. My work is on the financial side so I'm hardly prepared to give any spiritual suggestion."

"No verse you can think of?" he persisted. "This meeting is built around you, and you are the one who should suggest the theme."

O'Hara did not reply at once, then he asked, "Do you know *Bunyan*, Mr. Arthur?"

"Ah yes, very well. Don't tell me *you* do?"

"I had to read *Pilgrim's Progress* when I was a boy and more than that, I had to commit two of the short poems. The two best ones, I think."

"Yes, yes. *He that is down need fear no fall*, for instance?"

"That one and the other which I liked better. *Who would true valour see* . . ."

"And a fine one that is for any boy to learn. I must have my Academy students memorise that. So you still remember it?"

"Yes. Many and many a time as I rode along through the wilderness I recited it to myself. You see I had a feeling that there was a strong similarity between a *pilgrim* and a *pioneer*. But," he shrugged, "I doubt if this would have any bearing upon your problem."

"As a matter of fact," Mr. Arthur said slowly, "I think it might have an extraordinary one. You've given me an idea, General. Thank you!" And he turned abruptly and walked away.

Before he reached the church O'Hara was stopped again. This time a shabby man touched his hat and began to speak at once.

"I've been wantin' to run into you, General. Everybody's talkin' about the glass these days but I'm still thinkin' more about the *salt*. That's meant an awful lot to us. You know when you can get a good hunk of beef, a quarter mebbe, in the winter, it has to be salted to keep it, an' the brine has to be strong enough to *float an egg*. Did you know that, General?"

"I don't believe I did," he admitted.

"Well, that's the truth. An' before, we never could afford enough salt to do it an' so our meat never kept right. Now we're going to have good eatin' right along. I just wanted to thank you, General."

O'Hara reached his hand. "I'm glad you told me. I appreciate this."

As he went on he smiled to himself picturing the egg floating in a tub of brine. But that would be the rule and the recipe, he had no doubt, born of long pioneer experimentation. He must remember to tell that to Mary. But as he sat that night with her in the library, there was something more important of which he wished to speak.

"When we moved here," he began, "you said you wanted to go back sometimes and sleep in the old house just for old sake's sake. Do you remember?"

"Of course. And I would still like to. I wonder why we've never done it?"

"I thought perhaps this Thursday night might be a nice time after the meeting. It will be, I think, rather a memorable occasion, it's not long after our wedding anniversary . . ."

"And the apple trees are in blossom now. Did you notice?"

"Yes," he said, for the second time that day. "I never miss that. Then there's still another reason I would like to do it now. And that's because there is a definite connection between the guest room there which we would use, and my manufacture of glass."

"There *is?* What?"

"I'll tell you that night!"

"Oh James," she said earnestly, "I'm *so* glad you are sentimental. I don't think many men are, do you?"

"It's me Irish blood, darling," he said with a twinkle.

By Wednesday noon the work at the church was completed. From a central circle hung the immense glass chandelier with its double row of sperm candles. From their holders depended a myriad of crystals which gleamed even in the daylight. There had been less trouble than O'Hara had feared with curious onlookers during these last days. He had passed the word around that by Thursday night *and not until then* all would be welcome. So the wholesome respect in which he was held coupled with the human pleasure in anticipation of an ultimate surprise kept people away. General Neville wandered in once; Isaac Craig and Wentz came over and Tuesday afternoon John Scull, editor of the *Gazette*, entered the church, looked at the chandelier from all sides and left, saying nothing. O'Hara was slightly nettled by his silence but soon forgot it in the general excitement.

Thursday evening was one of May's finest, with a delicately fragrant warmth abroad and a lighthearted western breeze blowing. Eichbaum had promised to see to the lighting of the candles himself so the O'Hara carriage with all its family occupants rolled up to the stake-an'-rider fence enclosing the churchyard at exactly a quarter to eight, with the arrangement that the children would return home in it when the meeting was over. Even now the congregation was pouring in and at the door itself people were standing, waiting for a chance to enter. O'Hara glanced back to be sure the children were all close behind them and then as soon as was possible went inside with Mary on his arm. Once there they all stopped short. O'Hara, himself, had not seen his gift lighted until this moment, and his heart seemed to turn over in his breast. He could feel Mary's hand trembling as she looked first at the chandelier and then at him, for the sight was dazzling, unbelievable. Every tiny facet of the crystals caught and reflected the light of the hundred candles burning above them!

They all walked slowly up the aisle to their pew in the block of six to the left of the pulpit and from there could watch the congregation as they kept coming in. Some were awestruck, speechless, at the blaze of beauty before them; others kept exclaiming softly as though they could not stop. The church was soon full and still the people came. They stood in the side aisles and in the back, and when there was no more room they stood on the outer steps peering over each other's shoulders and changing position so that all had a chance to see the glory inside.

At last Mr. Barr and Mr. Arthur ascended the pulpit together and the meeting began, as, indeed, most services did, with the singing of the twenty-third psalm. For this there was no need of printed page nor precentor. Everyone had known the words from childhood. So now, strong and full the volume of voices rose:

> *"The Lord's my shepherd, I'll not want;*
> *He makes me down to lie*
> *In pastures green, he leadeth me*
> *The quiet waters by."*

When the singing was over, the Reverend Mr. Barr offered a prayer, a very lengthy one. During it at times O'Hara's lips twitched, for, as was his wont, the pastor gave detailed information to the Almighty which it was reasonable to assume He might already know. The little girls, sitting on either side of their father, grew restive and he put an arm around each to steady them. But at last the prayer was ended and Mr. Barr called upon General James O'Hara to make the presentation speech.

O'Hara moved out to the front of the pulpit, faced his townsmen and told briefly of his pleasure in conferring the gift, ending with the sentence he had thought of and written down months ago. "I give this," he concluded, "in token of a *glowing* desire to promote the *lustre* of this *enlightened* society."

There were some smiles. It was to be expected that the General's wit would in some small measure break through. Then John Wilkins, representing the Elders, accepted the gift on behalf of the congregation, reading from a resolution of thanks already prepared, which he then handed to O'Hara. It was now time for the address of the evening.

Mr. Arthur came slowly forward, leaned upon the big pulpit Bible, waited for silence, and then began very simply to tell a story. It was about a pilgrim who had set out on a hazardous journey to reach a Celestial city. He pictured vividly the dangers and tribulations with which the pilgrim had been beset: how he had been attacked by the dragon, Apollyon, been plunged into the Slough of Despond, overcome lions, fought with Giant Despair, languished in Doubting Castle.

"Oh," Mr. Arthur said, "according to the author of this story, '*the way was very wearisome.*' But what I want to emphasise now is that the pilgrim never once gave up until he had reached the end of his journey. Listen! Listen to the words which gave him courage!

> "*Who would true valour see,*
> *Let him come hither;*
> *One here will constant be,*
> *Come wind, come weather;*
> *There's no discouragement*
> *Shall make him once relent*
> *His first avowed intent*
> *To be a pilgrim.*

This that I've been telling you," the speaker went on, "was a fanciful tale written by John Bunyan over a hundred years ago. Now I wish to speak of the true story of another type of pilgrims."

He told then of how these, the pioneers, had crossed the mountains, a feat of incredible courage in itself; of the graves large and small which marked that terrible path over the Alleghenies; of the bitter privations and hardships in the little log cabins of the settlers; of the dangers from wild beasts; and at last he spoke of the deadly struggles with the Indians. As the word fell from his lips a quick breath, like a sigh, stirred the audience.

"But," Mr. Arthur continued, "you, too, and your fathers and mothers before you, never gave up even though 'the way was very wearisome.' You never went back. You pursued your avowed intent. And now here is our town, no more afraid of the destruction by night nor the arrow that flieth by day. All around is peace and growth and prosperity. And here to-night before us is this glorious, dazzling gift of beauty which we can accept as a symbol of the fact that those hardest times are past, and as an earnest of what Pittsburgh may one day become."

And then he closed with prayer. A very brief and quiet one but it seemed as though the congregation hushed its heart to listen.

He prayed that they might all remember that they were still pilgrims journeying to another, a heavenly city in which there would be no need of a candle, neither the sun to lighten it, for the Lord God was the light thereof.

For a long minute there was no sound, and then slowly the movements began and the voices, until all restraint was lifted and there was everywhere laughter and loud acclaim. O'Hara and Mary stood at the front and shook hands with the steady stream of men and women who came to express their thanks and admiration. Those who had had to remain outside during the service now came in and looked their fill. Everywhere there was manifest that exhilaration which comes from pure pleasure and satisfaction.

At last the church was emptied of all but a few. Eichbaum put out the candles, even as he had lighted them. Good nights were said and then O'Hara and Mary, arm in arm, walked slowly through the spring darkness. When they reached the King's Orchard she spoke suddenly.

"Oh, James, I have a lovely surprise for you!"

"You have? What is it?"

"The *Gazette* came to-day and I saw an editorial in it about your gift so I slipped it over here to the office when I came to arrange the bedroom. I thought it would make such a nice climax for the evening."

"An *editorial* about it?" he said. "Why, Scull came in the other day and looked it all over and never said a word!"

"Maybe he was just saving up for this. Oh, you'll like it!"

They sauntered along the lane between the blossoming trees. His arm was around her now as they neared the kitchen door. They went on through to the office where he made a light.

"Here it is!" Mary exclaimed, picking up a paper from the desk. "I have it folded at the place. Read it aloud, James. I can't wait."

He took the paper eyeing it with surprise. "An editorial, eh? *Splendid Present!* Well! Well!"

"Read on. It gets better the farther you go."

"A chandelier of elegant workmanship has been presented to the First Presbyterian Church of this place, by General James O'Hara. This beautiful ornament, which was imported at great expense and trouble, reflects as much credit on the taste as on the magnificence of the generous donor, and adds one more instance to the long list of liberal acts, performed during a most useful life by this worthy citizen."

"There!" Mary began. "Isn't that . . ." But she stopped short, seeing something she had never seen before. There were tears rolling down her husband's cheeks.

"This . . . this," he stammered, "touches me. To think of Scull's writing this way about . . . about *me!*"

Mary spoke quickly. "I feel it's beautiful, too, but it's not half of what you deserve. It would take a whole paper to tell of all your kindnesses, and the amazing work you have done, James. All the incredible things you, alone, have accomplished! I . . ."

"No," he said vehemently, "No!"

She looked at him, startled, as he crossed to where she was standing. Then with infinite tenderness he cupped her face between his hands, and gazed into her eyes.

"Not alone," he said. "Oh, my dear Delight, not *alone!*"

Epilogue

The following words are cut upon a flat stone which covers a grave on a gentle hillside in the old Allegheny Cemetery of Pittsburgh, Pennsylvania:

Here lies the body of James O'Hara who departed this life Dec. 16, 1819 in the 67th year of his age. Born in Ireland in 1752, came to America in 1772. Served in the War of the Revolution, was commissioned Quartermaster-General of the Army of the U.S. in 1792. As a pioneer he did much to develop the vast resources of this country And was highly esteemed by his contemporaries for his sagacity, intelligence and wit.

These lines are culled from *American Families of Historic Lineage*, The Americana Society, New York:

General O'Hara died in the sixty-seventh year of his age, on Dec. 16, 1819, at his home on Water Street, Pittsburgh, and the entire town mourned. It is said that the tears of the rich and the poor were commingled, for he had been the firm friend of both, treating all with justice.

First published in 2019 by Head of Zeus Ltd
This edition first published in 2020 by Head of Zeus Ltd

9 7 5 3 1 2 4 6 8

A catalogue record for this book is available from
the British Library.

ISBN (HB): 9781838932817
ISBN (ANZTPB): 9781838932824
ISBN (E): 9781838932848

Printed and bound by CPI Group (UK) Ltd, Croydon, CR0 4YY

Head of Zeus Ltd
First Floor East
5–8 Hardwick Street
London EC1R 4RG

WWW.HEADOFZEUS.COM

Place Names

Place names in Dark Ages Britain vary according to time, language, dialect and the scribe. I have not followed a strict convention when choosing the spelling to use for a given place. In most cases, I have chosen the name I believe to be the closest to that used in the ninth century, but like the scribes of all those centuries ago, I have taken artistic licence at times, and, when unsure, merely selected the one I liked most.

Bathum	Bath
Briuuetone	Bruton, Somerset
Briw	River Brue, Somerset
Cantmael	Queen Camel, Somerset
Carrum	Carhampton, Somerset
Centingas	Kent
Ceorleah Hill	Chorley Hill, Bruton, Somerset
Cernemude	Charmouth, Dorset
Cornwalum	Cornwall. The westernmost part of the older kingdom of Dumnonia. The people of Cornwalum were known as the Westwalas (West Welsh) by the men of Wessex.

Defnascire	Devon. The people of Devon were known as the Defnas.
Denemearc	Denmark
Dyfelin	Dublin, Ireland
Éastseaxe	Essex
Ellandun	Wroughton, Wiltshire
Exanceaster	Exeter, Devon
Frama	River Frome, Somerset
Hengestdūn	Hingston Down
Íraland	Ireland
Langtun	Langton Herring, Dorset
Mercia	One of the kingdoms of the Anglo-Saxon Heptarchy. It centred on the Trent valley in what is now known as the English Midlands.
Scirburne	Sherborne, Dorset
Sealhwudu	Selwood Forest. An ancient forest that ran approximately between Chippenham in Wiltshire and Gillingham in Dorset.
Somersæte	Somerset
Spercheforde	Sparkford, Somerset
Súpseaxe	Sussex
Súþríeg	Surrey
Tantun	Taunton, Somerset
Tweoxneam	Twynham (modern-day Christchurch, Dorset)
Wessex (Westseaxna rīce)	Kingdom of the West Saxons. In the ninth century, Wessex covered much of southern Britain, including modern-day Wiltshire, Somerset, Dorset and Hampshire. During the reign of King Ecgberht, Wessex conquered Surrey,

Sussex, Kent, Essex and Mercia, along with parts of Dumnonia. Ecgberht also obtained the overlordship of the Northumbrians. Supremacy over Mercia was brief however, with Mercian independence being restored in 830.

Wincaletone   Wincanton, Somerset

Witanceastre   Winchester

WOLF of WESSEX

N

CORNWALUM

DEFNASCIRE

SOMERSÆTE

Carrum

Tantun

Exanceaster

Hengestdun

Cernemude

R. Briw

Briuuet

Ceorleah H

Cantmael

Scirburne

Ba

S

La

0   20 miles
0   40 km

Ellandun

W E S T S E A X N A R I C E

W E S S E X

Hwitan
Sea
K. Frama

caletone

○Witanceastre

Tweoxneam

THE BRITISH ISLES
AD 838

NORTHUMBRIA

ÍRALAND
Dyfelin

MERCIA

ÉASTSEAXE
WESSEX
CENTINGAS
SÚPSEAXE
DEFNASCIRE
SÚPRÍEG
CORNWALUM

Anno Domini Nostri Iesu Christi
In the Year of Our Lord Jesus Christ
838

One

It had been a good morning until Dunston found the corpse.

When he'd left the hut, there had been nothing to suggest the grisly secret that was hiding deep within the forest. The weather was fine. A misty haze lingered in the folds of the land and along the winding course of the River Frama. There was a crisp bite to the air, but Dunston knew from the experience of many years that the mist would burn off as the sun climbed into the summer sky.

Sparrows scattered, bursting forth from the bracken as Odin, Dunston's rangy merle hound, sped off into the undergrowth. To see the dog run always lifted Dunston's spirits. The dog was close to seven years old, but seemed to think it was still a pup, such was its vigour and energy.

Dunston stretched his right leg and grimaced. Straightening, he winced as his back popped and cracked. He wished he could forget that he was no longer a young man, but his body would allow him no such fantasy. He'd suffered too many injuries, pushed his frame to the limits of endurance too many times for his muscles and joints not to protest. He ran his thick fingers through his beard and sighed. Sometimes he almost forgot the passing of the years. Each day was similar to the countless days before. But then he would catch a glimpse of himself in the polished plate that Eawynn had hung on the wall of his home and he would see that where his beard had once been as black as a winter's night, now it was streaked with silver frost. And the hair that had grown so thick and wavy was now thinning, receding back from his weather-lined brow.

Still, he was yet hale and strong and he strode off along the path, listening absently to the muffled crackle of Odin's passage through the leaf litter and undergrowth. After a few moments, silence fell on the forest and Dunston wondered whether the dog had picked up the scent of a deer. More than likely he would be rolling in some unspeakable dung. By God, if that dog returned covered in shit as he so often did, the stupid animal would be taking a dip in the river before heading home. And he'd be sleeping outside the hut until the stench abated. Christ alone knew what pleasure the hound took in lathering himself in excrement. Perhaps his instincts told him that in that way he would find it easier to stalk prey. Dunston thought it would be hard for any wild animal not to smell the dog's approach after he'd smeared himself liberally with manure. And yet, no matter how often he rebuked the beast, it never stopped him.

Dunston pursed his lips, meaning to whistle for Odin, but he paused before making a sound. Something was amiss.

He halted in a small glade, shaded beneath the surrounding trees and listened. He had lived with nobody but Odin for company for long enough to know better than to ignore his feelings. Breathing silently through his opened mouth, he noted his steaming breath billowing momentarily. There was no wind. He listened to the forest, straining to hear any indication of what might have unsettled him.

Silence. As absolute as a tomb.

Gone was the sound of Odin's bounding gait through the wood. No trees rustled their leaves. The birds, usually filling the forest with their twittering songs, had all hushed. The stillness was disquieting.

Alert now, Dunston moved stealthily into the brush beside the trail. With barely a glance he made out where Odin had passed. The fresh white wood of a broken twig. A bent fern. There, in the muddy earth between the boles of two gnarled oaks, a fresh paw print, claws dug in deeply where the dog had been running fast.

With scarcely a sound, the aches in his knee and back forgotten, Dunston followed Odin's trail. He stepped lithely and as quietly as a shade. He did not hurry, for to do so would be to make noise when he knew that the surprise of silence would serve him well against man and beast.

There were creatures that dwelt in these lands that it would do well to respect. He sometimes saw the spoor of bears and at times in winter, wolves would cause him trouble, ripping the flesh from the animals he snared. But he was not unduly concerned about bears or wolves. He was more worried that Odin might have stumbled upon one of the old boars that roamed the woodland. To face one openly could well spell death for a dog, no matter how strong. The larger boars had great, dagger-like tusks and he had seen hounds and once even an unlucky man, disembowelled by the furious wild pigs.

Dunston placed his hand on the large seax that was scabbarded at his belt. He had no spear, and if he was charged by a big boar, he knew the knife would do him little good. But the touch of its antler hilt reassured him. Barely breathing, he stalked forward, as silent as any woodland animal. He paused again, listening and sniffing the air. There was no sound. Surely if Odin had stumbled upon a boar, there would have been a cacophony of grunts and growls as the animals fought. Even the largest boar would not slay Odin without a fight. And yet, there was just the unnerving hush.

3

Light sliced through the leafy canopy, dappling the loam and leaf mould. Dunston dropped to one knee, the joint letting out a sharp report. He winced at the sudden sound, loud in the unnatural stillness. He peered at the ground, unsure for a moment what it was he saw. And then, the shapes of the trampled leaves and the scuffed mark on the moss-covered rock by the root of a linden tree all made sense in an instant of clarity. Odin had passed this way, but so too had several men. Large, heavy men, to judge from their tracks. Three of them. No, four. They had been travelling northward. Dunston examined the tracks closely. They were fresh. He did not recognise them. These were not the prints left by any of the men who came to the wood from Briuuetone. He would never mistake the tracks of the charcoal burners, the woodsmen or the swineherd leading his pigs in search of mast under the trees. No, these were strangers, he was sure of it. But what would four men be doing creeping around in his forest? Perhaps they were wolf-heads; men outside of the law, whose oaths were worthless. Such men could be dangerous. They had nothing to lose.

He pushed himself up and before setting off once more after Odin, he listened again. There was a whisper of a sound and an instant later, the grey, white and black hound loped into the lancing sunlight.

Odin, tongue lolling, panted. His chest heaved.

"Where have you been, boy?" asked Dunston in a hushed hiss. His heart soared at the animal's safe return and he let out a pent up breath, surprised at his own worry for the hound. He reached out a hand and Odin nudged it with his snout, licking his fingers. The dog's nose was wet and cool. Dunston rubbed absently at the dog's ear and was surprised to see a smudge of crimson on the beast's fur.

Blood.

He looked down at his hand and saw that it was slick with the stuff. Pushing Odin's head to one side so that it caught a ray of sunlight, he saw that the hound's mouth and muzzle were drenched in gore.

By Christ's bones, what had Odin discovered? Had he perhaps brought down a fawn? Odin was a good hunter and would often chase and slay animals. But somehow Dunston knew that this blood did not belong to any animal. The fresh prints of the men told him that much. That, and the unnerving quiet of the wood.

For the merest of instants Dunston considered turning away and walking back to his hut. A small voice whispered to him that he wanted no part of whatever it was Odin had found.

Later, on more than one occasion, he would regret not listening to that voice.

Yet as surely as he knew he wanted nothing to do with the strangers that were in his forest, nor to discover where the blood had come from, so he understood that it was not in his nature to walk away.

He sighed, blowing out air slowly so that his breath billowed about him for a moment in the early morning cool.

"Stay close, boy," he whispered. "Show me what you've found."

Odin looked up at him, its one eye dark and thoughtful, bearded mouth red and straggled. And then the dog spun around and padded silently back into the undergrowth. Dunston hurried behind, less concerned now with remaining silent as with finding the source of that blood.

It was closer than he had imagined. A few heartbeats later, Odin led him into a clearing surrounded by densely leafed linden trees. In the centre of the glade lay a corpse. He did not need to approach the body to know the man was dead.

The clearing was awash with blood. The man had been slain atop a fallen oak, the wood long dead and crumbling. The tree trunk was slimed with gore. The delicate white flowers of the dog rose that grew along the edge of the rotting tree were splattered with crimson. The moss that clung to the wood glistened darkly. Blood had spattered and smeared much of the clearing's green carpet of snakeweed and ivy. The corpse had been stripped to the waist. Where his skin was not daubed with his lifeblood, it was pallid; the blue-tinge of death. Dunston could not see the dead man's face. He had been left face down on the log. His greying hair dangled down, lank and blood-streaked, brushing the earth beneath his hanging head.

Dunston had seen death before. But the savagery of this man's slaughter made his breath catch in his throat. This was more than a murder, or a robbery of an unlucky traveller. There was evil here.

Dunston shuddered.

Odin padded forward into the glade.

"Stay," Dunston ordered, his voice harsh; a knife cut in the stillness of the forest.

The dog whimpered, but halted and sat on its haunches. Absently, Dunston reached out and placed a hand on the hound's head. The dog's warmth was comforting.

Dunston stroked the soft, warm fur behind Odin's ears, but all the while, his gaze remained fixed on the scene of slaughter before him.

The slain man's back had been split open. His ribs had been pried apart and his offal pulled from his flesh and splayed upon his back. Dunston did not need to get any closer to know that the bloody mess either side of the great wound in the centre of his back was made up of the man's lungs. They had been draped like crude, blood-drenched wings on the man's shoulder blades.

Dunston had heard of such things, but he had thought them the tales of scops to frighten children. Though why they felt the need to make the Norsemen any more terrifying than they were, he had never understood. In his experience, the men who came from the sea aboard the beast-prowed sea-dragons, oars beating as the wings of some giant bird, were fearsome enough. There was no need to invent stories of human sacrifice and ritual killings in the name of their one-eyed god.

Could it be that the tales were true? Had raiders landed nearby in their sleek ships, on the Frama perhaps? Surely the river was not large enough here to carry fighting ships? Were Norsemen even now creeping through the forest in search of prey?

And yet he had only seen the tracks of four men. And it was not the way of those heathen Norse to sneak around murdering men in the dark of the woodland. The people of the coast lived in constant fear of the coming of the dragon ships, he knew, but here? And why so few of them?

Whatever the truth of it, the remains of the poor man told him one thing. Danger was close.

Dunston dragged his gaze from the gory spectacle and cast around the clearing. Clothing was strewn about. A tawny-coloured cape. A ripped kirtle, tattered and flecked with dark stains. A single leather shoe. Dunston flicked his gaze back to the dead man and noted his left foot was bare.

An unusual shadow caught his attention. There was some-thing large just beyond the clearing. He took a couple of steps towards it. His hand rested on his seax handle and once again he was moving with the silent stealth of a woodland hunter. Two more steps and he was able to discern what the object was. A handcart. A simple, two-wheeled affair that could be pulled by one person. Walking to the cart, he tugged back the greased leather that covered its contents. He was surprised to find several sacks, a wooden box and a couple of small iron-hooped kegs, nestling safely and seemingly untouched beneath the cover. Teasing open one of the sacks he found long white goose feathers inside. A second, smaller bag held leather pouches. Each of the pouches was tightly tied, but they were not sealed well enough to disguise the heady aroma of pepper, cinnamon and mace. Dunston's head swam with the powerful scents of the spices. These were not the things that would bring Norse warriors battle-fame and have their names sung of in the halls of their northern lands, but the stuff was valuable enough. Pulling the leather back over the cart, he looked about him.

A light wind rustled the leaves high above. The summer sun was warming the land. Somewhere far off a wood pigeon called. The forest was returning to normal, breathing once again after the sudden violence that had happened within its depths.

Dunston sighed. When he had awoken that morning, he had meant to check his snares, and then return to his hut and the forge. The knife he was making for Oswold, the leatherworker from Briuuetone, was taking shape and it would easily have been finished by midsummer's eve. But now that would have to wait. He could not leave the man here. The easiest thing would be to bury him and just keep what was on the cart. He could sell the items over time, and some of the things might be of use to him.

Shaking his head, he returned to the clearing. He knew he would do no such thing. He was no thief, and besides, there were killers on the loose. Perhaps even Norsemen. No, he would take the cart and the man down to Briuuetone. Let Rothulf decide what must be done. Perhaps the reeve would know who the corpse was. Maybe the dead man had kin.

Dunston took in a deep breath and spat, readying himself for the task of wrestling the man's gore-slick remains onto the small cart. He once more searched the ground, as much to put off the task as anything else.

The same four men. They had all been here. He could clearly see where they had confronted the man with the cart and then dragged him to the fallen oak. The spray of the man's blood showed Dunston where they had first tortured him and then, with a great gouting fountain of dark arterial blood, they had taken his life. Dunston reached out to touch a bramble, pulling a small red woollen thread from a thorn. His hand shook. He could almost hear the screams of the dying man, the laughter and shouts of the men who had butchered him. Dunston was no stranger to death and he was accustomed to slaughtering, gutting and skinning animals small and large. But this torn tragedy, a mass of ripped flesh and offal, this was no way for a man to die.

Twisting the piece of wool between his forefinger and thumb, Dunston steeled himself for what he needed to do. But just as he pushed himself up, he noticed the slightest of prints in the soft earth in the shade of the dog rose. This was something else. No, someone else. Judging from the size and depth of the track, this belonged to a child or perhaps a woman. Had the four men taken her?

Dunston's heart pounded. Was there even now a defenceless child at the mercy of the brutes who had committed this act of savagery? He searched frantically about the glade for more sign, but the area was trampled. Flies and insects droned and hummed now about the corpse, gorging themselves on its blood and cooling flesh.

He could find no more tracks. Perhaps he should follow the clear trail of the killers in order to see whether they had carried the child off with them. He did not like the prospect. There were four of them and he wanted nothing to do with men capable of such atrocities. And yet, without a backward glance, he hitched up his belt and walked into the forest after them. He would have to come back for the poor man's body later.

Just as he stepped into the gloom beneath the linden trees, Odin let out a piercing bark. By the rood and all the saints, the stupid dog would get him killed. Dunston hissed at the hound for silence, but Odin ignored him, raising his snout as if scenting something on the breeze, and then bounding off into the undergrowth in the opposite direction to the killers' tracks.

Unsure for a moment, Dunston hesitated. Then, with a curse, he turned and ran after the dog.

Two

Aedwen tried not to breathe. She strained to hear any sign that the men had returned. But the wood was silent now. Gone was the terrible screaming. Before the inhuman shrieking that had come later, she had been able to recognise the sound of her father's voice. He had spoken in that infuriatingly calm manner of his; the tone that mother had said drove her mad.

Walking back from the stream, Aedwen had paused for a moment when she'd heard him speaking, wondering whether he was calling something to her. But then she had heard the other voices, hard and jagged, as different from father's tone as a flint is to silk. Absently wondering who the voices belonged to, she had started up the trail again. The bucket she carried was full and heavy, and she had wanted to relinquish its weight.

That was when the shouting had started. It had quickly been followed by screaming. For a moment she had stood there on the path, the forest still cold and gloomy in the dawn. The chill water from the bucket sloshed her hand, starting her into motion. She heard several coarse voices, and laughter.

And her father had let out a piteous wailing cry. Tears flooded down her cheeks at the sound, but she knew what he would have wanted her to do. They had talked about what to do if they were ever attacked by brigands on the road.

"If you can get away, you run, girl," he had said to her, as he had stirred the pot of stew over the smoking fire. That was on the first day after they had left the home she had known all her life. When this was still an adventure.

Father had often berated Aedwen for not obeying him, but that morning she did as she had been told. She spun on her heel and sprinted away. She had run without thought for her destination or direction. Branches whipped at her face, snagging her dress. Brambles scratched at her skin. All the while, father's screams echoed around the wood. His dying cries followed her until she was panting and breathless, sweat plastering her hair to her scalp.

At last, his screams ceased. Aedwen flung herself down in the lee of a broad-trunked old tree. She lay there, chest heaving and her face awash with great sheets of tears. She wondered whether she had merely run far enough not to hear him any longer, but deep down she knew the reason for his silence.

She tried to remember that first night when father had told her to run in the event of an attack. What had he said she should do after that? She could not recall any more of the conversation. The memory of his smile was clear though, his teeth shining in the firelight. Like all of his plans and schemes, there had been no thought to what happened next. By the Blessed Virgin, how she wished they had never embarked on this foolish escapade. But father had seemed so sure of himself. Wasn't he always?

If only she could have talked him out of it. But he was so assured, so convincing. Mother would have put a stop to his madness. She always did.

Aedwen sniffed and her tears fell as great sobs shook her body. How she missed her. And now she would miss him too.

Aedwen allowed herself to weep for a while, before wiping her nose and face on her sleeve. She was alone now. She needed to think. Holding the face of her mother in her mind's eye, she took stock. All she had with her were her clothes, the eating knife that hung from her belt, and the bucket that she yet gripped tightly. Most of the water had spilt from it as she had sprinted through the forest, but there were a couple of mouthfuls yet swilling at the bottom. She upended the pail and drank.

She had no idea who the men were who had attacked father, but everyone knew the forests were filled with those cast out from the law: wolf-heads. Men and women who had fled justice and could never return to their homes. They had no qualms in slaying innocent travellers. Their lives were already forfeit, and they could be killed like animals. And so they became as animals, savaging those who passed through their wooded home, eking out a living from robbery and murder.

If such men had killed her father, they might already be coming for her. She forced herself to breathe shallowly, listening intently for any sound of pursuit. But the forest was silent and calm once more. A bird cooed somewhere in the depth of the forest. The sound startled her.

It's just a bird, she told herself.

Think!

Could her father yet live? She scarcely believed that it could be so. Surely those screams were those of a dying man. And yet she could not flee, leaving him to God knew what fate. Perhaps even now, the outlaws had stolen the goods from their cart and had abandoned her father, allowing him to bleed to death, slowly succumbing to his wounds. The thought filled her with horror. Could he truly be lying in the clearing in need of her help?

She would have to find out. And if she found him alive, how could she help him? She was no healer. Perhaps with the help of the cart she could get him back to Briuuetone, the last village they had passed through. If she could find the clearing where they had camped, she thought she would be able to trace their steps back from there to the road and the village.

But what if the men were still there? She shuddered. Aedwen was no fool. She knew what would befall her at the hands of such brigands. Once more she listened. The sun had risen higher into the sky and spears of light stabbed through the leaf canopy. A wind whispered through the trees, sighing and making the branches shiver. The green-tinged light danced and dappled the earth around her. Far away the bird called again. But there was no sound of pursuit. No yelling and snapping of twigs and rustle of undergrowth. She let out her breath and drew in a great lungful of air. The woodland was redolent of growth, verdant and vigorous. Summer had brought bountiful life to the land. And yet, she feared that in a small glade surrounded by pale-leafed trees her only kin lay dead.

She had to know for sure.

She would creep back towards the glade where she had left her father. If she suspected the men who had attacked him were approaching, she would hide and slip away. She was fleet of foot and fast. She trembled, the light from the sun offered little warmth down here under the trees. And the ground was yet cold and wet from the rain that had fallen these last weeks. They had slept without a fire last night, cold and shivering, huddled together for warmth, as the woods creaked and murmured about them. She pulled her thin cloak about her shoulders. The wool was old and fraying and the garment offered little protection. Whether her father lived or not, she would need to find shelter before nightfall.

Much of the morning had already passed and the sun would soon be at its zenith. There was no time to waste. She would be cautious, but she must move.

Aedwen pushed herself to her feet, brushing ineffectually at the leaves and mud that clung to her dress. After a moment's hesitation she decided to carry the bucket. It could prove useful and she was not sure she would ever be able to find this spot in the forest again. Taking another deep breath of the heavy, rich air, she started north.

Scarcely had she taken five paces, than a dog's piercing bark sliced through the sylvan stillness. Aedwen stifled a cry of fear, but was unable to prevent her feet from carrying her back at a run to the bole of the tree where she had been hidden until moments before. She pressed her back against the rough bark, her breath coming as ragged and fast as when she had first arrived here after running for a long while.

Another bark. Was that a man's voice she heard too? She could not be certain. Sounds of passage through the brush grew louder.

"*Hal Wes ðu, Maria, mid gyfe gefylled, Drihten mid ðe. Ðu eart gebletsod on wifum and gebletsod ðines innoðes wæstm, se Hæland.*"

She began to whisper the words of the prayer urgently. All her brave ideas of returning to help her father, or fleeing from any pursuit, had vanished like smoke on the wind. She could not move. Fresh tears brimmed in her eyes, then fell unnoticed down her already streaked cheeks.

"*Halige Maria, Godes modor, gebide for us synfullum, nu and on ðære tide ures forðsiðes.*"

The movements in the forest were growing louder. There was no more barking, but she was sure that at least one hound and several men were crashing through the ferns and brambles, unerringly closing in on her.

What should she do? What could she do?

Her mind raced, the words of the prayer blurring into nonsense as her fear engulfed her.

She must move. Run or perhaps climb a tree. But she did nothing; paralysed by fear and the fresh memories of her father's echoing death-wails.

A huge mottled hound rounded the trunk of a tree. It halted, straight-legged, tongue flopping and hackles raised. Its teeth were white and very large. The dog fixed her with a baleful stare and she noticed it only had one eye. Was this a strange creature of the forest? Some devil hound of the Wild Hunt perhaps? It looked more wolf than dog, and its size was terrifying. It looked at her for a moment, as if it was as surprised as she was, and then it let out a peal of barking howls.

Someway off, Aedwen heard renewed sounds of people approaching. She could barely breathe now. The hound was still barking, but it had not attacked her yet. Her hand fell to the tiny eating knife at her belt. Perhaps, she would be able to halt the beast with the small blade. It only had one eye, so maybe she could blind it.

She pulled the knife from its worn leather sheath. The blade was scarcely the length of her finger. Still, it would take an eye out, if she could find her mark. She readied herself for the animal to launch at her. Gripping the knife tightly, she pressed her back to the tree's bark and prepared for the attack.

Before the beast could pounce, a man strode into sight. He was not tall, but he was broad of shoulder and there was a presence about him. He wore simple clothes of wool and leather. His hair was black streaked with silver like the wings of a jackdaw. His beard was a jutting white and black thatch. He looked ancient to her young eyes, much older than her father. But he was no wizened greybeard. No gum-sucking old man, who sat staring out to sea on long summer evenings. This man was powerful, the way a waterfall or the sea in a gale has power. The instant he entered the clearing, the dog fell silent.

The man's cool gaze took in everything in an instant. He must have been running to keep up with the dog, but he appeared to be barely out of breath.

"Well, girl," he said, his voice gruff and clipped, "who are you?"

Aedwen could not speak. She opened and closed her mouth, but no sound came.

"You'll not be needing that knife," the man said, indicating the blade in her trembling hand. "I think you would just anger him, if you prodded him with it anyway."

Seeming to sense her distress, the massive dog, quiet now, edged forward. She let out a whimper of alarm.

"Odin," snapped the man. "To me." His tone was commanding, but the dog ignored him and padded closer to Aedwen. She tried to push herself away from him, but the tree prevented her from moving further. She was crying uncontrollably now, tears flowing, mouth open and panting in terror.

The man frowned.

"Do not fear," he said. "Odin won't hurt you. Will you, boy?"

As if in answer, the dog licked her hand. Looking down, she saw the knife still clutched there. The dog looked up at her with its one, deep brown eye. It nuzzled its snout into her, inviting her to stroke it perhaps. Shakily, she sheathed the knife and reached out to caress the soft fur of the dog's ears. Odin sat down contentedly and once again nudged her with his head, encouraging her to continue.

Could the man be one of the heathen Norsemen to have named his dog thus? she wondered.

"By Christ's bones," said the man. "Disobedient and soft."

She noticed then that he had in his large hand a long seax. The blade of the knife glimmered dully as he moved. For an instant, her fear returned with a sudden icy chill. But as she watched, he slid the weapon into a scabbard that hung from his belt.

"Now," the old man said, "who are you and what are you doing in my forest?"

"I—" she stammered, her voice catching, "I am Aedwen, Lytelman's daughter."

"And where were you headed?"

"To find my father…" she swallowed, not wishing to put words to what had occurred. "He— He was attacked."

The man ran a callused hand over his face and beard. His eyes glittered, chips of ice in the crags of his face. She wondered if he ever smiled. His was a hard face, unyielding and unsmiling, so unlike her father's. He always appeared content with his lot in life. She recalled his screams and shuddered.

"You will come with me and Odin. My home is not far. We will rest there and then, tomorrow, we will go to Briuuetone."

"No," she replied, "I must go to my father. He might need me."

"He does not need you now, child," said the man, his voice as cold and hard as granite. "Your father is dead."

Three

Dunston stretched his feet out towards the fire. The flames had died, leaving writhing red embers that lit the small hut with a ruddy flickering glow. By Christ, he was tired. And yet he knew he would not sleep for a long while. He sipped the strong mead directly from the leather costrel. It was soothing, and he felt his shoulders relaxing.

He looked over the coals of the fire to where the girl lay. She was exhausted and he had needed to halt frequently on the journey through the woods. He wasn't sure how old she was, he hadn't thought to ask, but she was somewhere in that awkward time between a girl and woman. Something about her reminded him of Eawynn. Perhaps it was her determination. She had shown great strength when he had led her to the site of her father's murder.

"You do not wish to see your father as he is," he had told her.

She had argued, but he had been adamant, sending her to the cart to find something they could use to cover the man's corpse. He'd ended up using the man's cloak and the leather cover that had been on the cart. He had made her wait with Odin by the handcart and had set about tending to the girl's father. It was a terrible task, as he had known it would be, and after a time he was covered in sticky gore.

Aedwen's eyes had widened when she saw him step from the glade, arms and hands besmeared in blood. He had led her with him to the stream, where he had washed himself as best he could in the bitterly cold water, picking up handfuls of sand and rubbing away the grime. Then he had filled the girl's bucket and carried it back to the glade.

"Wait a short while more," he had said when she asked if now she could see her father.

He had wrapped the butchered man tightly in the leather and cloth, shrouding his body from view. He left his face visible, using a scrap of the man's kirtle dipped in the bucket to wipe his cheeks, chin and forehead clean. Then he cut a long strip of woollen cloth from the cloak and bound it about his head, over the crown and beneath the chin to hold the mouth shut.

Only then, when he was sure he had done all he could to make Aedwen's father look at peace, had Dunston heaved the man's corpse up and carried him to the cart. They had cleared the bed of the cart and Dunston had laid the man down as softly as he was able. The girl had gazed at her father's face for a long while.

Dunston had been nervous, peering into the forest and listening for any sign that the men who had done this thing might be returning. But they had disappeared and now that he had found the girl, he did not regret letting them be on their way. Nothing he did would bring Aedwen's father back. And men capable of this kind of violence would meet a bloody end themselves one day, of that he was certain. Sweat-drenched and breathless from his exertions, Dunston drank cool water from the bucket while Aedwen cried silently.

They had piled the goods from the cart around Lytelman's corpse, even placing a couple of sacks, one of feathers and one of smoked mackerel, on his chest. Dunston had said they could leave the contents of the cart hidden and return for it, but Aedwen would not hear of it.

"This is all that is left of my father's dreams," she had said, sniffing. "I will not leave it or throw it away."

Dunston had not replied, merely helping her to arrange the sacks. The cart creaked and groaned and was difficult to coax along the root-snarled paths to his hut, but Dunston understood Aedwen's anxiety at leaving the things untended in the wood. He had asked about her kin and found she had none. She was an orphan now, and this was all she owned. It was not much, but it was better than nothing at all.

Taking another swig of mead, he looked down at the girl where she slept in the fire-glow. In sleep, her face was soft, trouble-free. How would such a young child survive in this world? Well, that was no concern of his. He would do his duty and take her to Briuuetone. Let Rothulf there find a home for the orphan. Not for the first time, Dunston wished he had not left his hut that morning. Nothing but trouble had come his way. Everything had changed when he'd stumbled upon the blood-soaked corpse of the girl's father. Well, as Guthlaf had so often told him over the years, there were only two things you could ever be sure of in life: the passage of time and the unexpected. Today, he had been reminded of both. He twisted his head around and his neck gave an audible click. He grunted, feeling his age of close to fifty summers.

Odin let out a suppressed growling bark, dreaming of the shade of some woodland creature no doubt. His legs twitched as he ran in his slumber. The animal was stretched out beside Aedwen and one of his huge paws rested on her arm. Dunston snorted and sipped again from the costrel. He had never seen the hound take to someone in this way. The dog was friendly enough with him, and fiercely loyal, but he usually slept alone beside the fire, or curled up close to the door. He never came close to Dunston's bed at the rear of the hut.

The foolish beast would miss the girl when they left her at Briuuetone. All the more reason to be done with it. At first light they would set out. He could not have the poor girl weeping and complaining around the place.

Dunston awoke with a start. He yet sat in the high-backed chair he had carved many years ago. He made to rise and his spine cried out in agony at having rested so long against the hard oak of the seat. The half-full flask of mead toppled from where it had perched atop his belly. Cursing, he lunged for the falling costrel, sending fresh stabs of pain down his back and neck. Too slow, his fingers brushed the leather and it fell to the packed earth floor.

"By all that is holy," shouted Dunston, angrily heaving himself to his feet and snatching up the flask before all the mead had been spilt.

Light streamed in through the hut's open door and at the sound of his voice, Odin padded inside to gaze up quizzically at his master. The sun had risen long ago and Dunston could scarcely believe how long he had slept. The exertions of the day before must have taken their toll on his body more than he had imagined. Thank you, Lord, for yet another reminder of how old he was becoming.

Beside the hearth knelt Aedwen. She had rekindled the flames and was now placing oatcakes on a griddle. The smell of cooking brought saliva rushing into his mouth. They had been too tired to prepare food when they had arrived the previous night and his stomach grumbled now at the prospect of eating.

Odin nudged Dunston's hand with his cold wet snout. To Dunston, it looked as though the dog was grinning at him.

"What are you looking at, fool of a dog?" he growled.

Aedwen looked up from where she was cooking. Her eyes were red-rimmed and sparkling. Dunston noticed that she had brushed her hair, and it shimmered in the morning sunlight from the doorway.

"You're awake," she said. "The oatcakes are almost ready."

"You should have woken me," Dunston said, pushing himself up from the chair and stretching. He winced as his body protested. "I wanted to be gone long before now."

"You looked tired."

"There's strength enough in these old bones to get you and your father to Briuuetone."

She cast her gaze down to the griddle, poking at the cakes with a stick to check whether they were done.

"Well, I thought it best if I fed you first. Neither of us ate yesterday, and you'll need to keep that strength up." She decided that the cake closest to the flames was ready and prised it from the metal and scooped it onto a wooden platter. Dunston recognised the plate as one he had made. She handed it to him and, after a slight hesitation, he accepted it. The oat cake smelt good. He broke a piece of it off and the warm fragrance wafted up to him. He tested it with his tongue. It was hot, but his hunger got the better of him and he popped it into his mouth. The crisp outer shell broke under his bite, exposing the steaming soft centre. Gasping, he breathed through his mouth, waving his hand to indicate he was burning.

Aedwen smirked and handed him a wooden cup of ale.

He filled his mouth with the cool liquid, sighing as it lessened the scalding and dissolved the mouthful of oat cake.

"You've certainly made yourself at home," he said, frowning.

"I thought you would be happy for me to cook. It is the least I can do. You have been kind to me."

Dunston grunted and took another bite of the cake.

"These are good," he said grudgingly, taking a second draught of ale.

"My mother taught me," said Aedwen, before falling silent. She busied herself with the griddle, flicking more of the oatcakes onto another plate.

"I'll have another," Dunston said, suddenly awkward. "And I thank you."

Aedwen beamed and slid two more cakes onto his plate. Then she nibbled one herself and nodded, seemingly content with her handiwork.

"Do you live here alone?" she asked.

Dunston nodded.

"Just me and Odin." At the sound of his name, Odin raised his head. Dunston glowered at the dog for a moment, before breaking one of the cakes in two and tossing half to the hound. Odin caught the offering and in a heartbeat the food had vanished.

Aedwen watched the dog, a small smile tugging at her lips despite the horror and loss she had suffered.

"You have no kin?"

For a moment, Dunston chewed in silence. He glanced over to where the girl had laid out the cooking utensils neatly beside the hearth. Everything was just so, ordered and tidy. How long had it been since a woman had been in this hut? It seemed like a lifetime. His gaze flicked to Eawynn's silver plate, hanging on the far wall, where it reflected the light from the fire.

"I have a brother," Dunston replied at last. "But I have not seen him since Michaelmas this past year."

"Nobody else?"

"No. No one else, damn your nosiness, girl." He crammed the rest of the oat cake into his mouth and chewed sullenly. The girl said nothing, but her eyes brimmed with tears as she finished her food and set about clearing the things away.

"I am sorry," Dunston said. "You are right, I was tired. And hungry."

"It is no matter. Father was always ill-tempered in the morning before he broke his fast."

"Ill-tempered, am I?" he said, unable to keep the smile from his face. "I suppose I am at that. I am not used to having company." He wiped his hands through his beard. "And what of you, do you have kin..." he hesitated, "... beyond your father?"

The girl's face crumpled, her lower lip quivering. She stood, picking up the soiled cooking things.

He felt a pang of guilt at her reaction. Damn his clumsiness. He understood as well as anyone the anguish of grief.

"I do not wish to cause you more pain," he said, stumbling over the words, unsure of himself. "I have never been good with words." He held up his hands. They were thick-fingered and callused. "I only have skill with these," he said. "It has ever been so. Whenever I speak, I cause offence."

"What do you make?" Aedwen said, her voice small.

Dunston was confused. He grunted, leaning his head to one side. Surprisingly, Aedwen grinned.

"What is so funny, girl?" Dunston said, suddenly annoyed once more.

Aedwen bit her lip.

"I beg your pardon, it is just..." her voice trailed off.

"Just what?"

When she did not reply immediately, he continued. "You had better tell me. One thing I like worse than waking up late are secrets."

Aedwen took a deep breath, but still she hesitated.

"Well?" he said, his voice taking on an edge of iron.

With a sigh, Aedwen said, "The way you looked at me just then, with your head to one side, you looked just like Odin."

For a long while Dunston stared at the girl. To his surprise and her credit she held his gaze, until at last, he allowed himself to smile.

"Like Odin, you say?" The hound looked up at him and cocked its head at an angle. Dunston let out a guffaw and he was pleased to see that Aedwen was laughing too. "Well," he said, through his chuckles, "it would seem I have been too long in the company of this hound. As we walk to Briuuetone you will have to teach me once again the ways of mankind."

They laughed together as they cleaned the plates with some of the water from a barrel by the door. For a moment it was almost as though the previous day, with its blood and terror, had never happened. But when they returned to the hut, they both looked upon the shadowed shape of Aedwen's father, wrapped in the makeshift shroud.

"Have you any inkling of who the attackers were?" he asked, unable to avoid returning to the dark subject of her father's murder.

"No," she said, "I thought they must be wolf-heads."

Dunston nodded, saying nothing of the cart laden with goods that had been left behind.

"But I have been thinking about that," she continued. "Men living outside the law would be desperate for anything of value. They would never leave the cart."

Dunston said nothing. The girl impressed him. She was sharp and thoughtful.

"In answer to your question," she said, "I have no close kin. My father had two sisters, but they married and moved away before I was born. I know nothing of my mother's family. She never talked of them."

"It seems we are both alone," he said, feeling a stab of pity. It was one thing for a man of his age to look at a future devoid of companionship and family, but for one so young... Aedwen must be terrified of what her life would be now.

"You are not alone," she said. "You have Odin."

Dunston grunted.

"And I am not truly alone," she said. "While I was hiding in the forest, I prayed." Aedwen's voice grew wistful. "I prayed to the Blessed Virgin." Her eyes burnt with a new passion. "And the Mother of God answered me. She sent me you."

"I don't know about that, girl," said Dunston, uneasy at the thought of being part of some sacred plan.

"The Virgin Mary sent you to help me."

"Well," he said, lifting up one of the sacks that belonged to Aedwen and carrying it out to the waiting handcart, "I am happy to help you to reach Briuuetone. You will not be alone there. The reeve will know what to do with you. His wife is kindly and he has daughters too. Perhaps you can stay with them."

She followed him out into the warming daylight.

"I do not wish to go to Briuuetone. I have been praying and I believe you were sent to me for a purpose."

Dunston did not like the sound of this, or the direction that the conversation was headed. He returned inside for another sack. Aedwen followed him.

"And what purpose would that be?" he asked, unsure that he wanted to hear what this child would answer.

"You are adept at following tracks in the forest, are you not?"

He dropped the sack into the bed of the cart and its timbers creaked.

"I am a hunter. I can see where beasts or men have trod," he allowed.

"And you are clearly a strong man. A warrior."

Dunston bridled, not liking one bit the turn this morning had taken.

"I am no warrior," he spat and stalked back inside.

Aedwen ignored his protestations.

"I think you are," she said, "and I think the Virgin answered my pleas by sending you, and in the night, while you slept, I understood what we should do next."

"We?" he said, his tone incredulous. "There is no 'we', girl. I will take you to the reeve at Briuuetone and then you can pray to the Virgin all you want. But whatever you pray for, think not that I will be part of your prayers."

"I do not believe you are a man who would allow something like the brutal murder of my father to go unpunished."

"It is not my place to seek justice. I am not the reeve and I am no warrior."

"And yet you have not denied my words. You would see the men who killed my father punished."

Anger began to bubble within Dunston. The girl's words raked through the embers of his ire at seeing her father's ripped and savaged corpse.

He bent to lift the heavy form of the dead man onto his shoulder. He noticed how blood had soaked through the cloak. The burden was cumbersome and his back once again cried in pain, but he wrestled the corpse up and walked stiffly towards the sunlight and the cart.

"Of course I would have the men who did this thing brought before the moot and tried," he gasped, breathless from the exertion. "But I am but one old man." The words threatened to catch in his throat, but he knew the truth of them. He knew that years before, he would have swung the corpse up and onto his back with barely a thought. Now his bones and joints screamed out in protest. "What would you have me do?"

Aedwen placed a small hand on his burly forearm. He halted and looked into her limpid eyes.

"I would have you track the savages who did this to my father. You say you are a hunter. I want you to hunt them. And when you find them, I want you to kill them all."

Four

They walked in sullen silence.

Aedwen watched as Odin bounded before them, flitting into the trees and then returning sometime later, tongue flopping, tail held high. She wished she could be as carefree. It would be wonderful to be content to run through the forest, in and out of the pools of sunshine that dotted the path beneath the trees. But her mind was a turmoil of emotions. After the initial fear and horror of her father's death, she had set to thinking and praying. She had awoken deep in the darkest part of the night and had been sure she had the solution. She had lain there and listened to Dunston's snoring, comforted by the sound that reminded her of her father. She had tried to turn her thoughts away from her father's body, shrouded, still and stiff in the hut, but no matter how hard she prayed, her mind kept on going back to her father's corpse. She had cried then, silent tears rolling down her cheeks in the darkness, but when the first light of dawn drew a grey line beneath the door of the hut, she had been resolved. She knew what she must do and she had been certain that the grey-bearded man who had found her would accept her challenge.

How wrong she had been.

They had barely spoken since his refusal to seek out her father's killers. He had said that her idea was foolish. He would stick to his plan to take her and her father to Briuuetone and then he would leave. She had felt the fury building within her, like the tension in the air before a thunderstorm. She had been about to scream her anger at Dunston, but something in the set of his jaw and the furrow of his brow, gave her pause. She recalled the last time she had raised her voice to father. She could barely remember what she had been angry about, but her ire had been sudden and terrible. When she had calmed down, father had said something she would never forget, and she thought on those words now.

"I am your father, and I love you. But make no mistake, if you speak to others the way you have spoken to me today, things will go badly for you. Only kin will put up with that kind of foolish rudeness and even then, a father's patience has its limits."

And so, rather than scream and yell at Dunston, she had fallen into step behind him, sour and bitter resentment washing off her like a stink. For his part, he had seemed to be pleased not to speak, conserving his energy for pulling the heavy cart that creaked and groaned over the rutted ground.

More than once, she had needed to help him, lending her small weight to his considerable bulk to heave the cart over a thick tree root, or around a boulder jutting into their path. Not once did she say a word to him, instead doing what was necessary, and then resuming her brooding; an ill-tempered shadow trudging in his wake.

They saw nobody else all that morning. The forest was teeming with wildlife. Magpies chattered and wood pigeons cooed in the canopy and once Odin frightened a partridge from where it rested in the bracken. The bird burst from the undergrowth in a fluster of beating wings and narrowly avoided becoming the hound's meal. But despite the numerous animal denizens of the woods, no humans crossed their path.

Dunston led them unerringly through barely visible deer tracks until they eventually reached the road. Aedwen began to understand how lucky she was that Dunston had found her. Without his aid she would have surely been lost forever in this dense world of twisted trees and clinging brambles. Again she thanked the Virgin for sending him to her, and like someone going back to scratch at an annoying nettle rash, she once more pondered how to have the man do her bidding.

The sun was high in the sky when they came to a fast-flowing brook that the road crossed over by way of a simple timber bridge. The cart clattered over the mossy boards of the bridge and on the far side, Dunston eased the cart's shafts down and stretched, reaching his hands to the small of his back. He grunted as he massaged at his aches and he winced as he bent his right knee to sit with his back to the cart wheel. His forehead was beaded with sweat, but he seemed hale enough. She produced the remainder of the oatcakes from where she had stored them in a bag and handed him one.

He nodded his thanks, broke off a piece and chewed for a time before washing it down with water from a leathern flask. She ate in silence, and accepted the flask from him. The day was warm, and she was thirsty.

Odin gnawed contentedly at a bone he had found somewhere in the depths of the wood.

"I understand that you are filled with anger at the men who did this to your father," Dunston said, breaking the hush that had fallen over them. "But it would be madness to chase after them as you wish." He took back the water bottle from her and drew another deep draught.

"I cannot bear the thought of those men roaming free."

"If I could track them, what then? A girl and an old man against four men."

"You are not so old," she said, a glimmer of mischief in her eye. "You look like you would be able to defend yourself in a fight."

Was that a slight smile nestled within his beard? He snorted.

"Defend, perhaps. But to seek out a fight with men like that would be foolhardy. As I said, I am no longer young and I am no warrior."

She had been watching him closely all that morning, the way he carried himself. Walking lightly on the balls of his feet, his blue eyes never missing anything. She had noticed that his muscled forearms bore many scars, a pale cross-hatching of lines against the tanned skin. She tried to imagine how he might have come across such wounds and could only conclude they were from cuts delivered by enemies standing against him in a shieldwall. Then there was the large axe he had picked up and placed into the cart before they had left his hut. It was a broad-headed, wicked-looking thing; a weapon more than a tool used by a woodsman, she thought. The axe's dark iron head was swirled with intricate patterns of silver, which had been cunningly forged into the metal, and the long ash haft was carved with runes and symbols. The lower end of the shaft was tightly bound in old, worn leather.

He had said nothing when he had fetched it from a trunk. It had seemed almost as an afterthought. But he handled the hefty weapon as if it weighed nothing and as he had strode from his hut, axe-head gleaming in the morning sun, a sudden chill had run through her. He was certainly not young, but he looked like a warrior to her.

More than that, he looked like a killer.

She reached out her hand for the water flask again and he tipped it up to show her it was empty. Pushing herself up, she made her way down to the water's edge. It was cool in the shade of the bridge and the water was clear and cold. Silver daces darted and snaked languidly beneath the surface. She plunged the flask's neck into the water and watched the stream of silver bubbles gurgle up from the opening.

"I understand," she called back to Dunston. "This is not your fight. Why would you put yourself at risk for me..."

"Do not besmirch me as a craven, girl," the old man growled. "To what end would we hunt these men? To slay them, you say. Even if we could do such a thing, you will find no peace from revenge." He heaved himself to his feet with a grunted groan of pain. He tested his knee, flexing it and grimacing at what he felt. "Trust me on this. No," he said, once more lifting the shafts of the cart and setting off again southward. "We will go to Rothulf, the reeve. He is a friend and a wiser man than me. He'll know what to do. Besides, justice is his job."

Aedwen drank deeply, the cold water doing nothing to dampen the anger she felt. Refilling the flask, she hammered the stopper back in place with the heel of her hand and followed behind Dunston, once more too upset and disappointed to speak.

Five

They barely spoke for the rest of the day and the sun was low in the sky when finally they saw the cluster of houses known as Briuuetone. They had followed the course of the River Briw as it wound its way towards the settlement. As it progressed downhill, the river grew ever faster, its water changing from a burbling stream to a churning torrent. The Briw was ever fast-flowing, but after the recent rains, it was a raging, white-frothed deluge by the time it reached Briuuetone.

A few times during the afternoon Dunston glanced at Aedwen and was unsurprised to see her face set, her lips pressed tightly together in an expression of disapproving anger. If her situation had not been so dire, her childish rage might have amused him. As it was, he was saddened. He understood her desire for vengeance. She must feel lost and impotent in a world that had suddenly become frightening and more violent than she had ever known. But he was sure of his decision. To chase after the men who had slain her father would have been madness and almost certainly would have spelt his and Aedwen's deaths.

For his part, he did not mind walking in silence. The path grew smoother as they approached the village, but it was still hard work to push the cart over the rutted track and he had little inclination to talk. Besides, he was accustomed to the hushed voice of the forest. The creak of tall linden and oak when the wind caught their highest boughs. A far-off cry of a sparrow hawk. The chatter of sparrows and finches. Odin's panting breath when he ran past, flitting in and out of the undergrowth. All of the natural sounds of woodland life calmed him, giving him time to listen to his own thoughts. He pondered again who might have done this thing. He was convinced now that it could not have been Norsemen. It made no sense for such a small band to be here, deep within the kingdom of Wessex. But then why mutilate the man's body in such a horrific fashion? What sort of men committed such an act if it were not in the name of their heathen gods?

Dunston walked on, brooding on that, his mind filled with dark memories of blood and screams. He knew all too well what sort of man took pleasure from torture and killing. He had believed he would never again need to face such men. Well, after he'd got the girl and her unlucky father to Rothulf, he would return to his home and try to forget this fresh horror he had witnessed. He knew Aedwen's father's blood-slathered and broken body would plague his dreams, just as so many other corpses did. Each pallid face of the dead had its own place in his nightmares. Lytelman was another innocent to join their ranks.

Aedwen stumbled. She was tired. It had been a long, hard day.

"We are almost there," he said, making his tone soft.

The girl glared at him, still refusing to speak. With a flick of her hair, she turned away and strode with renewed determination down towards the smoke-wreathed settlement.

Despite himself, Dunston smiled. Eawynn would have liked the girl. They were both haughty and stubborn as mules when angered. With a grunt of effort, Dunston set the cart to moving faster to keep up with her. He thought about calling for her to slow her pace, but thought better of it. He would have to shout over the roaring rush of the river that flowed alongside the path. And anyway, she was heading in the right direction.

The road twisted around an outcrop of rock up ahead. Without looking back, Aedwen disappeared from view. Dunston felt an unexpected twinge of anxiety. Foolishness, he told himself. They were almost in the shadow of the thatched houses of Briuuetone. He could smell the woodsmoke from the haze of cooking fires. These were Rothulf's folk. Good people. Nothing could befall the girl here. Surely.

As if he too felt nervous to have lost sight of the girl, Odin burst from the brush beside the path and sped past Dunston, running around the bend in Aedwen's wake.

The Briw, fast and deep, churned and crashed over boulders. Dunston could hear nothing over the river's rocky roar.

The cart's left wheel caught on a protruding chunk of flint. Aedwen's father's shrouded body began to slip. Dunston lashed out a strong hand, hauling the corpse back onto the bed of the cart, where it nestled amongst all of Aedwen's possessions. Dunston spied the leather-wrapped haft of DeaÞangenga and briefly he placed his hand upon it. He wondered what had made him pick up the great axe. He had scarcely touched it since Eawynn's passing. Whenever he saw the weapon, it reminded him of why he had never been good enough for her.

"In love with your king and killing," she had said to him once. He'd argued with her, unable to accept her words. But now, looking back across the dark frontier of time, he admitted she had been right.

He frowned. Pushing aside his memories, he turned his attention once more to the cart and with a great heave it was over the stone that had impeded its movements and was once again trundling on.

At last he rounded the bend in the road and brought the cart up short. It was quieter here, the outcrop and its encompassing blanket of sedge, nettles and butter dock muting the river sound to a rumble. Before him, several stocky kine were lumbering down the lane. The cattle lowed and rolled their huge bovine eyes at Odin, but the hound seemed oblivious to their unease, and he trotted along beside them, ignoring their baleful stares.

Behind the cows walked a slender man with a hazel switch that he used to goad the beasts forward. Aedwen walked close by and it appeared the two of them were deep in conversation.

"Hail, Ceolwald," said Dunston, raising his voice more than he'd intended.

The slim drover turned and stared at Dunston. Placing his hands on his hips, he halted, waiting for him to catch up. The cart was cumbersome and it took Dunston some time to reach them. Neither Aedwen nor Ceolwald offered to help him.

"It's early in the season for you to be down this way, Dunston," said Ceolwald. "It's not even St Vitus' Day yet."

"I know what day it is, and what day it isn't," growled Dunston.

The drover nodded, as if that explained everything.

"Well," he said, "this young lady tells me she is walking to Briuuetone. I was just saying as to how she has just about reached there. We don't often get visitors unless it's a holy day. Funny you are walking that way too. I suppose we might as well all walk together." He looked disappointed.

"The girl and I are travelling together," said Dunston.

"Oh." Ceolwald looked from Aedwen to Dunston and back again, as if he were trying to understand something unfathomable. After a moment, his gaze settled on the cart and its gruesome burden. His eyes widened, and he snatched off the woollen cap he wore, wringing it in his hands. "What's this then?" he asked.

"The girl's father."

"Oh," the drover said and made the sign of the cross. "You taking him to Godrum for a proper burial?" Before Dunston could reply, Ceolwald looked over his shoulder at the cows that were now some distance away. "Whoa there, girls," he called, but the animals ignored him and continued trudging along the muddy path.

Shaking his head, Ceolwald said, "They know the way to the Bartons right enough. If we stand here dillydallying they'll be there long before me and they won't be happy. This time of year they need milking before they're put out for the night. They'll make a devil of a noise if they don't get milked sharpish."

He set off to hurry after the beasts. Dunston sighed and pushed his weight into the cart, getting it rolling again. His knee ached and a fresh pain lanced down his back. He grimaced, but said nothing. He would be there soon and he could be done with this burden and the troublesome child. Let her talk to the idiot drover all she liked.

But Ceolwald had only walked a few paces when he halted and came back to Dunston.

"Let me help you with that," he said. "Otherwise, you'll still be pushing it down the path come nightfall and all the kine've been milked."

And you would have missed the gossip about the dead man and his daughter, thought Dunston. He offered the drover a thin smile of thanks and moved to one side to allow him room to add his weight behind the cart. With the two men shoving the creaking cart along, the going was much smoother and Dunston was pleased for the easing of the pressure on his joints.

After a brief spell, Ceolwald asked, "Well, are you?"

"Am I what?"

"Taking him," he indicated with his chin at the shrouded corpse on the cart, "to Godrum? It's a good time for a burial. The ground is soft and easily dug."

Dunston glanced over at Aedwen and noted her downcast gaze. Her eyes shone.

"Have care with your words," he snapped. "You are talking about the child's father."

"I beg pardon," Ceolwald replied, bobbing his head and swallowing. "Well, are you?"

Dunston sighed. He rarely visited Briuuetone and when he did he barely spoke to its inhabitants. Save for Rothulf and his family, he had no friends in the village. They liked him well enough to accept his furs and knives in trade, but he didn't think they missed him when he went back to his solitary life in the forest. At times, when the winter wind bit the skin, and food was scarce; when the nights were long and the days short and brittle with ice and snow, Dunston would ask himself if he had chosen the right path for his life. Wouldn't he have been better off finding a new wife to tend to his needs? At moments like that he yearned for the company of others. Now, listening to Ceolwald's inane and incessant chatter, he was sure he had chosen wisely when he had made his home amongst the trees of Sealhwudu.

They pushed the cart along and Dunston did not reply. Perhaps it would have been better to have pushed the cart alone.

"Well?" Ceolwald asked again.

At last, Dunston capitulated.

"He will need a Christian burial," he said, pausing to wipe the sweat from his forehead with the back of his hand. Ceolwald nodded, as though he had been proven right in his answer to a particularly twisted riddle. "But," continued Dunston, finding himself increasingly irritated by the drover's demeanour, "I do not plan to take him to the church first."

"Well, you'll not be burying him anywhere else than in holy ground," he laughed at the idea, before growing suddenly grave. "Or is he such a sinner that he cannot be laid to rest with the good folk of Briuuetone?"

"My father was a sinner, like all men," said Aedwen, wheeling on the drover, her eyes ablaze. "But he was a good man and he will be given a Christian burial."

Ceolwald swallowed, unable to meet Aedwen's glare. Again Dunston thought how the girl reminded him of Eawynn.

"Of course, maid," Ceolwald said, "I meant nothing by it." They walked along in silence for a few moments before he spoke again. "So what is it you plan for him?"

"I am taking both Aedwen and her father to Rothulf, that he may determine the correct course of action. The girl is without kin now, and her father was slain most cruelly. The killers will need to be caught and brought before the moot."

Ceolwald was looking at him with a strange expression. He opened his mouth to speak and then snapped it shut once more.

"What is it, man?" asked Dunston.

Again the drover made as if to speak, but then hesitated.

"Speak, man," growled Dunston. "You want to say something, so say it. God knows until now nothing has stopped you from uttering the first thing that pops into your thought-cage."

"Well," said Ceolwald, his voice uncertain now, sweat beading his brow, "it's just that you won't be taking him to Rothulf."

Dunston gave the man a sharp look. He felt a scratch of unease down his spine.

"Why is that?" he asked.

Ceolwald's throat bobbed as he swallowed.

"He is dead. That's why."

Six

Aedwen could see the tidings of the reeve's death had rocked Dunston. Tears welled in her own eyes. She was angry that he had not chosen to do her bidding and seek revenge on her father's killers, but in that very act of defiance to her, Dunston had shown her he was in control. He had a plan and she had fallen into step with him, allowing him to lead. She had argued at first and then shown him her displeasure with her stubborn silence, and yet she had been comforted by his commanding presence. In response to her ill temper, the old man had ignored her, marking a fast pace through the forest without offering her a word. She could cope with his brooding silence. But now, she saw his face contorted in confusion and grief and this show of weakness frightened her.

The sun was touching the top of the trees across the river now. The thatch of the buildings was aglow with the golden light, stark shadows heightening the details in everything in the last rays of the day.

"How?" Dunston asked.

"It was the damnedest thing," Ceolwald said, seemingly torn between the need to maintain a dour expression at the dire news he was imparting, and wishing to grin at bearing that most compelling of gossip: a death. "He was drowned."

41

"Drowned?" asked Dunston, his tone incredulous.

"Yes, sir," Ceolwald said, again tugging off his cap and screwing it up in his bony hands. "They found him in the river, down by the mill. White as a fish, he was. Nobody saw what happened, but there had been a frost that morning. It seems he must have slipped, maybe banged his head. Still, when God calls your name, it's your time, and that's that."

Dunston frowned and Aedwen could see him thinking hard, pushing the dismay at his friend's death to one side and fighting to understand what had happened; regaining control.

"When did this happen?" he asked.

"Not two months ago."

"And he was alone? Nobody saw him fall?"

"No. But it was just his time. Bad luck, that's all. We held a hall-moot with the new reeve and all these questions were asked, and answered."

"New reeve?"

"Oh yes, Lord Ælfgar appointed one not a week after Rothulf's passing. Can't be long without someone to uphold the law, he said."

Dunston, face devoid of emotion now, started pushing the cart again. After a moment, Ceolwald joined him and they continued along the path in the last warm rays of sunshine.

Aedwen was silent. Odin padded close to her and she placed a hand on his head, running her fingers through the warm fur of his neck and ears. Despite the warmth of the sun on her skin, and the peaceful gold-licked beauty of the village before them, she pulled her cloak about her and shivered. The river flowed deep and fast beside the road. Its dark waters were high, lapping halfway up the trunks of some sallows that grew on the river's banks. In the distance she could make out a watermill, its great wheel still now, but able to revolve with the power of the water alone. To think that those same chill waters could grind corn for life-giving bread and also drown a man, pulling him down away from the air and the light until he was forced to take in great lungfuls of liquid, slaying him as surely as a knife to the heart. For a moment, she fancied that she had been caught in the swirl of some invisible river's flow. Her life had careened away from all she had known and now, here she was, in a village she barely knew, surrounded by strangers.

"What of Rothulf's goodwife, Gytha?" Dunston enquired. "And the children?"

"They are back at Gytha's family's farm. Up Ceorleah Hill way."

Dunston nodded absently.

"The new reeve has taken up in the hall then?"

"Yes, sir." They were almost at the first buildings of Briuuetone now. As Ceolwald had predicted, his cattle knew the way and they were trotting towards a gap between two thatched houses. Beyond the houses, cloaked in the smoke of the cooking fires, loomed the shingled roof of a stone building. A crucifix projected from the apex of the roof. A group of horsemen came into sight, trotting their mounts between the cows.

"There were many in the village," Ceolwald went on, "who were not happy with the treatment of Widow Gytha and her daughters. Rothulf was barely in the ground and they were turfed out and sent packing to make way for the new reeve and his household."

Dunston said nothing. He stopped pushing the cart, and stepped to the left, all the while watching the approaching riders with his cool blue eyes. Aedwen noted that his right hand rested on the haft of the great axe that was hidden beside her father's body amongst the sacks on the cart. Ceolwald watched Dunston in confusion for a moment before following his gaze and finally noticing the riders. He gripped his cap tightly before him, fidgeting uncomfortably.

The horsemen had almost reached them now. There were five of them. They came on fine horses, the animals' Harnesses clanking and jangling, gleaming in the fiery light of the setting sun. The men wore colourful, expensive clothes and boots of supple leather. Their jackets were trimmed with intricate embroidery and their cloaks were held in place with large silver brooches. At the head of the band rode a young, handsome man. His cheeks were shaven and his fair hair was brushed so that it glimmered in the ruddy sunlight like metal heated on a forge. His mouth was partially hidden by a lustrous moustache. He reined in his mount, a well-muscled, dappled grey stallion, and stared down at them for a moment.

Odin growled, low and deep, like distant thunder.

"Odin, hush," said Dunston, his tone quiet but firm. The hound grew silent, and sat protectively beside Aedwen.

The lead rider raised an eyebrow at the dog's name.

"So, what have we here, Ceolwald?" he asked, his voice smooth and friendly.

"This... this is Dunston," stammered Ceolwald. "He lives nearabouts. I was just bringing my cows down from the pasture for milking when I came across them on the road." After a pause he added, "We are not together." He looked longingly to where the last of the cattle had disappeared between the buildings. Their lowing came to them faintly on the breeze. "I really must be after the foolish beasts. They will make a terrible fuss if they are not milked soon." The rider looked down at the drover imperiously. "If it please you, lord," Ceolwald said, dipping his head and twisting his hat so much Aedwen thought he might rip it. The horseman waved his hand. Without looking back, Ceolwald scampered past the riders and ran after his cows.

"Well, well, well," said the horseman, shifting his attention to Dunston, "so you are the famous Dunston."

"Dunston is my name," the old man said. He stood, legs apart and shoulders set. His hand yet rested in the cart's bed.

Aedwen did not think she had seen him standing so tall and straight since she had met him.

To Aedwen's eyes there was more communication going on between the men than the words spoken. They were weighing each other up, assessing and gauging the threat posed by the other.

"You are modest," the rider said, smiling beneath his moustache. "Are you not the one known as Dunston the Bold?"

"I have not been called that for many years."

"No. I can see many years have passed since you were a bold man. Not so much bold now, as old, eh?"

One of his men, a swarthy-skinned fellow, gaudy in blue jacket and red breeches, laughed. The others took up the laughter dutifully. Dunston did not laugh.

"Well, you have me at a loss," Dunston said, his voice cutting through the riders' mirth like an axe through soft flesh. "You know my name, and I know not yours."

The rider's nostrils flared and he glowered down at Dunston for a moment before replying.

"Ah, yes. I am Hunfrith, and I am the new reeve of the Briuuetone Hundred."

Seven

"It is not right, Hunfrith," said Dunston, his voice raising in anger. "I will not allow it."

Just when Dunston thought this day could get no worse, now the fool of a new reeve was demanding to see Aedwen's father's corpse.

"You will show me the body," said Hunfrith. "I would witness with my own eyes the truth of what you say." He had dismounted and handed his steed's reins to the dark-bearded rider in the garish attire. The reeve strode towards Dunston. He was tall, a head or more taller than Dunston. The man's youth and height only served to further anger Dunston.

The sun had set now, and the sky was a deep pink. The shadows of the buildings grew deeper and cooler. Soon it would be dark.

"Listen," Dunston said, softening his voice with a force of will. "I will show you the corpse, but not in front of the girl." He stepped close to the reeve and lowered his voice to a whisper. "I went to much effort to conceal the true nature of her father's wounds from her. The man was butchered."

Hunfrith glanced back at the mounted men behind him, as if assuring himself he had the strength of numbers to push his demands.

"Conceal the truth, you say?"

"Only from the child. His passing must have been awful."

Hunfrith waved his hand, swatting Dunston's words away.

"I would see the wounds you mean to hide from the girl."

"By the love of God, no!" For an instant, Dunston imagined leaping back to the cart for DeaÞangenga. In a past life, when he had been known as bold, he might have done so. But it would have been folly then, as it would be foolish now. He had nothing to hide, and this man was the reeve. He had a right to see the crime that had been committed.

Sighing, Dunston walked slowly back to the cart.

"Quickly, man," said Hunfrith. "While there is still light."

Dunston ignored him.

"Aedwen," he said, staring into the girl's eyes. They were wide and dark. "Do not look."

She held his gaze for several heartbeats before nodding and turning her back on the cart.

Satisfied that she would not see the destruction of her father's body, Dunston turned to the task of unwinding the shroud. He could not risk Aedwen's father slipping to the ground so, taking a deep breath, he pulled the corpse half out of the cart and onto his shoulder. His back screamed at him, but he did not acknowledge the pain. As carefully as he could, he lowered the shrouded figure to the grass that grew at the verge of the path.

Unwrapping the corpse was not easy. It was stiff now, and the cloak and leather he had used to swaddle the body were sticky and rigid from blood and ichor. Dunston suppressed a shudder as his fingers brushed the man's face, revealing the blotchy pallor of the cheeks that he had wiped clean in the clearing where he had been murdered. The poor man's eyes were open, staring accusingly at Dunston in blind reproach for disturbing him.

"Turn him over."

Dunston flinched. He had not noticed Hunfrith coming so close. The young reeve leaned over the cadaver, eyes gleaming, mouth open with expectation. A couple of his men had also dismounted and crowded around to witness the grisly spectacle.

Dunston drew in a deep breath. This was wrong. The man should be left in peace, not stripped and uncovered for men to gawp at.

"Do it," snapped Hunfrith.

Dunston sighed. There was nothing for it. Perhaps when they saw the terrible wounds the man had suffered, they would feel compelled to seek justice.

Reaching out, Dunston gingerly rolled the man's corpse over onto his front. One of the men gasped at the horror of Lytelman's back. Dunston had made no effort to close the wounds, but he had bound the shroud tightly about him, and now, released from the constraining material, the split ribs yawned open slowly, like the maw of some unspeakable beast of hell. The butchered lungs and innards oozed and seemed to writhe as the body settled. Someone let out a nervous laugh. Another swore, turning away to spit.

Dunston gazed down at the ruin of the girl's father and felt anew his anger at the man's killers being allowed to roam the land after committing such an atrocity. It had been folly to think of pursuing them with the girl, but perhaps he could help Hunfrith and his men to track them. He had wished to return directly to his hut and be done with the girl and her troubles, but looking down at her father's corpse he knew that he could never turn his back on Aedwen. He could almost hear the sound of Eawynn's shade laughing at him for even considering such a thing. She had always known him better than he knew himself. And she had always seen the best in him.

"By God," said Hunfrith, his voice breathy, "you truly did a job on the poor bastard, didn't you?"

"I did my best to shroud him with what I had to hand. I knew not what else to do."

"Shroud him?" replied Hunfrith, taking a step away from the gore-smeared corpse. "Oh, I am sure your wrapping of his corpse was good enough. I was talking about the blood-eagle. To rip the man's lungs out like that. You must be a true savage."

Dunston's mind reeled.

"I did not do this thing to him," he said, his tone flat and shocked.

"What murderer admits his crime?"

"I am no murderer!" Dunston took a step towards the cart. Two of the reeve's men blocked his way. Their hands rested on the hilts of their seaxes. He halted. "Why would I do such a thing? It is madness."

"Most would call this madness, it is true," replied Hunfrith. "But what about one who worships the heathen gods? Would not a man who names his own beasts after the father of the old gods also require blood sacrifice? And look, the man is killed in the manner of the Norse."

Dunston looked at the shadowed faces of the men around him. Was this some form of jest? How could they think he had done this? But their faces were sombre and serious, with no sign of humour.

"I did not do this," he said, and he was angered to hear the note of panic in his own voice. "Ask the girl." He looked over to where Aedwen yet stood beside Odin. She had turned to face them and her features were pale in the gathering gloaming. Dunston was pleased to see that the cart blocked her view of her father's corpse. That was something at least.

"Well, child," said Hunfrith, walking towards Aedwen, his countenance and voice soft with compassion. "Did you see your father's killers?"

For a long while Aedwen looked from Hunfrith to Dunston.

"Tell me the truth, child," Hunfrith encouraged her. "Did you witness your father's slaying?"

"No," she answered at last.

Dunston let out a breath.

"And so it could have been this man who killed him, could it not?"

Tears trickled down her cheeks.

"But he helped me. It makes no sense."

Hunfrith stepped close to her. Odin snarled, his hackles raised.

"Odin, no," said Dunston, acutely aware of how his use of the name would sound to the listeners. "Lie down, boy."

The dog grumbled and growled, but slouched down to lie beside Aedwen.

"You are safe now, child," Hunfrith said, reaching a hand out to touch the girl's shoulder.

"Do not fear, Aedwen," said Dunston. The look of abject dismay on her face filled him with sadness. "All will be well. You know I did not do this."

"But it seems she really knows no such thing," said Hunfrith.

"Well, I know it, and there are many here who will vouch for me; who know me to be a man of my word. Men will swear oaths for me."

"Good. I hope for your sake things are as you say. But you will need to appear before the moot and there you can explain how it is you came to have the butchered sacrifice to a heathen god on a stolen cart."

Dunston's rage boiled up within him. His eyes narrowed as he took in the positions of the men around him. He could disarm the man closest to him, taking his seax and then moving on to the next. From there, he could snatch up DeaÞangenga and lay about him. With only a small amount of luck he would put an end to this madness and be done with it. But after that? What then? He would become a wulfesheáfod, a wolf-head, cast out from the law, to be hunted and shunned for the rest of his life.

Many years ago, he had been one of the feared Wulfas Westseaxna. He could become a Wolf of Wessex once more; dispatch these fools and be gone into the forest. But why do such a thing? To not stand before the men of Briuuetone and declare his innocence? Surely enough men would come forward to swear oaths to his good character. There was no plaintiff after all. Nobody could speak against him and his word was respected. All he had to do was attend the moot and declare his innocence and all would be well.

But what if he were made to face the ordeals? He had seen enough of them in his time to know they did not rest in any divine power. A chill ran through him.

Hunfrith, perhaps sensing Dunston's building anger, put his arm about Aedwen's shoulders. Dunston noted how the reeve's other hand dropped to rest on the handle of his seax. The threat was clear.

"I cannot have you free to flee from justice or to commit any further acts of violence, Dunston," Hunfrith said, almost apologetically. "You understand that, I am sure. So will you surrender your weapons and yourself without causing trouble?"

Dunston glowered at the man, for an instant imagining how easily DeaÞangenga would split his pretty skull. And yet he knew he would not risk Aedwen's life, even if he wished to risk his own. Besides, what of the promises he had sworn to Eawynn? He could not throw away his oaths so easily. He let his shoulders slump. Pulling his sharp seax from its scabbard, he tossed it without warning at the closest man. Caught unawares, the man fumbled the catch, dropping the blade to the ground with a curse. As the man stooped to retrieve the knife, he sucked at a finger where the blade had nicked him. Dunston smiled grimly at the small victory.

"I will go with you, Hunfrith, but this is wrong. While you waste your time with me, the real killers are free and surely travelling further from Briuuetone as we speak."

"We shall see," said Hunfrith. "We shall see."

And with that, the reeve went to his horse and swung effortlessly into the saddle.

Dunston left it to Hunfrith's men to deal with the cart and the corpse and in the closing gloom of dusk he looked to Aedwen. She walked along behind the horses. Her head was lowered and she moved like a beaten cur, defeated and broken of spirit. He knew how she felt.

She did not look at back at him.

"Do not fear, girl," Dunston called to her, as the men herded him towards the village. "All will be well."

The wind picked up, whispering secrets in the trees and Dunston shuddered. He wished he could believe his own words.

Eight

Aedwen lay in the absolute darkness and listened to the night sounds of the house as it settled its wooden bones. There was rustling in the thatch somewhere above her and she wondered whether there were mice dwelling in the roof. She was warm, but she found herself shivering beneath the blankets Gytha had placed over her and the other girls. Either side of her, Gytha's two daughters, Maethild and Godgifu, had finally fallen asleep. They were friendly and had welcomed her into their home and even their bed, and Aedwen had basked in the warmth brought by unexpected kindness. The world was a place filled with evil and despair, and yet, here were complete strangers treating her as one of their own family.

When the reeve's man had brought her to the widow's door, the woman had been wary, fearful of what might bring one of Hunfrith's bullies out to the farm after nightfall, but when she had heard the girl's tale and seen Aedwen standing there, pale and trembling from shock and exhaustion, she had shooed the man away and pulled the girl into the cosy interior of the cottage.

Despite the shroud of sadness that wrapped about her, Aedwen smiled to recall the meal that had followed.

"Where are you from?" Godgifu, the younger of the widow's daughters had asked, watching with wide eyes as Aedwen hungrily spooned the pottage into her mouth. Despite everything, she was ravenous and the stew, thick with onion, cabbage and peas and seasoned with parsley and sage, was deliciously warming and hearty.

"Let the poor girl eat," Gytha said.

"I don't mind," Aedwen said, dipping some dark bread into the dregs in the bowl and mopping up the last drops. "I am from Langtun."

"Where is that?" asked Godgifu.

"You don't know anything," snapped Maethild, who must have been the same age as Aedwen.

"Well, if you're so clever, where is it then?"

Maethild frowned at having been caught out by her younger sibling and Aedwen smiled at the bickering rivalry between them. She would have liked to have had a sister, she thought, someone who had always known her, and she had always known. If she had a sister, she wouldn't be alone now.

Godgifu was taunting her sister though, making Aedwen quickly re-evaluate her idea.

"You don't know! You don't know!" sang Godgifu, twisting her face into the contorted features of a simpleton.

"Girls! Enough," said Gytha in a tone that brooked no argument. "Aedwen has been through enough, without having to listen to your silliness." The girls fell quiet as Gytha fixed them with a stern stare. "You both know what it is to lose your father," she said softly. "Remember, Aedwen's father was killed only yesterday morning. Think about how you felt when you heard the news about father." The girls looked aghast and Godgifu sniffed, tears welling in her bright eyes.

"I beg your pardon, mother," muttered Maethild.

"It is not from me that you need to seek pardon," replied Gytha.

Maethild sat in dejected silence for a time, but Godgifu seemed to forget her self-pity soon enough.

"Is it true that old Dunston found you?"

"Yes," said Aedwen. Her mind had been in turmoil ever since Hunfrith had accused Dunston of her father's murder. It was true that she had not seen the killers, but she was sure she had heard many of them. And if it had been Dunston, why would he then tend to her father's corpse, feed her and bring her here? No, there was no sense to it, and she was certain that Hunfrith knew as much.

When she had seen the reeve, a tremor of fear had run through her. She could not say why, but the man frightened her. And the strangest thing was that she had recognised him. When they had passed through Briuuetone, her father had sought him out. It had been drizzling and she had been tired and so, as she had often done before, she had curled up to snooze beneath the leather cover of the handcart. Her father must have believed she had drifted off to sleep and so he had not disturbed her when he had approached the reeve. From beneath the leather sheet, she had watched as her father had asked to speak to the reeve. She'd heard him say he had urgent tidings for him. From her hidden vantage point in the cart, she had seen the handsome face of the reeve when he came to the door of his hall to listen to her father's words, though what he'd had to say, she could not imagine. Her father was but a poor peddler after all. Perhaps this was one of his schemes, a new way to get rich quick, she'd thought. But she'd never found out. With a glance back at the cart, her father, seemingly content that she was dry beneath the cover, had entered the hall. The steady drumming of the rain had lulled her to sleep then, and she'd awoken to the movement of the cart as her father pushed it up the hill out of the village.

When the reeve had approached her and Dunston she had recognised the man immediately. And yet, she was equally certain he did not know her. Indeed he seemed to have no knowledge of her existence. She had thought it strange that he had not mentioned to Dunston that he had known her father, that they had conversed at length just a couple of days before. And something had made her keep silent about what she had witnessed. But the more she thought about the events of the last days, her certainty grew that her father's death was not a random savage act perpetrated by wolf-heads. And after seeing Hunfrith, and hearing the man so quickly accuse Dunston of murder, she was sure the reeve had some part in it. But what, and why, she had no idea.

"They say he eats raw flesh," said Godgifu, voice filled with terrified wonder. "That he chews on children's bones in the forest."

"Who says such things?" asked Gytha, her disapproval clear in her tone.

"Everyone. Wulfwyn's mother told her that if she didn't go to sleep when she was told, old Dunston would come down from his forest lair and eat her!"

Gytha shook her head.

"Wulfwyn's mother was always a foolish girl. Dunston is no monster of the woods. He has never been anything but good to us. He was your father's friend."

"His dog scares me," said Maethild.

At the mention of Odin, Aedwen had begun to weep.

Now, lying in the hushed darkness, with the body warmth of Maethild and Godgifu pressing either side of her, tears rolled down her cheeks again as she remembered what had befallen the merle hound. The dog had padded beside her, every now and then glancing over its shoulder at its master. Dunston, flanked by a couple of the reeve's men, had trudged along head down and silent. They had been some way behind the mounted Hunfrith.

They passed houses, their shadows puddled cold around them like dark skirts. Ceolwald's cattle lowed from the animal pens she could just make out in the gloom. The village had the mingled scent of cow dung, woodsmoke, roasting meat and boiling vegetables.

Upon reaching a grand hall, Hunfrith had dismounted, throwing the reins to one of his men. Aedwen had needed to trot to keep up with the reeve and she was puffing. Odin matched her pace, mouth agape and tongue dangling between sharp white teeth.

"We cannot have the girl stay here, Raegnold," Hunfrith said to his mounted companion. "I don't want my rest interrupted by her snivelling. Take her to Widow Gytha. She will take the child in." He looked sidelong at Aedwen. "Until we get to the bottom of all this."

Raegnold, the tallest of the riders, with hair of crow black and a face as sharp as a seax, dismounted. He shot a furious look at Hunfrith's back, but quickly seemed to resign himself to becoming the child's escort. Snatching up a spear that stood propped by the hall's entrance, he set off southward, using the spear's haft as a walking staff.

Aedwen, dazed and shocked at the recent revelations, mutely followed the tall man up the hill as the dark drew the night about them. Odin seemed to have decided he would be her protector, and he shadowed them as they walked past gloomed houses and the silent mill, leaving the silhouette of the church and the moaning of the cows behind them.

"Get away," Raegnold shouted at the dog, angered by the animal's attention or perhaps taking out his annoyance at Hunfrith on the dumb beast. Odin flinched, turning its head askance to better see with his one eye. After a moment, the dog continued to follow them.

The man grew angrier and scooped up pebbles from the road. He flung one at Odin, but the stone missed, skittering away into the shadows. His second stone found its mark, hitting the dog squarely on the snout. Odin cried out in anguish, shaking his head against the sudden pain. But he was soon once more walking in their wake.

"I said get away," shouted the man, throwing another stone, which made Odin jump back a pace, wary now.

Aedwen could not bear to see the beast hurt any more.

"Go home, Odin," she said. At the sound of her voice, the dog cocked its head to one side, gazing at her with its one deep thoughtful eye.

The man used the moment of distraction to leap forward, lunging with his spear. The thrust would have spitted the hound, had it not been for the speed of its instincts. Odin jumped to the side and the sharp blade tore a gash down his flank. The animal yelped and snarled, snapping its jaws towards the spear that had caused him such pain. Blood ran down its side and soaked its fur black in the dusk.

"Odin!" Aedwen cried out.

The dog locked its great maw on the spear's ash haft and shook its head with all the strength of its muscled neck. The man clung onto the spear with difficulty, unable to dislodge the animal.

"Odin, no!" Aedwen screamed. "Run, boy! Run!"

For the merest moment, the dog's eye looked directly at her. And then, as if it understood her words, it heaved the spear out of the man's grasp. An instant later it dropped the weapon with a clatter and darted into the shadows of the trees that grew further up the slope. The hound did not look back and it ran effortlessly, as though it were the start of a new day; as if it had not been wounded. It did not cry out as it ran, and Aedwen began to wonder if the cut was shallower than she'd imagined. Surely it had just been a scratch.

But when Raegnold retrieved his spear from the ground the blade was smeared dark and Aedwen had seen splashes of blood in the mud of the path.

The house grumbled its timbered thoughts around her and Maethild muttered something in her sleep, rolling over and then becoming still. Aedwen's tears soaked into the blanket the way Odin's blood had soaked into his fur. By the Blessed Virgin, she prayed the dog was safe; that it had found its way back to its home in the forest.

But what of the dog's master? The last she had seen of Dunston, they had been leading him to a barn near the cattle pens. What would become of him? She could not dispel the image of his bearded face from her mind. He had taken care of her since her father's death and she was sure he was not his killer. And what was Hunfrith's part in all this? What did he gain from locking Dunston away and bringing him before the moot?

Her confused thoughts beat inside her head, as ever-changing as a murmuration of starlings. She wiped away the tears that had grown cold on her face.

For a long while she lay there, hoping that sleep would claim her. Perhaps she would awaken and find it had all been a nightmare. But the warmth and the soft sounds of the night did not lull her to slumber. She could not escape the terror of having to face the morning alone once more. Her mother and father had both been so cruelly snatched from her. And now, when she had found someone to guide and protect her, he too had been taken away. Gytha and her daughters had been good to her, but Aedwen knew she could not stay here. She could work for her keep, but even if they were able to spare the food, would she just begin a new life with these strangers?

Why not? What else could she do? She was young and alone. If Gytha would have her, to live here in Briuuetone on this steading would be better than almost anything she could have imagined.

And yet her thoughts kept on returning to Hunfrith. What had her father told him? And why had he kept his knowledge of Lytelman silent? And what did he hope to gain by accusing Dunston of this crime?

At last, resigning herself to a night of wakefulness, she rolled out of the bed, careful not to wake the girls who yet slept peacefully.

The cottage was cool now that the fire had died down and Aedwen picked up her cloak from where she had left it. Wrapping it about her shoulders, she tiptoed towards the hearth, hoping to glean some heat from the embers. As she neared the fire, small flames flowered and the coals glowed as someone blew life into them. The light flickered red on Gytha's face where she sat at the edge of the hearth, a blanket wrapped about her shoulders.

"You couldn't sleep either?" the widow asked in a whisper. The shadows from the flames contorted her features. Aedwen could not make out whether she was smiling or scowling in the gloom. "Come, sit," Gytha continued, patting the stool near her. Aedwen sat.

"I am not surprised you are unable to find peace," Gytha muttered. "You have been through so many trials these past days. Poor child."

"I cannot stop my thoughts," replied Aedwen. Her voice threatened to choke her, and she fought back the tears that suddenly welled in her eyes.

Gytha smiled sadly.

"Whosoever could do such a thing as keep themselves from thinking would be able to find peace indeed," she said.

Aedwen frowned in the darkness. It seemed to her only death would release her from the burden of her thoughts and fears. But she had no desire to join her parents.

"I keep asking myself questions. Questions about the reeve. About my father's murder. About Dunston. Questions that I cannot hope to answer."

Gytha gazed at her in the darkness, unspeaking for a long while, her flame-lit face haggard.

"I too have been pondering how all of this makes sense. Something is not right. I feel like the world shifted when my Rothulf died and now I do not stand on steady ground." Gytha's voice cracked and Aedwen realised they were not so different. Separated by many years of age, but they both grieved and the two of them were sitting awake and confused in the dark marches of the night.

Aedwen took a deep breath then and told Gytha about her father's meeting with Hunfrith and how the reeve had kept the meeting secret.

Gytha stared at her, the embers reflecting red in her dark eyes. After what seemed a long while, she spoke.

"We need to talk," she said.

Nine

Dunston tried to make himself comfortable. But no matter how much he stretched and turned, he could not find a position that would allow him to rest. His back was stiff and despite the hay and straw he had piled up to lay upon, his spine cried out if he lay flat on his back. When he turned on his side, his knee was agony, twisting if he bent it, and seizing up if he straightened it. In the dark of the barn he sighed to himself, a grim smile playing on his lips at the irony of his predicament.

He could almost hear the voice of Guthlaf speaking to him through the veil of time.

"The best trait of any warrior is to be able to sleep anywhere and anytime," the grizzled warrior had said to him. "You, Dunston, are deadly with a blade, but your ability to sleep in an instant makes you a truly great warrior." They had been resting beside a cracked old Roman road. They'd marched for two days already and Dunston had been exhausted. It had seemed as nothing to sleep on the verge, even as rain fell and thunder rolled over them.

Now, despite the relative comfort of the straw beneath him and the shelter provided by the barn's roof and walls, he was unable to find the relief of sleep. Guthlaf would have not thought him such a great warrior if he could see him now. But

Guthlaf was long in his grave, and it had been many years since Dunston had considered himself to be a warrior.

He had never thought of himself as great.

Sighing, he rolled over onto his back, staring up into the blackness of the roof space.

Again he regretted finding the corpse and the girl. If only he had chosen a different path, he would now be asleep in his hut, far from here and the machinations of men. And yet, would he truly wish for Aedwen to have been left, alone and defenceless in the great forest of Sealhwudu? She might have survived, he supposed. Perhaps she would have even found her way back here, to Briuuetone. But then what? What would have become of her?

He snorted in the darkness. What had become of her anyway? Yes, he had seen her safely here, but she had been taken away and here he was, locked inside a barn, with no prospect of freedom for at least three weeks.

Three weeks!

He ground his teeth in the gloom as he recalled Hunfrith's words.

"You will remain in my care until the next meeting of the Hundred-moot," he'd said.

"When will that be?" asked Dunston.

"The next meeting will be on the feast of Saint John the Baptist."

"But that is nearly a month from now," Dunston had raged.

"Indeed. Do not fear, you will be fed. No harm will befall you."

Dismissing him then, Hunfrith had left three of his retinue to lead Dunston to this barn. They had opened the door and ushered him inside, and after a moment's hesitation, he had entered without further complaint.

He had already begun to think of ways in which he could prove his innocence. Who would swear oaths for him before the moot? Would Aedwen speak out in his favour? Would anyone listen to her. She was a stranger and a child. If he was found guilty, he would need to face the trials by ordeal. Which did he believe he might survive? He had shuddered to recall others tried by the ordeal of iron, forced to grip a rod of glowing hot metal. This was then wrapped and, if after three days the wound was not healing well, the tried man was found to be guilty. Dunston was a smith of some renown and worked his forge on most days, so he had suffered many burns. But he doubted there was justice to be had from seeing how quickly such wounds healed or whether they became elf-shot.

Still, fire and iron he could face. The ordeal of cold water, where the accused was thrown into the river after drinking holy water, terrified him beyond anything he had ever confronted. If the accused floated, he was deemed to be guilty. If he sank, he was found innocent. Dunston was no swimmer. He imagined the cold water washing over his face, his breath running out and his lungs burning, while he prayed frantically that he would be dragged from the water and saved.

No, he must prove his innocence. He was no coward, but the thought of facing the ordeals filled him with dread.

Left alone in the dark, Dunston's mind had turned to Hunfrith's last words to him. He had not thought that he was in any immediate danger; that he had weeks to think of the means to secure his release and prove his innocence. That was until he heard those words. Now he was not so sure.

"No harm will befall you."

Why say such a thing? Unless...

By the bones of Christ. Three weeks cooped up in here. And what of Odin? The dog had gone with Aedwen. Dunston hoped she would feed him. Still, the hound could take care of himself. He was a good hunter. But what would happen to Wudugát, his goat? He had left the poor creature tethered. There was plenty of food and water for her for the time being, but he had never intended to be gone for more than a couple of days at most. Dunston's mind turned then to the snares left untended in the forest. His heart twisted to think of the animals that would be caught, only to die lingering deaths and then have their carcasses consumed by foxes and other carrion feeders. What a waste of good skins.

Dunston shifted again in the straw and groaned at the ache between his shoulder blades. The pain was in just the place where Lytelman had been hacked open.

What was happening here? Dunston felt like a child watching a game of tafl being played. He knew strategies were in place, could feel the shift and slide of the pieces, but he did not understand the rules of the game.

There was some dark contest afoot here, something that he was not aware of. Nothing else made any sense. The manner of Lytelman's slaying, and then Hunfrith's instant accusation. And what of Rothulf? Was his death somehow connected to all this? Perhaps there was no link. Dunston could certainly see none. But he was sure that the recent events he had become embroiled in held some dark secret.

He could barely believe that Rothulf was no longer alive. The old reeve would have known how to approach this problem. He was an astute man, able to unravel the most tangled of problems. Dunston sighed. By God, he would miss him. He had looked forward to their meetings. They would sit up late into the night drinking and talking of the past. And yet, while much of their chatter had been reminiscing over years gone by, they often spoke of the present and the future. Rothulf travelled widely and he listened wherever he went. And so he had become Dunston's only source of tidings of the lands beyond Briuuetone and Sealhwudu. Dunston had chosen to hide himself away from the day-to-day life of Wessex, but it would not do to completely shut himself off from the world.

He wondered now at the state of the kingdom. He had heard from Rothulf of the increasing frequency of raids from the Norsemen in their dragon-prowed ships. As the king's ally in Frankia, King Louis, had become embroiled in a vicious civil war with his sons, so the Frankish ships had ceased to patrol the waters that surrounded Britain. This had soon led to the Norse becoming emboldened, and not a year went by without some of their number striking along the coast, snatching what treasures and slaves they could, and then fleeing before the fyrd could be assembled and brought to the defence of the realm.

Only two years previously, Rothulf had recounted to Dunston how thirty-five Vikingr ships had landed at Carrum. The king had gathered his hearth warriors and the fyrds of the local hundreds and set upon them. The men of Wessex had been crushed, the king fleeing westward leaving the heathens to sack the lands there about with impunity.

Dunston had been saddened by the tale. Could this be the same King Ecgberht who had defeated the Mercians at Ellandun? The proud and wise man who had expanded Wessex to encompass the people of the Centingas, Éastseaxe, Súþríeg and Súpseaxe. Who had even taken the oath of Eanred, king of the Northumbrians, making Ecgberht the ruler of all of the Anglisc?

Dunston pulled up his knee and massaged it, wincing as his probing fingers pressed into the joint. No man remained young for ever. Even kings grew old.

Even warriors who once basked in battle-fame and were renowned as being bold.

From outside the door, came the muffled sound of voices. Earlier, one of the reeve's men had brought him a bowl of pottage and a hunk of dark, gritty bread. Perhaps he had been just outside ever since and was now, halfway through the night, being relieved of his duty.

The barn was stoutly built from planks of oak and the door was barred from without. But it seemed Hunfrith had taken the extra precaution of having his men guard the exit. Dunston thought on his situation for a moment. Would he attempt to flee if he could? Again his mind turned to the trials he might face, and the uncertainty of being judged by this new reeve and the people of Briuuetone without the guiding hand of Rothulf who was not only wise, but as honest as any man Dunston had known. Yes, Hunfrith was probably right to guard against his escape. Dunston knew he could survive in the forest for the rest of his days, he was not so sure of the outcome of the moot.

Perhaps his chance to run had already passed; the moment when he could have yet fought his way out, standing face to face with the reeve and his men. He was old and stiff, it was true, but armed he was still dangerous. He could have slain them and fled, he was certain. But Aedwen had watched on and she might have been hurt.

And he was innocent.

He had only ever fought his king's enemies. He was, or had been, a warrior, not a murderer. No, he would face the justice of the moot and pray that the people of Briuuetone would vouch for him.

The voices outside became louder. One laughed, a jagged harsh sound in the stillness of the night. Dunston strained to hear what was being said.

"... sliced the great bastard open like a..." The voices became muffled once more, then louder again. "... almost bit me... got my spear instead. Jaws like iron." Dunston didn't breathe, waiting for confirmation of what he was hearing. After a few more words that he was unable to make out, the louder of the two said, "No. The one-eyed beast was as fast as the Devil. It ran off, but I cut it good."

They must have moved further from the door then, for their words became unintelligible.

Dunston lay in the darkness and thought of interpretations of the words he had heard. He could think of none save that the bastards had cut Odin, and badly from the sound of it. He wondered whether the dog had attacked them. Had he been trying to protect Aedwen?

For a long time Dunston imagined the many ways he would hurt the man who had struck Odin. Whatever secrets were being hidden by the death of the peddler, and no matter the outcome of the moot, Dunston swore a silent oath in the darkness that he would make the man pay for hurting his dog.

At long last, with thoughts of vengeance spiralling in his mind, the fatigue from the day finally took its toll, pulling him down towards the welcome respite of sleep. His eyes closed and he was beginning to snore, when a sudden loud shouting woke him with a jolt.

"Fire!" screamed a woman's voice, splintering the still of the night.

Dunston pushed himself up with a groan. Through the cracks between the planks that made up the barn's door, the crimson flicker of flames was clear.

Ten

"I cannot believe Dunston is a killer," said Aedwen. Her voice quavered as once more the pain of her father's death washed over her.

Gytha gently placed a small log onto the fire, careful not to disturb the embers. The fire-glow painted her features the hue of fresh blood.

"Oh, he is a killer all right." She sat back in her chair and gazed at the tongues of flame that licked hungrily at the dry wood. "Or he was."

"He was a warrior?" asked Aedwen.

"One of the deadliest ever to walk the earth, Rothulf used to say. Though my husband was prone to exaggeration and he loved Dunston like a brother." Gytha fell silent for a time, perhaps thinking of the husband she had lost. "Still, Rothulf had seen the old man fight, years ago. They stood together in the shieldwall at Ellandun and Rothulf always said he had never seen a man so destined to slay others as Dunston. As men do when they are in their cups, he had boasted of how the corpses of the Mercians lay heaped before Dunston that day. How his axe had scythed through their ranks as if they were so many ripe heads of barley. To listen to Rothulf you would think nobody else had fought that day. But many brave men gave their lives on both sides."

Gytha looked wistfully into the fire, lost in the past and the sadness of remembered loss.

The flames and embers swam before Aedwen, and she cuffed angrily at the tears that brimmed in her eyes. It was as she had surmised when she'd seen Dunston standing beside the cart with his hand on his axe. If he was a great warrior, a slayer of countless foe-men, then surely he could have killed her father without a thought. She shuddered. Had she been so wrong?

As if the girl's movement had awoken Gytha from a dream, the widow started and turned her attention to Aedwen.

"Dunston may not have been the hero my Rothulf liked to brag about, but he was a killer. Of that there is no doubt."

Aedwen sighed.

"But make no mistake, child," Gytha continued. "I do not believe for one moment that Dunston slew your father. Woe betide any man who crosses him, even now, but the old man is no murderer."

Aedwen sighed again, but now with relief, not despair.

"Who do you think killed him?" she asked.

"I know not. But I think you are right to question Hunfrith's part in this. I fear that what your father spoke of with the new reeve was what led to him being killed."

"But what could they have talked about? My father knew nobody in these parts. This is the first time we have travelled this way." Aedwen didn't mention how she had argued against the trip. How she had warned her father against the folly of this new scheme of his. If only she had been more persuasive. But nothing could change the past.

"I do not know," said Gytha rubbing her fingers distractedly against her temples. "But I can only think that their meeting and his murder are connected in some way."

"Could it be that Hunfrith ordered my father to be slain?" Aedwen whispered, scared to voice her fear.

Gytha thought for a moment.

"I do not know," she repeated. "But Briuuetone has changed these past months. Nothing is as it was. It no longer feels safe."

"Why? What has happened?"

"Two things. First my husband drowned and then Hunfrith moved in as the new reeve."

Aedwen stared at the widow, sensing a deeper meaning in her words.

"You think Hunfrith murdered your husband," she said.

"Quiet, girl," Gytha hissed, as if the very sound of the words stung her. For a time, they were both silent. Aedwen watched as Gytha composed herself, smoothing her dress over her thighs. At last, Gytha nodded, the movement barely visible in the dim light from the embers. "I have no proof, and I have not spoken of this to anyone." She let out a long breath. "I fear for my girls."

"Why do you think Hunfrith would do such a thing? He is the reeve."

Gytha sighed.

"I have long thought on these matters. It is like a riddle that I cannot unravel." She looked down at her hands. She was rubbing them as if seeking to rid them of dirt. "Something had made Rothulf anxious, and he was not a nervous man. I asked him about it, but he said he would not talk of it until he had spoken to Lord Ælfgar."

Aedwen frowned.

"What tidings were so unsettling, so important?" she asked. "And why not tell you?"

"I know not," replied Gytha, her voice catching in her throat. "I like to think he was protecting us. He travelled to Ælfgar's hall, and then... I never saw him alive again."

Aedwen understood.

"You think his death was no accident?"

Gytha drew in a deep breath, as if girding herself for what she was about to say.

"I fear he was murdered." She sighed and smoothed her dress over her thighs. "There, I have said it."

"But why? What could Rothulf have said to Ælfgar that would have got him killed?"

For a moment, Gytha was silent, perhaps thinking whether she should continue.

"I have heard rumours," she said at last.

"Rumours?"

"That Hunfrith was born out of wedlock."

"I do not understand."

"Ealdorman Ælfgar appointed Hunfrith to be reeve of this hundred. Hunfrith is very young for such a post. He has no experience."

Aedwen thought for a moment, trying to deduce the meaning of what Gytha was saying.

"Ælfgar is his father?"

The widow nodded.

"That is what some say."

"You think Rothulf heard this rumour. That it was these tidings that he took to Ælfgar?"

"Maybe." She sighed. "But it makes no sense. Such a thing is not uncommon. There must be dozens of bastards in every hundred in every shire in the kingdom."

"But why then kill Rothulf?"

Gytha shrugged.

"All I know is that my husband went to Ælfgar with some news that had troubled him. The next day, he was dead. And then, Hunfrith came."

"What do you think Hunfrith will do with Dunston?"

"I know not, but I do not believe he means him well. Perhaps he will put him before the moot, as he says. But without you as a plaintiff, I see no point."

"But if Hunfrith killed Rothulf and my father. He could mean to slay Dunston too." The thought terrified her. Was it possible that a reeve could be so evil, so corrupt? A man trusted to dispatch justice by the lord of the shire and, through him, by the king himself.

"We have not one jot of evidence that Hunfrith had anything to do with my husband's or your father's deaths."

"But why not say that he knew my father then? Why keep that secret?"

Gytha shook her head in the gloom.

"And why," Aedwen went on, anger tinging her words, "lock up Dunston when he has shown me nothing but kindness?"

They went around and around these questions, circling and herding their thoughts the way dogs round up wayward sheep until there was nowhere else for them to go.

After a time, they grew silent and listened to the soft night-time hush. The crackle of the fire; the quiet snoring of one of the girls; the creaking of the timbers as a gust of wind shook the house.

Gytha got up and walked silently to a chest that rested beside the small table where they had eaten. She opened it and brought something out and returned to Aedwen beside the fire. She carried a flask and two wooden cups. She handed a cup to Aedwen, unstopped the flask and poured liquid into each vessel.

Aedwen sniffed the contents and was surprised to smell the pungent bite of strong mead. She had only sipped mead before, at the end of the Crístesmæsse fast.

"I do not like mead," she said quietly, not wishing to appear rude to her hostess.

"Neither do I," replied Gytha with a bleak smirk. "But I think we could both use some fortification if we are going to do what I think we must. So drink it down, and let us get on with preparations, before I change my mind."

With that, the widow tossed the liquid into her mouth and swallowed it down with a grimace.

Confused, Aedwen raised the cup slowly up to her own lips and hesitated, unsure of whether to sip it, or just to swallow it quickly as the older woman had done.

"But what is it we are going to do?" she asked.

"It seems we have convinced ourselves of Dunston's innocence and Hunfrith's guilt, at least in keeping a secret, and at worst of having a hand in my husband's death and your father's murder."

"But what are we to do about that?" Aedwen asked, tentatively sipping a tiny amount of mead into her mouth. It was sweet and she was surprised to find it not unpleasant. It was warm as it trickled down her throat.

"Why, we are going to free Dunston, of course," said Gytha.

Eleven

Dunston snapped instantly awake. He pushed himself to his feet, his aches and pains forgotten as the sounds of alarm from outside grew more intense and increasingly insistent. A hollow clangour echoed in the village as someone beat on something, an empty barrel perhaps. Shouts and yells of anguish drifted to where Dunston stood. He bunched his hands into fists, forcing himself to remain calm, despite the blood rushing through his veins. He recognised the sensation of his skin tingling, his limbs thrumming with tension. This was how he had always felt before battle.

But was there a battle taking place outside? Or was this something less dire? An abandoned rush light, or a stray ember tumbled from a hearth on the dry rushes of a floor perhaps. He breathed deeply, taking in the night-cool air that smelt of straw and dust and the animals that had previously inhabited the barn. Underlying these scents, he half-imagined he could detect the slightest trace of smoke.

Just outside the barn door, his guard called out to someone. "What is that?"

Dunston could not make out the reply muffled as it was by distance, the barn's timber walls and the noise of many people hollering in the night.

Could it be that the village was under attack from the Norsemen? Was it possible that the blood-eagling of Aedwen's father had presaged the arrival of the sea wolves this far inland? Were the people of Briuuetone even now being slaughtered by savage heathens? By Christ, if that were so, what would befall Aedwen? And Gytha and her daughters?

Dunston trembled. How he wished he had hold of Deaþangenga. The axe's sharp blade would make short work of this wooden gaol.

"What is happening out there?" he bellowed. No answer came to him.

He stumbled to the door in the gloom and placed his ear to its rough-hewn oak. Men and women shouted. Dogs barked, loud and insistent in the night. For a fleeting, sad moment he thought of Odin. There was no clash of metal on metal. The constant echoing drum beat had ceased.

He knelt and peered through a knot hole in the planking. Shadows flitted before the light of flickering flames. But he was unable to make out any details of the events beyond the door.

Standing, he beat on the door with a fist.

"Hey! Let me out of here. I can help."

He paused to listen for a reply.

To his amazement, he heard the bar being removed with a clatter. The door swung open, letting in the noise and light of the night. The cold air was redolent of smoke. Dunston blinked, trying to make sense of what he saw. Some distance away, in the Bartons, the alleys that led to the animal enclosures, a fire was raging. Long, dark shadows danced from the men and women who had flocked about the flames and were doing their best to douse them.

In the doorway, shadowed by the distant conflagration, stood two figures. After a moment, their shapes became clearer to him, their features limned by the silvery light of the full moon.

"Aedwen?" he said, bewilderment in his voice. "Gytha? What is this?"

"There is no time to talk," said Gytha. Despite the obvious urgency, Dunston could not help but notice how the woman had aged. She was, as ever, a handsome woman, and yet she looked as though a decade had passed since last they had met, rather than a few months. "You must flee," she said. "You are not safe here."

"What? Why?" Dunston felt stupid, unable to understand the meaning behind her simple words. The flames behind her seemed to be under control now, the shrillness of the voices in the darkness replaced with determined shouts and commands.

"There's no time, Dunston. You must run."

"I've done nothing wrong."

"I know that, but Hunfrith is keeping things secret. We think he means you harm."

"But why? I have done nothing." Dunston repeated the sentiment of his innocence, but even as he spoke, he could hear the shallowness of his words. Did he truly believe justice would be done here? He was being held for a crime he did not commit, by a man who would not listen to reason. And here was a girl and woman who had risked much to see him freed.

Gytha placed a hand upon his shoulder.

"That fire will not burn for long, Dunston. I must be gone from here and home with my girls before anyone suspects my involvement." She gripped his arm tightly for a moment. Her face was shadowed, but he could sense her terror of being found here. "You are a good man," she said, her voice hissing in the dark. "But you must go. Now. Godspeed." Without awaiting a reply, she turned and ran into the night, away from the now waning blaze. In an eye-blink she was swallowed by the darkness.

An instant later, his mind was made up. He trusted Rothulf's widow. She was a clever woman, honest and true, and if she had taken this action, there must be good reason. Casting about for his belongings, he saw none. That could not be helped. He would have to make do with what the forest provided. He wished he had a knife at least, but he would manage. He began to make his way around the barn, away from the noise and tumult surrounding the fire. Aedwen followed at his side.

Wheeling on her, he hissed, "You cannot come with me, child. Go after Gytha. You will be safe with her." He made to turn, but her small hand gripped his arm, pulling him back.

"No. I will go with you."

"By Christ's bone's, girl, do what you are bidden." He felt exposed out here. If someone should look in this direction they would see him arguing with Aedwen, lit up against the side of the barn by the dying flames of the fire.

"No," replied Aedwen.

By God, the girl was infuriating.

Dunston was about to snap an angry retort, when a large figure loomed in the darkness. It was a tall man, easily a head taller than Dunston, with a dark shock of hair and a mordant, angular face.

Without thinking, Dunston shoved Aedwen behind him. She was light and his strength flung her against the barn with a clatter.

"Well, well," said the newcomer. "If it isn't Dunston, the famous warrior. You don't look so bold now." He sneered, raising the weapon he held in both hands. The far-off fire gleamed from the familiar silver-threaded axe-head.

DeaÞangenga.

His eyes flicked towards Aedwen, who was pushing herself to her feet from where she had fallen. "Oh," he leered, "after I've cut you up, perhaps I can have some fun with the filly. I like them slim and tight."

If the reeve's man had expected Dunston to respond to his taunts, he was quickly disappointed.

Without a word, Dunston closed with the man. The man's eyes widened, but he was young and quick. He stepped backward and raised the great axe, just as Dunston had known he would. Dunston did not stop, instead he increased his speed, forcing the man to react. Dunston knew that most men will think twice before dealing a killing blow, especially against an unarmed man. He hoped to keep him off balance, but his adversary was no peasant and it seemed had no qualms about striking an opponent who bore no weapon.

He raised DeaÞangenga high in the air and swung a huge blow downward aimed at Dunston's head. If the axe had connected it would have killed the older man as quickly as lightning striking from a summer storm. But, Dunston was a veteran of many battles, and, unlike his enemy, he had used DeaÞangenga, the long hafted axe, in combat so often that he knew its heft intimately. He knew that such a powerful swing would slay any man, but he also understood that if it were to miss, the wielder would be unable to halt the weapon's progress.

Belying his advanced years, Dunston skipped backward, allowing the axe to slice the air a hand's breadth before him. His attacker was unbalanced. He stumbled as the axe-head struck the earth, burying itself deeply into the mud, Dunston sprang forward. Placing his left hand atop DeaÞangenga's haft, he drove his meaty right fist into his assailant's face. The man relinquished his grip on the axe's handle and staggered back, arms flailing. Dunston had struck him with all his weight behind the blow and was surprised that the man did not fall to the ground. He was a tough one, of that there was no doubt.

Shouts from the Bartons told of how others had seen the men fighting by the barn. There was no more time.

Tugging the axe out of the ground, Dunston swung it in a vicious arc, connecting with the blunt side of the iron head with a thudding crunch into the man's jaw. He dropped without uttering another sound.

Dunston scanned the gloom. His senses were sharpened now, the battle-fire flooding his body. He felt younger than he had in years. Several figures were approaching cautiously from where the fire was now almost completely extinguished.

Looking grimly at the collapsed man, Dunston prayed he would live. He had not meant to kill him, but perhaps he had hit him harder than needed. There was nothing for it now. His life was in Christ's hands.

DeaÞangenga was warm and comforting in Dunston's grip. Bending to the man's immobile body, he tugged the seax from the scabbard that hung from his belt. As he rose, his eye caught on a leather flask that was propped against the side of the barn. No doubt it held ale or mead that his guard had been drinking before the night exploded into fire and chaos. Without hesitation, Dunston snatched up the container.

Someone shouted out.

"Hey, you there!"

Quickly, Dunston decided which way he would run. He knew this land well and the night held no fear for him. He would make his way quickly down to the river's edge where the water's rush would mask any noise he made. Then he would head south for a time, away from his hut. In the opposite direction to that which the people of Briuuetone would likely expect. The thought of the tithing-men coming after him turned his stomach. The tithing-men would be simple folk of Briuuetone, doing their duty, as they saw it. Helping to bring a miscreant to justice. The villagers were known to him. He had no quarrel with them and did not wish to face them. He would flee deep into the forest where they would never be able to find him.

He sprinted into the darkness, the shouts of pursuers growing louder behind him. A moment later, he became aware of the slender shape of Aedwen, running along beside him. He halted and turned on the girl.

"You cannot come with me. It is too dangerous. You will become a wolf-head."

"I know you do not want me with you," she said, her voice high and trembling. "But think. The reeve's man saw me. If I stay, they will say I freed you. If I go, they will believe I acted alone and Gytha and her girls will be safe."

New voices had joined the shouting now. The crowd had found the fallen guard and from the sound of the yells and insults in the dark, the man's friends were not happy.

Dunston stared at Aedwen for a moment, her eyes glittered. She looked like Eawynn when he had first met her.

"Over there!" came the cry from one of the pursuers.

Dunston growled. There was no time to argue.

"Very well then," he said. "Try to keep up."

And with that, he sped into the black of the night and the willow-slender form of Aedwen followed.

Twelve

Dawn was not even tinging the eastern horizon and Aedwen's breath was ragged and wheezing. She was utterly exhausted, but she vowed not to admit weakness to Dunston. The grey-bearded man seemed not to feel fatigue as they trudged on into the night. Twice, soon after they had left Briuuetone, he had grabbed her shoulder and pulled her down, indicating for her to be silent. The first time he had done this, they had hunkered down beside the bole of a beech tree, hidden in the moon shadow beneath its boughs. They had remained there for a long time, but Aedwen was unsure of who it was that Dunston believed would hear them. The night was silent save for the breeze-whisper in the trees and the burble of the river, which ran broader and more slowly now they had moved south from Briuuetone. After a time, the light from the moon dimmed and, looking up through the branches, she had seen the darkness swallow up half of the great orb in the sky. She had trembled and when Dunston had followed her gaze, he had frowned.

"What is it?" she'd whispered, but Dunston had shaken his head and held a finger to his lips.

Moments later, the night had brightened once more and the moon was whole again.

They had waited so long like that, hushed and cramped beneath the beech that her limbs had become stiff and Aedwen had begun to fall into a doze. But then Dunston had pulled her roughly to her feet and was once again setting such a fast pace that she was barely able to keep up. Her legs were numb from the lack of movement and tingled unpleasantly as the blood flowed back into her abused muscles.

Dunston had appeared oblivious or uncaring of her discomfort.

The second time he had caught hold of her, guiding her into the lee of a stand of alder. She had shaken off his touch.

"What now?" she'd hissed, not wishing to again crouch in the cold and damp while her legs seized up. "And what happened to the moon?"

He had pulled her down roughly with an unyielding strength.

She opened her mouth to complain at his treatment, but before she could utter a sound, he clamped a large harsh hand over her mouth. She squirmed, but he held her tightly. She had been contemplating trying to bite his hand when she heard them. They must have been only ten paces from Dunston and Aedwen's hiding place.

Several men walked quietly past. From time to time one of them would whisper something, but they were travelling quietly, stealthily.

After a while, Dunston had released her, and they had both sat in silence for a very long time. Eventually, Dunston had been sure that their pursuers had moved on and he stood.

"Sorry," she whispered.

"Don't be sorry," he had replied, his voice the hiss of a blade being drawn from a scabbard. "Be obedient. Do what I say without hesitation and we both might live."

She had swallowed back a reply and merely nodded, unsure whether he could see her movement in the dark.

For the rest of the night they had walked in silence and had no further encounters.

Aedwen could not tell how Dunston was navigating. They were not walking on any roads or paths she could discern in the dark, and yet he appeared to be leading them with unerring conviction. Though to where, she had no idea.

She stumbled, her toe stubbing a root that ran across the track they followed. Dunston reached out with uncanny speed, grabbing the back of her dress and righting her. She could scarcely believe what she had witnessed in Briuuetone. Perhaps Gytha's husband had not been spinning tall tales about Dunston's prowess in battle. He had dispatched the younger, armed Raegnold in a heartbeat and it had all happened so quickly, she was hardly certain of what had occurred. One moment the tall man had been threatening them, the next he was slumped on the earth unconscious or dead. Dunston seemed to care not which.

"We will rest soon," he whispered in the darkness. She noticed with a start that she could make out his features. Dawn was not far off and the wolf-light that came before the sun was beginning to colour the land. Dunston had led them out of the dense woods and across some open grassland. It was colder here, the sky clear of clouds.

Aedwen's senses swam. Her legs ached as she climbed up an incline. She was barely awake and had been walking in a daze. Now, she was suddenly afraid.

"Will they find us?" she asked.

"Not where I am taking us," he replied. His voice was soft now, gentle. She nodded in the pre-dawn dark and stumbled along behind him. She believed him.

He led them to a cave. The entrance was scarcely wide enough for them to squeeze inside, and she felt a tremor of fear at being trapped in the earth. But she was too tired now to worry and so she followed Dunston in to the black gloom.

She sensed him moving, as he sat down, propping his back against the wall.

"You will be safe here, Aedwen," he said, his voice echoing quietly in the darkness. "Lie down and rest. Nothing will befall you here."

His voice was soothing, and the solidity of his presence comforting. She wrapped her cloak about her and sat down on the hard floor of the cave.

"You can rest your head on me," Dunston whispered. Without thinking, Aedwen did just that. She lowered herself down and placed her head on the old warrior's outstretched legs.

He patted her arm gently. She shivered.

Aedwen's mind was filled with visions of fire and blood and a moon being consumed by darkness. The face of her mother came to her as sleep embraced her, and in her dreams she was sure she could feel the warmth of Odin the hound stretched out beside her.

Thirteen

Dunston opened his eyes slowly, as if he were scared that the lids would ache like the rest of his body. Light lanced through the open doorway of the mound. He had not meant to sleep, but he supposed it had been foolish pride to think he would be able to stay awake for the whole night. Gone were those days of youth when he could ignore the desire for sleep and still be fresh and alert the next day.

During the night, he had sat for a time, the warm weight of Aedwen's head against his leg, and his mind running ceaselessly over recent events. Like Aedwen, he had been shocked at the moon partially vanishing in the sky above them. He had seen similar before, but had never understood the meaning of such things. Omens, he supposed. But of what, who could tell? Unable to answer any of the questions swarming in his mind, he had, at last, drifted into a deep sleep.

He looked down at where Aedwen slept. She had curled up on her side, resting her head on her arm now rather than his thigh. Her face was serene. Dirt smudged her cheek and her hair was dishevelled, but she slept with the carefree abandon of the young. At some point in the night she had placed her faith in him completely. He knew that she looked to him for protection and he felt acutely the weight of that responsibility.

She should have stayed with Gytha. By Christ's teeth, what had Rothulf's widow been thinking? Now both he and the girl were outlawed. He would never be able to return to Briuuetone. Still, he supposed there was not much for him there now that Rothulf was gone. He could find a new place to live, somewhere in the forest where nobody would find him. He would be content to live alone, with Odin for company.

With a pang of pain, he remembered that Odin was gone. He had wished to ask Aedwen about the hound the night before, but he had pushed the thought away. It was not the moment to converse. There would be time enough in the daylight for speaking, and waiting a while longer for tidings of Odin's fate would change nothing.

Aedwen stirred, mumbling something under her breath before growing still once more.

With an effort, Dunston pushed himself to his feet. His knee was a burning agony and his back popped and clicked painfully as he stood. To think that for a moment in the night he had thought he'd felt young again, able to fight and wield DeaÞangenga as though the last twenty summers had not passed. By God, who was he trying to fool? He gazed down for a moment at the sleeping girl. He had forced them to walk fast all night and she had done well, keeping up without complaint. Now, as his joints cracked and his muscles throbbed, he wished he had not pushed them so hard. If he was not careful, he would be the one unable to keep up the pace.

He snorted, looking to his side for where Odin usually stood. He stopped his hand as he reached for where the dog's head would have been. Stupid old man. It would take him some time to grow accustomed to living without the company of the dog.

Shaking his head, he moved silently to the entrance. He glanced back at Aedwen before he stepped out into the daylight. What was he to do with the girl? Perhaps he could take her to her distant kin. But where did the aunts she had mentioned live? And would they take her in if he found them?

Frowning, he held his hand over his eyes and scanned the horizon. The sun was high in the sky and the day was blessedly warm and dry. Thin trails of smoke rose in the distance to the north, but there were no other signs of men.

Setting off down the hill, he checked that the seax he had taken was still tucked in his belt. In his left hand he carried DeaÞangenga. His body's pains began to lessen as he walked. He would have to give some thought about what their next steps should be, but first, they needed water and something to eat. There was nothing to be gained from worrying about the problems of tomorrow.

Fourteen

Aedwen awoke to the smell of woodsmoke and for an instant she was back in Briuuetone in the dark, the fire Maethild and Godgifu had lit in the handcart spouting flames and billowing clouds of thick smoke. She sat up quickly, staring about her in fear. Where was she? It was dark, but sufficient light washed in from the entrance of the cave that she could make out the details of her surroundings well enough.

The walls and ceiling were too straight to be a cave. This was no natural cavern, gouged from the rock by aeons of rainfall and the flow of underground streams. The stone surrounding her was smooth, fashioned by man.

She saw Dunston then, looking much less like a warrior of legend and more like the old greybeards who sat hunched over their hearths in the long winter months. He was leaning over a small fire, feeding the flames with twigs.

Glancing over at her, he smiled. He looked tired, eyes dark-rimmed and skin wan.

"Ah, you're awake at last," he said. "We have much to talk about. But first, you should eat and drink. It isn't much, but better than nothing." He nodded to where a handful of cowberries glistened on a large leaf.

"How?" she asked, looking from the fire, to the berries, and finally to the trout Dunston was now skewering on a slender branch, which he had sharpened for the purpose.

"The land provides much, if you know where to look," he replied, with a twisted smile. "Everything seems better with a fire, and some food in your belly. It will be even better once this fish is cooked." He positioned the fish over the smoking fire and sat back, looking at her through the haze of smoke. "Drink," he said, handing her the leather flask he had taken from Raegnold at Briuuetone.

She unstopped it and sipped. It was water, with the faint tang of mead and leather. Aedwen suddenly realised how thirsty she was. She took several gulps of the cool liquid before handing the vessel back to Dunston.

"Eat," he said, nudging the leaf with the cowberries towards her.

She picked up a small red berry, nibbling it. It was good. Her stomach grumbled. The smell of the cooking fish made her mouth flood with saliva.

After she had eaten a few of the berries and Dunston had done likewise, he wiped his beard with his hand and looked at her with those penetrating ice blue eyes of his.

"First thing first," he said, "what happened to Odin?"

She told him of how Hunfrith's man had attacked the dog. She blinked back the tears that threatened to fall as she spoke.

Dunston sighed. Picking up a stick, he busied himself poking and prodding the fire. Not wishing to intrude on the man's grief, Aedwen looked down at the berries. They were the red of blood.

After a time, Dunston looked up. His eyes shone in the firelight.

"Now, why did you and Gytha see fit to rescue me from that barn?"

Aedwen recounted the conversation she had had with the widow; about her father meeting with Hunfrith but the reeve not mentioning it to anyone. She told him that Gytha believed Rothulf had been murdered, that he had unearthed something that had led to his death. She described how they had worried at the possibilities, going around the different reasons for the reeve's secrecy, Rothulf's drowning and her father's murder until they had become convinced that Hunfrith was somehow involved and, if that were the case, Dunston would not be safe in his custody.

Dunston turned the trout, holding the branch so that the other side of the fish would cook.

"So you think Hunfrith ordered your father murdered? And that he might have killed Rothulf too?"

"We don't know, but it seemed possible." Aedwen felt foolish, as if Dunston were judging her words and finding them wanting. It had all seemed so plausible in the black of night.

Dunston stared into the flames for a long time, his eyes pinched, looking beyond the fire. At last he nodded.

"I agree. It would make sense. But why? What did Rothulf and your father know? Even if the rumours Gytha spoke of are true, why kill for that? Bastards are as common as ticks on sheep."

"I know not," Aedwen said. It always came back to this. What reason could Hunfrith have for killing the old reeve and her father? "Father was but a peddler."

"Peddlers travel widely," said Dunston, his voice trailing off, perhaps lost in his thoughts. "Who did he trade with?" he asked after a pause. "Did you go to the houses of any ealdormen or thegns?"

She shook her head.

"No. We had only been on the road for a couple of weeks. Father had little idea of how to make money at the best of times. But he was a freeman and proud. And he had always wanted to travel." She wanted to say that she wished he had not been so proud. That he had been a fool to lead them north on dangerous roads with all of their goods on one small handcart. She longed to tell him of how she wished her mother had not died; that if she yet lived, her father would never have put his plan into practice and he would still be alive. But she said none of these things. Instead, she said, "He knew nobody of import. He was not important. A nobody." She felt ashamed at the words. Disloyal. He had been her nobody. Her voice cracked.

"You say he had not always been a peddler?" Dunston asked.

"No, until recently, he had worked the land."

Dunston nodded.

"An admirable labour. What changed?"

"My mother. She died." Aedwen could hear the tremor in her voice as the memory of her mother's passing rushed back, the pain as raw and sudden as a scab ripped off a graze.

Dunston turned the fish again, before adding a few fresh twigs to the small blaze. His firelit face did not give away his thoughts.

"I can only think of two ways to find out what your father spoke of to Hunfrith," he said after a time. "One would be to go back to Briuuetone and ask Hunfrith, but I think we can agree, that is not where we wish to be headed right now."

"And the other?"

"When you lose something, the best way to find it is to go back over the ground you have covered. I say we travel the route you took with your father and we speak with those he traded with. Perhaps one of the people he spoke to will give us the information we need to unravel this riddle."

Aedwen could think of no better suggestion.

"And then what?" she asked, wondering what Dunston hoped to do if he got to the bottom of the mystery of her father's murder.

Dunston squinted at her through the wafting smoke.

"If we find out why your father was killed our way will be clear," he said.

"Clear?"

"Of course," he said, lifting the trout and examining it to ascertain whether it was cooked. "I would rather not live out the rest of my days as a wulfeshéafod. I say we find your father's killers, and bring them to justice."

Aedwen stared at Dunston. Was he like her father? A dreamer. It was easy to have ideas, but quite another to see them through. She could see from the stern set of his jaw that he spoke in earnest. And this greybeard was not her father. She had seen Dunston fight, and he had brought them here to safety, finding food where they had none. No, Dunston was nothing like her father. And yet this was madness. How could an old man and a girl find the truth of all this? They scarcely knew where to start and they were outlaws, probably hunted even as they sat here in this cave. She looked about her again at the cut stone of the walls.

"Where is this place?" she asked. "I thought it was a cave, but these walls are shaped by man, not God."

Dunston busied himself with the fish that he had replaced over the fire.

"We are safe here," he said. "We'll rest for the remainder of the day, then set off south once again at dusk. I do not wish to meet travellers on the roads."

"But where are we?"

"Do you trust me?" Dunston asked, looking her squarely in the eye.

She thought for a moment. He was dour and irascible, but he was strong and honest, and she was certain he meant her no harm.

"Yes," she answered at last.

"Then trust me when I say we are safe."

"Very well, I believe you. But what is this place, if not a cavern?"

Dunston let out a long breath.

"It is a barrow."

"A barrow..." she repeated, the word not making sense for a moment. And then, cold claws of dread scratched down her spine and she sprang to her feet. "We cannot stay here any longer," she said in a hushed whisper, as if the sound of her voice might awaken the dead that slept deep within the crevices of the ancient burial chambers.

"Hush, Aedwen," Dunston said, but she noted that he did not move to impede her should she wish to leave. "I assure you that we are safer here than we would be out in the open. The day is bright and if anyone should be looking for us, they would likely find us up here on the hills."

"But the dead..." she stammered.

"Are long gone and still resting. They mean us no harm and I have oft slept in these places. No harm has ever befallen me."

Aedwen thought of his solitary existence, with only a dog for company, a dog that was quite probably dead. How he had been imprisoned by Hunfrith and was now a wolf-head, to be shunned by all men as outside the law.

He raised an eyebrow, perhaps reading the thoughts on her face.

"I have slept safely many times in barrows and the dead have never disturbed me. Now, sit, the trout is done."

She sat down slowly, unable to hide the fear that had now gripped her. She peered into the dark depths of the barrow, but she could not penetrate the gloom. She imagined the corpses of long dead kings lying there, listening to the echoes of the voices of the living, feeling the warmth from the fire. Smelling with dried cadaverous nostrils the delicious aroma of the sizzling fish. Did they miss being in the world of the living? Would they come crawling out of their ancient tomb, reaching for her young flesh with their skeletal, grasping fingers?

She shivered, and shifted her position so that she was closer to the fire and angled to be looking into the barrow and not towards the light. She would rather one of the tithing-men of Briuuetone found her than some nameless horror from the black interior of the barrow.

Dunston did not speak, and if he noticed it, he ignored her trembling fear. He placed the fish on a slab of wood he had cut to act as a trencher. With deft actions, he used the seax he had taken to pull the fish's meat from the thin bones. He offered her a piece of the trout. It was soft and succulent and tasted earthy and wholesome. The warmth of the food seeped through her, even as her skin prickled, the hairs on her arms rising as if she were cold. She could not shake the feeling that the dead were watching them, lying in wait for them to let their guard down.

"Are we truly safe here?" she asked.

"From the dead?" he asked.

She nodded.

"They will not disturb us," he said. "You know, the first time I stayed in one of these old burial mounds I was frightened too."

"So why did you go inside?"

"That is easy," he said with a shrug. "To remain outside would have meant my death. I had been caught in a terrible blizzard," he explained. "I was younger then, and less wise to the ways of the wild. I should have seen the signs in the sky, but by the time I realised the storm was going to catch me, it was too late to get home. Night was drawing in and the snow came down so thick I could barely see my hand in front of my face. I'd noticed one of the sacred mounds before the weather closed in, so I headed for it. They are dotted all over the land on the hills and the plains, but I'd never ventured into one before. I'd been too scared. But I knew enough about cold to know that if I stayed outside all night, I would not live to see the sunrise, so I swallowed my fear and I went inside."

She watched him as she savoured the fish. He prodded the fire and the flames jumped and danced.

"I trembled like a child," he said. He stared into the fire, lost to his memories. "As much from the fear of the ghosts that might inhabit the place as from the cold. And yet there was nothing for it. If I stayed outside, I would perish, so I entered the dark belly of the mound, praying all the while that the Lord would protect me."

"What happened?"

"Nothing." He laughed, looking up from the flames. "Eventually, I grew too tired to worry and I slept. When I awoke, the snow had stopped falling and it was day. The shelter of that barrow had saved my life and the dead did not seem to mind my intrusion." He scratched at his beard. "No evil befell me that night, but when I left, I made sure to place a silver penny in the barrow and I offered a prayer of thanks to the spirits of those who lived in this land long before you or I were born."

"You prayed to the spirits? Is that not blasphemy?" she asked.

"Maybe, but I don't think it does any harm to be respectful. Just in case. Whenever I've stayed in one of these old caves, I have always left a gift. And the spirits have never troubled me." He offered her a lopsided smile.

Did the dead truly live on in some way, she wondered? Her mother had been dead for nearly a year, and sometimes she could almost sense her touch or hear her voice. And yet she knew that her body lay deep in the earth, wearing her favourite blue dress and the necklace her father had given her as her morgengifu. Aedwen had placed the pendant around her cold pale neck herself.

"What will they do with my father?" she asked suddenly.

Dunston handed her another slice of fish and pondered for a moment.

"I daresay they will give him a Christian burial. They are good people in Briuuetone."

Aedwen thought of Gytha and her girls, but just as quickly recalled Raegnold lashing out at Odin, and then attacking them as they fled from the barn. She was not so sure.

"Godrum is a good man," said Dunston. "He will see to your father."

Chewing the fish she prayed to the Blessed Virgin that Dunston was right. Her father had been foolhardy and unsuited to the life of a peddler. And he had never been a good farmer, his mind was always on something else, far off in some half-imagined fantasy of his. But despite his faults he was not a bad man and he deserved to be buried correctly. A sudden searing anger ripped through her. She was taken aback by the ferocity of the rage that engulfed her. Her father deserved a decent burial, but more than that, he had done nothing to deserve torture and death in a lonely forest glade.

"I don't know how we can do it," she said, her voice trembling with the force of her emotion, "but you are right."

Dunston returned her gaze, sombre and unblinking.

"Right?"

"We must retrace our steps and try to find the truth."

Dunston's face was grim.

"Whatever your father knew, someone thought it was worth killing for," he said.

"Yes," Aedwen said, calm now that she had made up her mind, "and we must find out what that was and who his killers were. And then..." She faltered, unsure of the words she wanted to say.

"And then?"

Aedwen drew in a deep breath, conjuring up her father's guileless face in her mind's eye.

"And then," she said, staring directly into Dunston's icy eyes, "we make the bastards pay."

Fifteen

Dunston dozed by the barrow's entrance as the sun slid into the west. Aedwen had curled up once more, resting her head on her forearm. For a time she had turned and fidgeted, unable to sleep, casting furtive glances into the shadows at the back of the barrow, but Dunston had whispered that she was safe and eventually she had found sleep again.

Clouds had gathered all that afternoon, so as dusk approached, darkness was already creeping over the land. Within the barrow it was dark when Dunston woke Aedwen. He had only ventured out of the barrow to relieve himself and to find some more food. He didn't wish to risk discovery, so he had not returned to the river to fish, instead limiting himself to foraging for some more berries in a thick stand of alder and hawthorn.

He had also cut some linden bark and withies with which he fashioned a bag for any food they might pick up along the way. Into this bag he placed the leather flask.

Near the entrance to the barrow, Dunston pulled up some long grass. This, along with the fire-making materials that he had made earlier in the day, he wrapped in some of the linden bark and slipped the parcel inside his kirtle.

Finally, he had found a stout branch of oak, which he had cut to length and smoothed.

He handed the meagre handful of berries to Aedwen, who took them bleary-eyed and yawning.

"We will follow the road," he said. "We will make better time that way and it should be safe enough. Nobody will be abroad at night, save for outlaws and brigands." He smiled without humour.

He passed her the oak staff he had made.

"It will help with the walking," he said. "And, if we do run into any wolf-heads, that staff is thick enough to break a skull."

She accepted it without comment and together they walked into the gloaming.

As the night before, Dunston set a brisk pace, but he was careful not to push them too hard. His knee throbbed and he was already favouring his left leg, limping slightly. He would be of no use to Aedwen if he could not walk.

They stomped down the hill, through long damp grass, leaving the yawning black opening of the barrow behind them. Aedwen crossed herself as they looked back. Dunston had nothing to leave the spirits that dwelt there, but he vowed that if he were able to return, he would give them a small offering as a token of his thanks. Soon, the mound on the hill and the dark doorway were lost in the gloom of dusk.

When they reached the road, it was full dark and the rising gibbous moon cast but a dull glow through the roiling clouds.

Staring up, face pale in the moonlight, Aedwen whispered, "What happened to the moon last night? It looked as though it was being eaten." She shivered.

"I have thought long about what we saw," he replied. "But I have no answers."

"Could it be an omen?"

"Perhaps, but of what, I know not."

They walked on for a time. The stones of the road were cracked and pitted, ravaged by centuries of passing seasons. But the path was easy enough to follow, even in the darkness.

Without warning, Dunston broke the silence.

"Whatever the sign meant, the moon is whole again now, as it should be. It seems that if it was being eaten, it was quickly spat out again." She glanced up, perhaps to check that his words were true. "Put thoughts of the moon from your mind. We have more pressing matters to be concerned about."

A light rain began to fall, making the road slick and treacherous underfoot. They trudged on in silence, each lost in their own thoughts. Now that they had decided on a course, Dunston was calm and less concerned with what might happen to him. He could fend for himself and defend himself, and, if things went badly and the tithing-men came after them and caught them, he would be taken before the moot. Was that so bad? Even if they found him to be guilty of murder, the only thing he truly valued that would be lost would be his honour, and that was his alone. Should they take his life, that would not be so terrible. He was content enough with his existence of hunting, trapping and forging. But he had not been truly happy for many years. Not since Eawynn. No, the idea of death did not concern him. He had walked with death for so many years when he had served his king, it held no fear for him now.

But what of the girl? She was innocent in all this. As he had sat in the barrow during the quiet calm of the summer afternoon, his hands nimbly bending and softening the withies to tie up the edges of the bark bag, his mind had turned to Aedwen's father. For a moment he could only picture him as he had seen him, bloodied and broken, fish-pallid skin splattered with gore. But then he began to imagine the man Aedwen had talked about with such a mixture of emotions – grief, longing, sadness, exasperation, pity, but above all, love. And he had started to see Lytelman as he must have been in life. A man with desires and dreams, weaknesses and strengths, and with the responsibility for the life of a young girl. It seemed to Dunston that when he had stumbled upon the man's corpse, when he had looked into those unseeing, staring, horrified eyes, he had somehow taken on that responsibility. And he was not one to shirk from his duty.

"Very well, Lytelman," he whispered into the night, "I will keep her safe, or I will give my life trying. You can ask no more of me than that."

The rain fell heavily then in a squalling gust of wind that shook the boughs of the oaks that grew at either side of the road. Dunston shuddered before nodding at the dark sky. Aedwen glanced at him, peering through the darkness and the sheets of rain. Had she heard him? He could not tell, but if she had, she said nothing, merely pulling her cloak about her, lowering her head against the chill of the rain and trudging on.

He decided to make camp well before dawn. They were both wet, cold and miserable. Despite her cloak, Aedwen was shivering and Dunston had only his kirtle for warmth. It provided none, as it was sopping and plastered against his skin.

In spite of the season and the warmth of the previous day, the nights were cool, and the rain fell relentlessly, soaking them and leaching the heat from their bodies. Cold was a killer, Dunston knew. They needed a fire and shelter.

Leading Aedwen away from the road and beneath the dense canopy of the forest Dunston cast about in the gloom until he saw the familiar shape of a young sallow. The moon was high in the sky now, and some of its silver light filtered through the clouds and rain.

"We will make camp there," he said, pointing.

Aedwen did not reply. She was stooped against the cold, arms wrapped tightly around her in an effort to ward off the chill. Reaching the tree, Dunston pointed to its trunk, beneath the thickest foliage.

"Sit there. I'll make a shelter."

He went about constructing a rough shelter as quickly as he was able. First he used DeaÞangenga to cut several branches from the sallow. These he then piled up at an angle around the bole of the tree, using the branches there for support. In this way, very quickly he had a steep roof of branches and leaves, that whilst not affording complete protection from the rain, prevented most of it from reaching Aedwen where she sat against the tree's trunk.

"Now, help me collect bracken," he said, offering his hand and, when she grasped it, pulling her up to her feet.

Bracken grew thick around them and it didn't take them long to pull up an armful each of the stuff.

"Pile it up under the shelter," he said. "It will be our bed, so make it thick enough to keep us off the ground." She did as she was told. He looked at the small mound of bracken for a moment. "Fetch some more, while I start on a fire."

"Fire?" she asked, incredulous. "But how? Everything is so wet and we have nothing to provide a spark."

"It won't be easy in this weather," he said, "that's for sure, but with a bit of luck, I'll get a fire lit." I had better, he thought. Without the warming heat of a fire, they would get colder as their wet clothes drew the heat from their limbs.

She set to ripping up more of the ferns, while he took up his axe and quickly chopped into the lichen-covered trunk of a fallen alder. Within moments he had cut a few sizeable logs, splitting the trunk to get at the dry heartwood. Snatching up a couple of the branches he had cut for the shelter, he set to work on them with his stolen seax. It was not as sharp as he would have liked, but it would serve. His hands were numb with wet and cold, and in the dark it was clumsy work at best, but he worked with care. He knew that to rush would be to risk cutting himself, and so he went slowly, slicing into the wood of the branches and cutting along its length. Long curls of wood wound up from the seax blade. When he was close to the end of the branch, where the sliver of wood would be separated from the limb, he stopped, leaving the thin spiral of sap-rich wood exposed. He repeated the process several times until he had created something that resembled a wooden feather which would burn fast and well to get the fire going.

Aedwen carried over more bracken and placed it in the shelter. And then she sat on the leaves, out of the wind and rain and watched him. It was dark and he could not see her face, but her eyes glimmered in the moonlight.

Positioning himself in the wind shadow and partially under the sheltering branches, he reached inside his kirtle for where he had stored his fire-making items, wrapped in linden bark against the wet. He prayed they were dry enough. It would be nigh impossible to create a flame with wet tinder and wood.

Carefully opening the small packet, he withdrew the fire-lighting utensils he had fashioned the previous morning. He placed a sliver of wood on the ground and atop that, a larger flat piece of linden that would serve as the hearth. Then he took up a straight stick, as thick as his thumb and cut to a rounded point. He knelt, using his body to further protect the wood that would hopefully give them a fire. Holding the wooden board on the ground with one of his feet, he placed the dowel in the darkened groove that was already there from where he had created an ember to light the fire the previous day while Aedwen had slept. Placing the stick between the palms of his straight-fingered hands he began to rotate it rapidly. Rubbing his hands together with the stick between them, he pushed downward, forcing the dowel into the darkened depression.

The stick rotated against the wooden board as his hands descended. When they reached the bottom of the stick, Dunston quickly pulled his hands to the top and repeated the motion. Before long, his palms were warm. He carried on, more vigorously.

Was that smoke he smelt?

He knew not to stop too soon. This was a delicate process and on such a night as this, he could easily lose the precious ember after all his efforts. He continued until he was sure. A tendril of smoke rose from the depression where wood dust had accumulated and he detected a tiny glow, like a ruby in a distant cave. Quickly, careful not to lose it, he lifted the hearth block, discarded the stick and picked up the sliver of wood and its glowing ember and smouldering wood dust. With the utmost care, he gently tipped the ember onto the grass and lichen he had carried within the bark parcel.

Tenderly, he wrapped the tinder about the ember, like a father swaddling a tiny baby. Raising it to his lips, as if he were going to kiss it, he blew gently. Softly, he breathed life into the ember, blowing and then pulling the tinder ball away from his face. Then, blowing again, and a third time. The ball smoked profusely now and he knew the instant the flame would come.

After the fifth lungful of air that he offered the spark enshrouded in its grass and lichen, the ball of tinder burst into flaming life. The flames lit Aedwen's pale face. Her eyes flickered, reflecting bright tongues of fire. With haste he placed the burning tinder on the earth, positioning the first of the feather sticks over it. He held the stick delicately, dangling the wooden feathers into the hottest part of the new flame. They smouldered and blackened and for a sinking moment Dunston thought that perhaps the wood was too damp, that the tinder would not burn for long enough for the larger feathers of wood to catch. And then, just as it looked as though the tinder flame was about to die, a sudden brightness leapt up from the feathered wood. The flames crackled, giving off varied hues as the sap caught.

Dunston let out a long breath. By Christ, how a fire lifted the spirits.

He placed the second feather stick on top of the first, feeding the newborn fire's insatiable appetite. When it was burning hot, he carefully added some twigs and slivers of wood from the boughs he had cut down, before finally adding one of the logs. The fire was not large, but it was burning well now, and it would not be extinguished easily, as long as he continued to feed it.

Rising, he stretched, working out the aches from his back and rubbing his fingers into his stiff right knee. Being careful not to disturb the fire or to topple into the shelter's sloping roof branches, he slid in beside Aedwen. She was half asleep, but she moved enough to make room for him, and then rested her head on his shoulder.

Warmth from the fire washed over him. He had sat thus, enjoying the heat from a campfire in the wilderness countless times before, but it was something that always filled him with pleasure and wonder. To conjure the flames from nothing was a special magic and when it was cold a fire was not only a balm for strained nerves, it was life-giving warmth.

They sat in silence for a long while, staring into the ever-changing dancing tongues of flame.

Aedwen's shivering slowly abated.

"I am glad you know how to make fire from nothing," she said, her voice thick with sleep.

He gazed into the flames, enjoying the movement and randomness of them. Their vitality.

"So am I," he said at last. He recalled sitting in just such a shelter as this so many years before that he was uncertain whether he truly recalled it, or if he had created the story for himself, to think of on lonely nights. Still, the memory was vivid and it always pleased him. He remembered sitting beside a thickset man. Dunston had been a child then, and the man had placed his arm about his thin shoulders. They had sat in pleasant silence and watched the flames that the boy-Dunston had kindled. The man of his memories was grey-bearded and broad-shouldered; old, but wise and still powerful. Dunston smiled. He must look the same to Aedwen.

"My grandfather taught me how to kindle a fire," he said. He sighed, stretching out his hands to capture the warmth from the flames. Christ, he had loved that old man. "I could teach you, if you'd like."

Aedwen did not reply. After a moment he looked down at her and smiled ruefully. The firelight gave the girl's face a ruddy glow. Her eyes were closed and she was sleeping peacefully.

Around them, beyond the glow from the small fire, the night was impenetrable. The forest whispered and rustled out there in the dark. Somewhere far off, a vixen shrieked. A tawny owl lent its haunting voice to the forest music. Leaning forward he placed a fresh log on the flames and settled back next to Aedwen.

He was sure that nobody would be on the road now, and the glow from the fire would not be visible. But he knew that the smell of the smoke would be noticeable from quite some distance. Still, there was nothing for it. The fire would keep them alive. Tiredness engulfed him with its heavy, silent cloak and Dunston's eyelids drooped. He rested his right hand on DeaÞangenga's haft and offered up a prayer that nobody would stumble on them while they slept. Then, placing another chunk of wood onto the fire, he allowed sleep to overcome him.

Sixteen

Aedwen awoke when the sun was high in the sky. She stretched and was surprised to find she was warm. She had become so cold in the long wet miserable night she had thought she might perish. Her teeth had begun to chatter and her head had ached by the time Dunston had made the shelter in the shadow of the sallow tree.

She opened her eyes and saw that the fire was still burning and there were more logs piled nearby. There was no sign of Dunston. For an instant she felt panic rise within her. What would she do if he had left her? But just as quickly as the fear of being abandoned had come upon her, so it fled; dispelled by the warmth from the small campfire. She sat up and found that Dunston had covered her with a thick layer of bracken. The old man was surly at times, and he scared her, but no, she was certain he would not leave her to her fate alone in the forest.

The fire was burning low, so she took one of the logs and placed it carefully onto the embers. The rain had ceased falling but the sky was heavy and overcast. The day was hushed and the woodland dripped and murmured.

Aedwen's stomach grumbled. She hoped Dunston had gone in search of something to eat. He seemed to be able to find food anywhere. She picked up a twig and poked at the fire. She frowned to think of the cold nights she had spent with her father on the road. If only they'd had Dunston for a travelling companion, they would never have been hungry or without warmth. She thought of his huge axe and how quickly he had felled the man in Briuuetone. If Dunston had travelled with them, she thought, her father would probably still be alive. The questions around why he had been killed still plagued her thoughts, but she pushed them aside with an effort. She could not bear to spend the day gnawing on the same bones of ideas. They had plucked all the meat from them and they would glean no further information by chewing over them again. She hoped they would learn some useful piece of information when they spoke to those who had traded with her father as they had made their way northward. Until then, she vowed to try to think of happier things than her father's murder.

Running her fingers through her hair, she felt tangles and knots. When was the last time she had given it a proper brush? Could it be only the night before last? Maethild and Godgifu had both combed her long tresses, each plaiting her hair into long braids. Aedwen had revelled in the soft touch from the sisters' delicate hands, missing her mother terribly with each pull of the antler comb. At some point in the nights and day since then, the leather thongs they had used to tie her hair up had worked loose and she had lost them. The hair fell around her shoulders now in an unruly mess. She dreaded to think of how she must look.

She smiled to herself. Her mother had always despaired at Aedwen's lack of care with her hair and appearance in general. She would fuss about her, rubbing Aedwen's face with a cloth until her cheeks were red and smarting. And when she had finished with her hair and face, she would go to work on her hands and nails. Aedwen had always complained, trying to escape her mother's clutches at the first opportunity, to flee out into the fields, or woods, or to run along the beach, where she would quickly undo her mother's work.

She sniffed at her kirtle. It stank of woodsmoke, sweat and fear.

How she longed for a bowl of hot water and a linen cloth with which to clean herself. And how she missed her mother.

A quiet rustle in the trees made her think that a breeze was picking up. But a heartbeat later, Dunston stepped into the clearing. She noted that his limp seemed less pronounced than the day before. He carried his axe in one hand and in his other there dangled the carcass of a squirrel.

He smiled at her through his wiry silver-streaked beard.

"Awake at last, I see," he said. "How are you feeling?"

"Well," she said, "thanks to you. I don't know what I would have done without you."

He shrugged, but said nothing. Pulling the seax from his belt he set about skinning and gutting the squirrel.

"You have brought us food again," she said, her voice filled with awe. "I do not know how you do it."

"I have learnt the ways of the forest. She will feed you well enough, if you know where to look."

"How did you catch the squirrel?"

He grunted as he pulled the skin from the animal, as though it were a tight-fitting jacket. The flesh that was left looked long and scrawny, but Aedwen's stomach groaned at the thought of roasted meat.

"I found where the animals travel and I placed a snare there. I did not have to wait for long."

Working deftly and with the alacrity that comes from many years of experience, Dunston tugged the entrails from the game and began threading the animal onto a spit of wood. Aedwen watched carefully, trying to remember everything.

"After we've eaten, we should carry on to Spercheforde," Dunston said. "I have been up to the road and know where we are. We will be able to reach the settlement before dusk."

"Do you think someone there will be able to help us?" she asked.

"I do not know," said Dunston, placing the spitted squirrel over the fire's embers. "But you said you and your father had travelled through, so someone might have spoken to him. Perhaps the meeting with Hunfrith was not the only thing he kept from you."

His words held no reproach or judgement and yet Aedwen felt a keen stab of an emotion she could not define. There was no doubt that her father had been holding a secret from her. A secret that might have got him killed. And the fact he had not told her hurt her more than she cared to admit, even to herself.

Dunston stood and inspected his handiwork.

"There is a stream down there, if you would like to drink or wash." He pointed beyond a copse of alder. "I'll keep an eye on this."

She must indeed look terrible if the old man who lived alone in the forest thought she should wash.

"Is it far?" she asked, anxiety gripping her.

"No, Aedwen," he replied, his voice softening, "it is not far. And that way is away from the road. You will encounter nobody."

She let out a breath and nodded.

Aedwen shook off the rest of the bracken that covered her legs and made her way past the alders. The stream was nearby. Fast-flowing, clear water flowed over a bed of shiny pebbles. She drank and the water was sweet and fresh. Then, scooping up handfuls of water, she scrubbed her face and did her best to wash the grime from her hands and arms.

When she returned to their camp, the smell of cooking meat was strong. Her stomach complained at its emptiness once more, and she swallowed the saliva that flooded her mouth.

"The meat will be ready soon," Dunston said. "Better?"

She nodded.

"Yes, I am," she said. "I can scarcely believe I slept so well in such a shelter."

"The body does not need much to be happy," Dunston said. "But it is the things we do not need that cause us most pain."

She pondered his words.

"What do you mean?" she asked, at last.

He turned the squirrel. Its flesh was dark now, sizzling and bubbling fat dropped into the embers making them flare and flash.

"Men always strive for what they do not have. But to reach the object of their desire does not make them content. When a man attains his goals, he merely looks further to the horizon, for the next prize. It is why men will never be happy and why we will never know peace."

Aedwen's brow furrowed. Dunston's bleak words made her sad.

"Do you truly believe that?"

Dunston nodded.

"The Norsemen see our lands and come to steal our riches, and so we fight."

"But they are pagans. They know not the love of the Lord. I pray that one day the Norse will become followers of Christ, and then surely we will know peace."

Dunston snorted and his amusement at her words angered her.

"Does not the Christian king of Wessex seek to control Mercia?" he said. "Do not the Christian Wéalas fight us Anglisc for our land and our livestock? No, the priests may say that Christ is the God of love, but He does not make men content with their lot in life. Perhaps one day the Norse will worship Him too, but if they do and even if they live in peace with us, others will come, seeking what the Vikingr once sought – land and riches. Just as our forebears came to these lands to take the land from the Wéalas."

He lifted the squirrel from the fire and cut a small sliver of meat. He proffered it to her, skewered on the tip of the seax. She took it, blew to cool it and then placed it in her mouth.

"It is good," she said, speaking around the food. She was glad of the change of topic away from Dunston's dark vision of the world. She could not believe in such a grim future, where nobody was ever contented and war would constantly ravage the land. She needed to cling to the hope that Christ and His mother, the Blessed Virgin, would bring happiness and tranquillity to all mankind.

They ate quietly. Dunston cut up the squirrel and shared out the pieces between them. The outside of the meat was dark and crisp, but parts of the flesh near the bone were almost raw, pink and still dripping blood. This was no matter to Aedwen. She had been ravenous and chewed the meat until the bones were clean. Then she sucked the marrow from the thicker ones.

They talked little as they struck camp. There was not much to do apart from see that the fire was safely extinguished. Very soon, with the sun beginning its downward journey into the west, they clambered up through the dense woodland and back onto the road.

Aedwen held the staff Dunston had given her. It already felt natural in her hand and she walked along beside him with purpose. Despite the cold and wet of the previous night, they were both rested and filled with renewed vigour.

"If we hear horses on the road, we will hide," Dunston said.

Aedwen said nothing, but nodded.

"Horses," Dunston explained, "can only mean trouble for us as far as I see it, so it is not worth taking any chances."

Aedwen nodded again and they walked on in silence beneath the canopy of beech and oak.

As it turned out, they neither heard nor saw any horses, or indeed anybody at all, until they left the shadow of the wood. The sun was well into the west now, but still high enough in the sky for them to have ample light left to reach Spercheforde.

The road led them down between ploughed fields and hedgerows. Strips of farmland stretched out before them. In the distance, a man was busy plucking weeds from between the rows of a crop of wheat.

A cluster of houses, barns and a small timber church nestled in the valley.

"I am known here," said Dunston, breaking the silence that had fallen between them. "I sometimes trade pelts and knives with the folk. We should have no trouble."

Despite his words, Aedwen noted how he seemed to grow in stature and how his gaze darted about, as if looking for threats.

The man halted his weeding, shading his hands to better see who approached the village. Then, he slung his weed hook and stick over his shoulder and set a course that would intercept theirs as they reached the houses. Dunston did not slow his pace.

For a time the man was lost from sight behind a hedgerow that was a-chatter with sparrows. Then, just as the path sloped down into the shallows of the river, he stepped from a break in the hedge.

Aedwen held her breath, ready to flee, but Dunston halted, lowering his axe's patterned iron head to rest on the earth.

The man was slender and wore a wide-brimmed hat woven from straw like a basket. His sinewy arms were bare, weather-beaten and smeared with mud.

"Well met, Snell," said Dunston.

The man peered at him and then at Aedwen from under the shade of his hat. He sniffed and wiped the back of his hand under his nose.

"I did not know you had any children," Snell said, nodding in Aedwen's direction.

"She is not my daughter," replied Dunston.

"New wife, is she? Got tired of cooking your own pottage? You must get lonely out in Sealhwudu."

"No," replied Dunston, an edge of annoyance in his tone.

"Thrall then?"

"She is not my child, my wife or my slave, Snell. Her father was killed. She has nobody."

Snell removed his hat and scratched his thatch of curly, greying hair.

"Oh yes," he said, replacing the hat and examining something he had found on his scalp, "I heard about that." He squeezed the nails of his thumb and forefinger together. He grunted, evidently content with the fate he had delivered to the louse.

"Heard what?" asked Dunston.

"That you killed a girl's father and then stole her away and fled justice."

Dunston stepped back slightly, perhaps to better swing his axe should it come to that, thought Aedwen.

"What you have heard is not true."

"P'rhaps," said Snell, looking askance at Aedwen, "but here you are, with the girl they spoke of."

"Dunston did not kill my father," Aedwen said.

Snell stared at her for several heartbeats, rubbing his chin. He sniffed again.

"P'rhaps," he said at last. "Mayhap he did, mayhap he didn't. Those that came here seemed to think he did." He turned his attention back to Dunston. "They had nothing good to say of you."

Dunston snorted and Aedwen was surprised to see Snell smirk.

"Who were they?" Dunston asked.

"Well, I didn't get all of their names, but they were a rum-looking lot. Said they were sent by the new reeve of Briuuetone. One of them had really been in the wars, looked like he'd fought a Mercian warband and lost. His face was a state – blue and black like a stormy day in January. Swollen too. Though it wasn't he who did the talking, seems someone broke his jaw when they were escaping."

"How many were there and when did they come through?"

"Five of them rode up this morning asking if I'd seen you and the girl."

"And what did you tell them?"

"Said I hadn't seen you since before Crístesmæsse."

"Good man," said Dunston.

"Well, it was the truth." Snell seemed awkward all of a sudden. He craned his neck, scanning the hills and woodlands surrounding the settlement, as if he expected the riders to return at any moment. "What shall I tell them if they come back?"

"You can tell them what you wish, but you have known me for many years, Snell and I tell you I am innocent of this crime. All we seek now is to find out who slew this poor girl's father."

"Well, I am sure it weren't nobody from Spercheforde. The closest to a killer you'll find here is Herelufu. Her ale is so strong you feel like death after drinking more than a cupful."

Dunston snorted.

"I do not think the man's murderer is from here."

"So what are you doing here?"

"We are looking for anyone he might have spoken to. We are hoping we might be able to find some indication of why he was killed."

Snell removed his hat again and scratched frantically at his head. He peered at Aedwen. He seemed agitated.

"What is it?"

"I remember the girl and her father now. They came through here a few days ago, but he had nothing that the likes of me or Herelufu needed, and so we sent him up to Beornmod's hall at Cantmael."

"That's right," said Aedwen. "I remember the hall at Cantmael." It had been the last time she had felt safe. "It was warm and they let me sleep in the bed chamber with the womenfolk. Father stayed up late drinking. He sold a bolt of linen, but he drank too much of the ale. The next day he was pale and we had to stop several times for him to rest."

"We will go and speak to Beornmod and see what he can tell us."

"You had best tread with care, Dunston."

"What do you mean?"

"The reeve's men asked the same questions as you. Asked who the girl's father had spoken to. I sent them to Beornmod's hall."

Dunston frowned.

"The hall is not far from here, and they are mounted. With any luck, they will be gone by now."

"I've been in the field all day and no riders have come back down the road."

Seventeen

Dunston knew something was amiss before they could see the hall. The sky was a flat, iron grey, but behind the clouds the sun was low in the sky. Long shadows trailed out from the ash trees that lined the path and the hill that dominated the skyline was huge and foreboding. Some long-forgotten men had sculpted out steps into the hillside, creating terraces in the grass and lending the mound a strange, unnatural quality.

Cantmael was not far from Spercheforde and so they had not tarried long there. There had still been enough light in the day for them to reach Beornmod's hall and so, after convincing Snell to give them a bowl of the pottage that he had left simmering over the embers on his hearth, they had set off once more.

Now, as they approached the steading in the lee of the looming, stepped hill, Dunston halted and held up his hand for Aedwen to do likewise. He shrugged off the hemp bag he now carried slung over his shoulder. He had persuaded Snell to part with it and also an earthenware pot in exchange for the promise of forging him a knife when all this was done.

Snell had smiled grimly, clearly wondering how likely Dunston was to be able to fulfil his promise, but he had agreed without quibbling. Dunston had thanked him. He knew it was no small thing to trust a man at his word, and he was grateful to the wiry ceorl.

In the cool shade of the great hill at Cantmael, Dunston sniffed the air. Smoke and manure, and rain somewhere far off. Nothing untoward. And yet...

He took a few more steps towards their destination. The hall and its outbuildings would be visible when they rounded the next bend in the path he knew. He halted again, listening, straining to hear anything that might suggest to him what to expect at Beornmod's hall. He crouched in the path, examining the furrows and tracks in the mud, turning his head this way and that in order to pick out anything unusual in the churned surface.

Several horses had come this way recently, and earlier in the day, oxen had pulled a cart with a wobble in the rear left wheel. There were prints from the shoes of ceorls going to and from the fields. He could clearly discern where the men had jumped over the numerous puddles, where they had placed their feet close to tussocks of grass, trying to keep dry. Two dogs, large ones, had padded along the path too, but unlike the men, they had cared nothing about muddying their paws.

He saw no indication of the horsemen returning along this path.

Without a word he handed the bag to Aedwen.

"Go there," he indicated a hawthorn that was flanked by huddled downy willows, "and hide. Wait for me to call or to come for you."

"What if you don't come back?" she whispered, terror in her voice.

For an instant he was going to lie to her, to tell her that of course he would be back. But then he thought of the girl's father, and all of the man's broken promises. He pictured Lytelman's back split open like a butchered boar. He would not lie to Aedwen.

"If I do not return, wait till nightfall and then make your way back to Snell. He is a good man and he would help you."

He could see she did not much care for his answer, but she merely nodded and scampered away into the undergrowth. After a moment, she was hidden from sight.

Glancing down at the muddy path once more, he saw again the indentations made from the clawed, padded paws of the two hounds. His breath caught in his throat and for a moment, he thought one of the dogs might be Odin. He bent to get a closer look and realised his mistake. These were not the tracks of his dog. Odin was surely dead somewhere in the forest where he had run after being injured.

Dunston set his jaw and, gripping DeaÞangenga tightly, he walked down the incline and around the bend in the path. The shapes of the buildings came into view. All was still and with a jolt Dunston realised what had alerted him that something was not right. This was the end of the day, when thralls and servants would be bustling about the steading, preparing for the evening meal. The last chores of the day should be under way. The small hall, barn and two outbuildings should be abustle with activity.

And yet there was no sound. No movement at all.

A crow croaked from where it was perched, dark and brooding, in the grizzled old oak that gave shadow to the ground between the buildings. It was the first bird he had heard or seen since arriving here, and its doleful call made his skin prickle.

And then he saw what the crow was resting upon.

Two men in simple clothing dangled from a high branch of the oak. Ropes had been thrown over the bough and secured around the bole. The men's faces were mottled, dark swollen tongues protruding from fish-pale lips. Their breeches were stained where they had soiled themselves in death. Dunston sighed and spat. Would he never be free from death and killing? He yearned to be left alone, to live out his days in peace.

The crow cried out again and to Dunston it sounded like a harsh bark of laughter.

The moment he had found Lytelman, his chance of a straw death, growing old and dying in his bed, had fled. Everywhere he turned now, he stumbled on more blood and murder. He felt his anger brimming within him. He fought to keep it in check, but he recognised the call of the old beast. It had been sleeping within him for such a long time that he had thought it was gone, but it seemed all it had been waiting for was the right food to give it strength once more.

Strength and purpose.

Skirting the hanging men, he moved stealthily towards the hall. There were no sounds from within. No smoke drifted from the hole cut into the thatch. The stillness was unnatural. This was the pure quiet of a tomb. All he might find here were ghosts.

Close to the hall's open doorway lay the corpse of a large tan-coloured dog. Its head had been almost severed from its neck, its mouth pulled back in a defiant snarl from its white, dagger-like fangs.

Hefting DeaÞangenga, Dunston took a deep breath and stepped through the dark maw of the hall's door. Inside was gloom-laden, the air stale. Cold soot, sour beer, the acrid scent of shit and, beneath it all, the metallic tang of blood.

Squinting and blinking against the darkness, he looked around the hall. It was a modest building, with a high table that would sit four and enough room at the benches for perhaps twenty men in total.

Three women and an elderly man lay dead on the floor near the cold hearth. They had been cut down by swords or long seaxes. Great gashes had opened their flesh and their blood had soaked the rushes black.

The other dog was dead beneath its master's feet. It must have tried to defend Beornmod, but it had been pierced by spears and then hacked into a mess of muscle, bone, sinew and fur. And blood, so much blood. The huge pools of the stuff mingled with the gore that had run from the board where Beornmod's corpse was draped.

Dunston instantly recognised the handiwork of Lytelman's murderer. Beornmod lay face down on the board, blood-splattered arms hanging down, flaccid and mottled in death. The man's kirtle had been torn asunder and it was the sight of his back that brought the gorge rising in Dunston's throat. The ribs had been shattered and wrenched apart and the man's entrails and lungs draped on his back, like wings of offal.

He turned away from the corpse. Beornmod would tell them nothing. They had come to this hall hoping for answers and instead they had found more death.

"Is that how my father was slain?" said a voice. It was small and empty-sounding, but it was loud in the complete still of the hall. Despite himself, Dunston started, letting out a tiny sound of alarm.

"I told you to stay hidden," he said, his voice harsh and as brittle as slate. "God, girl, you promised to do as I said." He grabbed hold of her shoulders, spun her round and shoved her out of the doorway, away from the mutilated remains of Beornmod. "It could have been dangerous."

Outside, she turned to face him. Finding an outlet for his anger now, his ire bubbled up and he jabbed a finger into Aedwen's sternum. She staggered backwards with the force of his stabbing blows. He was only using his thick forefinger, and yet she was unable to hold her ground.

"What if the men who did this were still here?" he asked, his finger prodding out the beat of the words.

Aedwen's eyes filled with tears, and they started to roll down her cheeks. She let out a sob, and as quickly as they had been kindled, so the flames of his anger were doused. After a moment of hesitation, he pulled the girl close to him with his left hand. In his right he held his great axe and all the while he scanned the other buildings for signs of danger. Aedwen shook and trembled against him.

"I need to know you are safe," he whispered to her, "or else I will not be able to protect you."

She sobbed and sniffed, and at last she pulled away from him. She swiped at her face, brushing away her tears.

She mumbled something under her breath. He could not make out the words. Perhaps she was apologising, but his anger still simmered.

"If you mean to say sorry," he hissed, "save your words. I need to know you will obey me. When I tell you to do something, you do it. No questions. No arguing. You just do it! Understand?"

Aedwen nodded, her face a mask of misery.

"Well, you have chosen to defy me, and now there is nothing for it. I did not want you to see such things, but maybe it is for the best that you do. Perhaps then you will comprehend what it is we are dealing with."

Aedwen's gaze flicked to the oak and its dangling corpses, then she peered, wide-eyed, into the darkness of the hall, as if she wished to see the mutilated corpse in more detail.

"You think the men who did this were the ones who killed my father?" she asked. Her voice was so quiet it was almost lost beneath the cawing of the crow.

"Who else?" Dunston replied. "Now, stay close and keep your eyes open."

They moved through the steading, searching every building, but the men who had massacred Beornmod's folk had left. They found two more bodies. A young man, and a girl. The man seemed to have come running from the fields. There was a hoe and two weed hooks near his corpse, but if he had tried to use them as weapons he had clearly been no match for the horsemen. Spear points had pierced his chest, and he had been left to wail and bleed out his lifeblood into the soil.

The girl had been dragged into one of the storerooms. Her clothes were ripped, exposing pallid skin. Beneath her dark staring eyes, her throat had been opened in a terrible wound. Dunston read what had happened inside the small shed as clearly as if he had been there to witness the atrocious last moments of the poor girl's life. After the men had done with her, they had cut her like a pig for slaughter. Blood had fountained, gushing and pumping as her heart fought to keep her alive. She had been young and vital and now she was no more than a carcass, cold meat on the packed earthen floor of a storeroom.

Dunston turned away, closing the door of the hut behind him. He sighed. Christ, to think he had hoped to be done with death.

Aedwen had grown very quiet and he noted the pallor of her skin. He placed a hand on her shoulder and for a heartbeat, he thought she was going to run from him. But then she trembled, letting out a strangled sob.

"Sorry," she said.

"Come," he said, ushering her towards one of the buildings that was devoid of corpses. "I'll light a fire and we can eat and rest."

"Here?"

"It will soon be dark and I don't think the men who did this will be back."

"Are you sure?"

"I cannot be certain, but the tracks of their horses lead south and west. If I am not mistaken, and I rarely am when it comes to reading sign, they are in pursuit of something. Or someone. They were riding hard, pushing the horses."

He led her into a small house. Like the hall its walls were whitewashed daub and its roof was thatched. Inside it was comfortably furnished. The small hearth was circled by stools and chairs. Chests lined the walls and ham and sausages hung from the rafters. To the rear, a curtain hung to separate the sleeping quarters from the main space. Thankfully nobody had been slain inside this abode and the riders had not plundered its contents.

Indicating to Aedwen to sit on one of the carved chairs, Dunston set about kindling a fire on the hearthstone. The ashes were still warm and there was dry wood in a basket. Dunston found a flint and steel in a small wooden box beside the basket of logs and in moments, he had a small blaze burning.

He placed the tinder box in the bag Snell had given him.

It was dark within the house, but the flickering light from the fire showed Aedwen's frown well enough.

"That is not yours," she said.

"You are right, of course, but we have more need of it than Beornmod's folk now, don't you think?"

Aedwen scowled, but said nothing.

"Make no mistake, Aedwen," Dunston said, "I am no thief. But I will take from these poor people whatever I can to help us. I think that is what they would have wanted. I know I would not begrudge someone taking my things after my death. Especially if they were hunting my killers."

"Is that what we are doing now then? Hunting these killers?"

For a while Dunston did not reply. He picked up a split log and placed it carefully on the flames. The truth of the matter was he did not know what they should do next. He was but an old man and Aedwen was a child. What could they do in the face of such ruthless barbarity? But what alternative did they have? If they could somehow unearth the reason for these murders and unmask the perpetrators, perhaps he could return to his life in Sealhwudu. Far from the evil of men. He had seen enough of that for a lifetime and more.

"What else can we do?" he said at last. "I would wager these are the same men who killed your father, and they are clearly searching for something. I think we will need to follow them. And, with luck, we can find out what they are about before they kill again."

"They told Snell they were the reeve's men," Aedwen said. "Surely that cannot be true. The reeve's men would not kill all of these people."

Dunston had been thinking about this, and he had his suspicions about what had happened here. He ran his fingers over his thick beard.

"Perhaps they lied to Snell, or mayhap they are Hunfrith's men."

"But how could that be so? To kill so many..."

"Maybe the first kill was an accident. But after that first one, the only way to avoid justice would be to kill everyone. I think that is what happened. From the marks in the mud outside, I believe the workers were speared first, then the horsemen, reeve's men or not, moved on to the others."

"And the girl?"

"Once such men are on the course of blood and killing, they would think nothing of taking their pleasure with an innocent."

Dunston glanced at Aedwen and saw she was staring into the flames.

"Why didn't they burn the hall with the people inside?" she asked after a time. "Surely that would have hidden the nature of their crimes. And people might have believed it to have been an accident. Fires happen all the time."

"True," replied Dunston, strangely proud of the girl for looking at the situation and analysing the possibilities. "But the smoke would have drawn neighbours, and they might have been caught here and found they needed to answer difficult questions. In this way, they must have hoped that when the bodies were found, nobody would be able to say who had done these foul acts."

"Just like my father, killed deep in the forest."

"Yes, Aedwen. If there are no witnesses to a crime, it is much more difficult to prove who did it."

Now it was Aedwen's turn to fall silent, as she pondered his words. After a time, she nodded, her face pale and doleful in the firelight.

"We should bury Beornmod's people," she said. "Before we go. We cannot leave them like that." She shuddered, and Dunston could imagine her thinking of the girl lying cold and alone in the store. The men, dark tongues poking from blue-tinged lips, swinging stiffly from the oak. The other corpses, brutally cut down by savage men. The bloody, mutilated butchered remains of Beornmod himself.

"There is no time for that," he said. "If we remain here, we will lose the men who did this. Worse, others will come and blame us for what has happened." He glowered in the gloom, recalling the madness of being accused of Lytelman's murder. But without witnesses or those to swear oaths for him, who knew what men would make of him being found in Cantmael surrounded by corpses?

"But it is not right to leave them..." she hesitated. "To leave them like that."

Before Dunston could reply, a mournful moan came to them from outside in the gloaming. It was a doleful sound, full of pain and torment.

Aedwen stiffened and horror filled her eyes.

But Dunston smiled.

"Do not fear, child," he said. "That is not a bad sound to hear. Listen."

Again came the droning moan and as Dunston saw the truth dawning on Aedwen's features, he stood and said, "Bring that bucket," indicating a wooden pail that rested in the corner.

Outside in the gathering dusk, the sound was louder and clearer. They followed it to its source, Aedwen trotting along beside Dunston. By the door of one of the barns they found the creature that was lowing pitifully as darkness draped the land.

It was a large cow with twisted horns and distended udders painfully full of milk. Inside the barn, Dunston found a stool and another bucket. He tethered the beast, and set down the stool.

"We will have fresh warm milk tonight," he said, smiling in the gloom.

He could not make out Aedwen's expression, but he was pleased when she sat and proceeded to milk the cow effortlessly, sending warm streams of liquid squirting unerringly into the bucket. It didn't take long until the first bucket was full. Dunston passed Aedwen the second pail.

"Poor girl," he said, patting the cow's shoulder. The beast had stopped lowing now, and was content to be milked, relieving the pressure from her udders. "Looks like we'll have more milk than we can drink," he said.

"Perhaps you could spare some for me then," said a voice from the darkness behind him.

Aedwen leapt up, overturning the stool and spilling the milk from the half-filled bucket.

Dunston spun around, dropping his hand to the small seax he yet carried in his belt. By God, how could he have been so foolish as to leave DeaÞangenga back in the house next to the fire? Pushing himself in front of Aedwen, he tried to discern the features of the newcomer.

The figure stepped closer and Dunston's eyes widened in surprise.

Eighteen

Aedwen sipped at the still-warm milk. Its creamy richness coated her mouth and throat. The flavour was comforting and she could feel her body relaxing in the glow of the hearth fire.

Across from Aedwen, face lit from beneath by the flames, sat a girl not much older than her. When she had approached them in the milk shed, Aedwen had been terrified that the men who had murdered the residents of the farmstead had returned. Dunston had pushed himself forward, crowding the girl who had stepped from the gloom and Aedwen had thought how lucky the girl had been that he had not thought to carry his huge axe with him. He was as taut as a bowstring and Aedwen wondered whether he would have been able to prevent himself from killing the girl where she stood, if he had borne the weapon in his hand. As it was, he soon realised this was no killer striding from the dusk, rather a timid, slender and frightened young woman. Her hair was dark and her face had angular cheeks and a pointed chin that reminded Aedwen of a fox. Her skin was smeared with mud and grime.

Nothgyth was her name and she said she was one of Beornmod's house thralls. They had made their way back to the house, where Dunston placed more wood on the fire. Aedwen noted how he positioned himself beside the door, but not with his back to the opening. He placed his silver-threaded axe within easy reach.

Nothgyth had quickly produced wooden trenchers, some cheese, hard bread and some ale from the shadows in the hut. She unhooked the ham from where it hung from a beam and sliced off thick slabs of salty, greasy meat. She clearly knew where things were kept and soon the three of them were seated around the fire, eating food that until that day had been destined for Beornmod's folk's bellies.

Dunston drained his cup of milk and then refilled it with ale. He took a deep draught, grimaced, and then emptied the cup again before pouring yet more ale. He sat back, stretching his legs out before him. He winced slightly as he straightened his right knee.

"So, Nothgyth," he said. "What happened here? How is it that you alone survived?"

Nothgyth stared into the fire for a time, chewing a morsel of bread which eventually she washed down with a mouthful of milk. Dunston waited patiently for her to answer, but Aedwen had begun to wonder whether the woman had heard the question by the time the thrall spoke at last.

"I hid. Under the store." The store shed where they had found the murdered girl was raised from the earth on wooden posts in an effort to keep rats away from the grain and food stored within. "I was round the back picking some fresh summer sætherie when I heard them come. The number of them and how they came on horses frightened me. I've never seen so many riders before in one place." She gazed wistfully into the flames. Her eyes glimmered.

"So you hid," prompted Dunston.

"Not at first," she replied, as if he'd awoken her from a dream. "I just stood there listening to start with. Wanted to hear who they were. Thought they must have been the king's men. Perhaps the king himself had come to the master's hall."

"There were so many of them?" asked Dunston.

"Oh, many riders. Must have been five at least."

Dunston frowned, but nodded.

"So what happened?"

"They talked for a moment to Frithstan. I couldn't hear what they said. Something about a peddler. It made no sense." She grew silent then. She nibbled on her bread, lost in her memories of that afternoon's chaos and violence.

"What happened next?" Aedwen asked.

"The men spotted Wynflaed. And they said things about her. Bad things. Frithstan grew angry and shouted at them, and one of them struck him. That is when Eohric and Tilwulf came back from the lower field. Eohric told the men to be gone..." Nothgyth's voice trailed off, as she relived the moment. "One of them speared him, without a word. As if Eohric was an animal. He didn't even have time to scream. He just fell into the mud and was dead. One of them laughed then, even though the others were angry with him."

"Angry?" asked Dunston.

"Yes. They said they weren't supposed to kill them. I couldn't hear much of what they said then though, because Wynflaed was screaming. A couple of them pushed her inside the store. For later, they said." Nothgyth's voice caught in her throat. "They bound her and left her there while they went to the hall. That is when I hid. I could see their feet and the hooves of their horses, and I heard how they hanged Tilwulf and Frithstan and the screams from the hall were so loud. But all the while I could hear Wynflaed crying just above me. I should have helped her," a sudden sob racked her. "I just hid there. Even while they..." Tears streaked through the dirt on her cheeks.

"No, girl," said Dunston, his deep voice soothing in the

darkness. "You did what you needed to do. You could not have saved her and what good would it have done for you to suffer her fate too?"

"Perhaps God kept you safe for a reason," said Aedwen.

"Truly?" asked Nothgyth, her tone pleading and desperate.

"Truly," replied Aedwen. Surely God and the Virgin must have some purpose in all this. To think otherwise was too much to contemplate. "We mean to find these men," she continued, "and see they are brought to justice. God must have spared you so that you can help us."

"Help you?" Nothgyth looked terrified. "How could I do that?"

"You can tell us all you know about them," said Dunston, leaning forward, so that his jutting beard shadowed his face from the firelight. His eyes shone in the gloom.

"I know nothing," she wailed. "I was hiding."

"Think, tell us all you heard. Did you hear any of their names?"

Nothgyth furrowed her brow and took another sip of milk. Slowly, she shook her head.

"I don't know. I just heard them shouting at my master. And then I heard them laughing while Wynflaed screamed." She shuddered.

"If I am able, Nothgyth," Dunston rumbled in the dark, "I will see these men killed for what they have done. Men who do such things do not deserve to live. Now," he reached over and gripped her arm. She flinched, but he held firm, looking directly into her eyes. "What can you tell us about who they were or what they were looking for."

And then, her eyes widened as a fresh memory came to her.

"I don't know who they are, but I know where they are going."

"Tell me," Dunston said, his voice cold and hard.

"They have gone after Ithamar."

Nineteen

Dunston forced himself to loosen his grip on Nothgyth's arm. The girl was frightened enough without her fearing him too.

"Who is Ithamar?" he asked.

"A monk," Nothgyth said, her tone implying that everybody knew who Ithamar was.

Dunston frowned.

"And what did these men want with a monk?"

"I don't know. One of them was shouting at my master over and over. They were both yelling, but I didn't really understand what they spoke of."

"What were they saying?" Dunston asked, willing his tone to remain calm.

Nothgyth took a sip from her cup of milk, lifting it to her lips with trembling hands.

"They were asking about the peddler."

Dunston glanced at Aedwen. Her eyes were shadowed, but she was staring intently at Nothgyth.

"What about the peddler?" Aedwen asked, her voice rasping in her throat.

"I couldn't hear. I don't know." Nothgyth hesitated and Dunston began to wonder whether they would learn anything of value from this poor, frightened girl. "It made no sense to me," she went on. "They just kept asking him how the peddler had known."

"Known?" said Dunston. "Known what?"

"I do not know," exclaimed Nothgyth. "I told you, it made no sense to me."

For a time they sat in silence, each thinking of what they had witnessed that day and of Nothgyth's tale of torture and murder. A log shifted on the embers and sparks drifted upwards to wink out amongst the rafters and the hanging meat.

After a time Aedwen spoke.

"And Beornmod told them that Ithamar was the one they sought?"

"I think he just wanted them to stop," Nothgyth hesitated, unsure now. "To stop what they were doing and he shouted that the monk had carried a message."

"A message?" Dunston asked.

But before Nothgyth could respond, Aedwen said, "I remember the monk. He too had stopped here at the hall for rest. He'd only meant to stay one night, but there was a sick traveller and Ithamar was tending to him. My father and the monk spoke together long into the night, after I had gone to sleep."

"That traveller died in the end," Nothgyth said, crossing herself. "We were all frightened it was the pestilence. The Lady had been terrified his illness would kill us all. She had me and Wynflaed burn all his belongings and Tilwulf and Frithstan buried him right out by the great elm in the top field. Far from the house." She sniffed. "It weren't the pestilence that got them in the end though. Goes to show."

Dunston thought on what the girl had said. Could it be that Ithamar and Lytelman had learnt some terrible secret from this sickly traveller?

Nothgyth was peering at Aedwen in the firelight.

"I remember you now," she said. "The Lady let you sleep with us in the back of the hall." And then her eyes widened. "Your father is the peddler they spoke of."

"That's right," said Aedwen. "He was."

"I thought this one was your father," said Nothgyth, nodding towards Dunston.

"No. My father's dead."

"Killed by the same men?"

"We think so," Aedwen said.

"But why?" asked Nothgyth.

"We do not know, child," said Dunston. "But we mean to find out. And when we do, we will make them pay." She was no fool this one, Dunston thought, and he could see her thoughts clearly on her face. First confusion, then inquisitiveness and then, finally, a sudden dawning fear.

"If they find that I am alive and I saw the things that happened here, they will return and slay me." She spoke in a matter-of-fact monotone. And there could be no arguing with the sense of her words.

"You must be gone from this place at first light," said Dunston. "And never speak of what you have seen here."

"But where will I go?"

"Do you have kin?" he asked.

Tears tumbled down her dirt-smeared face and she sniffed.

"These were my kin," she said, her voice desolate. "I have no others."

"Take what you can of value and head east. Make your way towards Witanceastre. The land is safer there and a clever girl like you will find a way."

Nothgyth stared at him, frowning in the ember glow of the fire. She swiped at the tears on her face with the back of her hands.

"And what of you?" she asked.

135

Dunston drained the ale from his cup and stood. His knee ached and his back was stiff. But he would walk around the settlement before he slept. He was sure the riders would not return and yet he could not shake the feeling that despite hunting these men, he too was their prey. Who would be first to bring their quarry to ground he could not tell. But of one thing he was sure. There would be more blood spilt before the end.

"We will continue with our quest to find the truth," he said.

"And how will you do that?"

"We must try and find this Ithamar before the others."

And with that he picked up his axe and stepped out into the cool darkness of the night, leaving the two grieving girls alone in the flickering firelight of the house.

Twenty

Aedwen was surprised that she slept so well. As she had lain in the quiet warmth of the hut the night before, her mind had thronged with the horrors she had seen. She had fought against sleep, fearing that her dreams would be filled with the swollen faces of the hanged men, the blood-streaked corpses of the bondsmen in the yard, the pale skin of the dead in the hall and the mutilated, butchered body of Beornmod. But worse than all of these fearful apparitions in her mind had been the sightless eyes of the girl in the storeroom, throat gaping like a hideous, monstrous, impossibly wide grin.

Aedwen had prayed to the Blessed Virgin for the girl's soul. And she had prayed for Nothgyth, that the girl would find a safe haven, far from all this tragedy. Somewhere she might find people she could call her kin once more. And, as Dunston had returned from his patrol of the steading, she had prayed for herself. She asked the Virgin that She might help them find her father's killers so that they would be able to avenge him and the poor people of Cantmael. Aedwen was not sure that the prayer was worthy of the Virgin, for surely the Mother of Christ would frown upon one of her own seeking vengeance instead of spreading love and forgiveness. But Aedwen could find no space in her heart for love. Her thoughts were dark and twisted, and so, she had thought, would be her dreams.

But she had dreamt of a warm summer's day. In her dream her mother, fit and hale and full of life, had embraced her and brushed her hair. Aedwen had awoken refreshed and relaxed. For a time she had lain silently with her eyes closed, clinging to the feeling of her mother's warmth against her. She could hear Dunston quietly rekindling the fire and moving about the house. But she did not wish to open her eyes, for when she did she knew that the world would be as it had been the day before, her mother would yet be dead, as would her father. And she was sure that her future would not be warm and full of light, but dark and filled with death.

The illusion of lying in her mother's embrace was shattered when Nothgyth, who had slept beside her and had wrapped her arms about her in the night, awoke and rose to her feet, coughing.

As much as Aedwen felt rested, so Dunston seemed all the more tired. The skin beneath his eyes was dark and bruised-looking and despite his broad shoulders and muscled arms, she thought his face looked slimmer, his cheekbones more pronounced.

He looked old.

Dunston had been up early and had already milked the cow, so they had fresh milk and the remainder of the bread and some cheese to break their fast.

"You must take the cow with you," Dunston said to Nothgyth. When she protested, saying she was no thief, he had raised up his hands and told her that without her to milk it the cow would grow ill. "You said the people here were your kin, or as good as." Nothgyth nodded. "So then," Dunston continued, "you are merely taking what your kin have left you. They would want you to do well with your life and I'm sure they would not want the cow to go un-milked and

abandoned. That animal has been well-loved and cared for."
Nothgyth acquiesced in the end and they waved her farewell
as she forlornly led the beast along the path back towards
Spercheforde.

Aedwen noted that the corpses no longer hung from the tree
in the yard. And the farmhand who had lain in the mud in a
pool of congealing blood was gone. It seemed that Dunston
had done more than merely tend to the cow that morning. He
said nothing of the dead and so Aedwen did not speak of them
either. But she was thankful that she did not have to face the
staring eyes of the corpses in the bright summer sun.

There were only the merest wisps of cloud in the eggshell blue
of the sky as they set off following the path to the southwest.
Dunston had picked up a few things from the house, stuffing
them into his hemp bag, and he had told Aedwen to fill a sack
with food from the house. From somewhere he had found a
good seax, complete with a tooled red leather scabbard, and
a belt, which he fastened around his waist. For Aedwen he
produced a small eating knife. It had a polished antler handle
and when she pulled it from its plain leather sheath, she saw
that the blade had been sharpened many times. It was a short
blade, but it was wickedly sharp and even though Aedwen
had no idea what she would do with it in a fight, wearing it
from her belt made her feel somehow safer.

When they had walked a short way from the steading
Dunston knelt over the path, gazing at the mud and grass that
grew there. After a long while he rose to his feet and set off
with a determined stride.

Aedwen trotted to keep up.

"What do you see in the ground?" she asked.

"The signs are confused," he said, a tinge of annoyance in
his tone. "The horses went this way, but I had hoped to be
able to see the sign of the monk. But I was unable to discern
anything for certain."

"Well, Nothgyth did say that Ithamar left two days ago," said Aedwen.

"And it has rained," he said. "It would be much to ask that I would find his tracks easily on such a busy path."

As they walked along the track, leaving the looming hill of Cantmael and Beornmod's hall behind them, Aedwen watched as Dunston continued to survey the ground. Sparrows and finches twittered in the bushes to their left and a crow flapped lazily overhead. Dunston glanced at the birds, nodding as if they too spoke to him, telling him what they saw from their lofty positions.

"How did you learn?" she asked.

"Learn?"

"To read the tracks of men and animals."

"My grandfather taught me first," he said. "And after him my father." They walked on for a time without speaking and when Aedwen looked at Dunston she saw a wistful glint in his eye. She supposed his grandfather and father must have died many years before. She wondered what it would be like for her as she grew old, when her parents would be nothing but a distant memory, half-forgotten ghosts that had at one time been her whole world.

Reaching the brow of a rise Dunston halted and lowered himself down onto his left knee with a grunt. His pale ice blue eyes were surrounded by wrinkled skin and yet they were clear and bright, showing no sign of age. They flickered as his gaze took in the hidden details strewn before him in the muck.

"There," he pointed to a twig that had been snapped and pressed into the soft earth of the track. "See," he said, "I'd wager that's Ithamar's print. A soft leather sole. See how the horse's hoof snapped the twig when the riders passed yesterday?" He touched the print softly, rubbing a pinch of soil between thumb and forefinger. "It is as the girl said. The monk is two days ahead of the riders. But he is on foot and he does not know he is being pursued. If he sticks to the path, or if they have a woodsman in their number, one who can read sign, they will run him to ground before we can reach them."

He heaved himself to his feet and set off once more.

"Much of what I have learnt, the forest has taught me," he said after a pause. "You can learn much if you watch and listen. With patience and time the woodland will give up its secrets. All learning comes from being patient and thinking what you can glean of use from what is around you."

"It is as though you can see things in the ground that nobody else can see," said Aedwen.

"Anyone can learn the things I know. Would you like to learn?"

"Would you teach me?"

After a brief hesitation, Dunston said, "I will if you would like. We cannot tarry if we mean to find these men, but I can tell you some things as we go. Would you like that?"

Aedwen thought for a moment. She tried to remember the last time her father had taught her anything of value. Nothing came to mind.

"Yes," she said. "I think I'd like that very much."

And so as they walked briskly southwest, Dunston began to point out things of interest. They passed a thicket of linden trees and he told her of how the bark could be used to fashion containers and the inner bark produced good string. Spotting a fallen beech just off the path, Dunston led her to the rotting wood and showed her where dark, smooth lumps of fungus grew. He collected some, telling her how the charcoal-like fungus could be used to hold an ember when lighting a fire. He pulled a tuft of straggly lichen from a branch, explaining that it would easily catch fire with the merest of sparks. He plucked leaves from a sorrel and nibbled at them.

"These are good eating at this time of year," he said, passing a handful of the leaves to her.

She sniffed them. They smelt green and fresh.

"Go on," he said. "Try one."

Taking a deep breath, she bit off part of the leaf and chewed. It tasted sharp and sour, but pleasant and refreshing. She smiled.

Every now and then, when tracks joined the path they followed, Dunston paused and checked for sign of the monk and his hunters. But now, instead of silently scanning the ground, he explained to Aedwen what he saw. The depth of a print. The tiny prints of insects, rodents or birds could show the age of the impressions in the earth left by man and horse. There were many details that later she could not remember, but in this way, the long tiring day passed quickly and she had little time to dwell on the evil that had been done to her father and to the people of Cantmael.

During the morning they saw nobody save for some shepherds, glimpsed through a stand of hazel far in the distance on the slope of a hill. But sometime after midday the track they followed joined a larger road that ran north and south. The sky was clear, the day was warm and it seemed that many had decided to take advantage of the fair weather to travel and so in the afternoon, they crossed the path of drovers, shepherds and several individuals walking about their business that took them onto the roads of Wessex. They even passed a waggon that was escorted by four mounted warriors in byrnies of iron. The cart was well appointed, covered with a frame from which hung patterned curtains. Aedwen imagined it must have carried a noble woman, hidden behind the fine drapes. She was desperate to know the identity of the lady who rode within the covered waggon, but Dunston hushed her and pushed her into the long grass and nettles that grew in a tangle on the verge. The nettles stung Aedwen's legs and she rubbed at the rash as they carried on their way.

Dunston grew tense and taciturn with each traveller they passed.

"I don't like it," he grumbled. "Too many people have seen us. We are not a pair to be easily forgotten. And travellers talk."

For a while she did not reply. Her legs itched and she scratched at them, until he plucked a large dock leaf and handed it to her.

"Rub this on where it stings," he said. "It will help."

She did as he said.

He was right, of course. They would be remembered. The young girl accompanied by the hulking brute of a man with a bushy greying beard, a great battle-axe resting on his shoulder. As if he was not memorable enough, the iron head of his axe, embellished with whorls and symbols in silver inlay, certainly drew attention as it glinted in the afternoon sunlight.

"At least there is something good that comes of being on this road," she said with a grin. Her legs were feeling better already.

"And what is that?" he growled.

"We can travel faster."

"And how do you propose we do that?" he said, frowning. "Unless I'm not mistaken, our legs have not grown since this morning. And I do not believe either of us are ready to run."

She chuckled.

"No, that is true. But we can still move more quickly."

"How?"

"By not needing to stop to look for sign," she said. And then, when she saw the blank look on his face, she continued: "We can ask the people on the road whether they have seen a group of riders. They may even have seen Ithamar, if they have been travelling for a few days."

For a moment, Dunston did not reply and then he smirked, his smile twisted behind his beard.

"I am glad you have been paying attention to my teaching," he said.

"But you have been telling me about tracks, fungus and eating leaves."

"Yes, that is so. But the most important lesson of all was the first one I taught you this morning. That you can always learn new ways of doing things, if you listen and pay attention to what is around you."

Twenty-One

During the rest of that long warm day, they did as Aedwen had suggested and spoke to some of the travellers they passed. One man, who was leading a heavily laden cart drawn by two oxen, seemed pleased at the chance to stop and talk. He was accompanied by two thickset men who looked like brothers, or maybe cousins. They both had the same small piggy eyes and massive shoulders almost as broad as the oxen. Each of them carried a stout cudgel and Dunston thought they would be deterrent enough against all but the most determined brigands. When the carter halted, the two guards slumped into the grass at the edge of the path. They said nothing, but their gaze did not waver from Aedwen and Dunston.

The carter offered Dunston a drink of ale from a costrel which he took from the bed of the cart. He didn't offer any to his escorts, who just glowered from the shade of the verge. It was good ale, fresh and cool and despite his reservations about being seen on the road, Dunston found he trusted the carter implicitly. Unlike the cudgel-bearing louts, the man had an open face, a quick smile and guileless eyes.

He was taking a load of salt and smoked fish to Bathum and had been on the road for two days already. When asked whether he'd seen a large group of riders he answered immediately.

"I saw the king himself riding out to hunt with his nobles. A fine sight it was, all those horses trotting high-hoofed in the sunlight." He looked wistful at the memory. "Like something out of a song."

"The king, you say?" Dunston asked. "When was this?"

"That was on the morning I left Exanceaster. The king arrived a week ago with so many hearth warriors and thegns, they must have eaten all the meat in the city by now. Perhaps that's why they went hunting." He laughed.

"Have you seen any other riders more recently? A band of them?"

The carter took back the costrel from Dunston with a nod.

"Oh yes," he said, taking a draught of the ale. "A group of horsemen galloped past and I called out to them. Asked them whither they were headed in such a hurry. I didn't really expect a reply. They looked a rough sort, if you know what I mean. But the last one shouted out to me as he passed. He looked even more vicious than the rest. I'll never forget what he said."

"What was that?"

"He said, 'Just be thankful we're not looking for you.' Then he laughed. It sent a chill right through me, I can tell you. I pity whoever it is they are after. They looked fit to murder someone."

Dunston didn't tell the carter how right he was. Instead he asked him about the men.

"I can't tell you much," he answered, lifting the cap he wore and scratching beneath it at his sweaty hair. "They were driving those horses fast and they were past us in a flash." He thought for a moment and took a swig of ale. "All I can remember really is that they carried spears and I'm sure at least a couple of them had swords. I wondered whether the fyrd had been called, I've heard nothing. Have you?"

Dunston told the man he did not believe that the levies had been called to arms.

"May God be praised," the carter said finally, pushing the stopper into the mouth of his flask. "I was worried that perhaps the heathens had attacked again." The man crossed himself then and the talk of Norsemen had spoilt his good humour. "Well," he said, "Godspeed to you and your granddaughter. I'd best be getting on my way. Come along, you two."

Grumbling, his guards climbed to their feet.

As the red-faced carter goaded his oxen forward once more Dunston called after him.

"Have you seen by chance a monk travelling south on the road?"

"A monk?" the man replied. "No, I can't say that I have. Good day to you both now."

Dunston pondered over the information the carter had given them as they had walked southward.

"Perhaps Ithamar has already reached his destination," Aedwen said.

"Perhaps."

They trudged on through the heat of the afternoon. When they passed settlements and steadings Dunston could see the longing for rest in Aedwen's eyes. But he felt too exposed to stop. It was too dangerous and so they pressed on, hurrying past hamlets and thorpes that Dunston did not recognise. He had seldom travelled this way before and he'd been alone in his forest home for many years.

They had just left a small settlement behind them and Dunston could sense the reproach from Aedwen. The sun was lowering in the sky and by not seeking shelter at the farm, he had consigned them to another night in the forest.

"Where do you think Ithamar is?" Aedwen asked suddenly.

Dunston sighed, wiping sweat from his brow.

"If nobody has seen him on the road, I don't know."

"Can't you track him?" she asked.

He snorted.

"I can read sign better than most," he said. "But I'm not a miracle worker. Ithamar is two days ahead of us and this road is too well-travelled to find tracks. No, unless we find something to lead us to him, all I can think of is to continue following the horsemen." Even as he said the words the idea sounded mad to him. Five armed warriors on horseback. Even if he was able to catch up with them, what then? What good could come of catching this mounted, murderous quarry?

They walked on without speaking. Dunston brooded. This was madness. If only he had never found Lytelman. He could have been sitting back in his hut, resting after a day of forging or hunting, Odin sleeping at his feet. Now Odin was gone and as likely as not he would be dead soon too. He glanced at Aedwen and for a moment, the shape of her nose, the sunlight picking out the delicate sweep of her eyelashes, reminded him of Eawynn when they had first met all those summers ago. She had been not much older than Aedwen he realised with a start. He sighed. God's teeth, he had been young then too. How quickly the years washed by, sweeping away loved ones and youth and leaving only fading memories.

He shook his head and cursed silently at his own foolishness. Not because of the course they now followed, but at his dwelling on the past and bemoaning his decisions. There was no changing the past, just as there was no holding back the water in a raging river.

The path sloped down into a shaded vale. Alders encroached on the road to either side and it seemed as though a mist hung in the still air. There was nobody on the road now. Nobody apart from the two of them. Anyone with any sense had already sought shelter for the night or had made camp, he thought, with a rueful smile. They should get off the road and find a place to make a fire. He looked up at the sky and the shreds of cloud that floated high, tinged with the pink of sunset. It looked to be a clear night, it would be cold, but they had brought blankets and cloaks from Beornmod's hall, so they should be comfortable enough.

They entered the shadows beneath the alders and Dunston wondered about the mist. Could it be so cold down here? Perhaps there was a stream running through the woodland. Mist often formed over cool water, though not on sunny afternoons. He frowned and sniffed the air.

His mouth slowly stretched into a grin. By the rood and all the saints, he must be tired not to have realised what it was that he saw in the valley.

"What is it?" asked Aedwen.

"If my nose does not deceive me, we will not be cold this night and we will not camp alone."

Aedwen lifted her head and scented the hazy air.

"Smoke? Do you think it is safe for us to camp with other travellers?"

"That is smoke," he replied, with a broad smile. "But not from a traveller's campfire. Now, there should be a path somewhere into the wood. Come. Quickly, before it is too dark."

He led her on at a faster pace. The gloom under the trees grew thicker, as did the haze of smoke. It drifted across the road in a fug.

"Here," Dunston said at last, peering down at the ground and looking at the tracks in the mud where a path led off from the road into the shadows of the forest. He stood, with a slight frown on his face. Could that print of a soft leather shoe be from the same wearer as the track he had seen at Cantmael? Possibly. But it was getting dark and he could not be sure. He stepped over the muddy patch.

"Careful," he said, "don't step there."

"Where are we going?" asked Aedwen.

"Quiet now," he said, holding a finger to his lips. He held DeaÞangenga before him, just in case he was wrong. "Stay behind me," he whispered. "And with luck we will soon enough have warmth and company for the night."

He saw her questioning look in the gathering dark, but chose to say no more. He turned and walked silently into the woods, towards the source of the billowing smoke that now stung their eyes, and filled their throats.

Twenty-Two

Aedwen followed Dunston further into the forest. The boles of the trees loomed in the smoke-hazed darkness like giants. She hardly dared to breathe as she walked behind the old man. He moved without a sound, like a wraith flitting through mist. Despite her youth and slender form, she felt clumsy. With each step she snapped a branch or her cloak snagged on a bramble.

It was dark under the trees, and a feeling of dread seeped into her as they crept stealthily away from the road. If only at that last steading they'd passed they had asked the goodwife for some food and a warm place to sleep for the night. The portly woman had been friendly and had waved to Aedwen as they passed. She had been taking in the clothes she had left to dry on the bushes outside her neat, thatched house. Aedwen thought they could have been cosy by her hearth for the night. But no, Dunston had made them carry on and now it was dusk and they were deep in the forest, surrounded by smoke. She had no idea where it came from. For a moment, she thought of a great wyrm, coiled and waiting in a forest glade, breathing out acrid clouds of smoke, its feral eyes gleaming in the darkness as it lay in wait for its prey to come to him, lured from the road with promises of warmth and shelter.

A sound came to her then. A strange sound, that for a time, she could not fathom. A lilting warble accompanied by a rumbling thrum. The noise rose and fell and seemed to echo all about them, as if it emanated from the very smoke itself.

Dunston had almost been swallowed up by the haze and the gloom and with a start she realised she had stopped walking. Quickly, she sped after him, uncaring now whether she made a noise or not. The thought of being alone and lost in this smoky darkness, surrounded by the eerie music, filled her with terror.

Music.

Yes, that is what it was. She suddenly understood the sounds, and all at once she could hear more than one voice. And there were words too. Words of love and loss. She caught up with Dunston. He turned to her with a grin.

"Listen," he whispered.

They stood still and silent there in the forest and listened to the song. She did not recognise the melody, but it was achingly beautiful, as if the forest itself was singing of its loneliness. There were deep, bass tones, and higher counterpoints, but against it all, there was the throb of a chanted song of lovers, destined to be ever apart and only united in death.

When the singing ended, she found her face was wet with tears. Dunston cuffed at his cheeks, and placed a hand on her shoulder, leading her forward. It was almost full dark now, but she fancied she could make out a glow between the trees ahead.

"Hail, the camp," said Dunston in a low voice.

After a brief moment of silence, a voice came to them.

"Who goes there?"

"Friends," replied Dunston. "Just me and my grand-daughter." Aedwen glanced at him, but he did not return her gaze. "We heard your singing. One of my favourites. I have always loved the lay of Eowa and Cyneburg. We seek shelter for the night."

"Not many know our songs or would spend time with us," replied the voice. "What is your name?"

"My name is Dunston, son of Wilnoth."

Whispers in the darkness.

"Approach," said the voice.

They walked towards the glow. As they stepped from the forest path into a wide, open glade, Aedwen saw that the light came from a small fire, upon which hung a metal pot from a wooden tripod. The fire was much too small to have created all this smoke. Around the fire were several figures. Beyond them were five huge shadowy mounds and for a fleeting instant she thought again of the great coiled dragon lurking, awaiting its prey. Perhaps the creatures around the fire were the dragon's servants. Nihtgengas, night-walkers, for surely they could not be men.

They were black-garbed and black-skinned. Their eyes and teeth flashed bright in the dark. She shuddered, a terrible fear gripping her. What were these beasts? Why had Dunston brought her here? Was he in league with these goblins of the forest?

Dunston stepped forward and offered his hand to the nearest of the dark-skinned creatures, who was standing before the fire. His teeth showed as he smiled and gripped Dunston's forearm in the warrior grip.

The firelight fell on the goblin's smiling features and, in an instant, she felt her face flush at her own stupidity. These were no monsters. They were but men, blackened and grimed with soot and ash. The glade was thick with smoke that oozed from the mounds and she finally understood. These men were charcoal burners, outcasts from the world. They lived together, in their hot, smoke-filled world, tending the charcoal piles. Charcoal burners had the reputation of being devils, stinking of smoke and living surrounded by fire, as if in their own personal hell on earth. She had never seen any charcoal men before, and she felt trepidation at being here at night, surrounded by them.

But Dunston was smiling and slapping the man on the back.

"You are well come to our glade," the black-smeared man was saying. "We have cheese and we have ham."

"Smoked!" shouted one of the others, receiving a roar of laughter from all of the men. Aedwen could not believe this was the first time they had made this jest, but they laughed uproariously and she could not help but chuckle too, feeling the tension draining from her.

"We don't get many visitors here," the leader of the charcoal burners continued, "and then we have two in as many days. If this continues, we will have to send someone in search of more food."

"Or start charging for the pleasure of sleeping here!" shouted the jester, again receiving riotous guffaws in response.

"We share our camp and our food freely, Dearlaf," said the leader, with a scowl of reproach. "Come, sit with us, and tell us your tale. We are ever hungry for tidings of the world."

"We thank you," said Dunston. "We carry a small amount of provender and will gladly share what we have. Tidings too."

The men shuffled apart, making space for them by the fire and Aedwen sat beside Dunston. Grubby hands passed them food and a cup was thrust into her grasp. She sniffed at the liquid, but could smell nothing over the all-pervading stench of charcoal smoke. She drank and found it to be ale, bitter, and with an unsurprisingly smoky flavour. It was good.

After they had eaten some of the offered food, Dunston said, "You said you had a visitor a couple of days ago? That wouldn't have been a monk, by any chance, would it?"

The leader of the charcoal burners, whose name was Smoca, gaped at Dunston, eyes wide and bright.

"How did you know? And how is it you know of our songs and are unafraid to sit, eat and drink with us?"

Smoca was wary now, as though he was afraid he had allowed a predator into a flock of sheep.

Dunston swallowed a mouthful of the smoked cheese. Aedwen had thought the charcoal man to be jesting about all the food being smoked, but it seemed he had been in earnest.

"Those are two different questions," Dunston said, after he had washed the food down with a mouthful of ale. "In answer to the second question, I have often spent time with the charcoal men in Sealhwudu, where I live to the north of here. They have ever been kind and have never seemed like devils to me." He gave a wry smile. "I know many consider you less than them, as you are blackened by your fires, but I know that beneath the soot you are but men. And I need what you produce for my work."

"You are a smith?"

"I have a forge, yes. I produce blades and tools for the folk around Briuuetone."

Smoca nodded at Dunston's rune-decorated axe, where it rested on the earth by his right hand. The firelight glimmered on the silver threads that ran through its head.

"Your work?" he asked.

"Alas, no," replied Dunston. "I took her from the dead hand of a Norse warrior."

"So you are a warrior, as well as a smith?"

"I was, once."

"What do the carvings mean?" Smoca asked, gazing in wonder at the intricate runes and sigils on the haft.

Dunston shrugged.

"I do not know and I didn't think to ask the original owner before I sent him on his way." He lifted the axe and Smoca tensed. Dunston smiled and patted the weapon. "I cannot read the runes, but I named this beauty, DeaÞangenga."

Smoca swallowed. His eyes never left the blade as Dunston turned it to catch the flickering light.

"An apt name," the charcoal burner said. "I am sure death never walks far from that axe."

One of the other charcoal burners, a cadaverous man with a bald head and skin as wrinkled and tough-looking as leather, leaned forward, peering at Dunston through the dancing flames of the fire.

"Are you *the* Dunston? The one they called 'The Bold'?"

"I have been called that," Dunston replied, with a sigh. "Long ago."

"You don't look so bold now," said one of the other men. He was much stockier than the rest, and younger. He was the loud one who seemed always quick to jest. This time none of the men laughed.

But Dunston let out a bark of laughter.

"No, I don't suppose I do," he said. "If I am honest, I am not sure I ever truly warranted the name. But once a name is given to you, it often sticks and is impossible to shake off."

"How did you come by it?" the jester asked.

"Ah, that is a long story. Perhaps I will tell it later."

The young charcoal burner looked set to press Dunston for an answer, but the old man glowered at him, his eyes shining from beneath his heavy brows and the man clamped his mouth shut.

For an awkward moment, they all stared into the fire. One of the men leaned forward and added a log to the embers. Another coughed. Out in the forest, a vixen shrieked.

"You knew our song. You must have spent a lot of time with our kind to hear them sing."

"Yes, I have spent many nights over the years with them. I consider them my friends." He fell silent and took another sip of ale. Aedwen thought he would offer no more about his time with the charcoal burners when he said in a quiet voice, "I owe them much. They gave me my best friend."

"Your best friend is one of us?" asked Smoca.

"No," replied Dunston, offering the man a sad smile. "He is – no – was, a hound. I called him Odin." A couple of the men crossed themselves and Aedwen thought it strange that people thought of these men as heathen devils.

"Odin?"

"He only had one eye, you see. Like the god of the Norsemen. He was the runt of a litter, a tiny thing. Somehow he had scratched one of his eyes and it had grown putrid, full of pus. His mother had left him to die. And he would have done, had it not been for the charcoal men. They nursed him and tended to his eye. One of them walked for a day to my hut to ask for milk from my goat." He smiled at the memory. "By God, we all loved that pup. We fed him milk from the corner of a cloth dipped in the fresh milk. He was so small, we never thought he would live, but there was something about him, a look in his good eye. We just refused to let him die. And in a few days he began to put on weight and grow strong. When I eventually made my way back home, he followed me." Dunston held out his cup and one of the men filled it with ale. "I hadn't known it, but I was lonely, and Odin made a wonderful companion. He grew strong and spirited. A great hunter and a faithful friend."

Dunston fell silent, gazing into the flames as he drank from his cup.

"He sounds like a worthy companion for Dunston the Bold," said the jester, his tone now reverential.

Aedwen thought of the rangy one-eyed hound, and could scarcely believe he had once been a sickly puppy. Looking at the taciturn, gruff old man who had led her southward these last days, she also found it difficult to imagine him tending to a defenceless animal. And yet, had he not done the same with her? Like Odin, she had been alone and in need of succour. It seemed that Dunston, beneath his hard shell, would not turn away from a lost orphan.

"He was the best of dogs," she blurted out, surprised that she had spoken. The black faces of the gathered men turned to her. "He tried to protect me, but was cut down by a bad man."

"Which brings me to the answer to your other question," said Dunston, not waiting for a response to Aedwen's comment.

"The monk who stayed with us killed your dog?" asked Smoca.

"No, but we believe he is being pursued by the same men who struck down Odin."

"Why?"

"He has information that they seek."

"What information."

"We do not know."

"And you are looking for him too?"

"We are. This girl's father was slain in order to keep secret what this monk knows. They tortured and killed the inhabitants of Beornmod's steading to find out where her father had learnt of the tidings that got him killed." Smoca was clearly shocked by these tidings of murder. His mouth hung agape for a moment. He seemed poised to ask something, but Dunston did not pause. "They found that the monk, Ithamar, carried a message." He held up his hand to halt the query on Smoca's lips. "We do not know to whom, or what the message says, but we are sure they mean to hunt him and slay him. We hope to find him first, if we are able."

Smoca drew in a deep breath and pondered Dunston's words for a long time. A log popped in the fire. The vixen called again in the night. Aedwen tried to hear Dunston's words as they would sound to these men. It was hard to make sense of what had happened. Would they believe him? There were so many uncertainties in his story. And yet he spoke with conviction.

"How did you know the monk had sheltered with us?" Smoca said at last.

"I saw the print of his shoe on the path that led from the road."

Smoca nodded.

"A smith, a warrior and a woodsman," he said, raising his eyebrows. "And you say these killers are on his trail? How far ahead of you are they? We have seen nobody else since Ithamar came to us."

"We are a day behind them, but we are on foot, they have mounts." Dunston thought for a moment, running his thick fingers over his beard. "If Ithamar was here, and you have not seen his pursuers, all I can think is that they missed his tracks turning off the road. It was only by chance that I noticed the print of his foot, and from horseback, it would be easy to miss the path to your encampment."

Smoca nodded thoughtfully.

"Ithamar was scared of being seen on the road, busy as it is. We just thought it was because he travelled alone and was fearful of brigands and robbers. There are wolf-heads that will even stoop to attacking a man of the cloth."

"When a man has nothing to lose, he is as dangerous as a savage animal," said Dunston, his face grim. Aedwen wondered if he was referring to himself or to the brigands who preyed on travellers.

Something in Dunston's tone made Smoca hesitate.

"How do we know you do not mean the monk harm?" he said. "Perhaps he was running from you. He was good to us. Puttoc had a carbuncle and Ithamar lanced it for him and prayed over him. He prayed with all of us." He squinted at Dunston, trying to weigh him up.

"I can offer you no more than my word that we mean him no harm," Dunston said. "But the word of Dunston the Bold has never been doubted before."

Smoca met his gaze for several heartbeats, before finally nodding.

"Anyone who knows the song of Eowa and Cyneburg and breaks bread with charcoalers cannot be too bad. If you are right about the riders that hunt for Ithamar, and they have lost his trail on the road, they must have ridden for Exanceaster."

"Yes," said Dunston. "That seems most likely."

"But," said Smoca, with a glimmer in his eyes, "we know that he was not headed towards Exanceaster."

Dunston leaned forward eagerly.

"Where was he going?" he asked.

"He was making his way to Tantun."

"But this road leads to Exanceaster."

"That it surely does," said Smoca with a grin. "But we set him right. We put him on a path that leads through the woods. It joins a road to Tantun not far from here. If he has walked fast, he might be there already."

"Do you know why he was heading for Tantun?"

"As a matter of fact, I do. He said he wished to see the priest there. Come to think of it, he said he had a message for him."

Aedwen wondered whether the Blessed Virgin had heard her prayers. To bring them to this glade and now to be put on the trail of the monk, the Mother of Christ must be smiling upon them.

"Will you show us the path to Tantun?" asked Dunston.

"In the morning, I will take you there myself," said Smoca. "But first, rest. You look like you could use the sleep. One of us is awake all the night watching that the mounds burn well. No harm will befall you."

Dunston gave the man his thanks, and rolled up in his cloak and a blanket beside the fire and was soon snoring.

Aedwen lay down beside him and stared into the coruscating embers. Dunston seemed to trust these soot-smeared men, but she could not shake the lingering terror that the forest was the home of a sleeping dragon, the charcoal men its servants and she and Dunston its prey.

For a long while she fought against sleep, despite the tiredness of her limbs and mind. A light breeze whispered through the forest. A night bird screeched in the distance. And then, all around her, the black-faced men began to sing again, softly this time, their voices calming and achingly beautiful in the smoke-filled darkness. The melody washed over her, soothing her, allaying her fears, and soon, her eyelids drooped and closed.

Twenty-Three

Dunston awoke with the first lightening of the sky. The air of the clearing was hazed with the smoke that oozed and drifted from the mounds. Beside him, Aedwen slept, her childlike face soft and peaceful.

Pushing himself to his feet, he stretched. His back popped like a pine cone thrown onto a fire and his knee was stiff as he straightened it. But he felt rested and when Smoca offered him a cup of water, he took it gratefully with a muttered word of thanks. He swilled some of the cool liquid around his mouth and spat into the long grass that grew at the edge of the clearing. His mouth was dry and tasted of ash and woodsmoke. The flavour reminded him acutely of the time he had spent with the charcoal burners near his home when Odin had been a tiny pup. He looked down at Aedwen, half-expecting to see the hound stretched out beside her. He snorted at his foolish sentimentality.

The girl stirred and looked up at him with a smile. Dunston grunted and walked away from the charcoal mounds to piss.

He was glad his instinct about the charcoal men had proven to be accurate. The truth was he had been too tired to stay awake. They had been on the run now for three days and when they had sat beside the fire the night before he had been exhausted.

But now he felt rested and, despite the aches of his ageing body, he was ready to recommence the hunt. He allowed himself a small moment of hope. It appeared they had stumbled upon Ithamar's path, while the horsemen had carried on towards Exanceaster. With some luck, it was possible they might even find the monk before the hunters did. Perhaps then, they would be able to discover once and for all, why so many people had been killed. What could be so valuable?

He wondered what they would do if they found the monk, but then dismissed the idea. There was no point in thinking so far ahead. First they must find the man, and then they could decide on their next move.

They ate a few mouthfuls of fresh oatcakes that had been cooked on a griddle by the campfire. Like all the food the charcoal men gave them, these too tasted of smoke, but they were warm and wholesome.

Aedwen walked about the clearing, studying the charcoal piles and even asking the men about their work. She seemed much more animated than the previous night. There was colour in her cheeks and her eyes were bright. Dunston was pleased.

He picked up his scant belongings, calling out to her to do the same.

Smoca was waiting to lead them to the path that Ithamar had taken. Dunston thanked all the men for their hospitality and promised he would return one day, if he could, in better times. The charcoal burners nodded back at them, faces dark and serious, as they followed Smoca out of the smoke-thick camp.

He led them through dense forest, past hazel, ash and beech. The foliage was so snarled and the path so infrequently travelled that Dunston did not believe he would have found it on his own. But after a time, he began to notice signs of Ithamar's passing. Broken twigs, a scratch on the bark of a wych-elm, a print in the soft loam of a hollow were rainwater had puddled. He recognised the shape and weight of the tread and paused a moment to point out the sign to Aedwen.

She was a good student and he'd discovered that he enjoyed imparting his knowledge to her. He recalled words that his grandfather and father had spoken to him and he heard his own voice echoing theirs all these years later. It was as if they talked through him and he wondered whether their spirits were somehow present in this forest, in the dappled shade beneath the canopy of linden and oak.

They picked their way along the overgrown path until quite suddenly, as Smoca led them past a dense tangled mass of brambles, they came out onto a more clearly defined path. It was by no means a main thoroughfare. The trees and shrubs that lined its verges were packed close and grew tall and overhanging in places. The ground was bare earth. Dotted along the track were knotted roots that, along with the low branches of some of the trees that encroached on the path, would make it difficult for anyone attempting to travel the path on horseback.

"So this leads all the way to Tantun?" he asked, signalling to their left, westward.

"It comes out onto the road from Exanceaster," replied Smoca. "You'll be able to see Tantun's church tower from there."

"How far?"

Smoca thought for a moment.

"The best part of two days walking," he said, gazing up at the clear blue sky through the gaps in the boughs that stretched over the track. "But the weather looks set to hold fair. You two take care."

"We will," Dunston replied, clapping the man on the shoulder. "And thank you."

Smoca nodded in acknowledgement, but did not reply. He turned and made his way back into the thicket, disappearing quickly from view. For a moment, they listened to him retreating through the woodland, and then they were alone once more, the only sounds the wind rustling through the leaves and the twitter of the birds.

Dunston dropped to one knee and was pleased when Aedwen did the same without comment. Together they surveyed the earth of the track.

"There," said Aedwen, pointing to a small indentation in a soft, shadowed portion of the path. "Is that Ithamar's tread?"

Dunston moved closer with a grunt as his knee made an audible cracking sound. He peered at the soil for a moment.

"Good," he said, forcing himself to smile for the girl's benefit, despite his misgivings about their quest. "You have a good eye. It is as Smoca told us. Ithamar passed this way a couple of days ago."

They set out westward, pausing only occasionally when one of them noted a print of interest in the earth. Aedwen was growing in confidence and had a keen eye for the details that most people would miss. When they stopped at a stream to refill their skins, she found the tracks and spoor of deer and boar.

"Are they fresh?" she asked, taking a sip of water. The day was warm, even under the shade of the trees and Dunston could feel sweat trickling down his back. He wiped his forehead with the back of his hand.

"Three deer and a family of boar all stopped to drink here this morning," he said.

Aedwen grinned, clearly pleased with herself. He returned her smile. He remembered how excited he had been when he had first begun to understand the sign left by the forest's animal denizens.

A little later, Aedwen called him over to inspect another set of prints in the mud.

"Are these from a dog?" she asked. There was a catch in her voice and he knew she was thinking of Odin. He was touched by her tenderness. Placing a hand on her shoulder, he glanced at the marks in the earth.

"No," he said, straightening his back, "these are not from any dog."

"What are they then?"

"These are from the paws of wolves." He saw her eyes widen. "Don't be afraid," he said. "They will not bother us." But he thought of the deer and the boar that roamed the forest, and pictured the pack of wolves that stalked them. And his mind turned to the men who pursued Ithamar. They were also after him and the girl and now those killers were behind them. As they walked on through the dappled light of that clammy afternoon, Dunston could not shake the feeling that they had become prey to a hunting pack of wolves that slathered and bayed at their heels.

They saw no other people throughout that long day, and it was plain from his footprints that Ithamar had continued following the path that Smoca had set him upon. They found an area of flattened grass, some crumbs of dark bread and a thin rind from a slice of cheese, where the monk had sat and eaten.

They were making good progress and Dunston could imagine the monk walking the path before them at a more leisurely pace. His confidence grew that they might be able to close with him even before he reached Tantun.

And then, as they were passing a huge oak with a twisted trunk, Dunston held up a hand for Aedwen to halt.

"What?" she asked. He hushed her with a sharp hiss and a cutting gesture with his hand.

The hair on the back of his neck prickled. What had unnerved him? He could hear nothing untoward. He sniffed the air. It was rich with leaf mould and loam, but there was no hint of smoke. He knew not what had unsettled him, but Dunston had lived for too long in the forest not to pay heed to his intuition. Grabbing Aedwen by the arm, he pulled her away from the track and dragged her behind the massive, gnarled bole of the oak.

"What is it?" she hissed.

He did not reply, but held a finger to his lips.

He strained to hear anything out of the ordinary. The murmur of the wind, high in the leafy canopy. The chatter of magpies someway off. Then the sudden, panicked flapping of a flock of wood pigeons, flying up from their roosts into the cloud-flecked sky.

A heartbeat later, the first of the horsemen rounded the corner on the path. Dunston pushed Aedwen against the rough bark of the oak. He did not risk looking, instead he listened carefully. They came from the east and were leading their horses.

"Are you sure this is the way?" one said, his voice tired and irritable.

"Do you really think he would have lied to me?" answered another, tone harsh, an edge of cruel laughter tinging his words.

The first man did not answer. Dunston counted the horses passing until five horsemen had led their mounts past the oak. Dunston stared into Aedwen's eyes and saw terror there. He could hear his blood rushing in his ears and his right hand gripped DeaÞangenga's haft so tightly that his knuckles ached.

Off to the west, the lead rider called out.

"The path opens out here. We can ride for a while."

Sounds of men climbing into saddles. The creak of leather and the jingle of harness. Then the thrum of hoof beats on the soft earth of the track, as the men cantered into the west towards the lowering sun that slanted through the limbs of the forest.

Twenty-Four

Aedwen could not be certain, but she thought she recognised the voice of one of the horsemen as that of Raegnold, the tall man who had taken her to Gytha's house. The man who had stabbed Odin and then attacked them as they were escaping from Briuuetone.

His voice was muffled and muted, the injury he'd suffered at Dunston's hands evidently making speech difficult. But the sound of his voice had filled her with dread, bringing back the terrible sadness she had felt at seeing Dunston's dog hurt, the bleak terror of witnessing Dunston, the man who had led her safely from the forest, locked up. And, even though she had not heard Raegnold's voice before that evening in Briuuetone, somehow, the sound of it sent her mind reeling back to that morning in the forest when she had lost her father. When she had sprinted blindly into the woods, fleeing from his attackers and his screams.

Perhaps, she wondered, as Dunston led her back to the path, she had heard his voice amongst her father's screams for mercy. Maybe there was something in his tone that her memory was able to latch on to. Whether she had heard him or not all those days ago, there was no doubt now in her mind that he had been there when her father was killed. Her rage at the thought threatened to consume her. Her fear of the man and the rest of Hunfrith's men turned her stomach. Oh, that she were a man! That she could take up a weapon and strike down these monsters who had caused so much misery.

Looking down at the earth, she could easily make out the five sets of horse's hooves and the heavy, booted feet of the five riders who had been walking beside their steeds. Dunston touched her arm and she flinched.

"They are gone," he said. "They are not aware we are on their trail. They are solely focused on Ithamar."

"What will…" she had been about to ask what they would do to him when they caught up with the monk, but bit back the question. It was foolish. She knew all too well what lay in store for him if the horsemen ran him to ground. "What are we to do?" she asked instead.

"They are ahead of us now, so we must be wary. But they are travelling quickly, and I doubt they will suspect anyone is following them. Perhaps in their haste they will miss Ithamar. Or maybe he has already reached the priest and delivered his message. If he has, they will be able to do nothing to prevent it. I say we press on." He lifted his axe so that the sunlight caught its sharp edge. "With caution."

Aedwen took a slow calming breath and nodded. Her hands were shaking, but she grasped the staff Dunston had given her and set off in the wake of the riders.

They walked on in silence with none of the relaxed companionship they had enjoyed earlier that day. They were wary now, uninterested in the tracks of animals. All they cared about was that they were on the correct path and that they did not stumble upon Hunfrith's men.

The sun was low, glaring in sudden flashes from between the trees, when Aedwen saw the track. She might not have noticed it, if not for the angle of the sunlight. All that afternoon they had followed the fresh, deep prints of the horses, and there had been no other sign to follow. Any impression Ithamar's light tread might have made in the earth was trampled and obliterated by the passing of the five horsemen.

But just as they reached the top of a steep incline, where a lightning-shattered elm stood, she saw a strange shadow in the corner of her vision.

"Dunston," she whispered, still afraid to speak out loud, lest the horsemen might hear. She knew it was foolish, as they were surely far away by now, but fear had gripped her since the men had passed them. The old man halted and returned to her. "Is that Ithamar's print?" she asked, pointing at the slightest of marks in the mud.

Dunston squinted at the ground and then whistled quietly.

"You will be a better tracker than I soon enough," he said with a twisted smile. "The lowness of the sun has cast a shadow in it. I doubt either one of us would have noticed this at any other time." She wondered at that, and thought fleetingly again about the Blessed Virgin and her prayers.

"Look there," Dunston said, pointing at something on the elm. He plucked at the splintered trunk and showed her a thin thread. She took it and held it up to the light. Wool. And it was dark, like a monk's habit.

"It looks as though our friend left the path here," Dunston said, the thrill of the chase colouring his tone with excitement. "Let us see what he was about."

They followed the monk's tracks to a clearing some way from the path, but still within sight of the lightning-felled tree. Away from the churned mud of the track it was much easier to see where Ithamar had been. The snakeweed that grew thick on the floor of the glade had been crushed by his feet. Most of the leaves had sprung back, but his path was still clear to Aedwen, now that she had trained her eyes to look for any sign of disturbance on the ground.

Dunston cast about the clearing.

"Look, here," he said. "Ithamar did not leave this glade and go further into the forest. He retraced his steps back to the path."

Aedwen saw the tracks that Dunston was pointing out. She nodded, as she gazed about the clearing absently, unsure what it was she was looking for.

"Could he have come here to... you know?" she asked.

"To take a piss?" asked Dunston. "Or a shit?"

"Yes," she said, feeling her cheeks grow hot.

Dunston circled the clearing, sniffing and scrutinising the ground all around.

"There is no evidence he did anything here apart from walk about. And then go back to the track." He frowned, again moving about the clearing until he stood before a tree. There was nothing remarkable about it, as far as Aedwen could tell, and yet Dunston was staring at it.

"What is it?" she asked.

"An oak," Dunston replied, with a smirk, and despite herself, Aedwen laughed. Some of the tension ebbed from her. "He stopped here for a time," Dunston said.

She looked down at the ground, but she could not decipher the slight markings there that told Dunston that Ithamar had paused by this tree. And yet something did call out to her, snagging on her sight the way the unusual shadow had back at the path. Stooping down, she stared at the ground where the oak's roots rose from the earth. There was a large stone there, lichen-covered and almost buried in the loam. But some of the lichen had been scratched from its surface. The bright scrape of bare stone is what had caught her attention.

Bending down, she placed her fingers under the edges of the stone and tugged. It was heavy, but it came away from the ground easily. Much more easily than it should have, if it had not been prised from the earth recently.

Aedwen set aside the stone and Dunston dipped his hand into the insect-crawling space where the rock had been. He stood, holding something in his hands and turned to Aedwen.

"What is it?" she asked.

He showed her. It was a rolled up piece of thin calf's leather. The material had been scraped and stretched until it was smooth and thin enough to be written upon. It was tied up with a cord. Dunston untied it, letting the vellum fall open, exposing line after line of densely crabbed writing, scratched into the skin with the nib of a quill.

"What does it say?" asked Aedwen. The priest back in Langtun had taught her the letters that spelt out her name, but that was the sum of her knowledge of writing and reading.

Dunston looked back at her, bemused.

"I know not, child," he said. "I cannot read. I was a warrior in my youth, not a clergyman."

For a moment, they were both silent, gazing at one another. And then, despite the gravity of their situation and the blood-soaked journey they had travelled, they began to laugh. Deep belly-shaking guffaws racked Dunston and he bent over, resting his palms on his knees as he struggled for breath. Aedwen's eyes streamed with tears of mirth and she too found herself gasping for air, such was her merriment.

When at last, their laughter subsided, Dunston wiped his face with his hands.

"Well," he said, "whatever is written here, I suppose this must be the message that has got so many people killed."

His words were sobering and Aedwen stared at the sheet of vellum and wondered what on earth the words etched there might say.

But before she could reply to Dunston, a new sound came to them on the late afternoon breeze. All of their good humour was leached from them by the noise. It was a chilling sound that she had heard before. She had hoped never to hear its like again.

From the west, through the snarled undergrowth and moss-clad trunks of linden and oak, came the anguished, agonised wails of a man being tortured.

Twenty-Five

Dunston's breath rasped in his throat. Crouching behind the broad bole of an ancient oak, he tried to breathe silently, but was all too aware of his wheezing panting.

A howling scream. Loud. Harsh. Terrible. The forest was still all around them, as if it had been shocked into silence by the poor monk's pained cries.

Gruff laughter followed the piteous wail. Voices, but the words were muffled by distance and the woodland.

Dunston signalled for Aedwen to join him in the lee of the oak. Pale-faced and wide-eyed, she hunkered down beside him. She was trembling, but her mouth was a thin line, jaw set. She was not out of breath.

With a start, Dunston understood that his own laboured breathing was not from exertion, but from the horror of what he was hearing. The horrific sounds of the dying man's last moments conjured up dark memories. Often the faces of fallen enemies would come to him in his dreams. At such times, he would stoke up the fire in his hut until the flames burnt away the darkness. He would gulp down strong mead until at last he could no longer remember the faces of those he had seen die; no longer recall their screams and pleas for mercy.

But here, there was no escape from the cacophony of Ithamar's agony.

With an effort, Dunston slowed his breathing, taking long, drawn out breaths of the warm loamy air. It tasted verdant and full of the life of the forest.

Someone shouted. This time, the words were clear.

"Where is it?"

A pause. A sob. A mumbled answer. Then, another excruciating scream of pain.

Dunston wished Aedwen and he had not come closer. They should have run into the forest in the opposite direction, away from these murderers. But Aedwen had grasped his hand and stared up at him, eyes brimming with tears and compassion.

"We must help him," she had said.

And so, even though he knew there was nothing they could do for the monk, Dunston had led her through the dense foliage towards the sounds of torture. If only Ithamar had fallen silent in death before they had come so close. Then it would have been an easier matter to lead the girl away. And yet it seemed the man's tormentors had some skill in inflicting pain without causing death. For the monk yet lived, though there was no doubt in Dunston's mind he would join Lytelman, Beornmod and the rest in death as soon as he had given his torturers what they wanted.

The man he assumed was Ithamar screamed, and then groaned a reply. Louder now, more emphatic.

"Hidden!" he said, his voice rising into a shout. "Hidden, you sons of Satan!"

His angry answer was cut off by his renewed screaming, as one of his captors performed some unspeakable act of cruelty on the poor man.

Dunston half rose to his feet, hefting DeaÞangenga. By Christ's bones, he could stand this no longer. He would creep to where they were torturing the wretched monk and he would slay them all. He could not bear to hear the man suffer further. Aedwen gazed up at him as he stood. Her eyes were bright, her face expectant.

"Will you rescue him?" she asked.

In the distance, the monk's cries had dwindled to sobs and coughing. Harsh laughter echoed in the forest.

Slowly, Dunston lowered himself back down beside the girl. He placed a hand on her shoulder.

"I cannot," he whispered, fearful that any sound they made might be overheard in the preternaturally silent woodland. She open her mouth to reply and he held up a hand to silence her. "There are too many of them." As he said the words he heard the truth in them. There were five of them and he was but one old man. He might be able to kill a couple of the bastards, three with luck and surprise. If he had been alone, he would have taken his chances. It would not be a bad death to die trying to free an innocent monk from five murderers. It would be a death he would be proud of. Eawynn would have been proud of him too, he thought, despite the oath he had made to her long ago.

"I love that you always seek to defend the weak," she had told him once.

But as he looked at Aedwen's youthful, terrified face, he knew that his path had already been set. He would not rescue the monk. For if he fell in the attempt, what fate then would await Aedwen?

"Who else knew of the message?" came the sudden, furious shout from one of the torturers. "Who knew?"

"Nobody! Only the peddler..." Ithamar's words trailed off and were lost for a time. And then, with vehemence he cried out. "Forgive me, oh Lord, for speaking to the man, for his death is on my hands!"

"We cannot leave him at the mercy of these people," hissed Aedwen. Tears streamed down her face now, but she seemed oblivious to them. "We cannot."

When Dunston made no move to stand, Aedwen started to rise. He gripped her arm and yanked her down to the ground again. He longed to be able to act, to save the poor monk, but it would be folly.

"We must," he whispered. "We should never have come here. But now we know enough. We must take the message to someone able to read it."

Aedwen's expression changed from anguish to anger in a flash. She tried to shake off his grasp, but he was too strong.

"Let me go," she hissed, more loudly now. "We have to do something even if you are too craven!"

Her words stung, but he held her firm and would not allow her to move.

From the distant site of Ithamar's torment there came a strangely calm voice. After a moment, the words became clear.

"*Fæder ure þu þe eart on heofonum; Si þin nama gehalgod…*"

The voice must belong to Ithamar, but gone was his crying wail of pain, instead replaced with a tranquillity Dunston could scarcely believe. And he was reciting the prayer to the Lord. The man must have been incredibly strong of will.

"Stop that!" came a screeching scream and anger. "Answer me. Where is the message? Where have you hidden it?"

But the Lord's Prayer droned on and Ithamar did not miss a word.

"… *to becume þin rice, gewurþe ðin willa, on eorðan swa swa on heofonum.*"

It seemed the monk was done speaking to the men who had cut and tortured him. He had commended his soul to God and would pray until his demise.

Aedwen shuddered in Dunston's grasp. Sobs racked her frame and her face was wet with tears.

"Coward," she cried, her weeping making her voice catch in her throat. "Coward," she repeated and Dunston knew there was nothing he could say that would change her mind.

"Quiet," he hissed, shaking her. "Would you have us both killed too, foolish girl?"

His tone was sharp, and his words cut through her distraught anguish, for she bit back a retort and he could see her forcibly seeking to control her crying.

She stared into his eyes, unspeaking and unblinking, as they both listened to Ithamar's last moments of life.

"... *and forgyf us ure gyltas, swa swa we forgyfað urum gyltendum...*"

Ithamar continued chanting the words of the prayer, exhorting God to forgive him as he would those who did him ill. But before he could complete the prayer, his words were cut off.

"If you will not speak," came the coarse voice of Ithamar's tormentor, "then I will make you sing the song of the blood-eagle. Sing, you bastard. Sing!"

Whatever savagery was being dealt to Ithamar's body became too much for him to bear then, and he let out a moaning, keening squeal of pure agony.

This was a man they had known by name only. Hearing his howling cry cut off in a strangled gasp, Dunston knew they would never know the monk in this life. And yet in a short time of hearing him facing his attackers Dunston knew Ithamar was a brave man. He had been defiant till the end and had died as a true, devout follower of God.

Aedwen gazed up at him, her face contorted with fear, grief, anger. He shook her again, more gently this time.

"We must flee," he said in a hushed murmur, his mouth close to her ear. "We cannot have Ithamar's death be for nought." He touched the vellum that lay in the bag slung over his shoulder. "He gave his life for this message, we must carry it now."

"What can we do?" she said, her voice terribly loud in the stillness of the wood. "These men are monsters."

"Quiet, Aedwen," he whispered. "They might hear you."

Aedwen's eyes widened in sudden, abject terror and she pulled back from his grip, as though she thought he might be about to strike her. For a heartbeat, he was confused. Then he followed her gaze. She was no longer looking at him, but over his shoulder. Dunston's skin prickled as he heard a twig snap behind him.

"Too late," said a deep, husky voice. It held an edge of cruel humour. "One of them has already heard you."

Twenty-Six

Aedwen could not pull her gaze from the man's face. She recognised him as one of those who rode with Hunfrith. He was young, with a wispy beard and cheeks marked with the memory of the pox. But what caught her attention and would not allow her to look away, was the line of dots that ran all the way across his neck, chin, cheek and forehead.

The points were bright, red and glistening in the last light of the sun that filtered through the forest.

Her stomach lurched as she understood what she was seeing. Blood. Ithamar's lifeblood that must have sprayed up in a spatter of droplets as this man and his companions tortured and murdered him.

At last, she cast her eyes down, following the blood-splatter down the man's chest. In his right fist he held a long sword. The blade was clean; polished and deadly. The metal of the blade caught the sunlight. It glimmered with the patterns of a serpent's skin or the ripples of waves on the sea.

He gestured with the blade, twitching it, so that the point lifted.

"Well, old man," he said. "We've been looking for you and the girl for days. You've led us quite a merry dance."

MATTHEW HARFFY

Dunston did not reply. He fixed Aedwen with a steady look and gave the slightest of nods. She saw his hand tighten its grip on his great axe. The weapon was hidden from the swordsman's view.

"Come on, greybeard," the man said, stepping closer. "On your feet."

Without hesitation and with a speed that belied both his age and his bulk, Dunston surged to his feet and spun around in one fluid motion. At the same instant he swung his axe, flinging it at the young man's face. The axe was heavy and sharp and the throw was true. If it had connected it would have surely killed or mortally wounded the man. But the swordsman was fast and stood a few paces distant from Dunston. Moving nimbly to the side, he batted away the spinning axe with the flat of his sword.

But Dunston had never intended for the axe to slay the man. Using the momentum from turning around and standing, he threw himself forward, pulling Beornmod's seax from the scabbard at his waist.

The swordsman had not anticipated the old man's speed or his second attack. He was caught off balance, with his sword pointing to one side. Dunston did not slow his advance. He clattered into the slimmer man, knocking him from his feet. They landed heavily. The man grunted. Dunston made no sound as he plunged the seax into the man's guts. The blade came up bloody, droplets of gore flying from the wound. Again he hammered the seax into the man's stomach.

Aedwen watched on in amazement as Dunston grasped the man's throat in his meaty left hand. Dunston squeezed and the man's eyes bulged. Fighting for air, he struggled against the old man's grasp. In his panic and agony, he dropped his sword and fumbled at Dunston's wrist. It was like watching someone trying to prise the roots of a tree out of frost-hard ground. Dunston's grip was too strong. His fingers squeezed tighter. Two more times he drove the blood-drenched seax into the man's body.

With a juddering sigh, the light fled the man's eyes, and he grew limp. Blood bubbled and pumped from the savage rips in his midriff.

Dunston let out a long breath and he rose to his feet. Blood now flecked his face and stained his beard.

"Come, we must be gone from here," he hissed. "Now."

He retrieved his axe and the man's sword. Tugging off the dead man's belt, Dunston quickly fastened it about his own waist. He sheathed the sword, and spun to Aedwen once more.

She had not moved. She stared at him, eyes wide. She was not breathing. He had killed the man. It was all over so quickly, she could barely take in what she had seen. Her whole body trembled. She felt her gorge rising and feared she would puke.

"Come," he said again. "There is no time to waste." He reached out a hand to pull her to her feet.

She stared at the hand. It was large; thick fingers and callused palms. And it was covered in the brilliant crimson of the man's hot blood. She could not bear the thought of touching it. It would be warm and sticky, she knew. The scent of it was everywhere in the glade now. Metallic and hot on the back of her tongue.

"Come on!" Dunston implored. The sudden sounds of men calling out for their dead companion made Dunston rush forward, reaching for her with his huge hand. "We must flee!"

The sound of the monk's murderers' voices and Dunston's movement broke her moment of inaction. She did not wish to touch his blood-soaked hand, so she pushed herself to her feet.

"Follow me," Dunston said. "We need to be fast and silent."

She nodded, swallowing back her terror and the bile that burnt her throat.

Close by, on the path, the horsemen were approaching.

"Osulf," they called. "Where are you?"

Without waiting for her to reply, Dunston turned and ran southward, away from the path and deeper into the woods. For an instant, Aedwen glanced down at the dead man. Blood pooled in the gashes in his body. His mouth hung open in shocked silence. His unseeing eyes stared upwards into the canopy of the trees.

The men on the path were nearer now, their calls more urgent.

Leaving the bloody corpse of the young man behind her, Aedwen rushed into the forest following Dunston into the failing light.

It would be night soon.

Twenty-Seven

The night was quiet, the forest hushed, wrapped in the night-time cloak of darkness. Dunston was a shadow within the shadows; his footfalls silent on the leaf litter.

Through the trees, a campfire flickered, its light brilliant in the near absolute darkness of the forest. Even without the light to guide him, Dunston would have had no difficulty locating the men. They were whispering, their sibilant hisses strident in the stillness of the night. Despite not being able to make out the words, Dunston could hear the anxiety in their tone. The death of their comrade had unnerved them.

He smiled grimly.

These men had pursued them for some time as the sun went down. They had shouted and hollered, screaming abuse and threats after them as he had dragged Aedwen through bramble-choked gullies and bracken-thick ditches. There had been no time to cover their tracks or to attempt silence, and so he had decided his only option was to make their path impossible for horses, and difficult for men, to follow.

Thorns had scratched and snagged at their clothing. Nettles had stung them. For a time, their hunters had sounded very close behind and Dunston had feared he might need to stand and fight. But night had finally fallen and the forest was plunged into a darkness that reminded him of the depths of the barrow. They had stumbled on for some time, but when they had finally paused for breath, they could no longer hear the men.

Aedwen's face had been pallid, her eyes glistening in the gloom. Her cheeks were streaked with tears. Awkwardly, he had reached for her, meaning to offer her comfort. The girl must have been terrified after what they had heard and witnessing his killing of the man who had found their hiding place. Aedwen had shied away from his touch and Dunston had been shocked at the strength of emotion her reaction had caused in him. He felt powerless in the face of her sorrow. And her judgement.

He recognised the fear and revulsion Aedwen felt at seeing what he was capable of. Eawynn too had been terrified of the man he became when going into battle. Before her passing, he had promised her that he would die a peaceful death in their forest home. She had closed her eyes as he'd gripped her emaciated hand. He knew she worried that when she had gone, he would take up his axe and return to the ranks of the warriors who defended Wessex. She'd been scared that the darkness that brooded within him would engulf him, burying the light that had come from their love for each other. As he'd looked down at the once-beautiful face, Dunston had been filled with an all-encompassing feeling of terror. Perhaps if he swore the oath she wanted from him, promising to leave DeaÞangenga in the chest where he had hidden it, to never fight again, to not become the killer that frightened her so – perhaps then she would recover from the sickness that cruelly ate away the flesh from her bones. And so he had babbled pledges of peace to her, as tears streamed down his cheeks, soaking into his thick beard.

She had died the following morning.

But he had kept his oaths to her. All these long years.

Until now.

When they had recovered from their headlong run through the forest, he had pulled out from his bag a piece of cheese that Smoca had given them and a hunk of the ham they'd taken from Beornmod's hall. They had eaten in silence, each lost in their own troubled thoughts.

Now, with Aedwen secure in the dark sanctuary of the forest, Dunston crept closer towards his enemy's camp, threading his way wraith-like and silent between the ghostly shades of the trees. The men had camped close to the path, and he could make out the silhouettes of their mounts where they had tethered them in a widening of the track.

It had taken him a long time to make his way back here and he hoped that Aedwen would be all right where he had left her. She should be safe, he told himself. She was wrapped in their cloaks and blankets and covered by a layer of bracken. There could be no fire for them that night, but she would be warm enough. He had given her strict instructions not to move from where he had placed her.

He had explained what he planned to do, and all the while she had said nothing. But she had grabbed at his sleeve as he'd made to leave. Her touch had brought him up short.

"Promise me you will return to me," she had said then, her voice small, tremulous.

"I will return," he had said, and a chill had run down his spine. He knew he could not make such a promise. He recalled again his oaths to Eawynn. He would break at least one promise in the darkness that night, it seemed. Why then was he heading out into the night? Would it not be safer for them both to rest and then to press on away from the men who pursued them? He had thought much on this as he had stalked through the night and he had convinced himself that this was a sound course of action. If he could weaken the men further, they would be less of a threat to Aedwen. This is what he told himself, but if he was truthful, he did not believe this was his main reason for seeking out their camp.

What he had heard of Ithamar's last moments of life had filled him with a terrible rage. He thought about Lytelman's mutilated corpse. The man was just a peddler, a man of no consequence, but he had been Aedwen's father and not a bad man from what she had spoken of him. Then Dunston recalled the butchered inhabitants of Cantmael and the tale of rape and murder told by Nothgyth.

Perhaps it was true that to weaken the force that followed them would prove useful, but more than that, Dunston knew that now, despite his words to Aedwen and his promises to Eawynn, he sought revenge for what these men had done. With their acts of savagery they had awoken something in him he had believed long banished, and the realisation filled him with dismay.

He wanted to make them pay.

One of the men coughed and a horse stamped a hoof and snorted. The night air was cool on his cheeks. The flickering firelight and the sounds of the night brought back memories from long ago. For a moment, he could almost have believed he was a young man surrounded by his brother warriors, Guthlaf and the rest. Wulfas Westseaxna, Wolves of Wessex, they had called themselves. Many times they had sneaked up to enemy encampments, as silent as ghosts. He could not count how many men they had slain over the years. Norse, Wéalas, Mercians, Eastseaxna. Wherever their king had sent them, the Wolves would hunt. They had become feared by all of the enemies of Wessex. Some had thought them Nihtgengas, night-walkers, creatures of legend. Others had scoffed at the idea, saying they were but men. But wherever they were mentioned, people would cross themselves, and make the sign to ward off the evil eye, for the Wulfas Westseaxna, just like the hungry wolves in winter, would descend upon their prey and leave only bloody, ripped carcasses behind them.

Dunston drew in a deep breath of the forest air, tasting the smoke and the faint coppery tang of blood, whether from the man he had killed, or from Ithamar, or both, he could not tell.

He was the last of the Wolves now. But this Wolf, grey though its beard might be, still had teeth.

Stealthily moving closer to the fire, careful to avoid making any sound to give himself away, Dunston pushed all thoughts of Aedwen, Eawynn and his past out of his mind. The girl would be safe, and if she was not, worrying about her would do him no good. He took a deep breath, offering a silent prayer for Eawynn's forgiveness. He must not be distracted. He was a wolf stalking its quarry and he sensed that the moment to strike would be upon him soon.

He was very near to the fire now. So close that he could smell the dusty coat of the horses and the leather of the beasts' harness. He stood for a moment, pressed against the trunk of an oak, listening and watching. In his right hand was the familiar weight of DeaÞangenga. He had smeared mud from the bank of a stream over its silver-decorated head. He had rubbed more of the dark muck over his face and into his beard. If anyone had looked in his direction, they would have seen nothing but a shaded tree.

For a long while he stood thus; silently observing the men. Their whispers were loud in the night, but his hearing was not what it once had been and he could not discern their conversations. His right knee was stiff and when he shifted his posture, he was surprised to notice that his right elbow ached. He must have jarred it when stabbing the man, or perhaps when throwing DeaÞangenga. But these pains were as nothing to him. He had once fought with a spear jutting from his shoulder and still managed to take down four foe-men. The aches of old age would not slow him enough to blunt this Wolf's bite. This grey Wolf would still kill.

Three men sat close to the blaze. One threw a branch onto the fire and sparks flew high into the night sky before winking out. The sudden flash of light picked out the shape of the fourth man. He was some way off, outside of the fire's glow. He stood closer to the tethered horses and Dunston assumed he was supposed to be guarding them.

Dunston bared his teeth and, as silent as thought, drifted towards the guard. He propped DeaÞangenga against a wych-elm. And covered the last dozen paces to the unsuspecting man. Dunston was so close that he could smell the man's sweat and the sour stink of ale on his breath. It seemed that this Wolf still knew how to move silently in the night.

Clamping a hand over the man's mouth, Dunston plunged his seax into the small of his back. The steel penetrated the man's kidney and he went rigid in Dunston's grasp. He clung to him tightly. The man struggled as Dunston pulled out the seax, then shuddered when he slid the seax blade effortlessly into the man's throat. After a few moments of trembling, he at last grew limp. Dunston lowered the man to the ground and glanced over at the campfire. The three men still sat there, whispering and chuckling over some jest.

Dunston made his way to the horses. They stamped and blew at his approach. One whinnied. The smell of fresh blood always spooked horses. The element of surprise would soon be lost, so Dunston flitted quickly between the animals, using the bloody seax to slice through the ropes and reins with which they'd been tied to the trees that lined the path.

One of the horses, a large black stallion, tried to bite him, its white teeth snapping close to Dunston's face as he pulled back from it. Regaining his balance, he punched the steed hard on the snout and the animal shied away, whinnying angrily.

"Hey, Eadwig," came a voice from the fire, "what in the name of Christ are you doing?"

There was no time for anything more now. Dunston hurried back towards the wych-elm where he had left DeaÞangenga. As he passed the jittery horses, he prodded them with the sharp tip of his seax. They reared and kicked and the night was filled with their cries of pain and fear. In an instant, the path was a chaos of furious horseflesh.

One mare skittered in a circle, blocking Dunston's way. He slapped it hard on the rump, jabbing it with the seax for good measure, and the animal bounded away, galloping eastwards along the path.

The men from the camp were on their feet now, lending their shouts and calls to the madness that had descended on the small glade. All was confusion and Dunston grinned to himself in the darkness as he snatched up DeaÞangenga from where it lay. He watched for a moment as they tried to calm the horses, shouting insults at the man who had been set the task of watching the beasts.

He listened to them calling to each other in the darkness, as he slid back into the night. He did not worry about making noise now and he hurried away, sure-footed despite the black beneath the forest canopy. He heard their voices raised in fear and alarm as they found their fallen companion, and he grinned despite himself. For too long these men had believed themselves above justice, able to torture and kill as they pleased. And for what? A sheet of vellum that bore Christ knew what message.

Their voices receded and as he made his way unerringly back to where he had left Aedwen, Dunston was unable to suppress the warm feeling that flowed through him. What would Eawynn have thought of his actions? he wondered. She never understood him or the sheer joy and exhilaration that fighting could bring. But she had understood that sometimes the strong must stand up to defend the weak. And in killing one of their pursuers and scattering their horses, he had evened the odds against Aedwen and him.

That was so, but as he retraced his steps through the dense undergrowth of the wood towards the girl, there was one thing that troubled him. And he knew that it was this, more than the breaking of any vow, that would truly have upset Eawynn.

It had felt good to allow the long-sleeping Wolf out of its cage to kill once more.

Twenty-Eight

The forest whispered and murmured around Aedwen in the darkness. From where she lay under the thick blanket of cloaks and bracken she could make out a small patch of sky through the boughs of the great linden tree that spread its limbs above her. The light from the quarter moon silvered the leaves as they waved in the light breeze. Far beyond the tree, in the infinite expanse of the sky, the spray of stars was bright against the deep purple of the night's shroud.

Staring up at the moon, she wondered whether she would see it swallowed up before her eyes, as she had when they had fled from Briuuetone. But its light remained constant and cold in the sky.

An owl hooted far off. Aedwen half-imagined she heard the plaintive call of a wolf on the wind, but perhaps it was just a dog in a farmstead somewhere nearby. She recalled the prints that Dunston had told her belonged to a wolf and shuddered, despite feeling snug in her hiding place.

Something rattled and cracked out in the blackness of the woodland and she started, clutching tightly the small knife Dunston had given her. She shook her head. What use would such a weapon be should a wolf come upon her in the darkness? The thought of slavering jaws, full of drool-dripping sharp teeth filled her with terror.

She tried to push the thoughts away. No wild animal would attack her. No, she thought, it should not be the animals that frightened her. There were worse things in the woods that night.

She had watched in rapt silence as Dunston had daubed mud over his shiny axe and rubbed the mire on his face and beard. She knew he had once been a warrior, and she had watched him fight at Briuuetone, but now she had seen the true nature of the man. He had killed without thought, and then, painting his face so that he seemed more beast than man, he had slunk off into the night to kill again.

The sounds of Ithamar's torture had ripped at her soul, terrified her. After witnessing the aftermath of these men's tortures in Cantmael, she could well imagine what they had been doing to the monk.

When she had finally found the courage to ask Dunston what he meant to do, he had turned to her and she was sure there had been a savage gleam of hunger in his eyes.

"I am going to even the odds," he had said.

He had promised to return, but as she lay there in the darkness, she trembled to think of him coming back for her drenched in blood and stinking of death.

She tried to push such thoughts from her mind. It was unfair of her, she knew. He had shown her nothing but kindness and he was risking his life for her. And yet there had been something in his gaze since he had slain the man that unnerved her.

She awoke, surprised that she had slept at all. She was more shocked to find that the grey tinge of dawn illuminated the clearing. The clouds that drifted high in the sky above the linden were painted pink by the rising sun.

A rustling movement made her reach for her knife.

"Hush, Aedwen," said Dunston. "It is I. Here, drink some water." He handed her a flask. "We must be away from this place."

Gone was the blood and mud from his face and hands. He must have scrubbed himself clean in one of the many streams that trickled through the woods. His kirtle was stained. She chose not to wonder what substance had made the dark marks on the wool.

Shoving into her hand a piece of the hard cheese the charcoal burners had given them, Dunston rose and busied himself picking up their few belongings. She watched him as she chewed on the smoky cheese. He was moving with none of the grace and fluidity she had seen when he had faced their enemy. He grimaced as he bent to pick up his bag, pushing his hands into the small of his back and groaning as he straightened. With the grime and blood removed from his face his skin appeared sallow, his eyes bruised and tired. She could scarcely believe she had been so fearful of this old man.

She swallowed the cheese and drank the water. He turned to her as she sat up and his eyes seemed to glow in the dim light of the dawn. For a heartbeat she could not breathe under the force of that cold glare. She rose, mumbling that she needed to relieve herself. He did not move, merely nodding.

"Hurry," he said, his voice rasping like a blade drawn along a whetstone.

No, she had not imagined the savage fire that had consumed Dunston the night before.

When she returned, she had made up her mind about him. Dunston frightened her, but he had treated her well and she could think of nobody she would rather have at her side as they fled from Hunfrith's murderous men.

"How did you do? In the night?" she asked.

"Well enough," he replied, heading into the dense forest. She could not be certain, but she believed they were heading away from the path that led towards Tantun.

"Did you…" she hesitated. "Did you kill any of them?"

"One more," he answered without pause, as if slaying a man meant nothing to him. "And I dispersed their horses. It should take them a while to be after us. If we keep off the roads and paths I doubt they will find us."

"Did you sleep at all?" she asked.

"I closed my eyes for a few moments. I will sleep when we reach Exanceaster."

She had been right; they were heading south. She felt a flush of pride at keeping her sense of direction despite the rush in the darkness through the trees and foliage.

"Exanceaster?" she said. "Why should we go there?" She had never been to the place, but knew it to be the seat of power of Defnascire.

Dunston paused at the foot of a steep rise, peering upward into the dawn dark. The earth beneath the slope was boggy and clogged with sweet gale. A thin mist hung there, like webs of forgotten dreams. Evidently having made up his mind as to the best way to ascend, Dunston set off up the incline, using the slender trunks of birch saplings to pull himself up.

"Whatever is written on the vellum," he said, his breath ragged from the exertion of the climb, "it is something worth killing for." His foot slipped in the leaf mould and he cursed under his breath, catching hold of a sapling and hauling himself up. When he reached the summit, he turned and reached out his hand to her. She gripped it without hesitation and he pulled her slim form up to him easily.

"What do you mean to do with the message in Exanceaster? Tantun is closer and there would be priests and monks there who could read it."

"That is true, but those bastards know that Ithamar was heading to Tantun, and maybe they will believe we mean to carry it in the same direction. Besides, we must see that it gets into the hands of someone not only able to read, but also to see justice done."

They pushed on through a more sparsely forested area of sallow and elder. Aedwen welcomed the sense of openness, of air between the widely spaced trunks. To her left, the rising sun shone its rays deep under the leafy forest roof. She turned to the east, revelling in the warmth of the day on her face.

"You seek the king's reeve then?" she said.

"No," said Dunston. He let out a sigh and shook his head, as if to clear his thoughts. "I seek the king."

"The king?" she blurted out, unable to hide her incredulity. "Even if we could get to speak to him, why would he listen to us?" The thought of even seeing the king of Wessex seemed like madness to her. She glanced at Dunston, to see whether he was jesting. Perhaps this was his misguided way of trying to lift her spirits.

"He wouldn't listen to you," he said, raising an eyebrow. "But by God, he'll listen to me."

He picked up his pace and for a moment she looked at him, her head full of questions. She wanted to call after him, to ask him how he could be so sure that the king would grant him an audience. But as she opened her mouth to shout, the thought of the horsemen on their trail came to her. Her voice would carry far in the quiet dawn, cutting through the chorus of birdsong and leading their enemies to them, if they were near. She clamped her mouth shut and ran after Dunston.

Twenty-Nine

They made good progress as they trudged southward. Dunston had for a time contemplated setting snares and traps for their pursuers to stumble upon. He could rig traps that would injure them with sharpened stakes and sprung branches whipping forward when triggered by a clumsy footfall. But he quickly dismissed the idea as a waste of effort. To fashion such traps would take time and there was no way of knowing whether the men who followed would encounter them. He had seen nothing that made him believe they knew how to track them through the forest. And, encumbered by their valuable mounts, which would impede their progress through the foliage, he believed they would more than likely head to the main north–south road.

For a long while, Aedwen had walked beside him in silence. Whenever he glanced at her he saw her face set in a determined mask. Something had changed between them, he knew, but he could do nothing to alter that. He thought of Eawynn and how she had always said he was a better man than others saw.

"They see the great warrior," she had said. "I see the true man who hides behind his axe and fearsome face."

He smiled to himself at the memory.

"Fearsome am I?" he'd laughed, grabbing hold of her. She'd squirmed, pliant curves soft under his firm grip.

Giggling, she had kissed him.

"I do not see what frightens others," she'd said. "I only see my lovely bear of a man."

As always when he thought of Eawynn, the memory of her stirred and warmed him, but all too soon, the bitterness of her loss returned and he frowned.

Aedwen had seen in him what others had always seen. The warrior. The killer. The Wolf. He wondered whether the girl would ever believe that there was another side to his nature that only Eawynn had been able to coax from him.

"Do you think they are close behind us?" Aedwen asked, breaking the silence between them and bringing him back to the present.

They had walked for a long while. Dunston looked up at the sky that was visible between the limbs of the trees. The clouds had thickened and the warmth that the day had promised with the dawn had fled, replaced with a greying light and the scent of rain.

"They might be," he replied, "but I do not believe so. They won't be able to bring their horses this deep into the woods and they will not wish to leave them." He paused, listening to the sounds of the forest. There was no indication they were being followed. "No. I think they will have gone on towards Tantun, or at least the road that leads from Exanceaster to Bathum."

"If they have not followed us into the forest, how can they think to catch us?" she asked, hope of escape colouring her tone.

"They might send men along the road in both directions, hoping to hear news of our passing or to spy us when we leave the woodland." He set off once again, wincing at the constant ache in his knee. It hurt more when he was still, but all the same, he longed to sit and stretch out before a fire. Not much chance of that any time soon. Aedwen trotted along beside him, her youthful energy bringing the hint of a wistful smirk to his lips. By God, he missed being young.

"Won't they head towards Tantun?" she asked.

"They may well do that. But I think that they will soon fathom out that we have gone south and there is only one reasonable destination for us in this direction. After all, they must know we either have the message or know of it, so we need to take it somewhere. Knowledge is useless if it is not shared."

"And so we just plan to walk to Exanceaster and pray for the best?"

He shrugged.

"I would rather trust to our wits than rely on God to see us safe. We should head south of the town until we reach the River Exe. Then we can follow the river back to the walls of Exanceaster. In that way, with a bit of luck, we can avoid any prying eyes on the road."

They walked on for a time, following the course of a small river until it widened into a broad expanse of water. Aedwen held her oaken staff as if she had been born with it in her hand and Dunston smiled as he watched her halt for a moment to casually inspect the tracks of an animal in the mud beside the lake. Days ago she would not have noticed the small marks. She turned to him, eyes bright and inquisitive.

"What are these tracks?"

"Look about you," he answered. "What animal do you think might have made them?"

She gazed around her, forgetting about the men pursuing them, focusing solely on the matter at hand. Dunston lowered himself down, leaning his back against the trunk of a sallow. He turned his head this way and that, grunting as his neck popped. They needed to rest for a while and this place was as good as any. He pulled the ham and cheese from his bag, cutting off a slice and watching Aedwen as she thought.

She knelt on the earth and inspected the tracks carefully and methodically, before looking back at him.

"I don't know," she said. "I've never seen anything like this before. It looks as though a creature has dragged something behind it through the mud."

He grinned and took a drink from his leather flask.

"And so it has."

"But what?" she asked, confused.

"Animals do not only leave their prints in the earth," he said. "Look about you and take the time to really see. Think carefully and you will find the answer."

She got up and went close to the pool. A dense tangle of spearwort grew at its edge, the yellow flowers bright against the green of the leaves.

"Careful not to touch that plant," he called. "It will cause your skin to blister."

Moving warily past the flowering spearwort, Aedwen looked about her.

A large alder had fallen and its leafy boughs trailed into the still waters. Dunston broke the last of the smoked cheese into two pieces and ate his half. He was enjoying watching the girl discover the truth for herself. She moved to the toppled tree and touched the bright, fresh wood where its trunk had been split. Then she gazed out at the water, at last taking in that which Dunston had seen immediately.

She turned, pointing to a mound of branches that rose from the water.

"Is that where it lives?" she asked. Her face glowed with childish excitement.

"It is," he said, returning her smile. "So what left the tracks?"

"It is a beaver," she said. "The thing it is dragging behind is its tail."

When he nodded, she clapped her hands with delight.

After they had eaten, they continued on, leaving the beaver's dam and lodge behind them. Aedwen had been pleased with herself and Dunston had revelled in her simple pleasure. But their spirits were soon dampened when the rain that had been threatening to fall all morning finally began to waft down from the sky in a light, yet soaking drizzle. For a time, the tree cover kept them dry, but soon, the water trickled down to drench them. All about them the forest was dank, gloomy and wet. The birds that had filled the morning with song and cheer fell quiet and the only sound was that of the rain, pattering and dripping from leaf and limb. Where there were patches of open ground, the earth squelched underfoot.

There was still no sign they were being followed, but their conversation of that morning nagged at Dunston. They had followed the course of the river for a time, but now they had left it behind. Dunston pointed to a hill in the distance.

"Let us take a look at the land about from up there," he said, wiping the rain from his eyebrows and forehead.

The hill was bare, save for a stand of yew on its crown. If he judged rightly, the Bathum to Exanceaster road would lie someway off to the west.

"If we approach the rise from the east and head to the trees," he said, "we should get a good view of the road and the land to the north. Careful now, let us not be out in the open for too long."

It was steeper than it had looked and they both slipped and slid on the wet grass. All the while he worried that they might be seen. He felt exposed and began to question his decision to climb up here. Too late for that now. There was nothing for it but to press on. As they got higher and could see the rain-swept wooded hills of Somersæte rolling away to the north, he was relieved to see no movement.

Their clothes were sodden by the time they reached the shelter of the trees. After the exposed slopes of the hill, it felt almost warm beneath the branches.

"We will rest here awhile," he said, panting from the struggle up the hill.

They settled down under an old yew, beside the twisted skeletal remnants of a dead juniper bush. Old, brown needles crunched beneath them. They were wonderfully dry and it was good to be out of the rain even if only for a short time.

Below them, they could make out the unnatural straight line of the road, a shadow like a spear haft plunged through the undulating verdant curves of the forest. They sipped at the water from their flasks and watched, each silent and anxious. As if to speak would somehow give away their presence on the hill.

Thin trails of mist formed over parts of the woodland, like wisps of lamb's wool caught on thorns. Dunston drew in a deep breath, finally allowing himself to relax. He was rummaging in his bag, looking for the last of the ham, when Aedwen touched his arm. He followed her pointing finger. Far in the distance, where the road ran between two steep-sided hills, a great flock of birds was flapping into the misty sky, pale against the dark of the rain-slick leaves of the wood. His eyes were not as good as they had once been, but he thought the flock was a mixture of wood pigeons and doves.

As he watched, he noticed that the air was clearer now, making it easier to pick out details from afar. The rain had stopped and the wet land shone in a sudden blaze of golden afternoon light.

A croaking cry split the silence of the hill as half a dozen crows flapped into the sky from where they had been roosting on the branches of the yew trees.

Cursing silently, Dunston peered up and saw that the clouds had parted, sending brilliant sunlight down upon the trees and hills of Wessex. A flash of silver, as bright and flickering as distant lightning, drew his gaze back down to the road. He squinted.

"What is it?" he asked.

For a moment, Aedwen did not speak.

"I'm not sure how many," she replied at last, "but there are at least two horsemen down there on the road. The sun caught their horses' harness, I think."

Dunston spat.

"Riding south?"

"Yes," Aedwen said without hesitation.

By Christ's bones, he should not have brought them up here. He reached for her arm and pulled her back into the shade beneath the trees.

"Come, we must leave this place."

He led her through the copse, and then they proceeded to slip and slide down the southern slope, putting the hill between them and the riders on the road.

"You think they saw us?" she asked, her breath coming in ragged gasps.

"I do not know," he said. But he could not believe anyone could have missed the black-feathered crows that had taken to the wing above their vantage point. He hoped they were more foolish than he thought, but they would not have to be woodsmen to understand that something or someone had disturbed the birds from the trees.

He glanced at Aedwen and could see from the set of her jaw that she was thinking the same thing. She did not protest when he urged them into a trotting run southward, away from the hill and back under the canopy of the forest.

Thirty

They ran into the humid shade of the trees. They were both out of breath, but Dunston did not slow until they were deep within the woods once more, sheltered from the hill and the road by dense thickets of hazel and hawthorns. They pressed on. When Aedwen tried to speak with him, Dunston merely grunted. She wanted to say that it had not been his fault. He could not have known the men would ride into view at that moment, or that the crows would take wing, giving away their position. But after a time she kept quiet. Her words would not change how he felt. He was tense and irritable and clearly angry at himself for leading them up to the hilltop.

And so they walked in silence, and soon her sweat mingled with the damp from the rain as she struggled to keep up with him.

Such was the pace he set that soon her legs were burning and a blister on her left heel had burst, stabbing her with a jolt of pain at every step. She was on the verge of asking Dunston for a rest when he held up his hand, signalling her to be silent. He dropped into a crouch. She copied him, her aches and pains forgotten momentarily.

For a long while they remained thus, hunkered down on their haunches. She was about to ask him what was happening, but one glower from his blue eyes and she snapped her mouth shut.

A moment later, a skinny, dirt-smeared man stepped into the clearing. Aedwen had not heard him approach until the instant before he walked into sight. How Dunston knew he was coming, she had no idea.

Over his shoulder, the man carried a brace of pigeons and a plump hare. He held a bow in his hand, and a sheaf of white goose feather fletched arrows were thrust into his belt.

Dunston stepped from their hiding place. The man started, dropping the game to the leaf mould and snatching an arrow from his belt.

Before he nocked the arrow, Dunston stepped close.

"You'll not be needing that," he said, his voice deep and rumbling like far-off thunder. The man's eyes were wide and shining in the forest shadows, but Dunston moved back a pace, placing his axe on the ground. "I mean you no harm."

For a moment, Aedwen thought the man might run, but then he seemed to relax. Glancing past Dunston, he grinned at her, his teeth bright and surprisingly whole in his weathered and begrimed face.

Dunston asked him whether he had seen anyone else in the forest.

"Not since I left home yesterday morn," the man said, flicking his attention back to Dunston. "Not a soul. The only folk I ever see in these woods are wolf-heads." He looked at them askance then, and Dunston fixed him with his icy stare.

"Wolf-heads, you say?"

"Yes, but not today. Nobody today. Just the animals and me."

"And you have not seen us," said Dunston.

The man swallowed.

"Well, I have now," he stammered.

Dunston bent down and lifted his huge, besilvered axe. He swung it to rest upon his shoulder where the blade caught a ray of sunlight that lanced through the trees.

"You have not seen us," he repeated, his words slow and pointed.

The hunter's throat bobbed. He could not pull his gaze from the massive head of the long hafted axe. At last, he nodded.

"I haven't seen you."

Dunston waved his hand and the hunter snatched up the pigeons and the hare and hurried on, his shadow stretching out before him as he headed towards his home somewhere to the east.

When the man had disappeared and they could no longer hear his footfalls, Dunston strode off into the forest once more. Aedwen stumbled after him, her blistered foot squelching and rubbing with raw agony. She longed to be able to halt, to pull off her shoes, perhaps to bathe her feet in a cool stream. And yet she remained silent, not wishing to further anger Dunston.

The meeting with the hunter had done nothing to quell his nerves.

They walked along a barely perceptible path that had been made by some woodland creature. For a moment she paused, trying to discern what creatures' passing had worn this trail, but Dunston did not slow. Fearing she would be left behind, she abandoned her search for sign and limped after him. The track led south and east and Dunston seemed content to follow it as the sun fell. The shadows grew darker and colder, the light that filtered through the boles of the trees golden and blinding. The sun would soon set and they would be plunged into darkness. Aedwen shuddered. Her foot screamed in silent anguish.

"We should make camp soon," she offered.

Dunston ignored her. His pace did not falter. Aedwen did not like the thought of spending another night in the forest with no fire. She hurried after him, wincing and hobbling on her bleeding foot.

"Did you hear me?" she asked, raising her voice. "We should make—"

Dunston spun to face her, raising his hand. For the merest instant she thought he meant to strike her, such was the anger in his eyes. She flinched. Dunston's features softened and he pulled her in close and whispered.

"We cannot halt here. We are being stalked. Keep your eyes open and," he shook her shoulder, staring directly into her eyes, "no matter what happens, do exactly as I say."

Without waiting for an answer, he turned and continued along the path. She rushed after him, panicked thoughts tumbling in her mind. What did he mean? Who was stalking them? She had seen nobody.

They walked on without speaking. With every tree they passed, Aedwen found herself peering into the shadows, staring into tangles of brambles. They passed a holly tree, its leaves glistening in the sunset. A breeze shook the branches as the travellers drew near and Aedwen jumped back, certain that an unseen assailant was about to leap upon them from the mass of spiny leaves. Nobody sprang out of the undergrowth and Dunston did not slow. With her breath ragged from the exertion and the building fear, Aedwen ran after him.

When the men who hunted them finally showed themselves, they did not come crashing out of the foliage, but seemed to materialise from the shadows, like wraiths. The sun must have still been just above the horizon, but here, deep within the forest, little of its light penetrated. Without warning, Dunston halted and Aedwen almost collided with his broad back. Her eyes widened and panic rose in her throat as she saw three men had stepped into the glade before them. Glancing behind, she spotted the shadowy forms of three more.

Her breath came in short gasps and the blood pounded in her ears. How had their pursuers managed to follow them here, into the darkest part of the forest? Her stomach twisted as she thought what the men would do to them both. They would be furious at the old man. He had killed two of their own. And these men had tortured and slain for much less. Would they rip Dunston's lungs from his back? She trembled. Would they torture her too? Her mouth was dry and she felt faint.

"I told you before," said Dunston, "you do not need your bow."

The central man before them stepped into the failing light and she immediately realised her mistake. These were not the horsemen who had killed her father, raped and murdered the people of Cantmael and tortured to death the monk, Ithamar. The man confronting Dunston was the thin hunter. Relief flooded through her. They were safe. They would not be tortured and killed. The dirt-streaked hunter grinned at her with his unusually white teeth. There was something feral and disquieting in that smile. In his hands he held his bow, an arrow on the string. The wicked point of the hunting arrow was aimed squarely at Dunston's chest. As quickly as the relief had come, so it was washed away on a fresh tide of fear. There was no welcome in this man's eyes, only the wild hunger of a man who has nothing to lose.

"I suppose it is not surprising that you said you only saw wolf-heads in the forest," said Dunston, "as you are a wulfeshéafod yourself."

"You know nothing of me, or my friends of the greenwood," snarled the hunter.

"Well, that is not so, is it?" asked Dunston, taking a step towards the men who blocked their path.

"What do you mean, old man? You do not know me."

Dunston nodded and took another pace forward.

"I do not know your name, but I know much about you."

The archer raised his bow, pulling back on the string so that the yew wood creaked.

"Not another step," he hissed. Dunston halted. Swinging his axe down from where it rested on his shoulder, he grasped it in both hands, holding it across his body. The dying light of the sun made the silver threads in the blade glow in the gloaming.

"What is it that you think you know?" asked the archer.

"Why, I know that you are a wolf-head. Outside the law. I could kill you as I would a wolf and nobody would seek to take me to a moot. There would be no weregild to pay. Your life has no price."

"You know nothing of what I have done," said the archer, a cunning gleam in his eye. "Being a wulfeshéafod is a curse, but it is a blade that cuts both ways. My life has no worth to freemen or reeves, so I have nothing to lose. I could slay you where you stand, old man."

"You could try," growled Dunston, raising his great axe menacingly. "Do you truly believe your puny arrow could slay me before I could bury DeaÞangenga here in your skull?"

Aedwen could scarcely believe Dunston's words. Terror gripped her in its icy fist. She could barely move and yet Dunston seemed not only unafraid of these men, he appeared to be goading them into a fight. As she watched, she saw the bowman's gaze flit to the weapon in Dunston's massive hands and she realised she was not the only one frightened. Glancing past Dunston, the leather-faced wolf-head met her eyes for a heartbeat. Gone was the quick smile of before.

"Drop your axe," said the archer, "or we shall see just how deadly my arrows are." He tensed the string once more, the arrowhead aiming unerringly at Dunston's heart.

Dunston did not move.

"I will say this only once, boy," he said, his voice low and rasping. "Walk away now. Lead your friends away back to wherever you call home. If you threaten me or the girl again, you will regret it." He paused, glowering under his grey brows, his blue eyes flashing like chips of ice. "But not for long."

"Why not let them go, Strælbora?" said the man to the archer's left. Younger than the bowman, he was just as dishevelled, with the gaunt, wary look of a stray dog about him. "They have nothing of worth. They are probably fleeing from tithe-men. Perhaps they are being followed. It will be just our luck to have them bring the reeve down onto us."

"Silence, Wynstan," snapped the archer. "That axe of his is worth something. And when was the last time the camp had a young girl? That is worth more than a little."

Wynstan looked at Aedwen and licked his lips. She shuddered. She was sure this was how the hare must have felt before the man's arrow pierced its flesh.

"Drop the axe," repeated Strælbora, his tone harsh.

Dunston's shoulders slumped and with a sigh, he let the huge weapon fall to the loam at his feet.

With a smile of triumph, Strælbora said, "Wynstan, fetch that axe."

After a moment's hesitation, Wynstan scurried forward. Dunston stood, head down as if in defeat. Aedwen wanted to scream. These men would surely kill him and after that... She could not bear to think of what would become of her.

Wynstan bent quickly to lift the axe, clearly meaning to hurry back to Strælbora's side. But in the instant when he took his eyes from Dunston to retrieve the weapon, the grey-bearded warrior pounced. If she had not witnessed it with her own eyes, Aedwen would never have believed one so old could move with such speed. Like a striking serpent, Dunston's right hand lashed out and grabbed Wynstan by the neck of his grimy kirtle. Surging forward and stooping, he gripped the man's groin with his left hand. Wynstan let out a pitiful yelp.

For a heartbeat, nobody seemed able to move. Apart from Dunston. He hoisted Wynstan off the ground at the same moment that the unmistakable sound of an arrow being loosed sang out in the shadowed glade. The arrow thudded into flesh and for a terrible instant Aedwen believed Dunston had been struck. And yet it was Wynstan who howled in pain. Strælbora had let fly his arrow into his friend's back, and now, using the man's body as a shield, Dunston surged forward. He did not attempt to pick up his axe, instead he ran towards Strælbora, holding Wynstan as if he weighed little more than a child.

Suddenly, the clearing was filled with chaos. Men yelled and shouted. Somebody grabbed Aedwen roughly from behind, a strong arm encircled her chest and the stench of stale sweat and woodsmoke enveloped her.

Despite the horror that threatened to overwhelm her, Aedwen could not tear her gaze away from Dunston. He flung Wynstan's injured body at Strælbora. The archer was trying to free another arrow from his belt, and Wynstan clattered into him, sending him reeling backwards. Both men collapsed in a heap on the forest floor. Dunston did not slow his advance, instead speeding into the man who had been standing to Strælbora's right. The man had pulled a rusty knife, but Dunston seemed unperturbed by the blade. Catching the man's wrist in his left hand, he thundered a right hook into his jaw. The man fell to the ground as if dead. Perhaps he was, Aedwen thought, such was the power behind that punch.

"Halt!" shouted the man who held Aedwen. As if to reinforce his command, he shook her and pressed a cold blade against her throat. Aedwen felt her strength leaving her. She could barely breathe. Her legs trembled and she feared she might fall. "I'll kill her!" yelled the man, his voice hoarse and ugly. His warm breath, sour and stale, wafted against her cheek. His left hand was clamped over her chest. His touch made her want to squirm away, but even if she could have summoned the courage to move, his wiry strength would have held her firm.

Dunston showed no sign of hearing the man's threats. He did not turn or falter, instead he flung himself onto Wynstan and Strælbora. Wynstan screamed as the arrow was pushed further into his body before snapping from the pressure of Dunston's bulk. Strælbora was pinned beneath his injured comrade.

"You whoreson!" he bellowed, trying in vain to pull himself out from under Wynstan's stricken form and Dunston's considerable weight. "I will cut your eyes out and piss in your skull! I will cut off your manhood and—"

Dunston hammered a punch into his face, silencing him. Strælbora's head snapped back against the loam, his eyes vacant and unfocused. His mouth opened and closed like a beached trout, but no sound came. Dunston looked down at him for a moment, before thundering another blow into his nose. Blood blossomed, bubbling and flowing into Strælbora's dirty beard. His eyes rolled back and he lay still.

With a sigh, Dunston shoved himself up from the earth and the tangled forms of the wolf-heads. He rose to his feet with a grimace and turned to Aedwen and the three remaining outlaws.

As if remembering his role in this confrontation, the man who held her tightened his grip. The knife pressed against her throat and she gasped.

"I'll kill her," he said. Did she hear an edge of panic in his tone now?

Dunston ignored the man. He moved to his axe and lifted it from the earth.

"I will!" shouted the man, desperation in his voice now. Aedwen readied herself for the pain of the cut. How quickly would she die? She had seen plenty of pigs killed with their throats slit and they didn't seem to suffer for long after their initial squealing terror. Without being aware of what she was doing, she began to recite the prayer to Maria, Mother of God.

"If you harm her," said Dunston, his voice as cold and menacing as the huge axe in his grasp, "it will be the last thing you do on this earth. Even if you think you could kill me, I promise you I will take you with me. Death holds no fear for me. What about you, boy? Do you truly wish to stand before God in judgement of your sins before this day is out?"

Behind Dunston, Wynstan whimpered and panted.

For a long, drawn out moment, nobody spoke. Aedwen was aware of the man who held her wavering. She could almost hear his thoughts as he looked at the grey-bearded axe man and his three incapacitated companions sprawled on the forest floor. Could the three wolf-heads who remained standing defeat the old warrior? Was the prize worth the risk?

Dunston did not move. His cool eyes were unblinking as he glowered at the wolf-head. There was no doubt in Aedwen's mind that this was no idle threat. Dunston was prepared to kill them all, even if he died in the battle.

The tight grasp around her chest loosened. The wolf-head, it seemed, had decided to release her. Aedwen let out a ragged breath. Without warning, the blade was removed from her throat and the man pushed her away with such force that she stumbled and fell.

"Kill him!" he screamed.

The three wolf-heads surged forward, and Dunston widened his stance, swinging his war axe up to meet their attack.

Aedwen watched in horror from where she lay on the damp leaf mould. Death was in the late afternoon air and all that remained to be seen was who would survive. Surely Dunston could not hope to stand before the three outlaws and live.

The instant before the men met, a new voice rang out in the clearing.

"Halt! Put up your weapons!" the voice bellowed. It was loud and clear and carried the power of command in its tone.

Aedwen could not see who it was who spoke. The voice came from the shadows beneath the trees.

The wolf-heads evidently recognised the voice, for they responded by stepping back and lowering their blades. Dunston did not step after them, instead he lowered his axe and peered into the gloom of the forest, a quizzical expression on his face.

"Aculf?" he asked, his tone incredulous. "Is that you?"

Thirty-One

"Time has caught up with you, I see," said Aculf. He sat across the fire from Dunston, the flames lighting his face with a ruddy glow. It was full dark now, the forest black, the grey boles of the trees surrounding the camp crowding about the gathered band of wolf-heads.

Dunston offered a thin smile that didn't reach his eyes.

"Time is the hunter that always catches its prey," he said.

Beside him Aedwen leaned against his shoulder. The eyes of the outlaws glimmered in the gloom. All of the men were dirty and thin, with skin ravaged by the weather and years of living outside. Off to one side, Strælbora glowered at him. Huddled around the archer were the rest of the men Dunston had fought. Aculf, who had always been skilled with the ways of healing, had removed the arrow from Wynstan's back and now the injured man lay in a feverish doze. He had cried out like a child when Aculf had drawn the arrow point from his flesh, but despite the man's complaints, Aculf said he would more than likely live.

Strælbora's nose was broken, his eyes dark-ringed and bruised. The other man Dunston had punched had lost one of the few teeth he had left. The five of them did not cease to glare at Dunston and Aedwen, and he wondered whether he would be able to sleep that night.

"You may be old, but you are still as strong as an ox," said Aculf with a grin. "I cannot imagine any other man lifting Wynstan the way you did."

Dunston grunted. He did not feel strong. His back ached terribly and the pain in his elbow was worse than ever. You are not young any more, he rebuked himself after the fight. Lifting Wynstan was foolish. The moment he pulled him from his feet, Dunston had regretted it. His back screamed with the effort, but what else could he have done? He would not stand by while they raped Aedwen. You should have just killed them, a small, dark voice whispered deep within him. Perhaps he should have. They were outlaws, men who had lost their place in society. Why not simply strike them down with DeaÞangenga? It would have been faster and the chances were that if he had killed a couple, the others would have run. And yet he recalled slaying the man by the horses in the night, and how the thrill of the kill had coursed through him. He had made a solemn promise to Eawynn, he did not wish to forsake that vow. He had clung onto it for too long. He did not wish to admit to himself that he would resort to killing so effortlessly, as if the promise had never been made. Or that it meant nothing to him.

Looking over the fire at Aculf, Dunston felt his world shift about him. For a moment it was as if he had stepped back into his past. So easily had he returned to a life he'd believed gone forever, and now, to add to his discomfort and unease, ghosts were returning to the land of the living.

Aculf was thinner than he remembered him, his forehead bore a long scar Dunston did not recall, and his beard was dusted with frost, but the power of the man's character still shone in his dark eyes.

"I thought you long dead," said Dunston.

"I have come close," replied Aculf. "And now," he waved a hand to encompass their surroundings and the couple of dozen wolf-heads that were dotted about the clearing, "I am as good as dead to all but those outside of the law."

"What happened?" asked Dunston, accepting a leather flask from one of the other men sitting nearby. He took a tentative sip and was surprised to discover it was mead. Good sweet mead. He filled his mouth and passed the skin to Aedwen who took a small gulp, grimaced and handed it back, shaking her head.

"What always happens," said Aculf. The shadows from the flames danced and writhed about his features. His eyes were black in the darkness. "Bad luck. War. And the accursed Norsemen."

Dunston took another mouthful of the mead, feeling his body relax and the warmth of the liquid sliding into his tired and aching limbs. Handing the flask back to the wolf-head with a nod of thanks, Dunston waited for Aculf to continue.

Aedwen moved to rest her head in his lap. Her eyes were closed. She was exhausted. Aculf had given his word that no ill would befall either of them in the camp that night, but did Dunston truly know him? It must have been close to a score of years since he had last seen the man. They had been brothers in the Wulfas Westseaxna then. They had stood shoulder to shoulder in the shieldwall and they had walked together into the darkest of nights where the only certainty was death. Dunston remembered Aculf as a formidable swordsman and a man of honour. To find him here, outcast and living amongst brigands in the forest, filled him with pity. He snorted. Was he too not a wulfeshéafod? Who was he to judge this man he had long ago considered to be his friend? He would have trusted his life to Aculf once, he at least owed him the benefit of hearing his story.

"How is your woman?" Aculf asked. "Eawynn, isn't it?"

Dunston sighed. He did not wish to speak of Eawynn; of his loss. His expression must have been answer enough, for Aculf held up a hand. "I am sorry, my friend. How many children?"

Dunston shook his head.

"We were not so blessed."

Aculf raised his eyebrows and glanced down at the sleeping girl.

"I thought she was yours." He gave a twisted smirk. "Or your granddaughter, perhaps."

Dunston shook his head.

"She is not my kin, but I will not let any harm come to her."

Aculf nodded.

"You were always a good man," he said.

Dunston frowned, thinking of all the men he had killed. Had all of those men deserved death?

Aculf picked up a stick and prodded the embers of the fire.

"We had three, Inga and me," he said. "Two girls and a boy." His voice had taken on a distant, haunted tone. He poked at the fire and sparks drifted into the darkness. "All gone now."

"It is a terrible thing to lose loved ones."

Aculf sighed and threw another log onto the fire in a spray of embers and winking motes.

"I found my boy and Inga," Aculf said. "They had fought as best they could." He stared into the fire for a moment, his mind walking along the shadowed paths of memories. "I should have been there. I sometimes wonder what would have happened if I had been."

Dunston did not know the full tale of what had befallen Aculf's family, but he knew the folly and pain of such thoughts.

"You cannot change the past, old friend," he said, his voice barely a whisper. "To rake over those old coals will only cause you pain."

"You sound like Guthlaf," said Aculf. "He would always tell me how to think."

"I meant no harm."

"I know it. The pain is there whether you speak of it or not. I will never be rid of it, I fear."

Dunston said nothing.

Aculf sniffed, then reached out for the flask of mead.

"I never found my daughters," he said. He took a long draught from the skin and wiped his mouth with his hand. "I wonder if they are still alive somewhere. In Denemearc or Íraland. Perhaps they married strong Norsemen."

Dunston watched his old friend, but said nothing.

As if his memories had been held within a cask that had now been split, allowing its contents to pour forth, so Aculf's tale rushed out then. He spoke in a soft, distant voice of how he had been chopping timber in the woodland near Cernemude, the village where he had settled with his family, when he had seen smoke rising above the settlement. He had sprinted back through the trees, leading the other young men who had been with him. All of them desperate, all terrified of what they would find when they reached their homes. The Norsemen had left nothing behind except corpses and burning buildings.

He was not the only man bereaved that day. But the other men had not been of the Wulfas Westseaxna. They had wept and buried their dead and slowly rebuilt their homes and lives as best they could. Not Aculf. He had been filled with an all-consuming rage and a feeling of such helplessness that he had not been able to remain there, living the life of a farmer where all that remained for him were the memories of his dead wife and son and the daughters who had been snatched and borne away on the sleek sea-dragons of the Vikingr.

"We had become soft," said Aculf, his voice beginning to slur from the mead. "It had been years since the Norsemen had raided the coast. But when the Frankish ships stopped sailing the Narrow Sea, it was only a matter of time before the bastard Vikingrs returned. It was my bad luck that some of them spied Cernemude from the sea."

Dunston watched him through the flickering flames. He could hear the despair in Aculf's words. He recognised the feeling of impotence he felt at losing his family. For a man used to fighting, to cutting his way through the obstacles before him, it was a terrible thing to be powerless to protect those you loved. Dunston had sat and watched as sickness consumed Eawynn. The memories plagued him and he recalled the anger that had filled him after her death. But where should he direct his ire? At God? At the disease that had destroyed his beautiful wife? Such thoughts were foolish. Aculf knew there was an enemy responsible for his pain. He would never have been able to return to a life of peace while those men still lived.

Aculf continued with his tale and Dunston noted that many of the wolf-heads had fallen quiet, listening intently, their eyes glimmering in the dark as they watched their leader speak. He wondered whether this was a story he seldom told. Perhaps they had never heard it before. But now that he had started, he did not appear inclined to stop.

Unable to rest, and filled with the burning need for vengeance and the desperate hope of finding his daughters, Aculf joined the crew of a ship bound for Íraland. When they were attacked by a band of Norsemen aboard a dragon-prowed wave-steed, he had revelled in the fight, cutting them down and screaming the names of his daughters at them. But none of them knew of the attack on Cernemude, so they had been killed and thrown overboard. It was after that first trip that he began to realise that the men he travelled with were no better than the Vikingr he hated. They would set upon smaller vessels, killing the occupants and stealing their cargo.

"I was a fool," Aculf whispered. "I thought I could find my girls and bring them back. In the end, I knew I would never find them." He spat into the embers of the fire. "If I did, they would not recognise the man I had become." He sighed and took another drink of mead. He could not meet Dunston's gaze. "I left the ship, but on land I fared little better. Soon I had to come here, into the forest. Any reeve in the land would see me hanged for what I have done, so this is my life now."

Dunston stared at him for a long time.

"What happened?"

Aculf shook his head and waved his hand, dismissing the question.

"Bad luck," he said. "And not always just for me." He met Dunston's gaze for a moment and his meaning was clear. "I do not wish to speak of it any further. I am here, and this is my family now." A murmur came from the listeners. Strælbora and his knot of friends glowered at Dunston. "Now, Dunston, you must tell us how it is you have come to spend the night in our humble encampment."

Dunston sighed. He reached out and someone handed him the mead. He took a mouthful. Swallowing the liquid slowly, he pondered how much to tell. He cleared his throat, unable to think of a good reason not to tell Aculf everything. They were at his mercy after all. Dunston might have been able to kill three more in the fight that afternoon, but he could not hope to stand against two dozen.

And so he told them the whole story, leaving nothing out. At the mention of how Lytelman had been killed, Aculf glanced over at Strælbora, but it wasn't until Dunston described finding Beornmod's blood-eagled corpse and then how they had heard Ithamar tortured in the same way, that Aculf spoke.

"This sounds like the work of Bealowin, don't you think, Strælbora?"

"You know him?" asked Dunston.

Strælbora nodded, still scowling at Dunston.

"An evil whoreson," he said.

"With a taste for torture and inflicting pain," said Aculf. "You know the type."

Dunston nodded. Every group of fighting men attracted those who enjoyed the act of killing. Some such men became monsters, worse than any warrior they would have to face in battle.

"Bealowin travelled with us for a time," Aculf said. "I never knew his story, he would not speak of it. But his love for the ritual of the blood-eagle was unholy. Unnatural." Aculf stared into the flames and seemed to suppress a shudder. "We are wolf-heads, not animals. There are things even we will not abide."

"You turned him out?"

"Yes," Aculf said, smiling. "I can be quite persuasive, you know? I thought he would have got himself killed years ago, but if he yet lives, he is as deadly as a snake." He traced a finger along the puckered scar that ran across his forehead. "If you meet him, perhaps you could repay him for this."

Dunston thought of all the suffering the man had inflicted.

"He owes many for what he has done. I will collect the blood-price for what he did to you and much more besides."

Aculf stared at him for a moment and then laughed.

"I believe you will at that!" He chuckled. "This is Dunston the Bold, men! And he is even more persuasive than me!"

They spoke little of anything of import as the fire died down to embers. They reminisced over past battles and escapades and, despite their situation, Dunston found himself enjoying Aculf's company. It had been so many years and it was good to speak to one who had shared much of his youthful days of strength and battle-fame. Their mood seemed infectious, and soon, even Strælbora was smiling.

As the thin archer laid out his blanket on the ground, preparing for sleep, Dunston called out to him.

"There is no bad blood between us?"

Strælbora's face was dark in the ember glow. His eyes glinted and then his white teeth shone as he grinned.

"Very well, axe man," he said. "You can sleep easy."

"Good," replied Dunston. "I would hate to have to kill you before I break my fast."

Some of the men laughed.

"You have my word that no harm will befall you in my camp," slurred Aculf. "If any one of you touches him or the girl, and Dunston does not kill you, I will. Understand?" A rumble of assent. Dunston ached and was tired beyond anything he had felt for years. He hoped Aculf held sway over these outlaws, for he was sure they could slit his throat without him even waking.

Wrapping himself in his blanket, close to the fire and beside Aedwen's slumbering form, Dunston could feel sleep descending on him quickly.

"You seek the king tomorrow then?" asked Aculf, dragging Dunston from the welcoming embrace of sleep.

"I do," he replied, propping himself up on his right elbow and instantly regretting it, as it stabbed with pain. "I hope he will remember me and know what to do about all of this."

"Ecgberht will remember you, Dunston. Of that there is no doubt. We will see you safely to the edge of the forest. From there, it is a short walk to Exanceaster."

"I thank you," Dunston said, lying back.

"You have done no wrong," whispered Aculf in the darkness. "Perhaps old Ecgberht might pardon you."

Dunston had not thought so far ahead. He just wished to deliver the message and Aedwen safely to Exanceaster.

"Perhaps," he said, his voice softened by approaching sleep.

"Give me your word you will not speak of me," hissed Aculf, his whispering voice tinged with urgency. "Of us, here."

"Speak of you?" answered Dunston, confused with drink and tiredness. "In what way?"

"I know you could track a mouse across the forest. You could lead them to us."

"I would not do that. You have aided us. You are my friend."

"We were friends, weren't we? Long ago, in a different life."

"We each only have one life, Aculf. Perhaps I could speak of how you have helped us. The king would remember your service." A thought came to him. "He might pardon you."

"No!" hissed Aculf. "Promise me you will not speak to him of me. I would that he remembers me as the great warrior I once was."

Dunston sighed in the darkness, wondering what atrocities Aculf had committed in his past. But he knew he would not ask. He too would prefer to remember him as he had once been, full of power and honour.

"You have my word," he said.

Aculf said no more and soon the sounds of snoring and the soft whispers of the forest pulled Dunston into a deep and dreamless sleep.

Thirty-Two

"Look at that," said Aedwen, awe in her voice.

The River Exe was a wide thread of silver before them. Wherries and cogs dotted the water as fishermen and merchants plied their trades. To either side of the river were broad flat meadows of lush grass and summer flowers. Butterflies and insects fluttered and droned in the air. Nearer the water, the muddy banks were festooned with birds. Dunlins, sandpipers and redshanks dipped their slender bills into the dark muck in search of food. In the distance, to the northwest of their position, reared the walls of Exanceaster. They were crumbling in places, having been built many centuries ago by the long-vanished Romans, but the city was still an imposing sight to behold. And yet this was not what had excited Aedwen so. The sky above Exanceaster was a muddle of grey clouds, still heavy with rain, and before that drab backdrop, in a brilliant display of God's power, there arced a perfect rainbow. It reached high into the sky with one end seeming to touch the ground within the city's walls.

Dunston paused for a moment, but seemed unimpressed by the spectacle. He took the opportunity to scan the horizon for sign of any of their pursuers. Across the river, on the hills that rose there, sheep and goats grazed the slopes. All appeared calm. Aedwen sighed.

"It must be a sign that God is watching over us," Aedwen said, gazing raptly at the rainbow. It was so beautiful. After all the ugliness of these last days, it almost hurt to look at it. Her eyes prickled with tears and the vision of the vibrant colours swam.

Dunston grunted, he pressed on, walking determinedly along the meadow, the wet grasses soaking his leg bindings.

They had started the day dry. The rain had held off for much of the night and after her initial fear of the wolf-heads, Dunston's presence, the warmth from the outlaws' fire, and the drone of voices as the men spoke had lulled her to sleep. She had thought she would never be able to rest, with the hungry gaze of Strælbora and the others on her, but to her surprise sleep had found her quickly enough. As she had closed her eyes, her head resting on Dunston's thigh, Aedwen had begun to feel less frightened of what the future might hold. The rumble of his voice soothed her nerves. The way he had fought the wolf-heads filled her with awe. Dunston still frightened her, but she knew he would do anything, even risk his own life, to protect her.

She had awoken with a sense of wellbeing she had not felt for days. But that was as nothing when compared to the rapturous feeling she had now, looking upon the colourful arch of light in the sky.

Aedwen hurried to keep up with Dunston. She knew that he was nervous, more so now that they had left the cover of the forest and their destination was so close. The outlaws had led them to the river and then, with the briefest of farewells, they had vanished back into the gloom of the forest, like so much smoke.

Fear still scratched its fingers along her back and neck when she thought of the men who chased them, but she could not believe that the rainbow was not a good omen.

"The tale of Noah is my favourite story," she said. "Father Osbern told it often and he told it well."

Dunston said nothing.

"I always liked to think of all those animals in that great ship," she said. "I would picture the horses, cows, dogs, cats, chickens and such, but Osbern also spoke of other creatures. Lions and camels and other things I can't recall. Do you know what they look like?"

Dunston shook his head.

"I've never seen a lion or a camel," he answered gruffly.

They walked on. The clouds had once again drifted over the sun and the land was suddenly darker and cooler. Aedwen shivered.

"You know what the best part of the story is?" she asked.

Again, Dunston shook his head. His attention was elsewhere, and he reminded her of a sheepdog watching the land about its flock for wolves.

"It's when God placed a rainbow in the sky and promised never to send another great flood to kill His people."

"There are many other ways to die," Dunston said, his tone flat.

She did not know what to say to that. The old man had grown morose and looked more tired than ever.

"You know what the Norse call the rainbow?" he asked.

Now it was her turn to shake her head.

"I spoke to a captured raider once," he said. "I don't remember his name now." He snorted derisively at his bad memory. "How can I not remember his name? Anyway, it is no matter. Most of the Norse we captured shouted and spat at us until they were beaten senseless. This one, a great red-bearded giant of a man, was talkative. He'd sailed from Dyfelin with two shiploads of Vikingrs. They made the mistake of landing at Tweoxneam."

He fell silent for a moment, clearly remembering the events of years past.

"Mistake?" she said.

"Well, Tweoxneam is a rich port, with a wealthy church, so it was a good place to attack. But what the red-bearded bastard and his crews didn't know is that the king was there with his hearth warriors to celebrate the wedding of the son of Tweoxneam's ealdorman. Bad luck for the Norsemen. Good luck for the king."

"Or perhaps God helped the Christian king of Wessex to defend the land against the heathen."

Dunston gave her a strange look that she could not interpret.

"We met them on the beach, shieldwall to shieldwall." He grimaced at the memory. "It was a bloody business."

"You were in the shieldwall?"

"Oh yes, I was there all right. Got this scar on that beach." He pulled back the stained sleeve of his kirtle to show a long, thin white line running down the corded muscle of his right forearm. "It bled like a stuck pig," he said. "Looked worse than it was really. It stung like the Devil himself though. Funny that I can remember that so clearly but still cannot recall the name of that Norseman."

He scratched at his head, as if that might help him to remember. They were covering the ground leading to Exanceaster more quickly than she had expected. After the days of threading around trees, brambles and bushes, to walk in the open, with the wind and sun on her face, was a relief.

"Was Aculf there too?"

Dunston shook his head.

"No, he had left us before that." He paused, turning to face her. "When we reach Exanceaster, you are not to mention Aculf or the others. I gave my word." As if he needed to explain himself, he added, "We were friends, once."

She nodded, uncertain of what had been said in the night; what bonds connected the two old warriors.

"You have my word too," she said. Whatever Aculf had done to see him cast out from the law, he had helped them and he was a friend to Dunston. She thought he probably didn't have many. He held her gaze for a moment, then, seemingly satisfied, he continued walking through the long wet grass.

"Tell me of the Vikingr and the rainbow," she said.

Dunston looked up at the colourful arch of light against the rain-laden clouds, adjusting his huge axe on his shoulder.

"We drank ale together the night after that battle, that red-bearded warrior and I. As the sun went down, there was a rainbow over the Narrow Sea and he told me that his people called it Bifröst." Dunston let out a guffaw. "By God, I can remember that! What was the man's name? I should remember. Ah, it will come to me, I'm sure. I haven't thought of him for years. He said that Bifröst was the bridge that led to the afterlife, or to the kingdom of their gods, or some such nonsense."

They walked on, and Aedwen noted that Dunston had grown grim once more.

"He said that seeing the bridge was an omen that he would die and that his spirit would depart and travel to the feasting hall of the gods."

"What happened to him?"

Dunston sighed.

"The following morning, the king came to where we held the captives." Dunston stared up at the sky.

"What did the king do to the Vikingrs?" she asked, unsure whether she truly wished to hear the answer.

"He ordered them all hanged." Dunston spat. "They begged to be allowed to hold a weapon as they were killed. They said otherwise they would not go to the feasting hall of Valhalla."

"Did the king allow them their request?"

Dunston glanced at her.

"No," he said.

She pondered what he had told her as they continued across the meadow.

The men the king had ordered to be killed had attacked Wessex, had sailed intent on murder and theft. Was it not right they should be hanged? And yet she could sense Dunston's sadness at the memory of the death of the red-bearded Norseman and his Vikingr crews.

The rainbow had gone now, vanished as quickly as it had appeared. She watched Dunston stomping across the meadow, his great axe on his shoulder and his beard bristling from his jutting jaw. He looked more marauding Norseman than Christian. She would never look upon a rainbow with unbridled happiness again.

In the distance, a flock of green plovers burst from the grassland, filling the sky with flapping and squawking cries.

Dunston halted, raising his hand to shade his eyes, peering to see what had disturbed the birds.

And then, beneath the angry screeches of the birds, she heard something deep and resonant, like a far off peel of thunder. But this thunder did not dissipate, it grew until it was a thrumming rumble. She could feel it in her feet. The earth was shaking.

Dunston grabbed her shoulder.

"Run!" he shouted.

She could not make sense of what was happening. And then, in an instant of crashing terror, she saw what was making the thunderous roar. From beneath the swarming birds in flight came a line of some ten horsemen. Her eyes were young and keen and she picked out the glint of buckles on the mounts' bridles, the shine of sword blades slicing through the air. They came at a gallop and great clods of soft earth flew up behind them as they trampled the flowers and grass of the meadow. In an instant she recognised Raegnold, his sharp face mottled and swollen from where Dunston's axe had smashed into his jaw. At the sight of him she knew these men had only one purpose: to slay them; to silence them before they could deliver the message and its secrets to Exanceaster.

Dunston was shaking her, pointing away from the river. A copse of alder stood a spear's throw away.

"Run!" he repeated, thrusting his bag into her hands and shoving her towards the trees. "Climb a tree. I will fight these bastards."

"But… they are so many."

"Enough!" he bellowed and the strength of his voice alone spurred her into action. "Do as I say, or it has all been for nought."

She sprinted towards the trees, not looking back until she was in the shade beneath them. Her blood roared in her ears. As she ran she slung Dunston's bag over her shoulder. When she reached the trees, she leapt for the first low branch she saw and swung herself up. She could not carry her staff, so she let it fall. She still had the knife at her belt though. She prayed the horsemen did not have bows, and climbed as fast as she could, scrambling higher and higher. Her hands were raw and cut from scrabbling at the rough bark. Lichen and moss stained her pale soft skin.

When she was more than two men's height above the ground, she looked back at the meadow. She stifled a scream at what she saw.

The wall of horsemen were almost upon Dunston. They had not slowed and they bore down on him with weapons raised. Some carried spears, others swords, two wielded axes. The men screamed and shouted.

Before them, alone in the meadow, damp grass hiding his feet, stood Dunston. As immobile and resolute as a rock awaiting the incoming tide. His legs were set apart and in his strong hands he held DeaÞangenga. How could one old man stand before so many mounted warriors? It was folly. But what else could he do?

She offered up a prayer to the Blessed Virgin.

"Mother of God, please protect him," she implored.

And then the riders were upon him with bone-crunching force and Aedwen's tears prevented her from seeing clearly any more.

Thirty-Three

Dunston felt no fear as the riders charged towards him. There were too many of them for him to defeat alone, of that he had no doubt and he felt a pang of terrible sadness as he thought what they would do to Aedwen once they had finished with him. Hefting DeaÞangenga before him, he rolled his head, causing his neck to pop and crack. He would make them pay dearly for his life. Perhaps she would find a way to escape if he could hold them long enough. He knew that the idea was foolish, but he clung to it. He could not think of what might befall the girl. All he could do now was to kill as many of these bastards as he was able.

Glowering at the horsemen as they galloped towards him, he was filled with rage. Fury at his failure to protect Aedwen. Ire at the atrocities these men had performed on innocents. And anger at having to break his oath.

They were nearly upon him now, and he had already chosen the man he would kill first. A broad-shouldered man with blue cloak and a long, deadly spear. The spears were the most dangerous weapons in that first pass, so he would slay the largest spearman first.

"I am sorry, my love," he whispered, wondering whether Eawynn's shade could hear him. Well, they would be together soon. "I know that I promised, but I must break my oath to you once more, for it seems I will die fighting."

He thought she would have understood. What else could he do? He had to try and defend the girl. Surely that is what Eawynn had seen in him all those years before; what set him apart from other killers of men.

There was no more time for thinking. The thunder of the horses' hooves enveloped him. He stared into the eyes of the beast that carried his first target. It was a roan stallion, muscled and strong, but this was no warhorse. Its eyes were white-rimmed with terror as its rider urged it forward. The men screamed abuse at Dunston, but he ignored them all. There was nothing now save for the stallion and its rider. The man's spear dipped towards Dunston. In a heartbeat he would be skewered on the sharp steel point of the weapon. But in the last instant, he stepped to the right and raised DeaÞangenga high. The spear whistled harmlessly past his face, and the rider was powerless to adjust his aim. Even if he had been fast enough to do so, the horse's head and neck were in the way.

With a great roar that caused the horse beside the spearman to shy away from the axeman, Dunston swung DeaÞangenga in a great downward arc. Its silver-threaded head bit deeply into the roan's neck, splattering gore in the summer air. The animal let out a pitiful scream and collapsed, turning over itself in a flail of legs, hooves and mud. The rider was thrown.

But Dunston did not pause to see how the spearman tumbled into the long grass. Instead, he used the momentum from his great axe's swing to spin around and, crouching to avoid any strikes from the horsemen, he swung DeaÞangenga low. With a sickening splintering, and a jarring force that almost knocked the axe from his hands, DeaÞangenga's blade hacked into a second horse's forelegs. Bones shattered and the beast added its cries to those of the first animal. It ran on awkwardly for several paces, before toppling forward into the earth. Its rider leapt from the saddle, landing badly and sprawling on the ground.

The remainder of the horses rushed past, with no blow coming near Dunston.

In the time it took the horsemen to wheel their steeds around, Dunston ran past the first dying horse. The spearman was rising, half-dazed, from the long grass. Dunston's axe hammered into his neck. Blood fountained and the man fell back, to lie almost hidden from view in the meadow.

The second rider fared momentarily better. He clambered to his feet, sword in hand and advanced on Dunston. Perhaps he expected to be able to take the older man easily, while Dunston fought his comrade, but the axeman spun to face him a heartbeat later. Bright gore dripped from DeaÞangenga, and the man hesitated.

Dunston did not.

"Now you die, boy," he hissed and he sprang at his assailant.

The young warrior raised his sword, but Dunston batted it away with his axe before burying the blade into his opponent's chest. The young man collapsed to his knees and his eyes filled with tears. His face took on a look Dunston had seen countless times before: a dreadful mixture of despair and disbelief at how quickly death had come when moments before life had pumped hot and vibrant in his veins.

Dunston tugged his axe, but it was held fast between the man's ribs. The man keened. Wrenching harder, DeaÞangenga made an obscene sucking sound as it came free. Dunston kicked the man over and turned to face the rest of his attackers.

The riders had regained control of their mounts and were gathering for another charge now. But Dunston did not wait for them to come. He sprinted towards them, giving them no time to gain any momentum. Several of the riders' horses turned away, refusing to attack. Perhaps they were frightened by the screaming man rushing towards them, or maybe from the smell of fresh blood in the air. Dunston cared not, all he knew was that he had to keep moving, keep killing. To give them a moment to organise themselves would spell his doom.

Three of the men managed to spur their mounts forward. Dunston ran straight towards them. Only one, the man on his right, had a spear, the other two brandished swords. They built up speed, but they only reached a fast trot before Dunston was upon them. He laughed, filled with the glee of blood-letting, all thought of his broken oath now forgotten. The Wolf was no longer the hunted. This is what he had been born to do.

Feinting towards the spearman, Dunston swerved to the left, making it impossible for the man to bring the spear to bear without fear of striking his companions or their horses.

One of the swordsmen swiped at him, but Dunston dodged the blade easily. Reaching for the man with his left hand, he grabbed hold of his kirtle and hauled him from the saddle. The man's left foot caught in the stirrup and he was pulled away from Dunston. The horse, scared and confused by the unusual burden, bucked and shied, dragging the man away from the fight.

The second swordsman was evidently an accomplished rider, for he spun his mount around and aimed a strike at Dunston's neck. Dunston caught the sword's blade on DeaÞangenga's iron bit. The two weapons clanged together and Dunston half-expected the sword's blade to shatter. But despite the terrible blow against the axe's head, the sword was well-forged. Its patterned blade sang from the impact, but it did not break.

The man's steed reared, pawing the air with its hooves. Dunston jumped back and was surprised to see his assailant sliding from the saddle. He smacked his mount on the rump and the horse bounded away, happy to be distanced from the battling men.

"What are you doing?" called a heavy-set man on a splendid grey mare. He was richly dressed in fine linen and wool. A garnet-studded clasp held his cerulean cloak and a golden chain hung at his throat. He was older than the rest of the men and Dunston took him for their leader and clearly a man of worth. Dunston did not recognise him.

The dismounted warrior however was known to him. The man had been with Hunfrith at Briuuetone. It was impossible not to recall those ridiculous red breeches. The man swung his sword before him and grinned, his teeth white in his swarthy face and black beard.

"Just kill him and be done with it, Bealowin," shouted the leader. "We cannot tarry here. We are too close to Exanceaster."

So this was Bealowin. The torturer. The defiler. The murderer.

The swordsman was stepping lightly through the long grass and Dunston circled to follow his movement, unwilling to take his eyes off him for even a moment.

"I will slay him soon enough, lord," Bealowin said. "But this bastard has taken too many of my men. His life is mine. You would not deny me vengeance, would you?" He smirked at Dunston then, as if they were both party to some secret jest. The leader of the men was silent.

From the edge of his vision, Dunston could still make out the lord and the clump of horsemen gathered about him. He would have to hope that the man who had been pulled along by his stirrup had been dragged too far away to pose a threat.

Dunston took in a deep breath and swung DeaÞangenga in a wide arc, flexing the bunched muscles of his shoulders. Droplets of blood, as brilliant and red as the garnets in the lord's brooch, sprayed up in the sunlight. Sweat trickled down Dunston's forehead and stung his left eye.

"Feeling your age, Dunston the Old?" sneered Bealowin.

"At least I have grown old, boy. Just like Aculf. We both yet live. You must ask yourself how that is so."

If the mention of the wolf-head registered, Bealowin did not show it on his face. Without warning, he leapt forward and lashed out with his sword. He was fast and Dunston was barely able to step back from the attack. He felt the wind from the passing blade on his face. He recovered quickly. Taking advantage of Bealowin's lunge, he swiped across the man's chest. Bealowin's speed and agility saved him, and he danced away from Dunston, giggling.

"You are so slow," he chortled. "Just like Aculf. How you managed to kill so many of my men, I will never know. They say you were once one of the fabled Wolves of Wessex, but I cannot believe it. You are so very old now."

Dunston was out of breath, but willed himself to appear calm and poised. He could feel the sweat running in rivulets down his back.

"You will find out soon enough how easily I can kill," he said. "I am Dunston the Bold. Son of Wilnoth. I am yet a Wolf of Wessex, boy. And I will take your life."

"God," said Bealowin, stifling his laughter with difficulty, "how I wish I could have more time with you, old man. Your bleating amuses me. I would have liked to make you sing a merry song beneath the blood-eagle."

Dunston said nothing. The time for words was over.

This was the man who had performed the atrocious acts of butchery on Lytelman, Beornmod and Ithamar. Dunston thought of Nothgyth and the corpses at Cantmael. Who knew how many others Bealowin had tortured or killed? Dunston had met his kind before. Bealowin was one who took pleasure from the pain of others. And Dunston knew something with absolute certainty: Bealowin would die here today. Whatever the cost, Dunston would not allow the man who had inflicted such pain and misery to live.

As the thought hardened like tempered steel in his mind, Bealowin's expression changed, as if he too had come to the chilling notion that he might die here.

Without a sound, Bealowin sprang forward once more, slashing and scything his sword in a frenzied attack. It was all Dunston could do to parry and dodge the blows. All the while he was pushed back. Sweat drenched him now. His eyes smarted and his breath came in gasping wheezes. Step after step, Dunston retreated. DeaÞangenga was heavy in his grip now, and with each parry he seemed to be growing weaker and slower. Damn Bealowin. He had the one thing that Dunston could never regain: his youth.

A savage swing at his head made Dunston stagger, barely catching the sword's blade on his axe haft. Splinters flew from the rune-carved wood. The watching men let out a ragged cheer. But Dunston saw an opening in Bealowin's defences. The young man had over-stretched, leaving himself open to attack. Shifting his weight, Dunston sliced DeaÞangenga towards Bealowin's unprotected midriff.

Too late he saw the gleam of triumph in Bealowin's eyes. Dunston cursed himself for a fool. His mind must be growing as old and slow as his body to have fallen for such a ruse. For, in the instant that the axe swung towards Bealowin, the swordsman, clearly anticipating the attack, parried the blow, and then followed up with a vicious riposte. His sharp patterned blade scored a deep cut along Dunston's arm, following almost exactly the scar that a raiding Norseman had given him all those years before on the beach of Tweoxneam.

Dunston staggered back. His sleeve was in tatters and blood welled in the long cut.

Bealowin laughed.

"Finish him now, man," shouted the mounted lord.

The gathered horsemen jeered at Dunston, taunting him. They could see his death looming; imminent.

Dunston shook the sweat from his eyes. He could feel his strength sapping from him as the blood pumped from the wound. His arm throbbed with each beat of his heart.

"Come and finish it then, boy," he said to Bealowin. He opened his arms wide, holding DeaÞangenga out to the side in his bloody hand. This had to end now, he could not afford to grow any weaker. "You think you could make me sing? See if you can make me scream like those you tortured, you worm," he goaded. "Is that the only way you can make someone moan with your blade? To tie them up and cut them? Not man enough to make a woman moan with the weapon between your legs?"

With a bellow of anger at the old man's insults, Bealowin rushed in, lunging, jabbing, slicing with his blade. Dunston gritted his teeth against the burning pain in his arm and parried and dodged as Bealowin pressed his attack. Dunston's right hand was slick with blood and he could feel his axe slipping in his grasp. This could not go on much longer, and so, grasping the haft in both hands, Dunston smashed Bealowin's sword away and then followed with a powerful downward arc. If it had connected, it would have surely cut Bealowin from the crown of his head to his belly. But the blow did not make contact. Instead, Bealowin stepped back and Dunston's axe bit deeply into the soft earth.

Again the gleam of victory was in Bealowin's eyes. His foe was unarmed, his great axe embedded in the loam of the meadow. Bealowin roared and sprang at Dunston. He lunged with his deadly blade, meaning to spit the axeman on his sword.

But Dunston had not survived all these years and countless battles by strength alone. He knew when to bludgeon and batter an opponent, but sometimes guile was the way to win a fight.

Dunston released DeaÞangenga's haft, leaving the axe buried in the soil, as he had known it would when he'd made the swing, inviting Bealowin to believe him defenceless. Dunston spun, with the speed of a man half his age and Bealowin's sword did not plunge into his guts to deliver a death blow. And yet Dunston did not avoid the sword's bite altogether. The sharp blade ripped open his kirtle. Blood instantly streamed, hot and stinging, from a long slicing cut.

Dunston ignored the pain of the cut. It was not a killing wound. He gripped Bealowin's right wrist in his left hand, tugging him forward. At the same moment he pulled Beornmod's seax from the scabbard at his belt and drove it into Bealowin's stomach. He felt the younger man tremble in his grasp and he twisted the blade, pulling it out of the sucking wound and plunging it back into his flesh. Again he stabbed, and again, all the while watching the comprehension dawn in Bealowin's dimming eyes.

The man's blood gushed over Dunston's hand, mingling with his own that pumped from the wound on his forearm.

"Aculf sends you greetings," whispered Dunston, his face close to Bealowin's. "And now you understand."

"What?" the dying man gasped, lost confusion on his face.

"How I killed your men. Even an old wolf has fangs."

Bealowin let out a rattling, rasping breath and slumped. Dunston released him and let him fall to the ground.

Blinking away the sweat from his eyes, Dunston turned to face the horsemen. His kirtle was sodden with blood now, his stomach and arm a stinging agony.

"Who's next?" he shouted at the gathered men, disappointed that his voice cracked in his throat.

"What in the name of all that is holy is wrong with you all?" screamed the gold-chained lord. "He is but one old man!"

Dunston spat. He wished he had some water, but his flask was in the bag he had given to Aedwen.

"I would find some new men if I were you," he said, grinning despite the pain in his arm and stomach. "These ones are more like lambs than warriors."

"Kill him now!" yelled the men's leader. Spittle flew from his lips and his horse flinched at its rider's strident voice.

For a heartbeat, Dunston thought the man was giving the order to the riders around him. But then the thrumming of hooves reached his ears and penetrated through the rushing sound of his blood. The lord was not looking at Dunston, but behind him.

Dunston spun to face the new danger that came from his rear.

All was a blur. The glittering tip of a spear blade flickered towards Dunston. Instinctively, he leaned backward, allowing the steel to pass a hand's breadth from his face. But he was too slow to avoid the charging horse. The spearman who had passed him earlier spurred his steed onward and it hit Dunston with the force of a storm wave buffeting against a cliff.

Dunston was thrown into the waving grass. He tumbled over until he lay on his back. For a moment, he could not draw breath. He barely knew what had happened. The sky above him was grey. Was it growing darker? Sounds of a horse and a man shouting, muffled, as if from a great distance.

With a huge effort, Dunston finally sucked in a deep breath of the earthy air. His chest screamed out. A sharp stabbing agony made him groan, as he slowly climbed to his feet. He attempted another breath. The same searing pain engulfed him. The spearman had dismounted and was coming towards him. For a moment, Dunston's vision blurred and he thought he might faint. Then the man's features became clearer. It was Raegnold, the man he had fought outside the barn in Briuuetone. Raegnold's face was swollen and bruised.

Clenching his jaw against the pain, Dunston reached down and retrieved DeaÞangenga from the grass. Tears pricked his eyes from the pain. He could barely stand. Had his ribs pierced his lungs?

Raegnold was almost on him now. None of the other men came to aid him to dispatch Dunston. He was not surprised. He must have looked as though he might die soon anyway, soaked in blood and mud, and barely able to rise to his feet. He shook his head in an attempt to clear it. Judging from the intensity of the pain, he might well succumb with no further injuries, if he was given time. But Raegnold was clearly not going to allow that to happen.

"Come to let me finish what I started back in Briuuetone?" Dunston asked. His voice rasped, his breath scratched in his chest.

"You're dead, old man," hissed Raegnold through gritted teeth, unable to open his mouth any wider due to his broken jaw.

Dunston willed himself to stand upright.

"Speak up, I can barely hear you," he taunted. But he had heard the words well enough. And what was worse, he knew them to be true. He would die here, now. His body was aflame with pain and even if by some miracle he was able to defeat Raegnold, there were still six men here, hale and strong. He could not survive against them all.

Raegnold pulled his sword from its scabbard, but did not reply. Evidently speaking hurt too much. Dunston understood that feeling.

"Well, Eawynn, I will be with you soon," he whispered. "I hope I did not disappoint you too much by breaking my promises."

He hoped that Aedwen had run from her hiding place. Perhaps she would be able to reach the safety of Exanceaster before these brutes could capture her. He prayed it was so. For there was no more that he could do now.

"Come on then," he said, lifting his great axe in both hands. "Let's see if I can't improve that ugly face of yours."

Raegnold growled and rushed forward.
Dunston moved on leaden legs to meet him.
To meet him, and to die.

Thirty-Four

Aedwen clung to the branch and watched Dunston's stand against the riders with a mixture of awe and horror. She cuffed away bitter tears, smearing her cheeks with the green of lichen and moss. Despite the terror that she was about to witness the old man's death, she could not look away.

More than once she was certain that Dunston would be struck down, but each time he had emerged from the press of horses and weapon-wielding men. She watched in a daze of disbelief as the grey-bearded woodsman killed two of the riders in that first attack and left two mounts screaming and kicking in the grass. The sound of the animals' distress scratched at her nerves, echoing her own anguish. But she did not scream. She gripped the alder tightly until her muscles cramped while she willed Dunston on.

Surely he could not hope to face so many foe-men and survive. And yet, as some of the horses wheeled about, she gasped. The old man was rushing at them! His bellowing cry reached her and she shuddered. He pulled one rider from his saddle and the man was sent careening away over the meadow towards Exanceaster, dragged from his stirrup.

And then one of the horsemen dismounted. His sword flickered in the sunlight as he circled Dunston. The man was young and fast and Aedwen was certain that she was about to see the death of the man who had kept her alive these last days. She felt a hollow emptiness; was unable to think. She knew she should take advantage of the fact that all of the remaining men were watching the duel. She could slip down from the tree and sprint to the path that ran alongside the river. With luck, she could be at the woods the other side of the path before anyone noticed her. Perhaps then she would be able to make her way carefully and invisibly to Exanceaster. She patted the bag that was slung over her shoulder. The message was yet there. And surely that is why Dunston fought, so that she might have time to escape. He could not hope to live. She must flee. She knew it.

And yet she did not move. She shifted her position slightly so that she might see more clearly through the tree's leaves and she watched.

The two warriors, young and old, were speaking, but she could not hear the words from this distance. She held her breath as the dark-bearded warrior leapt at Dunston without warning. The clash of their blades reached her a moment later and she was shocked to see Dunston had avoided the man's attack.

Along with all of the riders, she watched raptly, unable to turn away as the two men fought. She let out a whimper when Dunston was cut, and wept with relief when finally he slew his younger and faster assailant.

But Dunston was wounded now, bleeding and struggling. She could barely imagine the fatigue and exhaustion he must feel, and yet she saw it in his gait, in the droop of his head and the slump of his shoulders.

Against all the odds, Dunston remained upright and Aedwen cursed herself for not running. He had bought her this time with his blood and his suffering. And, she was sure, with his death, which must come soon enough. And yet still she did not climb down from her vantage point.

She screamed out a warning when she saw the horse bearing down on him from behind. Perhaps this was how she repaid him, by saving him from a craven attack from the rear.

Dunston turned, but too slow and she could not stop her tears now as the horse clattered into him, sending him tumbling and sprawling to the soft earth of the meadow.

She sobbed, willing him to rise. And when he did, pushing himself painfully and slowly to his feet, her heart clenched. He was barely able to stand, his body broken and clearly in agony. The horseman who had hit Dunston dismounted. Despite the distance, she recognised him instantly and cursed at the cruelty of it. That the man who had slain Odin would now kill the dog's master.

The circle of horsemen watched on, anticipating the end of the great Dunston the Bold. Expecting to see his lifeblood pumping into the meadow grass here, beneath the crumbling walls of Exanceaster.

Aedwen watched too. Like the riders, she was entranced, unable to turn away. But from her lofty position in the alder she caught a movement in the corner of her vision. A stealthy rippling in the long grass. A grey shadow, slipping between the waving sedge and golden marigolds of the meadow.

Raegnold was close to Dunston now. The old man, holding himself awkwardly against the pain, said something to the advancing man, but she could not hear what it was.

Her blood rushed in her ears and she looked back for the approaching shadow in the grass, thinking she must have imagined it.

It was still there, creeping ever closer. Could it be a wolf? Her mind could make no sense of it.

And then, in an instant, all became clear.

For, at the moment that Raegnold rushed at Dunston, ready to hack him down, the grey shape sprang forward, abandoning stealth for speed.

Thirty-Five

Dunston blinked, unsure for a moment what he was witnessing. Had he lost his senses? His body screamed at him, his chest a burning agony with each breath, hot blood running in rivers down his arm and belly. He had seen men lose their minds at the end, delirious from the pain as their spirits fought to cling to life for just a few more heartbeats.

He shook his head to clear it.

He was not dead yet. His vision was clear.

And now there could be no doubt. The grey shape that had leapt from the tall grass was Odin, his great merle hound. The dog's snarling jaws snapped onto Raegnold's wrist and the tall man, completely taken by surprise, let out a wail of fear and pain and fell into the grass. Odin was a frenzy of snarling and growling. Raegnold screamed as the two of them rolled, half-hidden by the foliage.

Regaining his wits, Dunston staggered forward. He would not allow the bastard to kill his dog. Evidently he had not slain Odin in Briuuetone, Dunston was not about to let him now.

He had only taken a couple of steps, when Raegnold's screams abated suddenly. Odin rose, panting, chest heaving. Raegnold was still. The dog's tongue lolled and its maw was stained crimson. Dunston almost laughed to see the dog's grin, but then he saw the long, blackened wound that ran the length of Odin's body and his stomach tightened. No hair grew along the cut that appeared to have been stitched and then burnt to staunch the bleeding. Someone had tended to the dog's injury, but Dunston feared the mystery healer's work would be undone soon.

The leader of the riders was the colour of a ripe rosehip now, as he screamed at his remaining men.

"Kill him! Kill him! Kill him, you incompetent fools!"

Goaded on thus by their master, the men spurred their horses forward. Dunston saw fear in some of their faces. Much blood had been spilt in a matter of moments, and the old wolf still stood. And yet, there was resolve in his enemies' expressions too. The warriors urged their mounts closer. Their eyes were hard and their weapons' steel glimmered dully in the sunlight.

A light rain began to fall and Dunston welcomed its cooling touch on his brow.

"To me, Odin," he called.

The hound padded to his side. Dunston's hand dropped to the dog's head and scratched behind his ears affectionately. It was good to see the old boy one last time, though how he had come to this place Dunston could not guess.

The riders were hesitating now, unsure how to proceed. They were grim-faced and determined, and yet it seemed they had not contended with the prospect of attacking an armed killer and his huge hound, both covered in the blood of their fallen comrades.

"What are you waiting for?" yelled their leader. Dunston noticed that despite his anger at his men's ineffectiveness, he did not ride forward with them.

A horse snorted and stamped. Its rider sawed at the reins, struggling to keep the beast from galloping away.

Dunston scanned the men's faces. Their jaws were set and they still had the benefit of overwhelming numbers. They would attack soon enough, goaded on by their lord.

"Just you and me again, old friend," he whispered and patted Odin's head. The fur was wiry and wet. Odin gazed up at his master with his one eye and licked his hand.

Above the riders, a rainbow appeared in the cloud-embroiled sky. Dunston smiled, wondering at the sign. He drew in a deep breath. By Christ, his ribs hurt.

Well, whether the rainbow was God's promise or an omen from the Norse gods, he would find out soon enough.

Hefting DeaÞangenga before him, Dunston raised himself up to his full height. His teeth ground together and he winced at the pain. But he would not let it show on his face. He would meet these murderers standing tall, not cowed and broken like some old washer woman.

"Come on then, if you are coming, you cowardly whoresons," he bellowed without warning. The steeds shied at the volume of his voice. He grinned, his teeth flashing wolfishly. "Or are you too craven to kill an old man and his dog?"

He would die now, he knew, but he had resigned himself to that reality and had made peace with breaking his oaths to Eawynn. The thought of death held no fear for him.

"Come on then, you curs," he yelled, ignoring the agony in his chest and raising DeaÞangenga into the air so that the sun caught its silver-threaded blade. And at last, their leader's commands and Dunston's taunts made the men move. As if at some unspoken signal, they all touched their spurs to their horses' flanks as one, and approached him and Odin with a deep-throated growl rather than a roar of defiance.

Dunston lifted his axe and prepared to take as many of them with him before death claimed him.

"Goodbye, Odin, old friend," he said.

The riders were almost upon them when a sound cut through their ire-filled shouts and the thrum of their horses' hooves. It was a piercing wail of a hunting horn and it came from the direction of Exanceaster. The riders reined in their mounts, clearly pleased for an excuse not to attack the blood-soaked greybeard, with his death-dealing axe and his fanged companion.

They halted a few paces from Dunston and turned towards the sound of the horn.

Riding from the town, sending up more angry green plovers into the sky, came a large group of men. Their cloaks were bright and polished metal glittered from their clothing, weapons and horses' harness.

One of the men who had been about to attack Dunston cursed and spat. He wheeled his horse about and trotted back to his lord. A moment later, the other horsemen followed him.

The golden-chained lord who led Dunston's assailants had lost all of his bluster. He was pale now where he had been crimson with rage moments before.

Dunston placed his hand on Odin's head once more and let DeaÞangenga's blade rest on the earth. Smiling, he looked up at the many-coloured arc of the rainbow that still hung in the air. He wondered again at its meaning. Whichever god had sent it into the heavens, it would seem it was a good omen for him.

He leaned on DeaÞangenga and patted Odin as the new group of horsemen approached. The horses splashed through puddles, sending up showers of tiny rainbows into the air. He counted close to thirty men coming from Exanceaster. They rode good horses, and the men wore colourful cloaks. Spear-tips glinted. Silver and gold glistened at throats, shoulders and fingers. Dunston noted that several of the men bore bows. None were armoured.

Dunston watched as his erstwhile attackers drew together. They were agitated and there was much hushed conversation. Dunston could not hear what was said and he did not much care. His body screamed at him with every breath. He longed to slump down, to rest in the long wet grass. And yet he willed himself to remain upright. He did not know who these newcomers were and he would not face a potential enemy sitting down, not while he yet lived.

They came at a canter and once again the horn sounded, piercing and loud. Moments later, the large band of riders was reining in around them. Dunston met the gaze of the men who looked down from their well-groomed mounts. Most were young, fresh-faced and arrogant, with combed and trimmed beards and moustaches. Their expressions of disdain withered under the glare of his ice blue stare.

One of the riders, an old man, with full, grey beard and wolf fur trimming his cloak, despite the warmth of the day, nudged his steed forward. Two dour-faced, younger men, with swords at their belts, pushed forward to accompany him.

"So," said the old man, taking in the dead and dying men and horses scattered about the meadow, "this is what prevented you from joining me for the hunt, Ælfgar."

The gold-chained leader spurred his steed forward.

"My lord king," he said, "I thought you were planning on hunting to the north."

"I was drawn to the commotion to the south. I may be old, but I yet have eyes in my head and great flocks of birds taking to the wing seemed like good prospect for hunting." He paused, casting his gaze about, taking in each of the bloody corpses strewn about. With each passing moment, his expression grew darker. For several heartbeats, his eyes lingered on Dunston, blood-streaked, wounded and leaning on his gore-slick axe. "By all that is holy," the king raged suddenly at the ealdorman, causing the horses to stamp and blow. "What is the meaning of this?"

"My lord king," said Ælfgar, raising himself up proudly in his saddle. "This man fled imprisonment. He has broken your peace, as you can see." He waved a hand about him as evidence of Dunston's wrongdoing. "He has slain several of my men."

Ealdorman Ælfgar's voice trembled with barely contained emotion. "He is a killer and he must be punished."

The king shifted in his saddle. The leather creaked. He narrowed his eyes beneath his bushy brows and held Ealdorman Ælfgar in his stare. For a long while, he did not move. Men jostled and shuffled. Someone coughed. The ealdorman swallowed and, after a moment's hesitation, dropped his gaze. Seemingly satisfied, Ecgberht turned his attention to Dunston.

He peered down at him for a time. With an effort, Dunston stood straighter and met the king's gaze. Ecgberht nodded.

"Well," he said as last, "I know that this man is a killer."

Relief washed over Ælfgar's face.

"You are wise, lord king. Have your men take him and we will have him hanged forthwith."

"Do not presume to give your king orders, Ælfgar." Ecgberht's tone was as hard and sharp as a blade.

"No, lord," stammered Ælfgar, "of course not, I merely meant—"

Ecgberht cut him off.

"I said that I know this man is a killer," he said. Ælfgar nodded, uncertainly, waiting now for the king to elaborate. "But I have never known this man to slay any but the enemies of Wessex," the king continued. "What do you say on the matter, Dunston, son of Wilnoth?"

"But lord...!" blurted out Ælfgar. "The man is a murderer."

"Silence, Ælfgar," snapped Ecgberht and, despite the pain that racked him, Dunston could not help but smile thinly to hear the steel in the king's tone. The man had grown old, but this was the same Ecgberht who had led Wessex to so many victories over the years. Age had not diminished his spirit.

The ealdorman seemed about to continue to protest, but another glower from the king silenced him.

"I would hear the telling of this tale from the mouth of one I trust," Ecgberht said. "Dunston, speak."

And so, in spite of the pain throbbing in his arm and the burning agony stabbing his chest with each intake of breath, Dunston told the tale as best he could. When he mentioned Hunfrith the reeve, one of Ælfgar's sworn men, the ealdorman could keep himself silent no longer.

"Lord king, you cannot listen to any more of this wolf-head's lies. He is outside the law. He has no voice."

Ecgberht turned to the granite-faced man to his right.

"If the ealdorman speaks again without my permission, you are to bind and gag him."

The guard nodded.

"With pleasure, lord king."

"Continue, Dunston."

Dunston did his best to tell the story of how they had fled from Briuuetone, their plan to find out why Aedwen's father had been murdered, discovering the slaughter at Cantmael. He did not mention Nothgyth, instead saying he had picked up the tracks of the riders and followed them. He told of the torture of the monk and how they had found the message and decided to head for Exanceaster in the hope of finding the king.

"I thought that only you could bring justice, lord," Dunston said. "I am but a simple woodsman, but it seemed clear to me there was more to this whole affair than banditry and wanton thirst for blood."

"Indeed. If what you say is even half-true, then there is the stink of conspiracy and treason about it. Though to what end, I cannot fathom. Where now is the message? Without it, your word is pitted against that of the ealdorman's."

"The girl, Aedwen, has it."

"And where is she?"

"I sent her to hide in those trees," Dunston said. "I do not know if she remains there."

"Well, call her hither, man, and let us see if we can put an end to this."

Dunston raised his arm, wincing at the pain and waved towards the stand of trees. For a long while there was no movement and he began to think Aedwen must have fled, as he had hoped she would only moments before.

He waved again.

"Aedwen," he called, his chest screaming from the effort. "Come, all is well."

Still no sign of her. He sighed. His mouth was dry. The gathered men were growing impatient, no doubt imagining that his whole tale had been nothing but lies.

"Where are you, girl?" Dunston whispered. Sweat mingled with the blood staining his kirtle.

He raised his hand for a third time and was about to shout once more, when the slender figure of the girl stepped silently from the shadow of the trees.

At the sight of the girl, Ælfgar tensed. He seemed ready to ride away, but the king's stony-jawed guard rode forward and grabbed the ealdorman's reins.

Aedwen walked slowly towards them. Her eyes were wide as she scanned the mass of mounted men.

"Do not fear, child," said Dunston. "This is the king." Her eyes widened yet further.

"And you are Aedwen, daughter of Lytelman, I take it?" asked Ecgberht.

She nodded, but seemed unable to speak.

"I am sorry for the loss of your father," Ecgberht said. "Do you have the letter that Dunston has been telling us about?"

She nodded again.

"Yes, lord," she managed at last.

"I would read it," said Ecgberht, holding out his hand expectantly and clicking his fingers.

One of the young men jumped from his horse and moved to Aedwen's side. She glanced at Dunston.

"It's all right, lassie," he said. "The king must read it."

She rummaged in the bag and pulled out the rolled up vellum. She handed it to the man, who in turn carried it to the king.

Swaying on his feet from the effort of standing, Dunston shook his head. He blinked against the blurring of his vision and clutched tightly to DeaÞangenga's haft. The carved patterns and runes in the wood dug into his palms. He watched as Ecgberht read from the flimsy sheet of stretched calf hide. As the king's gaze drifted over the scratched markings, his face grew dark and thundery. Nobody spoke as he read. Ealdorman Ælfgar fidgeted uncomfortably in his saddle, glaring at the man holding his reins.

When he had finished reading, the king frowned and handed it to one of his retinue, a hawk-nosed man, with a prominent brow. The man read it more quickly than the king. On finishing, he lowered the vellum and looked with incredulity and scorn at Ealdorman Ælfgar. Without a word, he handed the note back to his king.

"Well," Ecgberht said, shaking the sheet of writing so that it flapped and snapped like a banner, "now I understand why you chose not to ride on the hunt with me. Retrieving this message was much more important." He shook his head sadly. "What a fool you are! For surely only a fool would commit treason and then have scribes put quill to vellum setting out that very treachery in ink for anyone able to see."

Without warning, Ælfgar tugged his reins free of Ecgberht's man's grip. Kicking his heels into his mount's flanks, he sought to gallop away. But, the grim-faced warrior had only been momentarily surprised and before Ælfgar could pull away from him, he reached out and took a firm grip of the ealdorman's cloak. The lord's horse bounded away from under him and he tumbled backwards, landing hard on the soft earth. As quick as a diving kingfisher, the warrior leapt from his own saddle and was beside the ealdorman, deadly long seax unsheathed and at his throat.

Ecgberht sighed.

"You really are a fool," he said, still shaking his head. "The rest of you," he said, looking at the face of each of the ealdorman's men, "drop your weapons. You will be judged in accordance with the dooms of Wessex and, if you are innocent, you have nothing to fear." Two of the men tossed their swords into the grass and held out their hands. The remaining three evidently did not think much of their chances of being found innocent. They swung their horses' heads to the south and spurred them into a gallop.

The hawk-faced man barked orders and several of the huntsmen galloped after them.

"Lord king," said Ælfgar, his tone pleading. "Show me clemency, I beseech you."

"Clemency?" spat Ecgberht. "I would no more offer mercy to an adder. You sought to conspire with my enemies, to see me slain and the kingdom invaded. And for what?" Spittle flew from the king's lips, and his face was crimson, such was his sudden fury. "For wealth? For power? What riches did the Westwalas promise you in exchange for your treachery?"

"Lord," whimpered Ælfgar, "let me explain."

"Silence him," commanded the king and his man cuffed the ealdorman about the head. Hard. "Gag him, I would hear no more of his villainy. I have enough here, in writing and his guilt is plain on his face for all to see."

The warrior who held Ælfgar pulled off the noble's belt, shoved it in his mouth and tightened it, so that the man could do nothing more than grunt and moan.

Ecgberht turned away from the scene as if it disgusted him. Slowly, with the careful movements of the old, he swung his leg over the back of his horse and slid to the ground. Dunston's head spun. How young he had been when he had first met

Ecgberht. The king had seemed old to him then. God, he must have been close to Dunston's age now. By Christ, the man must feel tired and stiff. It didn't seem all that long ago, since they had ridden into battle side by side, both strong and full of life. Hungry for glory and battle-fame. Not long ago. But a lifetime had come and gone since then. Many lifetimes. He thought of Eawynn. She had never liked Ecgberht. She had been overjoyed when he had left the king's service.

Strange that now, all these years later, he should be with Ecgberht once more, and Eawynn long gone.

"It's been a long time, old friend," Ecgberht said. He took in the blood that soaked Dunston's clothes, the tatters of his sleeve. "You look terrible."

Dunston laughed.

"I only came back for the compliments," he said, wincing as the pain in his chest intensified.

The king laughed too.

"By Christ, it is good to see you, even if you have grown old."

"We all grow old, lord king," replied Dunston. "At least I will always be younger than you. You must be over sixty summers now!"

"I don't need you to remind me of that." The king smiled ruefully and Dunston chuckled. His laughter promptly turned into a cough that sent paroxysms of pain through his chest. Ecgberht placed an arm about his shoulders until the coughing subsided.

"It seems," he said, "that as is usual with you, you come to my aid when I most need it. You know," Ecgberht said, shaking his head, "I had thought you dead long ago."

Dunston grimaced with each stabbing breath. His vision darkened. Ecgberht's voice sounded distant, echoing and strange, as though he were in a great cavern. Dunston tried to focus on the king's face, but he could not see him clearly.

Behind Ecgberht, the rainbow was still bright and vibrant in the grey sky.

"I'm not dead yet," Dunston said, and collapsed into the long, lush meadow grass.

Thirty-Six

Aedwen looked down at Dunston and whispered another prayer to the Blessed Virgin. Dunston's skin was grey and his cheeks hollow. The wounds he had sustained in the fight beneath the walls of Exanceaster had taken a cruel toll on his body.

"He is not a young man," Abbess Bebbe had told Aedwen when Dunston had been carried to the monastery and placed under her care. The abbess was a tiny woman, with a bird-like air of fragility about her. And yet she brimmed with energy and bustled about the wounded man, cleaning and binding his cuts, tying tight strips of linen about his ribs and probing with her twig-like fingers to ascertain how deep the damage was. Like Dunston, she was not young and to Aedwen, she seemed as old as the crumbling Roman walls of the town. But the woman was kindly and had set up a pallet for the girl in the room beside Dunston's. Aedwen had asked whether she might be allowed to sleep in the cell with the old man. She felt safe when she was near him and she could not bear the thought that he might die. At the suggestion, the abbess had tutted and shaken her head so vigorously that Aedwen had thought her wimple might fall off.

"That would not do," the elderly woman had said. "No, no, no. You are not even of his blood. It is not seemly."

The morning after they had arrived at Exanceaster, Aedwen had woken at dawn. She had gone outside to the courtyard where the nuns and monks were going about their tasks, trudging through the mud in a thick, drenching drizzle that fell relentlessly from an iron sky. Gone were the bursts of rainbow-bringing sunshine of the day before, replaced with this incessant, dreary downpour. Odin had been curled up in a doorway, half-sheltered from the rain, but wet and cold all the same. He'd stood on stiff legs and shaken himself, gazing up at her with his single brown eye. Abbess Bebbe had forbidden the hound's entry into the monastery, but Aedwen could not allow the animal to remain outside in the rain. He had been lost for so many days, alone and hurt. Yet he had still found them. Her eyes filled with tears whenever she looked at his blackened, cauterised wound, and the pain he must have felt. She wondered whether they would ever know who had saved him and tended to his wound.

Aedwen had brought the hound inside and led him to Dunston's bedside. There they had sat vigil together. The abbess had found them there and had shooed them out of the room.

"That beast cannot be in here," she had complained, but it seemed to Aedwen without much conviction. And the old woman seemed to have forgotten her own rule about the dog when she had changed Dunston's bandages and Odin was lying patiently outside the room beside Aedwen, waiting to be allowed back in to sit with his master. The old woman clucked her tongue disapprovingly, but later, when one of the young novice nuns, a pinched-looking girl called Agnes, whose nose reminded Aedwen of a weasel's, brought Aedwen some soup and bread, she also carried a ham bone that she tossed onto the rushes by Odin's paws.

That was four days ago and each day had passed in the same way. Aedwen had sat with Odin watching over Dunston, searching for some sign of improvement in his condition. Each day the abbess would come to clean the old warrior's wounds and to bind them with fresh linen. Every day the old nun would usher the girl and the dog out of the small cell, impatiently clapping her hands for them to hurry. And every day when Aedwen and Odin returned to Dunston's side, Aedwen would enquire about his state.

For the first three days, the abbess had shaken her head.

"He is not young, but he is strong. If it is God's will, he will live."

But to Aedwen's eye, with each passing day Dunston had looked more feeble, older, more fragile.

Closer to death.

She clung to Bebbe's words, taking comfort from the scant encouragement in them. Surely such a godly woman would only speak the truth. So Aedwen prayed and dozed. And when she slept, her dreams were filled with visions of death; the screams of horses, thrashing in long grass; Ithamar's heart-rending wails of agony in a forest glade. She longed to see the soft, smiling face of her mother in her dreams, but it seemed as though the horrors she had witnessed had burnt her mother's memory from her mind.

On the fourth day, something had changed in the atmosphere of the monastery and for a moment Aedwen lay on the straw-filled mattress and listened, trying to ascertain what was different. Bright light streamed through the small window, spearing the gloom of the room, the lance of light illuminating motes of dust that danced in the air.

That was the change: it had stopped raining. The day had dawned bright with the promise of warmth and sun. She felt her spirits lift. But, just as she was rising from the pallet, she heard sobbing from a nearby cell. Such sounds were not uncommon here. Many of the young novices were homesick and sad, and weeping was often heard, especially at night.

But now, the sounds of sadness struck Aedwen like an ill omen.

She rose, crossing herself and whispering the words of the prayer to Maria, Mother of God, under her breath. She hurried to the courtyard, to allow Odin in to the building. Abbess Bebbe's good nature had not stretched so far that she would permit the animal to sleep in the monastery overnight. Odin was not where he usually waited for her. She whistled, but he did not appear. Her unease grew. Could it be that he had fled, or been hurt somehow? Perhaps one of the monks or the city guards had beaten him, or worse, killed him. She had seen the corpse of a small dog in the river on the day they had arrived and ever since, she had worried that Odin might meet the same sad end.

Panic rising in her chest, she whistled again and called the dog's name, ever more urgently. After several heartbeats, the hound came bounding into the courtyard. His tongue dangled from the side of his huge maw and her fear disappeared in an instant. She laughed at his expression, for he seemed to be grinning. The warmth and sun must have pleased him. The beast seemed full of puppy-like energy.

She was still chuckling and scratching Odin's ears when they arrived at Dunston's cell. Unusually for this time of day, the abbess was there, and the slender woman's bleak expression sent a chill through Aedwen.

"Is he…?" she could not bring herself to voice her fear.

Bebbe shook her head and took one of Aedwen's hands in hers. The old woman's skin was cool and dry.

"He yet lives," she said. "But you must prepare for the worst, child. There is nothing more I can do for him. He is in the Lord's hands now."

Aedwen bit her lip and closed her eyes. Taking a deep breath, she thanked the abbess and entered the room.

She immediately sensed the change. The air was dank and Dunston's skin seemed to glow in the shadowed cell. She sat beside him, taking his huge hand in hers. His skin was hot. Odin sniffed at Dunston's face and licked his cheek, before whimpering and curling up on the rush-strewn floor.

Taking a clean piece of linen, Aedwen dipped it in a bowl of water. She used the wet cloth to drip cool water on Dunston's lips, then, wringing out the linen, she moistened his brow. He made no movement. Her heart lurched, suddenly certain that this was one fight too many for the old man, that he had given in to his wounds and left this world.

And yet his skin still burnt and, when she looked closely, she could see his chest slowly rising and falling.

She prayed to the Virgin, Christ and all His Saints, that they might spare Dunston. She babbled in her prayers, caring not for the words. She clutched his hand tightly and wept. Tears streamed down her cheeks and soaked into the blanket that covered Dunston.

"You cannot die," she sobbed. "You got me safely here, but it is not enough. I am alone. Would you just leave now? Leaving me alone to my fate? I do not wish to be a nun." She sobbed, uncaring that her words were unfair. Her anger swelled within her and she let it burst forth in an outpouring of ire directed at this frail, dying man. She was furious at her mother for her sickness, for leaving her alone with her father. Enraged at her father for leading her into peril and for allowing himself to be killed. For his inquisitiveness that had led him to discover the plot against the king and then for his sense of duty that had seen him tell the secret to one of the conspirators. Tears washed down her face and the words tumbled from her in a cataract of anguish and anger.

"I want to see the forest and learn your skills. You said you would teach me. Would you die now and break your promise to me? You are no different from my father. All promises that you never meant to keep." She sobbed, dragging in ragged lungfuls of air.

Dunston's leathery fingers pressed against her slim hands. She started, sniffing back the tears and the rage that had consumed her.

"Dunston?" she whispered, terrified now that this was his body's last convulsive movement before his spirit departed. Would the last words he heard in this life be hers rebuking him for having the temerity of succumbing to his wounds?

"I—" his voice croaked in his throat. She could barely hear him.

"What?" she asked, leaning forward, placing her ear over his mouth. "What is it?"

"I have broken enough promises," he whispered. "I will not break this one. Stop your crying and let me sleep, girl. I need to rest."

Scarcely believing her ears, she sat back and looked at him, but he was quiet once more. She stared for a long while at his chest. Was his breathing deeper than a moment ago? Yes, she was sure of it.

Leaning forward, she placed a soft kiss upon his brow. He was warm, but the feverish glow of sickness had fled.

He slept.

It seemed he would keep his promise to her after all.

When Agnes brought a bowl of pottage sometime after Terce, she found Aedwen standing by the window and looking out to the trees and the wide, silvered waters of the river. Aedwen turned to greet the young nun and saw that her face was blotched, her eyes puffy. Had she been the one weeping that morning?

Aedwen took the bowl from her with a broad smile. For the first time in many days, she felt as though she had come out of the darkness and chill of a cave, stepping from the cool, black shadows of a barrow and into the bright sunshine of a summer's day.

"Do not be sad, Agnes," she said.

Thirty-Seven

Dunston awoke slowly. With each passing moment, as he clawed his way back to consciousness, he wished that death had claimed him. For as his senses returned, so did the pain. His chest was a dull throb, then stabbing in agony with each breath. He raised his arm to touch gingerly at his ribs and found them bound tightly. His arm, too, was bandaged, and the sharp pain there as the skin stretched reminded him of the deep cut he had received from Bealowin. He let his arm drop back to the bed. He was so weak. That one motion made him gasp with the effort, sending fresh waves of pain through his chest.

Turning his head slightly, he observed his surroundings. He was in a small, plain room. The walls were whitewashed and blue sky gleamed through a single narrow window. Sitting on a stool by his bed was Aedwen. Despite the torment of his body, Dunston smiled. The girl's head was slumped forward to lean on her arms which rested on the mattress beside him. Her hair tumbled over her face and arms, leaving only one smooth, pale cheek visible. Relief and a strange calm came over him at the sight of her. So young. So alone. Brave and resourceful. He fought the urge to reach out and caress her face.

With a stifled grunt, he shifted his position a little and saw the shape of Odin, stretched out on the floor beside the bed.

Dunston sighed, as the memories of the journey south and then the confrontation on the water meadows came back to him. Images and thoughts flooded his mind and, as he lay there, staring at the pale sky outside the window, he tried to make sense of what had transpired. But his thoughts were muddled and all he knew for certain was that he had not broken his promise to Eawynn. And he had seen Aedwen to safety. With those thoughts bringing a contented smile to his lips, sleep engulfed him once more.

When he next awoke, the room was darker and the sky outside was the hue of fresh blood.

"Thank the Virgin and her holy son," breathed Aedwen, as Dunston opened his eyes. "I had started to think you would not live."

Dunston offered her a smile.

"It takes more than a dozen mounted men to slay me," he said. His words rasped, dry and cracking in his throat.

"There were but ten of them, I recall," Aedwen answered with a smirk.

He chuckled, but quickly his laughter changed to coughing. He grimaced at the pain as each cough felt as though a seax was being thrust between his ribs.

"Sorry," said Aedwen, lifting his head and offering him some water. He drank a few sips. The cool water tasted better than the finest wine, such was his thirst. The liquid trickled down his throat and he could feel it running down inside him, replenishing him like rainfall soaking into a field of barley after a drought.

"How long have I been here?" he whispered. He didn't attempt speaking normally for fear of starting the cough again.

"Four days." Aedwen offered him more water, and he drank again. "Not too much," Aedwen said after he had taken several mouthfuls. "Abbess Bebbe says you must drink and eat sparingly to build up the balance of your humours."

"We are in a nunnery?"

Aedwen nodded.

"The monastery in Exanceaster. Both nuns and monks live and worship here. The abbess has tended to your wounds. She is very skilled."

Dunston touched the wrappings about his chest and winced.

"I must thank her," he said. He knew he owed his life to this Abbess Bebbe whom Aedwen spoke of and yet all he wanted was to be whole again, to leave Exanceaster and return to his home. He was as weak as a newborn lamb, but he longed to be able to stride away up the path and into the forest. He was done with the lies and conspiracies of nobles. He frowned. He had ever been thus. Eawynn had said he was a dreadful patient, always keen to undo what those nursing him had done to make him well. He supposed some things never changed. Just like the mendacity of some ealdormen and the ever-present plots that swirled around kings.

"You can thank the abbess soon enough," said Aedwen. "I will fetch her and bring you some broth too. You must be terribly hungry."

Odin rose from the rushes, stretched with a whining yawn, then nuzzled at Dunston's face. Dunston pushed Odin's snout away and scratched the hound's ears.

"I missed you too, boy," he said.

Dunston's stomach grumbled and he realised that he was ravenous. His belly felt drawn and painfully empty.

"Food would be good," he said, but, as Aedwen made to leave the room, he called her back. "But first, I would know of the message. What was in it, and what has our lord, King Ecgberht, done in these four days I have been abed? We carried that message for so long without knowing its meaning, and so many died to keep it secret, I must know. I wonder if I didn't die so that I wouldn't go to my grave without discovering the truth."

Aedwen's expression darkened, but she sat once more on the stool.

"It would seem that the message was from one Ealhstan to Ealdorman Ælfgar."

"The Ealhstan? Bishop of Scirburne?"

"The same."

Dunston whistled softly.

"But what of the message itself? What did it say?"

"I do not know exactly, but from what I have heard from the novices and the guards at the gate, the bishop and the ealdorman were discussing ways in which Ecgberht could be distracted away from the southwest of the kingdom."

"To what end?"

"So that a combined attacked between Norsemen and Wéalas could strike from Cornwalum."

"The Westwalas of Cornwalum have allied with the Norse?" Dunston asked, amazement in his tone.

Aedwen nodded.

"Such a thing goes against God," she said. "I know the Westwalas are our enemies, but I believed they were good Christian folk all the same."

"Greed has no honour and prays to no god. Both the Norse and the Westwalas are our enemies and they have their eyes set on the rich lands of Wessex. Together, a well-organised host could take Defnascire and Somersæte, especially if the king's forces were weakened in some way."

He scratched at his beard. It felt greasy and matted.

"Where is the king now?" he asked.

"Gone. He gathered his hearth warriors and the warbands of the ealdormen from these parts and sent out riders to call the fyrd. They have ridden west into Defnascire. The letter gave the date of the attack as the feast of Saint John the Baptist." When she saw Dunston's blank expression, she added, "Only a week ago."

Dunston's head was spinning. Ecgberht had been right. The men must have been fools to write such treason.

"What of Ealdorman Ælfgar?"

"Imprisoned, along with his men. They will face the king's justice when he returns."

If he returns, thought Dunston, but he merely nodded. Even now the king and his men might be facing a horde of Norsemen and Wéalas. Dunston could well imagine the scene, the fluttering banners and standards, the thickets of spears. He could almost hear the screams of anger and pain and the clash of the boards in the shieldwall. Men would be slaughtered and their blood would turn the earth to a quagmire, and for what? If the bishop and the ealdorman had succeeded in their treachery, the host of Wessex's enemies would have marched into the land unimpeded, plunging them into war and chaos. And all in the name of greed. For surely it must have been gold and power that they had been promised should Wessex fall and a new Norse or Wéalas king be seated on the throne of Witanceastre. Dunston sighed. Sadly, the men's avarice did not surprise him, but their lack of guile did. Ecgberht had governed Wessex for well over thirty years. He had expanded the borders of the kingdom and repelled enemies from all sides. While he lived, Wessex would remain strong. But even as he thought this, he recalled hearing of Ecgberht's defeat at Carrum two years previously. And the king was old now. He had seen as much with his own eyes. And an old, weakened king opened the doors to plots and emboldened the kingdom's enemies.

The room had grown silent, and with a start, Dunston opened his eyes. Slumber had sneaked up on him, stealthy as any hunter.

The sky was dark now, and the room was lit with guttering rush lights. The warm glow caught in Aedwen's eyes, softened the lines of worry that had formed on her brow. She smiled to see him awake once more.

"I have some soup. It will be cold now, but I did not wish to wake you. The abbess said it was best to let you rest. She is pleased with your progress."

"I will have to thank her tomorrow, it seems," he said, returning her smile.

He longed to snatch the spoon from her hand, to sit up and feed himself, but he allowed her to prop pillows beneath his head and then to spoon the cold broth into his mouth. It was thin, with the vaguest taste of meat and a hint of salt, but he could feel it restoring his strength by moments.

When the bowl was empty, Dunston belched and was glad that action did not hurt his ribs.

"Where is Odin?" he asked, noticing that the dog was not at his side.

"The abbess does not allow him to sleep inside at night."

He raised an eyebrow.

"How is he?" he said. "His wound had been tended by someone. Stitched and burnt, it looked to me."

"Yes," she said, and he noticed her eyes gleaming as tears welled there. "He seems well enough. Though he will be scarred there forever, and no hair grows now around the wound."

"Poor boy," said Dunston. "It must have been agony. I can think of few people Odin would allow near him when injured and fewer still he would let treat him so. And two of them are in this room." He felt his own eyes prickle with the threat of tears at the thought of the dog's suffering. He blinked them back. "Perhaps one day we will find out who patched him up. I would like to reward them somehow. Kindness is all too often accepted and not repaid. Whoever they were, they might not have done a pretty job, but they did a good one. The boy can still hunt." Dunston grinned wolfishly, recalling how Odin had leapt out of the grass and slain Raegnold. "And he can fight."

For a time, they were quiet, each lost in their memories. Finally, the pressure in his bladder made Dunston break the silence.

"I need a pot," he said.

Aedwen looked embarrassed.

"There is one beneath the bed," she said. She rose. "I'll leave you to relieve yourself."

"Aedwen, I do not think I can climb from the bed unaided."

She hesitated, then moved to help him up. He groaned as his ribs twisted, but he thought the pain was less than it had been earlier that day. After a few moments, he had his feet on the floor. Aedwen pulled out the earthenware pot and placed it beside the bed.

"Can you manage?" she asked.

"Yes, Aedwen," he answered, and smiled at her sigh of relief. "Thank you. I will call you when I am done."

She left the room and Dunston soon realised he was not certain he could cope unaided. His body ached and he felt so weak he was worried that he might fall. Grunting with the effort, he was at last able to position himself in such a way that he could piss into the bowl while half-sitting on the bed. The liquid gushed from him, foul-smelling and dark, and he wondered how he could have so much piss in him when he had barely drunk in four days. When he was done, he fell back into the bed, too tired to worry about the jolt to his ribs.

"I am finished," he called out. His voice was feeble, the weakness of it filled him with dismay and shame. He might be younger than the king, but by God, he was old and weak.

Aedwen came in and took the bowl away without comment.

"Sorry," he muttered as she carried it carefully from the room. Though what he was sorry for, he was not sure.

When she returned a short while later, replacing the empty bowl beneath his bed, Dunston had regained his breath and was as comfortable as he could be.

"You never told me you knew the king," Aedwen said, as she sat on the stool once more.

"You never asked," he said.

"He likes you."

Dunston grunted.

"I don't know if I would go that far."

"Was it the king who gave you the name of 'Bold'?"

Dunston cast his thoughts back all those years. He could barely remember the events that had led to the title he was famous for. The tale had been told so many times, first by those who were there, and later by men who claimed to have been there, and then just by anyone wanting to tell a good yarn. He himself had heard the story many times and with each telling the story was different. And as the years went by, his memories became blurred and confused, as if the weft of the truth had been woven with the warp of the fanciful tales, so that it was impossible to tell which was which.

"I never liked the name. I was just a warrior, like any other. I did my duty, nothing more."

"But for the king to name you 'Dunston the Bold'," she said, her tone full of awe. "It is an honour."

"It does not feel like an honour." He gazed at the flickering flame of the rush light. Sometimes, the name the king had given him that day, all those long years before, felt more like a curse.

"But why did he call you that?" she asked. "What did you do?"

Dunston remembered the man he had been: strong, reckless, hungry for battle-glory and fame. And then he recalled how, moments before, he had trembled and moaned to fill a pot with stinking piss.

"Perhaps you should ask the king," he said. "I am tired now. I must sleep."

"Of course," she replied, and the sound of her disappointment stung him.

He closed his eyes and listened to her blow out the flame of one of the rush lights and then, carrying the other for guidance, leaving the room. With Aedwen gone, the room felt cold and lonely and Dunston lay awake for a long while, looking at the darkening sky outside the small window.

He listened to the sounds of the town and the monastery that came to him through the window. A dog barked from the distance, and he wondered whether it might be Odin. Somewhere far off a baby wailed. A bell rang and soon after came the thin voices of the holy men and women of the monastery singing Compline.

Dunston lay there, willing himself to find the solace and peace of sleep, but it refused to come for a long time. He thought of Ealdorman Ælfgar and Bishop Ealhstan, of Hunfrith, Raegnold and Bealowin, who had tortured and slain all those people. Who would bring themselves to do such things? To betray their people for greed, to torture and kill? What manner of men were they?

And a small voice within him whispered a question that had often kept him awake in the darkest reaches of so many nights throughout his life.

What manner of man was he?

Thirty-Eight

Aedwen went down to Exanceaster's western gate to watch the king and the fyrd return. She hadn't really wanted to, but Agnes had begged her to go.

Ever since she had shown the girl some kindness, the novice nun would often seek her out, sneaking into her room long after she was supposed to be asleep. There, hidden beneath the blankets, the two girls would whisper and share their secrets and fears. Agnes was sad most of the time. She missed her brothers and sisters and felt so lonely in the monastery. When she had heard that the king had called the fyrd to arms she had grown certain that her brothers would join the defence of the realm. Her family's steading lay to the southwest and so, as the two were old enough to bear shield and spear, it seemed likely they would join the levies of their hundred and march to stop the Norse and Wéalas force.

She had become convinced that they would either be dead or return in glory, basking in the favour of the king, and so had begged Aedwen to look out for them when the men came back to the city.

Aedwen had pointed out that she did not know what Agnes's brothers looked like and also that they would more than likely have returned to the family farm, as they would pass it on the way back to Exanceaster, but Agnes would hear none of it.

"The abbess does not permit any of us to leave the monastery," she had whispered, her breath hot against Aedwen's cheek in the cool dark of the room. "So you must be my eyes. Twicga looks just like me, but taller, and a boy, of course." Agnes giggled. "Leofwig is broader and shorter and looks more like my father."

When Aedwen had commented that she had no inkling of Agnes's father's appearance, Agnes had waved her hands in annoyance.

"You will recognise Twicga sure enough," she'd said. "We are like two beans from the same husk. And Leofwig will be with him."

Aedwen had been very doubtful she would see the young men, or even that they would enter Exanceaster, but Agnes had been so insistent, that in the end, she had relented and joined the crowds awaiting the fyrd's triumphal homecoming.

It was a warm day and the sun was high in the sky when the mounted nobles and their hearth guards splashed across the wide expanse of the Exe. The people had gathered, awaiting the moment when the tide would make the crossing possible, and now the horses sent up great sheets of spray as the thegns and ealdormen trotted their mounts through the shallow river. They rode up the dry slope and clattered between the stone columns of the gate into the city. The streets were thronged with people. Tidings of Ecgberht's victory over Wessex's enemies had reached Exanceaster two days previously and the town had been abuzz with thankful chatter and bustling with preparations for the fyrd's return.

The smells of cooking and brewing hung over the settlement like a cloud, and now the women who lined the streets held out bread, cakes and pies to the men who had defended their land. Young women smiled and looked through their lashes at the dashing thegns, bedecked in iron-knit shirts, riding proudly in the king's retinue. Many of the warriors returned the smiles of the girls and called out to them suggestions of how they might repay their bravery in battle. Flirtatious laughter rippled amongst the young women.

Aedwen did not understand the attraction of these men. They had the hard faces of the horsemen who had attacked Dunston. They were younger versions of Dunston himself, she thought. Tough, unyielding, dour and steadfast.

These past few days, the old warrior had regained much of his strength. He was able to rise and walk for short distances. He revelled in the fresh air and had taken to walking around the walls with Odin. Each day he managed to go a little further before he grew tired and needed to rest. The abbess had been dismayed at his stubbornness, telling Aedwen that she needed to ensure that Dunston did not overexert himself. One grey drizzled day, Dunston had set out to walk with his dog and the abbess had confronted him.

"Would you undo that which the Lord has repaired?" she had asked. "You will catch cold. If it goes to your chest, then what?"

"Then the Lord will have to heal me again," Dunston had said. The abbess had trembled and it seemed as though the old lady might scream with fury, but Dunston had placed a hand on her shoulder and looked directly into her eyes. His ice-chip blue eyes glinted. "Lady Abbess," he'd said, holding her gaze. "Bebbe. You know that I am indebted to you for healing me. But I will surely die if I am not allowed to feel the fresh wind on my face or the rain in my hair. I will be well."

He had stepped out into the rain, wrapping his cloak about him.

The abbess had wheeled on Aedwen, as if Dunston's behaviour were her fault.

"The man is insufferable!" she hissed. She was flustered and smoothed her habit with nervous strokes of her bony hands. "You must talk sense into him. If he grows sick and dies, I will not be held responsible. But I would not be sorry to see the end of the cantankerous fool."

But Aedwen had noted the frequency of the abbess's visits to check on Dunston. She had seen how the old lady's face lit up when he spoke to her. Once, Aedwen had even heard Bebbe giggling at something Dunston had said, like one of the girls who mooned over the returning thegns. No, Aedwen thought, the abbess would be very sorry if anything were to happen to Dunston. And yet, despite her warnings that he would fall ill once again, Dunston did not cease in his activities, and with each passing day, his strength grew. He would be ready to leave soon, she knew, and a shiver of anxiety ran through her at the thought. She was alone now, and did not know what the future would hold for her. The thought of losing Dunston terrified her. He may be an ill-tempered old man, but he had protected her and had proven himself a man of honour.

Carts and waggons, pulled by oxen and mules, were trundling into the town now. The mood of the crowds altered. These were the wounded; those too badly hurt to ride or walk. The onlookers grew sombre. Many wept at the sight of so many injured men. As the waggons passed, Aedwen glimpsed pallid skin, blood-soaked linen, vacant, staring eyes.

One woman, her eyes dark and cheeks flushed, rushed forward, calling out the name of her man. The carters shook their heads and waved her away. After a moment, another woman pulled her back, away from the wounded. The first woman sobbed, clearly convinced her husband had been slain. Aedwen scanned the faces of the other women gathered there. All were pinched and guarded. Some wept, but most held on to their hope with dignity.

After some time, the fyrdmen, bedraggled, dirt-smeared, wet-legged from their crossing of the river and leaning tiredly on their spears, made their way into the city. Soon the air rang with the happy laughter and joyful weeping of women being reunited with their loved ones. Aedwen watched as the woman who had been inconsolable moments before now laughed with abandon, clinging to an embarrassed-looking man who patted her head awkwardly. Aedwen looked away, suddenly angry with the woman. She had someone to worry about, a man to hold and to fuss over.

Nearby, a plump woman called out to a warrior she clearly recognised.

"Hey, Bumoth. What of Edgar?"

Bumoth's face was ashen and he would not meet the woman's gaze. He looked down at the worn Roman cobbles of the street and shook his head. His meaning was clear, and the woman wailed, her face crumpling in grief as tears washed over her cheeks.

Aedwen turned away. It was too much. She didn't know what she had expected when she came to witness the return of the Wessex fyrd, but she had not been prepared for this outpouring of emotions. She had her own grief and sorrow that weighed on her heavily enough without watching others learn of the deaths of their kin.

Pushing through the crowds, she wandered the shadowed streets, her head teeming with dark thoughts. The sounds of the people at the gate receded and she found much of Exanceaster quiet and strangely peaceful. Most of the populace had gone to welcome the triumphant men home. She gave little thought to where she walked, but after some time, she found her way back to the monastery.

She could hear the sound of singing coming from the chapel and she prayed that Agnes was at Vespers. Aedwen could imagine how she would react when she told the novice she had not seen her brothers. She could not face the girl and her weeping.

Aedwen's stomach growled and she wished she had asked one of the goodwives for a pie or some bread. She could have shared it with Dunston. Perhaps they could find some food and eat together. She would like nothing more now than to sit quietly with the old man and his dog. She felt safe when she was with them. Perhaps the time had come to broach the subject of her future.

But when she arrived at Dunston's small cell, she knew she would find no peace any time soon. Two grim-faced warriors, cloaks and boots still muddy from the road, stood in the room. Their bulk all but filled the space.

"Ah, Aedwen," said Dunston, noticing her. "It is good that you have come."

Aedwen said nothing, but she knew her expression must have been one of anxiety. Her nerves had become as taut as a bowstring.

"It is nothing to fear," the old woodsman said. "The king has returned, victorious from Defnascire. And we are summoned."

"Summoned?"

"To an audience with the king. We are to attend him at the great hall."

The thought of an audience with Ecgberht and his nobles in the grand hall filled her with dread. In the silence, her stomach grumbled noisily.

Dunston smiled.

"I am sure the king will be hungry too after his journey. There will be food in the hall, no doubt. Come, let us go. The sooner we have spoken to the king, the sooner we can be gone from this place."

The warriors led the way out of the cell and Aedwen followed behind Dunston. She knew he was keen to be gone, to return to the forest and his old life. But what of her?

Walking behind the two broad-shouldered guards, she wondered for how much longer she could avoid confronting her next steps.

Thirty-Nine

Dunston looked over to where Aedwen sat surrounded by young women of the court. These were the daughters and wives of the king's retinue. Aedwen's features were tight, skin pale with flourishes of colour high on her cheeks. A beautiful raven-haired girl tittered at something. She was about the same age as Aedwen, but with silver pins glinting in her coiled plaits and a silken girdle of the deepest red around her slender waist. Aedwen smiled, but Dunston could see she was even more uncomfortable than he felt.

He had thought nothing of the girl's clothes and hair as they had been led to the hall. Aedwen was clean enough and wore a simple dress of drab brown that Bebbe had given her. But when they had entered the hall, which was lively with rushing servants and already filling rapidly with men and women come to celebrate the king's victory, Dunston had felt a needling of guilt. He could almost hear Eawynn rebuking his thoughtlessness, bringing a girl to a royal celebration without seeing that she had something finer than coarse-spun wool to wear.

He sighed. There was nothing for it now. He thought longingly of the peace of Sealhwudu. The forest was simpler. The trees and the animals cared nought for what clothes people wore.

Nevertheless, he recalled that Eawynn had always brushed her hair until it shone and had adorned her clothes with trinkets and jewels, even though they rarely entertained anyone in their woodland home. He had never understood why she wasted time on such things, though he could not deny that he enjoyed to gaze upon her when he came home from a day's work.

Pushing his fists into the small of his back, Dunston stretched. He winced. His chest still troubled him, but less so with each passing day. His daily walks were restoring his strength and the constant aches of the knitting bones and mottled bruises were receding. It was when he was sitting that his healing ribs bothered him the most. And he had been seated now for a long while. He reached for the cup before him. A servant, a comely, round-faced woman, had just refilled it with a delicious Frankish red wine. Dunston did not miss his previous life in service to the king. He was not made for great halls, small talk, speeches and the conniving plots of court. No, he thought, taking a sip of the rich, spicy wine. He did not regret living his simple life in the forest, but he did miss the wine.

With a thin smile playing on his lips, he looked about the great hall of Exanceaster. It rang with the hubbub of celebration. Conversations, laughter, the clatter of trenchers and cups. It was a large hall, roofed in wooden shingles, and painted in bright patterns without. Inside, it was spacious and well-appointed. Embroidered tapestries hung along the walls, depicting scenes of hunting and what Dunston supposed were stories of Christ's life and miracles. Most of the images he did not recognise, but one in particular was clear. A figure, head crowned in light, walking on the blue threads of a sea, while a sinking man reached out pitifully from the waves.

It had been many years since he had sat at the board in such a fine hall. From the awe in Aedwen's eyes as they had entered the building, he presumed the girl had never been in such a grand place and again he felt the stab of guilt at not having thought of her comfort. It could have been worse, he told himself, taking another warming mouthful of wine. They could have been in Witanceastre. Now there was a lavish hall that would have truly intimidated Aedwen, with its paintings, carvings and stone-flagged flooring. Even the seats there were finely carved with the intertwining images of animals and plants. He had never been in a finer hall than that of Witanceastre, and he had been in many halls. Several had been larger and richer than this one. He thought of the hall of Baldred of the Centingas. And the long, dark hall of Sigered of Éastseaxe. He shivered, pushing those distant memories from his mind and signalling to a passing servant to replenish his cup.

Yes, he had been in many halls over the years, and they all had some things in common. They were always filled with too many people and too much noise. And no matter how high the rafters, or how long the benches of a hall, it always felt to Dunston that the walls were slowly pushing in on him. The pretty servant returned to him and poured fresh wine into the cup he held out for her. She smiled. He muttered his thanks and she was gone.

He sipped at the wine. He must be careful not to drink too much too soon. If he was not mistaken, this feast would go on for some time. But despite his good intentions, the afternoon slipped into evening and Dunston's cup was rarely empty. The servant seemed to have taken a shine to him, and saw that he had food and drink aplenty throughout the long feast.

Dunston had been seated at a linen-covered board near to the high table, where the king sat with his closest ealdormen and thegns. Ecgberht had raised a hand to him in welcome when he'd noticed him, but other than that brief recognition, Dunston began to wonder why he had been ordered to attend the feast. The wine was wonderful, it was true, but he would rather have taken a jug of that back to his room and drunk it by himself. Instead, here he was surrounded by loud-voiced men and women he did not know. He shifted uncomfortably, attempting to relieve the pressure on his bound ribs. However he sat, he could not get comfortable.

By his feet, Odin stretched out onto his back, opening his rear legs in an undignified display of absolute relaxation. It seemed the hound was quicker to adapt than his master. Dunston reached down to stroke the dog and immediately regretted the movement.

"Your wounds yet trouble you?" said the man to his left. They had spoken but briefly before when the younger man, a thegn of Somersæte called Osgood had sat beside him and introduced himself. Since then, Osgood, perhaps sensing that Dunston did not wish to talk, had directed his conversation at other diners.

Dunston winced and straightened. Frowning, he turned slowly to the man. Osgood was fair-haired, with clear skin and an honest face. His shoulders were broad, hands strong and Dunston had noted the grace of his movements when he had slipped down onto the bench beside him.

"Well, I am getting no younger," Dunston said, his tone gruff.

Osgood smiled.

"I fear that even the mighty Dunston cannot turn back the tide of time."

Dunston stiffened. Was the thegn making fun of him? He took another swig of wine. Perhaps he was at that, but the man's grin was open and seemed to hold no malice.

Dunston snorted and returned the smirk.

"I certainly do not feel mighty."

"But bold perhaps?"

Dunston groaned.

"Not really. I don't think I have ever understood why the king named me thus."

"Like most men, I have heard the tales," replied Osgood. "If they are even half-true, then you were bold indeed."

Dunston shrugged.

"Perhaps I was once. Long ago."

"The man I saw surrounded by the corpses of his enemies a few days ago looked bold to me."

"You were there? With the king?"

"Yes, and I think if you do not like to be known as bold, you must stop acting quite so boldly."

Dunston laughed. His chest tightened and he willed himself not to cough.

"That sounds like fair advice." Still smiling, pleased that the wine had softened his anxiety at being here, surrounded by strangers and the oppressive walls of the hall, Dunston asked, "You fought with the king?"

"I did," Osgood replied, and his gaze shifted, took on the glaze of memory.

"Tell me," said Dunston.

And so Osgood told him of how they had waylaid the approaching host of Westwalas and Norsemen at a place called Hengestdūn.

"Our scouts had come back with tidings of their movements and so we were able to position the fyrd across the path between the hills. Ecgberht ordered those of us who were mounted to conceal ourselves in the forest on the slopes overlooking the road."

Dunston nodded. When he had been in the king's warband, they had used a similar tactic on more than one occasion and it had served them well.

"How many were they?"

"There must have been well over a score of crews of Norsemen joined by the same number of Wéalas."

Dunston blew out.

"A war host indeed," he said, picturing in his mind the size of such a force, how they would sound, the crash and thunder of their shields, the roar of their battle cries.

"Yes, but they were poorly organised. They faced our fyrd, but before they could summon up the courage to act, Ecgberht ordered the Wessex men to attack. And the moment after the shieldwalls clashed, we galloped down from the woods and hit them hard."

Osgood grew quiet and took a long draught of ale. Dunston knew what it was to relive battles and so did not press the younger man for more detail.

After a time, as though he felt he owed Dunston further explanation, Osgood continued.

"We slaughtered many of them," he said, and his pale face and set jaw told Dunston much. "And then they scattered. We chased them, riding after them and cutting them down. When the sun set, we had killed more than half their number and the rest had fled like whipped curs."

Dunston patted Osgood on the shoulder.

"You did what was needed of you. They were marching to kill our people, to steal our land and riches."

Osgood nodded, but his eyes were dark and clouded.

They grew silent then, allowing the waves of the celebration to wash over them.

"Does it get any easier?" Osgood asked, suddenly.

"What?"

"The killing," said Osgood, his voice lowered to not much more than a whisper.

Dunston looked at him sharply.

"This was your first battle?"

Osgood nodded.

Dunston swallowed, casting his mind back to the first time he had faced armed foe-men. The first time he had plunged his blade into the flesh of a living man, watched the life ebb from him, as the hot blood pumped into the mud. He sometimes saw that man's pleading eyes in his dreams, heard his desperate wails for mercy.

"The taking of a life should never be easy." He thought of the ripped and rent corpses of Bealowin's victims, Ithamar's screams. "Killing in the defence of the weak is honourable, but it should never be taken lightly. And an honourable man must never seek to inflict pain and suffering, for that is the way of the weakly coward. But to answer your question, killing can become easy, but you will have to live with the memories of your actions forever. And God will surely judge you for them when you stand before Him, so make sure you are acting for the right reasons."

Osgood stared at him for a long while, his expression grave. At last, he nodded and raised his cup.

"I thank you for your honesty, Dunston," he said.

"It is all I have," he replied with a thin smile, lifting his own cup and tapping it against Osgood's. "Now," he said, "let us talk of happier things. This is supposed to be a celebration."

And so the evening passed more pleasantly than Dunston had expected. To his surprise he found Osgood to be good company and they talked of all manner of things. From time to time Dunston glanced over at Aedwen and was pleased to see her seeming to relax. Perhaps she too had drunk the wine, he thought and smiled. One thing that had been worrying her was soon dealt with when plentiful dishes of all types of delicacy were carried into the hall. There was roasted hare, succulent mackerel, glutinous stews and freshly baked bread. Dunston saw that Aedwen, whether she felt embarrassed or shy in the company of these rich nobles, had decided to eat her fill. Her trencher was heaped with food and at one point in the evening, as the lowering sun cast golden rays through the hall's unshuttered windows, Aedwen grinned at him, her mouth full of meat. To see her thus, smiling and contented, warmed him and he felt as though an invisible weight had been lifted from his shoulders. Whether from this lightening of his burden or the dulling effects of the wine, his ribs pained him less as the sun set.

Candles were lit and the feast continued, increasingly raucous, as the ale, wine and mead flowed. Laughter stabbed through the general hubbub from time to time, like flashes of sunlight through thick cloud.

Dunston rose stiffly with a groan and a grimace. His belly was full and so was his bladder. On his way outside, he passed Aedwen. She looked up at him.

"All well?" he asked.

"Yes," she said. "At least I am not hungry now." She smiled, but he could see there was more she wanted to say. He patted her arm. Now was not the time or place. They could speak about whatever was troubling her later, or on the morrow.

When he returned from the midden, he made his way to his place beside Osgood, who welcomed him back with a broad grin and a refilled cup of wine. The atmosphere in the hall had changed. Dunston looked to the high table.

Ecgberht, resplendent in a gold-trimmed purple gown, stood and surveyed those gathered in the hall. Slowly, a hush fell over the room.

"Friends," he said, his voice strong and carrying. "Country-men. Folk of Wessex. As you know, we have returned victorious from battle with a host of Wéalas and Norse."

"Praise the Lord," exclaimed a dark-robed priest who sat to Ecgberht's right.

The king glanced at the priest slowly and pointedly. His meaning was clear. Interruptions were not something he tolerated.

"The brave men of Wessex fought with the strength of wild boars. Many gave their lives, but it would have been much, much worse for us if we had not been forewarned of the treachery that had festered in our midst. There will be time for gift-giving soon. You know that I am a generous king and I reward those who stand by my side."

This received a loud roar of approval and the gathered men, intoxicated on drink and life, pounded the boards with their fists and stamped their feet on the ground until the hall reverberated as if with thunder.

Ecgberht smiled, seemingly happy with this interruption. The small priest pursed his lips and swept his gaze about the room, as if he were judging all those gathered there.

When the cheering abated, Ecgberht nodded.

"Yes, there will be gifts soon for my trusty thegns and ealdormen. But first I must give my everlasting thanks to one man, without whom we might well have been doomed." He held his hand out to indicate Dunston. All eyes turned to him and he glowered back. He could feel the men weighing the worth of him. They might well know his name, but to see him, old and grey, must surely have rankled some, who would begrudge him the king's praise. "You have my undying gratitude, Dunston the Bold," the king said. "Without the boldness of your actions, it is likely our enemies would have prevailed. Because of your warning, we were able to lie in wait and ambush them at Hengestdūn. If not for you, Dunston, Ælfgar and Ealhstan might very well at this moment have been accepting your new Norse or Westwalas king with open arms." The king's face was dark now. "And for what? Some extra land and gold? Am I not generous enough?"

The hall again echoed with the acclamation of their king's generosity, but Ecgberht did not seem to pay them heed. Instead he was staring fixedly at the figure seated to his left. A timber pillar had been blocking the man from Dunston's view but now he shifted to see who had so caught Ecgberht's attention. He started when he recognised the man. It was Ælfgar, grim-faced and dismal, but dressed in expensive linen and silks, with his gold chain at his throat.

The hall grew silent.

"Well," Ecgberht said, his voice dripping with venom, "was I not a generous enough lord for you, Ælfgar?"

Ælfgar said nothing.

"Answer your king," screamed Ecgberht, fury bursting from him.

"You have always been generous, lord king," Ælfgar said, his voice tiny in the silence of the hall.

"And yet this is how you repay me," said the king. "And now I expect you would seek mercy from me."

Hope lit Ælfgar's face.

"Lord king," he said, his tone pleading. "You have always been the best of lords. Wrathful in battle. Just and merciful in victory."

"Was it mercy you would have offered me when the Norse and Westwalas marched over the Exe?"

"Lord—"

"Shut your treacherous mouth," Ecgberht snapped. "Dunston, what would you do with Ælfgar?"

Dunston's mouth felt suddenly as dry as dust.

"Lord, it is not for me to say," he said. "He should stand trial."

"He is before the king. And we know of his guilt. Do you deny it, Ælfgar?"

The ealdorman looked from the king to Dunston, two old men with grey beards and piercing stares. He swallowed.

"I do not," he said.

"There you have it, Dunston," Ecgberht continued, his voice as cold and hard as iron. "He is guilty. What would you have me do with him?"

Dunston sighed. He met Ecgberht's gaze and saw the rage there. He had known the king for many years and knew there was one thing he despised above all else: disloyalty.

"I would have him put to death, lord king," he said at last.

Ecgberht grinned and nodded.

"Quite so," he said. "I hope you have enjoyed the feast, Ælfgar. For it will be your last."

Ælfgar had grown very pale, but he did not weep or whimper. He held himself rigid and listened as his king pronounced sentence over him.

"Tomorrow," Ecgberht said, his voice loud and clear, "Ealdorman Ælfgar will be hanged and his body left for all my subjects to see. It must be known that infamy and betrayal of one's king brings nothing but death."

Ælfgar lowered his head, but remained silent.

"His family," the king continued, "will be stripped of all titles and lands and they will be exiled from Wessex. If they should ever be found in the kingdom, they are to be treated as traitors and slain. Take him out of my sight."

Two guards, who had clearly been awaiting the order, stepped forward. The ealdorman stood and offered the slightest of nods to the king before he was led from the hall.

"What of Bishop Ealhstan?" asked Dunston.

Ecgberht turned to the priest who sat at his side.

"Yes, that is a good question, is it not, Inwona?" he asked. "The Church would not have the king try one of their number, Dunston. A matter for God, it would seem." The priest squirmed beneath the king's glare. "But I sent men to fetch him anyway. I would have liked to look the weasel in the eye. But alas, it seems that news travels faster than a horse can carry a man, for when my men arrived at Scirburne, the good bishop had fled. To Frankia, if one is to believe what Inwona here says, isn't that right?"

The diminutive cleric looked up. Dunston was shocked to see a glint of defiance in the man's eyes.

"That is so, lord king," Inwona said. "I have sent word that he is to be detained and he will receive the justice meted out by the Holy Father of Rome himself."

"I would rather a noose about his neck," grumbled Ecgberht, "but no matter. I shall have to bow to the wisdom of the Pope in this matter. So," he said, suddenly jovial, "what of you, Dunston?"

"Me, lord?"

"Your reward. I owe you my kingdom and perhaps my life."

"Seeing you hale and triumphant over our enemies is reward enough. I want nothing but to return to my home in Sealhwudu."

Ecgberht shook his head. Dunston was aware that every person in the hall was staring at him. Many would be thinking of what they would ask of their king should they be in the same position. But he had spoken the truth, all he wanted was to go home.

"No, Dunston," said the king. "I cannot allow you to go unrewarded. What would the people think?"

"I want for nothing, lord king. I merely wish to live out the rest of my days in peace."

"Ah, peace. Yes, that would be nice. But I fear we will not be so lucky, old friend. With Frankia forgetting her allies, our enemies are circling Wessex like flies around horse dung."

The thought of more enemies attacking Wessex, and warfare becoming ever more commonplace, filled Dunston with dread. If only he could return to Sealhwudu, he could be free of fighting, leaving the shieldwalls to younger men such as Osgood. He had played his part in the defence of the realm.

"I need no reward," he said, stubbornly refusing to acknowledge what he knew to be true. Ecgberht was determined and intractable. He was also the king. Dunston recognised the jut of Ecgberht's jaw and knew that when the king was in this frame of mind, it was impossible to dissuade him.

"Nonsense, man," the king said, laughing, as if he knew what Dunston had been thinking. "I have a gift for you, which I insist you will accept."

Dunston nodded.

"Very well, lord king," he said with a sigh. "What is this gift you would give me?"

Grinning, King Ecgberht told him.

Forty

Aedwen breathed in deeply, taking in the warm summer scent of the land. The sun had shone these past days and the air was redolent of lush life, verdant and brimming with energy. She'd felt it herself, the summer heat seeping into her body as they'd ridden northward. The dark days of pursuit, fear and death had vanished, replaced with a comforting sensation of safety and contentment. On the light breeze she could make out the distant lowing of the cattle that were being led down the path on the other side of the valley. There was a figure walking with the animals, too far to discern the features, but she thought it must surely be Ceolwald, leading the cows down to the Bartons for their evening milking.

The houses of Briuuetone were peaceful and inviting as the golden light of the late sunshine gilded the thatched roofs and hazed the smoke that drifted from dozens of cooking fires. The hint of woodsmoke reached her and Aedwen's smile faltered. For a moment, she recalled the last time she had been in this place. The night had been aflame and filled with screams. Raegnold had attacked Dunston and threatened her. The men of the village had chased them out into the night. A tremor of trepidation rippled along her spine. She shuddered. Perhaps she was wrong to have come back here.

Reining in her horse, a small, placid mare from the steward of Exanceaster's own stable, she glanced back along the road. Dunston raised his hand in friendly greeting. His presence settled her nerves somewhat. She knew he was not overly happy with the gift that the king had bestowed upon him. But the tension he had carried in his every movement seemed to uncoil the further they rode from Exanceaster. He spoke little as they travelled, seemingly lost in his own thoughts. When they halted to rest and when they made camp at night, he had resumed his teaching of her. He pointed out the signs of animals and set her challenges. Could she find leaves of sorrel? What about burdock? And each night he had insisted that she build and light the fire, while their escort looked on impatiently waiting for her to kindle a spark that would catch.

She returned Dunston's wave with a smile. He was a good man. If he was ready to bring her back to Briuuetone, it must be safe. He would not allow any harm to befall her.

Out of the bushes that grew in a jumble beside the road, bounded Odin. His sudden appearance caused one of the king's hearth warriors' mounts to shy and stamp. The rider, a stern-faced warrior by the name of Eadric, cursed.

"Keep your damned hound under control," he shouted, tugging at his reins in an effort to control his startled steed.

"Learn to control a horse," said Dunston. "After all, you are riding it. I am not seated on a saddle atop Odin's back."

Eadric scowled and the other men laughed. This was a long-running feud between the two men and it was well-meaning enough. The escort of six horsemen had been forced upon them by the king.

"We do not need to be protected," Dunston had said.

"Nonsense," Ecgberht had replied. "I will not have you set upon by brigands on the road. No, Eadric will go with you to Briuuetone, and that is the end of the matter."

Aedwen had seen the resignation on his face, and Dunston had not argued. He knew the king well, it seemed. They had an easy camaraderie when they spoke that told of many shared years of campaigning in the past. And what good would arguing do anyway? No man could challenge the king's will. But as they had ridden along the north road, Aedwen began to wonder whether the king had truly had their safety in mind when he sent the armed men to accompany them.

At night, when the moon rose and the land grew dark and still, Aedwen would look at Dunston and see him staring into the flames of the fire. The shadows danced and writhed about his face, his eyes glinting and haunted in the darkness. When she awoke in the cool of the mornings, Dunston would have risen before the dawn and be gone from the camp.

The first time this happened Eadric had grown anxious, pacing around the rekindled fire as his men cooked oatcakes. As the sun had risen high into the cloud-free sky, he had cursed Dunston.

"We'll never find him now," he'd said. "The king warned me he might do this."

"Do what?" asked Dunston, stepping from the shadow of the lindens and oaks of the forest, Odin at his side. Over his shoulder, Dunston carried a hare. The cut along its stomach showed where it had been gutted. "I thought I would catch us some meat for tonight's meal."

"We have been waiting for you for what seems an eternity," Eadric said. "By the nails of the rood, man, we have wasted most of the morning."

"I have wasted nothing," Dunston said, flopping the plump animal over the rump of his horse, where he secured it with a leather thong. "And you have rested. We are in no hurry to reach Briuuetone, are we? We will be there soon enough."

Dunston had called many stops on the journey.

"I am an old man, and I need to rest," he would say, with a wink to Aedwen. "And my wounds are not yet fully healed."

She was sure that his ribs still pained him, but she was equally certain that he was more than strong enough to ride without so many halts, that he was merely slowing their progress, prolonging the moment when they would arrive here, at the settlement on the River Briw.

She did not mind that the journey had taken them a day longer than Eadric had anticipated. She had enjoyed the sensation of riding, even though at the end of the first day her backside and thighs had ached terribly. She found the gait of the mare soothing, and the sure-footed steed needed little guidance, allowing Aedwen to stare out at the rolling hills and woodland that they rode through. She also relished the time spent with Dunston learning further secrets of the forest. After they reached their destination, she did not know how often she might be able to have his undivided attention.

The lowering sun glimmered on the fast-flowing waters of the Briw. Dunston caught up with her and turned his horse's head to the left, away from the river and along a narrow path leading uphill. Aedwen's mare did not wait to be steered in the same way. The beast fell into step beside Dunston's mount and together, with the armed escort riding at their rear, they approached the small steading that nestled at the knap of the hill. The sun was in their eyes as they rode up, the front of the hut shaded, and cool after the warmth of the afternoon.

Dunston was swinging himself down from the saddle when the door opened and Gytha emerged, wiping her hands on a rag and smoothing her apron over her thighs. Behind her, Aedwen could see the pale faces of Maethild and Godgifu. Godgifu waved at Aedwen, beaming.

Aedwen smiled back, but she could not halt the roiling sensation of anxiety in her gut. She had thought that she had been contented and relaxed as they had travelled from Exanceaster, but now she realised that in her own way she too had been dreading arriving here, at this door.

Gytha took in the mounted warriors with a glance. She held her face still, unsure of what was happening here. Aedwen thought back to the night she had fled from Briuuetone with Dunston. Gytha must live in fear of a visit from the reeve for her involvement in the woodsman's escape. Despite her anxiety, Aedwen let out a sharp bark of laughter.

Both Dunston and Gytha stared at her. She felt her cheeks grow hot. She dismounted to cover her embarrassment.

Gytha stepped towards Dunston, placing her hands on her hips and meeting his gaze.

"What brings you to my door, Dunston, son of Wilnoth?" she asked, her tone flat.

"I come bearing a gift and a request."

"Do you indeed?" she asked, glancing at the warriors who remained mounted behind the grey-bearded man. "The last I heard, you were a wulfeshéafod, having escaped from the reeve's custody, injuring one of his men in the process."

"That was a dark day," Dunston said. "When Rothulf died, justice died in this hundred. But I am no longer an outlaw."

Gytha looked thoughtfully at him, weighing the meaning in his words.

"So these men are not your guards?"

Dunston gave a crooked smile.

"Perhaps they are, in one manner of speaking. But I have been pardoned by the king himself."

Gytha could not hide her astonishment at this pronouncement. Such was the confusion on her face that Aedwen was unable to stifle another burst of laughter. For a moment, Gytha said nothing, and then, seeming to have made up her mind, she said, "In that case, you must come inside and tell us all of your tidings. It seems much has happened in these last weeks. You men," she indicated the mounted guards, "will need to stay without the house. There is not enough room for all of you inside. But if you wait for a moment, I will bring out some ale, bread and cheese for you."

Without awaiting a reply, she walked back into the house.

It was not long before they were sitting at the small table with plates of cheese, bread and some good ham in front of them. Godgifu and Maethild sat either side of Aedwen and for a moment she remembered the warmth of their bodies pressed against her comfortingly when she had shared the girls' bed. While their mother had prepared food, the two girls had chattered like finches fluttering around a bramble hedge in autumn, bombarding Aedwen with questions. She had told them of the journey to Exanceaster, deciding to leave out much of the story, but giving enough for Gytha's daughters to gaze at her, awestruck, as they heard tales of sleeping in a barrow, spending a night in the charcoal burners' camp and another with dangerous wolf-heads and then meeting the king himself in the great hall of Exanceaster.

All the while Dunston talked in hushed tones with Gytha and Aedwen noticed that the woman's gaze flicked in her direction several times. What she was thinking though, Aedwen could not tell.

As they had sat at the table, the girls had fallen silent. Godgifu stared with undisguised fear at Dunston until Gytha snapped her fingers.

"Dunston is a guest under our roof, girls," she said. "Show some respect."

Godgifu lowered her gaze and Maethild sniggered at her discomfort.

"Girls," Gytha said, after they had eaten in silence for a few moments. "I have some tidings." She paused, and looked at Aedwen for a moment. Aedwen's stomach clenched, but Gytha smiled at her and she quickly remembered the warmth of the widow's welcome when she had first come to this small house, lost and terrified in the dark of night. Gytha nodded in reassurance and turned to her daughters. "Aedwen is going to stay with us."

With the words spoken, Aedwen's eyes blurred. Her heart hammered and she feared she might weep. What would Gytha's daughters think of this turn of events?

"Oh, mother," said Maethild, "that is wonderful. Finally, I can have a sensible sister to talk to."

Godgifu leaned across and pinched her older sister, who slapped her hand in return.

"Girls!" Gytha's tone cut through their sport. "Aedwen will be treated as kin, and I will have no fighting. You must all learn to get along, or I will bang your heads together until you see sense. Is that clear?"

Gytha glowered at them in turn, and each girl nodded and bowed her head. Aedwen wondered for the briefest of moments whether she would have been better off with Dunston, but then, as if the two girls could sense her disquiet, each of them reached for her hands under the board. She grasped their hands and blinked at the tears that threatened to fall.

"Well, this is a gift indeed," said Gytha. "A new daughter."

"She is a good girl," replied Dunston. "But to accept Aedwen into your care was the request I had for you."

"And the gift then? What would that be?"

"Ecgberht has offered a gift of coin for Aedwen's upkeep. You will want for nothing."

Gytha was rendered speechless. This news was clearly a surprise and such was the look of amazement on her face, that the three girls burst out laughing.

Gytha wiped her eyes and then drank some ale.

Aedwen's hands trembled with the force of emotions that ran through her. Tears of joy rolled down her cheeks. She wished to dry her face, but did not want to relinquish the hold on the girls' hands. So she gripped them tightly, sniffing and blinking.

"Well," said Gytha, laughing. "What a fine to do. Now we are all crying. But still we do not know how it is that you both have returned to us. And not only free, but with the king's favour."

Dunston drained his cup of ale, wiping his mouth with the back of his rough hand. And in the warm gloom of the house, with the hearth fire and rush lights providing scant, flickering light, he told their tale. The womenfolk watched on, wide-eyed, as they heard tell of the pursuit through the forest and the hardships Aedwen and Dunston had been forced to endure. Dunston was no scop, not a poet from a lord's hall, but his words spun a stark picture of the terrible days they had spent in the forest. Unlike a tale-spinner, who sought to shock his audience, Dunston did not dwell on the moments when they had found corpses, or when he had stood and fought against their attackers. But somehow, the sparseness and simple nature of the telling made the tale more captivating. Gytha had grown pale. Godgifu and Maethild clung to Aedwen.

She shuddered as Dunston's words brought back the horrors they had faced. It was strange, she thought, that even though she had lived through the events he described, she found herself moved by the story, as one who is hearing it for the first time. Again she felt the bitter sting of the loss of her father. The terror of being caught by the savage men on the road. And then the breathless anxiety of seeing Dunston facing a line of charging, mounted men, as they threw up great clods of mud and sprays of water from the meadow. Dunston did not mention the rainbow that had shone in the darkened, clouded sky above Exanceaster, but she recalled its colours vividly and how the red of blood had been both darker and brighter than God's promise in the heavens.

At the end of the telling her face was again wet with tears. The girls at her side were snivelling and tears also streaked Gytha's face.

The widow reached out a hand and gently touched Dunston's shoulder. He started, as if woken from a reverie.

"You are a brave man, Dunston," she said, her voice quiet.

He grunted.

"Aedwen owes you her life, and it seems the king owes you his kingdom." Dunston picked up his cup to hide his embarrassment and found it empty. Gytha lifted the pitcher and filled it, smiling. "Perhaps we all owe you our lives. For who knows what would have happened if the king had not learnt of the ealdorman's treachery?"

"I merely did my duty," he said, his tone gruff.

It was clear that the praise was making him feel awkward, so Gytha rose and fetched a small wooden box, which she placed upon the table. She lifted the lid and inside there was a parcel wrapped in linen.

"Would you care for a honey cake?"

Her daughters, tears forgotten now, sat up expectantly.

"Dunston?" Gytha said, peeling back the linen and proffering the box to him.

Dunston peered inside and plucked out one of the small cakes. Sniffing it, he grinned.

"Better than the fare from the king's own board," he said and took a bite. "And certainly better company." A few crumbs sprayed out of his mouth and he quickly rubbed at his beard, abashed.

But Gytha beamed at the praise and offered the cakes to the girls. They each took one. Maethild and Godgifu made short work of theirs, but Aedwen savoured hers. It was sweet and chewy and perhaps the nicest thing she had ever eaten. She thought then of her mother, and how she would sometimes bake honey cakes. They were not as good as

Gytha's, she thought guiltily, and once more tears threatened to fall.

"So, Dunston," Gytha said after she had finished her own cake. "I suppose you will go back now to your home in Sealhwudu?"

Was there a hint of sorrow in Gytha's tone?

Dunston washed down the last of his cake with a swig of ale and stifled a belch.

"I would like nothing more," he said. Did Gytha frown at his words? "But it seems my days of peace in the forest are over."

"But you said that Ecgberht King offered you a gift. Surely with gold you can live comfortably any way you please."

Dunston scratched his beard and looked sidelong at Aedwen.

"Ah," he said, a rueful expression on his face, "but it was not gold or silver that our lord king gave to me."

"No?" replied Gytha, surprised. "What then?"

"Why, for my sins he has made me his reeve of the Briuuetone Hundred."

Forty-One

Sweat dripped into Dunston's eyes. It was a hot day and he had set a fast pace along the familiar forest paths. Sunlight slanted down through the summer-heavy canopy, dappling the hard, root-twisted ground before him. Taking out his water skin, he took a long pull. The cool water soothed his parched mouth. By Christ's bones, how he'd missed being out in the woods, free from the troubles of the folk of Briuuetone, away from the concerns of upholding Ecgberht's many laws. Who would have ever thought there would be so many disputes over the boundaries between men's plots of land? Dunston longed to return to the life he had known before, where he was able to hunt, forage and forge as the whim took him.

He smiled at the irony of the king's "gift". The position of reeve was one of standing, which came with a stipend and status, and Ecgberht had also rewarded him handsomely with a bag of silver scillings so large that he doubted he would ever be able to spend all the money. And yet the very thing that had been gifted to him prevented him from leading the life he craved.

But he was a man of honour, and he had long ago sworn his oath to Ecgberht. So while the king yet lived, his word was his bond. And Dunston knew that, though he would rather not be given the task of upholding the law, the king's choice had merit. Dunston was diligent and honest. The people of Briuuetone and the surrounding hundred could rest easy that he would do the job to the best of his ability.

But how he pined for the quiet of the forest. The wind rustled the leaves of the lindens above his head and he drew in a deep breath of the heavy, loamy air. He was almost at his destination. Just past that fallen beech, then a short way until the mossy outcrop on the left and the clearing he had called home for so many years would open in front of him. His back was hot and drenched in sweat beneath the empty pack he carried there. Now, as he drew close to his old home, he wished he had brought a cart. There was so much he would like to carry back to his new house in Briuuetone. Well, there was nothing for that now. He would have to make do with just taking a few small items; Eawynn's plate, his favourite hammer, the small seax he had been working on for Oswold, perhaps a couple of the cheeses he had stored, if the mice hadn't got to them. He had worried that Wudugát, his goat, would have come to harm. He had left the poor girl tethered and had hoped she would have managed to chew through the rope easily enough. And yet, he had still fretted. There were wolves out here, and he had assumed the worst.

He still could barely believe he had found her hale and whole that morning roaming a small enclosure on the edge of the charcoal burners' encampment. These were the men who had helped him to raise Odin when he was a pup and they welcomed Dunston like a long lost son. They had slapped him on the back, which made him wince, as his ribs were still tender. They laughed to see him, their blackened, soot-smeared faces lined and wrinkled with their happiness. When Dunston had enquired about the effusive nature of their welcome, the response they gave him answered a quandary that had been bothering him for some time.

"We thought you were dead," said the oldest of the men. "Thought you'd gone the way of all things, these many weeks past."

Dunston had shaken his head, confused.

"People often make the mistake of thinking I am dead it seems," he'd said, with a crooked smile. "But what made you think such a thing?"

"Why, when old Odin limped in here with half his back hanging off and covered in blood, we thought perhaps a boar had got you and him. You weren't with him, so we figured as like you were mouldering in the forest somewhere. Botulf sewed up the cut on Odin and burnt the flesh so that the rot wouldn't set in. That hound is as tough as they come. He barely whimpered and didn't snap at Botulf, not one bit. I thought he'd as likely bite his hand off, but it was like he understood that Botulf was just trying to help."

"Botulf," Dunston called to a younger man. "I thank you for saving my dog. If you had not done so, I might be dead after all."

"Odin lives yet then?" asked Botulf. "I thought he must have surely died by now. For when we woke the next morning, he had run off into the forest and no matter how much we called, he did not return. Gone off to die in peace, we thought."

"He lives, all right. He is out hunting with a new friend. A girl."

"Oh, a girl," said Botulf, with a wink. "About time you took a wife again, if you ask me."

"I didn't ask you," replied Dunston. "And she is not my wife. She is not much more than a child."

He had told the charcoal burners of their adventures then. They thirsted for knowledge of the world beyond their smoke-wreathed clearings and it seemed the least he could do after they had tended to Odin. It transpired that, after Odin had vanished, fearing for Dunston, they had gone to his hut to see if he might be there and in need of help. Instead, they found Wudugát. Realising she would perish if left alone, they brought the goat back to their camp.

"She has been well looked after," said Botulf, "and we have been glad of the milk, I can tell you. But, of course, you must take her with you now."

"No. Wudugát is yours," Dunston had said. "You saved my dog and in doing so, you saved me and maybe the kingdom, so I would have you supplied with fresh milk."

He smiled to himself as he remembered the charcoal burners' delight at first finding him alive, and then learning that Odin was well. And after that, they were even more pleased that they could keep the goat when they had thought they would have to give her back. It is the simple things that bring the most pleasure, he thought.

Pushing the stopper back into his flask, he set off on the last stretch of the path that would lead him to his hut in the clearing.

He had looked forward to getting away from Briuuetone for several days now. He was staying in the hall that Rothulf had built. It was comfortable and spacious; much too large for his needs apart from one day each month when the hall-moot was held there. On the day of the moot, it became the centre of life of the people of the village and the surrounding area of the hundred. He had been prepared for the busy nature of the day, but had found himself unable to sleep the night before. His mind kept jolting him awake with dark thoughts that he might need to preside over a suit involving murder. He knew he could face an armed man in combat and take his life in an eye-blink, but to have someone stand before him, to speak with them, to listen to the charges made against them, and then to mete out justice, took a different type of bravery.

As it turned out, his first moot at Briuuetone was a tedious affair, with the most arduous of the suits being that in which

Eappa had struck Cuthbald over some drunken squabble. Eappa had broken Cuthbald's nose, and Cuthbald demanded restitution. Dunston had conferred with Godrum, the priest, who had read through the dooms and informed him of the weregild that must be paid. Eappa had grumbled and complained when he was told to pay Cuthbald three scillings, but Dunston had stood up, and glared at him until he had meekly nodded and left the hall. The rest of the day had been filled with petty disputes over land rights and some minor thefts. Dunston relied on Godrum to provide him with good counsel and to pore over the vellum sheets of dooms. He found the priest to be methodical and patient and, despite the tedium of the day, his initial fears had been misplaced. He was sure his concerns had been due in no small part to having witnessed the trial of the traitors in Exanceaster just a few weeks previously.

By God, that had been harrowing, and Dunston was glad that he did not have to deal with anything as dire as treachery and murder.

After Ælfgar had been hanged unceremoniously from the east gate of the city walls, Ecgberht had ordered the men who had ridden with the ealdorman to be brought before him. The king had insisted that Dunston attend the trial, as he was a witness to many of the acts the men stood accused of.

Most of the accused, certain of their fate, were sullen and refused to speak. But one, a lank-haired man with stooped shoulders, by the name of Lutan, had seemed convinced that he could escape his punishment by telling everything he knew of what they had done. The others glowered at him, and one spat in his direction and swore he would seek him out in the afterlife and cut out his tongue. A guard had beaten the man into silence, and the greasy-haired Lutan had been allowed to speak.

The king nodded and urged Lutan to tell them all he knew.

"If you tell me the truth, man," the king said in a quiet voice, "I will see to it that you are treated better than your comrades in arms."

Lutan had dipped his head, swallowing and grovelling pitifully, while his companions looked on. Hatred burnt in their eyes at his betrayal.

Prompted by questions from Ecgberht, Lutan told of more than the incidents Dunston knew of. Much of what he told, Dunston had already deduced. Lytelman had somehow learnt of the message from Ithamar and then sought to bring the news of treason to one in power. He visited the reeve of Briuuetone. But, unbeknown to Aedwen's father, Hunfrith was party to the plans of Ealdorman Ælfgar and so had ordered the peddler silenced.

"Why was Hunfrith involved?" Dunston had asked, interrupting Lutan's snivelling whine. "Surely Ælfgar did not take lowly reeves into his confidence."

Lutan had stared at him for a moment, a sly expression on his ugly face.

"You do not know?" he asked incredulously.

"Know what?"

"Hunfrith is Ælfgar's son. A bastard from a milkmaid in Wincaletone. When Ælfgar learnt of Rothulf's meddling, he sent Hunfrith to take care of it. If you know what I mean."

He had smirked then at Dunston, and it had been hard not to rush at the man and knock him to the ground. Dunston had clenched his fists at his side, holding himself rigidly still. So, the rumours Gytha had heard were true, but it was not this knowledge that had led to Rothulf's murder.

"Meddling?" Dunston had asked. "How so?"

Lutan's eyes had darted about as his mind worked, seeking some advantage for himself from his knowledge. At last he turned to the king.

"If I tell you of more crimes, it will go easier for me?" he asked.

Ecgberht inclined his head slowly.

"I give you my word."

Lutan licked his lips.

"Rothulf had somehow heard tell of the plans to attack Wessex," he said. "I don't know how. But just after Easter he came to see Ælfgar and told him what he knew. Ælfgar thanked him and sent him back to Briuuetone. But no sooner had he gone than he sent Hunfrith, me and the others after him. It was Hunfrith's idea to drown him. Wouldn't look like a murder that way, he said. Once he was dead, Hunfrith took over as reeve. That way he could help stop any more rumours. And we would all share in the spoils once war came."

Dunston had grown cold at hearing Lutan's words.

"So Hunfrith murdered Rothulf?" he asked, his voice barely more than a whisper, but heard by all in the great hall of Exanceaster.

"He did," Lutan answered. He sounded somehow pleased with himself.

"Where is this Hunfrith now?" asked the king.

"The last we saw him, he was still at Briuuetone," replied Dunston.

The king ordered riders to go with all haste to Briuuetone and to seek out Hunfrith.

"He must be held accountable for his crimes," he said, and his face was thunder. "Rothulf was a good man."

But when the riders returned a few days later, it was to tell the king that there was no sign of Hunfrith at Briuuetone. It seemed he had fled when word had reached him of his father's capture. The news had weighed heavily on Dunston. He had not truly expected Hunfrith to still be in his hall, awaiting his fate, but the idea that the man had evaded justice after committing such foul crimes was almost more than he could bear. He had told Aedwen that vengeance did not bring happiness, but since Hunfrith's involvement in Rothulf's death had been confirmed, he had prayed that the man would be found and that he might witness his death, for there could be no other sentence for such as him.

But Hunfrith had run and now he would never have to pay for Rothulf's murder, for ordering the slaying of Lytelman, for abetting his father's treachery.

Dunston had resigned himself to taking some consolation in the downfall of Ælfgar and his men. And yet, witnessing their deaths by hanging, their tongues swollen and black as they danced on the end of a rope, had left him feeling as empty as if he had watched animals being slaughtered before winter.

He had felt something akin to a twinge of grim amusement as Lutan met his fate. True to his word, the king had made the man's sentence easier than that of his cohort of traitors; instead of hanging, which could be long and painful, Ecgberht had ordered the man beheaded. There had been a twisted sense of justice at hearing Lutan's anguished cries as he was forced to watch his friends pulled, choking, kicking and strangling into the air, before he met his own, mercifully quick ending.

But none of the killing had provided Dunston with any release. He had brought Gytha the news that Rothulf had indeed been murdered, but Hunfrith had vanished, leaving Dunston bitter and angry. He now wished that he had not told Gytha the truth. She had suspected, but in time she would have made peace with her husband's death. Learning of the certainty of his murder and the lack of justice for his killer had sowed dark seeds of despair in her soul. Dunston felt responsible for Gytha's new sorrow, though he knew in truth he was not to blame; he had loved Rothulf as a brother.

There had been many dark days since they had returned to Briuuetone. The summer days were bright and warm, but the shadow of recent events still hung over them, as if a storm cloud had drifted before the sun. And yet, there was much to celebrate in his new life. He had invited Gytha, her daughters and Aedwen to live in the hall with him. He needed someone to run the place and Gytha had been the lady of the hall until recently. And, though sometimes he found the noise of the girls' chatter grated on his nerves, he thought the time for silence in the forest was over for him. Better to be surrounded by the laughter of youth than the silence of approaching decrepitude and death.

And yet, when the opportunity to head into the forest had arisen, he had not hesitated. Dunston knew that he would settle in well enough over time, but some days the constant companionship of Gytha, the girls and the ever-present folk of Briuuetone became too much and he longed for the peace of nature to embrace him.

Stepping out into the glade where he had built the stout house he had shared happily with Eawynn, Dunston paused to take in the scene. The grass was faded and dried as it often became in late summer. The ground was parched, and he noted how fissures and cracks had opened up in the earth due to the long dry spell. The lindens that overshadowed the house were thick with leaf and heavy with fragrant yellow blossom. The trees whispered, as if in greeting and their voice was as familiar as his own breath. Dunston sniffed the air. The summer would be on the turn soon and those glossy green leaves would become ochre and russet. They would fall, forming a thick blanket on the ground. The nights would grow longer. It was then, he knew, when he would most miss this place. Every year the summers seemed shorter and winter's icy fingers scratched over the land more quickly. With each passing year, time seemed to flow faster, and with a maudlin frown, Dunston wondered how many more passing seasons he would witness.

Shaking his head at such thoughts, he moved to the forge that stood under a lean-to timber shelter beside the hut. He looked about the grimy surfaces, the charcoal that nestled cold and grey in the fire pit. His gaze fell on a scrap of leather on the anvil. He could scarcely believe it was still there, but other than the charcoal men, who else would have come here? Picking up the greased leather, he let it fall open to expose what was wrapped within. He smiled. It was just as he remembered it, not even a spot of rust. It was the fine blade and tang of the knife he had been working on for Oswold. There was still some fine hammering to do, it was not sharp and was still a piece of iron without a handle, but it would be beautiful when it was finished. He had left it out here on the morning when he had found Lytelman and Aedwen, meaning to work on it when he returned from checking his traps and snares. He would take it back to Briuuetone and finish the knife there. He had just the right piece of antler that would serve as a handle. Wrapping the blade back in the leather, he tucked it into his belt and with a last longing look at the forge, he turned to the house.

He opened the oak door that he had fashioned what seemed a lifetime before. It creaked on the leather straps that held it in place. He had often contemplated forging iron hinges, but had never been able to justify the extravagance. He snorted. Now he had enough silver not to worry about such things, but he would no longer be living here to care about the door's hinges.

The instant that Dunston walked into the hut, he knew something was wrong. At first he was uncertain what had alerted him that all was not well. The air was not as still as it should be, the house less quiet somehow, though when he paused by the door to listen, there was no sound. He took a slow breath and then it struck him. A faint scent of sweat, wool, leather and sour mead. Someone had been there.

He moved to the hearth, holding his hand over the thick layer of grey ash. Still hot. How had he not smelt the smoke before? He had been too distracted reminiscing about the past to notice. Cursing himself for a fool, he stood, his senses sharp and alert once more. He had grown soft in just a few weeks living in luxury in a warm hall. This was still wild land. There were beasts that could kill a man in Sealhwudu, and as he well knew, there were outlaws who would not think twice about killing him to take the clothes from his corpse. His hand dropped to the seax sheathed at his belt and he regretted bitterly not bringing DeaÞangenga. But he had come to hunt and to visit his old home, not to battle. He was done with fighting and killing. It was time to keep his oath to Eawynn.

A rustle outside gave him an instant's warning, but when the door swung open with a rasp, Dunston started. The sound was loud in the small hut.

Without turning, Dunston looked up at Eawynn's silver plate where it hung on the far wall. Within the burnished metal he saw the reflection of the shadowed figure that hesitated in the doorway. It was a tall man, but Dunston could not make out his features with the light from outside behind him.

"Well, come in, if you are going to," Dunston said. "It seems you have made yourself quite at home in my house, so there is no point being shy now."

For a moment, the man did not move, then he stepped quickly into the hut. The light from the open door fell on his face and Dunston's breath caught in his throat.

"You!" he said, turning to face the man. For the second time he regretted not bringing his axe. It seemed even now it was not his wyrd to fulfil his oath to Eawynn and lay down his weapons. For sure as the leaves would fall from the trees in the autumn, there would be a fight here today.

Hunfrith, thinner and with sharper cheekbones than Dunston remembered, slowly pulled his long sword from the scabbard at his side.

"I could scarcely believe my eyes when I saw you come down the path," he said. His sword glimmered in the sunlight spilling in through the doorway. The metal was clean and polished. It appeared that Hunfrith had at least not forgotten to tend to his weapon. His clothing was a different matter. His cloak was threadbare and ripped, stained with mud and lichen. The kirtle he wore was streaked and filthy. His moustache and beard, once so well-tended and clipped, were now an unruly and straggled thatch. His eyes held a febrile glint. His smell was overpowering in the small confines of the hut and again Dunston could not believe he had failed to notice the man's presence earlier.

Holding his sword menacingly before him, Hunfrith took a step towards Dunston.

"You ruined everything, old man," he spat.

Dunston kept his hands loose at his sides, ready to react in an instant. He only had the seax he had taken from Beornmod. It would be difficult to fight against a sword, but he had no other weapon to hand.

"I did nothing, Hunfrith, save see a young girl to safety after you ordered her father murdered."

Hunfrith's eyes narrowed and Dunston knew that he would strike soon.

"I should have killed you when I had the chance," Hunfrith said.

"We all live with regrets," Dunston replied, edging around the hearth and away from Hunfrith.

Hunfrith sneered.

"Your time for living is over, old man."

He swung his sword at Dunston's head. Dunston ducked and, scooping up a stool from beside the fireplace, flung it at Hunfrith. The stool's leg's tangled with Hunfrith's blade and Dunston rushed out of the open doorway and into the bright light of the summer afternoon.

Blinking against the sunlight, he ran as fast as he could across the clearing. His ribs, still not fully healed, were already paining him. He could not keep this up. Besides, even without his recent wounds, Hunfrith was younger and taller and would catch him soon enough.

Behind him, Hunfrith roared and sped out of the hut.

Dunston slid to a halt only a dozen paces away. There was nothing to be gained from running. All that would happen is that he would be out of breath and struggling when he had to confront Hunfrith's sword. Better to stand now while he was fresh and had some small chance of victory.

Turning to face the younger man, Dunston slid his seax from its sheath. Hunfrith sped towards him, the long blade of his sword gleaming. Dunston could see instantly that the younger man was no novice with a blade. Facing a skilled swordsman, without a shield and with only a seax, Dunston's only chance would come from luck. Or a cool head, if he could only make his adversary lose his.

"Your father's corpse is decorating the gate at Exanceaster," Dunston shouted. "All his men are dead too. Some I slew, others were hanged by the king. You are the last one left. The pathetic bastard who doesn't know when he is defeated."

Dunston had hoped to goad Hunfrith into a reckless attack, but the erstwhile reeve slowed his charging pace before reaching Dunston. Crouching into the warrior stance, he spat.

"They may be dead, but you will join them soon enough. You may think me pathetic, old man, but like you say, I don't know I am defeated, because I am yet standing and I have a sword in my hand. That doesn't feel like defeat to me."

Without warning, and with none of the tell-tale signs Dunston had grown to expect from warriors who faced him, Hunfrith leapt forward. He feinted at Dunston's head, and as the old warrior brought up the short blade of his seax to parry the blow, Hunfrith altered the trajectory of his blade. Unarmoured as he was, the sword would have disembowelled Dunston, if it had connected. But at the last instant, Dunston threw himself backwards to avoid the blow. His foot sank into one of the deep clefts in the earth caused by the recent lack of rain and he tumbled to the hard earth of the clearing. Dunston grunted with the pain as the fall jarred his ribs.

Sensing victory, Hunfrith pressed forward, swinging his sword down. Dunston threw his seax up with nothing but instinct to guide his hand. He parried the strike, and sparks flew. His hand throbbed at the force of the collision and his fingers grew numb. He could not survive more than a few heartbeats, but he could see no way of saving himself. He scrabbled back in the dirt, and Hunfrith came on, grinning at the sight of his foe lying prostrate before him.

"Now you will die, cowering in the muck. Not so bold now, are you, old man? Who's the pathetic bastard now?"

Leering, he sliced his sword down at Dunston's exposed legs. Dunston twisted away from the attack and his ribs screamed from the effort. Hunfrith's blade bit into the earth. Dunston tried to regain his feet, but he was too slow; his old injured frame not as lithe as it had once been. Before he was able to rise, Hunfrith had recovered his balance and his wickedly fast sword flickered down again.

Again Dunston managed to intercept the swing with his seax, but as the two blades clanged together, the weight of the heavier sword sent a wave of shock up his wrist, numbing his hand completely and Beornmod's seax skittered out of his grasp. It fell in the grass a few paces away, but it might as well have been in Exanceaster, for all the help it would do him now.

Hunfrith raised his sword. Dunston could only watch in dismay. He was not afraid of death, but to be killed by this treacherous cur rankled. By Christ's bones, how he wished he had brought DeaÞangenga with him. No matter his promise to Eawynn, he had never truly believed he would die without a weapon in his hand.

"Now you die, old man!" screamed Hunfrith.

A flash of inspiration came to Dunston then, as Hunfrith's blade glittered in the afternoon sun. With numb fingers, Dunston scrabbled at the leather-wrapped knife at his belt. He would yet die with a blade in his grasp.

Hunfrith's sword sang through the air as it sliced downward. Dunston roared and surged up, ramming Oswold's unfinished blade into Hunfrith's groin. The knife was unquenched and blunt, but it still had a point. Hunfrith's eyes opened wide as hot blood drenched Dunston's fist. With his left hand, Dunston grabbed Hunfrith's quickly weakening sword arm.

Aghast, Hunfrith stared down in confusion and disbelief as his blood pumped over Dunston's arm.

Dunston rose to his feet, grinding the bones in Hunfrith's right wrist in his powerful left fist. He shoved the younger man away from him and Hunfrith staggered, but did not fall.

"What?" said Hunfrith, stupidly. His eyes followed Dunston's movements, but he seemed incapable of action.

Dunston snatched up the fallen seax from the grass and advanced towards Hunfrith. At last, Hunfrith understood the threat and shook off his shock. He attempted to defend himself, to lift his sword. He stumbled back, away from Dunston. His face crumpled in agony; Oswold's knife yet jutted from his body. Again, he tried to raise his sword, but once more the effort proved too much. His breath was coming in wheezing gasps now. Blood gushed down his legs soaking his breeches.

Taking three quick steps forward, Dunston batted the sword away, slapping the flat of the blade with the palm of his left hand. His right fist punched forward and Hunfrith's eyes widened in horror. Dunston twisted the seax blade. It snagged on one of Hunfrith's ribs. The man juddered. Savagely, Dunston withdrew the steel from his flesh and then, without pause, drove it in again, probing with the point until it penetrated Hunfrith's heart. The man's stench filled his nostrils. Hunfrith let out a moaning, rattling breath, fetid with old mead and meat, and sagged against Dunston.

Stepping back, Dunston let his foe slump to the earth. Blood pumped from his wounds, staining the grass and the clover. Dunston was breathing heavily. His ribs ached and his hands shook. Looking down at Hunfrith's bleeding corpse, he thought absently how the grass would grow lush there, fed with the man's lifeblood.

The feeling slowly returned to his numbed right hand. His breathing came fast and ragged for a time and he slumped down in the grass, content to allow the afternoon breeze to cool the sweat on his brow. Eventually, his breathing slowed and he looked at the corpse in the grass. He could not tarry. Aedwen would be here soon. He had not been sure about letting her hunt alone, but in the end she had convinced him.

"Odin will protect me, won't you, boy?" she'd said, stroking the hound's ears.

Gazing at Hunfrith's crumpled form, Dunston felt a cold fear grip him. The forest was too dangerous for Aedwen alone, even with the dog. He would never allow such folly again. He stood with a groaning wince.

Dunston knew what he should do, but for a moment, he was filled with unease and uncertainty. He was the reeve now. It was his duty to uphold the law. Should he not take Hunfrith's body back to Briuuetone? Surely it was not right to merely leave him out here for the foxes, wolves and the woodland creatures to feast upon.

Dunston looked at his old house and remembered the day, only weeks earlier when he had set out one morning to check his snares and had instead found a mutilated corpse in a glade. He thought of how taking Lytelman's body to the village had sparked the dreadful events that followed. Of course, had he not found the man's body and taken it to Briuuetone, Wessex might now be overrun by Norsemen and Wéalas.

He sighed.

If there was a doom in Godrum's books forbidding what he meant to do, he did not know of it. Besides, Hunfrith was a wolf-head, his life forfeit. He would not be missed.

Hunfrith was a large man, and Dunston's ribs throbbed terribly as he dragged the corpse into the forest, far from the house.

Later, when he returned to the glade, smoke drifted from the hut's thatch and the smell of roasting game wafted to him on the warm summer breeze. As he drew near, he could hear Aedwen humming a tune to herself and relief flooded through him.

She was safe.

Her singing reminded him of Eawynn. Unbidden, tears filled his eyes. He stood there for some time, listening to her. The summer sun soaked into his skin and he closed his eyes, allowing himself to imagine, just for a moment, that the years had not passed. That he was not now an old man. That Eawynn yet lived.

Then, Odin barked and came bounding out of the hut. Dunston smiled at the hound and cuffed away the tears from his cheeks.

Stepping into the smoky darkness of the hut, he said, "Is that partridge I smell? Let's eat and then, let's go home. We have hunted enough for one day."

Historical Note

Novels often grow from the smallest seed of inspiration. So it was with *Wolf of Wessex*.

I stumbled upon the account in the *Anglo-Saxon Chronicle* for 21 June in the year 838. On that day King Ecgberht of Wessex defeated a joint force of Cornish and Danish at a place called Hingston Down (Hengestdūn). This got me thinking. How did Ecgberht know the enemy forces had gathered deep within Cornwall with enough time to muster his troops and march them all the way to the Tamar, where it is assumed the Danes had landed and the battle is traditionally thought to have taken place? I can't imagine the Cornish and Danish leaders would have amassed and then tarried for long enough to allow word of their impending attack to reach Wessex, so perhaps Ecgberht had been forewarned. We don't know where the Danes that joined the Cornish had come from, but it is very likely they were based in Ireland, which was by this time a Norse stronghold. But wherever they came from, if this was a planned joint assault, there must have been some communication beforehand that could have been intercepted. Now, it could well be that all communication had been verbal, but what if some of the missives about the attack had been written down?

And that was enough for me to start coming up with the plot of *Wolf of Wessex*.

Most of the characters in the novel are fictitious, but they are placed within the tapestry of real events and places. The very late eighth and early ninth centuries were years of upheaval after a period of relative stability for Britain. Following the first account of Norsemen landing on the coast of Wessex in 787, over the subsequent decade there followed a series of brutal raids all around the coastline of the British Isles. Infamously, the raiders, known now as Vikings (*vikingr* in the novel, the Old Norse word for people travelling to raid and seek adventure), sacked Christian monasteries such as Lindisfarne in Northumbria and Iona in the Hebrides. These Christian sites were situated in exposed locations, with access to the sea and no armed guards, and they also housed many rich artefacts which were ripe for the taking. These Scandinavian pirates were not Christian, so cared nothing for the supposed eternal damnation they might face for defiling the sanctity of monasteries and churches. And so it was that the Viking Age began. A time where the sleek dragon-prowed ships of the Norsemen were a constant threat to anyone living near the coast or navigable rivers in Britain and northern Europe.

For a time in the early ninth century, the number of attacks seems to have reduced, thanks in no small part to Frankish ships patrolling the English Channel. Like so many monarchs in the Anglo-Saxon period, Ecgberht had been exiled in his early life. He spent those years in the court of Charlemagne, the Frankish king, the greatest king of the age. There Ecgberht learnt much of how to be a statesman and how to govern a Christian country. This knowledge would serve him well and the alliance with the powerful Frankish royal family must certainly have aided him when he returned to claim his place as the king of Wessex.

Under Ecgberht, and with Frankish support, Wessex quickly became the most powerful kingdom in Britain. While the Frankish navy kept the southern coast relatively safe from plundering Norsemen, Ecgberht focused on conquest and expansion. In 813 and then again in 825 he led campaigns against the "West Welsh", conquering what is now known as Devon and subjugating Cornwall to the status of vassal state. Soon he had defeated the Mercians at the Battle of Ellandun (probably Wroughton in Wiltshire) and then swallowed up Kent, Essex, Surrey and Sussex. According to the *Anglo-Saxon Chronicle*, he even took the oath of Eanred, king of the Northumbrians, leading Ecgberht to be called the ruler of all of the English.

But as with all kingdoms, things didn't run smoothly for long. Mercia, Wessex's enemy number one, quickly regained independence in 830. And the Vikings posed an increasing threat along the coast of Wessex. This was due to a civil war breaking out in Frankia between the sons of Louis the Pious. As the bloody civil war raged, thoughts of protecting the Channel from Norse ships vanished, and the navy was disbanded.

So, with his continental European allies otherwise engaged and removing their support, Ecgberht found himself having to fend for himself. In 836, a fleet of thirty-five Danish marauders landed at Carrum (Carhampton). Ecgberht summoned his levies and they attacked the Vikings. But the Danes defeated the men of Wessex and "had the place of slaughter".

Ecgberht was getting old by this time and the threat of attack by Vikings must have been an ever-present worry for him. There was always the possibility of treachery from within too, of course. Which brings us back to the planning of the joint attack in 838. If messages were being sent to arrange times and places, perhaps they would be written down. This would be much more likely if Ecclesiastics were involved.

Perhaps they would be arrogant enough to think that so few people could read, their plots would not be found out.

There are several instances of bishops conspiring against kings for their own personal gain. Bishop Wulfstan in the tenth century, for example, switched allegiances between the Northumbrians and the Vikings as was expedient at any given time. Another example is Wulfheard, Bishop of Hereford. He had some very public spats with King Offa and went as far as to forge land grants to gain riches and power.

Ealhstan was the Bishop of Sherbourne in 838, but the only evidence for his duplicitous nature comes from Asser's *Life of King Alfred*, where he states that Ealhstan was involved in a plot to prevent King Aethelwulf (Ecgberht's son and Alfred's father) from regaining his crown when he returned from his pilgrimage to Rome.

As to nobles plotting against their kings for their own advancement, such a thing is all too commonplace. Even today the idea of powerful politicians betraying their nation for personal gain is met with resigned acceptance rather than outraged shock. One historic event that partly inspired Ealdorman Ælfgar and his bastard son, Hunfrith, is that of Huga (or Hugh), the Frenchman who had been made reeve of Exeter. In 1003 he betrayed the city to a great army of Danes led by Swein Forkbeard. The city was taken and destroyed and much of Wessex was invaded and plundered as a result.

Dunston is all fiction, but I liked the idea of a warrior looking back at the life he had led, believing he has served his purpose, only to find he still has a role to play, and perhaps a reason to strive for more than simply existing.

The location of his home, Sealhwudu (Selwood Forest), is real. In the ninth century the woodland covered the land between Chippenham in modern-day Wiltshire to Gillingham in Dorset. It was an important natural boundary between east and west Wessex. The name derives from Sallow Wood. Sallow is an archaic name for willow. A small part of this ancient forest remains to this day at Clanger Wood in Yarnbrook, Wiltshire.

Briuuetone (Bruton) gets its name from the river that flows through the town. Briw means vigorous and describes the fast-flowing water of the River Brue in spate.

The idea of a Christian of the ninth century having a dog named Odin, after the one-eyed father of the Norse gods, may seem far-fetched. However, the idea comes from my own family history. My paternal grandfather had a black Labrador called Satan, which I believe was named by my father (who incidentally went on to become a missionary and then a Baptist minister!). You can imagine the strange looks my grandfather would get in the 1960s and 1970s calling out for his dog.

The partial lunar eclipse of the full moon on the night of 11 June 838 was something I discovered while writing and seemed like a detail I had to include in the story.

The land of Wessex has been populated for millennia and is the home to Stonehenge and the larger stone circle of Avebury. It is also dotted with ancient burial mounds and barrows. The barrow where Dunston and Aedwen spend the night is loosely based on Stoney Littleton Long Barrow, which is maintained by English Heritage and open to the public. It can be entered free of charge.

Much of Dunston and Aedwen's story centres around the legal concepts of Anglo-Saxon Wessex. I have taken a rather loose approach to the legal system of the first half of the ninth century, incorporating elements that were not documented until later. However, I believe this leads to an authentic feeling of the legal process of the time, and does not detract from the novel or stray too far from the reality of what would have been.

The kingdom was broken down into areas called hundreds. These hundreds were probably comprised of a hundred hides

---

of land. Each hundred was further broken down into tithings of ten hides each. The terms, hundreds and tithings, were first recorded in the laws of Edmund I in the tenth century, but they may well have been in use for much longer and I think they give a good framework of understanding for how the law worked.

Each hundred held a monthly hundred court (or moot) where legal disputes would be heard. Any case that could not be settled could be taken to the shire court. The reeve of each hundred was a powerful man and responsible for the administration of the law and keeping of the peace. When a miscreant fled justice, or someone was accused of a violent crime and needed to be apprehended, the men of the tithing where the criminal resided were responsible for bringing him in to face justice.

Above the hundred was the shire, and difficult cases could be taken to the shire reeve (where we get the word sheriff). The shire court was held less frequently, perhaps every six months. The highest court of the land was the King's court, where the king himself dispensed justice.

The Church had its own Ecclesiastical courts where cases against the clergy were heard.

The trial system was based on oaths being made. If a defendant could find enough people to swear oaths to their innocence, they would be exonerated. If found guilty, the accused could seek to face trial by ordeal to prove their innocence by divine providence. However, this must always have been a last resort, due to the grisly, painful and sometimes deadly nature of the ordeals!

Most crimes had a price, or weregild, that needed to be paid to the aggrieved party and sometimes the reeve and king too. These penalties were set down in lists of laws, or dooms. Alfred the Great of Wessex, Ecgberht's grandson, codified the laws of Wessex into a single book. *The Doom Book* or *Code of Alfred* compiled three previous lists of dooms – those of Athelberht of Kent, Ine of Wessex and Offa of Mercia. For the weregild in this novel, I have used the dooms of Ine of Wessex.

The concept of the wulfeshéafod, or wolf's head, or wolf-head (caput lupinum in Latin) referred to a person being outside the law, and, like a lone wolf, they were open to attack by anyone. A wolf-head had lost all rights and so could be harmed by anyone with impunity. Such outlaws must have been truly desperate individuals, as they could expect no quarter if captured.

Dunston's axe is inspired by the axe found in Mammen, near Viborg in Denmark. The head of the Mammen axe is iron with intricate patterns of silver thread inlaid. It is not as large as DeaÞangenga, and it is not known whether it was used in battle or merely for ceremonial purposes. DeaÞangenga means Deathwalker in Old English, and seemed a very apt name for Dunston's huge axe with which he has sent so many men to their deaths.

The crossing of the River Exe by the warriors on their return from Hingston Down may have surprised readers familiar with the area. There had been a Roman timber bridge over the Exe, but that would have decayed and washed away by the ninth century. However, before the later stone bridge over the river was built in the thirteenth century, there are accounts that the Exe could be forded at low tide.

The generally accepted location of the battle of Hingston Down is near the Tamar River, in Cornwall. However, there is another Hingston Down, in Devon. It seemed more likely to me that, rather than striking deep into hostile territory, Ecgberht would gather his troops and waylay the approaching host of Vikings and Cornish. The Devon Hingston Down is near Moretonhampstead and on the route from the Tamar, where the Vikings landed, to Exeter, so it seems like a perfect location for an ambush.

At the end of this story, Dunston has somewhat reluctantly accepted the mantle of responsibility gifted to him by his king and Aedwen has found people who have welcomed her as if she were kin. For the time being, they are at peace. But King Ecgberht is old and his reign cannot last much longer. And when a king dies, chaos often ensues. And when the ruler of a kingdom as rich as Wessex dies, war is never far away. The power of the Norsemen is on the rise and Britain will soon see itself beset with an ever-increasing number of invaders.

How will Dunston and Aedwen cope with the upheavals that will shape the island of Britain and the history of the English people?

That is for another day, and other books.

Acknowledgements

As always, my first thanks go to you, dear reader, for using some of your valuable time to read my writing. Without you, there would be no books. I hope you have enjoyed *Wolf of Wessex*. If you have, please consider taking a moment to leave a review on your online store of choice and spread the word to friends and family. In a world awash with content, with so many things vying for people's attention, it is hard to stand out from the crowd and word of mouth is everything.

As with every book, there are a lot of people who have helped in getting *Wolf of Wessex* into the finished, published product.

Thank you to my trusty friends and test readers, Gareth Jones, Simon Blunsdon, Shane Smart, Rich Ward and Alex Forbes. They always provide me with invaluable input that helps me to polish the manuscripts before anyone else sees them and I make too much of a fool of myself!

Special thanks to Christopher Monk for his help with the Old English.

Thanks to Robyn Young, for her ideas for a title (even though in the end, I went with something else!).

Thanks to Steven A. McKay for reading an early draft and giving me some extremely useful feedback. I'd also like to thank

Steven and the rest of the online community of authors for all their support. These include, in no particular order, Martin Lake, Giles Kristian, E. M. Powell, Justin Hill, Stephanie Churchill, Gordon Doherty, Angus Donald, Jemahl Evans, Ian Ross, Ben Kane, Sharon Bennett Connolly, Paul Fraser Collard, Christian Cameron, Simon Turney and Griff Hosker. This is not an exhaustive list of all the writers who have helped me in one way or another, and I apologise unreservedly to those I have forgotten to include here!

I am indebted to Chris Bailey, founder and administrator of the Bernard Cornwell Fan Club group on Facebook. Not only has he been extremely supportive of my writing efforts, he also produced my very own customised axe, based on the description of Dunston's DeaÞangenga. It is a thing of exquisite craftsmanship and beauty and there is nothing like holding a Viking axe in your hands to get you in the mood to write some rip-roaring fight scenes!

Thanks to my editor, Nicolas Cheetham, and all of the team at Aria and Head of Zeus for their hard work and dedication to producing great books.

And lastly, but certainly not least, extra special thanks to my wonderful wife, Maite (Maria, to her work colleagues!), and our daughters, Elora and Iona. They all have to put up with me every day and I know I can sometimes (often) be grumpy when the writing isn't going according to plan. But I also know that without loved ones to share my highs and lows, whatever I wrote would be meaningless.

About the author

MATTHEW HARFFY grew up in Northumberland, England, where the rugged terrain, ruined castles and rocky coastline had a huge impact on him. He now lives in Wiltshire, with his wife and their two daughters.